THE DEVENSHIRE CHRONICLES

BOOK ONE

THE STONES OF ANDARUS

TOM SECHRIST

COPYRIGHT © 2012 Tom E. Sechrist, Jr.
The Devenshire Chronicles, The Stones of Andarus
By Tom Sechrist
ISBN: 978-0615943817
ISBN: 0615943810

www.tomsechrist.com

Editing and Formatting Services provided by
Literary Editor Rogena Mitchell-Jones
Rogena Mitchell-Jones Manuscript Service.
www.rogenamitchell.com

For me. For once... for me.

I love you, Renee!

Contents

PROLOGUE

CALEB KNEW HE WAS DYING. It wasn't the frantic, fear riddled last minute revelation of a sudden incident but rather the calm acceptance of an event he knew he was powerless to stop. He sagged against an ice-covered boulder and squinted into the blinding fury of the blizzard, acceptance began to sink in; he was lost.

The wind howled in all its natural fury at this intruder who dared to enter its land. As it screamed at him, it tossed up curtains of snow and ice that were nearly impossible to see through, while pummeling his chilled body as punishment for his naïve insolence.

The Wastelands were a desolate, mountainous range far north of any hint of civilization. Just as the name implied, there was nothing in this frozen tundra save for ice, snow, wind and death for any living thing that dared to journey too far inside its boundaries.

If the treacherous terrain wasn't enough to dissuade exploration of its vast expanse, the constant blizzard was. Only the very brave or the very foolish tempted their fates against this giant expanse of untamed wilderness.

Caleb was tired, more so than he had ever been in his life. The weariness soaked into every fiber of his being and seemed to team with the elements to sap his resolve to keep going. The journey had been long and treacherous, fraught with danger and death. Of the original six members of the quest, only he was left, the others having fallen to one pitfall after another along the way.

As he considered the white, cold, void around him, he asked himself what madness had brought him here. Why in the world would anyone venture into the Wastelands? Nothing lived here; not bird, insect, animal, and certainly not a man, who in all likelihood, never existed in the first place. He had lost his wife, craft, and all that had ever mattered to him because of this quest—this insane search for the one man who could help him. It would be inconceivable if that man were still alive after all of this time. If he lived, he would be very old and of little help. Much to his anguish, Caleb had no answers for these questions.

Almost without his being aware, he slid down the boulder to settle deep into the snow, the weariness whispering to him, softly coaxing him to rest for a while.

Tiny icicles clung to his eyelashes, beard, and mustache. The frost that covered his body cracked as he moved, threatening to freeze him solid. He promised himself that the rest would be brief. He could not stop, not now, not when he had come so far and lost so much. To give up now would make all the trials he had endured meaningless. He couldn't accept this, not when it was all he had left.

The quest had begun with six men a year ago with him leading the way; searching for the man of the myths. A man that not one scholar believed had ever existed, for whom there was not one shred of written proof. Yet there were hints, stories, tales of his adventures and his life. It was these hints, stories, and tales that instilled an almost insane conviction that the man of the myths had existed, and some shred of his life could have survived to the present day.

Along the way, each member would fall victim to one hazard after another. With each death, the remaining members of the quest resolved to complete the journey, find the proof, and make sure their deaths weren't empty.

Now only Caleb was left, having reached the borders of the Wastelands alone and more determined than he had ever been to complete this quest. But now, several weeks into his lonely journey, he found himself questioning his resolution. Was it worth it? Was what he had lost worth this search for the ethereal man?

He had been a well-respected member of his village. Through years of hard work, sacrifice, blind dedication, and with a steel-like resolution, he had built a solid craft under him and with it had come an even more solid reputation. A very comfortable life soon followed.

He attacked everything in his life with the same unwavering, rock-hard determination, and he did not stop until he was successful. No obstacle was too difficult for him to overcome. He was renowned for his steel will and determination. It was that determination that made him so successful in his craft, and with a young lady in his village that had caught his eye.

Cassandra. Just her name was enough to force a bittersweet smile to his frozen lips. She was more beautiful than anything he had ever seen. There were no words to describe her angelic presence. No sunset, no forest expanse, and no mountain range view could compare to her beauty, both inside and out.

He had pursued her with the same grit and determination that he used on everything he wanted. She had been unsure at first. She was young and not sure what her path in life was to be. She was strongly attracted to this brash young man who seemed to always gain that which he sought. She was also very aware that there was no shortage of women who sought his attention.

Most of these women were more interested in his growing fortune than in his honest, hardworking qualities. There were those who are attracted to him because of his rugged good looks and good qualities, but his focus was on her and her alone. When they would talk or meet each other in the street, she had the very distinct impression that, to him, she was the only woman in all of creation, and she had been extremely flattered.

Theirs had been a romance that made even the harshest heart warm. He had spared no expense in wooing her. She had no need that was not filled. She had no day that passed without him in it—either in flesh or in thought. He had vowed to spend the rest of his life making sure she was the most cherished, most loved woman in the history of the realm, and in short order, she agreed to become his wife.

The warm memories faded as a sharp blade of frozen wind slashed across his face, forcing his mind back to the present. He could no longer feel his legs, and his hands were quickly vanishing from his perceptions, as well. He was dead, and he knew it. All that remained was for his body to surrender to the inevitable. He had sacrificed it all: his craft, his life, his love. All for the search for the man of the myths. How could he have been so insane? What madness had driven him to this end? He had no answers for these questions, and he knew it really didn't matter in the end.

A puzzling thought pierced the frozen blanket permeating his brain. He wondered if his body would ever be found. Surely a very curious thing to be thinking at a time like this. If it were found, what would those who found him think? As they gazed upon his frozen remains, would they think of him as a brave explorer, seeking to tame this massive beast of nature? Or would they look upon him as a foolish knave who had been stupid enough to venture into the Wastelands, and do so alone?

A harsh, bitter chuckle rattled his throat as he closed his eyes. It really didn't matter what they thought. He knew it sure as hell wouldn't matter to him. He noticed that his body had stopped shivering. The violent shaking of his body fighting back against the bitter cold had been his only companion for weeks, to the point that his muscles had grown very sore. Now, even his body had abandoned him, as well.

Caleb relaxed. It was time. It pleased him that Cassandra would not know of his death. She would probably assume that he had found what he had been looking for, and she would be free to continue her life and, with a twinge of pain deep in his heart, find someone to share in her beautiful existence.

A sound reached his ears, and he paused. It was a sound different from the endless howl of the wind, and so faint that he wasn't sure he actually heard anything. Again, the faint sound came. It was a distinct crunching sound followed by a slight pause, and then it would repeat as though someone was walking through the snow.

He forced his eyes to open, which was a difficult task given the layer of ice that coated his eyelids. He turned his head in the direction of the noise, which was becoming louder with each occurrence. He actually found himself holding his breath to make sure he could hear the sound and make sure it was actually happening and not some trick of his dying brain.

Again the sound came—louder and closer. Squinting against his failing vision and through the endless swirling mist, he sought out the source of the noise. At first, he saw nothing but the blurred white of his soon-to-be tomb. Then a silhouette came into focus. It was a person walking toward him. For the first time in weeks, he felt a tiny spark of hope. Perhaps not all was lost after all.

As the shadowy form drew close, he found himself squinting hard, blinking rapidly to clear his vision, attempting to see who had come to his rescue. A small shred of strength returned as he pushed himself upright.

He tried to call out, but his throat was raw. Weeks of breathing hard in the frozen air had taken its toll. For a moment, he feared the silhouette would either be a trick of his faltering mind, or it would pass him by altogether, but it grew in size as it approached.

There was something familiar in the way the silhouette moved. The person was small in stature and walked with a gate he had seen before. His brow furrowed as he studied the approaching figure. Whoever it was wore little more than a cloak against the elements for their outline was easy to make out rather than the bulk of someone who had piled on layers of clothing. In fact, the form beneath the dancing cloak had the distinctive curves of a woman.

She moved with an unbelievable grace, almost as though she were floating over the snow instead of struggling to walk through it. He found a detached part of his mind admiring her grace and balance under the most difficult conditions. Again, the sway of her hips, the gracefulness of her step strummed a familiar chord in his mind. He knew her, but the memory was deep in the frozen mire of his brain.

"Hello..." he was finally able to rasp out, but he knew the sound had been caught by the vicious wind and whipped away long before it could have reached the woman's ears.

The shadowy figure stopped and gazed down upon him. He raised his arm to try to shield his eyes from the pelting snow and ice to see her, but her face was deep in the shadows of the cloaks' hood.

"Who... who are... you?" he croaked out, unsure if his voice had enough volume to reach her even at this close distance.

"You know me, Caleb." The soft tones of her voice replied, and in an instant, he was slammed back with the realization of who she was.

Of course, it was her. Who else could it be?

"Cassandra?" he asked weakly, barely able to comprehend how this could be happening.

She reached up and drew back the hood of her cloak, revealing a face that had haunted his dreams every night since their separation. A warm, loving smile parted her thick, red lips, and her hazel eyes twinkled with a light and love he had thought to never see again.

"Yes, my love. It is I."

"By the Fates..." he whispered as tears began pooling in his eyes. "How? How are you here?"

She knelt down into the snow beside him and ran her hands through the frozen bangs of hair that hung from under his cap. He was vaguely aware that her hands were bare, her skin as pink and healthy as he remembered and with no telltale signs of being exposed to the harsh environment. In fact, where her fingertips touched his forehead they were remarkably warm.

"I love you..." he croaked out. "I have always loved you."

Her smile widened, and she nodded slowly, "As I have you. Always and forever."

A tear slipped from his eye and trickled a short distance down his cheek before being frozen, adding to the layer of ice that already coated his entire body.

He became aware of her hands trailing down his face to the closures of his furs. He felt her begin to unfasten them. A spike of panic pierced his frozen perceptions as he felt a colder gust of air blast his chest.

"Cassandra! Wh-what are you doing?" he squeaked out. His furs were the last line of defense from the elements. To remove them would surely finish him.

"I have missed you," she said softly. So softly that he wasn't entirely sure if she had actually spoken or if it had been a trick of the howling wind. Whichever was the case, the soft warm tones of her voice soothed his panic.

"I want to join with you, to feel you inside me, to rejoice in the love we have always known, and have not felt in so very long."

Yes! To have her yield to him again. To join with her in love as they had so often, each time leaving him feeling completely awash with emotions he wasn't sure he could deal with. To have her again, to feel complete with her again, to feel things that had only been specters of his haunted spirit for so long made the cold, the emptiness of his being, the impending end of his life, seem so far below his notice.

"Yes, my sweet Cassandra! I have missed you! I have yearned for you with a passion I did not fathom could exist! I am yours. I always have been... I always will be!"

She smiled even wider as her warm hands slipped inside his shirt, caressing his chest with a love and warmth he had resigned himself to never know again. He closed his eyes and laid his head back against the boulder. Nothing mattered now, except this moment. None of the loss, pain, and suffering mattered. The man of the myths vanished from his mind. The comrades he had lost in the search for him faded. He had his precious Cassandra at his side again. She did still love him. She did still desire him.

Nothing else mattered.

He raised his aching, frozen arms, intent on parting her cloak. His hands hungered to touch her flesh, to feel the softness that no silk could ever match. It took him a moment to realize that he felt nothing under his hands. He moved his hands around, searching for her, but found nothing.

That was when he noticed that her hands had stopped rubbing his chest and stomach. Again, he forced his eyes open and looked down to find his furs undisturbed, the coating of ice over them intact.

His eyes snapped up, searching for her and found nothing but the white empty void of ice, snow, wind, cold, and death. With a growing fear and panic, he studied the blanket of white surrounding his body and found it as undisturbed as the ice coating his furs. She was gone... if she had ever truly been there at all.

"NOOOOOOOOO!!!" he screamed out at the wilderness with an intensity that even overpowered the howl of the wind for a moment.

Tears flooded his eyes as he fought against the incredible power of his despair. Not even the Fates would be so cruel as to show him his life's love and then whisk her away like this.

"Nooooooo!" he cried out again, much weaker this time, his now useless arms dropping to his sides.

To hell with it! To hell with the struggle! To hell with those who had been foolish enough to follow him on this stupid quest! To hell with the man of the myths! Most importantly... to hell with himself!

He sagged back against the boulder, resigned to die as quickly as possible — to end this sad, pitiful, useless existence! Tears flowed from his eyes, freezing to his face. He squeezed his eyes shut to force them from his eyes, and the harsh wind froze them shut. To hell with that, too! Where he was going, he wouldn't need eyes!

His perceptions began pulling even further in on themselves, preparing for his final journey. As the black abyss opened up before him, he felt no fear. It was time. It was past time. He opened his arms to embrace the emptiness, to dissolve him into the blackness.

As he spiraled down into the emptiness, he forced his mind to Cassandra and locked it there. He wished to perish with her being the last thought he had.

"I love you Cassandra! I'm sorry I failed you as a husband. May you find happiness in your life that I failed to give to you. May you someday understand what drove me. My love is yours... now and forever!"

~~*

Caleb had heard many tales of what happened when the soul traversed the border from the land of the living to the Afterlife. Of what to expect when the toils and troubles of life were left behind, and an eternity of peace lie ahead. Excruciating pain was not among the things he had expected to feel upon the completion of his journey.

He felt warmth. A welcome sensation after weeks of bone-numbing cold. The warmth came from furs piled upon him, and that struck him as odd. *Why would one need furs in the afterlife?* He had heard that the afterlife was a place where such things were no longer necessary.

His muscles ached, and his bones throbbed with a pain he could not even begin to believe was possible. His head felt as though it were encased in stone with someone attempting to shatter the rock with a sledgehammer.

His limbs burned with intensity unmatched by any flame. Never before, while he had been alive, had he ever experienced this kind of pain and suffering. Indeed, he found himself wondering if, perhaps, he had been banished to the depths of hell instead of being allowed passage into the Afterlife.

Through the ringing in his ears, he picked up the faint sound of a crackling fire and felt the distinct sensation of warmth. Yet, as the warmth soaked into his frozen body, it awoke with a new, more intense pain. The sound of the crackling fire only reinforced his fear that perhaps he was in hell.

He opened his eyes to take in his fate, finding nothing but darkness. With a sharp stab of panic, he realized he was blind. But that made no sense. Why would the Lord of Hell deprive himself of another tool with which to punish his prisoners? Surely, he would use his hellish powers to conjure up all manner of illusions to torture his unwilling subjects.

Blinking several times, Caleb was then awarded a new stab of pain within his skull. He then found a muddy pool of swirling darkness that hinted at the faint possibility that perhaps he wasn't blind, after all. Perhaps the Dark Lord was utilizing the threat of blindness, or the hope of restored vision, to torture him.

He felt as though the Fates had conspired to cheat him once again. All through his life, they had tricked and teased him with possibilities, only to dash them away. His craft, his love, his very life, seemed to be nothing but a plaything for their amusement. Now, even in death, they continued to taunt and torture him.

With a soft groan that grated across the raw meat of his throat, Caleb realized that even in death he would be the eternal plaything of the Fates. They would satiate their sadistic pleasures upon his twisted soul for the remainder of all time.

"I fear you blame the Fates for far more than they are guilty of, Caleb." A voice resounded over the ringing in his ears and the crackle of the fire. "At least in this instance."

Caleb did not recognize the voice. It was old, very old indeed. Yet, in the fragile cracking of the voice, he could hear power and authority. He tried to move his head so that he could look upon the source. His eyes could register nothing, and his head barely obeyed the commands of his mind.

"Save your strength."

How had he known what I was trying to do? How had he known my thoughts?

"W-where am I?" Caleb managed to speak, surprised by the coarseness of his voice.

"You are safe for the moment. Do not concern yourself with details. Simply rest and heal." replied the voice. "However, I am afraid I must disappoint you. You are not in the afterlife. You are still very much alive."

"Why should that disappoint me? Is it not the desire of every man to live?"

A harsh cackling laugh erupted in response. The laugh lapsed into a ragged cough that made Caleb's lungs ache and burn. Whoever owned the voice was not well.

"I have said something that amuses you?" Caleb asked weakly.

"What man would not want to live?" mimicked the voice after the hacking cough had subsided. "As I recall, you were seeking death, were you not?"

"I do not wish to die!" Caleb stated boldly, but knew that the statement sounded hollow.

"Indeed?"

Caleb felt as if the old man had looked into his mind and had seen his resolution to die. The sounds of shuffling feet came, and Caleb tried to track the source and direction. His brain, though, couldn't focus correctly.

"Tell me, Caleb, what brings a man who so dearly loves life to the Wastelands?"

"How do you know my name?"

"Why do you insist on wasting time with meaningless questions? Is it so important that you discover how I know it?" The ancient voice shot back with irritation.

"Yes, it is important. Have we met before?" he insisted.

An irritated sigh whispered into the air. The old man muttered incomprehensible words before saying. "Why must the young always hop about on one foot, while demanding answers to every mystery of the universe? If you must know, you spoke your name several times during your delirium. Satisfied?"

The explanation didn't ring true to Caleb, but lacking any evidence with which to doubt the old man's claim, he decided to let it stand for now.

"Where am I?" he asked tentatively, fearful of sending his aged benefactor into another rant.

"In my home!" came the curt reply accompanied by the stirring of cloth and shuffling footsteps.

Caleb screwed his eyes into the muddy mess that had become his vision, and he was just able to make out the hunched over shadow of the old man ambling across the floor. Just as the sight would begin to coalesce into something resembling focus, he would have to blink, which would send the image back into an unsubstantial blur.

The man stopped before the fire and bent over. Caleb's hearing was improving much faster than his vision, and he could make out the clank of something metal followed by the distinctive slurp of liquid being poured.

After a moment, the faint image of the old man straightened and began ambling toward him. The steps were hesitant and slow.

"Here!" the old man snapped as his trembling hand extended toward him through the murky darkness of his vision.

With a supreme effort, Caleb was able to push, pull, and twist his damaged body into something of an upright position. It amazed him how hard the most simple of tasks were. It took all of what little strength he had to move. Each movement brought another sharp stab of pain, another wave of nausea, and another fragment of belief that he had been sent to hell after all.

Breathing heavily from the effort and the pain, he raised his head up to focus on what the old man was handing him. Through the swirling muck and pounding pain in his head, he could make out a tin cup with a dark steaming liquid within.

Slowly, he forced his arms up and then took the cup from the old man's trembling hand. The cup was very hot, but it felt good against what seemed like the eternal chill that had permeated his being. He wrapped both hands around the cup and closed his eyes as the heat soaked into and thawed his frozen fingers.

While enjoying the warmth, he could make out the shuffling steps retreating away from him. Fighting back the urge to retch and cry out from the intense pain, Caleb forced his eyes open and considered the dark liquid within the cup. The steam wafted up around him, and the aroma was woodsy with a hint of bitterness at its edges.

"What is this?" he squeaked out.

"Poison!" was the snapped reply. "I rescued you from the blizzard so I could kill you with poison!"

Caleb blinked several times and looked deeper into the cup. "Poison?" he asked with confusion. The pounding throb in his brain made it hard to concentrate.

"Oh my lords!" the old man exclaimed. "How did someone so dense make it this far into the Wastelands? It's hot tea, you fool! Drink it while it's hot, or it will do you no good!"

Caleb, again feeling like a small, reprimanded child, slowly raised the tin to his lips and took a tentative sip. The tea was very hot and very bitter. In fact, Caleb was relatively sure that he had never tasted anything so vile in his life. For a moment, he wondered if the tea were, in fact, poison.

The heat from the tea coated his throat and soothed the rawness. He took another sip and found it even worse than the first, but he could not deny how good it felt going over his ravaged throat and the hint of warmth that touched his belly. A third, larger sip rewarded him with a distinct sensation of soothing warmth that spread from his stomach with a caressing hint of promised relief from his suffering.

Caleb cleared his throat and looked up, surprised by how much his vision had cleared in the past few moments. While his vision was still swirling at the edges with incoherent fuzz, the center was growing clearer. He could see his ancient benefactor lowering himself down into a high-backed chair situated next to the fireplace.

The man was old, indeed. Far older than even his crackling voice hinted. In his youth, he had been a tall man, but now appeared short due to his hunched posture. A stringy mane of bright white hair hung from his head to drape down his shoulders and back. A thick white beard covered the lower half of his craggy face, hanging nearly to his lap. His eyebrows were massive tufts of white that threw his cold gray eyes into shadows.

The parts of his face not covered by the beard were crisscrossed with deep crevasses of flesh that served as a map of the years that had passed across his features. The overall appearance of his face gave support to his cranky disposition and yet, there was the fleeting hinting glimpse of the vast experience and knowledge that he possessed. Even in his current decrepit state, Caleb could tell he was not a man to be trifled with. He was dressed in a dark blue robe that looked to be very thick, possibly to insulate his frail frame from the eternal cold.

"What is your name?" Caleb asked tentatively.

Cold, grey eyes regarded him briefly, before he answered. "You may call me sir."

The old man reached to his left and hefted a pipe from a hand-carved stand fashioned into the shape of a dragon's claw. The craftsmanship of the carver was clear in the intricate detail of each scale, each claw. Next, the old man removed the lid from a glass bowl and began packing the pipe with tobacco. The rich aroma reached Caleb and, though he was not a smoker, he found himself enjoying the fragrance.

A skinny, boney finger packed the tobacco deep into the bowl before he absently replaced the lid to the bowl.

"Tell me, Caleb. What brings a man who claims to cherish life so dearly to the Wastelands?" the old man asked as he leaned forward to take a burning stick from the edge of fire. He brought the flame up to kiss the tobacco, and he began drawing in, pulling the fire down into the bowl. Very soon, a thick grayish cloud of aromatic smoke began to drift from the bowl and from the old man's lips as he puffed the pipe to life.

"I came here on a quest," he replied, amazed how much his voice had improved. Despite the foul taste of the tea, he could not argue that each sip eased his suffering and seemed to be speeding his recovery.

The man paused in the act of tossing the stick back into the fireplace at the mention of the word. "A quest?"

"Yes," Caleb replied as he raised the tin to his lips for another sip.

"A quest." The old man repeated the word as the stick landed back in the fire. "A quest." The old man repeated for a third time, as though he were rolling the word over and over in his mind.

"Now there is a word I have not heard in a great many seasons," the man said with just the faintest edge of fondness in his voice. His use of the word seasons served to remind Caleb just how old the man truly was.

The passage of time was now referred to as years. In the past, a vast majority of the realm's economy was based in agriculture so the passing of the seasons was used to measure time.

"What brings you here on this noble quest?" the old man asked with a hint of sarcasm and yet, genuine curiosity, in his voice.

"I search for a man," Caleb replied slowly, taking a moment to squeeze his eyes tightly shut against another wave of nausea and throbbing pain behind his eyes.

"A man? He must be someone very special for you to risk the life you claim to cherish so dearly," the old man retorted. The layers of sarcasm were evident in his voice as he puffed on the pipe.

Caleb nodded slowly in response as he took another sip of tea. The war he was fighting with his own body made the sarcasm lost to his perceptions.

"Well?" the old man asked impatiently after a lengthy pause. "Does this man have a name or did you venture into the Wastelands without even that bit of information?" the old man snapped in impatience.

"He has a name." Caleb replied softly, gazing deeply into the dark tea, as if he could find some form of resolution there since it was growing more and more evident that there may be none elsewhere.

"Well? What is it?" the old man snapped.

Caleb paused. Did he dare speak that name? It was a name that had cost him so much. It had ruined his entire life and he found himself wondering if perhaps there were some form of curse associated with it.

He shook his head slightly. He was being maudlin. He had ventured so far, lost so much, there couldn't possibly be any more harm now than the first time he had spoken it.

"Daimion Devenshire."

A silence suddenly filled the room — a silence so profound that the crackling of the fire grew to a roar within it. What was it about that name that always seemed to inspire such a silence?

Caleb slowly lifted his aching eyes from the depths of the tin cup to find the old man staring at him in stunned disbelief. The pipe hung loosely from his lips, while the gray smoke trickled from his partly opened mouth.

"What did you say?" the old man whispered, his voice very faint.

"Daimion Devenshire. He is the one I seek," Caleb repeated, transfixed by the old man's reaction.

"Daimion Devenshire..." the old man repeated faintly, and in that one instant, Caleb felt his entire existence begin to spin. Only one thing could cause this type or reaction. The old man had known Devenshire, and from the stunned reaction, he had known him very well.

Very quickly, as though he had just been caught doing something horrible, the old man recovered his composure.

"He is a myth!" he snapped. However, the lack of conviction in his tone told Caleb that the old man was playing down his knowledge.

"So I have heard. Yet, there is proof that he did exist... once."

"It does not matter. I have not heard that name in a very long time, and I think it best that the world leave him as a myth."

"But I have come so far and lost so much in my search. If you know something, I beg of you to tell me!" Caleb pleaded.

The old man leveled a harsh glare at the younger man. "You have done what you have done of your own free will. No one asked you to begin this quest, or jeopardize all that you hold dear to achieve it. The mess of your life is of your own doing!"

"Devenshire did exist! I know it. I feel it! He is the only one who can help me, to restore to me what I have lost and give me what I have searched for all my life." Caleb said, seeming to ignore the old man's retort.

A faint, ancient chuckle echoed off the walls. "Then, my wayward friend, you are indeed a lost soul. Devenshire cannot help anyone anymore."

In that one sentence, Caleb felt his entire world begin to spin. The old man had all but confirmed that Devenshire had existed at one time or another, within the old man's lifetime. His heart raced faster as he realized that all had not been in vain. The sacrifices he had made, the friends he had lost, and the turmoil of his soul had not been for nothing. Devenshire had been a real person.

"Then he *did* exist. He had lived at one time!" Caleb said with conviction.

"Yes, he did live once, a very long time ago." The old man replied slowly, reluctantly.

"Did you know him?" Although it took longer than it should have, Caleb managed to bring himself up into a more upright position.

"I knew him. He and I were very close, we fought many battles together." The man paused for a moment and then shook his head in exasperation.

"That time has passed! Time marches forward, my young friend, not backward. We are all just pieces of driftwood caught in the currents of the river of time." The old head shook slowly, sadly. "There is no going back. One era must eventually pass and make room for another. Those who cannot let go of one will have the hardest time living in the other."

Caleb cocked his head to one side and winced under the sharp stab of pain the movement struck inside his skull. "I don't understand."

"Of course you don't!" the old man snapped in irritation. "That is because you have your mind set on one thing and refuse to see, consider, or even acknowledge, anything else!

"The era of fantasy is passing. The world is turning in on itself and is thinking of little else. There is no longer any need for beings like Devenshire. The world no longer believes in magic, in mighty warriors, powerful wizards, fair maidens, vicious dragons, or any other creature of that time." The man slowly shook his head and slumped forward as if the recollection had drained him.

"No one believes in other realms, in other worlds, or that one can cross from one to the other. No, Devenshire, and beings like him are nothing more than fairy tales, and soon, so shall be the period in which they had lived.

"There are those of us who still believe," Caleb argued softly.

The ancient head shook slowly again. "Not enough to warrant keeping the relics of the old time around. All will be as it should be in the fullness of time. Devenshire and the time he lived in will be embraced as a fond memory and then forgotten." A deep sigh passed through the bearded lips. "Perhaps that is as it should be."

"But the world needs to remember Devenshire and the time he lived in! They need the lessons he can teach, the wisdom of his life!" Caleb replied urgently.

"The wisdom of his life?" The man chuckled before shaking his head. "The myths that have grown around Devenshire have clouded the image of the actual man. Let me tell you something: Daimion Devenshire was not a god. He was not some celestial being with awe-inspiring powers. He was a mortal man. Granted, he had a few mystical powers, but for the most part, he was flesh and blood, capable of making just as bloody a mess of his life as you or I."

"Perhaps, but we can all learn from the way he lived, the great deeds he performed. The legends are replete with the many fantastic and noble deeds Devenshire performed in his life. There are no such men alive in this time with the gallantry, the power, and the wisdom that Devenshire possessed."

The man regarded Caleb for a handful of moments before turning his gray eyes to the crackling fire. For a moment, Caleb thought the old man had lapsed into some form of trance, for his eyes seemed to be looking at something far beyond the burning logs as if he were reliving something in the past.

He took the moment to consider his surroundings now that his eyesight was improving. He found himself in a cave that had been converted from cold rock into a warm dwelling complete with touches of the old man's personality.

Caleb was on a pallet of furs in front of a large fireplace, complete with a stone hearth, which looked to have been hewn from the wall of the cave. He briefly regarded his cantankerous benefactor and wondered how the frail old man had managed to engineer a working fireplace out of solid rock.

To the left of the fireplace was a simple wooden box that held kindling. To the right was the high-backed chair in which the old man sat. Between the chair and the wall was a neatly stacked pile of wood. He wondered how many hours the old man spent in that chair, feeding the fire log after log.

On the opposite side of the old man's chair was a round end table, which held a goblet, the small wooden statue of a dragon's claw that served as the pipe holder, a blown glass bowl with a wooden lid that held tobacco. A small brass candleholder completed the table's contents.

Behind the old man's chair sat a hand-carved oak desk with a design that indicated a style that hadn't been used in many years. The desk was neat and tidy, holding a sheaf of parchment, an ink well and a writing quill. Small wooden statues lined the upper shelf of the desk, each appearing to have been hand carved with intricate attention to detail. There were several statues of dragons as well as a buck and a very detailed carving of a sword with three serpents coiled around the blade. The coils ended with the three snakes rearing their heads at one another at the pommel of the sword.

Following the irregular curve of the wall around the room Caleb found that he sat between the fireplace and an elegantly constructed couch, which was flanked by two mahogany end tables. Each table held a very old dagger nestled into a hand carved wooden stand. The talent of the artist who had fashioned the holders awed him. He reasoned that the daggers must hold some sort of significance to the old man for him to display them in this way.

"It never ceases to amaze me how a few noble deeds can be transformed into feats that no mortal man could have ever accomplished," the aged man finally said, emerging from his reverie and leaning back into the chair. His eyes turned to the back wall of the cave and a breathtaking armoire.

The large cabinet appeared to have been constructed of oak with intricate carvings of dragons and serpents on the double doors and then stained to a deep, satiny finish. Small brass hoops on each door served as the openers. Caleb sorely wished to see what the armoire held, what secrets of the old man he would find.

"Surely, not all the tales are exaggerated," Caleb replied.

The old man chuckled dryly. "More so than you would think. The older the story, the greater its tale." His eyes never left the armoire as he spoke, and Caleb wondered what significance it played in the old man's story.

Caleb noticed two very large paintings graced the room. Above the rock hewn mantle of the fireplace, hung an ancient oil portrait of a woman. Her beauty was beyond compare and, for a moment, he felt that he could have even forgotten his precious Cassandra should he had found himself in the blonde-haired woman's embrace.

Across the room next to the armoire was the other painting and it, too, was of a very beautiful woman. The second painting didn't appear to be as old as the one over the fireplace, but it did speak of the incredible passage of time since the last brush stroke had been completed. This woman was stunning but in a different way from the first woman. He would have been hard-pressed to say which woman was more striking.

The woman in the first portrait was small in stature, almost child-like. Her hair hung loose to her shoulders, and the gown she wore hung off her shoulders in a very provocative style. Her face was beautiful except for a hint of sadness in her eyes. He wondered what horrible tragedy had marred her beauty with such sadness.

The second woman had a thick mane of black hair, which also hung loosely to her shoulders. She sat with her right side facing the artist. Her back was straight, her shoulders back, and her head turned to look directly at the artist. Her deep green eyes bespoke of wisdom and insight. Although her smile was only slight in the portrait, Caleb got the impression of a free, fun-loving spirit.

Like the woman in the painting over the mantle, there was something about her that spoke of an incredible inner strength, a force of will that was something to be reckoned with.

There was something else, something in both paintings that took him several moments to realize. The looks in their eyes, the carriage of their heads and straightness of their shoulders... something different. Then he realized what it was... Caleb had never met a woman who, with only a look, portrayed such confidence and inner strength. The caliber of womanhood represented in these two very old portraits simply did not exist in this time. There are incredibly beautiful women in this time, but none who carried themselves with the absolute air of self-assuredness that these two women possessed. Yet another indication of how time changes and people along with it.

"I have heard of the many great deeds that Devenshire was supposed to have accomplished." The man shook his head as he continued. A half-smile lifted the corner of his mouth as he gazed into the fire. "Very little of what the legends say of him is true."

Caleb tore his eyes from the woman in the second portrait so that he could focus on what the man was saying. He doubted that he could look upon either woman and hear the man at the same time.

"I know how history can defuse and dilute the truth surrounding great men," replied Caleb. "However, if only a small fraction of what I have heard about Devenshire is true, then he was a great man with a great deal to offer. Not only to his time, but mine, as well."

Again, the old man chuckled. "I fear that the truth about Devenshire would leave your sterling image of him quite tarnished. That is why I say it is better that the world continue thinking of him as a legend and a myth. I am sure Daimion would much rather be remembered the way you think of him rather than the way I remember him."

Caleb looked down at the furs and took a moment to consider this. He had always known that the stories surrounding Devenshire had to be exaggerated, but to hear the man tell it, Devenshire was nothing like what the legends portrayed. And who would know better than a person who had actually known him? He had to honestly ask himself if he were prepared to learn that his hero was actually as flawed as this man would have him believe.

The old man pulled the pipe from his lips and glanced down at the pipe, his heavily calloused finger gently packing the smoldering tobacco deeper into the bowl. A slight grin lifted the corners of his lips.

"I see hesitation in you, Caleb. Are you not prepared to learn that Daimion was just as human, just as flawed, as you or I?"

Caleb looked up at the old man, defiance flashing in his eyes. "Devenshire and those like him were great individuals. True, the stories about them may be exaggerated, but the core of their stories serves to remind all of us of the kind of people we should be."

The man laughed again, which sparked another series of deep coughs. Caleb tried not to make a sour face at the sounds of the fluids gurgling deep in the old man's lungs. As the ragged coughing reached its pinnacle, the man retrieved a cloth from within the folds of his robes and dabbed at the red that had suddenly appeared to stain the white of his thick beard. The old man was much worse off than Caleb had originally thought.

The old man slumped in the chair, breathing hard to recover from the coughing fit. After several moments, his faint voice asked, "Tell me, my impressionable young friend, what do the stories of Devenshire lead you to believe?"

"That Devenshire was a brave man, a great warrior, and holder of great magical powers." Caleb spoke with pride, daring the man to discount that impression.

Much to his dismay, the man took his dare.

One snow white, puffed eyebrow arched up over the other one, as his gray eyes looked deep into Caleb's eyes. A grin spread across the craggy features.

"A brave man? I will agree with you on that. Daimion was indeed a very brave man. A great warrior?" the old man nodded. "He could hold his own in nearly any fight, be it with fists, swords, or staffs. Great mystical powers?" He shook his head. "Daimion had studied the Mystical Arts for some time in his youth, but he had tired of the intense and time-consuming discipline that mastering the Mystical Arts required. He was not, by any means, a great mage. He was capable of some basic magic, no more."

"But he was, without a doubt, the shaper of the time he lived in!" Caleb said proudly in defense of his idol.

Again, the aged man laughed and looked up at the ceiling of the cave. "Do you hear this, Daimion? A shaper of the time you lived in?

Have you ever heard of such?"

Suddenly, the laughter turned to deep coughs accompanied by a more intense gurgling sound coming from deep in the man's lungs. The coughs wracked the frail body with waves of pain that were evident by the contortion of the aged features.

The old man dropped his pipe as both arms wrapped around his midsection, in an effort to support his body from the onslaught. Caleb's face twisted in an expression comprised of sympathy and disgust as the sound of the fluids in his lungs intensified.

"Are you alright?" he asked carefully.

The old man ignored the question as he continued to fight against the coughing fit. He turned sideways in the ample room of the armchair and curled his legs up until he was in something that resembled a fetal position. The coughs were deep, hard, and twisted the small frame with an intensity that made Caleb's suffering more pronounced.

Finally, the coughs began to subside, as the old man was finally able to dab at the fresh wave of blood that had been expelled from his lungs.

As the last cough came, and the old man was released from the attack, he collapsed into the chair, breathing hard from the attack. His heavy breaths rattling his chest and continued to swish the liquids around in his lungs.

"Is there anything I can do?" Caleb asked.

"You... you can remain silent... silent for a moment..." the man wheezed out between deep, painful breaths.

"You are ill," Caleb observed.

"Your powers... of observation... are staggering..." came the wheezed reply.

The old man slowly sat upright in the chair, his right hand pressed tightly against his chest as his trembling left hand reached out to the table next to his chair to retrieve the large golden goblet. As he brought the goblet to his lips, he used both hands to steady it as he drank deeply. He lowered the goblet, closed his eyes, and leaned his head back, his mouth stained with a deep purple color.

Several moments passed as the old man continued to recover from the attack. Caleb found himself understanding why the man would avoid laughter if this were the results. After a time, the old man took another sip from the goblet before returning it to the table. He sat forward in the chair, his elbows resting on his knees, as he continued to recover.

With his breath slowing, and the rattling sounds subsiding, the old man retrieved his pipe from the floor and slowly returned it to the dragon claw stand. He returned to resting his elbows on his knees, his head hanging low, and his eyes closed against the continued onslaught of pain.

Finally, the old man raised his head, and Caleb could see the pain etched deep in the man's face. He gently cleared his throat and eased back in the comfort of the chair, fixing Caleb with a tired, pain-tinged stare. "Let me tell you something about this great shaper of time. He drank too much on occasion, had a short temper, and had too fond an eye for the ladies. He was known to go off on tangents at the slightest whim, and for no other reason than it suited his fancy at the time. I would have to say that time was the shaper of the man, not the reverse."

The old man smiled weakly and chuckled gently as he whispered to himself, "Shaper of the time he lived in... good heavens."

"But he lived his life on his terms." Caleb defended, wondering if he were going to have to watch the old man die before his eyes.

A warm smile creased the old man's face as he nodded slowly. "Tis true. Daimion did as he damned well pleased, and whether others liked it or not, mattered not to him." One eyebrow hoisted up over the other as the old man's gaze bore deeper into Caleb. "And it got him into trouble on more occasions than not."

"That's what I want to learn from him. To live my life as he did. To take what I can from the realm and forget the things I cannot."

"You do not need Devenshire for these things. The teachers of your village should be able to teach you these things," the old man replied.

Caleb scoffed. "Teachers! They are brigands who teach only based on the coins you can place in front of them. What they have to offer is meaningless, empty, dribble that doesn't contain enough wisdom to fill a quill point."

"Then you should learn these lessons from your parents, your siblings."

Caleb's expression shifted into deep sadness as he gazed down into his now cold tin of tea. "My father despised children... even his own. He made sure each of them knew this, as well. My mother was a good mother, but she lacked the courage to stand up to my father. As for my siblings? I am the oldest of my parents' nine children. They looked to me for guidance I did not possess to share with them."

The old man was taken aback. "Has the realm truly turned this far in on itself?"

Caleb lifted his tired, sad expression to the old man. "You have been up here a long time. The realm is not as you left it. People care not for each other any longer. They take what they can from the realm and do so only to their own ends. Little regard is shown for others. The realm is very much a place where you fend for yourself, or you get lost in the press."

With a weary sigh, the man nodded. "Tis what happens with the passage of one era to the next. I have lived in the old era and have seen the roots of the new one take hold. But the basic human spirit will always live on, no matter how it is disguised. We all must take solace in that fact and face life as it is dealt to us."

Caleb shook his head slowly. "You do not understand. There are those who cannot do as you say. There are those who have learned of the old ways and yearn for them, and who feel as if they cannot survive in this world without them. I am one such person. I feel as if I were born in a time in which I do not belong."

The man smiled warmly. "I do understand such a feeling, Caleb. There were many in my time that yearned for the time before. Each era possesses those who wish they had lived in the previous time. So they learn as much as they can of that era and, in some small way, ensure that it will continue, and to serve as a reminder of how things used to be."

Caleb looked up at the old man and smiled slightly. "Exactly. That is why I seek Devenshire, to ensure that his time is not forgotten, to bring his life back to my world so that it is not forgotten."

"I have already told you, Devenshire is dead. He died many seasons ago. So, return to your village, win back your fair Cassandra, and get on with your life. Find a way to reconcile your past with your future and live a happy life."

Caleb shook his head as his eyes began to moisten. "I cannot win her back. The love she once held for me belongs to another. Nothing remains for me in the past."

"Then perhaps there is a message to be learned. Everything happens for a reason, Caleb. Perhaps it is destined for you to find another. I know the pain you suffer. I have felt it on more than one occasion; yet, I survived just as you will. The pain may never ease completely, but it will heal."

Caleb shook his head as he spoke, and the old man noticed it. "Right now, the wound is fresh and still bleeds, so it will hurt from time to time. But the wound will heal, and the pain will ease, trust me in this."

He regarded the old man with skepticism. Then his mind changed directions, and his eyes sparkled with a new hope.

"If Devenshire is no more, then might I look at his chronicles?"

A puzzled expression graced the old man's face. "Chronicles?"

"Yes. The Devenshire Chronicles. Do you have them? Do you know where they are?"

"There are no chronicles. Devenshire did not have the patience for writing." The old man paused as a genuinely confused expression etched further into his face. "Come to think of it, I am not even sure he knew how to write."

Caleb's eyes grew wide. "Impossible! The chronicles exist! They must exist! The legends speak of them!"

"And I am telling you that if Devenshire ever wrote anything down, I know nothing of it!" the old man snapped in return.

"No!" Caleb cried out. He believed in the chronicles even more deeply than he did in Devenshire himself. He had always known he would never actually find Devenshire the man, but he had believed firmly in the existence of his chronicles.

"There are no chronicles, Caleb," the old man said firmly, with only the smallest hint of sadness in his voice. He could see the conviction in the young man's beliefs. He knew that Caleb had honestly expected to find Devenshire's chronicles at the end of his journey. No other outcome had ever occurred to him.

He watched as Caleb's posture slumped under the crushing revelation, and he felt pity for the young man, regardless of how foolish he had been for abandoning everything for the quest.

Caleb felt despair return. Once again, he had come so close to realizing his dream, only to have it dashed from his hands. If Devenshire had made no permanent record of his life, then there was nothing. It had all been for naught. The sacrifices he had made, the friends and loved ones he had lost, all of it had been for nothing.

His head dropped, then his shoulders slumped, and he felt incredibly tired, as if the last flickering remnants of his will had been extinguished. When he spoke, his voice sounded dead, defeated.

"Then I have traveled this far for nothing. I have sacrificed my entire existence for nothing. All I have endured and forced those around me to endure, the friends who believed as I did, believed strongly enough that they risked their lives to accompany me on this quest, have died for nothing." Caleb simply stared down into the furs beneath him, his eyes unseeing. "My life has been for nothing."

The old man watched Caleb for several moments. His despair was as complete as any he had ever seen in his long life. Whatever weaknesses plagued the young man, lack of strength in his convictions was not one of them.

"I am sorry," he replied simply.

"What does it matter? Devenshire had become my last hope. He was the only one who could teach me what I needed to know and help restore to me what I had lost." Caleb grew more lifeless with each passing word.

The old man watched him for a few more moments and then, when he could bare the sadness within the young man no more, he turned his gaze to the fire. He tried to convince himself that Caleb's troubles where of his own design, that he was not obligated to help this practical stranger in any way.

Yet, his thoughts rang false in his mind, and he felt as though he were being watched. He slowly raised his ancient eyes to the portrait above the mantle, and the woman's eyes appeared to bore deeply into his. Then his attention was pulled toward the other portrait next to the hand-carved armoire. The deep green eyes gave him no quarter and appeared to chastise him as harshly as the eyes in the first portrait.

I have done all I am obligated to do by common courtesy! He said in his mind to the two women.

Would Daimion turn his back on such a tortured soul? The eyes in the portraits asked him.

*I am **not** Daimion Devenshire! I owe this man nothing more than shelter from the storm and time to regain his strength for his journey home!* The old man mentally screamed back at the women.

Give him what he seeks, what he needs. If you value Daimion's memory and that part of him that lives on in all who remember him, give Caleb what he seeks.

What would you have me do? Tell him of Devenshire? Destroy his lofty impression of him? It all happened a very long time ago, and I cannot remember enough to relay a very accurate story! He argued back.

What of your lofty words that the past should be remembered? To be carried on to remind the present and the future generations of how they came to be?

Empty words! Meaningless platitudes from an old man who should have already joined all of you! Besides, it all happened so long ago. I am not even sure I have reliable memories any longer! He answered with growing irritation.

Stop making excuses and keep Daimion's memory alive. You are the only one left who can. The true Daimion Devenshire will die with you. This is your chance to let this faltering new world see not only Daimion, but also the time we all lived in as it truly existed. If you let Daimion die with the past, then you condemn all of us to the same fate of being forgotten.

As angry as their words were making him, he could not argue with their logic. *Very well! For all the good it will do! Now go back to haunting brothels and leave me be, you wenches!*

Soft, ghostly laughter echoed though his mind as their presence faded from perception. The man fixed each portrait with an appropriate glare of irritation as he considered the thoughts. With an irritated sigh, he rose slowly and, with shuffling steps, moved behind his chair to the beautiful hand-carved oak desk. He retrieved a sheaf of parchment, an ink well, and a quill.

As he turned to face Caleb, he could see the complete, total, and utter destitution within the young man. His spirit was on the verge of being broken, if it hadn't been already. Again, the annoying pang of sympathy thumped his chest, and his irritation rose even higher. Such maudlin thoughts and emotions were a waste of time and served to foul his mood anytime they occurred. It was one of the many reasons he had retreated to this place as to spare himself the toil of having to deal with them.

With faltering, shuffling steps, he crossed to the pallet of furs and dropped the items in front of Caleb. The young man blinked out of his self-pity and focused on the items before him, looking up at the old man with confusion.

"Do you feel well enough to write?" the man asked, not even trying to hide the irritation in his voice.

"Write what?"

"The Devenshire Chronicles, what else?"

Caleb's eyes flew open wide as he looked from the man to the parchment and back again. "Me? Write the Devenshire Chronicles? I... I am not sure... I am not sure that I am worthy."

The old man rolled his eyes as he shook his head. "Stop being so damned melodramatic about it! I will tell Devenshire's story, and you will write it. I would do it myself, but my eyes are weak, and my hand trembles too badly. Do you want the story or not?"

Caleb slowly took up the parchment and writing equipment. He stared at the pages of parchment for a handful of seconds before looking back up to the man.

"I will write it as you relay it to me. I swear I will not embellish it in any way with my own thoughts. The story I take with me from this place will be as pure as you tell it."

The man stared deeply into Caleb's eyes with an intensity that should have made the younger person look away. Caleb held his gaze as if to let the ancient one see that he had meant every word. Finally, the man nodded once before he turned and shuffled toward his seat next to the fire.

"That is all I ask. There are enough fluffed up stories concerning Daimion as it is. Wherever he is, I am sure his head has swelled to three times its size with the myths concerning him." The old man smiled fondly as he set about fixing another pipe to smoke. "I am sure he will not like the truth about him being told, but he will just have to get over it."

While the old man knocked out the remnants of his last smoke from the bowl and set about packing fresh tobacco into it, Caleb pulled a nearby table over and set up the writing supplies. He was surprised at how his hands trembled from the prospect and wondered if he would be able to write with them trembling so.

The older man lit the pipe and puffed it to life. He leaned back into the chair and regarded the flames of the fire yet again, as if consulting them for some mystical purpose. It was several moments before he spoke, and when he did, Caleb got the impression that the man's mind was many miles and many years away. Even some of the age seemed to melt from his voice as he began to speak.

"I suppose the best place to start are with my earliest memories of him. No one knows where Devenshire came from. Some say from another realm, others say from another time. But one thing is sure... To some he was a gift from the heavens; to others he was the spawn of hell itself."

Caleb wrote quickly, the words spreading across the parchment and into his soul. This is what he had traveled halfway around the world to get, what he had risked his entire past, present, and future to obtain.

So the past conversed with the future, and the story of one man, tied directly to both, began taking shape between them. Reminding one of a life he had all but forgotten, while teaching another of times that were soon to be no more... save for the words scribbled on a piece of parchment.

Yet, when the story is told, both will be changed.

CHAPTER ONE

SHANTIRA BOLTED INTO THE CLEARING and slid to a stop. Leaning over, she rested her hands on her knees and sucked air into her starved lungs. She only allowed herself a moment to catch her breath before she straightened and slowed her breathing, straining to hear over the pounding of her pulse in her ears.

The distant crash of bodies through the underbrush told her that she had not eluded her pursuers. In fact, they were much closer than she would have imagined they would be. She had honestly thought she would be further ahead of them. Biting back at the wave of fear that tried to claim her focus, she forced herself to concentrate.

A quick glance around the clearing showed her a deeper section of the forest that would better facilitate her escape. She quickly broke into a dead run for the opposite side of the clearing, and the whispered hint of security offered by the deeper gloom of the forest beyond.

She had grown up in these woods, and she knew them like the back of her hand. She had little doubt that once she reached the other side of the clearing that she would make good her escape. Pumping her legs harder, she poured on all the speed she could muster. The edge of the tree line was close now.

That's when her plan went awry.

Something slammed into the back of her right leg with enough force to knock it out from under her. She quickly twisted her body to

THE DEVENSHIRE CHRONICLES

try to regain her balance, but she knew it was too late as the ground rushed up at her with sickening speed. She knew this was going to hurt. She squeezed her eyes shut and tried to brace for the impact.

She hit hard, much harder than she expected, and the wind left her already famished lungs in a loud gasped rush. The inside of her skull erupted in multi-colored sparkles of pain and disorientation. The force of her flat out run served to propel her body into a tumbling roll across the forest floor that her addled senses couldn't correct. She felt her body bounce and flop, each impact adding another stab of pain, which was quickly numbed by an ever-thickening layer of fog around her brain.

Her rolling, bouncing trip seemed to last for hours before she crashed into the base of a giant oak tree. A detached part of her brain knew the impact should have been incredibly painful, but her mind didn't register the impact. Her perceptions swam in a nauseating, stormy sea of disorientation. For a span of time that she couldn't even begin to measure, she lay at the base of the oak tree, her head spinning in one direction while her stomach spun in the other. Her lungs felt like they had collapsed. She gasped, desperately trying to suck in air. She forced one eye open and quickly shut it again as the sight of spinning tree tops churned the nausea in her stomach threatening to make her retch if she were foolish enough to try that again.

She suddenly remembered why she had been running through the woods and knew she couldn't afford the time to lay here and collect her wits. The bandits would be upon her quickly. Gritting her teeth against the waves of nausea she forced her eyes to open as she slowly pulled herself into a seated position against the tree, dragging her right leg across the ground as she moved it. A white-hot searing shaft of pain shot up her leg causing her to gasp before stifling a cry behind a harshly bitten bottom lip. Putting aside the recovery from falling, she looked down at the back of her leg and felt her blood run cold.

A crossbow bolt protruded from the muscle of her leg, blood gathering around the shaft and a trail already weaved its way down her chilling flesh. It took several moments for enough of the disorientation from her fall to clear for her to appreciate what her eyes were showing her. Deep inside her mind she knew she had to rise, to regain her feet and flee before the bandits caught up to her, but her limbs felt as though they were huge. Far too large for her to move, and they weren't responding to her mental commands to stir.

Breathing hard from having run so hard, having the wind knocked out of her, and the fight against the waves of pain that were starting to register with her clearing perceptions, she forced her limbs to move. Using the tree as a brace, she forced herself to her feet, keeping all her weight on her left leg. Panic tried to pierce her reasoning, but she forced it back. She knew she would need all her wits about her. There was no time for fear.

Just as that resolution settled in, she heard the snap of a twig and the rustle of brush heralding the arrival of her worst fear. The bandits had caught up to her. Swallowing hard against the knot of fear in her stomach, she raised her still swirling vision to see the six men enter the clearing from different points around its perimeter. Blinking back the waves in her eyes, she realized that not only had she not been outrunning them, but her course had been so obvious that they had been in the process of encircling her position.

Forcing her face into a mask of controlled defiance, she forced herself to remain calm. All was not lost, and she was certainly more than she appeared to be. To her left, a bandit emerged from the tree line carrying a crossbow. His smug expression, showing pride at his marksmanship, caused the pain in her leg to cry out in a throbbing protest of her iron control. Through his labored breathing, he set about casually reloading the crossbow.

"A valiant effort," the man directly in front of her said as he paused halfway into the clearing. He bent over, resting his hands on his knees as he took in some deep breaths. His comrades completed their journey into the clearing and formed an arch in front of her, sealing off any hopes of escape in that direction.

Using the large oak tree as a brace and as protection from an attack from behind, Shantira knew her only course of escape lay behind her. The throbbing, stabbing pain in her leg reminded her that she wouldn't stand a chance. She knew she would have to stand and fight and, while she was confident in her abilities, even she knew she was no match for six men.

The man directly in front of her stood upright again, his labored breathing having eased some, "but wasted nonetheless," he finished.

With revulsion, she noticed how he openly allowed his eyes to roam over her body. She saw duplicate expressions on the faces of the others. There was little doubt as to where their thoughts were going, and she felt her skin crawl under the thought.

She resisted the urge to cover herself. Such a tactic would be a waste of time and would only serve to bolster their already over-confident mindset. She was dressed in a dark gray cotton work dress and black sandals tied about her ankle and calves. The dress was short, coming to midway down her upper leg. It had no sleeves and was cut low at the neckline. It was designed to be light and cool in the heat of the fields, but it showed more of her body than she cared to at the moment. She could practically feel their eyes roam over every part of her body, the swell of her breasts, the curves of her hips and the toned muscles of her legs. A shudder passed through her as one of the men hungrily licked his lips, his eyes continuing their feast.

With a deft move of her right arm, she retrieved one of the two daggers she had tucked into one of the pockets of the dress. She quickly assumed a defensive stance with legs spread shoulder width apart, arms wide, and eyes open slightly wider in order to take advantage of her full field of vision. Her pierced leg screamed out in protest at having to support her weight, but she ignored it. She couldn't afford the distraction now. She held the dagger in front of her and poised herself, ready for what may come next.

The man who had spoken to her regarded the dagger with a great deal of humor in his face. His expression was the smuggest of the group; his attitude and the way he carried himself told her that he was the leader. With a cruel grin curling his lips, he regarded the dagger. "What do you intend to do with that?" he asked.

Shantira leveled a cold glare at him through the deep blue of her eyes. Her face was emotionless, but her voice carried a hard edge to it as she answered, "Defend myself."

The leader chuckled as he glanced at the men on his right. "I think all you will do is amuse us." As if on cue, the other four men laughed at her.

She ignored it. Let them underestimate her. It would give her an advantage. She silently thanked whatever it was that made a man automatically assume he was superior to a woman in combat.

The leader took in another deep breath to complete the task of bringing his labored breathing under control. He looked at her with something akin to softness.

"Surrender, little one. Who knows? Perhaps you will even enjoy it."

She felt her upper lip begin to curl in anger and disgust. The term "little one" was reserved for slave girls, and she was NOT a slave girl. She caught the snarl before it had a chance to manifest and forced her features to remain cold. "I would rather die than willingly give you any part of me," she replied curtly.

The sardonic grin that spread across the leaders face struck another chord of anger within her. "I do not believe your willingness will be an issue."

The other bandits broke into laughter in order to bolster their leaders' position. Again, fear, panic, and anger clawed at her, seeking to rend her self-control to shreds. The primal parts of her wanted control, to leap forward and cut those smug, arrogant expressions from their piggish faces. Again, she swallowed hard against the dry knot in her throat and the raging emotions that sought to take control.

She had been working in the fields of her village, like any other day, when the attack had come. Twelve bandits on horseback had exploded into the village from different directions and immediately set about wrecking havoc. Like the others toiling in the fields, Shantira, taking up her hoe and running from the fields, was intent on protecting her home.

During the course of the battle, Shantira watched several villagers fall under charging hooves and swinging swords. She also watched as one of the raiders were quickly dislodged from their mounts and dispatched in short order. While her village was made up of simple farming folk, they were determined to keep what little they had.

One bandit discovered this the hard way as a group of young boys swung out of a tree in order to pull him off his horse. A group of villagers quickly descended upon him, making sure this raid would be his last.

Shantira spied another raider spinning his mount around and spurring it in the direction of his screaming compatriot. His path would carry him right past her, and he didn't even acknowledge her presence. With a cruel grin, she tightened her grip on the hoe. So much the better.

The swing caught the bandit just under the breastbone, and the force lifted him clear off the saddle, causing him to land flat of his back. The impact caused his breath to explode from his lungs in a foul gale, and the dazed expression told her he was adequately stunned. She swung the hoe around and back over her shoulder to strike another blow, but a group of men piled upon him, his screams telling her that this was his last raid, as well.

She turned to see where she was needed next, when she spied two daggers in the dirt near her. They must have come from the bandit she had struck, and she quickly picked them up. She stuck one in the pocket of her work dress and gripped the other tightly in her right hand. She kept the hoe in her left hand, just in case.

At this point, some of the remaining raiders had dismounted and began closing in on the group who were attacking the man she had knocked from the saddle. She flipped the dagger over to grip it by the tip of the blade and then hurled it at the nearest attacker. The dagger struck with an audible thump as the blade sank deep into his chest. With a startled gasp, the raider clutched the dagger, stumbled, and fell. A moment later, a long wheezing breath signaled the end of his life.

The surviving raiders slowly lifted their shocked gazes from the dead man to Shantira, and their expressions turned harsh as though they saw her as the reason their raid was failing. Their angry stares gave her an idea of a way to spare her village from any further death or destruction. She began backing slowly away from the advancing men. They increased their pace to catch up to her, and she increased her speed accordingly. Convinced that she was the center of their attention, she turned and bolted into the forest. A quick backward glance had told her that all six were following.

That would leave two bandits. Two doomed bandits, Shantira had recalled with pleasure.

Now, facing off against six very angry bandits, she seriously questioned whom the true doomed one was.

"Surrender, little one! We will take what we want from you," the leader replied easily, putting a little more emphasis on the term *little one*. She realized that she had not completely concealed her earlier snarl at being called that.

"You will only be defiling a corpse, for I will take my own life before you touch me," she snapped.

The leader elbowed the raider to his left, "It would not be the first time, eh?"

The raider grinned and leaned on his leaders' shoulder with his right forearm. With a wolfish grin, he turned his lust filled gaze to her before nodding, "Me likes 'em cold and still."

Shantira felt her eyes narrow and her mouth drop open in shock and disgust. She felt the revulsion pound over her in waves. She didn't know if they were speaking the truth or simply trying to shock her, but the thought of these savages releasing their foul pleasures upon the dead was almost more than her mind could comprehend. She had never even imagined such evil wickedness could exist in the hearts of men.

Even with all of her will, she could not suppress the shudder of revulsion that rippled through her. "You are disgusting!" she hissed.

The leader smiled a truly evil grin and shook his head. "Little one, you have no idea. Stohl! Take her!" he shouted suddenly causing Shantira to jump in a start.

The bandit to the leaders' right smiled and began advancing on her. She shifted her position only slightly to face him, but kept the others in her peripherals. Again, her wounded leg screamed out at her while the fear and revulsion teamed in trying to distract her. She clenched her jaw tight and steeled her resolve. She became very aware that she might have to make good on her threat to kill herself before these savages could rape her. She mentally shook off the thought. It hadn't come to that yet.

Stohl slowly drew his sword and began advancing on her. She could tell by his expression and exaggerated movements that the show was supposed to intimidate her. It had quite the opposite effect. "Save yourself from unnecessary pain, pretty one. You cannot defeat me, and I sorely do not wish to mar that beautiful body."

"My body is none of your concern, and your pursuit of it will be your doom," she replied in tightly controlled tones.

The other bandits sounded up a chorus of "ooohhhs" and "aaahhhs" in mock fear of her. She didn't mind. The more they underestimated her, the better her odds of surviving the encounter.

As he drew closer, Shantira could smell the stench of his

unwashed body, and her revulsion doubled. His approach was slow and careful, but she could see the gaps in his defenses and knew that he did not seriously consider her a threat. He seemed to relax and Shantira found herself letting a little of her tenseness ease, as well. She almost didn't realize her mistake and the cleverness of his tactics. He suddenly leapt forward, slashing down and to his right, in a maneuver designed to surprise more than injure her. Fortunately, the move was sloppily executed, and Shantira was able to evade it.

The bandit pitched forward, off balance from the maneuver. It was just another indication of his lack of discipline and training. Shantira saw her opening. Stepping in as quickly as her wounded leg would allow, her left arm circled around the man's neck as though she were about to embrace him. As she stepped in, she buried the dagger deep into his gut. When the hilt of the dagger touched home, she twisted the blade and jerked back hard, ripping the blade from his body with a wet tearing sound. As the dagger was ripped free, she stepped back on her good leg and, with a savage snarl, quickly smashed him in the face with her left elbow, sending him staggering back, his sword tumbling from his hand.

Shantira wasted little time in taking up the sword and quickly resuming her defensive stance. The sword was a poorly made, off balance weapon, but it was preferable to the small dagger.

The entire encounter had happened so quickly that Stohl took several moments to assimilate what had happened. He blinked the tears from his eyes caused by having his nose smashed in. Blood trickled from each nostril as he reached up to see how badly it had been injured. It was broken. "You bitch!" he hissed as he took a step toward her. His angry expression said he had every intention of beating her thoroughly. It was then that the first tendrils of pain from his much more serious wound caught his attention. He looked down at the rapidly spreading red stain flowing across his midsection.

With growing panic, he ripped his shirt open to see the gaping wound. It had been torn open so far that parts of his intestines were protruding from the hole with a river of blood swirling out around them. "What?" he asked as his hands flew to the wound, trying to staunch the flow of blood. He laced his fingers together and pressed in as much as the pain would allow, but this only caused the blood to course out around his hands.

The other bandits were stuck fast to their places. The mock sounds of fear and laughter gone in the wake of the quick and very deadly attack. They watched in shock as Stohl turned away from Shantira and began a very slow, ambling walk toward them.

"Help me... please..." he whispered as each step grew less certain. Each bandit looked at the other, each knowing there was absolutely nothing they could do for him. He was already dead.

Stohl looked from one face to another, searching for some glimmer of hope that he would not die here, and each face telling him that he was, indeed, about to die. His paling, fear-filled features came to rest on the leader. "Doran... Help me... please..." he whispered as he stopped walking.

Doran simply stared at Stohl with a tightening look of dread and uncertainty. It was clear he had no idea what to do to help his man. He briefly looked to each member of the party, seeing if anyone had any idea about how to help. They held the same uncertain expression as their leader.

Stohl opened his mouth to say something, but all that came was a gurgling sound as he sank to his knees, his hands still desperately trying to stop the flow of his life from escaping the massive hole in his stomach. He swallowed hard, his eyes growing wide in fear. The expression froze on his face as he slowly pitched forward to the ground. A few moments later, a shuddering, wheezing breath signaled the end of his life.

The other men's faces told Shantira that none of them had been prepared for the outcome of the brief encounter. They all stared at the fallen Stohl with shock that slowly turned to anger as they realized that he was either dead, or very close to it. One by one, angry glares sought her out, and she forced her senses to a fine edge. They had been dangerous enough before but now, outraged by the death of one of their own, they were even more so. The leader must surely know the expensive nature of sending his men against her one at a time. She prepared herself for an all out rush from the remaining bandits. The dagger in her left hand called to her. If they rushed her, she would drive the dagger quickly and deeply into the center of her chest. A remote part of her mind was amazed at how calmly she faced her own demise. She had always imagined a greater fear at the prospect of the end of her life.

"You will pay for that dearly!" the leader hissed. "I was going to kill you quickly once we finished with you, but now your end will be more agonizing and longer than anything you have ever imagined!"

Shantira took a deep breath and steeled herself to her fate. This was it. She silently bid a fond farewell to all of her loved ones. She hoped her sacrifice made it possible for her village to survive. If just one home, just one life were saved by her act, her death would be more than worth it. Fear called to her again, tried to pull her into its ice-cold grip, but she resisted. She forced her breathing to calm, forced her thoughts to focus, and centered her attention on this moment.

Without a word or gesture from the leader, the raiders slowly began to move, not advancing on her directly, but spreading out to make it harder for her to watch all of them at once. Shantira tried to keep all of them in her field of vision, but knew that would soon be impossible.

There came a flash of movement from her right, and she turned slightly to face whatever threat might come from that direction. It was then that something hit her hard in the left side, just above the hip, and left a stinging, burning sensation behind.

At first, she thought one of the men had hit her with a stone, but the white-hot pain that lanced her side told her it was far more deadly than a stone. She looked down to see the hilt of a dagger quivering in her side at the top of her hip.

She fought panic as blood began to seep out around the blade and down her hip. She bit her bottom lip to stop the whimper of pain as the sword and dagger slipped from her hands. Without realizing it, she sank slowly to her knees as her hands wrapped around the blade where it entered her skin.

Too late, she realized that she had made a critical mistake by diverting her attention to her wound. Hands roughly grabbed her arms and pulled her savagely to her feet. She struggled against the two bandits who held her arms, but they held her fast. She was crudely slammed back against the tree as her arms were pulled back on either side of the trunk. The coarse bark bit mercilessly into her back, and her shoulders screamed in agony from being pulled so hard.

She hissed in anger as she struggled to free herself. She looked up just in time to see the leader step up and draw his right hand up and over his left shoulder. She knew what was coming, but there was nothing she could do to prevent it.

The leader backhanded her with such force that she feared she would black out. Sharp explosions of light and pain erupted inside her skull as her head was snapped to the side. She tasted blood, and her senses swirled on the rippling edge of unconsciousness.

"Now you will see what happens to those stupid enough to stand against us! We will take what we want from you, and when we are finished, you will die a slow and agonizing death!"

Shantira could barely make out his words through the loud ringing in her ears. Her head slumped forward, and she could barely open her eyes. The leader grabbed a handful of her thick hair and jerked her head up. "Do you hear me, bitch?"

She felt her eyes roll in their sockets as she winced against the savage pull of her hair. The throbbing in her head, which had just begun to fade, was brought back to full intensity. She felt nausea churn in her stomach and pain come in waves as her senses teetered on the edge of consciousness.

"You will beg for death! I promise you! But it will not come, not for a long time!" The leader growled as he released her hair, allowing her head to slump forward again. She blinked several times, trying to clear the sickening spin of her vision. She spat blood and tried to force her mind to clear, trying to find a way out. "Perhaps, if you beg for mercy, I can be persuaded to consider it," the leader said with thick sarcasm. "Do you wish to have mercy?"

Her tongue felt too thick to speak, and her head still swam with sickening ripples of disorientation. She felt his hand grab her chin and jerk her head up again, renewing the throbbing ache between her temples. "Well? Do you wish for mercy?" he growled. Then she felt his other hand grab her right breast and squeeze hard. "Do you?" he repeated savagely.

She clenched her teeth against the pain and fear. She knew what was to come, and it made her pray for unconsciousness. Perhaps, she reasoned, if she angered the leader enough, he would strike her again, rendering her unconscious.

"Oh, you like that?" he asked as he continued to knead her breast roughly. "Are you one of these girls that pretend to be all proper but, in reality, are nothing more than little whores?"

Anger began to seethe through her, and she forced her eyes open. She glared deep into his. Through bloody, clenched teeth she hissed, "Go to hell!"

As she had hoped, the leader became furious. He released her breast to cock his fist and smashed her in the mouth. Her head slammed back against the tree and, for a precious moment, she thought she would lose the curse of consciousness. She felt a sharp tug on the front of her dress and heard the material tear. Through swirling senses, she felt cool air on her chest and stomach, and she knew what had happened and was even more aware that there wasn't anything she could do about it.

Again, the feel of his hand came to her breast, but this time without the barrier of cloth. His hands were rough and made her skin crawl with revulsion. She heard his deep moan of satisfaction as his other hand found her left breast; stroking and kneading them with little thought to anything save his own disgusting pleasures.

"Very nice," he sighed heavily. "I may not kill you, after all. A body this perfect should be kept. I can see you warming my blankets for many nights to come."

Shantira struggled to fight back, to find a way to free herself and to make this arrogant bastard pay for his atrocities.

"It never ceases to amaze me how bold and brash even the lowliest of scum can sound when they have their opponent outnumbered five to one." A deep resonant voice sounded from behind the marauders.

Shantira felt the leader's hands suddenly leave her breasts as he spun around. She forced her head up and tried to focus on the owner of the new voice. Through the ringing in her ears, she heard the leader's angry voice once more. "Who are you?"

"My name is the least of your concerns at the moment," replied the deep voice, and for the first time since being pinned against the tree, Shantira found a sliver of hope. Finally, her vision began to clear, and the man across the clearing began to come into focus.

He was leaning casually against a tree, arms folded across his chest, and his expression was mildly amused. She felt her breath catch and her heart skip a beat as the last ripples of disorientation left her vision. He stood over six feet in height with thick jet-black hair that flowed to his shoulders. Deep-set blue-green eyes stared out from hooded lids that seemed on the border of being sleepy, yet aware of everything they took in. He was handsome, more so than any man she'd seen in recent memory.

He was dressed in black breeches tucked into the tops of black riding boots. An off-white pullover shirt was stretched across his broad chest and tucked into the breeches showing the flatness of his stomach. The collar of the shirt was open to the midpoint of his chest, revealing his bunched muscles. The sleeves of the shirt were partially rolled up to the middle of his muscular forearms. He also wore a black vest, which he left open. A black cloak was tied loosely around his neck with the hood down. A short sword was slung low on his left hip.

There was an air about him that Shantira was hard pressed to define. It was an ease of presence, yet, at the same time, a tension that seemed ready to explode at any moment. Shantira could not understand why, but the sight of him made some of her fears evaporate, and she found herself actually finding hope.

"The woman is ours! Go find you one of your own!" The lead raider shot back, assuming that this stranger had come to steal their newfound prize, and Shantira had to admit that she could not be sure of the newcomer's intentions. As her senses began to clear, she became aware that the two bandits holding her against the tree were diverting their attention to the stranger. Their grip on her was not as strong as before, and in that, she found another bit of hope. If her captors were distracted enough, then maybe she could free herself. She was also aware of how the front of her dress had been ripped open and how she was exposed. She felt embarrassed and angry, and desperately wanted to cover herself.

The dark-clad man chuckled and slowly shook his head as he looked down at the ground for a moment before returning his gaze to the raiders. "The Fates saw fit to give man two heads, and yet only enough blood to use one at a time. As is usual for those like you, you are thinking with the wrong one."

"What?" the bandit leader asked, not entirely sure he understood.

The stranger chuckled. It was a deep, rich sound. "Take your time."

The leader's face contorted into deep thought as he mulled over what the stranger had said. Suddenly, the meaning of what the stranger had said registered, and his face flushed crimson. "You are an arrogant bastard!" he snapped.

The stranger grinned and nodded, "Aye."

"You are either mad or suicidal," the leader replied with a controlled tone to his voice that told Shantira he was fighting anger. "I do not care which, but you only have one chance to save yourself by withdrawing now!"

The stranger's smile never wavered as he cocked his head to one side. "How odd. I was about to say the same thing to you."

The raider's eyes narrowed. "You are far too arrogant for your own good! Perhaps you need to be taught a lesson in respect."

One dark eyebrow arched slightly over the other as the stranger pretended to consider the statement. "Indeed. Perhaps I do. But I sorely doubt that you or your men will be the ones to teach me that lesson."

Shantira marveled at how poised the stranger was. There was no fear evident in his bearing, no trepidation. His arms were still folded casually across his chest as he continued to lean against the tree. He seemed relaxed as if he were merely passing the time of day with a new acquaintance. She wondered if this man were truly demented, or was he actually that sure of his abilities?

She felt the tension mount. The leader was trying to intimidate the man and was failing miserably. She knew that the situation was escalating; the leader would have to save face before his men by getting the better of the arrogant intruder, and knowing men, there was only one way to accomplish that.

A fight was coming, and she knew she needed to be ready. Tearing her gaze from the newcomer, she began looking around for weapons. The sword and dagger she'd held earlier were well within reach if she could just get free from the bandits holding her. The last of the fuzz was clearing from her mind, and she forced herself to concentrate, to be ready to move if and when the opportunity came.

"Izirra! Kill this pest!" the leader shouted angrily.

The raider, who had made the comment about liking his women cold and still, stepped away from the leader and grinned as he began moving slowly toward the stranger. In response, the black-cloaked man simply turned his head to watch the raider approach with an expression of boredom.

Izirra paused a moment when the sight of his approach failed to scare the intruder. He had expected to see fear or, at the very least, concern on the stranger's face. He wasn't prepared for boredom, and it angered him. With a scowl, he drew his sword and held it at the ready.

The stranger regarded the sword briefly before returning his bored expression to Izirra. "In case you are curious," the stranger said nodding toward the tip of the sword, "the pointed end goes into your opponent."

Izzira's eyes grew wide, at first, in shock and then in anger. He screamed a battle cry and charged. Shantira watched in awe, as the stranger did not so much as flinch as the raider charged toward him, sword raised high.

Just as the raider was upon him, the intruder exploded into action. Later, Shantira would recall the next events and wonder if they had truly happened as quickly as they had appeared.

As the sword came down, the stranger gracefully stepped aside as he reached up and grabbed the attacker's wrists, redirecting the swing downward and to the right. The stranger turned with the momentum of the swing until he was facing the same direction as the raider, and the end of his sword was buried in the ground. Before Izirra could react, the stranger savagely drove his right elbow back into his attacker's nose.

The bandit's head snapped back so hard and so fast that Shantira was sure that she would hear the snap of his neck. The raider pitched backwards as blood gushed from his shattered nose. He landed hard on his back, twitched once, and was still.

While Izirra fell, the stranger followed the momentum of his elbow smash and spun around, flinging his right arm toward the man with the crossbow, who had just raised the weapon in an attempt to draw a bead on him.

Shantira didn't wait to see what happened next, for just as the man spun around, the bandit holding her right arm released her in order to join the fight. The time had come, and she knew that if she had any hope of surviving, she had to act. In a single fluid movement, she stooped down and picked up the dagger just as the other bandit reacted to her sudden movement. He tried to wrench her wrist around to stop her movement, and the sharp stab of pain lanced her wrist, but it was too little too late.

Her dagger pierced his skin just below the breastbone, and she pushed for all she was worth, driving the blade deep. With a strangled gasp of surprise and pain, the bandit released her wrist and backed away, trying to put distance between himself and his captive who, in the span of a heartbeat, had become his attacker. The anger sprang to the surface as she allowed the bandit to pull himself off the dagger, and back away. It was only a momentary respite.

Ignoring the searing pain of her wounds, she advanced on the man who was suddenly much more interested in his wound than restraining her. The few seconds he took to understand what had happened were too many. As his pained and shocked expression rose to see what had become of her, she deftly reached up and slit his throat. Hot blood sprayed from the gaping wound, splashing in her face as the man gagged and clawed at his neck as if trying to remove something that was robbing him of air.

"Bastard!" she hissed as the man slowly fell to his knees, making horrible gurgling, gagging sounds. The blood continued to spray from his opened throat, and the sight brought her sadistic joy. She felt no pity for the man, and she hoped his death would be as horrible and terrifying as it appeared to be. She watched as the man fell to his side, his hands still trying to stop the geyser of red spewing from his neck.

As his struggles to live became weaker, she turned to see where the others were. The man with the crossbow was lying on his back, a dagger protruding from his chest. No doubt, the stranger had flung the dagger after downing Izirra. The other bandit who had been restraining her now stood at his leader's side. Neither man seemed aware that she had killed the other man.

She nodded to herself, *Good.*

The leader was looking at the crossbowman, and then his uncertain gaze shifted to the prone form of Izirra lying at the stranger's feet. Two of his men down and the man had yet to draw his sword. Doran's anger flashed to the surface. "You bastard child of a thousand whores!" he shouted as he drew his sword and advanced on the intruder.

Shantira saw the other bandit who had been holding her advance with his leader and was moving to attack him when she spied movement from the crossbowman. The man wasn't dead yet and was trying to slowly reach his crossbow without drawing attention to himself. With a dark grin, she changed directions and began moving toward the crossbowman while keeping an eye on the remaining two bandits and the stranger.

The leader had quickly advanced on the stranger, unleashing a vicious sword stroke that was supposed to remove his head. The stranger waited until the last possible second and then stooped low, going into a backwards leg sweep that took the leader's legs out from under him.

As she stooped to pick up the crossbow, she watched as the leg sweep brought the stranger's back to the other bandit. She watched in horror as the last raider quickly stepped up and swung his sword downward. She fully expected to see the handsome stranger cleaved by the raider's sword. What she did not expect was for the stranger to shift his weight back onto his knees and bring his sword up and over his back to deflect the blow. The sound of clashing steel echoed through the woods.

The stranger quickly brought his arms down, shifting his weight to them, and without wasting a moment, he unleashed a savage backward kick. His boot found the raider's kneecap and snapped the joint backwards in a direction it was never designed to go. With the wet popping snap of torn ligaments, the bandit went down in a screaming heap, both hands clutching his shattered knee.

The stranger bounced to his feet with a grace that surprised Shantira. With his height and build, she hadn't expected him to be as agile.

Doran quickly scrambled to his feet and turned. He was stunned to find the stranger waiting for him with that unnerving half smile. With a snarl and a growl, the leader launched into his attack.

She reached the downed crossbowman and absently reached to retrieve the crossbow. Over the clanging of swords smashing together, she could hear the bandit crying out with pain. He clutched his knee in both hands and rolled back and forth, trying to find any form of relief from the intense pain. A cruel smile touched her lips as she watched him writhe on the ground. Normally, she would have felt sympathy for the man, but the fact that he was ready to take his turn in defiling her body wiped out any trace of sympathy.

She shifted her attention back to the combatants just in time to see the leader feint a right side attack and then switched it around to a left slash. The stranger stepped back, using his blade to deflect the blow. The leader, in poor sword fighting etiquette, stepped forward and launched his left fist toward the stranger's face.

The stranger bobbed his head out of the path of the punch, returning the favor with a vicious left cross that smashed across the leader's jaw, sending him staggering backwards and loosening his grip on the sword.

The leader regained his balance and held his jaw in one hand while he glared at the stranger. With a smile, the stranger took several paces back, leaving the leader's sword in the dirt where it had fallen. For a moment, the leader's heated gaze alternated between the stranger and his sword. It was as if he weren't sure what he was supposed to do next for it was an act he would have never done in the stranger's place.

Slowly, the leader advanced and stooped low to retrieve his weapon, his angry glare never leaving the stranger. The stranger had his arms at his sides, not even bothering to assume a defensive stance.

Shantira was amazed. The air of the stranger spoke volumes to his conviction that he would win this encounter. She had never met a man who was so sure of his abilities.

The leader took up his sword and advanced on the stranger. In short order, the fight resumed with the leader attacking with growing brutality, and the stranger defending easily, passing up several opportunities to go on the offensive.

Suddenly she felt a hand grip her ankle. She spun around quickly to find the crossbowman looking up at her. "Give me that!" he rasped out, indicating the crossbow.

She quickly brought the weapon up to her shoulder and lined up the sights on his forehead. Instead of fear, the wounded bandit chuckled. "You are a woman and have no stomach for killing."

A cruel smile parted her blood stained lips. "Then allow me to expand your knowledge of women," and she touched the trigger.

The crossbow jumped in her grip as the bolt tore through the bandit's skull with a wet, meaty thump. The bandit's grip on her ankle instantly went limp as his astonished expression stared up through the trees.

With the raider dispatched, she turned her attention to the leader and the stranger, locked in a violent display of sword fighting. Shantira was in awe of the fluidity and grace of the movements of the stranger. The leader's face was a mask of fury and exertion. The stranger's expression was mildly amused, almost bored.

The leader saw the superiority in the stranger's expression. This man did not fear him in the least, and it showed in his actions and expressions. The insolent bastard was mocking him as surely as he was breathing. With a savage snarl, he launched into another attack.

Their swords collided, echoing their song through the clearing. The bandit leader feinted a left side swing and quickly changed it to a straight on thrust. The stranger easily stepped back and blocked the thrust with a counter clockwise downward arch. The leader quickly stepped forward and tried another vicious thrust aimed at the stranger's midsection. The stranger smiled and side stepped the thrust, which threw the leader off balance. He fully expected to feel the stranger's blade pierce his exposed side and was genuinely surprised when the stranger simply assumed a defense stance, waiting for the next attack.

The leader squared off again, studying his opponent and wondering if the man were truly this clever or just ignorant. The stranger watched the bandit leader intently, simply waiting for the next attack. His calm expression and relaxed manner infuriated the bandit. He was used to striking fear in his opponents.

The leader launched into a series of rapid short jabs that drove the stranger back as he defended. The stranger easily countered each jab as if they were the flailing's of an apprentice swordsman.

At the end of his series of short jabs, he feinted a straight in thrust and swung his sword around in an attempt to slice the stranger's sword arm. To his surprise, the stranger quickly spun his blade up to deflect the blow as he turned out of the leader's path of attack. Again, the leader found himself exposed and off balance. The stranger either did not see this opening or ignored it as he stepped clear and resumed a defensive stance.

The raider stepped back, his chest heaving from the exertion of his ineffective attacks. His eyes burned with a fury of embarrassment at the stranger, which was met with that same, nerve-wracking calm that seemed permanently etched into his face. With a shrill cry, he feinted a left side attack, which the stranger moved to counter, and then drove straight in for the very center of his opponent's chest.

Shantira closed her eyes, unable to watch what was the one and only mistake the stranger had made in the entire encounter, and the one she was sure would finish him. At that distance, there was hardly any way to counter the straight on attack. Although her eyes were closed, her ears picked up the unmistakable sound of a sword sinking deep into flesh. There was a very surprised gasp followed by a fading moan as a body collapsed to the forest floor.

She silently saluted the stranger and bid him farewell as well as her thanks for his assistance. At least now, even wounded, she stood a chance of surviving against one man rather than six. She opened her eyes, fully expecting to see the leader standing triumphantly over the body of the stranger with his sword buried deep into his chest. She was not prepared for the reverse.

With her eyes growing wide and her mouth hanging agape, she saw the stranger standing over the body of the leader with a grim, angry look on his face as he looked down at him. He squirmed weakly under the blade buried in his chest. His eyes were wide with panic. With another soft moan, the leader stopped struggling and relaxed into death, his eyes wide open and staring up into infinity.

The stranger simply turned leaving the sword in the leader, and then he strode across to the only bandit still alive. It was then that Shantira realized that he had never drawn his sword, fighting the entire encounter with Izzira's blade.

The bandit continued to writhe on the ground, crying out as the nerves of his shattered knee sent waves of pain through him. In one fluid motion, the stranger pinned the raider to his back with his left knee while producing another dagger with his right hand. As the sharp edge of the dagger touched the taut skin of the raider's throat, he stopped writhing and moaning. His focus was now fully on the dark, threatening countenance of the stranger. There was no longer any merriment or mischief in his blue-green eyes as they bored intently into the tear-laden ones of the bandit.

"I am feeling charitable this day, so I will not kill you. Let the lesson of your shattered knee remind you of this day, and do not be foolish enough to allow yourself to come into my sight again. I can promise you that the outcome will be more than permanent."

With tears and sweat streaming down his face, the raider nodded once, his already pale features seeming to grow even grayer than before. Despite the incredible pain of his crushed knee, he remained still and silent as the stranger continued to drive the truth of his words into the bandit with the intensity of his stare. Finally, he nodded once and rose smoothly to his feet, slipping the dagger back into its hiding place beneath his black cloak and allowing the bandit to lapse back into pitiful wails and moans of pain.

With the raiders dispatched, his attention finally came to rest on Shantira. She did not miss how his eyes, like those of the raiders before him, roamed openly over her body. Such open gazes always irritated her and made her feel as though she were some form of livestock set out for inspection at sale. It was then that she realized that the front of her dress was still open, and her breasts were exposed. She dropped the crossbow and simultaneously retrieved the dagger while pulling the torn dress together to cover herself. She was still not sure if the man were here to help her or simply take the bandits' prize away from them. It was a strange thing; while part of her despised the stranger for staring at her in such a manner, another part did not.

During his inspection of her, she saw his eyes pause at the dagger in her side and then the crossbow bolt protruding from her leg. His eyes finally returned to hers and lingered there a moment. "Are you all right?"

"I will live!" she answered a little more tersely than she would have liked. She was in shock, both from her wounds and from having been swept from a sure end to her life, and she was having a difficult time regaining her mental footing.

"I am not a healer, but I do have some limited experience in such matters," the stranger offered.

"No," Shantira replied as she moved back toward the tree where the sword lay. She wanted to be closer to the weapon should the need arise and to put some distance between herself and the man.

"Are you certain? I will be more than happy to aid you in any way I can," he repeated.

There was too much happening at once. The pain of her wounds continued to rake at her like fiery nails, her nerves were rattled, and she found she could not stop trembling. There were other emotions and sensations she couldn't understand, and the close proximity of the stranger was not helping those either. She needed time to sort through what had just happened, and what had almost happened.

She spun around to fix the stranger with a heated glare. "I said I would be fine! I have no need of your assistance. Your motives are probably of no more pure intent than those of the raiders before you!" Shantira shot back, fighting down a wave of dizziness.

Why was she being so short with the stranger? He had just saved her life and was offering to help her, yet she was angry and could find no way to contain her anger.

His only response was to arch his right eyebrow again and regard her with a curious expression. If her words had offended him, he gave no indication of it. He simply turned and raised his thumb and forefinger to his lips.

A shrill whistle cut through the clearing and echoed off through the woods. Within seconds, Shantira could hear the pounding of hooves and the crash of something large coming through the brush.

A great black Friesian exploded into the clearing and galloped up to the stranger. The creature was magnificent, and Shantira found herself admiring the beauty of the animal. He stood an easy 15 hands tall with a lean yet muscular frame. His mane was long and thick, hanging in loose curls to his chest. The tail was equally thick with long loose curls hanging almost to the ground. The abundantly long hair of his legs reached from the middle of the leg, completely obscuring his hooves.

The Friesian carried his head high, and his face was quite expressive, as was customary for the breed. He was a proud animal, and she somehow knew that the black-clad man did not own the horse, but rather theirs was a partnership.

Friesian's were usually used to pull carriages or for light agricultural work, but the stranger had obviously seen the majestic beauty of the animal as a saddle mount. The creature moved with a fluid grace that matched the grace of her benefactor. Each step the animal took was sure, and his muscles rippled smoothly beneath his black coat.

In the distance, she suddenly heard what sounded like a large number of people moving through the woods toward her. No doubt, it was a search party from her village, and the sound was a welcome one to her. It meant that the two remaining marauders had been dealt with, and her village was safe.

The stranger paused in the act of gathering the reins and tilted his head in the direction of the sound. With a barely perceptible nod, he reached up to grip the pommel of the saddle.

"Wait!"

The mysterious man had paused for only a heartbeat before releasing the pommel and turning to face her, the question clear in his features.

"What is your name?" she asked, trying to control the tremble both in her limbs and in her voice.

The mischief she had seen in his eyes earlier returned in full force, but it was different, almost seductive. With even strides, he began walking toward her, and she felt herself begin to tense. A sudden knot formed deep in her chest, and her stomach fluttered as though it were suddenly full of butterflies. She tightened her grip on the dagger and tried to raise it to the ready in a form of warning. To her shock, the weapon remained at her side. She felt her eyes grow wide as the stranger approached.

She wanted to stoop down and pick up the sword, but doing so would mean releasing the torn front of her dress and exposing herself to the stranger. He'd already seen more of her than she liked. Looking deep into his eyes, she tried to discern what his true intentions were. She, instead, found herself almost mesmerized by the odd color and rich warmth that radiated from them. She was amazed at the seductive way they remained locked tight to hers, never wavering.

With a hard swallow, she tried to wet her suddenly dry throat and realized how short her breath was. Her mind swam from the dizziness of her wounds and the strange eyes. How could this perfect stranger paralyze her limbs with nothing but a gaze? What was it about him that caused her heart to beat faster and her stomach to suddenly seem empty?

He stopped very close to her. She pressed herself further against the tree as he leaned down, bringing his face very close to hers. She tried to shrink back away from him, but found her path blocked by the tree.

His face was so close that she feared he would actually kiss her. Without her will, her eyes darted down to his thick lips before being pulled back to his eyes. His breath was warm on her face, and she found herself almost holding her breath as a strange duality suddenly tore through her. Part of her wanted to attack the man, force him back. Another part, a part she hadn't known existed within her, wanted to beg him to kiss her.

His eyes looked deeply into hers, not searching, simply looking. She saw his eyes drop slowly down her face to her trembling lips, pause there a moment, and then return to her eyes. She wondered how she was managing to remain on her feet given how badly her knees were trembling. Were her wounds that serious? Had the shock of her ordeal finally settled in? Or was it something else?

"If my deeds are unworthy of your notice," his deep voice drifted softly around her, almost as a blanket, "I feel my name would be equally so."

He held his intense gaze for a moment or two more. Then, without warning, he smiled, stepped back, turned, and began walking back to his mount. Shantira wanted nothing more than to sink to her knees, but she willed herself to remain standing. She had already shown this confident man more than she had cared to.

Without hesitation, the man swung himself up into the saddle, took up the reins, turned the animal, and buried his heels deep into the Friesian's flanks. With a grunted snort, the massive steed bolted from the clearing and into the woods. Shantira listened until the pounding of the hooves faded, and then could be heard no more.

She silently cursed herself for being so short with the stranger. She should not have been so quick to assume that his intentions had been anything but pure. She felt another wave of dizzying weakness sweep over her and let herself sink slowly to the ground to lean back against the giant oak tree. The sounds of the approaching search party eased some of her fears for she knew she could never make it back to the village on her own. She felt as weak as a newborn, and she knew it was past time for her wounds to be tended.

She leaned back against the tree and closed her eyes. The whimpering raider, and the sounds and shouts of the approaching villagers, only dimly registered on her mind as she considered the stranger, his actions, and with a touch of shame, her own. She wondered if she would ever see the handsome stranger again.

As her mind teetered on the edge of unconsciousness, a thought swam up... she sorely wished to thank him for his help.

CHAPTER TWO

SHANTIRA'S VILLAGE WAS ONE of the few fortunate enough to have a gifted healer, and he was very effective in helping heal her wounds. Her youth and inner strength played no small part in helping her regain her strength much sooner than many thought possible.

Once she was back on her feet, Shantira busied herself by helping to put her village back together. She took her turn at nursing the wounded, clearing debris, aiding in the repairs of homes, and trying to get life back to some semblance of normalcy. The hardest task before her was mourning the dead. Fortunately, there had not been many to mourn, but to Shantira, one life lost was too many. All things considered, her village had been very lucky. The damage and loss of life could have been much worse.

After three weeks, there was no trace of the raid left. The dead bandits were rounded up and buried in unmarked graves far out in the wilderness. Of course, the graves weren't very deep and, no doubt, all types of scavengers had discovered the villager's gift, and feasted well.

The only surviving bandit was taken back to the village and treated by the healer before the constable from Kahala came to take him to stand before a Tribunal for his crimes. Unfortunately, for him, since he was the lone surviving raider, he would endure the brunt of justice for the raid.

After three weeks of work, Shantira was weary and in need of a respite. She did not shirk her responsibilities to her village, but she also could not shirk her responsibility to herself. She needed one evening of fun and revelry, a release from the grueling task of putting the raid in the past.

Fresh from a bath, Shantira padded into her tiny room and paused before the full-length mirror against one wall. She removed her smock and took a moment to regard her reflection. It was the only vanity she allowed herself, but she took great pride in her appearance. Fortunately, she noted, the dagger and crossbow bolt scars would not be too unsightly, another tribute to the healer. Life in her village was very hard. The days of manual labor, and her battle practice, had toned her body to near lean perfection.

Her thick dark brown hair hung in loose ringlets to her shoulders and down her back to just between her shoulder blades. Her skin was tan from hours of toiling under the sun, her hands were heavily calloused from years of manual labor, and yet her skin was still soft and supple, a lingering advantage of her youth. It was an advantage the older women of the village warned her to enjoy for it would all too soon be gone.

She turned slightly to study her reflection in more detail. There were parts of her body that she had previously given very little thought. It was only in the past few seasons that she'd became aware of her breasts, and she wasn't entirely comfortable with them. They were full and stood straight out from her chest, another trait that the older women warned her that would soon pass with age and the inevitable effects of gravity. They weren't overly large, but they seemed to always be in the way. She had also noticed that the men of the village were constantly fixated on them, their lust-filled gazes irritating her. She found it increasingly annoying how men always seemed to be talking to her breasts for their eyes hardly left them. As the seasons had passed and her breast had grown larger, she had begun dressing in more loose fitting clothing, so as to hide them.

A shiver of revulsion rippled through her at the memory of the bandit leader's hands upon them. She squeezed her eyes shut against the onslaught of nightmarish images that flooded her mind from that day. In her mind, as had occurred in her nightmares, there had been no handsome stranger to save her. No one had intervened, and no one had stopped the bandits from raping her repeatedly. Using her body for every perverted sexual act their sordid minds could conjure.

She convulsed with the images and shook her head, trying desperately to clear the images from her mind. She had never known the touch of a man, and she was very grateful that an act she truly didn't fully understand wasn't at the hands of brute savages like the raiders. Drawing in a deep breath, she opened her eyes and forced herself to think of something else, anything else.

As had been the case over the past weeks, the handsome stranger was the first subject her mind chose to use to distract it. His casual air, the mischievous light in his eyes, the way he moved with such assuredness as if he knew the outcome of every action long before he took it.

As she gazed at herself in the mirror, her mind showed her the way he had walked up to her so brashly, so sure that he could do absolutely anything he wished, and she would be powerless to stop him. With such arrogance, he had lowered his face to hers, nearly kissing her. She slowly closed her eyes and could almost feel his warm breath on her face, and she felt an unfamiliar desire form deep within her body.

That was another new sensation that had come from that day. There were feelings and sensations associated with the stranger that she could not name, could not understand. The way her thighs would tremble, the feeling of a tight knot down deep in her belly, or the swarm of butterflies that swirled throughout her stomach. What was it about this man that conjured such things within her?

She had felt these feelings faintly before, when one of the young men of the village worked without his shirt on, or a particularly handsome man paid her some attention. She would feel physical reactions that made her want to do things she had been taught were evil. She had urges that she resisted valiantly, and until she had met the stranger, she had managed to ignore the temptation. But he stirred these things within her with an intensity that left her breathless, speechless, and unable to stop herself.

She shook her head to clear her mind and returned to her self-examination. The swell of her breasts gave way to a hard, flat stomach. The swell of her hips rounded into long legs with just enough rippling muscle to be attractive. At just over five feet nine inches tall, her body was sturdy, strong, and despite her best efforts to hide it, definitely feminine.

Feminine.

With a slight smile, she recalled the disdain the village elders had expressed with her lack of proper femininity. While most of the women her age were taking husbands and having babies, she spent her time honing fighting skills. There had been suitors in recent seasons, and she had skillfully avoided the subject of marriage. She did not know what her destiny would be, but she knew her path did not lie in the same direction as the one her friends were choosing.

On more than one occasion the village elders, or some of the older women, had taken her aside and tried to show her the folly of her ways. By practicing skills studied by the men, she would soon lose her appeal as a prospective mate. A woman's place should be in the home, supporting her husband and raising her children. On each occasion, she would respectfully and politely tell them that what she chose to do with her life was her business and concern.

After a time, they all seemed to realize that she was going to do as she pleased and simply left her to her own devices. The fact that

Shantira never shied away from any task, regardless of how hard or unpleasant, helped them accept her choices. She sensed a grudging respect from many of the village citizens and more than a touch of envy from many of the women.

Shantira slipped into a pair of tan breeches, followed by a loose white blouse, and black boots over the legs of her breeches. She reached up to tie the laces of the neckline of the blouse, and at the last minute, gave herself a naughty grin and left the neckline untied. She was feeling reckless this evening, a part of her wanting to gain as much freedom as she could, sensing a dropping of her guard.

As a final touch, she retrieved her dagger and slid it into the sheath on the inside of her right boot.

She glanced at the sword belt hanging from a hook above her cot and briefly considered wearing it tonight. She tucked in the lower corner of her bottom lip and chewed on it absently as she considered it. A look at her reflection convinced her that it would do little good to leave her neckline open to invite prospective male attention and then offset that with a sword swung low on her hip.

She reached up and ran her fingers through the thick ringlets of still damp, dark brown hair, trying to arrange it in something that didn't look like she had just crawled out of her grave.

After several moments, her hair finally cooperated a little bit. She turned her head to one side and then another. She wondered if the stranger would find her attractive now that she wasn't bleeding and covered with the blood of the bandits.

She frowned.

Why had that thought come to her mind? Why should she care what the nameless stranger thought of her? What was it about him that made it so easy for him to haunt her thoughts like this? Tonight, she vowed, she would not give the stranger a second thought. She was going to be with friends and have a merry evening.

Giving herself a small wink, she smiled and quickly took up her cloak on her way out the door.

She stepped out into the cool night air and made her way toward the side of her hut where one of the village mounts waited. She felt her hands tremble with anticipation of the night of revelry that lie ahead. She needed this. It was long overdue.

"And just where do you think you are going, young lady?" came a stern voice from behind her.

She suppressed a smile as she turned to see the elderly woman who stood with her arms folded across her chest and the harshest expression in the realm on her face. The torches that provided lighting at night only served to cast some of her aged features in shadows and making it even more severe than normal.

"To The Tavern, Auntie Lucinda," she replied gleefully.

"Off to carouse with the truly wicked of the realm, I see!" Lucinda scoffed.

Shantira's lips twitched as she resisted the urge to smile. "Were you not the one who taught me that creatures of the same breed run together?"

The old woman's eyes sparked, but not with anger. A suppressed smile spread across her ancient features. "And to think, all of these seasons I felt as if my lessons were falling upon deaf ears."

"Not deaf, Auntie. Merely inattentive on occasion." Shantira returned the old woman's smile.

Lucinda was the closest thing to a mother Shantira had known since the death of her own mother when she was very young. Lucinda had seemed incredibly old to her, and it was amazing how little the woman had changed in her twenty seasons.

With the passage of time, Shantira's memories of her mother and father were faint and growing fainter. She clung to the hazy images desperately, but as more time passed, the images grew dimmer.

She had once expressed her concern about this to Lucinda. The old woman had smiled softly. "*Child, they live here,*" she said as she tapped the center of Shantira's chest before reaching up to place her wrinkled hand at her temple. "*Not here. No amount of time can erase their memories from your heart. Your mental images of them may fade, but the love they had for you, and you for them, will continue for as long as your heart beats.*"

As she gazed upon the older woman, Shantira's mind traveled back to fond memories of Lucinda teaching her many things about the land, her heritage, and the history of her small village. Lucinda had also tried to teach the lessons about being an independent person and a strong, yet sensitive woman. The latter was a difficult lesson in a world where those two concepts seldom went together. Other memories surfaced, such as the many long walks the two of them had taken through the woods, and the very long talks they had shared when some new element of life had sprung up to confuse and frighten her.

"Inattentive on occasion?" Lucinda laced her voice with doubt.

"I was not that bad a student, Auntie," Shantira said in defense.

"Such is your view. Fortunately, I am not cursed with the ability to change my past to suit my conscience," Lucinda replied with humor.

Shantira chuckled as she realized that perhaps Lucinda did have a better view of the past and that it was entirely possible that she was altering her own memories in order to make herself feel better about it.

"Perhaps I was a tad difficult at times," Shantira finally admitted.

"*At times?*" Lucinda exclaimed incredulously.

Both women broke into laughter. It was an easy laughter, born of seasons of camaraderie and warm affection.

"Perhaps you wish to see the stranger who came to your aid?" Lucinda asked, softening her tone ever so slightly and jarring Shantira from her memories.

Shantira blushed as she dropped her eyes to the ground, tracing a small pattern in the dirt with the toe of her boot. "I do not even know his name. I had never seen him before and I seriously doubt I ever will again."

Lucinda reached out and cupped Shantira's chin, gently lifting it, forcing her to raise her face. "Do not ever hide such a beautiful face. The realm can be such an ugly place. It needs reminders of beauty such as the one you provide."

"Yes, ma'am," Shantira whispered in reply, the blush of her cheeks going into deeper shades of red.

"Besides," she said, her cranky disposition returning as she released Shantira's chin. "If this man has any sense about him at all, he will seek you out!" She paused and then shook her head. "Then again, a man with sense would be a rarity, indeed!"

Shantira laughed.

"Go on, child! I have chores to tend to, and I have little desire to be up to all hours of the night because I wasted precious time bantering with you!" Again, there was sternness, albeit good-natured, in her voice. Shantira stepped forward quickly and hugged the old woman.

"Please, be careful, child," Lucinda whispered into Shantira's ear.

"I will, Auntie. I will." Shantira released Lucinda and quickly mounted the horse. It was actually property of the whole village and was used primarily for agriculture or pulling wagons. The Council frowned on villagers using one of the four horses for personal use, but again, not every villager had Lucinda in their corner.

She had to ride the animal bare back for a saddle was a luxury the small village could ill afford. Taking up the reins, she used her knees to guide the mount out into the main lane and then off into the darkness.

Lucinda watched her fade into the darkness. Only when she was certain that the young woman was well out of sight, did she allow a warm smile to crease her face. With a soft chuckle, she shook her head and turned to finish her chores for the day before turning in.

"My little girl is growing up," she whispered softly.

~*~

It took nearly an hour to reach the city of Kahala. The trail from her village to the city was dark, lit only by the full moon overhead. The night air was cool and crisp, filled with the scents of pine, earth and a myriad collection of wild flowers. A faint breeze whispered through the trees and rustled her hair. She closed her eyes and breathed deep, letting the clean night air clear her senses.

In stark contrast, the streets of Kahala were lit by numerous torches scattered all along the main thoroughfare. She slowed her mount to a slow walk as she took in the sights and sounds.

It took another quarter hour for her to traverse the width of the city to the forest on the other side. Just before entering the forest, Shantira glanced up into the black sky and was delighted to find the swollen orb of a full moon had just begun its assent into the sky; the night was still young. By the time they reached The Tavern, the evening's festivities would be in full swing.

Perfect, she thought.

Once she settled onto the well-worn path through the forest, she knew her destination was close, and she felt her pulse quicken.

Following a frequently travelled path through the dense forest, she rode for nearly half an hour. Long before she reached the large clearing where The Tavern was located, she could hear music and see the glow of many lanterns.

Very soon, she rode into a massive clearing, which served as home to The Tavern. The building sat on a hill with rolling land down to the base of the clearing, which held a modest lake.

It may have seemed odd to put a tavern way out in the middle of nowhere, but this was the least of the oddities and mysteries surrounding The Tavern.

Shantira let her eyes dance fondly over the building and could already feel the sense of peace and the release begin to gather about her.

As she entered the large clearing, she pulled up rein next to the lake. The surface was as smooth as glass and reflected the light from the stars and moon overhead. Serenity surrounded the lake, and Shantira felt the urge to simply spend the evening on its banks, soaking in the peacefulness.

She shifted her gaze from the lake to the couples and lovers strolling along its edges. They held hands or had arms draped about each other, and she had always wondered at the strange way they seemed oblivious to everything around them. Was that love? Was that what it was like to be so enthralled with someone that nothing else seemed to matter?

In recent seasons, she had begun to feel differently about the vast mystery of love. Thoughts that only a short time ago had seemed alien and unimportant now vied for her attention with an intensity that surprised her. Once, she had snickered at these lovers and made jokes about their behavior. Lately, though, she found herself enthralled, fascinated by whatever unexplainable thing it was that drew a man and woman together in this way.

She wondered at her changing responses. The village boys always pursued her, and she had no interest in returning their vulgar attention. But suddenly, she found herself pondering the mystery of love with a new, but frightening interest.

The lovers were no longer a source of amusement. They were an enigma that caused her to lie awake in bed each night, her mind wondering what it would be like to have a lover to walk alongside her around the lake.

She had heard the older women speaking of such things, of the ways a man could bring pleasures of the heart and of the body. Both feelings were unknown to her, and she desperately wanted to experience them.

Then, as he had so often done in recent weeks, the stranger came to mind. Within her memories, she clearly saw the way he had smiled at her that day. She tried to shut out his image and the odd sensations that accompanied his memory. She did not even know his name. So, why should his memory haunt her? She shook her head and resigned herself to the knowledge that she would probably never see him again. Curiously, the thought of seeing him once more was soothing yet left her disquieted. Shantira shrugged off the memory and forced her eyes to the massive building beyond the lake.

The Tavern was a large two-story building that had been here for a very long time. None could remember exactly when it had opened its doors for business or what had been in its place before that time. It was known for miles around, and on any given night, the place was sure to be full of customers. Some of the more superstitious people thought that perhaps some mystical force had created the place to cover evil magic. Shantira was not one of them. True, many odd things had happened in The Tavern, but not so odd that Shantira would attribute them to something evil. The place had an atmosphere all to itself and Shantira accepted it's oddities with gratitude. On more than one occasion, it had eased many disturbances in her soul. This was a place she had come to release her inner fears, doubts, and qualms with ease.

She smiled as she nudged her mount onward. She rode up the well-worn path from the lake to the side of the building where many horses and carriages were parked. As she dismounted and tied her horse to the rail, she could see that business was good.

As she rounded the corner of the building, heading for the front door, Shantira let her gaze rise to the balcony where the soft yellow glow of lantern light spilled out into the night. The balcony was large, extending out from the second floor, and thereby providing an awning for the main entrance. Several couples could be seen leaning on the rail, and either gazing into each other's eyes or out into the night. She smiled, for she knew that if there were any magic at work within these walls, it was the magic of romance.

As soon as she crossed the threshold, she felt the sense of ease and peace she had sought settle over her like a warm cloak on a cold day.

The tension eased, and the troubles of her life faded away. As she entered The Tavern, she smiled at the throng of people inside. It never ceased to amaze her how the place always seemed able to accommodate many more people than were present.

People moved back and forth. Some were merely navigating from one side of the room to the other, either searching for a companion to last the evening, or reestablishing an old acquaintance.

Couples occupied the dance floor in the center of the room dancing to music from skilled minstrels situated on a bandstand to the left of the dance floor.

Tables and chairs were scattered around the dance floor, while booths lined the walls. Small candles occupied each table while oil lanterns were placed along the walls to provide a subdued lighting.

Through the throng of people, Shantira spotted the bar as it covered the entire back wall of The Tavern, and was well serviced by tenders along its length. To the left of the bar was a staircase leading to the second floor. Just beyond the staircase was a massive rock fireplace complete with a mahogany mantle. As always, a fire crackled in the fireplace. She couldn't recall a time that a very warm, inviting fire wasn't present.

Shantira took in a long breath as the sights, sounds, and smells of The Tavern continued to ease the burdens she had come here to displace. A feeling of peace descended upon her, and she felt like she had come home from a long journey.

Glancing upward, she could see most of the second floor. A series of rooms ringed the second floor save for the massive balcony. A handrail circled the ring of rooms and allowed someone from the second floor to gaze down onto the happenings of the first floor.

"Shantira?" a voice called from her left. She looked into the mass of people gathered there and began searching for the owner of the voice. Within moments, a man emerged from the crowd and advanced toward her, smiling.

"Luke!" she shouted in delight and rushed to greet him. They embraced for several moments, each enjoying the warm feeling of friendship. As they pulled away, he took her hands in his and smiled even broader than before.

"Shantira, how have you been? We have not seen you in a very long time."

"I have been very busy. My village was attacked by raiders, and we have all been busy cleaning up." Shantira spoke lightly, not wanting to let the memories ruin what was promising to be a wonderful night.

Luke's features darkened in concern and regret. "A raid? How bad was it?"

"There were a dozen of them, but the damage and loss of life were blessedly light."

"I am sorry, child. I had not heard of the raid."

"The raid failed, and only seven of our people were killed." Shantira did not want to talk about this, not now.

Luke nodded, staying silent for a moment in tribute to those who had died.

"Where is Rosalyn?" she asked.

Luke smiled. "Where else would she be?"

"Of course. Will you excuse me?" she asked.

Luke nodded. "Only if I have the promise of a dance later."

Shantira reached out and squeezed one of his hands. "Of course."

As she began working her way through the crowd, she noticed that to her far left, along the sidewall of the building, the tables and booths had been removed to make way for a huge table. Across this table was a massive feast.

On occasion, The Tavern would host a hearty feast as a way to thank the community and those who supported The Tavern. The sights and smells of roasted meats and steamed vegetables made Shantira's stomach growl. There was more food on that table in one night than her entire village would see in a season. Such extravagances always amazed her. She could not imagine that much food existed in the entire realm, let alone Prothtow Province.

She had not known a feast would be held this night, but that didn't make her any less thankful for her excellent timing. Her stomach was demanding that she make her way to the large serving table immediately. While she promised her empty stomach a proper feeding, she had someone else she had to see first.

As she weaved through the crowd, several familiar faces offered her warm greetings which she gladly accepted, and returned with every ounce of warmth they had been delivered. There was a sense of extended family with the regulars of The Tavern.

Once she reached the bar, it did not take long to spot Roslyn. She was laughing and chatting with bar patrons as she served up drink after drink, appearing to know what a particular person would want before they spoke their request. Gold coins passed from one side of the bar to the other as quickly as the drinks made the reverse trip. Roslyn kept up a jovial conversation with one customer while she served several others, never missing a word of her conversation, a drink order, or the payment. Shantira knew the demands on her concentration must be great, but Roslyn handled them with an ease that had become second nature.

"Roslyn!" Shantira shouted over the din of the crowd. For a moment, Roslyn gave no indication that she had heard her name called, and then her laughing eyes turned down the bar and locked onto Shantira. With an even wider smile, she stepped from behind the bar and crossed to the younger woman, embracing her warmly.

"Shantira! My lords, it is good to see you! Where have you been keeping yourself?"

Shantira held the hug for a long moment, gathering strength from the older woman.

"Our village was attacked by raiders. I have been busy cleaning up in the aftermath."

Roslyn's handsome features took on a rare moment of sadness as she looked down at the floor for a moment.

"I know, I heard. My sorrow is with you and those who lost loved ones. I also hear that you were wounded while defending your village. I trust you have recovered?"

Shantira was always amazed at how Roslyn seemed to be up on the latest news from around the countryside. It was said that if it were worth knowing, she knew it.

Roslyn was well into her fiftieth season, but her face still beamed with the wonder of youth. While the passing of the seasons had taken the taut youthfulness from her face, time had not removed her beauty. She was a beautiful woman, probably more so now than when she had been Shantira's age.

Roslyn's red hair, which in her youth had been a bright crimson, had faded into softer, subtler shades. Only the very light shade of red at her temples told of the approach of gray. Roslyn wore it piled upon her head in a very neat, very sensible fashion. Shantira often wondered how long her hair would be if she ever released it from the multitude of clips that held it rigidly in place.

She wore a midnight blue gown with a neckline that took a tasteful plunge. The gown was as practical as it was stylish. It was not to flaunt her wealth, of which there was rumored to be plenty, but to allow her to look elegant while carrying out the myriad of tasks she had to perform on a nightly basis.

"It was a near thing. I had drawn six of the raiders away from the village and had hoped to circle back to aid in the villages' defense, but I was caught off guard and captured by them. Had it not been for the intervention of a stranger, I would have surely died in the attack." Shantira tried not to let any of her inner feelings for the stranger surface.

Roslyn, though, was not only wise but also attentive, and caught the slight shift of Shantira's voice when she mentioned the stranger. "A stranger? He must have been a rare and unique stranger."

"What makes you say this?" she asked, trying valiantly to hide her feelings.

Roslyn fixed Shantira with a knowing smile. "Come now, child. Do not forget whom you are talking to… This stranger must have made quite an impact upon you."

Shantira allowed herself to smile shyly as she realized that there would be no deceiving Roslyn. "He was impressive."

"Indeed? Does this impressive stranger have a name?"

"I did not get his name." Shantira remembered how rudely she had dealt with the stranger after the attack.

"Why not?"

"I fear I was not myself. I had been wounded and was, I believe, in shock. He offered to help with my wounds, and I accused him of having less than pure intentions," Shantira answered with guilt.

Roslyn laughed softly before hugging Shantira again. "You poor girl. You really must learn to contain that temper of yours. Perhaps you will meet him again, and the Fates will allow you the chance to correct your earlier mistake."

Shantira sighed and smiled sadly. "I doubt it. I have never seen this man before."

"Roslyn! I need more ale!" a deep voice thundered from down the bar. Roslyn broke the embrace and looked over her shoulder at a rather large man, a warrior by his garb and attitude, and smiled sternly.

"Do NOT shout orders at me, Zandorth Krahl! You have already had more than your share of ale for this eve!"

The threat of having his supply of ale cut off seemed to have had the desired effect. The large man shook his head. "I was not shouting. I was simply making sure you could hear me over the racket of the crowd." While his face still held the harsh scowl of a moment ago, his words were considerably softer in tone and edge.

Rosalyn hid her smile and nodded. "Let me assure you my hearing is fine. I will be there in a moment." Zandorth gave a single curt nod before turning back to lean on the bar.

Because of her vast life experiences, her impressive will to succeed, or just a simple thirst for it, Rosalyn commanded respect from everyone who entered The Tavern.

"Excuse me, child. I must get back to work. Will you be here long?"

"All evening," she replied warmly.

"Good. Perhaps you and I can talk later." Roslyn hugged Shantira again and made her way back behind the bar, immediately resuming her endless tasks.

Shantira watched her for a handful of seconds before turning her attention to the massive gathering of people. She saw many faces she knew and many more that she did not. There were the regulars that always frequented The Tavern, and there was a constant flow of faces that were new.

Having seen and briefly talked to Rosalyn, Shantira turned her attention to the serving table. Her stomach rumbled again, and she knew it would not be denied much longer. Weaving through the crowd, she took up her place in the line of people waiting to get food.

At the head of the table, she found several stacks of wooden plates and a small pyramid of rolled napkins. Smiling warmly at one of The Tavern workers who stood ready to aid any guest, Shantira took up a plate and a napkin before beginning to work her way down the table.

First was a large plate with the remnants of a roasted pig upon it. Not much remained of the animal. Shantira wasted no time in using the large fork and knife, cutting out several hunks of meat from the carcass, and hefting them to her plate. Any kind of meat was a delicacy to her village. On occasion, during one of her village's festivals, a couple of pigs would be slaughtered for the feast, but the daily diet of her village was devoid of any type of meat. Hunting was banned in the forest of the kingdom. Anyone caught killing a wild animal was subject to harsh punishments as handed down from the King.

Of course, hunting occurred, and such ill-gotten gains were enjoyed by the entire village. It was a strange thing how the memory of the meat or where it had come from vanished as soon as the meal did. But such things were a rarity for one never knew when a King's patrol would be active.

Next to the pig was a large plate of smoked beef. Beef was even rarer than pork, and she took a healthy portion of it, as well. Smaller plates of fruits, raw vegetables, steamed vegetables, along with dates and nuts serving as both decoration and food. Shantira helped herself to healthy servings of each.

Next was a large rack with several loaves of freshly baked bread. Some of it was still warm, and the aroma only served to enrage her hunger. Forgetting some of the manners Auntie Lucinda had taught her, Shantira tore off two larges hunks of bread to add to her already loaded plate.

Shantira paused as she considered the massive amount of food on her plate. There was more food on this one plate than most of her neighbors saw in months. A twinge of quilt came over her as she thought of her neighbors settling down for the evening meal with a small bowl of pottage, a few vegetables from the village's fields, and if they were lucky, a stale chunk of bread.

Pottage was the staple food for her village and just about every other village in the realm. The people of the realm were exceedingly poor. They toiled at the fields to sell their crops at market. They would raise animals, but they were used for tilling the fields, or for milk, or for sale at market. Very little of what her village produced went to the village. Almost everything went to market for sale, the profits used to buy what few supplies they could not produce themselves, and to purchase more seeds and plants to replant the fields for the next harvest.

Pottage was a thick soup made by boiling vegetables, grains, and if available, meat or fish. Generally, there was a large cooking fire kept going in the center of the village. A large pot was suspended over the fire, and the ingredients were boiled for several hours until the entire mixture took on a homogeneous texture and flavor. When possible, loaves of bread were set out next to the pot, and that would comprise the meals they ate—day after day, season after season. As people came and took portions from the pot, more ingredients would be added making the meals slightly different. Her village also grew several grains such as barley, oats, and rye, which they would sell at market and use to bake breads.

On rare occasions, if a particular harvest was very profitable, her village would purchase hops and honey, both of which were quite expensive, and make mead. Mead was made by fermenting honey, water, and hops, which produced an alcoholic brew that was very enjoyable, and a delicacy in its own right.

At the end of the table was a large barrel of Mead with a spigot in it. Wooden goblets were lined up, and ready for use. Shantira took up a goblet, and filled it with mead. Shantira had tasted The TavernThe Tavern's mead before, and it was far superior to the brew her village produced.

At the very end of the table was a wooden box with a slot cut into the lid. This box was to collect any donations people wished to make. Again, she felt a pang of quilt for she had no money to give and a quick glance at her plate, and then at the long serving table, only sharpened the fact in her mind that a feast such as this one was very expensive.

Shantira looked up at the young woman tending to the donation box and other tasks associated with serving guests. She smiled warmly at Shantira in greeting.

"My apologies," Shantira said. "I have nothing to donate."

The young woman smiled wider. "Think nothing of it, Shantira. You have helped The Tavern many times over. Rosalyn would be angered if you tried to donate."

Shantira smiled her thanks to the woman and set about finding a place to sit and enjoy her meal. Suddenly the crowd parted near the dance floor, and she caught a glimpse of a welcome face, as welcome as Roslyn's face was to see. With a broad smile, she began working her way through the crowd toward the woman.

When she broke through the crowd to the tables, she found the woman sitting at a table by herself, writing in a journal.

Occasionally, without looking up from her writing, she would reach out and take her wine glass, sip from it, then return it to the table and resume her writing.

Shantira walked up to the table and smiled down at the woman. "I see that some things never change. No matter what surrounds you, you are constantly writing in that journal. I believe the building could fall down around you, and you would never notice it."

The woman never stopped writing, never looked up, but a fond smile crossed her lips. "Do not confuse concentration for a lack of attention. I am aware of far more than you would think, Shantira."

Shantira smiled easily. "How are you, Brianna?"

The woman finally laid her quill aside and looked up, merriment in her eyes. "I am fine. I trust you are well after your ordeal?" The Lady Brianna Standish closed her journal and capped her ink well. She indicated the chair across from her. "Please. Sit and enjoy your meal."

It did not surprise Shantira that Brianna would have heard of the raid on her village. As the governing Lord of Prothtow Province, it was her job to know of such things.

"I am recovering. The wounds have nearly healed." Shantira eased out a chair and sat down. As always, she was taken with the beauty of Lady Brianna.

Although she did not know her exact age, Shantira guessed her to be in her late twenties, perhaps early thirties. She had a massive mane of black hair that flowed about her shoulders and down her back. Her features were delicate and very feminine, yet they suggested an incredible inner strength.

Brianna was notoriously more independent than Shantira thought herself to be. Brianna had also decided not to follow the customary path of most women. She had no husband, no children, and gave no indication that she ever would. Brianna was a woman who valued her privacy and would defend it fiercely. She would, on occasion, seek out male companionship, but those relationships would not last very long. It was one of Brianna's mysteries that had always puzzled Shantira.

Brianna Standish had the unenviable task of being a woman in a position traditionally held by men. Her father, Lord Trenton Standish, had served as the Lord of Prothtow for many seasons and had left an undeniable mark on the province as one of the greatest leaders in recent memory.

He had been a veteran of the Goblin Wars as well as serving as chief advisor of diplomatic affairs for King Lorderon. After many successful campaigns against the enemies of the kingdom, Trenton Standish had been named as Lord of Prothtow, the largest province in the kingdom.

It was a fitting office for a war veteran and a decorated defender of the kingdom. Lord Standish served the citizens of Prothtow with honor and dignity for many seasons before his death.

Upon his death, by the laws of the land, the office of Lord of the

Province fell to his eldest child. Since Brianna had been his only child, the office fell to her. She quickly became known as The Lady Brianna Standish.

Of course, there had been no end of the complaints and protests sent to Castle Nightwind, home of King Lorderon. Many people were indignant that a woman would hold such a high office. It was believed that a woman was incapable of governing much more than her husband's household and then, even that was under his direct supervision. Many of the other Lords of bordering provinces had petitioned King Lorderon to strip Brianna of her title and lands, and award them to any number of other suitable, and noticeably male, candidates.

King Lorderon had patiently listened to each case, each protest and then reiterated what had been laid down in the doctorates of the Kingdom many seasons ago. There was no stipulation in the doctorates that said a woman could not serve as Lord or, for that matter, Queen of the Kingdom. The law was the law, and the law clearly stated that upon a Lord's death, his office, lands and estate would pass to his first born child. There had never been any distinction that the first-born child had to be male.

However, to appease the protestors, he had degreed that should Brianna ever marry, the title of Lord, the authority of the office, and all lands associated with the title would transfer to her husband.

There was definitely no shortage of potential suitors for Lady Brianna. True, some were driven by the prospect of becoming the Lord of Prothtow and all the power and wealth such an office promised.

The fact that Brianna Standish was an incredibly beautiful woman only sweetened the potential pot. She stood five feet nine with thick black hair that shone with a youthful luster. Tonight, she wore it loose, hanging around her face and down her back.

Piercing green eyes flashed out, taking in everything seemingly at once. Brianna had the uncanny ability to look at someone, giving that person the impression that their innermost secrets had, somehow, been revealed to her. There was an eternal light of youthful wonder in her eyes, as though she could find the brightest point of the darkest situation.

She had high cheekbones with a slender nose that came to a slightly upturned point. The gentle curve of her nose gave way to thick, naturally red full lips that always seemed to be on the verge of a smile, even when she was angry. Her rich, supple skin was a bit pale, but shone with a youthful glow that made guessing her exact age difficult.

Tonight, she wore a dark green satin gown of exquisite tailoring. Of course the gown was custom made for her and fit her perfectly at every point. The shoulders of the gown hung off the points of her shoulders, and then the neckline plunged low, showing off her ample cleavage. The gown fit tightly about her trim waist before tightly following the well-rounded curve of her hips to flair out to the floor. A slit had been tailored into the gown to show most of her right leg if she so wished to show it.

Brianna was not a vain woman. She was completely comfortable with her body, and very aware of the effects she had on most men. It was a flirty game she enjoyed playing and was unmatched in her skill at it.

Shantira smiled her thanks and quickly sat down, attacking the plate of food with a ravenous hunger that she was not aware of until she caught the mildly amused expression on Brianna's face as she watched her eat.

With a slightly wolfish grin, Shantira wiped her mouth with the back of her hand. "My apologies," she muttered through a mouth full of food. "My manners have escaped me."

Brianna laughed softly. "Think nothing of it. It is a pleasure watching someone enjoying their food." A mischievous light flared in her eyes as her lips lifted in a playful smile. "I understand you encountered a stranger during the attack."

Shantira knew she should have been surprised by Brianna's knowledge of what had happened during the raid, but she wasn't. Her long association with Brianna had taught her that there was very little she did not know.

"Yes," she answered as she quickly chewed the mouthful of food and began swallowing it. "I fear, had he not intervened, I would not be here today," she answered before taking a deep drink from the goblet to wash down the last of the food. The stranger returned to her mind once more, along with a sudden tightness deep in her stomach. She realized too late that she had let her emotions betray her when she caught the growing smile at the corners of Brianna's mouth.

"Yes. He must have been quite a man, indeed, to have captured your thoughts in this way," Brianna suggested with a twinkle in her eye.

"I was merely grateful for his assistance!" Shantira replied quickly, trying to cover her lapse in control.

Brianna laughed merrily, her voice light and musical. She regarded Shantira with knowing eyes. "You may expect others to believe this, but please do not expect it of me."

Shantira blushed slightly as she realized no amount of control on her part would have kept Brianna from knowing just how deeply the stranger had affected her. Feeling a sense of trepidation, she lowered her voice.

"Brianna, he was unlike any man I have ever known before. His calm demeanor during the encounter assured me, yet his confidence unnerved me. As if he were merely passing the time of day with strangers instead of being faced with odds that could have easily meant his death. Even during the battle, he never showed fear or even concern. It was as if he knew from the beginning that he would win, and do so easily.

"His skill with a sword is breath taking. I would venture to say that I would be hard pressed to best him in a duel."

Brianna's eyebrows rose slightly at that. "Indeed? Impressive, to say the least. Your skills with a sword are not child's play."

She then relayed the events following the battle, those of when the black-clad man had arrogantly pressed his face so close to hers and reprimanded her for her rude behavior. He'd done so in a way that Shantira had not even realized was a reprimand until days later.

A strange smile touched Brianna's full lips, and her eyes took on a distant gaze, as if Shantira's story had reminded her of someone she had known.

"Girl! That is not the way to endear yourself to someone who has saved your life!" Brianna scolded with merriment in her voice after Shantira had finished her tale.

"Tell me! I have often wished for that moment back so that I could correct my mistake," Shantira replied.

"Perhaps you will have the chance."

"I doubt it. I have never seen him before, and I sorely doubt I will ever see him again."

"The Fates work in strange ways, Shantira. Do not be surprised if you see him again. My advice is to be a little less rigid should that opportunity arise again."

"I am not rigid!" Shantira defended herself.

"Come, child. You, once again forget whom you are speaking with. I have watched you struggle against the stifling constraints of what is expected of women in this realm, and you have done a valiant job of establishing your independence. But you still need to learn that you can be strong and independent, and still be a woman."

Shantira could not argue her point. She lowered her gaze to her half empty plate, wondering just when her hunger had faded. "It matters little. I sorely doubt I will ever see him again."

"Never say never," Brianna replied as she took up her wine glass and drained the remnants. As she sat the glass down, a bar maid appeared, quickly removing the empty glass, and placing a full one before her.

Shantira sighed heavily and cast a look about the room. That was when something at the door caught her eye. She looked at the double doors, but the sea of bodies made it impossible to see what it had been that had caught her attention.

"How goes the rebuilding?" Brianna asked, mercifully changing the subject.

"It is nearly completed. Fortunately, the attack caused minor damage. Our losses were blessedly light, compared to what they could have been. We should be fully..."

She had been studying the throng of people around the door, looking for what had initially caught her eye, while she spoke. Now her voice trailed off as she searched harder.

"What is it, Shantira?" Brianna's voice grew dim as if coming from far away.

Shantira did not answer as she scanned the crowd around the door, hoping for another glimpse of what had caught her eye. She was vaguely aware of Brianna's head turning to follow the direction of Shantira's gaze.

The crowd parted, and there he was. The stranger. He stood just inside the door of the tavern, searching through the mass of people. Despite her best efforts, she felt her breath catch in her throat, and her heart began to race. She silently cursed herself for allowing these reactions to surface, but she knew that they were beyond her ability to control.

"My lords! It is *him!*" she breathed.

CHAPTER THREE

SHANTIRA FELT AS IF SHE HAD suddenly been addled. Her eyes were wide, her jaw hanging slack, and her heart about to beat out of her chest. Her reaction to seeing him again was much stronger than she was prepared for.

He stood just inside the entrance, dressed just as he had been that day in the clearing. His rugged features looking even more handsome than she remembered. His blue-green eyes looked about the interior of The Tavern with what she now assumed was the ever present air of mysterious mischief in them.

Several people near the door quickly walked up to greet him. Most of which, Shantira realized with a sharp stab of jealousy, were women. Each greeting was returned with an incredibly warm smile and nod. He began working his way through the crowd, heading in the general direction of the stone fireplace on the opposite corner of the building.

"I should have known," Brianna said.

Shantira tore her gaze from the stranger to look at her friend. Brianna was just turning back to face forward in her chair as she reached for her wine glass. Her face was beaming with a broad smile, and the look in her eyes twisted on the pang of jealousy in Shantira's chest.

"Should have known what?" Shantira asked, wondering why her question had sounded more like a demand.

"That he would be your *stranger*," Brianna answered as she turned her head to watch him walk through the crowd. If Shantira's tone of voice had registered, she gave no indication of it. The look in her eyes bothered Shantira more with each passing moment.

"You know him?" she asked, more careful this time to keep the edge from her voice.

Brianna nodded absently as she continued to watch him. "As well as anyone could, I suppose." She took another sip of wine followed by a deep breath before turning back to face Shantira.

"His name is Daimion Devenshire," she finished.

"I have never seen him here before. How is it you know him?" Shantira asked, trying not to look at him and failing.

Brianna didn't try to hide her visual admiration of Devenshire as he crossed the room. "He has been coming here for nearly a season now. He does not frequent The Tavern as much as the rest of us. In fact, this is the first time I have seen him here in a number of weeks."

Shantira forced herself to turn back to face Brianna and instantly regretted it. That annoying expression on her face and in her eyes as she watched him seemed to be growing in intensity. She had seen Brianna look at men like that before and it usually meant one thing, and that one thing threatened to crush her heart.

"He is yours," she whispered, not wanting to give the thought access, but realizing she must. She knew she was no match for Brianna's seductive charms. No man had ever been able to resist Brianna once she set her sights on him.

Another way that Brianna Standish was different from any other woman in the realm was the way she conducted herself with men. She cast aside societies accepted guidelines of proper female behavior. She had been involved in numerous relationships with men through the seasons Shantira had known her. At the moment that the relationship gave even the slightest inkling of heading in the direction of marriage, Brianna would sever ties with the man completely.

Brianna was not the type of woman to dedicate herself to one man. She enjoyed the wide and varied choices the men of Prothtow Province provided too much to settle for just one. Whether Brianna could not love or simply chose not to love, Shantira did not know, but love was one emotion that Brianna resolutely refused to consider.

Along with enjoying the variety of men in Prothtow, Shantira knew there had been some great tragedy that had befallen Brianna in her youth. It was something that Brianna never spoke of, but Shantira had learned enough to know that whatever it was had made love something she would not commit to, ever. While Shantira had questioned her about this on several occasions, Brianna would smile a lovely, warm smile and gently side step the subject as only Brianna could.

There were many in the province that viewed Brianna's promiscuity with men in great disdain and condemnation. They felt no woman should behave like a common bar wench or whore, but especially the governing Lord of the land. To that group, men and women alike, the governing Lord should be above reproach, and the image she portrayed at Court was a reflection of them all.

Such issues were lost on Brianna. She cared not what anyone else thought of her. She lived her life on her terms and made no apologies. She was a very good Lord, and treated her people well. Far better than most of her male counterparts treated their subjects.

Shantira had often heard Brianna's response to the objections to her lifestyle choices... "*I am a woman. I like men. Little else needs consideration.*"

Brianna laughed. It was a light musical sound that came from a deep joy within her.

"No. He is not mine. I have no hold over Daimion. No one does," She answered fondly as her green eyes, once again, sought him out.

"But you are with him," Shantira replied, looking down into the half-eaten plate of food. The food was so much less appealing than it had been before.

Brianna shifted her gaze to Shantira and could see the conflict within her young friend. "Shantira?" she said softly.

Shantira looked up at her, the pain in her eyes more clear than any spoken word could relay.

"I have been with him, yes. But I am not his nor is he mine. You will not offend me in the least if you choose to pursue him."

Shantira's expression shifted into confusion. It was an expression Brianna was used to seeing when such topics came up. It was a strange concept for anyone to handle. It was a concept that the current society was unwilling and unable to accept.

"I do not wish to interfere in your relationship with him. If he is your chance at happiness, then..."

Brianna smiled warmly. "You proceed from the false assumption that I need a man in my life to make me happy. I find all the happiness I need in my life. I do not need anyone, especially a man, to make me happy."

Shantira studied Brianna intently and saw nothing but the heartfelt truth of what she was saying. It always puzzled her how someone could maintain such a tight hold on their emotions. As she accepted Brianna's statement as truth, another train of thought began to form.

Brianna watched the thought form, and the smile faded a little from her face. "I must warn you though. Enjoy his company. Take what he will offer you, but do not make the mistake of falling in love with him, and do not try to win his heart, for you will surely fail."

Shantira's expression shifted into confusion as she turned in her chair to look at him. "Why?"

Brianna looked over at Devenshire. He had eased down into one of the high backed chairs near the fireplace. As he cradled a snifter of brandy, he sat gazing deeply into the fire. Given how busy The Tavern was, Shantira was amazed that he had been served so quickly.

"Love is something he will not commit to; his heart is fiercely guarded and no one granted access," she replied.

Shantira could suddenly see why the two of them would connect.

"In fact, that is one of the stipulations of our relationship," Brianna added.

Shantira looked back over her shoulder at her. "What do you mean?"

Brianna smiled. It was her usual warm smile, but Shantira could have sworn she caught the tiniest hint of sadness in her eyes. "Our relationship continues on the basis that neither of us is allowed to fall in love with the other. The moment that line is crossed," Brianna shrugged, "the relationship is over."

Shantira looked deeper into her eyes, searching for that faint trace of sadness, but just as quickly as it had seemed to appear, it was gone, replaced with the eternal light of genuine joy that always shone from her eyes.

"That is cruel!" Shantira said, a hard edge forming in her voice as she turned her head back to cast a hard look at Devenshire. "What kind of cold-hearted man would force a woman into such a relationship?"

Brianna laughed. "It was not Daimion's idea. It was mine."

Shantira turned back to her friend with shock and disbelief in her face. "What? Why?"

"Daimion is the first man I have met that hasn't wanted more from me than I was willing to give. He cares not about my office or wealth, he does not want to own me by marrying me, he takes me as I am and asks for nothing more. Do you know how incredibly refreshing that is?" she looked briefly at Devenshire as she took up her wine glass and took a sip. She tilted her head to one side while she studied his profile, accented by the roaring fire within the fireplace.

A warm smile touched her lips as she returned her wine glass to the table. "My boundaries for the relationship are my way of making sure neither one of us does anything stupid and ruin what has become a very rewarding encounter."

Shantira turned back to watch Devenshire. She found herself wondering if she could be like Brianna. Could she indulge in the purely physical and keep the emotional separate? Could she ignore all the lessons she had been taught about how the sanctity of marriage was a union sanctified by the Fates, and any physical interaction between men and women had to take place within the boundaries of that union? Watching Devenshire and feeling the myriad reactions he stirred within her, she found that she could not honestly answer that question.

"Would you like to meet him? Properly, this time?" Brianna asked.

Shantira turned back in her chair to face Brianna, suddenly uncomfortable with the prospect. The memories of how she had repaid his kindness the last time not the least of the reasons for her discomfort.

"I do not know…" she said, taking up the wooden goblet.

Without warning, Brianna looked over at the fireplace. "Devenshire!" she shouted loudly.

"What are you doing?" she hissed.

Brianna shifted her eyes just briefly, giving Shantira a wry grin before shifting them back to Devenshire.

For a moment, it appeared that he had not heard her, but then he slowly swung his head around to look at her through the crowd. One eyebrow arched over the other one, and a grin parted his lips as he waited for her to speak.

"Come here! There is someone I wish for you to meet."

Devenshire rose smoothly to his feet and began working his way over to them. Shantira suddenly had the urge to crawl under the table, or better yet, jump out of the nearest window.

As he reached their table, he gave Brianna an obvious head to toe perusal with his eyes, not even trying to hide his thoughts.

"That is a lovely gown you are *almost* wearing, Brianna," he said with that ever-present edge of mystery and mischief.

Shantira felt her jaw drop open. Only a select small number of people referred to her with just her name. Etiquette demanded that she be addressed as Lady Standish, or at the very least, Lady Brianna. Not only did he show complete disregard for her office, he practically undressed her with his eyes making such a comment about her attire. She looked over at Brianna's honor guard and was amazed that they took no action. They watched him, but did not react to his behavior.

She shifted her gaze to Brianna and was stunned to see her actually blush slightly. She placed her right hand on her chest and took a moment to compose herself. She then fixed Devenshire with a playfully hard look.

"Bastard!"

One thick dark brow arched as his thick lips curled in a seductive smile. "You would have me no other way."

For a moment, they locked eyes and a silent message, known only to them, passed between them. Shantira felt that annoying stab of jealousy surface again.

"I would like for you to meet a dear friend of mine. Daimion Devenshire, this is Shantira Dubrie."

To her own amazement, Shantira was able to look up at him. She saw the flash of recognition in his eyes, and it pleased her. He smiled warmly and gently took her right hand in his.

"We have already met, albeit briefly, and without the aid of introductions. Shantira. What an enchanting name." Bending low he lightly kissed the back of her hand. She felt the temperature of The Tavern suddenly rise and a wave of something akin to dizziness pass over her.

He released her hand and stood upright again. "I trust you are recovering from your ordeal?"

She nodded as she reached out for the wooden goblet again, nearly knocking it over in her unsettled state. "Thanks to your timely intervention, Sire Devenshire."

Devenshire shook his head. "Please. I hold no title and am not worthy of being called 'Sire'. Call me Daimion or Devenshire…"

"…or bastard," Brianna injected playfully which drew an equally playful glare from him.

Shantira smiled. "Very well then… Daimion." She took a long drink of the mead in an attempt to settle her very rattled nerves.

"Please, join us," Brianna said, her hand indicating the empty chair. Devenshire eased the chair out and lowered himself into it.

Silence reigned for a moment, and to Shantira it felt crushingly uncomfortable. She had been given the opportunity she had sorely wished for, and now she couldn't find her voice.

"So, Devenshire, what mischief have you been into?" Brianna asked.

A faint smile tugged on the corners of his lips. "And what makes you suspect I have been into mischief?"

Brianna's musical laughter floated into the air. "I know you. If you are not involving yourself in the mischief of others, then you are out creating some of your own."

Devenshire chuckled before turning to Shantira. "I know not what she has been telling you about me, but rest assured, it is probably a lie," he said pleasantly.

"I would wager that the fair Lady Brianna speaks nothing but truth about a brigand such as you!" came a thundering voice from behind Shantira. She turned quickly to find the massive man who had shouted at Rosalyn earlier standing there, a hard angry glare fixed squarely on Devenshire.

The pleasantness slowly left Devenshire's face as he turned his head to fix the large man with a bored expression tinged with hardness.

"Mind your tongue and business, Krahl!" he warned.

Zandorth Krahl's cold gray eyes bore into Devenshire as his granite features showed nothing but anger.

Krahl stood an easy six foot five inches tall with thick brown hair flowing to his shoulders. The man was massive with a heavily muscled frame. His tan shirt was stretched tightly over the bunched muscles beneath it, the seams straining to contain them. A massive broadsword hung low on his left hip, the buckle of the sword belt adorned with the crest of the Warriors' of the Ancient Class. Shantira's eyebrows rose a little.

The Warriors of the Ancient Class were a noble group of men whose charter it was to defend the realm from all manners of evil. They were not appointed by the king or any other governing body. They had formed nearly one hundred seasons ago, and since their inception, had been the last line of defense against any and all who posed a threat to the realm. The tales of their heroism, bravery, and unbending sense of right and wrong, were legendary.

For a Warrior of the Ancient Class to be challenging Devenshire gave Shantira a moment of pause. Perhaps he wasn't the brave defender of virtue she had previously thought.

Krahl briefly regarded Shantira before shifting his hard glare back to Devenshire. "I see you have found yet another woman to drown in your empty charms!"

Yet another woman? Just how many had there been? Shantira wondered.

One eyebrow arched upward as a glint of humor flared in his deep eyes. "Empty charms are far preferable to no charms at all."

"Brave words from such a gutless man. Are you prepared to back them?"

Devenshire smiled. "You know that I am. Shall we make it the usual wager, or do you feel compelled to lose more gold to me than usual?"

Shantira was confused and quickly looked at Brianna. Her friend's poorly concealed smile of amusement told her that something out of the ordinary was about to happen.

"You are an arrogant bastard! Deep within my soul, I feel that tonight you will finally be bested.

"Indeed? I find that incredibly fascinating," Devenshire replied with something that could pass for genuine surprise on his face.

"What? That I feel I can best you?" Krahl asked.

Devenshire shook his head slightly as a tight smile raised the corners of his lips. "No, that there is a soul somewhere within all that muscle."

The expression on Zandorth's face was identical to the one Shantira imagined he would have had someone slapped him across the face.

"I triple our usual wager!" he hissed.

Both of Devenshire's eyebrows rose at that. "Triple? You must surely be drunk this eve to make such a wager."

"*Ahh*...the yellow streak of your cowardice has finally shown itself. If the stakes are too high, all you need do is say, and I will claim victory!" Krahl snarled.

"Cowardice?" Devenshire asked incredulously, both brows rising. "Indeed. I accept your wager just as quickly as I will accept your gold once you have sobered." Devenshire stood and casually reached up to untie his cloak.

"Roslyn! The Ale of Battle, if you please!" Zandorth shouted over his shoulder, never taking his eyes from Devenshire.

Shantira looked over at Brianna again, her face showing her confusion.

Brianna answered her unspoken question. "Rest easy, girl. This is a game these two play frequently. It is foolish, dangerous, and typical male. They enjoy it, though, so let them be."

Shantira watched the patrons gather into a tight circle around the two men. Wagers flew back and forth across the room, some betting on Krahl and many more on Devenshire.

"Brianna, I do not understand. What is to happen? What is the Ale of Battle?"

"*Shh!* Watch, and be entertained," Brianna spoke without taking her eyes off the men. Then her eyes flared, and Shantira smiled, for she had seen that impish look before. Brianna had mischief of her own to add to tonight's festivities.

As the wagers flew back and forth, Brianna rose with graceful, cat-like movements to the edge of the circle. She regarded Krahl with a seductive smile.

"Tell me something, Zandorth. Do you really feel that you can best Devenshire this time?"

Zandorth nodded, his eyes never leaving Devenshire.

"And you, Devenshire?" she asked, fixing Devenshire with a truly seductive gaze.

His lips twitched with concealed laughter as he swung his sleepy, seductive gaze to her. "Not a snow storms chance in hell."

Brianna smiled widely, her face beaming with the pure joy she was feeling at the moment. She was genuinely enjoying herself. "Then I wish to enhance the wager. To the winner I will give a kiss."

Shantira did not miss the subtle moan that passed through the male members of the crowd as well as the widening of Zandorth's eyes. For a moment, his mouth hung open slightly in amazement. A quick look at her honor guard showed the Captain of the Guard shaking his head as he lowered it into this hand, a poorly concealed smile creasing his features.

Zandorth recovered his shock as a wolfish grin spread across his face, revealing strong, even, white teeth, "You have all but lost, Devenshire! The chance of a kiss from the lovely Lady Brianna has sealed your fate!"

Devenshire's eyes had never left Brianna's, and the expression in them left little doubt as to what he was thinking. There was an almost tangible heat between them, and Shantira found it quite irritating.

With a thick smile he answered, "I have tasted the sweet nectar of the Lady Brianna's kiss before. The chance to taste it again has only steeled my resolve to defeat you," he swung his wolfish grin to Zandorth to finish his sentence, "once again."

The crowd reacted to Devenshire's statement, and their reaction only added to the Warrior's growing anger. His mouth opened to say something and then quickly clamped shut. He had no reply.

Rosalyn appeared through the crowd carrying a tray with two large glass tankards upon it. The brew inside the tankards was dark with a hint of foam floating on top.

"As challenger, I claim first strike!" Zandorth proclaimed.

"As you wish," was Devenshire's reply.

The wagers continued flying back and forth across the room, even Brianna's honor guard was busy retrieving coins and placing bets.

Brianna slipped gracefully back into her chair and took up her wine glass, her eyes watching the combatants. Shantira shot her a playfully reproachful look for her addition to the festivities. Brianna caught the look and donned a poorly formed expression of innocence, "What?"

Devenshire stepped up, took up one of the tankards from the tray, and stepped back to his original spot.

"Try not to land him on a table this time, Daimion. They are quite expensive to replace," Rosalyn said. Her expression bore a look similar to that of a mother whose children's playing had turned too rough.

"It will be HE who lands this time!" Zandorth bellowed, indignant that she had already assumed Devenshire would win.

Rosalyn smiled up at the warrior and warmly patted his massive forearm. "Of course, my dear."

The crowd began to quiet down as they finished placing their wagers and inched in closer, eager for the festivities to begin. Shantira had no idea what was coming, but judging from the crowd's reaction and anticipation, it promised to be quite entertaining.

Devenshire glanced down into the tankard and took a deep breath, letting it out slowly. Then he brought the tankard to his lips and began to chug the contents in one long draw. Some of the ale seeped from the corners of his mouth and trailed down his jaw, and Shantira watched his throat as he gulped down swallow after swallow of the drink. Apparently, he had to drain the entire tankard at once.

Once the tankard was empty, he sat it down on a table and then raised his eyes to Zandorth. Shantira was sure his eyes were slightly glazed.

The warrior smiled a wicked grin before stepping up and

smashing Devenshire across the jaw. The right cross was crushing, and Shantira was sure it would take his head off. With a wet smack, flesh collided, and Devenshire was pitched sideways from the force of the blow.

Shantira felt her hands fly to her mouth to contain the gasp of shock and horror of such a vicious blow. She watched as Devenshire stumbled into the crowd, which quickly scattered, making room for him should he fall.

Just as it appeared that he would indeed topple to the floor, Devenshire caught himself and halted his sideways stumble. He sagged under the weight of the Ale of Battle and the crushing blow from Zandorth.

Shantira looked at Zandorth's heavily muscled arm and wondered what was keeping Devenshire's head attached. There was a graveyard-like silence hanging over The Tavern as it seemed as though everyone was holding their breath, waiting to see if Devenshire would fall. It was then that Shantira realized she, too, had been holding her breath. As she let it out slowly, her eyes riveted to Devenshire's sagging frame.

Finally, Devenshire gave his head a quick shake and rose slowly to his full height. He raised his glazed eyes up and fixed Zandorth with an appreciative nod as he reached up to touch his jaw. Already the skin was starting to discolor.

"Very nice, Zandorth. Your best effort to date," he said, and there was only the slightest slur to his voice.

The members of the crowd who had bet on Devenshire erupted into loud shouts, claps, and cheers as he crossed back to the spot he had occupied when Zandorth had struck him.

Krahl's eyes widened in disbelief. It was clear that he had put his all into the blow and had fully expected it to flatten the smaller man. He took several steps back to the spot he had occupied before, his disbelieving gaze still locked on Devenshire.

Devenshire glanced at the remaining tankard of the Ale of Battle on Rosalyn's tray and then raised an eyebrow as he looked at Zandorth. "Well? Are you waiting for an invitation from the King?" Devenshire teased, a good-natured smile spreading across his face. The discoloration on his jaw was rapidly turning darker, and she knew it was the beginnings of a nasty bruise.

"Yes! Your turn, Zandorth!" someone shouted from the crowd.

"Someone, remove that table behind him," another shouted and the crowd erupted into laughter.

"Get those reviving spirits ready, Rosalyn. Zandorth is about to take a nap!" another voice shouted which increased the pitch of the crowd's laughter.

"SILENCE!" Zandorth bellowed out in a thunderous voice that

instantly resulted in the crowd quieting down.

With a mixture of anger and trepidation, he took up the tankard. Unlike Devenshire, he took no time to prepare himself, and instantly, began to swallow down the contents.

Whatever the Ale of Battle was, it was potent. When Zandorth set the tankard aside, the effects of the brew were clear in the glazed expression. He blinked his eyes once and fixed his hard stare on Devenshire.

Devenshire stepped up, planted his feet, and let loose a savage uppercut that caught the warrior on the point of the chin, slamming his head backwards with a quick snap. But that was the only reaction to the punch as Devenshire stepped back. The warrior didn't even have to take a step back to absorb the power of the blow. There came a sharp, collective intake of collected breaths as the crowd watched in stunned silence.

Slowly, Zandorth lowered his head back to its' normal position and fixed Devenshire with a look of satisfaction.

"By the Fates!" someone exclaimed.

"He has done it! He has survived!" another patron shouted. This began a murmuring chorus of shocked exclamations.

"This has never happened!"

Shantira had to admit that she was stunned that Zandorth had taken the powerful shot with apparent ease. She looked at Devenshire, expecting to see a look of shocked disbelief on his face. What she saw was that Devenshire had crossed his arms across his chest and simply stood watching Zandorth. It was as if he were waiting for something.

Shantira leaned closer to Brianna, but didn't take her eyes off Zandorth, "What happens now?"

"They go again. This will continue until one of them falls." Brianna answered, and Shantira could hear the shocked disbelief in her voice, as well.

Zandorth leaned forward, and Shantira assumed he was about to take a step forward, but his feet never moved. Like a mighty tree, the Warrior of the Ancient Class careened forward to land hard on the floor at Devenshire's feet, the pleased smile still on his lips. The impact was hard, and Shantira could feel it in the soles of her feet.

The crowd exploded into shouts of victory and groans of defeat as the losers began paying the winners. Shantira spied the way Devenshire visibly relaxed, obviously very grateful that the contest was over, and she wondered just how the combination of ale and the punch had affected him.

Smiling a return to all the shouts of congratulations, Devenshire turned and walked back to the table with Shantira and Brianna. He stopped behind his chair, resting his hands on its back and locking his eyes to Brianna. The crowd hushed a little and inched in closer, waiting for the rest.

"I believe I have another part of the wager to collect, do I not?" he asked. All traces of being dazed were gone, replaced with that nearly unnerving air of mysterious charm that seemed to permeate his entire being.

Brianna smiled a wicked little smile as she rose gracefully to her feet and stood before Devenshire.

"Be careful, Devenshire! The kiss of a beautiful woman is far more powerful than any combination of ale and punches," someone shouted out from the crowd to the accompaniment of merry laughter.

"I assure you," he replied as his left arm snaked out to encircle her small waist and pull her to him, "it is taking all my will to remain on my feet."

"You are such a bastard," she said, but the tones of her voice were softer this time.

"Indeed," he replied as he lowered his lips to hers.

For a moment, they held the kiss and then it went deeper. Both of her arms slowly rose to encircle his neck, and their lips parted.

Shantira wanted to look away as the kiss tore at that unexplainable dagger of jealousy in her chest, but she could not. The passion that had already erupted between the two of them was powerful. Several of the women in the crowd began to fan themselves as several men licked their lips absently.

Finally, Shantira ripped her gaze from the passionate kiss and took up her goblet of mead. She took a long, healthy drink in an attempt to numb the pain in her chest. The temperature of The Tavern had most definitely gone up in the last few moments.

After what seemed like hours, the kiss ended. Devenshire pulled back and fixed Brianna with a smile that only she could understand. She replied with a veiled look in her eyes that said something only he could comprehend.

"Very nice, Devenshire. Your best effort to date," she said, mocking his response to Zandorth earlier. With a sultry parting look, she stepped out of his embrace and lowered herself back into her chair.

One of Devenshire's eyebrows arched upward and the smile grew into a full out grin. Several men stepped up and clapped him on the shoulder, congratulating him on far more than his victory over Zandorth.

Shantira watched Brianna as she picked up her wine glass to take a drink. She saw the way her hand trembled as the glass rose to her lips, and the length of the drink told her that she had felt the kiss and had felt it deeply.

"Come, Devenshire! Let me buy you a drink!" one man shouted.

"The next is on me!" another shouted.

Rosalyn stepped up and placed her hands on her hips, fixing Devenshire with a playfully reproachful look. "You two are going to kill one another one of these nights!" she scolded.

Devenshire shook his head, "I think not," he said as he looked down at Zandorth's unconscious form. "Neither of us wishes to journey to the afterlife and admit the other had sent us there."

Rosalyn chuckled softly and shook her head. "Alright. You four," she said pointing to four men beside her, "carry him to the back and let him sleep it off."

The four men laughed as they stepped up to hoist the warrior off the floor. They struggled under the considerable weight as they removed him. The crowd of well-wishers began trying to herd Devenshire toward the bar. He paused to address the two women at the table.

"Will you two lovely ladies excuse me for a moment?" he asked.

They both nodded, and he was quickly whisked away. The minstrels began playing again, and the crowd began breaking up into their own pursuits of entertainment.

Shantira watched Devenshire's back until it was swallowed up by the crowd. She turned back to Brianna to see her watching after him also, the look in her eyes speaking volumes to the level of arousal she was experiencing.

"That good?" she asked reluctantly, wanting to know, and yet not wanting to know.

Brianna let out a long breath through her pursed lips as she reached for her wine glass again. Just before the rim of the glass touched her lips, a wicked little smile twisted them. "Better than I remembered."

CHAPTER FOUR

THE EVENING OF FESTIVE enjoyment had quickly turned to a night of endless torture. Shantira sat slumped in her chair, cheek propped in her left hand while her right hand absently toyed with the remnants of her dinner. The sense of peace and release that she had come to find eluded her, which had never happened before.

Devenshire tortured her heart while his relationship with Brianna twisted her mind. She struggled under the burning weight of her jealousy and quickly discovered she was ill equipped to deal with these new emotions. She knew that Brianna had been nothing but sincere in her granting "permission" to pursue Devenshire if she wanted. Brianna had never lied to her before, and her reputation for being honest, brutally at times, was above reproach.

The truth of Brianna's wish to let Shantira pursue Devenshire was not the problem. The fact that Brianna was in a position to grant such a wish was.

Shantira found herself growing angry with Brianna, and she struggled to contain that anger while trying to understand it. She had little success with either. She had no claim to Devenshire, and therefore, no reason to be angry with her dear friend. That did not stop her mind from conjuring up all manner of images that involved Devenshire and Brianna entwined in steamy embraces, each one angering her more than the one before it.

She glanced up at Brianna and found her talking casually with another man who was an old acquaintance.

Has she had him also? She caught herself thinking and quickly snapped it back. She knew Brianna's free spirited nature with men, and it had never mattered to her before. Perhaps that was the point. There was no shortage of men in Brianna's life. She could have any man she chose, and usually did. Why could she not leave just one for her?

She shook her head sharply, trying valiantly to dispel the dark thoughts. Brianna was her closest friend and confidant. She had become involved with Devenshire before Shantira had ever laid eyes on him. She had every right to pursue any man she chose.

The thoughts made sense to her and angered her every bit for their logic. She sighed deeply, knowing she would have to get quick and complete control on these feelings before they drove her to do or say something foolish that she would deeply regret later.

"Are you well?"

Shantira snapped her head up, not realizing she had let her gaze and attention wander. Brianna was looking at her with concern on her face. The man she had been talking with had excused himself and was gone.

"I am fine," she replied with more of an edge to her voice than she wanted, and it registered on Brianna's features.

"Something possesses your thoughts," she said softly. "I have found that when dark thoughts occupy my mind, the best way to dispel them is with a bright ray of light from the counsel of a friend."

Shantira's brows angled downward in growing anger. "I said I am fine! It is of little consequence!"

The slight inching upward of one eyebrow was the only reaction from Brianna. She nodded slowly. "As you wish," she replied with a definite chill in her tone.

Shantira closed her eyes and took a deep breath. This was ridiculous. There was no reason to be so short and angry with Brianna. She opened her eyes and opened her mouth to issue the apology in her throat but stopped short as another man stepped up to the table.

"Milady Brianna. May I have the honor of a dance?"

Brianna glanced up at the man and quickly gave him a head to foot appraisal in that way that bordered on trampish and yet remained totally within the confines of a lady. It was an amazingly thin line to walk, and Brianna did it with ease.

Shantira noticed her guard tensing, several of them placing their hands casually, yet deliberately on the pommels of their swords. She did not envy their charges. To be responsible for the safety of a woman who continually insisted on putting herself in potentially dangerous situations had to be extraordinarily taxing.

"I would love to." Brianna's warm voice replied as she offered her right hand. The man smiled warmly, took her hand and escorted her to the dance floor. It was then that Shantira noticed the minstrels had begun playing a particularly slow, romantic tune.

The romantic in her soul, which had been given more exposure tonight than in the balance of her seasons, cried out for someone to dance with her. She watched the man put his left arm around Brianna's waist while his right hand gently held her right hand. He pulled her close, but not so much that it would be construed as inappropriate for a woman in Brianna's station. They moved easily through the strands of the song and the romantic in her soul went from crying to screaming.

She tore her eyes away from the couple on the floor and took up her mead. She took a deep drink, hoping to drown the irritating anger and the sappy romantic at the same time. She sat the goblet down and let the warmth of the mead hitting her stomach begin to spread. Perhaps she would violate her own resolution this night and become drunk. It seemed to be the only path of escape open to her at the moment.

She silenced the romantic with a mental scream. She was an independent woman. She made her own way. She did not need a man or the sentimental trappings of romance to be complete. She was her own person. It sickened her how hollow all of that sounded to her mind.

"May I have the honor and pleasure of this dance?" came a deep voice from behind Shantira. She let out a sigh of irritation and turned, rather curtly, to refuse the man's offer. The last thing her overactive romanticism needed at this moment was a dance. She looked up, the curt reply already forming on her lips. The reply stopped short as she saw Devenshire standing there, smiling warmly at her with that damned mysteriously seductive mischief glowing softly in his eyes. She felt her knees go weak and her mouth hang open slightly. How could he do this to her?

"I would love to," she heard herself answer.

What? I meant to say no thank you. Her mind screamed. To exasperate her amazement she felt her right hand rise to allow him to take it warmly in his. She tried valiantly to pull her hand back, but like that day in the forest clearing, her body ignored her.

Devenshire smiled, took her hand, and guided her to the dance floor. Much as the man had done with Brianna, he placed his left hand on the small of her back while his right took hers. He pulled her close to the heat of his body and began leading her through the dance.

Shantira felt her knees trembling and was sure Devenshire would feel it as well, but he showed no sign. Then, the hand he held firmly began to tremble, and she feared she'd been discovered. If he felt it, he gave no indication. He looked calmly into her eyes as he gracefully moved her slowly around the floor.

His intense gaze made her more than a little uncomfortable, and she tried to look elsewhere. She could not take her eyes from his, though, no more than she had been able to that day in the clearing. She could not understand what it was about his incredible eyes that made it impossible to look away. It was as if he were holding her gaze with some hypnotic power.

The odd feelings he stirred in her intensified as she found herself at the very center of his attention. Not once did his gaze flicker away, not even briefly. It was as if she, and only she, existed in that moment. His rapt attention was both pleasing and terrifying. She felt drawn into the depths of his soul and wondered if she would ever find her way out. She had to honestly ask herself, would she want to?

The music began to fade into the background of her perceptions, as did the other couples on the dance floor. Shantira feared that she was about to become lost in the moment, in her feelings, and into the beauty of those incredible eyes. Brianna's warning whispered into her mind, and she became fearful that if she did not break this hypnotic moment, she never would.

Something changed in his eyes. It was so subtle that, had she not been staring so deeply into them, she would have missed it. His head cocked slightly, and the intense, unexplainable expression on his features shifted ever so slightly. He appeared to understand and accept something that he had not known before.

"How goes the rebuilding of your village?" he asked softly.

"What...?" His lips moved. Had he spoken?

"I asked how the rebuilding of your village was proceeding," he repeated.

"Oh. It is going well. In fact, it is almost complete." She realized that he had sensed her mood and was trying to put her at ease.

He nodded. "That is good. I trust the losses were minimal."

"Yes, fortunately. I really would like to thank you again for your assistance." She was more than a little relieved that the intense moment had been dispelled. Yet, for all her relief, she could not deny the twinge of regret at having such a powerfully romantic moment cast aside.

"It was my pleasure. I am only thankful that I happened to be in the area and was able to help. I would hate to think of someone as lovely as you in the hands of ignorant savages who could not truly appreciate the beauty of what they held."

Shantira felt her jaw go slack as her knees threatened to revolt and refuse to support her weight any longer. No one had ever said such things to her. His words, his voice, and his eyes, combined to turn her inside to mush. Her heart skipped several beats, and her stomach began to tremble as though a thousand butterflies had suddenly taken flight within it.

Shantira felt a sharp jolt of yet another emotion racing through her. From any other man, she would have taken those words for false flattery. Though, from him, she knew the words to be sincere. Despite her best efforts, she blushed and lowered her eyes.

"Thank you. You are too kind," she whispered.

"You are most welcome," his warm voice answered softly.

The music faded away, and Shantira found herself wondering why the song had been so short. Or had her attention been otherwise occupied that she simply had not noticed the passing of time?

As the last strands of the song faded, Devenshire gave her hand a slight squeeze before releasing it.

"Thank you, fair lady." He bowed to her before escorting her back to her table.

When they reached it, he pulled her chair back and she sank into it, grateful to be off her shaking legs.

The gentleman was escorting Brianna back to the table. Sending him a pleasant smile, she said nothing and sat gracefully down. The man thanked her for the dance and departed.

"If you will excuse me for a moment, I left a most intriguing discussion unfinished at the bar." Devenshire bowed, and then he too disappeared into the crowd.

Shantira watched him leave until she lost sight of him in the crowd. Her heart was pounding hard in her chest, and her legs trembled with a sensation she had never known before.

She turned slowly back to the table and took up her goblet of mead, taking a long swallow, which drained the last of its contents. She needed all the help she could get to settle her raging emotions and rebellious body.

The goblet hit the table harder than she had wanted to set it. She looked up to see Brianna smiling at her with an expression similar to the mischievous glint she had seen in Devenshire's eyes. "What?" she asked, trying to throw up some sort of thin veneer of her normal control.

Brianna's chin jerked toward Devenshire's direction. "That good?"

Shantira smiled as she turned her head in his direction. "Better than I had hoped."

Brianna watched Shantira and saw the signs. She had seen many women look at Devenshire in the exact way Shantira was now. A feeling of trepidation crept in as she realized that Shantira was, in no way, equipped to handle him.

Devenshire had a very powerful personality, and he could be very seductive with very little effort. She, herself, had been surprised at just how remarkably easy it would be to lose herself in him. It was only her determination to never ever surrender her heart to a man again that kept her emotions in check.

If Shantira did not get control of her emotions concerning Devenshire, she was headed for heartache. What she would want from Devenshire was not possible. His determination to never surrender his heart was even more resolute than Brianna's.

Her natural instinct was anger with Devenshire, for he must surely know how Shantira felt, yet he ignored her. Brianna knew that becoming angry with Devenshire was a waste of time and energy. He held no qualms in the way he conducted himself. He neither encouraged nor discouraged a woman's attraction and attention and pursued whatever he could from the moment. Then he would seek out the next moment.

Brianna had to admit to a deeply buried twinge of jealousy at Devenshire's lack of attention toward herself. However, she had come to accept his behavior as simply another part of the man as a whole, and the thrilling, exotic adventure that he offered.

They had shared some very intimate moments that would forever be a part of her fondest memories. But, like her, Devenshire would not allow what they had shared to become muddled by love. Brianna was sure that Devenshire, in his own way, cared for her and treasured their unique relationship. She knew he would never pursue it to the next level, and for that, she was exceedingly grateful. She was not prepared to reciprocate any amorous feelings and was thankful that at least one man in her life would not have to be watched for the telltale signs that he was falling in love.

As she smiled to herself, she had to admit to an honest curiosity of what might happen if they both allowed themselves to fall in love. She often wondered if such thoughts ever entered Devenshire's mind. The thrill of not knowing only added to the excitement of their relationship.

"Shantira?" Brianna said softly, regretting what was to come.

The young village girl turned back in her chair and looked at her. "Yes?"

Brianna could see it in her eyes. She was already falling in love with him.

"You must gain control of your heart," She said softly.

"What do you mean?" Shantira asked, a bit of confusion showing in her expression. Brianna knew that the bulk of her consciousness was still fixed on Devenshire.

"Daimion is a very powerful personality. He has a way of making you feel many different pleasurable things," she said carefully, wanting to warn her without angering her.

Shantira smiled and turned her head in Devenshire's direction. "As I have seen."

"But these feelings will lead you to fall in love with him, and such a thing is folly."

Shantira frowned as that statement sunk in. She turned back to Brianna, confusion plain on her features. "What do you mean?"

"Devenshire will not love you," she shook her head slowly. "Such is not in his nature."

Shantira's frown deepened. "What are talking about? I am not in love with him. I have only just learned his name."

"True, but I see the emotions within you, and they are leading you down a dangerous path," Brianna warned.

Shantira turned back to find Devenshire at the bar. She spotted him leaning casually on the bar, engaged in conversation with a woman. That lingering spike of jealousy suddenly thrust itself into her mind as her eyes narrowed.

The woman was flirting with him with an intensity that sickened Shantira. She twirled her hair and batted her eyes, while she stood entirely too close to him. He said something humorous and she laughed, taking that opportunity to lay her hand on his bare forearm. He smiled at her laughter.

"Tramp!" she hissed at the woman.

Brianna looked up to see what had sparked the reaction from her. She knew the woman. She was one of the many whores of the province, and she was working Devenshire like a true professional. Of course, she knew that Devenshire knew exactly what was happening and was playing along. With an inward chuckle, she knew Devenshire would probably try to find a way to charm her services out of her for free. Knowing Devenshire's skill at seduction, he could probably pull it off.

Prostitutes were frowned upon by society, and their profession was generally considered illegal. Brianna knew that such a law was in place for Prothtow Province, put in place by her father seasons ago. She did not enforce it very strictly at all. There were some things that were simply too basic, too primal, and too essential to ever govern. Brianna felt it was a woman's choice what she did with her body, and if she chose to sell it to men, that was her business. There were far more important matters facing the province in general and the realm as a whole. She would, on occasion, take a token stand against prostitution, but it was an empty platitude designed to placate the more rigid minds of the province.

Prostitution was a business, and as long as these women conducted their business honestly, she would turn a blind eye to it. If, however, they chose to operate their business in an unethical way, they would face the full wrath of her power in the form of swift and decisive justice.

Rosalyn, herself, employed a number of skilled whores. It was the most poorly kept secret of the province. The rooms on the second floor of The Tavern were not designed for, nor were they hardly ever used for, overnight sleeping.

There were rumors that Rosalyn, herself, had been a prostitute in her youth, and she had wisely turned her earnings into the thriving business it was today. She kept a very tight rein on her girls, and they operated well within the unspoken guidelines of Brianna's liberal application of the laws of the land.

The woman at the bar with Devenshire was one of Rosalyn's girls, and she was, no doubt, trying to steer him to one of the rooms on the second floor.

Brianna turned her attention back to Shantira and saw the anger smoldering. "That is what I speak of, Shantira. You have no hold on him and no right to become angry at every woman who speaks to him. If you do not get control of your emotions, they will make you miserable."

Shantira watched as the woman glanced about them, as though making sure no one was within earshot before she leaned forward to whisper something in Devenshire's ear.

Whatever she said caused him to arch one eyebrow. It had piqued his interest. He moved his head around and whispered something back to her. Her eyes grew wide, and a wicked smile turned her lips upward. She laughed as she placed a hand on his shoulder.

"Look at her! She is acting like a whore!" Shantira hissed.

"That is because she is a whore, Shantira," Brianna replied.

Shantira spun around to glare at Brianna. "Then you should have her arrested! She is breaking the law!"

Brianna smiled sadly at her young friend. "Come now, Shantira. You know how that law works."

Shantira squeezed her eyes shut tightly against the raging fury growing rapidly within her. She knew she had absolutely no right to feel this way, but she could not contain the anger.

"Are you, or are you not, the Lord of the province?" Shantira demanded hotly. "There are laws against this, and you sit there and allow it to continue!"

Brianna's warm gaze turned suddenly hard, "Yes there are laws against it. There are also laws against hunting game in the forests, and yet your village hunts on a regular basis!"

Shantira's eyes narrowed. "That is for our survival!"

Brianna's gaze never wavered. "As it is for her!"

Shantira clenched her jaw and sighed heavily. There was no counter argument. She knew Brianna was right and that only served to anger her further.

Brianna saw that she was fighting a losing battle with her emotions. Fighting those feelings in such close proximity to Devenshire would only serve to ruin her evening. Brianna glanced at the door. A change of scenery would be in order.

"It is getting stale in here. Let us take a walk outside for some fresh air," she suggested.

Immediate relief flashed across Shantira's face. "That is an excellent idea!"

The two women rose from their table and began making their way toward the door.

As they stepped outside, they inhaled a deep breath of the crisp night air before setting off on the path toward the lake. Even though the sounds of The Tavern could still be heard, other sounds became evident to Shantira as they walked. There was the soft rustle of Brianna's silk gown, the whisper of her own clothing as she walked, the chirping song of the insects that mingled with the soft sigh of the breeze moving through the branches of the trees. As they neared the lake, even the soft lapping of the water against the bank found its way into the song of the night, adding to its beauty.

As the song played its melody upon her soul, Shantira found her tense emotions regarding Devenshire beginning to ease. She took another deep lung-full of the clean air and let her gaze drift out over the lake's glossy surface. Finally, the peace she had come here to find found her.

Brianna was lost in her own reverie as the spell of the night worked its magic on her, as well. It seemed nearly impossible that such a peace could exist when she considered the many trials she faced on a day-to-day basis. Unlike others, she would not question its source or meaning, but merely accept it and be thankful.

A few couples could be seen around the bank of the lake, and Brianna took a moment to watch each of them. They were either holding hands or had arms draped around each other. Some gazed out over the lake, the serenity of the place making conversation unnecessary. Others gazed into each other's eyes, oblivious to the lake or anything else. Brianna felt a twinge of regret deep inside for not having the luxury of such moments.

There had been times when she had walked these banks in the company of a man and had felt the thrill of romance, finally succumbing to its lure. But she knew then that such moments were temporary at best and would not lead anywhere. With a heavy sigh, she acknowledged her regrets and quickly packed them away. It was the price she was forced to pay for the management of her heart and emotions.

She looked at Shantira and could see the emotions on her friend's face. Although the peace and serenity of the lake had helped to ease Shantira's turmoil, Brianna could see that she still wrestled with her attraction to Devenshire.

"He does not intend to be insensitive," Brianna finally said.

Cocking her head, Shantira lost interest in the lake, but did not turn around. "What do you mean?"

"I know that many times he seems indifferent to those around him, but that is not the case. He maintains such a tight rein on his emotions, and in doing so, sometimes gives the appearance of indifference," Brianna explained.

"He did not appear to have trouble with his emotions earlier!" Shantira muttered angrily.

"Do not mistake composure for ease. In many ways, he and I are alike. I speak from personal experience, not from any detailed knowledge of Daimion. There are simply some things, emotional things, which we will not allow to happen."

Suddenly, Shantira spun around and fixed Brianna with a gaze so angry and intense that Brianna took a small step back.

"Why? I do not understand why you run from love! I do not understand why anyone would run from something that everyone else embraces with passion. You and Daimion are showered with amorous attention, yet you discard it disdainfully. There are those of us who would kill to have the passion of romance be sent our way, yet the two of you throw it easily away, run from it, hide from it. Why?"

Brianna's memories were awakened, and they were memories that were not welcomed. Shantira's intensity only increased her irritation at being forced to face those painful memories.

"Do not attempt to lecture me on my choice of lifestyle. I have never questioned or condemned you for yours, and I would expect the same courtesy in return!" Brianna replied in snipped tones. She took a moment to calm her anger before speaking again.

"You are still young and have not yet experienced all that I have. You speak of love as one who has never experienced it. All too easily, your ignorance will allow you to succumb to the perils of such a powerful emotion. I pray that you never have to experience that pain, and I hope that you are able to find the love and romance that you seek. But you must understand, there is nothing in all the realms that comes without a price, and the price for such an all-consuming love is very high."

She looked out across the lake, a flash of intense sadness crossing her eyes and melding with her voice as she continued... "Very high indeed."

Shantira heard the pain in Brianna's voice and was taken aback, for she had never heard it before. Whatever great tragedy had befallen the Lady Brianna, it had left her with deep scars. Shantira felt instant regret for having spoken so harshly.

"My apologies, Brianna. I fear that I am letting my own emotions get the better of me. Please forgive me."

Shantira waited anxiously until Brianna smiled. The night seemed to become brighter from the radiance. Whatever past phantom had surfaced to haunt Brianna, it was gone, and she was as cheerful as ever.

"Think nothing of it. I am not without understanding in such matters. I do not deny that the act of being in love is a wonderful thing. The varied emotions that it stirs are thrilling. But I simply choose to experience those emotions from a safe distance. Again, do not mistake composure for ease, in Daimion or in me."

Shantira nodded as her eyes strayed once again to the peaceful lake.

Brianna studied her friend's profile for several moments, watching the emotions play across her face. "Shantira, you and I have been fast friends for a long time. We have shared many deep secrets, and we have a rapport that few friends possess. I have found, during times of emotional sadness, it is best to seek the counsel of a friend," Brianna said finally.

Shantira's shoulders sagged and her gaze moved closer to the bank at her feet.

"What am I to do, Brianna? I cannot force him from my mind. Is it simply the mystery of him? Is it the power of this night, his charming smile, and his gallant behavior? Is it my gratitude at his intervention in saving my life? What is it?"

Brianna clasped her hands in front of her and shrugged softly. "Daimion has a charm that is hard to ignore. Your reaction to him is quite normal, but you must decide if you can accept a relationship with him on his terms. If you cannot, then you must put as much space between you and him as possible. I know that is a difficult choice, but you must find a way to deal with that truth."

"Has he ever loved? Does he even know what it is to love?" Shantira asked with more than a little desperation in her voice.

"I do not know with any certainty. But judging from my own experiences, I would have to speculate that, at some point in his past, Daimion has loved deeply. Then again, it could simply be that Daimion is not capable of reciprocating love. Which is the truth? I do not know," Brianna answered honestly.

"Then what am I to do?" Shantira asked, knowing her despair was plain.

"Hope," Brianna offered softly.

"Hope? Hope is not a very sturdy foundation on which to build tomorrow," Shantira said.

Brianna slowly shook her head. "No. But many times, it is all that we have."

"What is it that you have?" came Devenshire's deep-timbered voice. Both women turned to see him strolling toward them.

"Hope, Daimion," Brianna answered softly.

There was something in her tone that warned Devenshire that he had happened along at the end of a personal discussion. He showed the proper courtesy by not pursuing the subject further.

"Am I interrupting?" he asked.

Brianna did not answer, but simply looked at Shantira and waited.

Shantira suddenly found a spot on the ground to fix her gaze upon. As the weight of the silence grew as she looked up to find Devenshire and Brianna looking at her, their gazes' expectant. She realized that Brianna was giving her the opportunity to politely dismiss Devenshire by answering the question.

"Oh no, not at all," she answered lightly, forcing a smile to her lips. Despite the turmoil he caused within her, she found his presence very comforting.

"Has Zandorth woken?" Brianna asked, wanting to break the heaviness of the mood.

Devenshire chuckled as he reached up and touched the dark bruise on his jaw. "Not yet. Perhaps that is a good turn of fortune, for I have found his moods to be quite foul after losing our contests."

"Roslyn is right, you know. One of these nights you two are going to kill one another," Brianna said.

Again, Devenshire laughed and shook his head. "At least our journey to the Afterlife will have been at the hands of friends."

Shantira felt out of place. She was being given the opportunity to get to know Devenshire better, yet she could not find her tongue. He and Brianna talked so easily, as old friends would. She searched for something with which to include herself in the discussion. She had to honestly ask herself if her motivation was simply to have Devenshire's attention on her.

"What is the point of this contest?" she finally asked.

Devenshire grinned wickedly. "It is a very unique turn of events."

"Nonsense!" Brianna injected. "It is the product of male ego."

Devenshire fixed Brianna with a mock stern glance. "The contest is how Zandorth and I met. I had just started coming to The Tavern and Zandorth took it upon himself to test me. To be perfectly honest, I was drawing the attention of a young lady that had caught Zandorth's eye, and he was not at all pleased. He proceeded to inform me that I was interfering in his relationship with the young woman. I told him that the young woman was free to pursue whichever of us she chose. This did not set well with him, and he challenged me. I could hardly refuse," Devenshire explained.

"Zandorth had invented this contest seasons ago and was the reigning champion," Brianna injected. "He had never been defeated, and he took great pride in that fact."

Devenshire nodded in agreement. "He saw the contest as a way to humiliate me and win back the attention of the young lady in question. I defeated him that night. During the next several nights, he challenged me and lost. In between contests, somehow, we developed a friendship, or at the very least a grudging respect for each other. There have been many nights that I feared I was on the verge of losing. It has finally become a matter of pride. He is determined to beat me, and I am determined not to lose."

Shantira smiled and looked at Brianna. "You are right. It is a product of male ego."

Devenshire allowed a slightly shocked expression to cross his face before it lapsed into a bright smile. He nodded to Shantira. "You are right. It is a product of male ego. I cannot argue the point."

Shantira laughed and was joined by both Brianna and Devenshire. Despite the earlier turmoil, the mood was now much lighter. The laughter was easy, and Shantira found the warmth of his presence was more comforting now than torturous. Like the peace of the lake, she wrapped herself in the sensation and enjoyed it.

Suddenly, a horse broke through the tree line, galloping full out with a small boy on its back. The three of them turned and squinted into the darkness at the shadow running toward them. The full moon overhead provided some illumination, but it was still hard to make out whom the boy was.

"Ronan?" Shantira asked as she screwed her eyes into the darkness to see who was riding so recklessly in the dark. Running a horse full out in the darkness was a good way to break a horses' leg or a riders' neck.

"Who?" Brianna asked.

Shantira's focus was on the rider. "A boy from my village," she replied as she stepped away from them. As horse and rider drew closer, it was becoming clear that the boy was doing little in regards to guiding the animal. Shantira jogged toward the approaching horse, ready to try to stop the mount in case the boy could not. The horse suddenly saw her and locked its' legs to come to a sliding stop, throwing the boy from its' back. Shantira quickly scrambled to the side and caught the boy, easing him down to the ground. The horse, breathing very hard from the run, snorted and ambled off, its' head hung low in exhaustion.

Shantira was stunned by the appearance of the boy. He was pale, trembling, and his face bore a harsh mask of pure, absolute terror. His face was dirty, his clothing half on, half off, and his entire body shook as though he were freezing.

"Ronan? What is wrong?" she asked.

The terrified, tear-laden eyes looked up at her as if seeing her for the first time. "Sh-shantira?"

"Yes, dear, it is I. What is wrong? What has happened?" she asked, trying to be soothing but knowing something terrible had happened.

"Raiders! Bandits!" he cried out, hugging Shantira tightly and burying his face deep into her chest.

Devenshire and Brianna stepped up behind her, taken aback by the sheer terror gripping the young boy.

"What?" Shantira asked, not sure she understood what he said.

"The village... raiders! Cutting... hurting... burning... blood..." his trembling voice replied, muffled by his face being buried.

Shantira felt her blood run cold. Another attack? Or a continuation of the previous one?

"How many, Ronan? How many bandits?" she asked urgently, nearly demanding.

"Too... too many to count... they are everywhere... hurting... people screaming... fire... burning..." The boy's voice trailed off into incoherent mumbling.

Shantira looked up at Brianna, the color draining from her face as the brutal truth sunk in. "My lords, Brianna! My village!"

Brianna's face paled, as well, a hand lifting to cover her open mouth. "No," she whispered.

Shantira's wide eyes looked briefly about the clearing and stopped on the horse Ronan had ridden in on. She slowly rose, sliding the boy gently over to Brianna. "Brianna, take care of Ronan. I must go."

She did not wait for an answer as she quickly began jogging toward the horse.

"Shantira, wait! You cannot ride off without knowing what is happening." Devenshire called out to her.

"My home... my people!" Shantira replied as she swung herself up onto the horse's bare back. She quickly took up the reins, savagely turning the animal in the direction of her village before burying her heels deep into its flanks. The horse grunted in protest but broke into a full gallop. Within moments, horse and rider were gone, swallowed up by the shadows.

Brianna had lowered herself to the ground and cradled the small, terrified boy in her lap, gently rocking him. Her concerned gaze rose to find Devenshire staring at the point she had lost sight of Shantira.

"Daimion, she is not thinking clearly. She will get herself killed."

Devenshire didn't answer as he dropped the brandy snifter and turned back toward The Tavern. He raised his thumb and forefinger to his lips and let lose a shrill whistle.

Very quickly, his massive black Frisian came bounding down the hill from The Tavern. He slid to a stop as Devenshire gripped the pommel of the saddle and swung himself up into the saddle.

"Roust Zandorth! Tell him what has happened and that I need his help!"

"Daimion, wait! Do not go alone. You do not know what is happening," Brianna urged.

The Frisian shifted nervously under him, as though he sensed his master's urgency and was ready to move. Devenshire shook his head. "There is no time. Shantira will most certainly ride into certain death if she is not stopped.

"Be careful!" she said.

He looked down at her and smiled warmly. He gave her a quick wink before he snapped his head back in the direction Shantira had gone and kicked the horse into a full out gallop. The wind filled out his cloak and billowed it out behind him as he leaned low, gaining as much speed as possible.

Other people who had been at the lake were coming close, investigating what had happened. Brianna quickly turned the sobbing, terrified boy over to another woman before gathering her gown in her hands and running toward The Tavern.

CHAPTER FIVE

DEVENSHIRE EXPLODED FROM the woods into one of the streets of Kahla. His eyes quickly scanned the street for any sign of where Shantira may have gone. He was amazed that she had, on a tired mount, pulled so far ahead of him so quickly.

The Frisian pranced in a nervous circle as Devenshire continued to study the area for any indication of where she had gone. The pressure of passing time weighed down on him, and he knew she had a much bigger lead on him than he had originally thought. It would stand to reason. She had grown up in this area; she most certainly knew many routes to her home.

With a frown, he realized that if he had any hopes of catching up to her before she rode blindly into a full out attack, he would have to use other means. Using his knees and reins, he wrestled the anxious mount to stand still.

Dropping his head and closing his eyes, he focused his attention, while calling on his powers. He calmed his breathing and forced his mind to blot out all but calling on the mystical arts. He felt the faint tingle at the edges of his perceptions and reached out for it. Slowly, a distinct fog settled over his mind, cutting off the outside world.

A small sliver of his mind tried to panic at the disorienting fog floating about him, and he resisted. This was customary for a Spell of Knowledge, but still unsettling. Squeezing his eyes tightly shut, he relaxed, releasing his conscious grip on the physical realm, allowing his mind to float into the mystical realm.

Images began to coalesce in his mind. They were both familiar and unfamiliar at the same time. Configurations of rocks and trees, the curve of a path, the arrangement of a hill, all began to settle into his consciousness until the image of Shantira's village came into sharp focus.

The fog began to dissipate, and Devenshire opened his eyes slowly. It was an unsettling bit of spell work that always left him slightly disoriented and with a touch of a headache. He took a moment to allow the disorientation to pass.

He now knew the way to Shantira's village as well as he knew the way to his own dwelling. Shaking off the last remnants of spell, he jerked the reins, turning his mount and kicking it into a gallop. He didn't know how far ahead of him she was, but he knew he had to catch her before she reached her village.~*~

Even before she crested the ridge that overlooked her village, Shantira knew she was too late. She had seen the glow of several fires a few miles back, knowing what they meant, but she could not slow her approach.

Icy fear gripped her stomach and twisted it tighter with each step the horse made. The rational parts of her mind screamed at her to slow down, to use her combat training to gain some sort of advantage over her opponents. Yet her concern for the villagers caused her emotions to dictate her actions. She gave no thought to what would happen if she simply rode into the midst of the attack and was not concerned with how she would fight off such a large force. All that mattered was getting to the village.

She crested the ridge and pulled up hard on the reins, bringing the horse to a skidding halt. It snorted out in protest and pranced in agitation at its rough treatment. Shantira didn't notice. Her wide, shocked, and terrified gaze was locked on the massive annihilation laid out below her.

The devastation was total.

Not a single hut or building was untouched by fire; everything was burning that had not already burned to the ground. The fields to the north blazed brightly as the fires hungrily consumed the crops that remained. Shantira's mind reeled in the face of such absolute ruin. She was not aware of anything except the vivid glow of the raging conflagration that devoured her home. Her wide eyes swept over the obliteration refusing to accept the death of her village.

Images of people she had known her entire life rushed through her mind; times of laughter, great joy, and terrible sadness. There were other times when the entire village had pulled together to help one of their own. Visions came of backbreaking work, performed shoulder to shoulder to keep the village alive and prosperous. The festivals they had hosted had been small with their limited means, but had always been successful and joyous. The harsh winters that had left scarcely any food, yet no one had gone hungry.

Without realizing it, she urged her mount forward and the

fatigued animal began a slow descent off the ridge and down into the village. Shantira was vaguely aware of the contrast between the coolness of the night behind her and the heat of the fires before her. It felt as though it were burning her face and eyes as fiercely as it scorched the huts. The heat became too intense for the horse, and it simply came to a stop, lowering its head in sheer exhaustion. Shantira, her eyes never leaving the scene before her, dismounted absently and began walking slowly toward the inferno.

The toe of her boot hit something at her feet and for the first time since cresting the ridge, her eyes left the fires to see what she had walked upon. Blinking away the burning after-image of the fires, she squinted to see the body of an old woman laying face down in the dirt. Shantira knelt slowly and rolled the body over. The ancient face stared back at her, eyes wide open and mouth agape in the expression of surprise. In her stunned state, it took her a moment to put a name with the face and when she did, tears welled in her eyes at the memories of this old woman.

"Auntie Lucinda?" she asked in disbelief of what her eyes were showing her.

The old woman did not respond and continued to stare up into infinity. "No..." Shantira said, still refusing to believe what she saw.

She gently shook the woman, "Auntie Lucinda? Please... please wake up... please..." she softly begged, shaking the woman harder with each passing moment.

"No... you cannot leave me like this... Auntie Lucinda, please do not leave me like this..." she begged harder, the hot tears tracking down her cheeks.

"By the Fates... no..." The tears flowed and grief gripped her heart in a steel grip, threatening to crush it at any moment. She shook her head slowly at first, and then with growing intensity to match the dawning terrible truth, "NO!" she screamed at Lucinda. "Do not dare leave me here alone! Do you hear me?"

The first sob shook her body as she squeezed her eyes shut against the next wave of tears. She pulled the old woman's body close to her and squeezed. "Please do not leave me here like this!" she said in a softer tone. She searched the lifeless features for any sign that the woman had heard her. Through the veil of tears she desperately searched the depths of Lucinda's sightless eyes for any signs of the wonderful woman she had known her whole life.

There was nothing in the eyes. They were cold and empty and... dead.

"NO!!" she screamed again, shaking her head as if the act would dispel the truth. Finally, with the grief crushing her chest, and the tears burning her eyes, she threw her head up and released a soul-wrenching cry of pain into the night. It was a sound of pure anguish and pure defiance at what had been taken from her. Then she dropped her head and continued to rock the woman's chilling corpse. As the sobs racked her body, memories of this woman, the only mother she had ever really known, began playing through her mind.

Her face was one of the first to be etched into Shantira's dawning memories. She had only been a toddler when she tightly gripped Lucinda's finger as they walked through the village. As they walked, the old woman would talk of many things, teaching her the rich history of the village. She had told great tales of the young men who came to this place and tried to tame the land. How those men struggled to dominate the land, and eventually, learned to strike a pact with the land. They then carved out what was now the village they all called home. Those young men eventually became the ancient men who now made up the Council of Elders.

"But Auntie Lucinda..." the toddling Shantira had asked, confused on how the Elders had struck a pact with the land. "How do you talk to the land? The land is not alive."

"Oh, but it is, child. The land, in many ways, is much more alive than you or I." Lucinda had stopped and eased down onto a fallen log overlooking a valley near their village. She pulled the tiny child up onto her lap and took in the beautiful view laid out before them with a sweep of her hand.

"Many foolish men view it as something they can claim and own. But the land will not be owned. If forced into the service of man, it will eventually retaliate and yield naught. But when the land is treated with the respect it deserves, it is a valuable ally in the fight for our survival."

This had drawn only confusion from the little girl, which in turn had caused Lucinda to laugh merrily. "You do not understand, do you, Shantira?"

"No, Auntie, I do not."

Lucinda smiled lovingly and patted the girl's leg. "You will, child. In time, you will."

Shantira looked down into Lucinda's lifeless face and felt the tremendous grief rip at her heart.

"Shantira?" A voice called, but she ignored it. She couldn't summon the energy to worry if the voice were a friend or a foe. At this moment, she simply didn't care.

After a short time, a hand came to rest on her shoulder. The touch was gentle, strong, and offered consolation.

"She was the first person to take me in when my parents died," Shantira said over her shoulder. It did not matter who stood behind her, only that the person knew what the realm had lost with the death of this woman.

"She taught me things, showed me how things were," she paused to swallow hard against the lump in her throat. "She was the closest thing to a mother I had known since the passing of my own." Her voice shook with grief. The person behind her had the presence of mind not to say a single word.

"She stood up for me when the Council of Elders sought to make me conform to what *they* thought a young woman was supposed to be. They said I should take a husband, give him strong sons, and tend to his house." She sniffed and shook her head. "They did not count on Auntie Lucinda's iron will and hot temper." A sad smile crossed her face as a short, soulful laugh came. "She put them in their place in short order and told them that my path was my business. It never ceased to amaze me how the mighty Council of Elders could find a way to give in to her without ever agreeing with her."

The smile faded and more tears seeped from her grief stricken gaze that was locked on Lucinda. "She helped guide me when I came of age, and all the boys of the village sought me out. When the first feelings of young love touched me and left me so bewildered, it was she who tried to help me understand.

"When the frightening time of purification came upon me, it was she who helped me understand that I was becoming a woman. She taught me that I could be strong and independent and still be a woman." Shantira knew not how long she spoke, but she did become aware that the hand on her shoulder never wavered, never left.

"She taught me that the land is a living thing that you cannot treat like something to be owned." She sniffed and scrubbed at her face. "She said that if you treat it with anything other than respect, it will yield not what you seek from it, and survival is impossible."

She reached down with her free hand and gently swept aside a lock of gray hair from her face. "Why in name of the Fates would anyone wish to harm her? What manner of beast would be so empty inside that they would feel the need to rid this realm of one so wise?" she asked the unseen supporter behind her.

"My sorrow is with you in your grief, Shantira," the owner of the gentle hand on her shoulder said. She was finally able to look up, to see who had been kind enough to put an understanding hand to her shoulder. Through the blur of tears, she could make out Devenshire's face. She closed her eyes again and laid her cheek against his hand on her shoulder, soaking up his warmth and compassion.

"Thank you," she whispered.

"Rest assured that Lucinda has passed in body only. Her spirit will live on in all who knew her, in all who loved her. As long as you keep her memory alive, she will live on in your heart."

"I will never forget her! Ever!" Shantira growled through her choked throat, swiping away at her falling tears. Sobs of pain and grief wrestled to take control of her emotions.

"Then Lucinda will never be truly dead," he replied.

Despite her terrible grief, Shantira had to admit the words had brought her comfort. Finally able to regain some control over her emotions, she leaned forward and gazed into Lucinda's face. With a tearful smile, she silently said farewell to the body of her Auntie, but not to her spirit.

Devenshire knelt down beside her and examined the old woman. Death had come quickly. The dagger that protruded from her chest told him she had not suffered as the blade almost certainly had pierced her heart.

She slowly and gently lowered Lucinda's body to the ground and firmly pressed her fingertips to her eyes, closing the lids, closing her own eyes, as well.

"Remain here. I will check the rest of the village," Devenshire ordered softly.

Shantira's eyes snapped open, and her face became unreadable through the anger he had been waiting to surface.

"No! I must see what these bastards have done! I must know what manner of beast I must confront!" she snarled.

Devenshire recognized the need for vengeance forming within Shantira. At this moment, he knew that he did not possess the words to dissuade her from her course. Perhaps later, when the grief was not so strong, he could talk to her sensibly. Short of rendering her unconscious, there was nothing he could do to stop her.

"Very well. But the raiders may not have gone far and could very well return. You must put your grief and anger aside long enough to think clearly, or you will certainly join the others in death," he warned, hoping it would be enough to roust her, at least partially, from her grief.

Shantira nodded curtly before bending low to place a loving kiss to the old woman's forehead. "I love you, Auntie," she whispered.

She rose to her feet, lifting her gaze to the burning ruins of her home. The anger burned in her eyes with an intensity that surpassed the flames that consumed her village.

Devenshire looked about the community, noticing the damaged buildings and the bodies that littered the ground everywhere. Fighting back the intense heat of the flames, they walked through the village finding death with every step they took.

It did not take Devenshire long to realize how fortunate Lucinda had been to die so quickly. The raiders had not been as kind to the rest of the villagers, nor had they shown any regard for status in their grisly attack. Young and old, men and women alike, were mutilated, their body parts strewn everywhere. Devenshire fought down his own anger and revulsion at the terrible lack of regard for human life displayed before him. He realized that as difficult as it was for him to view this scene, it must be doubly so for Shantira, for she had actually known these people, had lived with them, shared their lives.

At the front of the remains of one smoldering hut, Devenshire saw the bloody body of a young woman sprawled on her back. Her legs were spread wide, and her clothing had been torn from her body and strewn around her. There were what appeared to be bite marks on her thighs, vagina, breasts, and neck. Her throat gaped open from a horrible slash from a very sharp blade and her wide, horror-filled eyes stared up into the night in a final expression of fear, forever frozen into her swollen, bloody features.

Judging from the bruises and swelling about her face, she had not only been raped, but beaten as well before her throat was slit. The body of a man lay sprawled, face down next to her. His hand was holding hers, and his badly beaten face was positioned to where she was the last thing he saw before the multiple stab wounds had claimed his life.

A few feet away from the couple was the horribly mutilated body of a young child. The body was so badly mangled, he could not honestly discern if the child had been a boy or a girl.

Devenshire's eyes narrowed and his brow furrowed as he took in the ghastly scene. A young family, attacked, beaten, and finally killed for nothing more than the savage pleasure of their attackers. His first impulse was to squeeze his eyes shut and turn away from the grotesque scene, but he forced himself to etch the image into his mind, to lock it there as a reminder of what had happened here. He silently swore that when he found those responsible for this atrocity, this image would dominate his mind as he paid them back for this young family's suffering.

He heard Shantira's steps behind him and quickly turned to block her view of the scene.

"Shantira, there is no need for you to see these things. Please reconsider and wait elsewhere." He said.

Shantira's face was a mask of rock. The only expression Devenshire could make out in the flickering reflection of flames upon her face was anger and grief. At the moment, her mind simply took in the grisly scene with the kind of acceptance that only intense anger mixed with deep grief could provide. He knew that she would grieve in her own way and in her own time, and that the grief would be soul rending.

"No!"

"Shantira, there is nothing to be gained by torturing yourself with these sights," Devenshire argued, firmly taking her shoulders in his hands.

Devenshire could see the battle raging in her eyes. She desperately wanted to flee this scene while at the same time, another part of her desired to see just how demonic the evil was that had swept through her home.

"These were my people. They were my family. I am the only one left who can avenge them! I have to see what these bastards have done." Her voice faltered only slightly as another wave of grief crashed over her and she sagged in Devenshire's grip for a brief moment. When she spoke again, her voice was small but laced with intense venom. "I must know what manner of beast it is that I will hunt."

"There will be time for hunting later. For the moment, you must give yourself time to recover from the shock and grief." Devenshire took in a deep breath and let it out slowly, shaking his head. "You cannot bring them back and torturing yourself with the visions of their remains will do nothing but increase your suffering. Please. Wait next to your mount."

Shantira straightened in his grip and the look of cold defiance came again. She took a deep shuttering breath and steeled herself. She leveled a hard glare deep into Devenshire's eyes, driving the absolute truth of her convictions into them. "I will avenge them."

At the first signs of the savagery of the raiders, Devenshire had clamped down on his emotions, tucking them away so that they could not interfere with what was to come. Seasons of experience had taught him how to keep his emotions from interfering with what he knew he had to do. The sight of the old woman named Lucinda, the young family behind him, and the other atrocities he was sure to see this night called to him and tried to wrest some form of reaction from him, but he refused and simply acknowledged what was laid out before him. But deep inside he knew that there would be a reckoning for this horrendous act... he swore it.

The sound of pounding hooves drew their attention to an approaching rider. Only a dim silhouette could be seen beyond the light of the various fires.

Devenshire recognized the silhouette as it drew nearer. Zandorth Krahl had answered his call for aid. Putting another layer of displacement between his emotions and the carnage before him, he turned and strode toward the approaching rider, gently pulling Shantira with him, trying to keep her from seeing more of the senseless, soulless destruction heaped upon her village.

Even before his horse came to a complete halt, Zandorth had leapt from the saddle. By the time he hit the ground, his broadsword was drawn and ready. Devenshire saw the stern look on his face and knew that Krahl was calling on his warrior training, preparing for battle.

"There is no trace of any remaining raiders. They have departed," Devenshire said as he approached.

Krahl did not relax as he took several strides into the village, and his eyes swept it finding the carnage that dominated the ground. His features hardened, as did his gray eyes as they took in the destruction.

"By the Lords of Kuvol! What manner of beast would do this!" he growled, cringing at the remains of what was once a small child. The tiny body had been battered and twisted, touching all of them very deeply. "What manner of honor can one gain from cutting down a child?"

Devenshire's features were grim as he contemplated the attack and who could have been behind it. Could these raiders be part of the smaller band that had attacked Shantira's village earlier? While bandits operated throughout the realm, Devenshire had never heard of one as large as this one appeared to be.

True, he reasoned, Shantira's village was small, but it would have still taken a great number of men to execute a raid on a scale of this magnitude. He took a moment to look about the village and tried to find any clue that would give him some form of an answer.

"It was a large attack," Krahl muttered as he also looked about the village, but with the trained eyes of a Warrior of the Ancient Class. He knelt and brushed his fingers through the dirt, examining things that would only make sense to a warrior. "Much larger than was necessary."

"Do you have any idea of how many?" Devenshire asked.

Krahl continued to study the ground, occasionally moving to another spot and studying it as well. Finally, he gave a short shake of his head. "Not yet," he muttered as he continued his search. "But I will."

Devenshire turned to see Shantira hugging herself against a chill that had nothing to do with the weather. She trembled, and her eyes seeped silent tears of a grief she had never known could exist within a human soul. He knew he would have to watch her closely. At this moment, her mind was as fragile as an eggshell. He reached up and untied his cloak, drawing it from his shoulders as he moved next to her.

"Here. This will keep you warm," he said softly as he gently settled the cloak about her shoulders.

She never looked at him, her eyes staring off into the night. She took the edges of his cloak and hugged it tighter about her.

"Why?" she whispered. "That is all I wish to know... Why?"

Devenshire left his hands on her shoulders after draping his cloak about her. "I wish I had that answer for you, Shantira. I truly do. If you can take no other comfort from me, take this—I will find those answers and those who are responsible will pay."

He felt her body stiffen and watched as the grief was swept aside again by the intense anger.

"Of that I am sure," she growled. She turned her bloodshot, tear-laden eyes to his and locked her conviction into his soul as surely as it was locked within hers. "Of that I am sure," she repeated.

He nodded, accepting all that she was saying without words. He understood her grief and her growing thirst for revenge. He had tasted it before, and he understood.

"There will be time for vengeance later. For now you must rest, and allow yourself time to grieve," he said gently.

She breathed another shuddering sigh and briefly closed her eyes. "Could you rest?"

That gave him a moment of pause. He knew exactly what his actions would have been had he been in Shantira's place. He tried to find another answer that would not be a flat out lie and failed. Finally, he shook his head.

"No," he whispered.

CHAPTER SIX

THE NIGHT OF JOYOUS FESTIVITY had quickly turned to soul-wrenching grief. The cold gray dawn found Devenshire, Shantira, and Zandorth busy with the sad task of gathering the dead from the ruins of the village. Soot and grime covered each of them, streaking their grim features with harsh lines of fatigue, and the heavy load of the task they had undertaken.

Many of the buildings still burned which made retrieval of the bodies within impossible for the moment. Perhaps that was a mixed blessing for each of the three had already dealt with more death than any of them cared to. Shantira took the brunt of the task as each new body discovered raised her hopes that at least someone in her village had survived the attack. Yet with each new body discovered, her hopes were dashed.

After several hours of the grisly work, Shantira's face took on the set features of one who no longer thought, but simply moved out of automatic response. Her deep blue eyes had glazed over and now took in each new sight of death and dismemberment without a hint of reaction. Odd lines traced down her cheeks where tears had fallen and washed away some of the soot, but even the tears had stopped flowing as her mind and soul became numb.

Devenshire had insisted on several occasions that she stop and allow him and Zandorth to finish this task, but she had refused. She had never shirked any task set before the village, why should she do so now.

Zandorth had found picks and shovels and set about digging graves, stopping only when massive pieces of debris needed to be moved to recover a body. As a Warrior of the Ancient Class, he had seen his fair share of death and the many horrid ways a body could be mutilated, but a majority of death he had seen in his life had befallen men. To see women and children hacked down so ruthlessly disturbed him to his very core, and he, like Shantira, now wore the expression of one who simply refused to acknowledge that such cruelty could exist.

Devenshire had just finished laying the body of a woman down next to the other bodies that had been recovered when he sensed the approach of a horse and carriage. He was surprised that his powers worked at all given his level of preoccupation of the task at hand. He turned his eyes to the trail that led into the village and summoned the mystical energies. With a tight, tired smile, he nodded. He should have known she would come. Her very nature would have demanded it.

"The Lady Brianna approaches," he said aloud. Shantira and Zandorth stopped working and joined Devenshire as the carriage came into view.

Despite her grief and fatigue, Shantira regarded Devenshire with confusion. "How do you know it is Brianna?"

Devenshire did not answer as he took several steps away from them to greet the carriage as it approached. His mind, body, and soul were heavily taxed from the work of the past night, and he did not wish to explain how he had known.

As he waited for the carriage to arrive, he took a moment to look out at the approaching dawn. This had always been his favorite time of day. There was something about the earliest sunrise that touched his soul. Each one gave the unspoken promise of a fresh beginning. It was a new start, a way to cancel out the trials of the previous day, which was now part of the past, never to return again.

It also marked the passing of another increment of time that put even more distance between him and the memory that he felt certain he would be seeking to flee for the rest of his life.

Each new dawn put that memory another notch into the past, and perhaps that, above any other poetic meaning of the occurrence of sunrise, was why he so enjoyed the birth of a new day.

However, he could find no such peace in the birth of this one. He was amazed that a new day would dare be born in the wake of such death, destruction, and sadness. However, he reflected, the Fates bore no regard for any single event and continued their business unabated.

The carriage, surrounded by Brianna's honor guard, rolled to a stop, and the driver stepped down from his high perch to open the door. For a moment, Devenshire considered stopping the driver, to spare The Lady Brianna the horrid knowledge of what had transpired here. Yet he knew such an attempt would be futile for once Brianna had set her mind to a course of action, there was little chance of altering it. Indeed, any attempt to alter her course of action would only steel her to it.

Devenshire could see the pale expression on the drivers' face as he took in the massive destruction and the line of bodies. He said nothing as he opened the carriage door, reached inside and took out a small stool that he placed on the ground underneath the door. Reaching inside, he took Brianna's hand as she stepped from the carriage. As the driver before her, she took in the scene and paled.

"Oh my Lords..." she whispered, her right hand lifting to cover her mouth, her eyes filling with tears at the magnitude of the destruction sprawled before her.

She stepped down from the carriage as her mortified eyes found Devenshire's dirty features. He stepped up and took her hands and squeezed, nodding in silent acceptance of what she was thinking.

"What happened?" she whispered, still not wanting to believe what her eyes were showing her.

Devenshire glanced over his shoulder to make sure Shantira was out of earshot. "The attack was complete, Brianna. It was well thought out, as well. This was no random act of raiders. Whoever did this, full intended that no one would survive."

Brianna's tear-filled eyes left his face to scan the smoldering remains. She saw Shantira and quickly pulled her hands from Devenshire's as she crossed to the young woman. The lost, dulled, grief-filled expression on her dirty face caused the tears to flow down Brianna's cheeks.

"Oh, Shantira!" she said as she gathered the trembling village girl in her arms. "I am so sorry," she whispered.

At first, Shantira stood rock-rigid, refusing the comfort being offered her. "Why, Brianna? Why?" she asked in a quivering voice,. "There were young... little boys and girls... old men and women. They are all gone... much worse than just killed... they were... were..." her voice broke, and she collapsed into Brianna's arms, the sobs racking her body.

"Just let your grief go, Shantira," Brianna whispered as she hugged the woman tight, tears flowing freely down her cheeks as she gazed skyward, not wanting to see any more of what she had already seen.

Devenshire reflected, as he watched Brianna comfort Shantira, that despite her bravado, despite her fierce independence, despite the distance she strove to place between herself and those around her, there was a strong warmth and compassion within the woman.

Zandorth watched the two women while Devenshire watched him. Devenshire could see the warrior was torn between wanting to help, and not knowing exactly how to do so. Finally, he slowly shook his head and returned to his task of digging graves.

With a heavy sigh, Devenshire realized that like Zandorth, there was nothing he could do for Shantira or her grief. Brianna had known her for some time and right now, she was the only person who could offer the comfort that Shantira so sorely needed.

He turned and walked back into the ruins of the village to search for another body and another reminder of just how frail the life force within each being truly is.

He was walking past a building when a tingling shiver ran down his spine. He paused and turned to face the building. Someone or something possessing mystical powers had recently been inside the building. It was a gift that nature had seen fit to grant him, the ability to know when people or objects possessing magical properties were in close proximity to him.

He placed his hands on his hips and studied the burned out hull. There were no distinguishing marks to tell him what the building had been, but judging from the layout of what was left of the building, it might have been the church. His eyes narrowed as he continued to study the building and regard the rippling sensation that continued to course down his spine. It was possible that their signs of faith had triggered his senses. It had been his experience that simple farming folk often had the strongest faith. The aura of religious faith always left him with a warm sensation. This sensation had the definite chill of evil associated with it. Whatever had triggered his senses, it wasn't religious in nature.

He took a deep breath and let it out in a sigh of dread. He knew he had to enter the building and investigate. He also knew that he had to perform the spell he should have performed hours ago. It was time to find answers to some of Shantira's questions.

With reverence, he walked slowly to the center of the building and paused a moment to collect his thoughts in preparation of performing the spell of Mystical Knowledge. The tingle in his spine grew in strength as he became closer to the source, or the location the source had occupied. He was so close that the tingle was almost painful. The cold sensation that spread through him left him in dread of discovering what manner of evil had been inside a church.

He knew what he would need to do. The Spell of Mystic Knowledge was a particularly difficult spell, and one that would leave him drained. He sat down on the floor and folded his legs as he lowered his head and closed his eyes. Forcing himself to concentrate on his breathing, he entered a trance where the outside world faded from his perceptions. He focused on his breathing and his heartbeat, breathing deeply.

The foul odor of burning death that prevailed throughout the village faded, the songs of the birds in the trees faded, Shantira's wracking sobs and Zandorth's digging also faded. His perceptions began folding in on themselves as his mind wrestled free of its earthly confines.

He saw himself seated on the floor of the church, but could no longer feel his body. His vision was clearer when he was in the trance, and the feelings that swam over him were hard to describe. It was a sense of freedom. There was no pain, no restraints of an earthly body. His consciousness had separated from his body and was now free to explore the many levels of the mystical realm.

Focusing more power into the spell, Devenshire began searching the countless streams of mystical energy, searching for the one that would lead him to the knowledge he sought. This was not like the spell he had performed to find Shantira's village. That had been a simple matter of locating the village and showing him the way to it.

This would involve seeking out the source of the energies he had detected in the church and finding their source, nature, and current location. It would involve a deeper probing of the mystical realm and, therefore, more energy.

At first, all Devenshire could ascertain was that something of magical origins had been in this building, but the nature and level of power of that magic eluded him. He doubled his concentration and mentally channeled more energy into the spell. Very slowly, images came to his mind.

Three stones... deep amber in color... crystalline in design. The energies within those three stones were formidable. Their ancient and almost limitless power had not been tapped in countless ages and even the Spell of Mystical Knowledge could not reveal exactly how to tap into the stones. What was clear was the deep-seated sense of dread that swept through his soul. The stones were evil, their power unholy.

Forcing even more energy into the spell, Devenshire dug deeper into the knowledge that hovered just out of his reach. He had to know the answers. He furrowed his brow tighter as he poured more concentration into the spell. Tiny beads of sweat popped out upon his brow and began to trickle down the sides of his face as he tried to force the mystic veil to part and reveal to him what he desired to know. Finally, the mist of ignorance began to lift, and the brutal truth of the stones began to reveal itself to Devenshire, and what he saw terrified him to the depths of his being.

~*~

Shantira's soul-wrenching sobs finally began to subside, and Brianna was grateful that she was able to vent at least some of the grief for she knew more was to come.

"Feeling better?" Brianna asked softly as Shantira's sobs dwindled to sniffs while she still clung tightly to her.

Shantira nodded slowly.

"Is there anything I can do?" Brianna asked in a soothing whisper.

"You have already done much," Shantira's shivering voice

answered weakly.

"What are friends for?" Brianna asked with a smile. The smile was not one of humor, but of comforting reassurance that the young woman would not have to face this burden alone.

Shantira finally found the strength to pull out of Brianna's embrace and stand on her own, but she kept her back to the village as she wiped the tears from her cheeks, smudging the soot and grime. She took several deep shuddering breaths as her eyes scanned the tree line of the forest behind Brianna.

"I do not understand. Why would anyone want to completely wipe out our village? We have nothing of value. We have done no harm to anyone, why?"

Brianna shrugged slowly as she exhaled in a sigh of sad knowledge. "I wish I had the answers for you. I have never understood random, unprovoked violence for the sheer pleasure of wreaking havoc and chaos."

Shantira sniffed and drew a shuddering breath as her tear-rimmed eyes continued to scan the trees, and Brianna saw the beginnings of the fire burning deep within Shantira. The grief was beginning to give way to anger again.

"The bastards will pay! I swear on all I consider holy that every single one involved in this deed will pay!" she hissed in a harsh whisper.

"More violence, Shantira?" Brianna asked calmly. There was no accusation in her voice, just a simple question designed to make Shantira consider what she had just said.

Shantira fixed her with a look that was comprised of anger, grief, and determination. "Violence begets violence! I will not rest until every single one of those who did this have suffered and paid for their atrocities! The souls of these people will not be able to rest until justice is done. Their phantoms will haunt me the rest of my days if I do not avenge their deaths."

"I understand your grief and your desire for vengeance, Shantira. But consider this: Revenge is a two-sided sword that can cut down the wielder as well as the target. These raiders killed your people, and now you seek revenge. You go out and strike down those who committed this horrid act. Then what? What will fill the rest of your days once you have lowered yourself to the level of those who have done this?"

Shantira seemed to digest this piece of advice, and for a moment, Brianna thought she might have actually gotten through to her grief-riddled mind.

But the look of vengeful determination returned. Her lips twisted into a snarl and through clenched teeth, she said, "A chance I am willing to take!"

Before Brianna could answer, there came the sound of crashing debris and staggering footsteps. She and Shantira spun to see Devenshire stumble over some rubble he had dislodged, almost falling as he exited a building. He caught himself on the charred doorframe and used it to hold himself up.

"Daimion?" Brianna asked as she began walking toward him.

He sagged against the frame, his head down and his eyes shut as if bearing some great weight. His breathing was ragged and fast. He seemed drained, almost to the point of exhaustion, and his face was very pale despite the layer of soot and grime that covered it.

Devenshire did not respond, he simply continued to lean against the doorframe. She felt a touch of concern. She had never seen him like this. Something had shaken him badly.

"Daimion, what is wrong?" she asked as she drew closer.

Finally, Devenshire looked up at her, as if seeing her for the first time. Brianna got the impression that, for a split second, he had no idea who she was or even where he was at that moment. His brow furrowed as he studied her face and then relaxed as the recognition came. He bowed his head again, eyes shutting out the images raging inside his mind.

"I am fine," he answered in a hushed tone, and she did not believe it for a second.

"What is happening? What have you seen?" she asked stopping before him.

Devenshire looked deep into her eyes, and she knew that whatever had happened, it did not bode well. So many times, she had looked deep into his eyes, searching for some indication of what motivated him, for what made him the man he was, and on each occasion, she had only seen whatever Devenshire saw fit to let her see.

Now, there was something else in the depths of his eyes. There was pain, confusion, uncertainty, and fear.

He gathered himself, pulled himself upright, and pushed off the doorframe, "I do not have much time... we do not have much time. We have to act quickly," he whispered.

"I do not understand, Daimion. What are you speaking of?" Brianna asked, realizing that she was speaking in the same hushed tones.

"What is wrong?" Shantira asked as she joined them. There was suspicion in her eyes and tone. Obviously, their hushed conversation had led her to believe that they now had some knowledge of why her village had been attacked.

Devenshire swung his gaze to Shantira and debated on how much, if any, of what he had learned he should tell them. The knowledge he had gained weighed heavily on him, and he feared that revealing that knowledge would only add unneeded weight to her already burdened soul.

"Forgive me, Shantira. I must depart now," Devenshire finally said as he stood straight again, his posture no longer showing the signs of fatigue. He turned to Brianna. "Round up as many people as you can to assist in the burials." With that, he began walking off.

"Wait! Where must you go? What is going on?" Shantira called out to him, but he did not answer, did not even slow his stride. It was as if he had not heard her.

Shantira gave Brianna a confused look before jogging off after Devenshire. She caught up to him and grabbed his arm halting him.

"What are you talking about? What is going on?" she demanded.

Devenshire looked down at her, and she could see the concern in his face. He regarded her for a handful of moments before placing a gentle hand on her shoulder. "Bury your dead. Mourn for them, and honor their memories. Do not concern yourself with anything else at the moment," he said softly.

"Devenshire! What have you discovered!" she demanded with her anger and rage circling, waiting for a target to attack.

Devenshire sighed heavily and gently pulled his arm from her grip. "I have business to attend to, and I am already late... very late."

"If you know something, I demand that you tell me!" Shantira shouted, her raw emotions breaking free of their tattered bonds.

Devenshire regarded her for several more moments, his expression blank, revealing nothing of what he was thinking or feeling, and that blankness irritated her. Without another word, he turned on his heel and began walking off again.

Shantira strode after him, anger building within her as she sensed that Devenshire held some piece of information that would help all of this senselessness make some small amount of sense.

"Damn you, Devenshire!! If you know something, you must tell me! Do not leave me here to wonder for the rest of my life! Do not curse me so! I must know why this happened!"

Devenshire did not reply as he stopped at the edge of the village and raised his hand to whistle for his mount. Before his thumb and forefinger could touch his lips, Shantira grabbed his arm and jerked it down violently, turning him partially toward her. Devenshire turned on her, his own anger flaring briefly, before he wrestled it back under control.

"There are things that are better left unknown. Ignorance, at times, can be a blessing in disguise. Trust me on this! Wrap yourself in the cloak of ignorance, and set about rebuilding your life!" he said with his voice low, his tone laced with an angry edge.

"How can I wrap myself in the cloak of true ignorance when some of the truth has already been revealed to me? By your very actions, you tell me enough to make true ignorance impossible!"

"She does have a point, Daimion," Brianna injected. Devenshire snapped his head around to look at her. In his preoccupation, he had not even heard her approach. For several long moments, he alternated his gaze between Brianna and Shantira. Neither woman could discern what was going through his mind.

"What is the point?" he finally asked, the anger and frustration just barely audible in his controlled tone. "What would you have me do, Brianna? Burden her already heavy soul with information she can do nothing about?"

"Do not speak of me as if I were not here!" Shantira injected hotly. "My village, my home, my very existence has been erased from the face of this realm, and you would have me simply bury the remains and go on about my existence as if this were something I could just forget about?

Her voice trembled in the harsh grip of her grief and anger. There was no rational direction for such raw emotions. "Perhaps you are capable of such coldness, such emptiness of soul, but I am not! These people were MY people, MY family! I *will* avenge their deaths if it takes me a lifetime!" Shantira shouted, her finger stabbing at the ground, accenting each word and trembling with uncontained emotion. Her swollen, bloodshot eyes welled up with even more tears of frustration and grief.

Devenshire looked at Shantira and instantly saw the conviction there. The absolute determination of a path she had set for herself. Though he knew little about this young woman, he knew her caliber and knew that there would be no deterring her from what she said she would do.

Zandorth stepped up, having heard the commotion. He regarded the three of them individually before turning his attention to Devenshire.

"What have you learned?"

"Too much and yet, not enough," was Devenshire's remote reply, his gaze locking to the ground. He briefly closed his eyes and gave his head a sharp shake to clear the last vestiges of what he had seen.

Brianna's eyes narrowed as she studied him intensely. Then it dawned on her why he was acting so strange. He had seen something that only someone with mystical abilities could have seen.

"You have performed a Spell of Mystic Knowledge," she said with no question in her voice.

"A what?" Shantira asked, the anger still churning beneath the surface, ready to explode at any moment.

"It is a spell," Krahl answered with disgust. Looking at Devenshire closely; finally realizing that he had performed the spell, and whatever he had learned was the reason behind his current behavior. "What did you learn?"

"A spell?" Shantira asked her eyes growing wide as the implication of that word sank into her mind. "You possess magic? You command the Mystical Arts?" Her tone was more accusing than questioning.

Devenshire regarded Shantira briefly before answering. "I have limited abilities in the Mystical Arts."

"Then you could have stopped this attack! You could have used your powers to save my people!"

Devenshire shook his head slowly, sadness tinting the edge of his eyes. "No. I could not have. Not with magic. I am not a mage."

Sadness, anger, regret, and a thousand other emotions wracked Shantira as she stood before Devenshire and contemplated this sudden revelation. Grief tore at her soul while anger chewed upon her mind. She was lost in a sea of contradicting emotions and could find nothing in any of them to anchor her to a solid footing of reasoning.

She struggled to make some semblance of order return to her thoughts but it stubbornly refused and that angered her. For one of the very few times in her life she felt completely out of control over the elements of her life and that angered her, as well.

The anger was the strongest of emotions that prevailed upon her senses, and in that heated embrace, she found a possible release for all the other emotions that assaulted her, and without her conscious effort, the anger struck out.

"Is that why I was so attracted to you? Did you cast a spell upon me? Is that how you gain your fleshly pleasures, by casting spells on women? Is that how you are able to win your childish contest with Krahl? Do you use your *limited* abilities in that area, as well?" she asked with an extreme sarcastic emphasis on *limited*.

Devenshire's eyes flashed in anger as he took the brunt of Shantira's verbal attack. The muscles of his jaw clenched, and his fists doubled as he fought to control the outrage of her accusations.

His voice was low, laced with anger and trembled slightly with the effort he was excreting to hold his temper. "I have been accused of many things in my life, but never that! I will not stand here and explain myself to a child!"

He turned and strode away, his posture rigid in the grip of his anger. Shantira moved to follow, but Brianna stayed her with a touch to her shoulder and a sad shake of her head.

"Let him go."

"No! He will tell me what he knows if I have to cut it from him a piece at a time!" she shouted. She turned to follow Devenshire and found her path blocked by Zandorth's massive frame.

"You have said enough already. Let him be!" he said his voice hard and his gaze even harder.

It was then that Shantira realized that she might have crossed some unseen line for when she looked at Brianna she saw a veiled look of disapproval. When Zandorth was sure that Shantira would not attempt to follow Devenshire, he looked briefly at Brianna, and then back at Shantira before turning and walking off in the direction of the graves he had been digging.

"Why do you two defend him? Do you not see how he has been manipulating you? He has used magic, not some mysterious charm he holds! How can you condone such behavior?" she demanded of Brianna.

"You are in grief and not thinking clearly. You have no idea how badly you just insulted him." Brianna said, and Shantira could hear the effort she was using to control the edge of her own anger.

"If you knew of what you speak of, you would know that most of what you accuse him of is not possible. Additionally, if you truly knew him you would know that for him to use his powers in such a way is simply beyond the realm of possibility. Despite his many faults, he is a man of honor. To accuse him of using his powers in such a way is the worst kind of insult you could do him or any other student of the Arts."

Shantira felt torn, torn between her grief, her anger, and now her guilt over having insulted Devenshire. The harder she tried to gain control over her emotions, the harder they assaulted her, ripped at her mind, confused and contorted her reasoning, and that infuriated her even more.

A part of her wanted to chase Devenshire down and apologize to the depths of her being while another part wished to chase him down and draw his hidden knowledge from him regardless of the methods required to do so. She wished to ask for forgiveness, and at the same time wished to give none.

The turmoil tore at her until she could stand it no longer. With a cold glare that followed Devenshire, she slowly turned toward the remains of her home and fixed Brianna with the same icy stare.

"To hell with all of you!"

Brianna watched her stride off and was compelled to go after her, in an attempt to help calm her anger, but she knew that such anger was better left to burn itself out.

Just as Shantira disappeared behind the smoldering remains of a hut, Devenshire steered his Frisian up to Brianna. She could see the anger and frustration in her friend and lover as clearly as if he had spoken them aloud.

"Do not be too angry with her, Daimion. She has been through much this past night," Brianna said softly, placing a warm hand on his leg.

Devenshire's angry gaze locked to the corner of the building Shantira had disappeared behind, and he opened his mouth to speak.

Brianna was sure some short, anger driven retort was on the way, but at the last moment he clamped his mouth closed sealing off words she was sure he would have regretted uttering later.

After several moments that she was sure Devenshire spent wrestling with his anger, his manner softened somewhat, and he looked down at her.

"Take care of her, Bri."

"You know that I will. Where are you going?"

"When her village was attacked the first time, one of the raiders survived. I will speak with him. If what I suspect is true, there is a great danger at hand," Devenshire replied.

"What kind of danger? Daimion, you must not hold this burden within yourself. What can be done?" Brianna pleaded. She could sense the burden Devenshire was under.

Devenshire watched her for several moments before his eyes lifted to take in the land around them. There was a strange expression on his face, as if he were looking at something that he truly did not ever expect to see again, and that expression, more than anything else, struck a chord of fear within her.

"I do not know. I am not certain anything can be done. But I must try."

"You are not alone, Daim. You must remember that," she said softly. She did not know why, but she suddenly had the distinct impression that Devenshire had always been alone.

Suddenly, memories of seeing him in The Tavern came to mind. Memories of him encircled by people, laughing and talking, flirting and carousing, and the one distant look in his eyes that she had never really understood. Now the meaning of that look solidified. Even among many people, Daimion Devenshire was alone, totally and utterly alone.

His eyes met hers, and some of the softness she was so used to seeing there returned. A slight smile tugged at the corners of his mouth, and he dropped a hand to cover hers before giving it a gentle squeeze.

"I know," he said softly before he took up the reins and urged his mount forward. As soon as he was clear of her, he urged his horse into a trot and then a gallop. Brianna watched him ride away.

She heard the heavy footfalls of Zandorth as he came up behind her. Although Zandorth professed a certain dislike of Devenshire, she could feel his concern for him.

"He is deeply troubled," Zandorth said as he joined her in watching Devenshire's retreating form.

"Aye, that he is," she replied not taking her eyes from Devenshire.

"I wonder what he learned. What terrible deed is at hand?" Zandorth asked.

"I do not know."

"Damn his stubbornness! Why will he not let us help? Why does he insist on taking on the entire realm single handedly?" Zandorth muttered through clenched teeth.

Despite the heaviness of the situation, Brianna could not help a small laugh as she turned and looked up into Zandorth's face.

"You may as well ask the sun to rise in the north. You would, no doubt, have better chances of success than asking Daimion to change his ways."

Brianna patted his massive forearm before moving off to direct her Honor Guard in the ghastly deeds that lay ahead of them. Zandorth did not watch her as she moved off, his gray eyes still watching the point where they had lost sight of Devenshire.

"Indeed!" he mumbled.

He would have sooner faced a thousand enemies unarmed than admit to any respect for Devenshire, but he could not deny that he felt a kinship with the mysterious black-clad man. There was a sense of honor within him that touched the same within himself. Over the season or so, that he had known Devenshire, he had found himself actually liking him.

Though he would never admit it to anyone... least of all Devenshire.

CHAPTER SEVEN

KAHLA WAS THE LARGEST CITY in Prothtow Province and served as the seat of power for the province. Like any large city, Kahla played host to a wide and varied sampling of humanity. There were the good, honest, hard-working, and law-abiding citizens and there were the not so good, not so honest, and definitely not so law-abiding individuals. The latter usually found themselves inside the building Devenshire now stood outside of: The Kahla Jail.

He regarded the building and wondered if gaining more information about the attack was worth walking into this building. For many seasons, he had given buildings such as this, as well as the people who worked within it, a wide berth and for good reason.

While the... misadventures... of his past were many miles and a few seasons away, a wanted notice with his name or description could have found its way to the Constables' desk. He had come to learn that word of misadventures such as his had a very annoying habit of following him around.

He glanced around at the city street slowly waking to the new day. The morning sun was still low in the sky, and the streets were just beginning to come to life. He took a moment to consider the people moving about, intent on their daily business. None of them knew of the terrible tragedy that had taken place in Shantira's village... at least not yet. It seemed a shame to burden them with the news.

Shaking himself out of the maudlin thoughts, he turned back to the jail. With a deep breath, he shoved his trepidation aside as he stepped up to the door and lifted the latch. There was no time to spare.

The outer office was tiny compared to the mass of the building that housed it. There was a simple wood burning stove, two desks, a large cabinet, and a few shelves. The office was bare except for the necessities of conducting the business of enforcing the laws of the land. Situated in the center of the back wall of the office was a heavy door with a large lock. Devenshire knew that beyond this door were the cells used to house prisoners awaiting either their day before a tribunal or transfer to another jurisdiction. If they had already had their day before the tribunal, then they were housed here until the execution of their sentence could be carried out.

Constable Reardon sat at one of the desks, sipping a mug of strong black coffee from a pot that gurgled atop the wood burning stove. His chair was positioned so that he could drink his coffee and look out the window at the waking city. As Devenshire stepped through the door, Reardon looked up at him. Devenshire watched as the constable took in the dirt and grime on his face as well as the distinct odor of smoke that emanated from his saturated clothing. No doubt, he presented a very odd appearance.

"Good morning to you, sir. How may I be of service?" Reardon asked pleasantly, albeit guarded given Devenshire's appearance.

"There has been a raid on a small village outside Kahla," Devenshire replied without preamble, wanting to divert the constable's attention to anything but his identity.

Reardon's brows furrowed in a look of trepidation and growing regret. "Which one?"

It was then that Devenshire realized he didn't even know the name of Shantira's village. With a touch of shame, he shook his head. "I do not know the name of it. It is situated ten miles to the southeast. One of its citizens is named Shantira Dubrie."

Reardon's face instantly lost color and his mouth hung agape in shock. "Nelton? Oh my lords, no! Not again!"

Devenshire regarded Reardon and wondered if he would be forced to endure another round of crushing grief. He had no idea that Shantira's village had been so well known. He also found it odd that a man in Reardon's position, who had undoubtedly seen just how cruel one man could be to another, would be so shocked at the attack on the village.

"How bad?" Reardon asked sitting up in his chair and setting his coffee mug on the desk.

Devenshire's features remained a soot streaked mask of grim determination to keep the horrors he had seen to himself. "Bad enough. The destruction was complete. Only Shantira and a boy survived the attack."

Reardon's face went slack for a moment as his mind reeled from the news. While raids on small villages were nothing new, to have an entire village eradicated was. Reardon's face paled even more as he considered what Devenshire's answer would mean. His eyes drifted down to his desktop without seeing it as he wrestled with the news.

"Those poor souls," he all but whispered.

Again, Devenshire was struck with the power of Reardon's grief. He was used to dealing with harder men in Reardon's position. While the Constable absorbed the horrible news, Devenshire studied the man. He was in his early to mid forties with graying brown hair. While he was a large man, he still appeared to be in good physical condition.

Reardon didn't look like a Constable. He looked more suited to farm life or some other occupation where his natural good nature would not be tarnished by the evil deeds that men were capable of. Devenshire wondered what it was about this man that would make Brianna appoint him to such a position.

"I will send sheriff's immediately," he said as he roused himself from his shock and reached for his sword belt hanging from a peg in the wall. He swung the belt around his hips and set about buckling it into place. "Are there any at the village now?"

"Zandorth Krahl, Shantira, The Lady Brianna, and her honor guard," Devenshire answered.

Reardon stopped buckling his belt and glanced up at Devenshire, shock clear in his features. "The Lady Brianna? What is she doing there? That is no place for her!"

Devenshire grinned slightly. "Indeed. But I would like to encounter the individual who would have prevented her from being there."

Reardon chuckled. "Aye. The Lady Standish can be a touch stubborn."

"Indeed," Devenshire answered.

Reardon's brows furrowed slightly as he regarded Devenshire. "Who are you?"

Devenshire's lips pursed slightly as he absorbed the question he knew was coming. Without realizing it, his eyes darted to Reardon's desk, checking to see if there was anything that would cause him trouble should Reardon learn his identity.

"My name is Devenshire. I am an acquaintance of Lady Brianna," he answered. There was no time for deception.

"I see. What can you tell me of this attack?" Reardon asked. Devenshire relaxed only a little. Just because Reardon had not recognized his name now did not mean that he would not recognize it later. He knew he would have to keep a very wary eye on the good Constable.

Devenshire quickly relayed the details from the night before, beginning at The Tavern when the boy had first arrived with news of the attack and ending with the arrival of Brianna and her entourage. He was careful to only give the Constable the barest details. The fact that he had sensed an evil magic within the church, and his ensuing Spell of Knowledge were left out.

When he finished his tale, Reardon shook his head, stunned by the brutality of the attack. "Senseless. Absolutely senseless. Those poor people have never done harm to anyone."

Devenshire nodded in agreement. "It is a tragedy."

"My thanks to you Sir Devenshire for bringing this matter to my attention. I will ride to the village with my sheriffs and see what can be done about finding the brigands responsible for this deed.

"I must ask that you remain in Kahla for the time being. I may have more questions for you once I return. How may I find you?"

"I will be staying at The Tavern for the time being," Devenshire answered.

Reardon nodded as he moved from behind his desk, heading for the door. Devenshire admired how he had been able to be mortified by the death of Nelton and then put that aside and launch himself into action.

"A moment, Constable. I have a request." Devenshire raised his hand to halt him.

"Yes?" Reardon asked, pausing at the door.

"The bandit captured after the last attack on Nelton. Is he still here?"

Reardon's brow furrowed, his mind already leaping to why Devenshire would have asked such a question. "Why do you ask?"

Devenshire mentally saluted the constable. He took the tiniest clue and was already thinking along the same lines as Devenshire was, even if he hadn't voiced it yet.

"I believe the two attacks are related," he answered simply.

"What brings you to this conclusion?" Reardon asked, already knowing the answer.

"The attacks were too close together to be the random acts of two separate bands of raiders."

Reardon nodded slowly as he considered the thought. "I can see your point. To answer your question, yes. He is still here."

"May I speak with him?" Devenshire asked.

"I am afraid not, Sir Devenshire. You are not an officer of the court, and your intervention in this matter, no matter how well intended, could be disruptive. I must decline your request." Reardon replied with what Devenshire sensed was genuine regret.

"There is no harm in asking. If I can be of any further assistance, please do not hesitate to let me know."

"Thank you again. Now if you will excuse me I must round up my sheriffs and set out for Nelton," Reardon said. He moved to the door, opened it, and stood to one side to allow Devenshire to exit.

"Of course," Devenshire replied and walked out of the jail

followed by Reardon. Devenshire made his way down the street while the Constable mounted his horse and set off in the opposite direction.

Devenshire waited until the Constable was out of sight before he quickly turned around and made his way back to the jail. No doubt Reardon would dispatch a sheriff back to the jail to watch over the prisoners. Devenshire knew he would have to act quickly.

While Reardon was, Devenshire sensed, a good man, he was not marred by a fault of being too trusting. He had been Constable long enough to learn his lessons about being too naive.

Entering the tiny office, Devenshire studied it again. This time, however, he was searching for the most likely location of the keys to the cells beyond the office. He knew his actions were illegal, but the Constable had no idea of the evil that was threatening the realm. There wasn't time for the tribunal courts to extract the information he needed.

A quick search of Reardon's desk rewarded Devenshire with the keys. While the constable may not be too trusting, he was very predictable. The desk was the last place Devenshire would have put the keys.

~*~

The bandit from the first attack on Shantira's village napped on the tiny cot inside his cell. The sound of keys rattling in the outer lock roused him, and the dull throb of his crippled knee returned. Over the past couple of weeks, the pain in his knee had gone from maddening to just infuriating. It throbbed and ached all the time, and the medicinal herbs the healer gave him did little to ease his suffering. His treatment at the hands of the constable and his sheriffs was less than gracious, but it really didn't matter. When the Master came to free him, they would all pay dearly.

As the outer door creaked open, he rose to a sitting position and prepared to be as belligerent and uncooperative as he had been since his capture. They had tried to draw information from him, and he had held true to the cause. He had not revealed anything about his Master or his plans. They thought that by constantly badgering him with angry questions and empty threats of impending justice that he would betray his band. They were fools. He would never betray his Master. He would die first.

First came the sounds of boots on floorboards, and he assumed a bored posture. The Constable and his silly sheriffs did not impress him, and he took great pains to make sure they knew it.

He lifted his bored gaze, preparing to greet the constable and his men with defiance. He was not prepared to see the one man aside from his Master, who terrified him. The black-clad man from the clearing was standing before his cell, staring at him. First his eyes widened in shock and then terror as his knee began to burn with pain similar to the pain he had felt when the man had snapped it.

"You!" The bandit gasped in disbelief.

"Greetings," Devenshire said but there was no pleasure, no warmth in his voice or features. His eyes were cold and dangerous as they bore into the bandit. His white shirt was nearly black from soot, and he reeked of smoke. His face was dirty which, in an ominous way, made him look even more dangerous than he had that day in the clearing.

"How did you get in here?" The bandit tried to sound defiant as he tried to control his fear. He quickly glanced around at the other cells to see the other prisoners peering through their bars to see what was happening. With only a marginal easing of his fear, he realized there were witnesses.

Devenshire raised his arm to show the keys dangling from his fingertips. "You and I have some unfinished business."

"I have nothing to say to you! Be gone!" The bandit snarled in reply.

Devenshire arched one eyebrow as he continued to stare intently into the bandit's eyes. "I would love nothing more than to depart this place and your foul presence. However, you have information I need. How soon I depart depends upon how cooperative you are."

"I will answer none of your questions! Where is the Constable?"

Devenshire gave the bandit a tight, dangerous grin. "If I were you? I would be more concerned with giving me the information I need before I am forced to come into that cell and take it."

The bandit's eyes began darting about the cell, much like a trapped animal searching desperately for a route of escape. "You will not assault me with so many witnesses present!"

"I see nothing. I know nothing!" one man called out from his cell.

"I am plagued with bouts of blindness and being struck deaf!" called out another.

A third man laughed. "The only thing I will bear witness to is my pleasure at seeing you beaten like the cowardly cur you are!"

Devenshire arched one brow at the comments and the ensuing look of growing terror in the bandits' eyes.

"You seek to hide amongst those like you and find they want nothing to do with you." A tight grin creased his features as he nodded slightly. "Poetic."

"You can all go to hell!" he shouted aloud before shifting his attention to Devenshire. "I have nothing to say to you! You would do well to be gone from this place before the Master comes for me. You will suffer horribly for what you have done to me!"

"Interesting," Devenshire commented as he set about unlocking the cell door. "Why should I fear your Master so? Who is he?"

The bandit seemed to press himself further into the bars at his back as if trying to press himself through them to escape.

"You will know him soon enough. You will taste his wrath and curse the day you were born. No one treats one of his like I have been treated." With each passing moment, the bravado in the bandit's voice grew fainter, while the fear increased.

Devenshire swung the cell door open and casually stepped inside, his eyes never leaving the bandit.

"Tell me, this Master of yours, why has he not come for you already? It has been weeks since your capture, and yet you are still here."

"No one dictates the Master's actions. He acts when he sees fit. He will come for me. He would not leave one of his loyal followers at the hands of brigands." While the bandits' words held the conviction of his belief, his eyes told a different story. Devenshire could see his question had made the bandit seriously wonder why his Master had not come for him.

Devenshire pulled up a small stool and sat down in front of the bandit.

"Well, until he arrives, and I am introduced to him, that gives us time to talk. I seriously want to know all about your Master."

"I am not afraid of you!" The bandit replied with almost none of the bravado he had used earlier.

Devenshire's right hand suddenly shot out and gripped the bandit's ruined knee, squeezing it very tightly. The joint was heavily bandaged but even through the bandages, he could feel the horrible swelling. The bandit screamed out in pure agony as searing waves of pain spiked up from the knee. He gritted his teeth as Devenshire put all the power he could into the squeeze. Devenshire quickly rose while maintaining his tight grip on the knee. With his left hand, he took a handful of the bandit's greasy hair and slammed his head back into the bars with a very hollow and metallic sound.

The howls of pain subsided as the bandit was momentarily dazed. He groaned as his eyes rolled in their sockets from the pain and shock of having his head rammed into the bars. With moans of intense pain, the bandit managed to get his eyes to focus, and what they saw chilled him to the bone.

Devenshire's eyes had turned almost black as they bore ruthlessly into his. He saw a very dark, very real danger in their depths as Devenshire's lips peeled back in a snarl.

"You should be."

CHAPTER EIGHT

WORD OF THE TRAGEDY SPREAD quickly, and by the time the sun had hit its high point in the sky, Nelton was full of people from Kahla and surrounding villages. All came willingly, taking their turn in retrieving the dead and assisting with burials.

Constable Reardon and his sheriffs arrived, asked the questions required of their office, and conducted a thorough investigation. Once done, they took up their place with the others, helping with the sad work of the day.

A priest from Kahla stood over each grave and gave as individual a eulogy as he could. Unfortunately, most of the bodies had either been burned or mutilated so badly that they could not be identified as man or woman let alone who they may have been in life. Most of the graves would have blank markers.

Shantira, her mind and body pushed to their absolute limits, stood solemnly by each grave, saying as an individual farewell as she could. She insisted on attending each burial.

At the end of one of the funerals, she turned to return to the village and stopped short. The hollowed out shell of her village teamed with many people; so many people. Men moved debris and retrieved bodies. Women set about keeping a steady supply of water and bread to those working. Occasionally, a rider from another village would arrive, bringing more bread and water to keep the people working hydrated and fed.

One man sat on a log, wiping the sweat from his soot-coated forehead. A woman, his wife undoubtedly, eased up beside him, passing him a tin of water and a chunk of bread. The man refused the bread but gulped the water down. As he handed the tin back to her, his haunted expression returned to the remains of the village. His head shook slowly with the level of devastation. His wife pulled him close to her, lovingly stroking his hair and planting a gentle kiss to his temple. He seemed to soak in her comfort for a moment before pulling from her embrace and giving her a warm, loving smile. He kissed her softly and gazed into her eyes, and a silent understanding passed between them. If any good at all could come from this day, it would be the harsh reminder of just how short life is and how quickly everything you know and love could be wiped from existence. He nodded softly and returned to the grisly tasks ahead.

Shantira felt new tears sting her eyes at the scene. Such love warmth and compassion between two people in the shadow of such death and destruction was touching. She closed her eyes to force the tears from them and to etch the scene into her troubled mind. She so wanted that kind of comfort again. To feel that warmth and love, and to know that no matter what the realm dealt out, there would always be a comforting hand to ease her burdens.

A comforting hand…

She remembered how Devenshire had laid a comforting hand on her shoulder when she had grieved over Lucinda's body. Her brow furrowed and a frown creased deeper into her features as a fresh wave of guilt washed over her. She deeply regretted losing her temper with him. She tried, unsuccessfully, to forget the horrible words of insult she had hurled at him. She didn't know why she had been so angry with him, but she had noticed that her emotions, this day, were completely beyond her control.

That was twice the man had tried to help her and twice she had lashed out at him. It was a very disturbing pattern that she sorely wished to change.

By the time the sun had begun its descent into the waiting arms of night, the last villager's body was lowered into the grave. The Priest, his faith and strength pushed to their limits, uttered the words he sincerely hoped would do the deceased honor. All who had gathered to lend aide attended the final funeral of this horrible day, and Shantira felt as if her life had ended with those of her fellow villagers. She was without a home, without anything to link her to the land she had loved so dearly.

As she tried to focus on what the Priest was saying, her mind began asking questions. What would she do now that her only link to this world had been so savagely cut? There were no answers to her mournful questions, just as there had been no answers to the questions she had been asking since discovering the destruction the night before. Her eternal, soulful cry of why, went unanswered.

The Priest uttered closure to his prayer of the deceased, and the group of people began to silently disperse, leaving Shantira to stand next to the grave alone. Several of the men began gathering wood for a fire and the women set about the task of preparing some sort of an evening meal. Shantira had already given them permission to use whatever food they could find in the village stores to feed all who had come to help.

She tried not to dwell on the irony of a second fire in as many nights being started within her village and for completely different purposes. One fire had destroyed life while the other would help sustain it.

Shantira shook her head to clear the thought from her mind. She was so very tired and yet the thought of rest was distasteful to her, as was the thought of eating or seeking the warmth of friends. If she had not insisted on going to The Tavern last night, she would have been here, perhaps would have been able to help turn back the wave of savagery that had flooded through her village.

"Shantira?"

She turned to see Brianna walking up to her. She was a far cry from the elegant lady with a heavy undertone of sexuality from the night before. Her beautiful emerald gown was tattered, filthy, and absolutely ruined. It had not taken Brianna long to rip the sleeves from the gown as well as cut the skirt down to something easier to work in.

Her thick black hair was a frayed mess, slipping from the multiple clips used to hold it in place. Her beautiful face was streaked with a mixture of dirt, soot, and sweat. Her deep green eyes appeared dull. Like everyone else, she had seen things that would be with her for the remainder of her days.

Despite her rank and status, she had toiled with the others, working side by side with those she ruled. It spoke volumes of her as a person and as a ruler.

Shantira smiled softly as she took Brianna's dirty, blistered hands in hers. "Brianna," she whispered as the ever-present tears in her eyes welled up again.

"How are you?" Brianna asked softly.

A single tear tracked down her filthy cheek as she slowly shook her head. "I sincerely wish to thank..." She was cut off by Brianna's shaking head.

"Do not thank me. I could have done no less and wish I could have done more. I have no doubt that you would do the same for me in the reverse."

Shantira's expression shifted to the last grave being filled. "I pray to the Fates that I never have to... for your sake."

The two men working to fill in the grave finished rounding off the mound and stuck their shovels into the ground next to the grave. They wiped the sweat from their foreheads and paused a moment to pay their final respects. They expressed their condolences to Shantira who accepted them with a tight smile and muttered gratitude. The men gave the appropriate bow to Brianna in respect and then moved off to join the others.

Left alone, the two women stood and watched as the day and the night exchanged places in the sky. As they slowly passed each other, the sky was on fire in the brilliant colors of the mixing of the two. Deep blues and purples mixed with a myriad shading of yellows to cast the few clouds in the sky with a magnificent highlight. It was a breathtaking scene and both women simply took in the vision, taking what solace they could from it.

After a while, Shantira drew in a shuttering breath. "Daimion said that they will never be truly dead, that as long as I remember them they will live on in me."

Brianna smiled tiredly and gave her hand a gentle squeeze. "He is right."

Shantira sighed. "I wish I had not been so harsh with him. I do not know what came over me."

"We have all said and done things we wish we could take back. It is part of the lessons of life we all must go through. It helps us learn what motivates us and helps us strive not to repeat the mistakes we have made. Besides, you have been through much this day. Do not be so harsh with yourself," Brianna replied softly, her eyes never leaving the sunset.

Shantira wanted to say so much, yet could find no words to give her thoughts flight. So she simply nodded and let the silence descend upon them. They watched the day and the night bid a brief greeting to each other as they exchanged places in the heavens. The shadows deepened, and a faint chill came to the air. The symphony of the night began warming up their instruments for this night's concerto.

She had always taken time to walk through her village at sunset, to witness the changing of the day with night and listen to the beautiful songs. The transition had always calmed her from the days' work and brought a peace to her.

As she stood in the midst of the graves and awaited the arrival of the night, she knew she would draw no peace from it this time and could not help but wonder if she ever would again.

Finally, Brianna spoke again. Although her voice was soft, the sudden sound of it startled Shantira.

"I am going to get something to eat. You should eat, as well and take time to rest."

Shantira gave a wan smile and nodded once. "I will join you shortly."

Shantira smiled and nodded, "I will join you shortly."

Brianna looked into Shantira's eyes and gave her a warm smile before giving her a hug. "You are not alone." she whispered.

"I know. Thank you," Shantira replied, drawing strength from her friend for hers felt as though it were at its ragged end.

Brianna pulled from the embrace and looked deep into Shantira's tear stained eyes, driving the truth of her statement home to her. She could not begin to imagine the pain and grief the young woman must be going through. She wanted to do so much to help her, but had no idea how.

Brianna nodded as she gave her hands a reassuring squeeze before turning and walking toward the campfire.

When Brianna entered the circle of people around the fire, someone offered her a plate of food and a tin of wine. She gratefully accepted them and found a log to sit upon next to the fire. She took a moment to search the faces of those around her and found each person battling the horrors they had seen this day. There was no light conversation, only the silence of those who wanted to speak, but could find no words that seemed appropriate for the moment.

"How is she?" Roslyn asked as she slipped next to Brianna. She had closed The Tavern down for the night, and it was the first time Brianna could ever remember The Tavern not being open. Like her, Roslyn had toiled and struggled alongside everyone else in the day's sad work and bore the same harried expression.

Brianna looked over her shoulder at the dark silhouette of Shantira and sighed. "She is holding up remarkably well considering the circumstances. I feel she will be fine, in time."

Roslyn watched the lonely silhouette, her face twisting into a sad expression of grief and regret. "Poor child. My heart grieves for her."

Brianna nodded slowly, watching Shantira for several more moments before the sadness bore too heavily upon her. She sighed and turned her attention to the plate of food before her.

Even though she was ravenous with hunger, she could not seem to force herself to eat. The village stores of food had been cleaned out in the attack, and it was with forethought by the women of other villages that food had been brought in. She felt compelled to eat, to show her gratitude for those who had brought the food, yet to eat in the midst of such death seemed an atrocity.

"Eat, Brianna," Roslyn said softly, sensing her hesitation. "Starving yourself will not bring the dead back. Do you not remember the festivals held here? How these good people opened their homes and hearts to all who would come? How the food, wine, and fellowship were offered without hesitation or condition?" She patted Brianna softly on the arm. "Do you really think they would want this situation to be any different?"

Brianna did recall the festivals this village had held. These people had offered all they had so their guests would be made welcome, and enjoy their hospitality. With a tight smile and brief nod, she slowly began to eat, more in tribute to the people than to quell her hunger.

~*~

From a distance, a dark figure watched the people below as they ate in solemn silence. He felt hunger growl at him and was hard pressed not to act on it. There was a different food below, and he could hear it call to him, rousing his primal need to feed. With a great effort, he stayed the hunger by sheer determination. Feeding was not his purpose for coming here.

A great evil had swept through here and, for a time, hell had reigned supreme. He had felt it call to him, and arouse him in ways he no longer thought possible. In his mind, he had seen the blood flow, had heard the screams of pain, had seen the ghostly images of terrified expressions of fear and anguish, and rejoiced in the sinister malevolence that caused them. He had heard the heartbeats rapidly thump in mind ripping fear, and then in soul rending pain, and then flutter and cease. He didn't have the words for the sensations that had coursed through him, but it was very much like being intoxicated on the finest of wines. The experience had been exquisite.

He had been too far away to discern the true nature of the evil power, but it had to be extraordinarily powerful to touch him from such a distance, and to convey the sensations and visions he had experienced.

This both delighted and troubled him. The fact that someone was capable of such evilness, of being able to strike such abject terror in its victims, was impressive and he admired the power.

Yet the same things that delighted him also troubled him. It had been a very long time since anything had been able to touch him in such a way, and he wished to know if this new presence of evil were something he would need to be on guard against, or welcome as an ally.

A robed figure entered the circle of people, and he felt instant revulsion rise up within him as he recognized the robes and adornments of a priest. Indeed, he would need to keep his distance from these people.

He stretched out his mind to gauge the intensity of the man's faith and was not surprised to find it quite high. On his many treks into this region, he had discovered that the priests here were devout in their faith, and therefore, a very real threat to him. He would have to be very cautious.

Keeping a wary eye on the priest, he reached out to seek any trace of the incredible evil presence he had sensed the night before. All he perceived were translucent after-images, fleeting, swirling glimpses, very much like the last wisp of smoke from an extinguished candle.

As he considered his next course of action, a face in the crowd below caught his attention. He had not bothered to study the faces of the people below for they were of little interest to him beyond what they could provide him in nourishment, but this face called to him. When he looked upon it, he felt his eyes grow wide in astonishment as something deep in his unmoving chest fluttered for the first time in many seasons.

Could it be?

Did he dare hope?

Did he dare allow himself to believe?

The woman was filthy. Her black hair was disheveled while her features were caked with dirt, soot, and dried sweat. Her green eyes were dulled by the things she had seen this day, and he could sense the exhaustion that weighed heavily upon her. Grief crushed down upon her even more than the exhaustion. A thousand other emotions assaulted him as he probed her mind, and he was forced to retreat to keep the emotions from overwhelming him. He was too shocked at finding her to be able to keep her emotions at bay. As if he had been pushed by an invisible hand, he took an involuntary step back.

As she turned her head to answer someone, he got a better look at her face and felt himself begin to tremble. He had known before getting a better look at her face, but any doubt was now removed.

He knew.

Her soul had returned yet again. Just as it had so many times before, to linger just out of his reach, just outside his ability to reclaim what once was his so long ago. The cruelty of the Fates was once again torturing him with her countenance, teasing him with images of a life he had left behind.

The great evil that had swept through here was now of little concern, an after-thought. He gazed upon her, helpless to stop the torrential flood of memories her face conjured. Along with the memories came another feeling he did not welcome—pain. He had thought that pain and suffering would be gone when he awoke in his new existence, and with the exception of her memory, he had been right. He knew the only way to eradicate the one last vestige of pain from his existence was to reclaim her.

Just as she had been before. Just as she would be again. This time he would not be denied—the Fates be damned!

It took every ounce of self-control he could muster not to immediately swoop down and take her. Now was not the time, and he would not take her by force. He had tried that once before and failed, just as he had failed in every attempt he had ever made to reclaim her since that fateful night so long ago.

She would give herself back to him willingly. He had learned the error of his previous attempts, and he now had the precious gift of patience. Sienna, Gwenna, Cianni, or whatever name she went by now... she would be his... he swore it.

The impact of finding her again, combined with his growing hunger, made him begin to lose control. He turned and silently slipped through the woods away from the ruins. He felt as if her presence were following him, to taunt and tease him with a reality that a part of him feared would never be. He violently dashed that feeling from him as he increased his pace. He would feed and then meditate before the rising sun came.

He would not fail this time.

CHAPTER NINE

AS ONE DARK FIGURE slipped away from the ruins of the village, another dark clad figure stepped to the edge of the light cast by the fire. He leaned against a tree, folding his arms across his chest as he watched the people eat and comfort each other in the wake of intense tragedy. He was impressed by their numbers. They had all set aside their own problems to come to the aid of another.

He was touched by the fact that they came from different places, different stations in life and led very different lives and yet they were all linked together in some intangible way that made them a sort of an extended family. He was also touched by the fact that although many of them knew him and had accepted him, he was not truly a part of them.

Devenshire's brows furrowed as he watched them, and he tried to recall a time that he actually felt as though he belonged. He instantly regretted it for it called to mind the very memory he spent each sunrise trying to outrun. With a heavy sigh, he realized that it would take many more sunrises to put the memory back where it had been.

He took in a deep breath and shook himself out of the maudlin thoughts. There was much to do and very little time to do it. He quickly scanned the crowd and found Zandorth's massive form seated on the ground, leaning against a boulder and eating. The warrior was just as dirty as the others were and bore the same weary, harried expression of having seen things no one should ever have to bear witness.

Devenshire cocked his head to one side as he studied Krahl. He sat off to the side of the others, not seeking the warmth of the crowd. He was, no doubt, dealing with the horrors he'd seen in his own unique, stubborn way. Devenshire knew him well enough to know that he would not dare show weakness to anyone.

Krahl looked up, and Devenshire got a good look at his eyes. The warrior was having a great deal of trouble dealing with what had happened. The death and waste of human life that had been savagely spread out before him had pushed him to the very brink of his endurance, and in many ways, Zandorth was harder hit by the tragedy than most.

Devenshire smiled slightly as he realized that, despite his massive size and gruff demeanor, Zandorth Krahl had a soft side. With a soft chuckle he shook his head. He'd be damned if he would point that out to him.

He focused his attention on Krahl and called on his powers, sending his thoughts to Krahl's mind and establishing a link that would allow them to converse without anyone else being aware.

Zandorth. I am in need of your assistance.

Krahl jerked in a start as he began looking around to see who had spoken to him. None of the people around him gave any indication that they had spoken to him.

Devenshire could sense his thoughts. It was disturbing him, to say the least. The non-verbal way of communicating could be very unsettling for those who were not used to it.

It is I, Daimion.

Devenshire? By the Lords! What manner of blackness are you working on me? came the warriors harsh, anger riddled thoughts.

Devenshire could not deny a certain level of amusement at watching Krahl's reaction. I am working no blackness on you. I am trying to get your attention without anyone else knowing. Now stop looking so mortified before someone notices. I am in the clearing to your left. Come here so that we may speak.

Krahl sat his plate of food to the side and rose, moving around the group of people at the fire. He went to the clearing and scanned the shadows, finding Devenshire under a tree. With a backward glance to ensure no one had followed him, he strode up to Devenshire, glaring down on him.

"Do not ever do that again! I feared the demons of hell had come for me!" he growled.

Devenshire fixed his gaze into Zandorth's eyes and smiled. "The demons of hell would not waste their time coming for you. I am quite certain that they would fear you would take over the rein of hell once you arrived."

"Then perhaps I will take you with me. I can see you being a useful servant to me in hell!" he growled in response.

Devenshire hid a smile. Had the situation not been so dire he would have liked to continue their usual banter. Time was a commodity that was in dangerously short supply.

"I spoke to the bandit from the first raid on the village," he stated flatly.

"What did he say?"

Devenshire's eyes had drifted off to the side as he contemplated what he had learned. At Krahl's question, he shifted his serious gaze back to the warrior. "Xavier and his followers have returned."

Zandorth's eyes grew wide. "What? Impossible! Xavier was destroyed, his Followers killed or disbanded. His depraved Order was eliminated seasons ago."

Devenshire shook his head. He was still having trouble believing what the weeping bandit had told him, and part of him seriously wished to not believe it. "The bandit I spoke to was a Follower of Xavier. There was no deception in his words or thoughts. Xavier is alive and well despite the stories to the contrary."

Krahl spat viciously into the dirt. "Xavier! Only the demons of hell would dare spawn life to such a vile creature!"

"Who is Xavier?" Shantira asked, stepping from another set of shadows. Both men spun to face her, startled by her sudden appearance. Sneaking up on either man was not an easy feat.

Devenshire regarded her, fighting down his anger at her from earlier in the morning. "You should not be here."

Shantira breathed softly, sadly, as she wrapped her arms about her. "I have nowhere else to be." She looked up at Devenshire, locking her gaze to his. "What have you learned of the attack? Who are the Followers and who is Xavier?"

"The spawn of hell itself!!" Zandorth growled, clearly unsettled by the prospect of Xavier still being alive.

Devenshire decided that she should at least have a name to give to her grief and suffering.

"Xavier was once a student of the Ancient Arts of Duvall. It was said that he could very well have become the next High Master Adept in time."

"What is the Ancient Arts of Duvall?" she asked.

"There are several orders that study the Mystical Arts, each one pursues the Arts in a different fashion. The Arts of Duvall are the most widely accepted study.

"People who have the promise of possessing the Mystical Arts are sent to retreats so that the Adepts can study and measure their abilities and train them in the use of the Arts," Devenshire explained.

"Magic! It is a tool of the Lord of the Underworld!" Zandorth spat.

"Not when it is taught and applied correctly," Devenshire replied evenly.

"Nonsense! Magic is a tool for those who are too lazy to carve out their own way in the realm!" He paused to slap the hilt of his massive broadsword. "This is all a man needs to make his way!"

Devenshire shook his head. He and Zandorth had debated this subject on many occasions, and they had yet to reach a middle ground. Zandorth had no tolerance for the Mystical Arts and very little use for its practitioners.

"Be that as it may, Xavier was a promising student. His level of power and mastery of the Arts was impressive, to say the least. His mastery of the Arts grew rapidly, some thought too rapidly. Some feared that he was gaining great power but with little discipline to use it properly."

Devenshire paused and took a deep breath. "Their fears were justified and confirmed.

"Xavier was expelled from the Retreat of Duvall for practicing what was deemed to be unethical magic. A season later, he returned with a veritable army of Followers and laid siege to the Retreat of Duvall."

"It was a massive battle." Zandorth picked up the story. "The people inside the Retreat fought bravely and with great honor, but the brigands Xavier had recruited to his foul bearing were lowly, unethical beings who knew nothing of honor or of the Codes of Battle.

"They finally breached the walls of the retreat and slaughtered all who were inside." Zandorth looked over his shoulder at the ruins of Shantira's village. "They bore no regard for their victims, and all died horrible deaths." He finished as he turned his head back, knowing that what he had seen this day all but confirmed the handy work of Xavier's Followers.

Devenshire nodded slowly, his eyes also gazed into the shadowed remains of Shantira's home. "The mystical battle between Xavier and the High Master Adept was said to have lasted for three days, with both casting incredible spells of power with which to best the other.

"In the end, Xavier called on the Dark Mystics and used their black magic to defeat and finally kill, the High Master Adept. Xavier converted the Retreat of Duvall into his own and formed The Order of Xavier. Only a sick and twisted mind such as his would have dared to pervert the Retreat into what it became."

Devenshire caught the brief flare of his anger and forced it down before continuing. "The Followers of Xavier are given to every pleasure of the flesh and the material wealth of this realm. They bear no regard or respect for the Fates or the Afterlife. There are tales of raids on villages for the purpose of harvesting young women to be taken back to Xavier's retreat where they were subjected to every torture and humiliation until their spirits were broken and they became slaves of the Followers."

They were silent for several moments, each wrestling with their own thoughts before Zandorth shook his head. "But Xavier was defeated ten seasons ago. The Warriors of the Ancient Class, The Warriors of Kintaid, and the Mystics of Soltolmi combined their powers and numbers and led a massive assault on the Followers. All were said to have been killed or absorbed in the great spells the Mystics had cast!"

Devenshire nodded slowly. "Yes, but Xavier's body was never counted among the dead, and the Mystics of Soltolmi were never able to confirm his souls' presence among the deceased. It would be foolish to simply assume that Xavier had perished in the battle. It would not be beyond the realm of possibility that he would use the bulk of his Followers as a shield to cover his escape, leaving them to their own fates."

"Are you suggesting that Xavier actually survived the battle and has returned to re-establish his Order?" Zandorth asked, not wanting to believe the Fates would permit such a thing.

Devenshire shrugged. "I suggest nothing. I simply state what the facts lead me to believe. I felt a powerful presence inside the church this morning, and my suspicions were confirmed by my discussion with the bandit from the first attack."

"Perhaps it was one of his previous Followers recreating the Order in some perverted memorial to Xavier," Zandorth offered.

Devenshire shook his head. "Only someone with tremendous Mystical powers could have left the presence I sensed this morning. There are only a small handful of beings in the realm capable of that. We must assume the worst."

Shantira regarded the two men and their reactions. "I have heard stories of that which you speak. I thought they were simply rumors, tales designed to frighten."

Devenshire let out a brief, bitter chuckle, his eyes staring off into the darkness. "If only that were true."

"So why would he attack my village? We had nothing of value to anyone but ourselves," she asked.

Devenshire glanced briefly at Zandorth, the unease in his expression saying he knew why the village had been attacked, and he really didn't want to reveal it. "The Stones of Andarus," he said so softly that it was almost a whisper.

Zandorth's eyes grew wide in disbelief. "You are mad! The Stones are a myth!"

Devenshire shifted his weight and took a deep breath. "They are no myth. They exist, and they were here, in this village."

Shantira looked confused. "The Stones of Andarus? Our priest had them. They were a religious artifact handed down to him through generations of his family. He said that the ancient power of the stones is what created the realm."

"They did not create the realm, but they could very well destroy it." Devenshire replied with trepidation.

"Great Lords of Kuvol!!" Zandorth exclaimed, and Shantira watched him pale as he looked at Devenshire. "If the Stones are real, and if Xavier has returned and resumed his macabre studies.... Lords, protect us all!"

"I do not understand. The Stones were a harmless religious artifact. What are you trying to say?" Shantira asked.

Devenshire shook his head. "I am saying that your Priest held three of the most evil artifacts in creation, and Xavier came for them. When the first raid he ordered against your village failed, he came for the Stones himself.

"The Stones are older than time and far more evil than any creation of the Underworld. For uncounted seasons, their whereabouts were unknown, and it was widely accepted that they had been separated and hidden away in the far corners of creation."

Devenshire paused to look out at the ruins of the village. "Apparently, the tales were wrong. I felt their presence in the church this morning... along with what I must now assume was Xavier's presence."

Zandorth leveled a hard look into Devenshire's eyes. "You are sure?"

Devenshire met and held the warrior's gaze. "I have never been more sure. Xavier has returned and he holds The Stones of Andarus."

"Xavier." Shantira whispered. She turned the name over in her mind. Finally, her rage, grief, and desire for vengeance had a name.

"Then the legends are true. The Stones of Andarus hold the power of creation, and the power to destroy creation," Zandorth said softly as if fearing to voice such a conclusion too loudly.

"I believe Xavier knows the depth of their power but not how to tap into it. However, he is an adept at the Mystical Arts and aligned with the Dark Mystics, as well. It would be foolish to assume that he could not discover how to gain access to that power. We must act quickly if we are to have any chance of stopping whatever plan Xavier has in his twisted mind."

Zandorth absorbed Devenshire's words silently and without comment. He regarded the shadow of Devenshire only briefly before he spoke. "I am with you!"

"As am I," came another voice, and both men turned to find the Lady Brianna standing in another shadow watching them.

"It will be a dangerous task," Devenshire stated flatly.

"And?" she asked, accepting his assessment of what lay ahead and reconfirming her commitment to join he and Zandorth.

Devenshire gave his head a quick shake. "Do not take this quest lightly, Brianna. The perils will be great, and I cannot say, with any certainty, that we will have any chance of success," Devenshire warned.

"What would you have me do, Daimion? Sit here knowing what I know and do nothing?" she asked.

"You could very well die," he replied.

"If what you fear is true, I shall die anyway. If I am to be forced into death, then I wish to face the hand that pushes me into the abyss," she replied, her green eyes unwavering as she stared into his.

Devenshire locked eyes with her, trying to find some way to discourage her from coming along. On the other hand, he could not argue with her on that point. He could not help but admire Brianna's courage in the face of what promised to be a most dangerous and deadly trek into uncertainty. As with her arrival to this place this morning, he knew that trying to talk her out of coming would be futile. He could see in the flash of her eyes that she had already made up her mind to come along.

Finally, he shrugged. "Do as you wish. I have warned you of the dangers, and the final decision must be yours."

"Will you grant me the same courtesy of choice?" Shantira asked boldly.

He turned to face her, one eyebrow arching above the other, "You do not understand the perils that lie ahead."

"By your own admission, neither do you," Shantira replied evenly.

Devenshire stepped from the shadows and crossed to stand before her. He looked down into the deep blue of her eyes that caught an occasional flicker of light from the distant fire and reflected it back. He saw the same level of determination there that he had seen earlier and knew, like Brianna, she had made up her mind.

"Are you sure you wish to pursue this path?" he asked softly.

"More so than perhaps any of you. My people were slaughtered for the whims of a madman intent on evil. Xavier gave little thought to life as he tore through my village and destroyed their existence..." Her eyes filled with tears as her gaze drifted downward. "My existence." She quickly shook herself out of another wave of grief and locked her determined gaze back into Devenshire's.

"If he is intent on more evil, then he must be stopped, and I feel compelled to do what I can, in honor of my people, to stop him." She looked deeply into Devenshire's eyes. "Please do not deny me this, Daimion. It is all I have left."

The urgency and passion of her words touched Devenshire, and for a moment, he put himself in her place and had to honestly ask himself what he would do if the situation had been reversed. The answer was almost instantaneous.

He slowly nodded. "Then join us, and let us all hope we are successful."

Shantira slowly closed her eyes and lowered her head slightly as an expression of gratitude came across her face. She wondered if Devenshire knew just how much he had just helped ease her suffering with his statement. For the first time since she had crested the ridge over her village, and saw what had happened, a sense of direction returned.

"What is the plan?" Zandorth asked.

"Gather whatever supplies you feel you will need for a long journey, but pack light. Meet me at The Tavern one night hence, and we will begin," Devenshire answered as he turned from Shantira and began walking toward the shadows of the woods.

"Where are we going?" Brianna asked.

Devenshire paused, and then turned to look at the three of them. "With Zandorth's skills, we will track them. There were too many of them for them to be able to adequately cover their trail."

"What if he used his powers to eradicate their trail?" Zandorth asked.

Devenshire sighed. "Then we will head to the region of Halitadous, to the retreat of Duvall."

"How can you be sure he has resumed his old retreat?" Zandorth asked.

Devenshire shook his head. "I cannot be. It is the only hope we have, at this point."

Zandorth locked gazes with him. "What if you are wrong?"

Devenshire didn't so much as blink. "Then we die."

Zandorth's features grew hard as he gave a quick, sharp nod, accepting Devenshire's blunt assessment of the situation. "You realize that going to Halitadous will take us through the Coledecci," he said.

Devenshire nodded slowly. "Aye. It will."

"I will bring my full Honor Guard," Brianna said.

Devenshire shook his head. "No. They may be your Honor Guard, but they owe their allegiance to King Lordoron. If you involve them, the Captain of your Honor Guard will be duty bound to report to the King and delay our departure. We cannot be delayed. We will have to recruit assistance along the way."

"My Honor Guard is loyal to me," Brianna argued.

"You and I both know better. You have let the warm friendship you have established with your Honor Guard cloud your judgment. You know what the Captain of your Honor Guard will be obliged to do once he learns what is at hand."

Brianna opened her mouth to argue the point with him, but she knew he was right. It was standard protocol within the Lordship. Her brow furrowed, and she frowned as she nodded. She hated to lose an argument, especially with a man, and specifically with Devenshire.

"Fine," she retorted.

Devenshire fixed each of them with a deep gaze before turning on his heel and vanishing into the night.

Zandorth and Brianna exchanged worried glances as Shantira stepped closer.

"What is the Coledecci?" she asked.

"It is a forest region many miles to the north. It is said that true Black Magic reigns there, and that many foul creatures of the Dark Mystic roam the area in search of souls to take to their Master," Zandorth replied.

"It is also said very few who have ever entered the Coledecci have ever left. Those who have left were not as they were when they entered," Brianna added crossing her arms about herself at a sudden chill.

"I do not understand. Who is this Dark Mystic you speak of?"

"Legend has it that he was once an adept of the Mystical Arts, a mage of great power. But he began dabbling in the Black Arts, and they claimed his soul, turning him forever to the darkness. It is said that he wields powers that go beyond the understanding of even the Dark Mages. It is said that he commands powers from the underworld itself, if not from the very depths of hell," Zandorth answered, and Shantira's look of fear did not go unnoticed. "Do you still wish to come with us?"

Shantira took a moment to ask herself if she truly desired to continue this voyage. The sights and sounds of this past day recalled why she had insisted on coming in the first place. She steeled her resolve and looked Zandorth straight in the eyes.

"More so now than ever," she replied.

"Very well," he said as he turned his attention to Brianna. "Give my regards to the others. I will depart now to begin preparations."

Brianna only nodded, as most of her attention was many miles to the north.

Zandorth nodded briefly to Shantira and then turned and strode away toward his own mount.

Shantira stepped up beside Brianna. "Is this as dangerous as they let on, or is this an attempt to dissuade me from going with them?"

Brianna looked at Shantira with an expression that caused her trepidation to double.

"It is more dangerous than you can imagine. Providing we survive the journey through the Coledecci, the evil that awaits us at the Retreat of Duvall will make the Coledecci pale in comparison."

CHAPTER TEN

THERE WAS LITTLE TIME FOR grief or mourning through the next day as Shantira and Brianna prepared for the long and dangerous journey ahead. She was very thankful for something to do; anything to do that would take her mind off the charred, horrific memories of less than a day ago.

She had found what little of her hut the fires had left and quickly discovered that the only possession that survived was her father's sword. There was some minor damage to the hilt, but it was easily repaired. The blade had been tarnished from smoke and soot, but she had been able to clean and polish it back to its former luster.

She found it quite symbolic that the only earthly possession she retained after the attack was her sword. She vowed that it would strike the blow that would avenge her people.

Brianna had offered, and Shantira had gratefully accepted, lodging at Brianna's Keep. It was not quite a castle but more than a simple dwelling. The rooms and halls of the Keep bore every indication of Brianna's unique personality. The day had been spent with the two preparing for the journey, and Shantira in the unusual situation of guiding Brianna. Through the bulk of their friendship, Brianna had always served as a sort of older sister, gently guiding the younger Shantira through the many twists and turns that life could hurl at someone.

Though Brianna was a woman of deep inner strength, and Shantira had no reservations about her making this journey, she was not used to extended travel without the luxury of being able to take everything she thought she might need. With considerable irritation, Brianna soon discovered that she would be allowed to carry far less than what she would have considered "necessary for survival."

Soon the considerable size of supplies Brianna had intended to carry had been reduced to only that which would fit in dual saddlebags. As she regarded the pile of discarded supplies, she had placed her hands on her hips and let her breath out in an irritated sigh while she shook her head. "This will be a most barbaric journey to say the least."

Shantira regarded the meager pile of supplies that would be taken and couldn't help but notice that Brianna's journal, an ink well, and writing quill were among the things that she absolutely refused to leave behind.

She had often wondered what was written in the pages of that journal, but Brianna guarded it fiercely, refusing any access to its pages.

"Perhaps you are too pampered for such a strenuous journey, Milady." Shantira said, only a small glint in her eyes betrayed her good-natured jab.

Brianna slowly rolled her eyes as she turned her head to fix her friend with a stern, albeit good-natured, glare, "I can see that you have already had too much exposure to Devenshire. You are becoming as big a brat as he."

Shantira let out a breathy, light chuckle as she smiled slightly and closed her eyes while shaking her head. Brianna laughed as well, relieved to see some flicker of Shantira's personality beginning to break through the grief.

Shantira felt a twinge of guilt at her ability to laugh so soon after the tragedy, but she did not voice this, as the sight of her laughter seemed to ease Brianna's concern for her well-being.

"I am going to change," Brianna commented as she turned and swept out of the room.

Shantira nodded as she turned to make sure her things were packed and ready. She took a moment to consider her own attire; black knee high boots, brown tweed breeches and tan, loose fitting blouse. A darker brown cloak with a hood was draped over a chair next to the door. These were borrowed from a woman in another village since what few clothes she owned had been destroyed in the fire. The clothes actually belonged to the woman's eldest son. The woman had apologized that she had nothing else to offer her in the way of clothing. It actually suited her to be wearing the more masculine clothing, especially in the face of the journey ahead.

She stepped before the full-length mirror and regarded her reflection. Her long, thick black hair had been pulled back and tied at the nape of her neck. She noticed her face looked even more haggard than before. Her red rimmed, swollen deep blue eyes stared back at her with deep-rooted grief and sadness. Her eyes looked hollow, empty, devoid of the light of life. She wondered if she were looking at her new, permanent reflection and felt another layer of sadness add itself to her soul.

She turned from the mirror, not wanting to look at that sad creature any longer. She busied herself to avoid the specter waiting for her in the mirror and retrieved her dagger from the nightstand. She slipped it into her right boot, and then checked the dagger in its sheath on the belt, which also carried her sword. Satisfied that all was ready, she sat down on the edge of the bed to wait for Brianna.

Her thoughts turned to Devenshire. The mystery surrounding the man had only deepened. Try as she might, she could not dispel the attraction she felt for him... and the physical and emotional reactions his memory stirred within her.

She felt deep regret for her harsh words to him. Now, in the wake of her intense grief and rage, she realized just how cruel she had been with him.

"Well?" Brianna's melodic voice asked from the doorway.

Shantira regarded her friend and couldn't help but smile. She wore black breeches that hugged her hips and legs tightly. The legs of the breeches disappeared into the tops of tight fitting black riding boots that also showed the curve of her lower legs. The heels of the boots were higher and thinner than the heels of normal riding boots. No doubt, Brianna had the boots custom made to her specifications.

A green satin blouse hugged her upper body. The blouse was pullover in design but with the neckline taking the same seductive, yet tasteful plunge to her cleavage. The neck of the blouse had ties, but Shantira was relatively sure they had never been used. The emerald of the blouse seemed to set off and enhance the deep piercing green of her eyes.

Her hair was, as Shantira's, tied back so that it would be out of the way. Brianna turned a slow circle so that Shantira could judge her entire ensemble, and she smiled to herself. Leave it to Brianna to find a way to dress for a rugged journey, yet lose none of her sexual appeal.

"Very nice. I am sure the men will appreciate your efforts," Shantira replied.

Brianna smiled and winked in her seductive way. "I would certainly hope so."

Shantira shook her head and laughed as she stood and strapped her sword belt around her hips. Brianna stepped back into the hallway and soon reappeared with her own sword, which she wore in a shoulder harness that put the hilt just over her right shoulder. Though Shantira could not see them, she was sure Brianna had at least two daggers hidden somewhere on her, though despite the tight fit of her clothing, she could not discern where they were.

"Are we ready?" Brianna asked hoisting her saddlebags to her shoulder.

Shantira looked about her room briefly before taking up her own saddlebags. "As ready as we are going to be."

They made their way through the lavishly decorated halls to the head of a grand spiral staircase that led to the ground floor.

Shantira had never been to Brianna's Keep before although Brianna had visited her simple dwelling many times over the course of their friendship. Standing in the midst of her home, Shantira wondered how the Lady Brianna could have lowered herself to enter a simple villagers' hut.

The entire residence radiated Brianna's unique personality and taste for the finer things her title and wealth offered. While the furnishings and decorations were lavish by Shantira's standards, they were modest when compared with the gluttony of the other members of the Lordship.

Brianna surrounded herself with the things that brought her comfort. Rich mahogany furniture, fine crystal chandeliers, and silver candelabras were just some of the furnishings and decorations to fill her home with a subtle statement of her position and yet, for all of its grandeur, there was warmth and radiance of a home. Drapes and tapestries of the finest design and craftsmanship adorned the walls and only deepened the sense that this was not just an exclamation of Brianna's holdings but also a tasteful extension of her warm personality.

When they reached the main foyer, they found Brianna's servants had gathered. As was customary when the Lord or Lady of the Keep departed, the servants gathered to bid them farewell.

While Standish Keep was large, the number of servants gathered was much higher than would be required to maintain the residence. Knowing Brianna as Shantira did, she suspected she used the pretense of needing staff to provide for those who were less fortunate.

Brianna's full Honor Guard was in attendance, standing at attention in respect. Their backs were straight, their shoulders back, their chins tilted upward, and their eyes locked on a spot just above Brianna's head. They were an impressive sight in their neat uniform tunics.

As they reached the ground floor, the Captain of her Honor Guard wasted no time in voicing his concerns over her plans. After approaching her and executing the customary bow, he launched into his protest.

"Milady Brianna, please reconsider your course of action. This trek you must undertake speaks of danger. You should allow your honor guard to accompany you."

Brianna smiled warmly at the older man. "Your concern is duly

THE DEVENSHIRE CHRONICLES

noted, Zeb. You have been a faithful servant and a diligent protector, but there comes a time when someone must act as their conscience guides them, regardless of the protocols of office."

Zebadiah Constance stood just over six feet in height and struck an imposing, impressive figure even for a man in his late forties. His once coal black hair had shifted to a salt and pepper blend, which he wore close, and cropped to his head. He was, if nothing else, a soldier to his core and was not at all eased by his mistress's words.

"I simply do not understand, Milady. All you will say is that you must depart for a time without even the tiniest hint of where you must go or why. While I serve you, I also serve His Majesty, and the dictates of my office are quite clear on this matter. Under no circumstances am I to allow you to be placed in harm's way."

Brianna's smile only warmed as she regarded Zebadiah with the sort of affection rarely shown subservient individuals. A deeper-rooted part of her felt disappointment that Devenshire's assessment the night before had been pinpoint accurate.

"I am sorry. I wish I could tell you more, but there are some things that I am not at liberty to discuss openly. Rest assured that I will be well watched over during this trek. Zandorth Krahl, a Warrior of the Ancient Class, will accompany me. Surely, that will make you feel better about the situation."

The tightening of the harsh lines of Zeb's weathered features said it did not. "Granted, a Warrior of the Ancient Class is a formidable opponent, but he is still just one man."

Brianna chuckled in her soft melodic way. "You obviously have never met Zandorth. From his size, I would say he is more like two men."

The harsh crevasses of his weathered features showed no sign of amusement nor did the hard glint of his brown eyes. "I see nothing humorous about this situation, Milady. You are putting me in a most uncomfortable position." Zebadiah replied tersely, more tersely than he should have given with whom he was speaking.

Some of the warm merriment left Brianna's features as she sensed a subtle underlying threat in his words. "Indeed? How so?" There was just enough edge in her voice to broadcast her disapproval of his sudden change of tone toward her.

"I am under very detailed orders from King Lordoron on matters such as this. My first and primary duty is to His Majesty and my duty is to see to your protection at all times, and at all costs."

Brianna's brow furrowed and the normal humorous light of her eyes began to dim in growing irritation. "Pray correct me, Zebadiah. Are you threatening me?"

He shook his head. "I would never do such, Milady. I am simply stating facts. My orders are to protect you. This is a dangerous realm, and many horrible things could happen to not only a member of the Lordship, but particularly to a female member of the Lordship. Do you not see the vulnerable position you are putting yourself in by this behavior?"

"So your loyalties do not lie with me?" Brianna asked, a definite edge forming in her voice.

"Of course they do, Milady. I would die in your service, and you know this. Do not take me to task for executing my duty." Zebadiah knew he was treading a very dangerous path and was trying valiantly to do so very carefully.

Brianna was silent for a moment as she leveled a hard look at the captain. She was considering her options. "You would defy my orders in allowing me to leave alone?" There was very little question in her tone or in her hardening gaze.

His face took on the subtle look of pained regret. "I wish you would not phrase it so bluntly."

"Let us be blunt, Zeb," Brianna shot back, her arms flying out to encompass the entire room. The irritation in her voice was as clear as the palpable anger brewing just beneath the surface.

All the gathered servants began to shuffle nervously. Although Shantira had never seen it, the fiery temper and ensuing wrath of Brianna Standish was legendary. It was said that while Brianna was slow to anger, once that fine line of anger was crossed, woe to the individual unfortunate enough to find themselves in her path. Shantira had heard Brianna's temper likened to a fierce storm that laid waste to all within its path.

Constance was very close to unleashing the storm, and none wished to be within range should he succeed. Shantira watched the assembled servants and could feel the tight knot of tension form. Even the brave Zebadiah seemed to sense just how precarious a position he had placed himself in, but his duty dictated his actions, and such men never shied from their charges. The only expressional shift Shantira could see in the captain was a slight tightening of the flesh around his jaws. At the same moment, there was a spark of his own growing irritation deep in his eyes.

"Very well then. If that is how you wish it," he replied, squaring his shoulders as though he were preparing for battle. His voice took on an edge of its own as he continued. "Yes. I would defy your orders to allow you to leave alone. I would do so with a heavy heart for I have found you a very fair and noble person to serve. I have grown to respect you as I respect few others. You have been a most fair and just ruler, and a generous mistress. Yet all of the respect and admiration within me cannot offset the dictates to my duty and my service to the crown."

Brianna's face became unreadable as she digested this. "I see." Her voice was laced with sharp icicles, layered with the effort she was exerting over her temper. Shantira felt herself begin to tense in anticipation of the horrible 'storm' brewing in the room.

"Forgive me, Milady. I mean no disrespect and would sooner face the demons of hell than say these things to you. You have your duties and responsibilities, and I have mine. To this point in time, they have always agreed with each other."

Brianna's darkening gaze studied the Captain for several moments, and Shantira was sure she saw the man wither under her heated gaze. But a soldier never shirks from such things, and Zebadiah Constance was nothing if not a soldier.

"I could dismiss you for such behavior!" Brianna finally said. There was no trace of the warm underlying tones that usually accompanied her beautiful voice. Shantira had never heard her use a tone of voice one would expect from someone in such a position of power. It was uncanny and completely unlike the woman she knew.

"Aye," he answered, but his honor kept him from reacting to the implied threat with cowardice. He was bound by his duty and he would see it out to its bitter conclusion. "If such is to be the case, then I can only hope my successor has the same value for your life and safety that I do."

Brianna lapsed into silence again, considering her options while her suddenly cold green eyes bore into him. Zebadiah took the silence as a sign that perhaps she was reconsidering. He found a tiny sliver of hope that he might survive the storm of Brianna's temper and used the opportunity to dive for the sliver.

"Surely, there is a way to reach a compromise here, Milady. Perhaps, if you are so intent on this journey, you will allow a small detachment to accompany you. Not your full honor guard, but a smaller group, say four men. In such a way both of our obligations are fulfilled."

Instead of seeing the promise of compromise in her eyes, he saw the sudden flash of growing anger.

"You are so sure that I need protecting! You are so sure that I am incapable of defending myself!" Brianna said without a hint of question in the growing chill of her voice. "I wonder if I were a man, would you be showing such a devotion to your duty?"

As Constance took in the implication of Brianna's accusation, his eyes widened, and he was honestly taken aback. "Gender has nothing to do with this, Milady. My dedication to my duty knows no difference. My resolution to not allow you to leave alone would be the same."

"I am sure," Brianna replied without any conviction in her words. "So my choices are to either allow you to saddle me with an honor guard, or dismiss you?"

He nodded solemnly, almost as if he were facing the gallows, "Aye, Milady."

Brianna's eyes narrowed as she studied his ramrod straight posture. His head was high, his shoulders squared, and his eyes defiant in that soldier's way. He was set in his determination, and not even the possibility of incurring the legendary wrath of the Lady Brianna Standish was enough to deter him. Shantira had to honestly ask herself if he was dedicated or demented.

"You would honestly force my hand? You would force me to dismiss you instead of simply looking the other way this one time? Would you honestly risk your post here for such a trivial matter as my wishing to take a few weeks of diversion?" Brianna asked with her face and voice showing her awe at what was obviously a depth of his honor that she had not known existed.

Constance didn't pause a heartbeat. "When it comes to the matter of your safety, Milady Brianna? There is no such thing as a trivial matter. To answer your questions, yes, I would."

Brianna studied her captain for several moments, searching his face and eyes intently. Her eyes narrowed and her lips parted. Shantira knew what was coming. She was going to dismiss him in short order and have him removed from her property. IF he were lucky, she wouldn't have him arrested for insubordination.

Suddenly, her expression shifted slightly and her lips closed; Brianna she saw something. Her eyes narrowed as her mind pursued the train of thought something in his bearing had triggered. She leaned slightly forward and continued to study the man's eyes. Slowly her hard expression began to soften, her eyes narrowed further as the thought solidified in her mind. A warm smile slowly spread across her face, dispelling the clouds of anger that had been there only moments before. "You old bastard!" She grinned. Gone were the growing clouds of anger.

"Milady?" Constance asked, his nervous expression saying he wasn't entirely sure what had just happened.

"Very clever, Zeb, very clever indeed," she replied.

"What do you mean, Milady?" Zeb asked, almost pulling off the act of appearing innocent of any subtle accusation Brianna was making.

"You old war horse! Do not play innocent with me! While I may be several years your junior, I am just as shrewd as you." She laughed pleasantly and the tension in the room suddenly vanished. "By forcing me to dismiss you, I would then be forced to remain here until your replacement arrived, thus preventing me from leaving without a guard."

His rock hard features never shifted, but Shantira was sure she saw a small glint of a smile in his eyes as he looked steadily into

Brianna's.

"I have no idea of what you speak, Milady."

Brianna's smile widened. "I am sure."

A silent understanding passed between the two of them, and Brianna finally surrendered gracefully. "Very well, Zeb. You win. I will not set out on the journey this eve. I will give you two days to assemble four of your best men. Have them ready to leave two nights hence. Is that fair enough?"

Constance desperately wanted to sag under the relief that his plush appointment to Brianna's Keep as Captain of the Guard would not be cut short, but he maintained his composure and discipline. "Fair enough, Milady."

Brianna studied him a few more moments before laughing and shaking her head. "I will have to keep a much closer eye on you. You are far too clever for your own good."

"Or yours, Milady," he answered with a crooked grin.

"Come, Shantira. It appears we have more time to prepare," Brianna said, and she turned to walk back to the spiral staircase. She reached the bottom step and turned to fix her smiling reproachful gaze on him.

"I trust this brash display of insubordination is not something I will be forced to endure on a regular basis."

Constance swung his arms behind him to clasp his hands at the small of his back. He tilted his head to her, his eyes smiling while his face remained neutral. "That would depend upon your continued proclivity for stubbornness, Milady."

Brianna arched one of her eyebrows, and her tight smile seemed to brighten the room. "Touché," she said as she turned and led Shantira up the staircase.

They made their way through the halls of the keep to arrive at Brianna's room.

Shantira felt her eyes and mouth open wide at the opulence of the bedroom. She was relatively sure half of her village could have lived comfortably in this one room.

A massive four-poster bed, complete with sheer canopy was centered on one wall. Elegant mahogany nightstands sat on each side of the bed complete with lanterns.

Across from the bed, on the opposite wall, was a large fireplace with a fire crackling softly within it. The mantle was adorned with small statuettes and other knick-knacks. Two solid silver candlesticks took up the outer most positions on the mantle.

Above the fireplace was a large painting of Brianna. It was the official portrait of her office, which normally hung in the foyer of the keep. Brianna had left her father's portrait in the foyer out of respect to him and had opted to hang her portrait of office in her room.

In the portrait, she sat with her right side toward the artist. Her back was straight, and her shoulders back with her head held high. Her head was turned toward the artist, and her expression bore the haughty countenance required of the portrait of office. Yet, even with the forced expression of feigned superiority, Shantira could see that the artist had done an impeccable job of capturing the wisdom and insight always present in Brianna's eyes. Although her smile was only slight in the portrait, Shantira could see Brianna's free, fun-loving spirit.

To the left of Brianna's bed were the double doors that led out onto a massive balcony. To the right of the bed, on another wall, was a massive desk adorned with other subtle indications of Brianna's impeccable taste in decorations.

A small table and two high-backed, thickly padded chairs sat off to one side of the fireplace, arranged so that the table was between the chairs, and the chairs were facing the fireplace.

As Shantira took in the opulence of the room, she slowly lowered her saddlebags to the floor. Brianna sat her bags down and quickly crossed to the desk.

"Daimion is expecting us at The Tavern. How will we let him know we will not be there?" she asked.

"Who says we will not be there?" Brianna asked as she pulled out a piece of parchment and uncapped an ink well. She took up a quill from a cup of the writing utensils on the desk, dipped it into the ink well, and quickly began writing.

"You told Captain Constance that you would wait until he gathered a small honor guard for you," Shantira replied.

Brianna smiled and nodded. "Aye."

Shantira stepped up behind Brianna. "So you lied to him?"

"That is such a harsh way to phrase it," Brianna said with a hint of laughter in her voice.

"So how would you phrase it?" Shantira asked.

Brianna looked up as if in thought thinking the question over, "Hmmm... I much prefer to think of it as a clever diversion rather than something as vulgar as a lie."

Shantira could only chuckle and shake her head as Brianna resumed writing her letter. Shantira looked up at a portrait over Brianna's desk and instantly felt her cheeks flush.

"Oh my..."

The portrait showed a nude Brianna laying on her right side on the bed in the room. She was propped up on her right elbow while her right arm was seductively draped over her bare hip. Her hair was heavily tousled, and her eyes were thick with seduction as she smiled invitingly at the artist.

There was absolutely no hint of modesty about the Lord of

Prothtow Province as her pose and posture left nothing to the imagination. This was Brianna at her most wild and free natured.

At the foot of the bed, a dress was draped across the footboard. It struck a spark of familiarity within Shantira, as though she had seen the dress before. She turned, her eyes seeking out the portrait of office to find that the dress draped across the bed was the same one she had worn in the first portrait.

"Ah yes... Andre," Brianna said fondly. Shantira turned back to find Brianna looking up at the nude portrait of herself.

"The artist?" Shantira asked.

Brianna's warm smile broadened as she nodded. "He was magnificent." Shantira was sure she was not referring to his skills as an artist.

"You had him?" she asked in hushed shock.

Brianna shifted her sultry gaze from the portrait to Shantira. "Oh yes, three times that night, if memory serves."

"Oh my..." Shantira repeated as her eyes drifted back to the portrait.

Brianna regarded the portrait once more and sighed fondly before resuming her letter.

Clearing her throat and wanting to divert her embarrassed attention elsewhere, she asked, "What are you writing?"

"Instructions. Zeb deserves that much," Brianna replied as she dipped the quill into the ink to finish off the letter with her signature.

She folded the letter. She opened one of the desk draws and pulled out a stick of deep red wax. Taking a candle from the upper shelf of the desk, she set about melting the end of the stick.

She moved the stick over the edge of the folded parchment and allowed a large pool of melted wax to form. Moving quickly, she pressed a ring on her right hand into the wax, stamping it with her seal. She returned the candle to the upper shelf and dropped the stick of wax back into the drawer before she stood and moved to the double doors leading out onto the balcony.

"What are you doing?" Shantira asked as she watched Brianna step out onto the balcony and look in both directions. When she came back into the room, her face was full of youthful light and mischief. She was a grown woman, the governing Lord of one of the largest Provinces in Caston, and yet, at this moment, she looked like a girl in her sixteenth season.

Brianna giggled. "Something my father would have beaten me for had he known I was doing it. Fortunately for me, he never found out."

"What?" Shantira asked.

"Sneaking out," Brianna whispered with a conspiratorial tone to her voice. She was immersed in an enthusiasm usually reserved for the young.

"Brianna!" Shantira gasped truly shocked that she was capable of such behavior. She looked back over her shoulder at the nude portrait and realized her shock was far misplaced. Such behavior was typically Brianna.

Brianna grinned, put her finger to her lips in a silencing motion, as she picked up her saddlebags, and then quickly ducked out the door.

Shantira stood still, not quite sure what she was supposed to be doing.

After a moment, Brianna's head appeared through the open door. "Are you coming? Surely you have snuck out before?"

All Shantira could manage was a slow shake of her head.

Brianna's eyes widened before she laughed again. "Oh, you poor girl, what a wasted youth you have had." Then her face twisted into an almost evil mischief. "Come. See how the other side lives." With that, Brianna giggled and vanished. Gone from Brianna was all the propriety of her office. Shantira found herself looking at a very young Brianna, and it was then that she understood how the Lord of Prothtow Province kept her youthful appearance... she had never lost her youth.

CHAPTER ELEVEN

BRIANNA AND SHANTIRA ARRIVED at The Tavern just after nightfall to find the festivities for the evening in full swing. As they rode past the lake, Shantira faced a moment she had dreaded since sneaking away from Brianna's Keep. She had wondered if the "magic" of The Tavern would ever be able to ease the burdens of her soul again.

Her eyes roamed the silhouette of The Tavern, searching desperately for the sense of peace this place had always brought to her and yet fearing she would find it. It seemed inappropriate for her to be seeking out peace and tranquility in the wake of the tragedy. Yet her tortured soul screamed for any form of relief… any source of peace it could find.

To her relief, a sliver of the tranquility this place had always brought her eased into the charred ruins of her soul, striking a tiny spark of healing. It wasn't the pronounced, all encompassing peace she had experienced before, but it was enough to make her believe that somehow, someday, the pain would become bearable.

They rode to the side of the building and tied their mounts to one of the rails before making their way to the main entrance of the building. As they walked through the double doors, they were almost instantly swarmed with people. Most of the men quickly encircled Brianna, vying for her attention and tripping over themselves to compliment her on her unusual attire.

Women, and the men who could not penetrate the wall surrounding Brianna, offered hugs and warm words of condolence to Shantira. She gratefully accepted all of them; it brought a form of soothing comfort to her.

After what seemed like an eternity, they were able to make their way to a table and seat themselves. A few of the people who could not get to either of them upon their entrance to The Tavern, made their way over to the table to offer condolences to Shantira and compliments to Brianna.

A barmaid appeared and Brianna ordered wine for both of them. Shantira found herself scanning the massive crowd of people for Devenshire. She sorely wanted to see him. As her eyes drifted by the staircase, she spied a man in the shadows under the stairs. She frowned. How odd that he would be standing in the shadows alone like that.

What struck her even more was his appearance. He was tall and thin in build. His face was extraordinarily pale, gave the appearance of illness, and yet, in his ice-blue eyes and gaunt features was a sense of incredible power. He had pitch-black, shoulder length hair with a distinct graying at the temples. His eyebrows were thick and angled slightly upward which gave his face an overall look of malevolence. A thin, well-groomed moustache draped over his upper lip while his squared chin was covered with a goatee.

He was dressed in finely tailored black breeches with the legs tucked into black boots. A blood red shirt of exquisite tailoring peeked out from underneath a black coat. Around his shoulders was draped a black cloak fastened by a gold chain. His overall appearance was very sinister, and it made the hair on the back of her neck stand on end. She knew absolutely nothing about this man, but she knew he was extraordinarily dangerous.

He looked out over the gathered throng of people with a haughty air of superiority. It was very much as though he believed himself to be far above anyone else in the room. It was a conceited air of superiority that went far beyond ego or arrogance; it was a deep-rooted belief.

Suddenly, his eyes shifted to her, and she felt a distinct chill run down her spine. His face remained expressionless as his cold stare bore into her. It was as if he had known she was staring at him. She quickly averted her gaze, wanting to be the absolute last thing the strange man noticed. She couldn't suppress the shudder that ran down her back and resisted the urge to look back at him. She wanted to keep an eye on him, but the thought of being the center of that stare was enough to keep her eyes averted.

Taking a deep breath to settle the unease the strange man had caused she searched the interior of The Tavern again for Devenshire, very careful to avoid the staircase.

"I do not see Daimion," she said.

"Nor do I. He has not arrived yet," Brianna answered as she also searched the crowd. Suddenly a strange expression came across her face, and her right hand lifted to her temple.

Shantira watched her for a moment. "Are you alright?"

Brianna suddenly appeared very nervous and on edge, as if she were being threatened. Her wide eyes slowly scanned the crowd around them, and Shantira got the distinct impression she wasn't looking for Devenshire.

"I am fine. Just a touch of a headache is all," Brianna replied absently and in a near whisper. Her fingertips rested against her temple as her pale, disconcerted expression continued to search the crowd intently.

"Are you sure?" Shantira asked. Whatever may be causing the sudden change in her behavior, Shantira did not believe it was a headache.

Brianna finally gave up her search and turned to face front. She shook her head and forced a warm smile. "Absolutely. I am just tired is all." Shantira heard the echo of falseness in her words and saw it in her demeanor. The strange man under the staircase suddenly came to mind, and Shantira casually shifted her eyes toward him. He was still in the shadows and still watching the crowd in general. He did not seem particularly interested in any one person. She quickly shifted her stare away from the man for fear that he would look at her again, bringing back that icy spike of fear that had claimed her earlier.

~*~

The wine arrived, and Brianna wasted no time in taking a large drink to calm her rattled nerves. The voice that rang out in her mind was deep and carried with it a strong sensual undercurrent, which had left her unsettled.

Devenshire's mind had communicated with hers on many occasions. It was odd the way he could project his thoughts into her mind and read her responses without a sound ever being uttered. He was very skilled at it, and she had often enjoyed it.

This voice had not been his, and Devenshire had never left her feeling uneasy and vulnerable. She continued to subtly scan the crowd for the source of the voice, but had no idea where its owner was located. She was trying to keep up a jovial front to keep Shantira from knowing just how deeply it had touched her and how shaken it had left her.

Greetings, Lady Brianna. It had said to her.

In those few words, she felt as if she should recognize that voice, yet she had never heard it before this night. There was a sensation that accompanied the voice, a warm sensual sensation that drew a very impassioned response from her. As the voice had echoed in her mind, she would have sworn that a pair of cool hands were resting on her shoulders. As the voice had faded from her mind, so did the sensation of touch, leaving Brianna shaken and wondering if it had truly happened or if she had imagined it.

Have you grown so rude as not to return a proper greeting when it is offered to you? The voice suddenly rang out in her mind, and the sensation of hands touching her returned drawing another quick breath. She struggled to keep her outward reactions from being seen by anyone as she called on the lessons Devenshire had given her on communicating without words.

I have not. I simply was not expecting your greeting. Who are you? She thought back.

The warm sensual sensation intensified, and she felt the heat of her blushing cheeks as her body reacted to the "touch" of the stranger. A chuckle resounded in her mind as the deep voice answered.

You know who I am. You have always known me. You simply do not remember me at the moment. Fear not. That is a situation that will soon be rectified.

Then perhaps you would be good enough to jar my memory with a name? She asked.

My name would mean little to you right now. But you will know it soon. Tell me, Brianna, does the nightmare still haunt your sleep?

Brianna's mind reeled in shock. No one knew of her nightmare. It had been torturing her sleep for most of her life, and she had yet to understand its meaning, or why it plagued her. No matter how many times she had it, it always woke her with a start, leaving her gasping for breath and soaked with a chilled sweat. To have this stranger speak of it unsettled her.

How do you know of it? Who are you? She mentally demanded.

The sensations began to fade, and despite the alarm they had caused, Brianna found herself wanting them to remain. Then she noticed the strangers' presence in her mind fading, as well.

Soon, Brianna. Soon. And as the last thought entered her mind, all trace of the strange mental touch was gone. She desperately searched the crowd again for any trace of the owner of the thoughts that had touched her in a way none ever had. But whoever it had been was skilled enough to project the thoughts without giving her any indication of where they had come from. She felt her body tremble in the aftershock of the very sexual touch, and she forced herself to absorb the sensations and quell her physical reaction.

"Who are you looking for?" Shantira asked, not missing the tremble in her hand as she reached for her nearly empty wine glass.

Brianna blew her breath out between pursed lips after lowering the wine glass, trying desperately to hold herself together. "Simply seeing if Daimion has arrived yet."

Shantira studied her. It was a lie and she knew it. Something had unsettled her, and she was trying valiantly to hide it.

"Are you sure you are well? You look very pale," she observed.

Brianna shifted her gaze to Shantira and warmed her with a dazzling smile. "You worry too much. I am fine... *Mother*."

Shantira's brows furrowed together as she continued to study Brianna. The smile looked normal for her, yet the trace of the haunted look in the depths of her eyes told Shantira that it wasn't normal. Her demeanor was exaggerated and forced. Only someone who knew her well would have noticed the deception.

She leaned forward, placing a hand on hers, and opened her mouth to voice her concerns when Brianna's head snapped toward the door. "Daimion is here!" she proclaimed and Shantira heard the heavy tones of relief in her voice. Brianna stood and began making her way toward the door where Devenshire stood, surrounded by several people, mostly women, welcoming him. Shantira watched Brianna nearly push herself through the crowd toward him and took note of another inconsistency in her behavior. Brianna never went to anyone. They came to her.

What had happened? Her brows continued to knit together as her mind tried to work through the puzzle. The sinister man beneath the stairs again came to her mind, and she carefully looked his direction.

He was gone.

A quick scan of the interior of The Tavern didn't reveal him anywhere. It was as if he had simply vanished into thin air. She stood and searched the crowd again for him and could not find him. She found it hard to believe that she would not have seen him leave. He was someone who stood out in a crowd. She moved toward the door and Devenshire, suddenly feeling the need to be near him as well. Not knowing where the man under the stairs had gone made her blood run cold.

As she moved through the crowd toward the door, she noticed how Devenshire appeared as he had the first time she had ever seen him. Gone were the haggard lines around his face, and the haunted look his eyes had taken on at the sight of the destruction of her village. His smile was warm as he exchanged pleasantries with people and his eyes twinkled with the seductive, mysterious mischief that seemed to always be there. A part of her couldn't help but feel a twinge of anger at his apparent ability to so easily sweep aside the horrors he had bore witness to not even a day in the past.

I know that many times he seems indifferent to those around him, but that is not the case. He maintains such a tight rein on his emotions, and in doing so, sometimes gives the appearance of indifference.

Brianna's words from last night echoed from her memory, and she suddenly understood. The horrors he had seen were haunting him, were tearing at his resolve. He just had such control on his emotions that he chose not to give them leverage on his bearing.

Understanding it didn't make it any easier to accept.

Devenshire made his way through the crowd surrounding the doorway and found himself face to face with Brianna. The merriment in his bearing dimmed somewhat as he saw the lingering traces that something had disturbed her deeply.

"Bri? Are you all right?" he asked.

"I am fine," she replied as she stepped close to him. Shantira was sure that she was on the verge of hugging him. "I was coming to see what had detained you. The hour is getting late."

Devenshire arched one eyebrow and looked over at Shantira, his expression asking the question. Shantira managed a subtle shrug to keep Brianna from seeing it.

"I am not late. You are early," he replied, testing her mood.

"You are a bastard, and a late one at that," she snipped in reply, trying to sound playful and failing. She turned and began walking back toward their table. "Come. We have much to discuss before we begin."

Devenshire stepped up beside Shantira. "What is wrong with her?"

Shantira continued to watch her as she shook her head. "I do not know. She only started acting this way a few moments ago."

"Indeed," he muttered as he followed Brianna.

Devenshire seated himself at the table with Shantira following suit. "Are you ready?" he asked, deciding not to pursue whatever it was that had unsettled Brianna.

"Yes. Are you?" Brianna replied.

Devenshire nodded as he made an odd gesture with his right hand. He then lifted a snifter that had not been there a moment before. "Yes. Zandorth should be arriving shortly."

Shantira watched him sip his drink and felt a hot poker of anger jab at her. He could use his powers to conjure a drink, but not save her village. She wanted to scream at him, to slap the drink from his hand and demand that he use his powers to turn back time, and save her people.

"Does Roslyn know you supply your own drinks?" she asked with more than just a touch of sarcasm.

Devenshire turned his gaze to her and leveled a hard look into her eyes. "What she does not know will not harm her. As I have already said, ignorance can be a true blessing."

It was as close to a warning as she was going to get. She could tell that he was still angry with her about her harsh accusations. and a part of her could not blame him. Yet the brutal, senseless death of one hundred thirty-eight men, women, and children did not lend itself to a calm understanding.

"But when true ignorance is not possible, the truth is a very jagged dagger that slashes the heart and soul without mercy," she snapped in reply.

"Enough!" Brianna all but shouted. "You two need to resolve this thing between you and do so now! We have enough ahead of us without having to deal with this! Daimion, take her to the balcony and talk this out."

Devenshire swung his head around slowly to settle his hard gaze on Brianna. "I will not explain myself to a petulant child."

Shantira's shocked expression could not have been more severe had Devenshire slapped her. Her eyes narrowed in anger, and she opened her mouth to reply, but was cut short by Brianna snapping her arm up, holding her hand up to silence her.

"That child just lost every last thing in this realm that connected her to it. Her ties to this life have been slashed until only a tiny thread is all that is left. Put aside your petty, bruised ego and reach out to her! If you cannot do that, then I must seriously ask who the bigger child is!" The hard look in her eyes as they bore into his gave no quarter.

Devenshire frowned as he felt the sting of her words. It was rare that anyone gained the upper hand with him in a debate, and Brianna was one of a very few who could do it consistently. He nodded slowly, acknowledging her words and the embarrassing truth of them. Shantira's accusations had hurt his ego, and he had not even realized how deeply until this moment.

After a long moment of contemplation, he arched one eyebrow and allowed a small grin to tug at the corners of his mouth. "You really are a bitch. You know this, do you not?"

She smiled while keeping the hard look in her eyes. "You would have me no other way."

He nodded as the silent understanding passed between them. He took in a deep breath and turned to Shantira's fury. "My apologies, Shantira. Let us retreat to the balcony and settle this."

"Why not just use your powers to..." she started but caught herself and clamped her mouth closed. In her peripherals, she could see that Brianna's hard, harsh gaze had shifted from Devenshire to her.

She closed her eyes and took in a long, deep breath. A moment later, she let it out slowly, seeking to calm herself and finding the tumultuous assault of raw emotions still raging deep within her.

"Very well," she finally answered tightly.

Devenshire downed the last of his drink and set the snifter down on the table before rising and standing aside to allow Shantira to rise.

She slowly stood and walked toward the staircase, every single move displaying her anger and indignation. Devenshire shook his head and turned back to Brianna.

"She will not listen. Anger still holds her tight," he said.

Brianna watched her walk away and nodded, sadness tinting her eyes. "It is all she has left for the time being."

She shifted her eyes to Devenshire and smiled warmly. "If anyone can rescue her from the all encompassing embrace of anger, it is you. Be patient with her, Daimion."

He nodded in understanding. He turned and followed Shantira, trying to compose his thoughts. He had encountered this type of anger before and had learned that when such anger was all that a person had left to hang on to, it was nearly impossible to loosen its hold on them.

They made their way up the stairs until they reached the second floor. The giant balcony loomed ahead. Shantira saw several couples scattered along the circular handrail at the edge of the balcony. Many gazed out into the night while others gazed into each other's eyes, the breathtaking sight of the lake and the beautiful night beyond lost on them.

She found a relatively secluded spot and leaned on the rail, looking down at the lake. She closed her eyes as the night breeze rustled the loose strands of hair around her face and brushed it gently. The scents of pine, earth, and jasmine wafted to her, and she could feel the tight knots of anger and her tension begin to relax.

She could feel that Devenshire had stepped up beside her. She cracked one eye open to see him leaning on his elbows on the rail, gazing out into the night sky.

"I spoke out of turn," she said hesitantly. She knew she was wrong, but she could not bring herself to be sorry for it. The anger was the only emotion that gave her the feeling that she had any control.

"As did I," he replied softly, gently. "You have my most sincere apology."

"I cannot believe they are all gone," she whispered, feeling the tears begin to sting her eyes as the empty pain swallowed her heart.

"I cannot imagine that you can. It has barely been a day. You must give yourself more time," he replied.

Shantira opened her tear-rimmed eyes and looked out into the night as she shook her head. "One day or a thousand days. I cannot imagine that it will ever go away."

Devenshire continue to gaze out at the stars. "It will never go away, Shantira. The pain will accompany you to your grave. It will get easier to bear, and there will be times that you almost forget it is there." He paused as he slowly, sadly shook his head. "But it will never, ever go away."

Shantira let out a bitter chuckle as a lone tear slipped from her eye to track down her cheek. She looked at his profile. "Is that supposed to make me feel better?"

Devenshire pursed his lips as he shook his head. "No. It was meant to help you understand the true state of things." He turned his head to fix his gaze into hers. "It is harsh. It is unfair. It is cruel. It is also the way of the realm. There are many things that will come our way during this journey called life. Some of them will be the most pleasant, most rewarding times your mind can imagine. Others will be cruel taskmasters who will show no mercy with their whip upon your soul. In this contradicting assault of good and evil, pleasure and pain, fair and unjust, it is how we deal with both that defines who we are."

Shantira scrubbed at another tear that had slipped down her cheek as she absorbed his words. They were harsh, almost as if he were pressing a red-hot dagger deep into a festered wound, and yet she could not deny the truth of them. While she did not feel any relief from her pain, she did feel as though she had gained something of a better understanding of it.

With that understanding, came the stark realization of just how unfair she had been to snap at him, to accuse him of things that she knew at her core he was incapable of. She lowered her eyes from him, unable to bear just how accurate his description of her as a petulant child had been.

"I am so sorry. I had no right to accuse you of such things," she whispered.

Devenshire nodded slowly as he looked back out into the night. "I do not like discussing my past. I do it very rarely. I only do it now to help you understand.

"When I was younger, I began studying the Mystical Arts. I was found to possess the potential and was sent to a retreat to evaluate my powers and train me in their use. But I did not complete my studies and have only a very rudimentary knowledge of manipulating the Arts. I am capable of some basic spells, no more. I do not have the power to force anyone's will to mine; I cannot make women fall in love with me. Indeed, such a feat is well beyond even the most Adept of practitioners. The emotion of love is a very powerful one, more powerful than even the Mystical Arts.

"Even if it were within my power to force the hearts of women to my will, I would not do so. I believe love should be given freely, not forced by magic. The reason there are so few truly skilled Mages is that to fully master them, one must be pure of intention. Those who seek to use the Mystical Arts for the things you accused me of are not disciplined enough to learn the very spells they seek to master. Do you understand?"

Shantira felt her shame deepen at just how crude she had been in her accusations toward him. She nodded slowly.

"I accept your apology. I understand you were under a great burden when you uttered those words. I just wish for you to understand that even if I possessed such abilities, I would not use them in that way. Had I the power you accused me of having, I would have surely used them to save your people. For the first time since leaving the retreat, I sorely wish I had completed my studies."

Shantira looked up to see his face had taken on a very solemn, sad expression, and she knew he spoke the absolute truth. This only made her shame run even deeper. She lowered her gaze in shame and closed her eyes against the onslaught of conflicting emotions.

"I am sorry," she repeated in a whisper.

He reached out and gently cupped her chin as he forced her head up so that she would have to look him in the eyes. A powerful sensation coursed through her at his touch, which intensified when she looked into his eyes.

"I admire your ability to see your short comings and your willingness to admit them. It tells of a maturity that belays your age. But you must never avert your eyes from anyone. If you are basking in the glory of victory, or sulking under the cloud of defeat, never allow anyone any superiority over you by averting your eyes. Face defeat with the same fierceness with which you accept victory," he said gently.

She smiled at him and nodded in understanding. He returned her smile and released her chin.

"Then let us speak of it no more. It is in the past, and there it shall remain," he said as he stepped back to allow her to lead the way back to the table.

A part of her sorely wished to remain on the balcony with him, to have his attention fully devoted to her. But she knew that there was more pressing business ahead, so she turned and began walking back toward the stairs.

When they returned to the table with Brianna, Devenshire noticed that she was more like her usual self, but there was still a haunted look deep in her eyes. With his brows furrowing he called on his powers to lightly tap into her mind.

Are you all right? He sent to her mind and saw her jump in a start. He sensed fear and trepidation from his mental touch and was tempted to delve deeper. Such a thing was considered rude in the etiquette of the Arts, and equally so given the unique nature of his relationship with Brianna. Besides, he mused, he was not nearly skilled enough to go deep enough to find any information of use.

I am fine. I have a touch of a headache. She replied.

He could detect the lie with ease, which meant it was a rather large one for him to be able to pick up on it so easily.

He pulled out Shantira's chair and continued to study Brianna as Shantira settled herself into it. Brianna looked back at him and tried to reassure him with a warm smile. He wasn't buying it for a moment.

Something had disturbed her deeply.

As tempting as it was to pursue the matter further, he knew that it was pointless to try to make Brianna discuss any subject she didn't want to as she could be extraordinarily stubborn when the mood struck her.

He nodded a silent acceptance of her response as he eased back into his chair. He conjured another brandy as a woman came up to the table. It was obviously someone both Brianna and Shantira knew, and they began a conversation that had nothing to do with him.

Free from the conversation, he continued to contemplate the journey ahead. Over the past day, he had plotted several options and outcomes that could form in the days and weeks ahead. He now began fleshing out his plans, counter plans and contingency plans. If what he feared were true, and he had no reason to believe it wasn't, he would need to be extremely diligent and very well prepared.

Please forgive the intrusion. May a stranger enter here? Came a soft melodic voice into his mind. They were not Brianna's thoughts, those he was very acquainted with, rather these thoughts were from someone new and from someone with a mastery of mental communication that far surpassed his. He calmly leaned back in his chair and did not attempt to search out the source of the new thoughts.

It is no intrusion at all. All are welcomed here at The Tavern. Enter, and be welcomed. He replied.

Thank you, kind sir. I am new to this area and was seeking a place to rest. The voice echoed within his mind, and Devenshire was taken by the gentleness of this woman's thoughts. Yet he could detect something beneath the surface veneer of calm. It was something that peeked out at him briefly, and he could not discern its true nature. He was intrigued, to say the least.

No thanks are necessary. I am not the owner of this place, but I know that you will be welcomed here. He replied.

May I know your name? She asked and Devenshire could not help but feel that the owner already knew his name. As an afterthought, he added a little more power to his own mental shields, just to make sure.

Daimion Devenshire. And yours?

Rachelle Tambrey. It is a pleasure to make your acquaintance.

The pleasure is mine, Milady.

I see that you are in the company of other ladies. I will trouble you no more. The voice softly stroked his mind.

They are only friends. You are not troubling me at all. He replied and he felt her mind try to pry a little deeper into his thoughts, to test the truth of his statement. It was not a direct probe, but more like a subtle nudging. It was right on the line of being inappropriate, yet seemed

THE STONES OF ANDARUS

totally within the etiquette of mental communications.

A slight smile crossed his features as her thoughts sought to pry a little deeper as she encountered his strengthened shields, realizing that she had been caught.

My apologies, sir. That was inappropriate of me.

I am not offended. It is only natural to seek more knowledge of a new acquaintance. Devenshire answered.

"What do you find so amusing?" Brianna asked, and he realized that he had let his conversation with the woman play across his face. He smiled a little wider as he looked to Brianna

"Just lost in my own thoughts."

"I see," she replied. "Care to share the humor?"

"Tis nothing. Just a childhood prank that suddenly came to mind." Devenshire lied. Brianna nodded, seeming to accept his answer. She returned to the conversation with the other woman and Shantira.

Where do you hail from? He asked her.

My dwelling is several miles to the east. I have heard stories of this place and decided to search out the truth for myself. I will admit to an ambiance here that goes well beyond the stories I had heard.

Yes. The Tavern does have an uncanny way of making everyone feel welcome.

Yes, it does. I was afraid my kind would not be welcomed here. She stated.

What kind is that? He asked.

There was a hesitation in her thoughts, and Devenshire knew she was adding to her own mental shields in the event that he sought to pry as she had before. He did not attempt to pry and simply waited for her to answer.

Let us just say that I am not like any other person here. She replied finally.

I see.

Your name. I find it interesting. What are its origins? She asked, intentionally changing the subject.

My surname comes from a land far away from here. I know very little about it since I was not born there. I fear that I have little knowledge of my heritage. My memories of my childhood before the fifth season are vague and shrouded in mystery.

How unfortunate. Have you attempted to learn of your heritage? She asked and Devenshire sensed nothing but a sincere curiosity in her questions.

Long ago, I tried to learn more, but my entrance to the realm seems to be lost. It is of little consequence. I know who I am now, and that is all that concerns me. If it is in the Fates that I learn of my origins, then I am sure I will.

A very noble approach to such a large mystery. If I may be so bold,

TOM SECHRIST | 163

you are not like any I have encountered in a very long time.

Since I do not originally hail from this region, I am not surprised. I have had a unique life.

As have I. She replied. Devenshire could detect the many underlying meanings to that statement and found his curiosity piqued. There was a touch of sadness in her thoughts that surfaced from time to time, despite what he sensed were her best efforts to conceal it. There was something very different about his woman, and he found himself wanting to learn more about her.

Since you seem to know my physical identity, may I ask to know yours? He asked.

Of course. I am in the booth to your left.

It took a considerable amount of control not to spin instantly to look at her. He calmly and casually turned his head to his left, and instantly knew where she was. He found himself wondering how he had missed her entrance to The Tavern.

She sat in a shadowy booth alone. She was beautiful, breathtakingly so. He fought the impulsive urge to gasp as her beauty swept forward to surround him. She was small in stature, yet there was something in her posture that spoke of great inner strength. He knew what a mistake it would be to underestimate her simply because of her slender build.

Thick blond hair cascaded around her delicate, yet strong features. There was paleness to her skin that reminded him of illness. Her eyes danced in a strange light all their own, as if the light that reflected off the moisture of her eyes came from some deep inner source rather than the lanterns of The Tavern.

There was something in her bearing that Devenshire could not put into words, could not find a way to explain. Then she turned her head and their eyes met. A strange feeling surged through him, and he was hard pressed to understand what it was. There was something mesmerizing about those eyes... those delicately beautiful features... the full lips that always seemed on the verge of a smile without actually ever smiling. The eyes... always the eyes... there was a hint of knowledge and wisdom there that spanned many more seasons than had passed across her face. There was also sadness deep inside them... almost as if she had accepted some terrible fate long ago and was now simply living with the sadness as though it were a part of her.

He watched her eyes lock with his, her gaze hesitant and searching all at the same time. For a span of time he could not even begin to measure, they simply sat and stared across the room into each other's eyes. Her head tilted slightly, and her mind caressed his...

There is a deep sadness within you, Daimion.

As there is within you, Milady Rachelle. He replied and saw the flicker in her eyes as she realized that she had shown him more of her than she had intended to. The flicker was so slight that had Devenshire not been staring into their depths, he was sure he would have missed it.

Aye. I suppose there is such sadness within each of us.

He nodded slowly, his eyes still locked with hers. True, but not like what I sense within you. It seems such a cruel trick of the Fates that a countenance as lovely as yours would be marred by such a deep sadness.

You flatter me, sir, and I am unworthy of such. She replied mentally while a very small smile played briefly across her pale lips.

I am not in the habit of dishing out empty compliments, Milady. I truly find you very beautiful, sadness and all. He replied.

Then I thank you for your compliment and accept it as you have given it. I sensed such about you. In so many others, I have found that compliments are given out of some hidden desire to gain something. But within you, I sense no such emptiness. She replied softly, deep warmth coming to her thoughts.

I have found that our lives are entirely too short for empty words of mere flattery. If my eyes find something of beauty, I make every attempt to appreciate that beauty for what it is, not for what I can take from it. He replied, finding himself wondering if he could ever tear his eyes from hers. Again, there was a very slight flicker deep within her eyes that told him he had touched a sensitive nerve somewhere deep inside, yet what that was he could not know for her control over her emotions rivaled his.

You are indeed a unique individual, Daimion Devenshire.

As are you, Rachelle Tambrey. I am truly thankful for this opportunity to make your acquaintance. I trust we can learn more of each other.

Again, her eyes flickered with some hidden thoughts, and Devenshire caught the faintest whisper of her deeper thoughts. There was a genuine desire to get to know him better, which was quickly and violently dashed aside by something else, some deeper conviction that getting closer to him, or anyone, was simply not possible.

I do not think that would be possible. She replied.

Why?

You see the surface, Sir Devenshire. What lies beneath is not as beautiful. I think I would rather you continue to think of me as you do now, not as you would if you saw beneath.

You seem to be under the impression that I would react as those you have encountered before. Have you not said that I am unlike any you have encountered in a long time? We all have phantoms that we hide from the light of reality. I have demons within me that would, no doubt, terrify and repulse you. Yet I am not willing to deny myself a new acquaintance simply because of my fear that these specters would drive one away.

He saw the warm smile grace her lips at the same time it caressed his mind within her thoughts.

You speak with a wisdom that is not customary for someone of your age. But you do not understand the true nature of my demons, as you phrased it. They are not the common demons most people carry within them. There was the slightest impression in her thoughts that hers were, indeed, more terrible than most.

I see, He replied gently. Since I struck you as unique enough for you to begin this conversation with, would it not be interesting to test for yourself if I am as unique as I appear to be? What would be the harm in letting me decide for myself if your demons are too horrid for me to deal with? Is it not a bit presumptuous of you to impose your reactions to your phantoms upon what my reaction might be?

He caught only the fleeting edge of anger flaring within her, yet he could not understand where that anger had come from. He felt her mental presence pull back, as if she were about to severe the link between them.

You are indeed different from any I have encountered recently. But you are mortal, human, and there are certain absolutes that reside within mortals. Your reaction to my phantoms or demons would be beyond your control as they are part of what makes you human.

What have you to lose by allowing me to be the judge of that? He asked gently.

There was a long pause before her voice in his mind sighed sadly.

A friend.

Would it not stand to reason that, if we became friends, I would eventually learn the nature of what you hide so deeply inside? Why risk the heartache of losing a friend later when you could simply lose an acquaintance now?

Devenshire sensed a good-humored laugh within her thoughts as a broader smile crossed her physical lips. Her eyes sparkled with the humor she felt inside, and Devenshire feared he was about to tip headlong into those strange eyes and be lost forever. He quickly pulled in rein on his emotions and sought out his control again.

You put forth an excellent argument, Sir Devenshire. You intrigue me, and I will give your proposal consideration. I must depart for now. I look forward to speaking with you again.

"Daimion?" a voice sounded in his physical ears and he was startled as he realized that his surroundings had faded from him while he had been mentally conversing with Rachelle. He spun his head around to see Brianna looking at him with a touch of concern in her eyes.

"Yes?" he asked, trying to cover his start.

"What are you thinking of? I have never seen you so deep in

thought."

"My apologies. I was simply lost in random thoughts. What were you saying?"

"I said that Zandorth has arrived," she said pointing to the doorway.

Devenshire looked up to see Zandorth weaving his way through the crowd toward them. It troubled him that Rachelle Tambrey had been able to hold his attention so well that so much had happened around him without his knowing. Such lapses could be deadly and he chastised himself for allowing his concentration to lapse.

"Good," He replied a little more curtly than he would have liked to, and his terseness did not go unnoticed by Brianna. The concern did not diminish in her eyes. In fact, it grew, and he saw her head begin to turn in the direction he had been looking. He stole a glance toward the shadowy booth and was both surprised and disappointed to find it empty. He quickly scanned the room and could find no trace of the woman. He reached out with his mind and could find only the shadowy after images of her mind's touch on his. Again, that strange sensation coursed through him, but this time it was tinged with a sadness that he was unprepared to feel.

Rachelle? His mind asked hopefully. He had not expected an answer, and he was truly surprised when one came. It was not as clear as her earlier thoughts had been, but it was understandable.

I will consider what you have said, Daimion. We will meet again.

As Zandorth seated himself at their table and talk of the preparations for their journey began, Devenshire could not deny the sheer thrill that he would meet Rachelle Tambrey again.

CHAPTER TWELVE

DARKNESS.

It was feared by so many, and yet he took his greatest comfort from it. The deeper the night, the more complete his solace. It was in shadows that visions came to him and that the pleasures of his earthly body were taken as he wished. In darkness, his power was complete, near absolute.

The light of day was far too distressing. There were too many things seen, too many things known. Its harsh beams threw everything into nauseating clarity, a clarity that was unwelcomed and akin to poison to his resolution. Only in darkness could his true self emerge, a self that bore no regard for anything but that which brought him pleasure.

He could vaguely recall when he, like the pathetic beings around him, took delight in the light and dreaded the fall of night. He had since come to know the power of darkness and knew that it far exceeded the paltry power of light. He embraced it as one would a lover. Only the vampire had a more intimate relationship with the dark, and on many levels, he envied the undead for their relationship with the night.

With a deep smile of satisfaction, he rose from the bed and slipped his nude form into a thick robe, leaving it open in the front. Padding across the tight confines of the tent, he moved to the center post and turned up the wick on the oil lantern hanging there, casting the interior of the tent in pale yellow light.

At the base of the post was a table holding a decanter of his favorite whiskey. His dark blue eyes gazed off into the distance while he absently pulled the cork from the decanter and poured a healthy amount of the dark brown liquor into an elegantly etched tumbler.

The young woman bound to the bed continued to weep in pain and shame, her mind struggling to come to terms with what had been done to her over the past several hours. She had never known such depravity could exist in one human being.

"Please… release me… do not hurt me anymore," she pleaded softly through her sobs.

He ignored her as he took a large drink from the tumbler, a tight grimace coming across his bearded features as the alcohol bit the back of his throat. After the swallow, he breathed out a soft sigh of satisfaction as the liquor slammed into his stomach, and instantly releasing vaporous warmth that only added to the satisfaction of sexual release.

He moved to another table, which held an elegantly crafted small wooden chest. With a reverence that bordered on religious, he slowly lifted the lid to reveal three stones. They were oblong in shape with a deep amber tinge from incredible age. Small cracks crisscrossed their ancient surfaces, and small chunks were missing from some areas. It was another testament to their incredible age. The ancient runes carved into their surfaces were deep red in color, but the patina didn't come from paint. It was almost as if the Stones bled from where the runes had been carved into them. They almost hummed with the incredible power housed within them. Of course, only a skilled practitioner of the Arts would be able to detect the throb of power.

"Finally," he whispered as his eyes swept across the three of them. A hard smile twisted his lips. As he looked at them, memories of the raid he had led to claim them returned. What an intoxicating night of mayhem, sheer terror, death, and bloodlust that had been.

He vividly recalled the intoxicating sounds of blood curdling screams, the visions of blood, and the sweet sense of terror from the villagers. He reveled at the sights of bodies being rent beyond recognition, and the sheer exhilaration at the screams of those who had been bound inside a hut that was set afire. He remembered watching each one, savoring their terror, as death approached them slowly, intently, wanting just one thing from each of them. The memories aroused his senses to the point of intoxication.

The fight, although one-sided, had been exhilarating, and he made a mental note that future raids would have to be conducted, perhaps against larger villages where a greater amount of resistance could be expected. The thrill of battle, when you're winning, can be quite exciting.

"Such power," he whispered, and he lovingly brushed his fingertips across each of the three Stones.

"What?" the young woman asked through choking sobs.

He turned to gaze at her bruised, naked form. Her wrists were bound together and lashed to a stake driven deep into the ground at the head of the bed. The bindings were so tight that her long fingers had turned purple from lack of blood circulation. Her ankles were lashed tightly to each corner of the footboard.

"Do you understand what true power is?" he asked with a very deep timbered voice. His thick black hair trailed down his shoulders. Thick black eyebrows arched upwardly over each of his deep-set dark blue eyes to lend his hard features an evil appearance. An elegantly trimmed goatee framed his thick red lips and hard chiseled chin.

"I do... do not understand," she wept. "Please let me go. I have done no harm to you, and you have taken what you wanted from me. Please let me go. Please?"

He smiled and shook his head. "You do not understand. Most like you do not." He looked down at the dirt floor of the tent and chuckled softly. "You have experienced such power this night. I have used my physical power over you to take what I wanted from you. You lay there now, bruised, battered, and aching from me exerting my power over you. There is no part of your body that I have not touched or explored to my heart's content, and all the while, you were absolutely powerless to stop me."

She closed her bruised eyes to force more tears from them as another series of sobs wracked her wrecked body. "I just wish to go home..."

"That is power," he whispered with passion as he turned back to the chest housing the stones. "When I stormed into that paltry village to reclaim what was rightfully mine," he reached out to lovingly caress the stones again, "the silly little villagers were powerless to stop me. I came, I took what I wanted, and laid waste to the rest."

He turned back to her. "THAT is power! Yet it pales in comparison to the power housed in these three stones. Power that is mine! Power that has been hidden away for countless seasons! Power that is finally within my grasp!" His voice rose to a near shout as the passion swelled within him.

He glared at her with an incredible passion in his eyes and a near insane glee in his voice. "Once I have mastered their power? I will do to this realm what I have done to you this night!"

There came a hesitant rapping at the post near the tent flap. He ignored it, continuing to stare into the woman's terrified, tear-swollen, bruised eyes. He felt himself begin to swell in excitement at the thought of the power of the stones combined with her naked, helpless body laid out before him. He considered taking her again, dominating her again as he had since kidnapping her from a nearby village as she tended the crops.

"Master?" came a hesitant voice from beyond the canvas flap.

Xavier blinked, breaking himself out of his power induced trance. He smiled a harsh smile at the woman before turning to face the tent flap. "Come!"

While the tent flap opened and one of his men entered timidly, he took another swallow from the tumbler.

The man bowed and said, "My life is yours to command, Master."

"I was not to be disturbed," he said. It didn't matter that he was finished with the village girl, but his men knew that when he was with one of his conquests, he was not to be disturbed.

"Yes, Master. Our rear guard has returned with distressing news," The Follower said softly, his posture hunched, his eyes stuck fast to the dirt.

Harshness began to form on his features as he regarded the Follower with growing tension. "What news?"

"A small group of people know of your raid on the village. They know you possess the Stones of Andarus, and they are setting out in pursuit of you this very night."

Xavier frowned. "Impossible! I left none alive! How could they know such things?"

"I do not know, Master. The rear guard is waiting to give you his report."

"I will hear his report!" Xavier hissed as he drained the contents of the tumbler. His anger was rising quickly and he knew he had to gain control of it for the time being, at least until he heard the report.

The Follower raised the tent flap and motioned to the man standing outside. The rear guard entered meekly, executed the bow that Xavier demanded of all of his Followers upon entering his presence, and issued the greeting also demanded of Xavier.

"My life is yours to command, Master."

Xavier moved back to the decanter and poured himself another drink. He could feel a tingling remoteness begin to form to his perceptions as the whiskey took a hold. After taking a more moderate sip from the tumbler, he fixed the rear guard with a dark look of foreboding.

"Report!"

"Master, a group of people know of your possession of the Stones. They intend to set out in pursuit of you this very night."

"How do they know these things? I left no one within the village alive!" Xavier demanded, the growing edge of his anger becoming evident in the deep tones of his voice.

"One who lived in the village was not there when we attacked. She came upon the remains. Another who came to her aid possesses mystical powers and was able to discern that the village priest held the Stones and that you have claimed them."

Xavier's face became hard as he absorbed the news. He had planned the raid in every detail since he had sensed the failure and ensuing death of his men on the first raid. The three weeks on the trail to the village had been spent with his strongest warriors, planning out every detail of the raid to ensure no one would survive to tell the tale.

Again, the Fates had intervened to throw his best-laid plans to waste. He vowed that once he had control of the Stones, the Fates would pay dearly for their repeated interference in his life.

"Why are they not now rotting into the foul earth they were spawn from?" he asked with tight, harsh tones of anger.

"Master?" the rear guard asked, not entirely sure what Xavier meant.

"Your life is mine to allow continuing or ending as I see fit. Correct?" Xavier asked.

The guard paled. "Yes, Master."

"I grant you all the earthly pleasures this realm has to offer, do I not?"

"Yes, Master," the guard replied, careful to keep his gaze averted from him.

"I make it possible for you to live above the silly laws of the paltry mortals around us, do I not?"

"Yes, Master. You are the most gracious, generous leader I could ever ask for."

"Then I ask, again, why are these people not dead instead of planning to come after me?"

"I sought your counsel, Master. I wished to make sure your wishes were carried out exactly as you would have them," he replied, suddenly realizing where this line of questioning was going.

Xavier's eyes darkened until they were pitch-black. He slowly raised his left hand with the index and middle finger extended while the other fingers curled to his palm and his thumb stuck out from the rest of his hand. He made a sweeping gesture with his hand, and the rear guard was instantly encompassed in a glowing red light.

The guard was alarmed at first, not sure what to make of the red light. Then the pain came. Thousands of invisible needles stabbing him at alternating intervals all over his body. The man grimaced at first, and then began to grunt in pain as he tried to brush away the stinging stabs that he couldn't see.

The first man to enter the tent stepped as far back as the tent canvas would allow. He sorely wished to be as far from this situation as possible.

"You need not seek my counsel to deal with those who oppose me! You know full well what my orders would have been!"

"Yes, Master," he grunted.

"What would my orders have been?" Xavier asked through tightly clenched teeth as he increased the power of the spell and the pain being dealt to the man. The man began to whimper out, his face showing the fear and pain as the assault intensified.

"You would have me kill them," he grunted out between gasps of pain.

"So why is your useless carcass here, wasting my time and energy with a problem YOU should have dealt with?"

Xavier gestured again, and the red glow intensified. The man screamed out in agony as he clutched his mid-section, falling to his knees from the incredible throbbing that ripped through his body, stabbing at all parts of his body at once, from inside as well as out. His screams rang out through the tent, and Xavier allowed a small smile to crease the hard set of his features. He could feel the man's terror, and it was pleasing to him.

Even the young woman tied to his bed had stopped weeping to watch the horrific scene playing out before her. For a moment, even her suffering was placed aside.

"I will not tolerate failure!" Xavier said in low, dangerous tones. "Our greatest moment... MY greatest moment is at hand, and I will brook no interference from anyone!" he shouted as he applied more power to the spell. The man's cries of agony intensified and he slumped over.

"Please Master... I will not fail you again..." the man begged, trying to keep from retching from the intense pain.

A cruel smile twisted Xavier's lips as he nodded. "Oh... I know you will not." He swung his black gaze to the first man to enter the tent. "Remember what you see here! Let the word go forth amongst all my Followers..." He turned his gaze back to the rear guard and allowed his left hand to relax until all of his fingers were extended and his hand made a cupping shape. His eyes began to glow with the same red light that encompassed the man. Suddenly, the man stopped screaming and writhing around. He shot straight up on his knees, his bloodied eyes wide in terror and a pain so intense that he could not even utter a sound. His skull began to swell and contract with the incredible energies of the spell that twisted his brain in a savage grip. Blood trickled from his eyes, nose, mouth, and ears as the pressure of the spell increased even further. He clawed at the sides of his head, trying to tear away the skin and bone to rip whatever the source of the pain was from inside his head.

"...failure means death!" he hissed as he suddenly clenched his fist tightly shut. There was so much power behind the gesture that the clenched fist trembled.

At the same instant, the man's skull exploded, spraying blood, brain, and bone in a wide radius around his twitching body as it collapsed upon the dirt floor.

For a long time, there was no sound save for Xavier's excited breathing. The first Follower was rooted to the spot, his wide eyes unable to look away from the disfigured corpse that had, only a moment before, been a friend of his.

The young village woman was silent as well, suddenly terrified to even make a sound in the wake of what she had just witnessed. She felt her stomach convulse and knew that had she not been so terrified, she would have surely vomited.

Xavier relaxed slowly, letting the powers he had gathered about him dissipate, leaving him feeling taxed, but exhilarated. He closed his eyes to soak in the moment of pleasure and to allow his heightened senses settle. When he opened his eyes again, they had returned to their normal color.

With another deep sigh, he drained the contents of his tumbler and sat it aside before moving to a large chest near his bed. He opened the chest and removed a large canvas bag from within. He tied his robe about him, took the bag, and closed the chest.

He made his way toward the tent flap, careful to avoid the bloody mess that had been the rear guard's head.

He paused at the flap and addressed the first Follower, taking great delight in his pale, fear-filled expression as he stared at the remains, "Clean this mess up! I want no trace of this fool to remain when I return!"

The Follower bowed. "Yes, Master."

Nodding once, Xavier stepped out of his tent into the camp his men had set up. The night was cool and clear with a sliver of a moon overhead. He would have preferred a full moon. He took a deep breath of the night air, letting the breeze blow through his hair. The tensions of his anger and the attack on the Follower drained away, leaving his mood high.

He noticed the bulk of his Followers gathered around a campfire. He strode over to it. As they noticed his approach, they all shot to their feet and executed the customary bow.

"My life is yours to command, Master," they said in near perfect unison.

He smiled in satisfaction. His Followers were well trained, and they knew what he expected. They needed to be rewarded for the valiant performance during the raid, and with their swift efficiency in making and breaking camp to keep them moving back toward the retreat.

"There is a woman tied to my bed. She is young, tender and has many favors to experience. You may have what is left of her."

The gathered men began to smile in anticipation of releasing their pleasures upon the woman. Xavier motioned to two men near him. "You two. You may enter my tent to retrieve your prize. Take her with my compliments and my blessings."

Xavier turned to walk away. He was feeling pleased with himself. He didn't normally share his women with his men, leaving them to find their own. Of course, if their prizes were more attractive than his were, then he would claim her as his own.

On rare occasions, he would share his prizes with them. It was a treat for them, a token of his gratitude for their devotion. Despite the shortcoming of his rear guard, his men were loyal and worked very hard to keep him pleased. They deserved an occasional scrap from the Master's table.

As the two Followers scurried off to claim their prize, another man stepped up. "Master?"

Xavier turned back to face the man, his hard expression asking the question.

"What do we do with her once we have finished? Do you want her back?"

Xavier's expression shifted into annoyed revulsion. "Take her after you have had her? I think not! Slit her throat and leave her with the waste of the camp."

The Follower nodded enthusiastically. The two men emerged from the tent with the naked woman, her wrists still bound together. She screamed out in protest, begging them not to rape her again.

Xavier moved to the edge of the campfire light and turned back to watch for a moment. The woman quickly vanished into the sea of men, and her screams quickly rose as the first man took her.

With another twisted smile, he turned and made his way into the woods. As the woman's screams and cries echoed off into the night, he smiled. Not so much at the suffering of the young village girl, but for the chaos and mayhem he would soon unleash on this realm.

CHAPTER THIRTEEN

XAVIER WALKED CASUALLY through the pitch-blackness of the forest, his mind lost in the incredible power of the night, and his powers guiding him. He always enjoyed taking long walks through the darkness. it gave him a sense of power he could never duplicate in any other setting. During these walks, he felt most connected to the darkness and all the power it held.

There was danger in the darkness. There was any number of things in the night that could end his life in a single moment of blind, soul numbing terror. Even now, he sensed all manner of beasts that stalked him, measuring his ability to evade them or fight back, and injure them. In their primitive minds, they assessed the rewards and the risks of attacking. With a twisted smile, he sent out a subtle mental sign that attacking would be foolhardy at best. The smile broadened as he sensed the creatures scurrying away.

He lost track of how long he walked, his mind in the embrace of his dark mistress. Such power, such beauty, such absolute solitude; how could anyone not love the night?

He suddenly found himself in a clearing and decided this would be the best place for him to use the Orb and answer the questions his inept rear guard could not. He sat the heavy canvas bag down next to a fallen log and set about gathering wood. While he could easily use his powers to perform the menial task, he knew he would need a considerable amount of his power to manipulate the Orb of Vision with any degree of success. It was a taxing bit of spell work and took a great deal of power and concentration.

Very soon, he had a small pile of wood gathered. He fixed his stare into the center of the small pile of wood, calling on his powers to gather about him. With a couple of small hand gestures, he suddenly thrust his right hand, palm out, toward the wood. A split second later, a small fireball erupted from deep in the pile, igniting the kindling underneath. Very soon, a small fire crackled, pushing back the chill and the darkness of the night. Xavier blinked several times, his eyes having adjusted to the darkness.

He retrieved the canvas bag and sat on the ground near the fire. He untied the bags' closures and slowly drew a large statue from the bag.

The base of the statue was formed from a ring of bronze. The pedestal rose from the base ring to taper slightly to a smaller bronze ring. The pedestal was fashioned from granite that had been stained repeatedly until the surface was a smooth glossy black color that was almost reflective.

Atop the pedestal was a pile of human skulls, each one chiseled out of marble with exceptional skill and attention to detail. Various individual skulls were scattered about the top of the pedestal from the main pile.

Straddled atop the skulls was a winged demon figure, also carved with intricate detail. The creature was very thin, almost skeletal. It was a deep red color and was adorned with only a ragged loincloth to cover it. The bulge of its ribcage, hipbones, knees, and elbows pressing against the skin added to its emaciated appearance.

The demon was bent over, its arms raised and bent at the elbow while its lower arms reached up behind its head, its claws splayed wide to help support the enormous globe of white crystal. The demon's wingspan joined with its arms to serve as the cradle for the snow-white globe. The demon's head was turned to its left, its woeful expression a mixture of intense pain and grief. Its eyes sagged downward, its mouth hung agape in a sigh of desolation, and hopelessness as it was forced to be frozen in time to eternally support the large globe.

Xavier let his eyes dance over the statue with reverence. White crystal was exceptionally rare and known for its unique mystical qualities. The Master Adept of the Duvall Retreat had held the artifact for many seasons, rarely utilizing its powers. He had been a fool, Xavier felt. Such an item could make someone nearly invincible if they could discipline themselves enough to use it.

The Orb of Vision had been the only thing, aside from the Duval Retreat, that he had taken from the High Master Adept that had been of any use. He had taken great delight in raiding the High Master Adepts' chambers and claiming the fool's belongings for himself.

It had taken a long time for Xavier to learn how to manipulate the mystical properties of the white crystal orb and even longer to learn how to control it. Even now, he had to make sure his concentration was drawn to a razor's edge and absolute. Any distraction would allow the contrary energies of the Orb to spin off into any number of unpredictable directions.

He sat the Orb on the ground and slid back a little bit. He folded his legs under him and slowly lowered his head, letting his breath out in a long slow release. He pulled his concentration inward, forced his mind to turn in on itself. He concentrated on his breath, which slowed with each cycle. He forced all thoughts from his mind, willing it to be clear of any thought save drawing his concentration to a fine point.

Slowly he raised his head, his eyes still closed. His arms rose, his hands curling into the necessary hand gestures. Slowly his arms moved through the movements that would call his powers to him and then channel them into the artifact, making contact with the magic deep inside the white crystal.

It emitted a low-pitched whine, and Xavier ignored it. The first time he had been able to connect with the energies of the globe and the whine had come, he lost control of his thoughts in the excitement, and the resulting backlash of power had left him with a splitting headache for many days.

Slowly the white color began to change, to shift from solid white to a cloudier, insubstantial color. It now appeared that the sphere was transparent with a rolling white cloud inside of it. Parts of the white cloud rolled around the circumference of the orb while other parts rolled in on itself.

Xavier's hands moved around it, never touching, shifting his aura of power and force of concentration into it. The whine rose in pitch and volume while Xavier continued to connect with its energies. Once he had completed his connection with the artifact, the next daunting task would be forcing the energies to his bidding.

The shifting patterns became impossible to follow as they moved, shifted, rolled, and then began a completely new and random pattern. A sheen of sweat covered Xavier's forehead from the intense concentration as he slowly opened his eyes to gaze into the depths of the globe. All color was gone from his eyes as they took on the stark, solid white color of the relic. Slowly, the very center of the sphere began to clear to reveal an image of a Tavern.

The room was full of people. Many sat around tables drinking and laughing. Many more milled about the room, striking up conversations with others. Even more became visible dancing to the strains of a small band of minstrels. Xavier repressed the disgust that rose within him at the sight of them carrying on as if they believed themselves worthy of such pleasures. Only he and his most loyal of Followers were allowed to taste the pleasures of this realm. They were the only ones worthy.

The others? Xavier honestly believed that the others had been created and placed here for his service, amusement or whatever other task he could call to mind.

He forced more concentration into the object, and the view within it shifted. It rotated within the tavern and centered on a single table seating four humans. Xavier manipulated his powers and forced the globe to move the image closer so that he could see each face clearly.

The first face to fill the sphere was unknown to Xavier. He was a large muscular man. He stood six feet, six or seven inches tall and probably weighed well over three hundred pounds. The weight came from rock hard muscle, not the soft flab of fat. Xavier doubted that there was an ounce of fat anywhere on the man's body.

A warrior or barbarian to be sure. Whatever he was, Xavier knew he would be a very formidable opponent. The thick muscles of his large frame and the air of confidence that radiated from him confirmed it. He would have to send only his most skilled warriors to face this massive brute. Xavier may not know the thug, but he knew his type. The man's skill with his fists would only be surpassed by the massive broadsword he spied on his hip. Men such as this were known for their resolute spirits. Xavier felt such men were simply too ignorant to know when defeat was inevitable. Men like this would die before surrendering. Defeat was not in their limited vocabularies.

Xavier mentally shrugged. So much the better.

The next face to fill the orb was that of a woman, a very beautiful woman to say the least. Her thick black hair, green eyes, full lips, and equally full figure all came together to fill the artifact with a vision of seductive beauty. He did not recognize her, but he knew the moment he laid eyes upon her that she would grace his bedchamber for many nights after her capture. He hoped she struggled as valiantly as her appearance promised. It would be sheer pleasure to slowly break her will to his.

A brunette beauty replaced the first one. She was younger than the first woman, and in her own way, just as stunning. Her deep blue eyes appeared to burn with a passionate fire unlike any Xavier had encountered in a long while. It pleased him to know that he would have two new women, eventually broken in, to add to his stables.

Once he had forcefully bedded them a few times and taken away their control, they would gladly open their arms and, he smiled, legs for him at his slightest beckoning. Xavier was unsure which he would enjoy more, taking the willing pleasures from these women or the very act of forcefully breaking their wills. Either way, his plans for the beauties promised him many months of pleasure.

Finally, the Orb shifted, and the last face came into view. Xavier felt his eyes grow wide and his breath catch in his throat. The force of recognition caused him to freeze, even his breathing stopped in stunned silence.

No. How can this be? He thought. He died seasons ago. I killed him myself!

Yet the *very much* living features of Daimion Devenshire filled the interior of the Orb. He smiled warmly as he exchanged words with the black haired, green-eyed beauty. Xavier had not yet mastered the relic well enough to be able to hear sounds of what was being shown to him.

Xavier's white, wide eyes gazed intently into the face as trepidation coursed through him. It was a startling thing to realize that he could still feel fear, even after all of the seasons he'd spent working to eradicate it. Yet, he could not deny the horrible emotion. At this moment, the icy fingers of fear traced a pattern up his spine, and his entire body shivered in response.

Could Devenshire know? Was it possible that my one dark secret has somehow been revealed?

Impossible! He had taken all the steps necessary to keep it hidden from all. The secrets of the Ancient Scrolls were his and his alone. Only a small handful of practitioners had ever read the Scrolls contents. There was no way Devenshire could know.

However, it would be sheer folly to discount any possibility with a man who had obviously survived a certain death plunge from a castle tower. If the Scrolls were correct, then a way had to be found to eliminate Devenshire before he could reach his retreat. He was quite possibly the only human who could prevent him from completing his plans.

Xavier fought down the panic that tried to intrude upon his orderly thoughts. Now was not the time. He must be calm, think rationally, and plan diligently. Devenshire would have to be killed. Only upon his death could Xavier continue with his plan.

Devenshire's face still hovered within the depths of the Orb, despite his break in concentration. The magic of the White Crystal had a will of its own at times, and Xavier began calling on a counter spell to wipe the man's face from it. The act forced his mind back into orderly thought, and he was thankful, this time, for the Orb's insolence. As the shifting white of the crystal slowly covered the man's face, he allowed a small part of his mind to picture the same happening in reality to Daimion Devenshire.

~*~

"I say we leave at first light," Zandorth said as he tossed back the last remnants of his third tankard of mead. He wiped his mouth with the back of his massive hand before belching loudly. "Traveling at night is dangerous," he amended.

Brianna and Shantira's faces twisted into expressions of disgust at the warrior's lack of manners, which Zandorth either didn't notice or didn't care to notice. Devenshire smiled as a slight chuckle rattled his throat.

"We are only a day behind Xavier. Surely a few more hours will not make that much difference," Brianna added, moving a little further away from Zandorth.

Devenshire lifted his brandy and took a swallow from the snifter, savoring the flavor and aroma wafting about his senses. "You are assuming that he will wait until he gains his retreat to begin to try to manipulate the Stones."

"Certainly he would wait until he was safely within the walls of his retreat, where he knows he would be the most secure," Shantira replied.

"From all the stories I have heard of Xavier, the only thing you can count on him to do is the one thing you did not count on him to do," Devenshire replied setting his snifter back to the table before folding his arms across his chest.

"I do not claim to know a great deal about these Stones, but if they are as powerful as you indicate, would it not take Xavier time to study them? To learn their secrets?" Brianna asked.

"Indeed. Legend has it that no one has ever been able to tap into the power of the Stones since their creation. Even someone as powerful in the Mystical Arts as Xavier will need time to learn their secrets," he replied, rocking his chair up onto the two back legs and rocking gently.

"I would not think that the trail is a place for such study," Shantira offered.

"More mead!" Zandorth bellowed out loudly to any barmaid within earshot.

"Zandorth!" Roslyn's voice shouted back over the crowd. "What have I told you about shouting orders?"

"More mead… please!" Zandorth grumbled out in reply, his brows furrowing in agitated frustration over having to alter his behavior at a woman's command.

Devenshire looked at Zandorth, at first, in amazement, but then in amusement, with one eyebrow cocking up over the other and a mischievous grin spreading across his lips.

Zandorth glared at him in warning. "Say one word, Devenshire. Just one, and I will show you what your insides look like from your arse!"

Devenshire held up his hands in mock surrender as he chuckled. "Not a word."

Brianna laughed as she shook her head. It never ceased to entertain and amaze her how two men who professed such an intense dislike of each other, and never passed up an opportunity to enjoy the suffering of the other, had not killed each other by this point.

"Can we please get back to the task at hand?" Shantira said with more than a little irritation in her voice. How could they carry on such? Had they already forgotten what had happened just one night ago? Were their hearts so hard that not even the complete annihilation of a village could penetrate them with some form of grief?

"Of course," Devenshire replied as he lowered his chair to all four legs and leaned forward on the table. "To answer your question, Xavier's powers are strong, and his determination even stronger. It would be safe to assume that he has already begun his study of the Stones." Devenshire shook his head slowly. "The promise of the kind of power the Stones are supposed to possess would be far too enticing for him to ignore. Every moment we waste is another moment he has to study the Stones and how to tap into them."

He paused to fix each of them with an intense gaze. "Would you not wish for these moments back if we were to reach the front gates of the Retreat of Duvall only to witness the unleashing of his powers?"

Despite the usual sounds of The Tavern, a deadly silence fell around the four of them. Each took a moment to mentally call up the image Devenshire had given them. The despair and regret that would prevail sent a brief shudder through them.

Devenshire leaned back in his chair and took up his brandy, watching the other three absorb his words. As he let the fiery liquid trickle down his throat, he had the sensation of being watched. A tingling down his spine warned him that magic was at work nearby. As he let his eyes casually scan the room over the rim of his snifter, he opened his mind to locate the source of the magic.

No one appeared to be looking at him directly, and for a moment, he considered the possibility that Rachelle had returned and was seeking his attention. He felt no trace of her anywhere and quickly dismissed the feeling. Then he realized where he had encountered this sensation before. It had come from the aura he had sensed within the burned out church of Shantira's village.

Xavier.

Devenshire concentrated harder, trying to learn what manner of magic Xavier was using, but the sensation was fading rapidly. *Some sort of observation spell?* Devenshire realized that it had to be; it would explain the sensation of being watched. A cold needle of dread pierced him as he realized that Xavier knew of them, which meant he had to know they were planning to stop him. The danger of the quest, he realized, just doubled. He had been counting on the element of surprise and now, obviously, that was lost.

He decided not to tell the others what he feared. There were enough challenges for them ahead as it was. He saw no point in adding to their burden.

"We should depart," Devenshire said.

"Which path shall we follow?" Zandorth asked.

"Did you not say the bandits left Shantira's village heading north?" Devenshire asked.

"Aye." Zandorth nodded.

He nodded again. "Then we must first travel to Lirpa."

Brianna's brow furrowed, and she leaned forward. "Why Lirpa?"

"An old friend of mine resides there, someone who could be of aid to us on this journey." Devenshire stood, letting his cloak flutter and drape about his shoulders and body.

"It will take us the rest of the night and well into early morning to reach Lirpa. It will also involve traveling through the fringes of bandit territory," Brianna observed calmly.

"I will not deny Zandorth's claim that traveling by night will be dangerous, but we have no other choice. If any wish to remain behind, no word of cowardice will be said of you, at least not from me. Yet if you decide to proceed, know this: once the journey begins, I will not argue or attempt to justify any decision I make." He gazed at each person with sincerity. After several moments, Devenshire walked toward the door, his mind made up. If they wished to follow him, or if they wished to remain behind mattered not. By the time he had whistled for his steed and mounted, he noticed with a touch of pride that his three companions had already mounted and were ready to follow him. With a brief nod, he turned the horse about sharply and urged it into a steady gait northward.

~*~

A set of eyes watched from the shadows as the four riders galloped away. The eyes regarded each rider in turn before settling on the man clad in black in the lead. There was something about him that would not leave her mind. He was the reason she decided to follow, at least for a while.

CHAPTER FOURTEEN

ZANDORTH HAD BEEN EXPECTING an attack. By the very laws of human nature, especially as it pertained to bandits, an attack would have been impossible to avoid. Four lone riders, two of which were attractive women, taking a hazardous path in the darkness would be too tempting a target to overlook.

The warrior had detected their movement through the woods long before they struck. His warriors' senses told him that there were at least eight or nine of them, their unwashed bodies and almost clumsy movements through the surrounding trees announcing their presence loud and clear. The horses sensed them as well. They snorted and he could just make out his mounts' ears twitching, listening for the direction the danger would come from.

They moved with the blundering ignorance of those who honestly thought they were keeping their presence hidden when in all actuality, they were broadcasting their number and location to any who were perceptive enough to notice.

Krahl looked ahead and tried to see if Devenshire had noticed the fact that they were not alone on the trail. In the dim moonlight, all he could make out was Devenshire's shadowy silhouette. He did appear to be sitting a little taller in the saddle, and Krahl was sure he saw his head turn casually, yet intently, back and forth. His posture was rigid, as if he were preparing himself for what was to come.

Krahl shifted his gaze to Shantira who was riding behind Devenshire. She also rode as if she knew they had unwanted visitors approaching.

Behind her was Brianna and probably Krahl's biggest concern. He had little doubt as to Devenshire's abilities in battle, and he had heard of Shantira's training in the art of battle, but Brianna was a different story. She was the governing lord of the province, a rich woman, and a member of the Lordship. He seriously doubted she possessed any battle skills at all. He made a mental note to try to stay close to her once the battle began.

Despite his unease at having Brianna present during a battle, he did notice that she seemed tense and alert. Could the pampered ruler of Prothtow actually sense trouble coming?

The tension in the air began to build until Zandorth was sure that even the bandits must know their presence had been discovered. Krahl glanced upward and was disappointed that only a sliver of a moon shone above. Not ideal fighting conditions, but they would have to do.

The attack came in a flurry of crashing movements and shrill battle screams as the bandits exploded from the trees on either side of them. They had picked their spot of attack well, Zandorth reflected. The thin trail they had been following passed through a very narrow passage of the forest, the perfect bottleneck for an attack.

As the first twig snapped, Zandorth had drawn his broadsword. Seconds later, Brianna reached up to free her sword and quickly lowered her body against her horse, making herself a harder target to hit.

In a simultaneous move, Devenshire shifted the reins to his left hand and crossed his right hand to his short sword. It sang clear of its scabbard and whistled through the air as he brought it to the ready.

In one fluid movement, Shantira drew her sword, and like Brianna, bent very low, making her shadow meld with the thick neck of her mount.

The first raider launched himself into the air toward Shantira just as she ducked low against her mount. Her sudden movement sent the bandit sailing over his target. Flying over Shantira's back, the bandit made a final attempt to dislodge her by forcing his feet down, catching her in the side, and dragging her from the saddle.

Zandorth knew that the bandits would first try to dismount them. Being mounted on horseback gave them a tremendous advantage.

He tried to see where Shantira and the bandit had landed, but the ground was a sea of blackness in the dim moonlight. He started to urge his mount in her direction when a body slammed into his left side, knocking him from the saddle. As he hit the ground, stars exploded inside his head from the impact and he growled a curse at the attacking raider.

Devenshire spun his mount around as raiders charged from opposite sides. The first raider gathered himself to leap at the mounted target and found his plans interrupted by the point of Devenshire's sword piercing his chest.

As he screamed out in pain, the second raider shifted his position and tried to come up on Devenshire from the rear. A tight squeeze of his knees on the Friesian's shoulders caused the massive steed to kick out with his back legs, catching the raider square in the chest. With the sound of cracking bone, and a shriek of startled pain, the bandit flew backwards into the shadows. There came the crashing sound of his body hitting brush and then no other sound came from that direction.

Riding the momentum of his mount's kick, Devenshire slipped his feet free of the stirrups and swung his body upward into a side somersault. Landing on his feet, his sword still buried deep in the bandit's chest, he jerked the sword free. As the bandit sank to the ground, he spun to face another bandit.

As he turned, he heard the sound of someone running upon him from behind. Instinct caused him to jerk to the left just as the point of a sword sliced through empty air that had, only a heartbeat ago, held his body.

He quickly grabbed the raider's arm and pulled while, at the same time, turning to face his would-be attacker. While he couldn't see the man, he could smell his foul breath and the stench of his unwashed body. Using the momentum of his pull on the bandit's wrist, Devenshire drove his left knee deep into the man's gut.

The rush of air suddenly leaving the bandit's lungs in a gale as foul as his unclean body rewarded him. The man sank to his knees, trying to suck air back into his lungs. Devenshire sent him into blissful slumber with the pommel of his sword.

Brianna spun her mount around in a tight circle, thwarting two bandits' attempts to take her down. As her horse circled, she widened her eyes to take advantage of the small amount of light available. She saw the dim silhouette of a man crouched low, waiting for an opening. His patience was rewarded by a gash across his chest as Brianna leaned out to slash at his silhouette. He screamed in pain and staggered back.

Watching him stumble backwards, Brianna wasted no time in launching herself in his direction. Landing on the balls of her feet in a low crouch, she immediately moved toward the bandit, who had abandoned his sword to hold his bleeding chest. When the man felt he was far enough away, he paused to see how badly he had been wounded.

"That small wound should not concern you," Brianna said. The man jerked his head up, his eyes growing wide as saucers. Her low voice hissed at him, "This wound shall be far more deadly." She swung her sword quickly and accurately in a long arch.

A hot flash of pain sliced deeply through his midsection and the warmth of his blood spilled down his groin and legs.

Brianna watched the bandit sink to his knees, one hand clutching his chest, the other his stomach. The man looked down at his body, then back to her. Though she couldn't see his eyes, she knew he would not rise to strike again. Without a sound, the bandit pitched forward.

Just as she turned to rejoin the fight, something smashed into the side of her head causing an explosion of sparks inside her skull. The force of the blow carried her off her feet and sent her sword spinning out of her grip. A strange numbness descended upon her, and by the time she hit the ground, her senses had deserted her completely.

Zandorth had just dispatched the bandit who had carried him from the saddle and was getting back to his feet when he spied the shadowy images of three bandits in mid-leap. Before he could form a defense, he was carried back to the ground and quickly piled upon by the bandits. They punched and gouged him with determination. As the pain raced through his body, he fully expected to feel the sharp point of a dagger or sword piercing his skin. They pummeled at him with their fists and the pommels of their swords and his vision swam as tiny sparkles of light popped in and out, making him dizzy. Obviously, they were intent on capture, not murder.

"Enough of this!" he growled in irritation. His massive hand shot out in a direction guided by instinct rather than conscious thought. His palm encountered the throat of a bandit and instantly closed around it. He was rewarded by the sound of gagging. Smaller hands clutched at his arm, and then frantically clawed at his hand, trying to break the grip on his throat.

With a snarl of rage, Zandorth quickly twisted his wrist and heard the distinct crack of breaking bones. The raider's body twitched once in his grasp and then became dead weight. With a howl of rage, he hurled the lifeless body from him and quickly rose to his feet, carrying the other two bandits with him. The warrior's hand found the arm of another bandit and hurled the man away from him. No sooner had the second bandit been sent flying through the air, and then the warrior spun and drove a massive fist into the center of the third raider's silhouetted head. Both hearing the crack of bone and feeling it under the course knuckles of his fist, he felt the last bandit's hand fall away from him as the force of the blow carried him off into the darkness.

Shantira struggled beneath the weight of the man who knocked her from the saddle. A fear of death came as she hit the ground and found herself under the man's crushing weight. Anger rushed forth to overshadow her fear.

The man tried to knock her unconscious, but the blow only stunned her. Her attacker had known she was a woman and had not put his full strength behind the punch.

Shantira's lips peeled back into a snarl as she called upon her strength to twist her body, tossing the man from her. She rolled clear, and into a crouched position, waiting for his next attack. She did not have time or room to retrieve her sword, so she consoled herself with the weight of the dagger she had drawn from her boot.

The bandit swore and rushed toward her. At the last moment, she lunged forward with her dagger. She felt the jarring impact along her arm as their combined momentum drove the dagger deep into his stomach. She followed the momentum, and they both rose to a full upright position, her left arm encircling the man's neck in a deadly embrace, holding the dagger at the depth it had penetrated. With a violent twist, she jerked the dagger free, then stepped back to allow the man room to fall.

Finding himself without an opponent, Devenshire started to go to someone else's aid. Too late, he realized another bandit had singled him out for attack. Something solid collided with the back of his head, and his senses left him like a wisp of smoke from an extinguished candle. He pitched forward to his knees, his mind swimming in a thick mass of swirling explosions of color and pain. He knew he had to regain his footing, but he could not force his suddenly numbed limbs to move. He was dimly aware of someone roughly hauling him to his feet and holding him there.

"You son of a bitch!" A savage voice snarled before a fist caught Devenshire across the jaw, sending him pitching backwards onto his back within the brush. What tiny amount of coherence he had left was swept away, a cold blackness tried to drag him under. He forced his mind to hold on to the failing edges of consciousness.

He tried to focus his vision, but all he was able to see were the spinning treetops, stars and moon, making him feel sick. A silhouette entered his vision, and he knew it was his attacker. Unless Zandorth or one of the others came soon, Devenshire knew his journey would end here. He had pondered his death many times over the seasons and had wondered what his final moments of life would be like. He felt a touch of disappointment that it would end in a less than glorious fashion.

Devenshire watched, powerless, as the silhouette raised his sword high, preparing to deliver the final blow.

He heard a sound, one he had not expected to hear. To his dulled senses, it sounded very much like a crossbow being fired. The silhouette towering over him suddenly went rigid. Devenshire could not be sure, but he could have sworn he saw a thin shaft suddenly protrude from the silhouette's neck. His attacker swayed until he disappeared from sight. Seconds later, he heard something heavy landing beside him. The bandit made a brief gurgling and choking sound before lapsing into the silence of death.

Devenshire tried to clear his mind and force his body to move, but the force of the two blows to his skull kept his senses from returning.

Two very cool hands suddenly touched each side of his face. The touch was soft, yet held none of the warmth of human hands. For a brief moment, he feared that the very specter of death had finally captured him, but the hands began to warm, as if something within them was generating great heat. The warmth penetrated his incoherence, and he found he was, once again, aware of his body. In the same moment, his vision began to clear and solidify.

Moaning softly, he rolled his hips sideways and bent his knee. He could move again! He reached up to touch one of the hands on his face, but his fingertips came in contact with his own skin. He bolted upright and turned his head quickly, looking behind him, but he saw nothing. Had it not been for the warmth still on his face, he would have thought the gentle hands had been a product of his imagination.

The sounds of battle called to him and he knew he had no time to ponder this mystery. He gave silent mental thanks to whomever or whatever had aided him and quickly took up his sword to rejoin the fight.

Brianna struggled to fight off the effects of the blow. She knew that at any moment her attacker would close in to kill her. She staggered back to her feet and tried to blink her vision clear and find her opponent. She heard an evil chuckle and could smell the man's rancid breath upon her skin as she swayed. She shook her head and some of her senses returned. A hand grabbed her roughly by the shoulder and spun her around. She tried to bring her arms up to ward off another punch, but her reflexes were slow and she tensed, preparing to absorb the blow.

What she was not prepared for was the very savage, evil, animal-like snarl that sounded from somewhere behind and above her. Something very cold swept past her at incredible speed. There came another savage snarl, a scream of fear, and then Brianna found herself suddenly standing alone. She blinked and turned in a slow circle, searching for any trace of whatever had come to her aid. She found neither her attacker nor benefactor.

"Brianna… Shantira?" Devenshire called.

"I am here, Daimion!" Brianna answered, her voice shaking with bewilderment.

"Here!" Shantira replied, her voice broken by her heavy breathing.

"Zandorth?"

"Is that all of them? Surely not! I was just beginning to enjoy myself." Krahl's angry voice returned.

Devenshire moved through the darkness and found Brianna. He gently laid a hand on her shoulder. "Is anyone injured?"

Brianna could hear the crashing retreat of at least two bandits. Obviously, they had decided to abandon this fight.

"A little rattled, but unhurt," Brianna answered lightly. She was still confused by her sudden, unexplained rescue.

"Were those Followers?" Shantira asked.

"No, they were far too undisciplined for Followers." Devenshire scanned the area around them. He did not expect to see anything with his eyes, but his internal instincts told him that there were no more attackers in the immediate area.

"True. This fight was won far too easily," Zandorth grunted. He felt disappointed that the fight had been so brief.

"Speak for yourself!" Brianna grumbled as she rubbed her swelling jaw and could still hear a slight ringing in her ears. The memory of something rushing past her at incredible speed returned, and she recalled how very cold the sensation had been. A deeply buried memory tugged at her consciousness. Though she felt certain she should remember it, she could not quite put a finger on the subdued memory.

"We should go. I doubt they will return, but we cannot be certain." Devenshire spoke suddenly as if he too had been lost in some puzzling thought. He turned and whistled for his mount. It took the others several minutes to find their own since they had scattered during the battle.

The night sounds began to return, washing over the silence left behind by the battle. The four riders faded into the shadows.

~*~

As the four riders vanished into the night, a pair of small-booted feet stepped up next to the body of the bandit with the crossbow bolt protruding from his neck. Sharp eyes, well accustomed to the dark, watched the riders for a moment before looking down at the corpse. The dark silhouette knelt down, and with a savage jerk, ripped the crossbow bolt free from the warm body. The female gave little notice that she had nearly severed the head from the dead man's body. A fresh fountain of blood poured onto the ground, smothering the earth with a rich aroma that caused her to take an involuntary step backward.

She hungered, and the smell only intensified her hunger. Drawing from an ability she had acquired from many seasons of long practice and concentration, she quelled the hunger pangs slightly.

She was nervous, weary, and not from the act of subduing her hunger. There was another like her nearby, and they were feeding. It was a gift of her kind, the ability to sense when another like her was near. She was shaken from her own need to feed and in no condition to battle one like her. Retreat was her best option at the moment.

With little more than a soft whisper of movement, she was gone; absorbed into the night, the realm of her existence.

CHAPTER FIFTEEN

LIRPA WAS THE LARGEST CITY in Lakira Province, sitting nearly on the border between Lakira and Prothtow. While Kahla was the largest city in Prothtow Province, it was only half the size of Lirpa. It was a massive, sprawling collection of huts, houses, and buildings that attempted to portray an epitome of civilization for the entire kingdom to admire.

The offered illusion was only a thin veil of deception that bore no resemblance to what lay hidden underneath.

By day, the city of Lirpa was a center of civilization in the swirling wildness of the land around it. The light of day kept the darker aspects of the city at bay. With sunset, though, the night took control, and these dark aspects swept forth from the shadows to claim their hold on the city, sending the denizens of daylight scampering away.

It was a very old story, one that had been told in large cities for ages, and would continue for ages to come. When prosperity brought large numbers of people together in one place, this duality was nothing more than a simple by-product.

The four weary travelers paused on the edge of a hill on the outskirts of Lirpa in the chilled gray dawn to survey the city. Lantern light spilled from many windows along the edge of the city as smoke curled from chimneys. No doubt, these were the dwellings of the day people of Lirpa, setting about with their daily routines.

The streets they could see from their vantage point were deserted. Devenshire, Brianna, and Zandorth knew that only a short span of time ago the streets had been packed with people. This was the dead zone, the time in the course of the cycle in which neither night nor day ruled the city streets, as though it were some form of a natural barrier between the two.

Shantira took in the massiveness of Lirpa with wide-eyed wonder. She had never seen a city of this size. Kahla had been the largest city she had ever ventured to, and she had thought it massive. However, now, sitting on the edge of Lirpa, she was amazed at how small it now seemed by comparison. She had heard stories of Lirpa and had always wanted to travel here to see for herself if the tales of grandeur were true. She wondered how so many people could possibly know closeness, like that of her own village. Surely, it would take a very long time to get to know each person.

"Lirpa," Devenshire whispered more to himself than to anyone else. There was a fondness in his voice that matched the expression on his face as his eyes roamed over the huddled collection of rooftops.

Shantira turned toward him. "You have been here before?"

"Indeed, I have," Devenshire answered affectionately, his eyes still slowly scanning the city laid out before them.

There was something in his voice that spoke of warm memories, and Shantira wondered exactly what Devenshire had encountered here.

"Who is it we have come to find?" Brianna swept her gaze across the expanse of the sprawling city, feeling the rebel in her soul wanting to dive headfirst into the deepest night this city could throw at her.

"Raven Darkseed," Devenshire answered simply, as if the man's name should be explanation enough.

"Who is he?" Shantira asked.

Devenshire smiled slightly, continuing to take in the city. "A Mage. He and I began the study of the Mystical Arts together seasons ago."

"I take it that he completed *his* studies?" Brianna asked with a touch of criticism in her tone.

"Yes, he did." Devenshire gave no indication that her veiled criticism had even registered.

Krahl raised his arm, pointing toward the city. "Where, in all of *that*, will we find this magician friend of yours?"

"He is not a magician, Zandorth. He is an Adept Mage."

"Magician, Mage, Sorcerer, Wizard, they are all brigands, as far as I am concerned," Zandorth grumbled in reply. "Magic! It is nothing more than a tool of those who are too weak to take up a sword!" he amended.

It was no secret that Zandorth had little use for the Mystical Arts or those who practiced them. In his opinion, a man should carve out his existence with a sword, not mumbled words, and odd hand gestures.

Devenshire smiled again as he realized that Zandorth was attempting to draw him into a debate.

"Let us seek out an Inn. We will rest today. We will not be able to find Darkseed until tonight," Devenshire said, sidestepping Krahl's attempt to bait him.

"How will you find him in such a large city?" Shantira asked in awe as she swept the view of the city with her hand.

Another fond smile, mixed with mischief, touched his lips as he nudged his horse onward.

"I know exactly where he will be."

~*~

As the first fingers of dawn began tracing their patterns upon the ebony canvas of night, he knew he would have to break off his pursuit of Brianna. With a snarl, he began moving toward a cave he had found in previous treks into this area.

For all his powers, for all his might, he was still cursed by a weakness that he could not overcome. He hoped that once night returned, he would be able to catch up to her and continue watching over her, slowly and methodically preparing her for the moment when he would reveal the truth.

He had been able to think of little else since he had discovered her that night in the ruins of the small village. Even the great evil that had originally drawn him to that place seemed of little importance. Memories flooded through his mind, so many images of her from the past. Though each beautiful image was quickly replaced by the horror he had felt each time he had lost her. Anger coursed through him as the memories replayed themselves over and over again, tormenting him, teasing him with a promise that it seemed would never be fulfilled. But this time would be different. he swore on his very existence that she would be his again, as she had been so very long ago.

The cave entrance was directly ahead and he quickened his pace. He felt his power ebb as the blackness of the night sky turned lighter shades of gray. As he reached it, he paused to turn his icy blue eyes toward the sky. The blackness was gone, shifting into ever lightening shades as more stars winked out of existence. Deep within his mind he recalled a time when a blooming sky would have thrilled him, would have rooted him to the spot so that he could take in the approaching sunrise in all of its beauty. But that was a very long time ago and such things were not allowed to him any longer. The only thing of beauty left to him was Brianna, and he vowed he would have her again.

With a sigh of longing for a woman still out of his reach and disgust for another day without her, he made his way deep inside the cave where no light could possibly penetrate. As the strange sleep claimed him, his thoughts naturally turned to Brianna. Closing his eyes, he envisioned her beauty and let the promise of being with her carry him away.

~*~

"Bonzwa, if this is another of your jests, I shall cleave your heart out myself!" Lordal growled as he trudged through the brush, his breath heaving in his chest from the exertion. He was getting on in seasons and had put on much weight. This trek through the woods taxed him more than he cared to admit.

For many seasons, he had reigned as leader of the largest group of bandits in this region. He had not noticed how he had let himself lapse into inactivity in his duties as leader, which for the most part, consisted of counting the spoils of his carefully planned raids and wallowing in his growing, sizeable wealth.

He remembered how he used to be a tall strapping man with a body of granite muscle and boundless energy. He had fallen into considerable favor with the old leader, and upon his passing, assumed his throne, so to speak. The seasons had quickly turned his granite muscles to soft flab and tapped his stores of energy. This, above losing seven of his better men, served to anger him considerably.

"Lordal, if all is not as I have told you, I shall cleave my own heart out and present it to you." Bonzwa led Lordal and ten men to the place where he and his men had met defeat only hours before.

"How is it that two men and two women were able to so completely defeat you and nine of your men?" Lordal demanded for the third time since Bonzwa had first returned to their lair and relayed his story.

"I do not know. They fought as demons, like those possessed of the Black Arts," Bonzwa replied nervously. His tension did not stem from his leader's disbelief or by the lack of evidence to support his story. What terrified Bonzwa was that whatever dark evil had claimed one of his men would still be there, waiting to claim him as well.

Bonzwa remembered how one of his men had stunned one of the women travelers. Bonzwa had come up behind him when the man had pulled the woman back to her feet to finish rendering her unconscious. Then a terrifying sound filled the air and echoed through the woods. It was followed by a damp, chilled wind. His man screamed, a sound drenched with horror, and then... nothing. The chilled silence, reminiscent of a graveyard, remained.

Fear had him taking flight into the woods, dimly aware that another of his men was running behind him.

Along with Lordal, the bandits trudged through the woods, the morning dew coating their heavy cloaks as they brushed by low-hanging limbs and underbrush. The light of dawn was beginning to dispel the fog that had formed and their vision improved. Early morning smells wafted up around them, the freshness of the new day's air and the damp fragrance of pine and oak. The chill of the morning — that had begun to dispel with the rising sun and their own exertion — returned to swirl around their bones at the sight of a body. The group of bandits gathered around as Bonzwa knelt down beside the dead man.

"This was Gerritt," Bonzwa whispered. No one missed how Gerritt's chest was horribly caved in. Gerritt had been the bandit that Devenshire's horse had brutally kicked in the chest at the onset of the battle.

There was a brief moment of silence before the group moved on, Bonzwa in the lead again. They would return and collect the body later. Bonzwa led them a short distance where a break in the forest revealed the road where last night's battle had taken place. There they found the evidence to back up Bonzwa's story. One man lay in a heap in the thick brush on their side of the road. Lordal knelt beside the man and could see the marks left by a massive hand that had gripped his throat. He could also see the odd angle in which the head lay in relation to the rest of the body. There was no doubt that his neck had been broken.

A few feet away lay the body of another man. Lordal moved to him and even before reaching it, he could see the slight distortion of his face. Something very large had been driven into the man's face with considerable force.

Lordal kept his features emotionless. As he stood and looked at the other bodies that littered the battle site, his anger was nearly beyond his control. Yet, from the outside, his expression was no different from if he were looking at a field of crops. He stepped across to the first body on the other side of the road. The body lay face down in a pool of blood. Lordal rolled the body over with the toe of his boot and found a deep gash had been cut across the man's chest and another, deeper gash, transversely through his abdomen allowing his intestines to spill out onto the ground.

The fourth body had a gaping hole in his stomach from the thrust and twist of a blade. The fifth body's head had nearly been severed. Lordal took in the scene of death around him, and his features turned grim as he wrestled with his anger and even a touch of humiliation. Never, since he had assumed the mantle of command over these men, had he ever suffered such a total defeat.

"There are two bodies missing," Lordal said with a forced control.

"Rotalla." Bonzwa had known his body would be missing. Rotalla had been the one to be swept away into the night, accompanied by a savage snarl. He had not told Lordal that part of the story. Partly due to fear of Lordal's reaction, and partly from the hope that he had imagined the entire incident. He had half expected the light of day would return Rotalla to their numbers.

"And the other?" Lordal asked in tight tones of the control he was exerting over his growing anger.

"Twayne," Bonzwa pronounced his name. "I know not what became of him. He was part of a group that was sent after the lead rider."

"I want their bodies found!" Lordal ordered. With a sweep of his hand, he sectioned off his men. "Five of you search the woods, the rest of you begin preparing the bodies to be moved."

The assembled bandits quickly spread out, and each began their assigned tasks.

"What manner of beings were these?" Lordal asked as his eyes took in the carnage around him.

"They appeared to be normal humans. I had no idea that they would fight as they did." Bonzwa made a point not to look at the bodies. As a member of Lordal's inner circle it was to him that Lordal would lay out the details of a raid. Then he, in turn, would pick the men he considered most able to handle the task and execute the raid. Bonzwa had lead many successful raids for Lordal, and they had all watched their share of the wealth grow. To suffer such a defeat as this made Bonzwa wonder how long he would remain in the inner circle of Lordal's lieutenants. Indeed, if he would even continue to be a part of Lordal's very lucrative 'army' at all.

In hindsight, it had been a terribly planned affair. Bonzwa and his men had been returning to their lair after scouting out a village as a possible target when they had spied the four travelers.

The itch to rob and plunder had been growing in recent weeks, and Bonzwa found himself anxious, ready for action. The four travelers had seemed like easy targets, and he had quickly formulated a loose plan for relieving them of what wealth they may be carrying.

Lordal's thoughts were well hidden as he slowly paced the short area of road, his eyes squinting, searching the dirt as if to find some explanation for what had happened.

Bonzwa watched his leader carefully, hoping to find some indication of which direction his anger would go once released.

"Appearances can be very deceiving, Bonzwa," Lordal said in low, controlled voice. "You should already know this."

"Yes, sir." Bonzwa lowered his gaze to his feet. "The night was dark, the moon was only a sliver in the sky," he managed to whisper.

"Even more reason not to execute an attack. The darkness of night can conceal a great many facts."

"Yes, sir." Bonzwa's voice grew hoarse, fearing for his own life. Lordal had little patience for failure, especially when coupled with gross ignorance.

Lordal's richly tailored robes fluttered about his considerable bulk as he moved around the area. It appeared that at any moment he would draw his sword and force Bonzwa to pay for his severe lack of judgment.

"Did any of them display any mystical powers?" Lordal asked.

"Not that I saw, sir." Bonzwa answered.

Lordal nodded as he reached up to stroke his beard, another indication that he was considering what course of action to follow. Lordal's crisp brown hair was cut short, and possessed a natural curl that kept the locks tightly wound. The chilled morning air rustled the curls, as the bandit king's brown eyes were lost in deep thought.

After many minutes of pacing, Lordal stopped in front of Bonzwa and fixed the smaller man with an unwavering gaze.

Bonzwa forced himself not to cringe, wondering if his body would be among those to be carried back to their lair.

"You know what the penalty is for such a blundering failure, do you not?"

Bonzwa began to tremble, but he locked his eyes with Lordal's and never flinched as he answered, "Yes sir."

"You have served me well in the past, Bonzwa. I have come to rely upon you when a particular task seems difficult. For that reason I will offer you a chance to redeem yourself."

The penalty for failure was unpleasant. It consisted of the condemned being tied to a post with the other bandits passing by the condemned, and each cutting the man with their sword. Once each member had passed the condemned, Lordal would step forward and remove his head. It was a brutal ritual, but it served to remind the others that such gross ignorance and incompetence would not be tolerated.

Bonzwa remembered the times he had taken his turn at stepping past a bound man and drawing his sword across the man's body, adding to the man's screams of agony and pleas for mercy. He had vowed, each time, that he would never end up tied to that post. How had he so swiftly been forced to face that very prospect?

"How may I redeem myself, Lordal?" Bonzwa could not keep the pleading in his voice.

"Find these four individuals. Track them down and bring them to me... alive. Beat them, torture them if you wish, but they must be dragged before me alive and with their senses intact. I have a special punishment planned for them. The death of any one of them will result in you taking their place."

"I hear you, sir." Bonzwa fought down the wave of relief and sudden urge to sink to his knees with gratitude for this second chance. The fear he had felt swiftly turned to anger at the four travelers who had nearly cost him his life. He vowed to hunt them down and drag their beaten and broken bodies before Lordal.

"Sir Lordal!" came a horrified shriek from deep in the woods. Lordal's head jerked in that direction an instant before he bolted toward the woods, Bonzwa close on his heels.

"Bartol! What is it?" Lordal yelled searching frantically for the man until he finally found him.

"May the Fates protect us!" Bartol whispered, staring above his head into the trees.

Lordal and Bonzwa followed his gaze and found the missing body of Rotalla. It was high up in the tree, draped backwards over a limb. His dead eyes and mouth were wide open in an expression of intense fear. The color of his skin was the white ashen of death.

"His throat, sir!" Bonzwa whispered. "My lords!"

Lordal screwed his eyes to focus on the distant throat and saw what had caused Bartol's soul-rending fear. Under the left ear were two jagged puncture marks, a tiny trail of blood traced from each one. Lordal quickly scanned the bark of the tree all the way down to the base and saw not a single drop of blood anywhere. The implications of the punctures, position of the body and the lack of excess blood slammed the revelation home. The bandit leader felt his fear mount.

"By the Saints of..." Lordal began, but lost his voice.

"A vampire!" Bonzwa whispered so low that he was not sure it could have been heard. He was not sure he wanted it heard, as if uttering that foul word aloud would bring the un-dead demon down upon them all.

"Impossible! There are no vampires in this region!" Lordal hissed, his own voice seeming small in light of the massive evidence before their eyes.

"It would appear one has come here," Bartol whispered the obvious. Like the others, he was unable to take his eyes from the horrified expression on Rotalla's face. He wondered what terror had torn through the man's mind as the beast's fangs had sunk deep into his throat.

Lordal shook his head. "A Dark One would not dare move into this region. The priests here are true of faith, and their holy powers would keep the demon at bay."

"But sir... a vampire? How can we possibly defeat a creature that is already dead?" Bonzwa tore his gaze from the corpse in the tree. Regardless of the power and faith of the priests, the evidence was laid out in sickening clarity.

"There are those who hunt the un-dead and are knowledgeable in the ways of how to destroy them." Lordal turned his gaze to Bonzwa and noted how pale the man had become, as pale as the corpse in the tree above them. "We will find the creature that did this and destroy it! If I find that the four travelers are in league with this demon, their fate will be as horrific as the one that awaits the un-dead!" Lordal turned on his heel and strode back toward the road.

"Sir, what of Rotalla?" Bonzwa called.

Lordal paused, and then turned to regard the corpse again. "Get him down. Severe his head then burn the body to ashes. Package the ashes and bring them with us. We will have to have the ashes blessed by a priest before dispersing them to the winds. We will take no chances. Do not delay! We must move out by mid-day if we are to overtake the four travelers."

"*We*, sir?" Bonzwa asked carefully.

Lordal fixed his gaze on Bonzwa. "Yes, we. I will lead this hunt myself." Lordal turned abruptly and strode away.

Bonzwa watched Lordal leave, and then turned his attention to the body high above him. His gaze traveled down the tree to find Bartol who appeared terrified by the prospect of having to retrieve the body.

With a heavy sigh, Bonzwa unbuckled his sword belt and began the slow climb. Most likely, he would also have to be the one to behead Rotalla's corpse and set the fire that would burn the remains to ash. He could have ordered Bartol to do it all, but Rotalla had been a friend. He owed it to the man to, hopefully, free his soul from the grip of the Dark One. Bonzwa had no doubt in his mind that Rotalla would have done the same for him.

CHAPTER SIXTEEN

DEVENSHIRE ENTERED HIS TINY room at the inn and closed the door. He leaned back against the door and laid his head back against the chipping paint, closing his eyes and letting his breath out in a tired sigh. His head still throbbed from the blows he had taken the night before, and he was very tired. He had not slept much since the destruction of Shantira's village.

Latching the door, he sat his saddlebags down, realizing that it was past time for him to sleep. The quest ahead was fraught with danger, and he would need all of his senses about him to stay one step ahead of Xavier.

He slipped his cloak from his shoulders and draped it across the room's only rickety chair. Next, he unbuckled his sword belt and laid it in the chair's seat. He crossed to the bed and sat down on the edge of it, letting a yawn come.

He pulled his boots off, dropping each one onto the warped floorboards with a loud thud. Flexing his toes in the sudden freedom, he dropped his head and simply enjoyed a moment of inactivity. His long hair dropped down around his face as he closed his eyes and simply took a moment to exist. No thought. No action. Just to sit and not do anything.

His mind could be a most contrary thing, however, and his moment of quiet solitude quickly turned to intense thoughts about the night before. He wasn't too concerned about the attack itself, such a thing was almost expected. It was the unknown person who had come to his aid. Whoever it had been, was a deadly shot with a crossbow. To have shot the bandit in the neck, just below the left ear in near total darkness was no easy feat.

None of his party carried a crossbow, so that meant someone else had been present during the attack, someone who was following them, mirroring their movements.

Xavier?

Unlikely. If it had been Xavier, or more likely, one of his Followers, they would have most certainly dispatched him in short order.

Then whom?

Devenshire shook his head slowly. There wasn't enough information to make even a wild speculation. Was the person with the crossbow the same one who had touched his face and helped restore his addled senses? The memory of the chilled hands touching either side of his face and then warming was vivid. So, too, was the way the gentle heat dispelled the fog that had engulfed his senses. He could almost feel the soft chilled flesh begin to warm rapidly even now.

He briefly considered performing a Spell of Mystic Knowledge, but he seriously doubted he would have any success. His body was tired, his mind fatigued. He doubted he could draw enough concentration to focus his limited abilities into a strong enough spell. Perhaps after he rested he would make the attempt.

There were too many questions, and not nearly enough answers readily presenting themselves. With another yawn, he lay back on the small bed and swung his feet up on the bed.

It was more like a cot. It was barely wide enough to support his shoulders, his feet hung off the end of the bed, and the mattress was barely more than a sack full of something that might pass for padding. At the moment, though, Devenshire was extremely grateful for it. A third yawn came, and he stretched his entire frame, forcing tensed muscles to bunch once more before relaxing.

As he released the stretch, he could feel the feathery fingers of sleep begin to stroke his eyelids, drawing them closed with each stroke, making it harder to open them again. His mind let go of the mysteries, the tension of the quest ahead, and all the other concerns that had held his attention the last days. His muscles relaxed as the outside world began to fade from his perceptions.

The knock was tentative, hesitant, and barely audible.

For a moment, Devenshire remained motionless, his eyes closed and his breathing slow and steady. Perhaps if he ignored the knock, whoever it was would move along.

The knock sounded again, stronger this time followed by a hushed voice, "Daimion?"

Devenshire's eyes snapped open, and the tiny bit of sleep that had begun to overtake his mind was instantly swept away.

Brianna.

There was something wrong. He could hear it in her voice. She had something on her mind, had since the previous night in The Tavern.

Perhaps she would finally talk about it. He rolled off the bed, crossed the room, and opened the door.

Brianna stood in the hallway looking uncomfortable. Only someone who knew her as intimately as Devenshire would notice her preoccupation. It was subtle things about her that told him this — the tilt of her head, the faint echo of troubling thoughts in the back of her eyes, the way she clasped her hands before her in a most un-Brianna-ish display of modesty.

"Bri?" he asked.

"Am I disturbing you?" she asked softly. She quickly stole a glance up and down both ends of the hallway, as if she were trying to keep her visit to his room a secret. Another display that was totally out of character for her.

He gave her his warmest smile. "Your type of disturbance is always welcome."

She smiled and lowered her head slightly as her right hand quickly tucked an errant strand of black hair behind her ear. "You are trying to be charming," she almost whispered.

"Am I succeeding?" he asked warmly.

She looked up into his eyes and her smile broadened. "You know that you are."

He nodded and stepped aside. "Do you wish to come in?"

She looked relieved at his invitation, and he got the distinct impression it had nothing to do with their exchange. Something was most definitely troubling her, and it was putting her on edge.

As she entered the room, he closed the door and latched it again. He extended his hand toward the bed. "Please. Be seated."

Brianna quickly crossed the tiny room and sat down on the edge of the bed. She busied herself with her fingernails, the thumbnail of one hand grating across the edge of the thumbnail on the other hand.

Devenshire cleared the chair, pulled it over to swing it around, back facing Brianna. He straddled the back of the chair, propped his arms on the back and fixed his gaze on her.

"What is troubling you?" he asked without preamble.

"Is it that obvious?" she asked, trying to make the statement sound lighthearted and failing.

"It is to me," he answered evenly. "You have been troubled since last eve in The Tavern. What is wrong?"

She curled her bottom lip in to bite on it absently as she focused on fidgeting with her nails. He didn't say anything, letting her come to the decision to confide in him on her own.

"Have you sensed anything... unusual?" she finally asked, not looking at him

"Such as?" he asked.

"Any strange magic at work or any unusual individuals close by."

Devenshire lowered his eyes to the floor, carefully considering her question. He focused his attention to last night's strange incident, even the brief exchange with Rachelle Tambrey. But none of this would have any impact on Brianna, and he finally shook his head, returning his eyes to hers.

"No, nothing out of the ordinary. Why?"

"Someone communicated with me last night in The Tavern, the way you and I do at times. Mentally."

"Who?"

Brianna's eyes took on a far away gaze, as she stared off into the distance, briefly shaking her head. "I do not know. Whoever it was shielded their identity."

"Did you recognize the mental pattern?" Devenshire spoke quickly, narrowing his eyes on her face, searching for answers.

Brianna bit her bottom lip again as her eyes dropped to the floor, shaking her head. "No, I had never heard their thoughts before last night. But it was more than mere thoughts." Her hands rose and gestured as she spoke, as if she could conjure up the exact thought and feeling she was having for him to inspect. "There were sensations, impressions with familiar feelings. I felt I should know the person, but do not."

Devenshire's brow furrowed as he considered the implications. Projecting thoughts into another person's mind was simple enough. It took very little training and concentration to do. But to attach sensations and impressions with the thoughts took considerable effort, training, and discipline. "Please, explain."

Brianna was silent for several moments before her right hand traveled up to tuck the ever-errant strand of hair behind her ear. Her deep green eyes were troubled. Devenshire had to admit that while he had seen her upset before, he had never seen her preoccupied with any one problem. Finally, she took a deep breath and launched into an explanation.

"I could nearly feel this person's hands on me and felt a very strong sexual undercurrent to his thoughts. I felt as if I should know this person, but I did not." Brianna searched for a better explanation and finally sighed in frustration. She could not find adequate words to convey what she had felt.

Devenshire reached out and placed his hand over Brianna's folded ones. "It is all right. Take your time. Relax, and tell me what you can."

"He knew things about me that no one knows, not even you. He spoke to me as if he knew me very, very well. At least that was the impression he left in my mind. I tell you, Daimion, I was more than a little unsettled by the whole incident."

"I can imagine. The kind of mental communication you are describing is very difficult and takes a great deal of discipline to accomplish."

Brianna was silent for a few more moments before her confusion forced an explosive sigh of frustration from her lips. She rose from the bed and crossed to the window. She folded her arms across her chest and leaned against the window frame, letting her troubled gaze sweep across the crowded streets below.

"I cannot get it out of my mind. The harder I try to forget it, the more it plagues me."

Devenshire watched her back for several moments before he rose to his feet and began walking toward her.

"Perhaps it is someone from your past. Someone you knew a long time ago, and they have resurfaced. Perhaps they are merely playing an exaggerated jest upon you."

Brianna shook her head slowly. "I have considered that possibility and dismissed it. No one I have ever known would do this to me. Besides, you are the only one I know who can communicate mentally."

Devenshire digested this news before offering another alternative. "Then an enemy, perhaps. Someone you may have angered in the past."

"I suppose such a thing is possible, but I strongly doubt it. Do not ask me why, I simply do. Something within tells me that I should know this person, and knew him at some point in my past. But I cannot remember anyone who has affected me in this way," Brianna whispered the last.

Devenshire considered her words as he stepped behind her, gazing over her shoulder to the street below. The sights went largely unnoticed as his mind wrestled with her problem.

It was possible to delve deep enough into someone's mind and retrieve hidden information to use against them. Though, only an adept of the Mystical Arts could do such a thing without being detected. If such a person had been present at The Tavern last night, he would have sensed it. Then an idea came to mind, and he quickly shifted his gaze to Brianna's profile.

"Was this person male or female?"

Brianna turned her head and gave him a puzzled look. "Male."

Devenshire's brow furrowed as he nodded. It was possible that Rachelle Tambrey could be the person responsible. Even though Brianna was sure the person had been male, a skilled practitioner of the Arts could make their mental presence appear as either sex.

"Why do you ask?" Brianna inquired.

"Just trying to narrow down the suspect list," he lied in response. "If someone of this level of skill had been at The Tavern last eve, I would have sensed their presence."

"But obviously, someone of that skill was present," she answered and then caught herself. "Wait! The communication happened before you arrived."

Devenshire nodded. "Then it is very possible that this person was long gone before I arrived." He discounted Rachelle's involvement in this little mystery. He wasn't exactly sure why he didn't believe her to be the one, but he just had a gut feeling.

"I do not know what to say, Brianna. Obviously, someone is trying to gain your attention. Did you ever feel as if this person was prying into your mind?"

Brianna shook her head slowly.

"Yet, they knew things that no one else would know."

She nodded as she turned her troubled gaze back out the window, biting absently on her bottom lip. It was a sign of just how nervous the incident had left her.

"Odd, to say the least," he commented.

After several long moments of silence, Brianna turned from the window to face Devenshire, her troubled eyes seeking his.

"I have a very unusual request of you, Daimion."

It was Devenshire's turn to adopt a confused expression. "Continue."

"Can you read the hidden mind? Are you able to go deep enough into my mind and see if there is something I am not considering, not remembering?"

Devenshire was silent for many moments. He knew where she was going with the conversation.

"I can, to some limited degree. But you must realize exactly what that would mean. I would be exposed to things within your mind that you may have wished to keep secret. Once inside, I cannot simply pick and choose what I discover. Indeed, the answer you seek may be beyond my abilities and reach."

Brianna was silent, considering his warning. Was she willing to risk the opening of her mind? Was she willing to allow him to see things that she otherwise would keep secret? Could she risk it?

"What might you see?" Brianna had to know if her secret would be revealed.

"It would depend on that person. Each mind is arranged differently. I cannot say with any certainty what things I would be exposed to once I began probing your mind." He leveled a serious gaze into hers. "There are no lies within your mind."

Brianna nodded slowly. There was little that Devenshire didn't already know about her, but there were things that she kept hidden from him and would continue to do so. There were also things in her mind that she was obligated to keep from Devenshire, such as Shantira's true feelings for him. There were simply too many things that he did not know. She could not risk letting him discover these truths.

"I understand. Perhaps I will simply have to find another way." She released her breath slowly, her gaze stuck fast to the warped floorboards of the room.

Devenshire nodded slowly in agreement. He had not revealed that the link was often two ways. As much as he would learn from her, she would learn from him. He was not skilled enough to keep his thoughts from intruding upon her mind as he accepted hers. He acknowledged a few things that he did not wish for her to discover.

"I am sorry that I cannot be of more help," Devenshire said slowly.

Brianna smiled warmly and gazed up into his eyes, conveying her gratitude. "Do not be sorry. I am grateful that you told me what you have, rather than take advantage of an opportunity to delve into my mind for secret thoughts and desires. It is why I came to you. I know I can trust you."

Devenshire returned her smile, and for several moments, they stood in silence, their eyes locked together.

Brianna watched his eyes and tried to discern what thoughts were going through his mind. There was something about his eyes that always seemed to mesmerize her to some degree. She often wondered precisely what secrets she would learn if she could read his mind.

Her skin began to tingle with heat, and the sensations heightened. Staring into Devenshire's eyes always seemed to arouse her deepest desires. The odd mixture of heat and the chill down her spine, signaling awareness, swam around her body and made her shiver delicately.

Devenshire's low voice became laced with seduction. "What are you thinking?"

"Why do you ask?" Brianna found herself unable to look away.

"You give the appearance of a woman with something on her mind," he said, and there was a slight change in his overall appearance. It was something that heightened her already raging desires.

The troubles that had brought her here seemed to fade with her rush of desire, and she quickly embraced those feelings. She allowed a slightly seductive smile to play across her full lips. "Only thinking random thoughts, nothing in particular," she replied with a slight purr to her words.

"*Ahh*, I see," His deep-throated reply was simple as he began moving toward her.

Brianna willed herself to remain absolutely still, to not betray what she was feeling. As he stepped closer, she could not help but admire the ease with which he moved, so steady, so sure of each step. The sleepy seduction of his eyes bore deeply into hers, making her body tremble.

She tried to hide her reactions every time they became intimate, but she never doubted for a second that he knew exactly what she was thinking.

He stepped very close to her yet they did not touch. He looked down into her eyes and smiled softly. "Is there any chance you might share a few of those random thoughts?"

Brianna tilted her head back so that she faced him fully, and then smiled. She let her eyes echo the heat and meaning in his. Her smile deepened, as did her husky voice. "There is always a chance, Devenshire. All you need do is to ask the right questions."

Devenshire arched one eyebrow, as he looked deeper into her eyes. Without breaking contact, he wrapped one arm about her waist and pulled her close. Once her body was pressed hard against his, he reached up with his free hand to trace a gentle trail down the side of her face with warm fingertips.

As soft and warm as Devenshire's touch had been, it ignited the smoldering embers of her passions. It took all her will not to let the moan in her throat pass her lips. A part of her always enjoyed suppressing her reactions to him at first, simply to see what new method he would come up with to invoke a response. She was never disappointed with his efforts.

His fingers trailed down her cheek, then lightly up her jaw line to slip beneath the blanket of her thick hair. They came forward until they arrived at the hollow directly behind her ear. After tracing a light pattern there, his fingertips slid softly down the side of her neck to the collar of her blouse before following the edge of the material to the upper slope of her breast.

With no control to stop it, a shudder of pleasure rippled through her sensitive skin. She could tell by the faint glint in his eyes that he had indeed felt it. Her lips parted slightly as the tip of her tongue darted out to moisten them. When, exactly, had they gone dry? She saw his eyes dart quickly down to her parted lips. She wanted to kiss him deeply.

She rose up on her toes to entice him into kissing her, but she saw the flicker of mischief in his eyes and realized that had been the exact response he had anticipated.

He pulled his head back only slightly, and she yearned for him to close the distance between them with a smoldering kiss, but she knew that he would not kiss her until he was ready. It was a game they played often and one she had always considered herself proficient at playing... except with him. Had any other man pulled back from her kiss, she would have simply pulled out of the embrace and walked away. But she had quickly found with Devenshire, such a tactic would be met with apparent indifference.

With that delicious sensual mischief flaring in his eyes, he slipped his arm from around her waist and stepped casually behind her, placing his hands firmly on her hips as his lips drifted to her ear.

"Hmm, the right questions? Would you care to give me a hint?" His husky voice and warm breath whispered over her ear.

He was playing with her, and she knew it. How could he not know his effect on her? Surely he could feel the heat flowing from her body, could sense the tiny trembles that raced along her spine.

"And spoil the game?" she teased in a near-whisper as she slowly closed her eyes and tilted her head slightly to the side, exposing her neck for his tasting pleasure. Sensual heat wafted up around her, fogging her mind with a very familiar, but still exciting, sensual cloud.

Very slowly, his lips drifted around to her ear, barely grazing it in a slow circular motion. In the same moment, his strong hands gently pulled her hips back to press against his. She could feel the stiffness of his arousal press into her firm buttocks, which caused her to whimper softly. Her head drifted back to rest against his shoulder.

"A game?" His thick voice caressed her earlobe.

"Y-yes... a game..." she replied breathlessly.

His lips brushed across her earlobe before he gently drew it in to suckle on it. She tried to stifle the moan that rose up in her throat, but could not stop it from whispering past her lips—no more than she could stop her hips from gently gyrating back into his. To her delighted surprise, his hips met hers, and he drove his shaft forward, harder against her. Another ripple of raw sexual hunger tore into the very center of her body. It formed a tiny knot deep in her belly that would quickly grow into the deliciously painful promise of release.

He released her earlobe only to gently caress it with a teasing flick from his tongue. "A game would imply rules. I have never been very good with rules," he growled softly.

As he spoke, his hands left her hips to circle around to her hard, flat stomach. She was only dimly aware of his hands pulling her blouse free from her breeches. With surprising swiftness, his hands slipped beneath the blouse and found her heated flesh, tracing intricate patterns on her stomach. A searing jolt of pleasure stroked her. As her knees began to tremble, she was grateful for his support.

"No... no rules, Devenshire," she whispered huskily as her right arm snaked slowly up to coil around his neck. Her fingers entwined in his thick black hair.

A throaty chuckle sent his hot breath across her neck an instant before his lips found the juncture where her shoulder and neck joined. His lips and tongue danced across the silken flesh, kissing and licking a hot, intricate trail up the side of her neck, deftly working to the soft spot behind her ear.

She groaned as his ministrations found one of her sensitive areas. She wondered exactly when she had lost control of her vocal cords?

Her body was responding from impulses that came from somewhere other than her conscious mind. She became aware of their bodies moving together, swaying, and gyrating in perfect rhythm with one another. As she moved her hips back, he thrust his forward, crushing his growing shaft between them.

His hands roamed the smooth flatness of her stomach, inching slowly upward. Brianna became impatient for more of his touch. She wanted his hands upon her breasts, between her leg, and all over her body, yet he was moving with agonizing slowness. It was torture. Delicious torture, but torture nonetheless.

Suddenly, her eyes flew open as his teeth sank into the soft flesh of her neck. He had never bitten her before, and the sharp pain of his teeth coming together on her skin caused her to tremble in anticipation of the giant release building within her.

"Oh gods...." she murmured. "W-w-what are you doing?"

His teeth released her neck, and he gently kissed the bitten area. Harshly, he replied, "Breaking the rules." Suddenly, he bit her again, harder than before. Her belly and upper thighs trembled as the knot of pent up release doubled in size. She sagged against him, unable to stand on her shaking legs.

As she began to slide down his body, his hands found her bare breasts beneath her blouse. His strong hands cupped them sending hot desire and renewed strength raging fiercely through her, more so than she had ever experienced with him before. By the Fates, how could he do this? How could he always find some new way to drive her to the brink of insanity with such pleasure?

He took her hardened nipples between each thumb and forefinger before gently rolling them. Wave upon wave of pleasure crashed over her, threatening to drown her senses in a sea of boiling desire. She had wanted him before stepping into this room. Now she felt as though she would swell and burst if she did not have him immediately.

"Take me, Devenshire! Take me now!" she commanded breathlessly.

Suddenly, he squeezed both sensitive nipples hard and twisted them between his thumb and forefinger. At the same instant, he took another loving bite of her neck so hard that she feared the skin would split. A shocking wave of raw pleasure slammed her upright, causing her muscles to tense in anticipation of the release that stubbornly refused to come.

He released her swollen nipples and removed his hands from beneath her blouse, much to her dismay. Taking both of her delicate shoulders in his firm grip, he turned her to face him, his eyes smoldered down into hers with the fire of passion. When her jaw went slack and her wide, glazed eyes found his, she could have sworn she saw actual flames flickering in their depths. Sweat glistened on her forehead and upper lip.

Before she could say anything, his lips came down to crush against hers, his tongue stabbing past her lips to entwine with hers in a sexual dance. With an animal grunt of pure pleasure, she slammed her hips into him and hooked one leg around his, pulling herself as close to him as possible.

She did not know how long the ravenous kiss lasted, but he pulled away too soon for her liking. Without realizing it, she rose up on her toes, trying to draw his delicious lips back down to hers.

"To take you now could be viewed as a rule," he whispered with a teasing smile.

"You..." she began, but had to stop to draw in a deep breath and swallow hard, "...you really are a bastard. You know this, do you not?" she panted huskily.

Devenshire's features became so much softer than she had ever seen them before.

"You would have me no other way," he answered softly.

He slowly lowered his lips to hers, and as they touched, time lost all meaning. The purpose of their journey, even the very reason she had come to his room, was gone from her conscious mind, replaced by an all-consuming fire.

As her hands slipped beneath his shirt and her nails lightly scraped up his bare back, she felt the very thick cords of odd crisscrossed scars. She had felt the scars and had actually seen them on a few occasions. They were horrible, ugly, thick masses of scar tissue that formed a hideous pattern on his back. She had asked him about them on several occasions, and each time he had skillfully evaded the question and the issue, replying with some typical Devenshire whimsical remark.

As her fingers gently rubbed across the thick cords, she felt his body tremble beneath her touch. Despite his best plays at keeping his reactions hidden, she knew his passion was rising beyond his control. His lips slipped down to the silken skin of her neck and throat, and she allowed another moan of pleasure to softly caress his ear.

Strong hands continued to roam her body, and she allowed herself to sink into the flames of their passions. Her eyes fluttered closed when she felt him lift her clear off the floor and move toward the bed.

She smiled a secret smile as the flames of her desire consumed the last of her rigid self-control. For a while, she could be herself, her true abandoned self, and she reveled in it.

CHAPTER SEVENTEEN

SHANTIRA TOSSED FITFULLY ON her bed as she tried to sleep but found her efforts wasted. The harder she tried to relax her mind and body, the more overwrought they became. She knew she needed rest, to conserve her strength for the journey ahead, but sleep refused her call, and she found herself staring at the ceiling of her tiny room. The fact that sunlight still streamed through her window compounded the problem. She was accustomed to being up and about, performing work of some kind during the day.

She finally gave up the effort and sat up on the side of the bed. The fight last night still played on her mind, as well as the excitement of being in this giant city. Also, as she was beginning to become accustomed to, Devenshire drifted through the shadows of her thoughts. Of course, the loss of her village was never, ever far from her feelings. The pain and the grief continued to smear it's blackness upon her soul as though it were a canvas for the pain and grief to use to paint some twisted dark portrait of suffering.

The bandit's attack had taken her completely by surprise. When the bandit had knocked her from the saddle, she had feared for her life. Though her fear had been intense, the exhilaration of the fight had been equally so. She could not find the words to describe her feelings. Her emotions were many, and not one stood out from another. Like a caged animal, Shantira circled the stifling confines of her small room as if that would ease her restlessness.

It didn't.

Her bare feet did not feel the cool wooden floor as she paced back and forth, searching for a direction. Shantira shook out strong arms that demanded action.

Restless. That's precisely what she was feeling.

Sounds came to her from the window. She quietly padded over to gaze out at the quickly filling streets below. Lirpa was awe-inspiring. Never in her wildest imagination could she have believed a place like this existed. The sheer size of the city numbed her mind, as did the possibilities that waited below. All of her life had been spent in her tiny village where the barest of necessities were a struggle to obtain. But from here, she could see that was not the case in Lirpa.

Life flowed and ebbed like the tides of the ocean, and she felt a part of her call out to be caught up in it. For the first time, she realized that there was so much more to life than tending crops, building huts, toiling the earth to coax from it what was needed to survive.

There were so many things, she now realized, that she did not know, things in life that she desperately wanted to experience. It was as if a secret part of her had awakened, and it called for all the knowledge it had been deprived of for so long. For the first time, she found herself coming closer to truly understanding Brianna. Brianna was free-spirited and sought out all that life had to offer.

Shantira felt the sheer excitement of discovery as she looked out over the tiny part of the city she could see from her window. The city called to her, inviting to teach her so many things if she would only loosen her rigid control and let herself experience them. She had always been concerned with her duty to the village, and to those who had helped raise her. She only allowed herself the small self-indulgences of battle training and thought herself a free spirit for defying the Council of Elders.

Lirpa, though, whispered seductively to her, showing her exactly how tightly bound she had kept her spirit all of these seasons. Her village was forever gone. She still felt remorse and grief, feeling certain a part of it would always be with her. But beneath the grief lay something else — an awakening of sorts.

She had no home, and her future was no longer set in granite.

Free.

The word slammed into her mind, and she gasped as it finally dawned on her. She was free. Free to go where she pleased, do what she pleased. Her newly found freedom both exhilarated and frightened her, and she reveled in the combination.

Devenshire. As always, he came to her mind. A faint smile touched her lips as she remembered the first time she had seen him in the woods, leaning so casually against a tree. She remembered the sensation that had stirred within her. The look of mischief about him, the dark mystery that seemed to permeate him at all times.

That night in The Tavern when he had held her so close in a dance that she had wanted to refuse, and yet she would not have missed for the world... The seemingly endless emotions and sensations had stirred within her, had tortured her… Could she do what Brianna had said she must? Could she surrender to the physical, discarding the emotional? She was not sure. Yet she had to acknowledge the purely physical responses he drew from her and her desire to experience them. She had toyed with these thoughts before with other men who had caught her attention, but she had never given in to her bodily desires. Devenshire was different. The desires he spawned in her raged and boiled within her, refusing to be ignored or suppressed.

Then she remembered her newfound desire to experience all that life had to offer alongside the mental image of Devenshire and her perceptions were altered. Why should she deny herself the experience of being touched, of being made love to, simply because of her fear of not being able to capture his heart or his refusing to capture hers? Who was to say that she could not be the one exception to his rigid rules?

These questions scared and excited her, and she knew she would give them very careful attention while seeking the answers. The deaths in her village reminded her that time in this realm could be cut short with nothing more than the slash of a sword. Could she face the afterlife with all of these questions left unanswered? The thought chilled her, and she quickly sought out the image of Devenshire again to soak in the strange warmth his memory brought her.

As her eyes took in the sights of the city below, she vowed to herself that she would not stand at the portal of the afterlife, looking back and sighing sadly at the opportunities she had denied herself.

~*~

Devenshire slowly opened his eyes as the last vestiges of sleep withdrew from his mind. The first thing he became aware of was the weight on his right shoulder. He smiled fondly, tightening his arm ever so slightly around Brianna's sleeping form. She sighed softly in her sleep as a wicked smile crossed her features before snuggling deeper into his shoulder.

Devenshire looked down into her face. She was as beautiful in sleep as she was while awake. Even asleep, she had a feminine air about her that he was at a loss to describe. There was a strength that belayed her softness, a sense of will that dominated her, even in a deep sleep. Her ability to maintain that mixture of strength and softness constantly amazed him. There were times when he could not imagine Brianna needing anyone to make her life complete. Then times, like now, when she seemed so dependent upon him. He knew this was a façade designed to stroke his ego, to make him feel needed.

He reached up and very carefully swept a strand of black hair from her forehead. Her face a few hours ago had borne the ravages of her pleasure. Yet, even during the most heated moments of their passion, when she had seemed completely out of control and abandoned to the moment, there had been that sense that she was in complete control of her emotions. It was a very intriguing mixture that Devenshire had yet to understand, but found incredibly exciting.

There were times when he was hard pressed not to allow his heart to dominate his thinking. He had admitted a long time ago that it would be exceedingly easy to fall in love with Brianna. With a touch of sadness, he knew that such a thing could never be allowed to happen. For his sake as well as hers.

As his thoughts roamed the tightly fenced plains of his mind, faces arose from his memory. Women he had known, made love to, and yet had never loved. Women who had sought to capture his heart and give him theirs, and each time he had refused. Those same faces went from the coy glances and subtle smiles after first meeting, to veiled desire and passion. Then, as they always were destined to, tears came as the realization hit home that they could never possess of him what they sought.

Each face had touched him in a different way, and each face would forever be a part of his memories, but none of them stirred the cold dead embers of love that would burn no more within his breast. Brianna came closer to any to stirring the ashes, but not even she could strike a spark there. How much of this was due to a lack of ability on her part, and how much was due to his own determination, he did not know.

He could not deny that he cared for Brianna. He would even be brave enough to admit that she was only one of two women to ever inspire such caring within him. He was relieved that he could still care for someone without being in love with them. Although, it terrified him that caring for her would lead to him falling in love.

Devenshire searched his emotions for any signs that such a thing was happening. Though his concern and friendship for her were strong, he felt secure that he was in no danger of falling in love with her... at least not yet. He felt a sharp warning deep inside, cautioning him to guard his feelings for Brianna. One day he would be forced to part from her in order to prevent himself from falling in love.

Love was a very tricky emotion—it could sneak upon you and take you unawares. It was madness. Madness. With a fond smile, he remembered the man that had given him the wisest words he had ever heard.

Sir Elbert had been a friend from his youth. He had been the governing lord of a province in a kingdom far south of Caston. The name of the kingdom escaped him, as most names from that time in his life tended to. Back then, he drank heavily and had no real preference, as long as it would numb his mind.

He had met Sir Elbert in his twenty-fifth season. The man was large, larger even than Zandorth, but unlike the warrior, Sir Elbert was a jovial, good-natured man of incredible wisdom and mirth. He found humor and delight in almost any situation and was incredibly slow to anger. Devenshire recalled that in the three seasons he had been in Sir Elbert's company, he had never even seen the giant of a man so much as annoyed.

He was a man who enjoyed every pleasurable aspect of life and his position as Lord of the Province allowed him to indulge in anything he chose. Good food, good, strong drink, good friendship, and of course, beautiful women, were among his favorite indulgences.

He loved to laugh and had a deep, mellow laugh that was quite infectious. Even if one didn't hear the jest, hearing Elbert's deep-bellied laugh would often cause more laughter than the original comment.

The large black man was probably the closest thing Devenshire had to a true friend at that time in his life. One day had found them in a tavern, drinking heavily and discussing philosophical questions of life and love.

Another one of Elbert's qualities was that he could be falling down drunk, and yet appear the perfect portrait of sobriety. No glazed eyes, no slack expression, and no slurred words. The more he had to drink, it seemed, the more sober he became.

Such was not the case for Devenshire, especially in those days. He spent each day attempting to drown the dark memory with as much alcohol as he could consume. If his mood had been foul before he began drinking, then he was certain to be a holy terror by the end of the night.

On this particular night, Devenshire's mood had been quite dark, and the alcohol he had consumed had only served to make it darker. Very quickly, he was looking for someone to fight, to take out all of his frustrations upon. Back then, he enjoyed a good fight. The more challenging his opponent, the better. One man at the bar had quickly drawn Devenshire's attention, and he set about finding some excuse to initiate an opportunity to beat him into an unconscious and very bloody pulp.

"Your mood seems even more foul than usual, Daimion," Elbert had observed. Elbert knew the dark memory that haunted him and knew how his thirst for combat was only an outlet for the pain and agony. He was also one of the only people who could keep Devenshire in control when his alcohol-induced desire for vengeance appeared.

"You are far more intelligent than I first thought. Your powers of observation are staggering for such a fat bastard," Devenshire had slurred in reply. "I forget your brain can move quickly even if your massive bulk cannot."

Elbert chuckled warmly. He knew that Devenshire was merely

venting his grief. "Perhaps you would like to test my speed. I see you are looking for a fight this night. Perhaps your grand opponent is not so far away." The warm smile never left his dark features.

"I would reduce you to a quivering pile of wasted lard without breaking a sweat," he sloppily snarled in reply. At least he had intended it to be a snarl, but it had come out as drooling, curled lip expression that looked like he was having a seizure.

"Indeed?" asked Elbert, the broad smile still spread across his face. "Then it is a fortuitous turn of events that finds you incapable of making good on your threat."

Devenshire slugged back nearly half his tankard of mead and set it loudly back on the table. He turned his bleary gaze to Elbert, blinking slowly as he sloppily wiped the foam from his lips. "And what makes you so certain that I am not capable?"

"Two things."

"And those are?" Devenshire asked after a deep belch.

"Fear and your feet," Elbert replied with a deep chuckle, which at Devenshire's slack expression, turned to a deep laugh.

After a moment, Devenshire could not restrain himself and started laughing, also. Shaking his head as he realized Elbert had broken the tense moment with ease. "You fat bastard!"

"Tell me, my mead soaked friend. What has your spirits so low this eve?"

Devenshire made a sputtering noise that sent spittle across the table, "Life in general!"

"Hmmm. That is quite a broad topic to be so angry about. Perhaps you have a particular aspect or two of life that has you angrier than the others?"

"Love! It is a curse of the Fates, of the underworld! It is a complete waste of time and perfectly good energy! The Fates should ban it from existence!"

"Do you really feel such?" Elbert had asked.

"Indeed, I do!" Devenshire took another deep swallow from his tankard before looking at him. "Go ahead Elbert! Tell me how wrong I am! Tell me what a beautiful gift from the heavens love is and how I should exhaust every ounce of strength within me in pursuit of it.

"I would never do such. I am in complete agreement with you on this point."

"You are?" Devenshire had asked incredulously. "I would have thought you would proceed to shower me with all the philosophical babble about how great love is and what a gift from the heavens love is and all that other meaningless dribble!" he had replied, and he sloppily drew another healthy swallow from his rapidly emptying tankard.

Elbert had chuckled in that incredibly rich bass voice, and shaking his head, said, "Not I. I know exactly what love is. We are quite fortunate that we two, you and I, have discovered the true nature of love and can live out our days without being burdened by it."

Devenshire blinked again, his brain swimming so badly that he wasn't entirely sure he was truly hearing Elbert's words or if some trick of his pickled mind was simply filling in the gaps he could not hear over the ringing in his ears.

"We have discovered this great truth? You and I?" he asked slowly.

Elbert looked up at Devenshire and smiled warmly, nodding, "Of course."

Devenshire had no bloody idea what he was talking about. He searched his swishing mind for the memory of the conversation they had shared in which this awesome truth had been discovered. After several moments, he could not recall what the truth was, or when they had discovered it.

Clumsily looking about to make sure no one was listening, he leaned closer to Elbert, motioning for him to come closer. "Remind me of this great truth one more time."

Elbert laughed heartily. He had never shared this pearl of wisdom with Devenshire before, and the young man's attempt to save face while completely drunk was very endearing and damn funny.

He took another sip of his brandy and smiled at Devenshire. "Love is nothing more than an over romanticized state of insanity."

Devenshire pulled his mind from the past as a smile spread across his face. Those words had brought him a sense of clarity, a weapon to fight back against the pain, and the potential of making that mistake again.

The more seasons that passed between him and that statement, the more he found the deep-rooted truth within it. Only through constant, diligent attention to his true feelings could Devenshire maintain a tight lock on the very powerful emotion. Once it took hold, it would rage out of control, stir the insanity, and lead him down a path he had visited long ago. The toll for such a path was entirely too high.

Forcing his thoughts from the unpleasant memories, he directed his attention elsewhere. With a slight shake of his head, he turned it toward the window across the room and saw that it was near mid-day.

There were several hours before sunset, and he would be in need of more sleep. Since nothing could be gained from remaining awake, and Brianna was lost in a deep exhausted sleep, he closed his eyes to the silken fingers of sleep, drawing him back into their warm folds.

Before his mind left the conscious realm, another delicate face entered his memory. The face of a small-framed blonde woman had touched him and left him completely shaken. Nearly asleep, he wondered if he would ever encounter the mysterious Rachelle Tambrey again.

~*~

A few miles outside of Lirpa, in a deep underground cavern, all was silent and dark, as it had been for uncounted seasons. No human had ever seen the interior of this cavern. In fact, a physical entrance did not exist. The only way into the cavern were the small holes designed for the animal inhabitants. Neither man, nor the light of day had ever seen its interior, save for a few very thin shafts of sunshine that penetrated natural vents from the surface.

A few rodents scurried about in the pitch black, searching for some bit of food. Their tiny black eyes scanned the dirt floor as their noses twitched, searching for anything edible. A strange new odor met their noses, and they instantly froze, sampling the air for more information from the new scent.

A few of the rodents raised up on their hind legs in the hopes of reaching the scent, while others inched closer to the dim silhouette that lay propped against the back wall of the cavern. The odor was not one of food. In fact, it spoke of something that caused many of the rodents to scurry away in fear. The braver ones, or the ones more hungry than the others, inched even closer. There was something in the odor that spoke of death. But the ravages of starvation canceled out their instinctual fear of the unknown and caused them to forge ahead.

There were no signs of life from the silhouette. The scent of death lingered heavily around the form. Two of the rats decided that their hunger outweighed any danger from something that was obviously dead and decaying and advanced to sniff at the cloth that covered the form.

In a flash of movement, the two rats paid for their hunger and curiosity with their lives. Before the remainder of the rodents could flee, their two companions were snatched up. To the accompaniment of squeals and a very hungry snarl, their bodies were pierced and their warm blood flowed into hungry lips. The form drew their life's force from one, then the other.

As the two drained, lifeless bodies dropped into the dust, the small form rose from its resting place and began moving toward the tiny natural vent shaft that led to the surface. With an inaudible sigh, the form dissipated into smoke that was sucked up through the tiny opening.

On the surface, in the growing darkness, a wisp of smoke rose from the ground like a thin stream of fog. The fog hovered above the ground for a moment before it began to shift and take on the shape of a human body. Within moments, the smoke solidified, and a small body stood on the hillside, eyes scanning the darkness for any signs of anything that did not belong.

Taking a deep breath of the crisp night air, the form felt the ravages of hunger still calling. The rats' blood would not be nearly enough to satiate the demands of her eternal hunger, but it had taken the edge from it. No creature was within her sight or within hearing range. She sighed heavily. The rats would have to do for now.

Forcing her concentration to quell the hunger pangs, she turned and strode up the hillside to its peak. From this vantage point, she could see the flecks of yellow light from Lirpa. The object of her journey was somewhere in the city; she could feel his presence even from this distance.

A fond smile touched her bright red, moist lips as she thought of him. She set out for the city and the source of her curiosity. Moving easily through the darkness, as though she were a part of it, she questioned her intentions concerning this journey. It was dangerous, even for one such as her, to be this far away from her own area. There were hunters who delighted in finding her kind and eliminating them without thought. But something about this man called to her, had piqued her curiosity, and compelled her to follow. She had decided to learn more about him.

She acknowledged a part of her that the man had aroused, a part that should have died long ago. He was attractive in the purest romantic sense of the word. The sensations he had stirred caused her to remember a time when she had taken such sensations for granted. She had feared such feelings would be forever gone. To have them stirring again caused a flush of heady excitement to pass through her, much like a breath of fresh air.

Or a walk in the sunshine, she thought sadly.

Many dangers could lie along the path she had chosen to pursue, both to her and to the man. The feelings he spawned within her could put the man in mortal danger... or worse. If she had any concern for him at all, she knew she should abandon this foolish trek at once. Simply turn around and return to her region, a known territory where she knew where to find food, where to hide from hunters, where to find shelter from the day.

Yet, even as she acknowledged this logic, she moved steadily forward, toward the city.

And the man.

~*~

Brianna felt consciousness call to her and she swam slowly toward the light. She became aware of the feel of sheets against her bare skin, the soft comfort of a feather mattress beneath her, the smell of the soap used to launder the linens and the unmistakable smell of Devenshire. She had grown accustomed to his smell and loved waking to it. Her eyes fluttered, opened slowly, and then closed again as a smile spread across her face. She felt content. The turmoil caused by the stranger's mental touch was gone, as were the tensions caused by the destruction of Shantira's village and the attack from the bandits last night. All of it was lost in the sweet memories of Devenshire's embrace.

Devenshire had a way of making love that made her feel her wants and needs were primary to him, above even his own pleasures. The way he touched her, the things he did to her spoke of his drive to please her before seeking his own release.

With a sleepy smile, she recalled precisely how good he was at drawing out her releases, long before taking his own. She remembered once, after a fiery embrace, she had asked him about this. His reply had been very simple and straightforward. He had told her that the more pleasure she took from their embrace, the more pleasure he took from it.

With a long, cat-like stretch, she opened her eyes, the smile still spread across her face. But the smile faded when her eyes rested on the empty pillow beside her. She propped herself up on one elbow and looked around the small room only to find that he was gone. She tried to ward off the disappointment that he would have risen, dressed, and left without waking her. But such was Devenshire's way and it was one of the few aspects of him that she still had trouble reconciling. Each time it happened it troubled her a little more. The few times that he had remained were her fondest memories. He would hold her, softly stroke her hair or shoulder, and they would talk. The subject did not matter; only the act of talking and touching made their lovemaking complete. These few rare moments made her current disappointment more pronounced.

Fighting off her displeasure and clinging to the deep satisfaction and contentment he had given her, she rose and dressed quickly. A glance outside told her that night had nearly fallen. No doubt, Devenshire had already left to find Darkseed. She had been to Lirpa on several occasions and knew the lay of the city fairly well, so finding Devenshire should pose no problem.

Brianna arrived in the tiny lobby of the inn to find Zandorth standing at the door, looking out at the darkened street. She stepped up beside him and followed the direction of his gaze. The city's transition from day life to nightlife was nearly complete. The people wore darker clothing, they skulked around, eyes down and constantly darting about as if expecting attack from each corner. The others were likely the ones who stayed hidden, waiting to strike.

The smells that drifted toward them were different from the ones they had encountered this morning. Meats were being cooked over open flames along the street. Mixed with these odors were those of many ales and wines. Some concoctions could not be placed, but were definitely alcoholic in nature.

Scantily clad women moved about the street, tempting men with their trade. Though they were somewhat attractive, they wore false smiles and there was no light in their eyes. To Brianna and Zandorth, it was as if these women had surrendered their souls to a destiny of endless, meaningless nights.

"Where is Devenshire?"

Brianna smiled tightly, hiding her disappointment that she was not able to say exactly where he was. "I do not know. I stopped by his room, but he had gone."

"It would stand to reason that he would set out on this search of his alone. I assume that he took Shantira with him." Zandorth grumbled in reply.

"If he would not take you or me, I doubt he would take Shantira," Brianna replied tartly.

"He must have taken her with him. She is not in her room for I checked before coming down."

Brianna felt a sliver of alarm penetrate her mind as she considered what Zandorth had said. She or Zandorth were accustomed to large cities and the dangers that lie in their darkened streets, but Shantira was not. She was an innocent and perfect prey for the unsavory types that inhabited the nightlife in cities such as Lirpa. Devenshire would not have burdened himself with having to watch over her while he searched for Darkseed.

"You are sure she was not in her room?" Brianna searched the lobby as she asked.

"I am sure. The door was not locked and when she did not answer my summons, I opened the door. She was not in her room."

Brianna gave Zandorth a look that communicated her concern for the young woman before she turned and crossed to the front desk and the aging clerk there.

"Excuse me, sir?"

"Yes, Milady? How may I be of service?" the man asked.

"Have you seen a man leave recently? He is tall with long black hair. Clean shaven and dressed in black breeches, a white shirt and a black vest with a black cloak."

"Ah, Sir Devenshire. Yes, Milady. He left about an hour ago. He asked me to relay a message to the other members of his party."

"What is the message?"

"He said that he would return as soon as his task for the evening is completed. He also instructed me to inform you that none should leave the inn before his return."

"Did he leave with anyone? Perhaps a young woman?" Brianna leaned in closer against the clerk's desk.

The clerk considered her question for a moment before he shook his head. "No, Milady. Sir Devenshire left alone."

Brianna looked up at Zandorth, her concern deepening as it became apparent that Shantira had done the worst thing possible.

"Have you seen a young woman with black hair and blue eyes? She was dressed in travel attire.," Zandorth inquired.

The clerk, again, considered the question carefully before answering. His face brightened slightly as a memory surfaced. "As a matter of fact, yes I have. Such a woman departed only a short while ago."

Zandorth muttered a curse as he turned away from the desk to begin an agitated pace of the small room. The clerk's good-natured expression darkened slightly at Zandorth's reaction. He looked from Zandorth to Brianna, his eyes asking if he had made some sort of mistake.

"The woman has never been to a city such as this. Her entire life has been spent in the confines of a small village, south of here." Brianna explained and watched as the older man's face paled.

"The night streets of Lirpa are no place for such an innocent. There are many dangers for those who do not know what to expect."

Brianna nodded in agreement, as she considered what to do next. There was a chance that Shantira was aware enough, with her battle training, to avoid the more serious dangers of this city. Though, she had seen Shantira's wide-eyed wonder at seeing the massiveness of the city, she also knew that the sights and sounds would dull her trained instincts. She could be lured into danger more easily than normal. It was simply not a chance Brianna was willing to take.

"Thank you, sir. If Sir Devenshire should return before us, please inform him of what has happened and that we will return as soon as we are able," Brianna said as she turned to leave, moving across the room quickly.

"We must find her!" Zandorth growled as he stood at the doors of the inn, staring into the darker streets of the city.

Brianna could hear the concern behind his massive growl. "I agree. I left word for Daimion should he return before us."

"Then let us go and pray to the Fates that we are not too late." Zandorth strode through the door with long strides that Brianna nearly had to run to match.

They stepped out into the street and paused to consider which direction to search first. After a brief debate, they decided on a direction and set out after Shantira.

~*~

Bonzwa paused next to his horse, letting the cramps of his legs ease from the hard hours spent in the saddle. His legs, back, and especially his backside ached from the punishment of having ridden hard to try to overtake the four individuals who had humiliated him so completely the night before.

Lordal stood in the center of the street and looked as though he had recently arrived fresh from a restful sleep. It had been a very long time since the leader had undertaken such a journey, and yet the toll of the hard ride did not show on him. Bonzwa was amazed by the older man's resilience and began to understand why he was the leader. But he was concerned by Lordal's change in manner. He was a calm man, not easily angered, not one given to bouts of irrational behavior. Though, as the miles had passed, Lordal's temper had grown ever shorter. Each request to stop and rest had been more harshly refused than the previous one. Eventually, no one had dared to even hint that they stop.

Bonzwa could find no reason for this sudden change in his leader. Lordal had known defeat before. Mislaid or poorly executed plans had thwarted many a raid, but never before had Lordal displayed the outrage he had after last night's utter failure.

Perhaps it was the discovery that a vampire could be among the travelers. Bonzwa knew that at some point in Lordal's past he had been a Hunter, that noble group who dedicated their lives to searching out the un-dead and eradicating their foul existence from the world. Why he had left that group to lead a band of raiders was unknown to Bonzwa, and he was not about to be the one to question him about it, especially in his current state.

Lordal scanned both sides of the streets carefully before turning and joining his men. "We will check all of the inns first. If the demons have stopped here, then that will be the most likely place to begin our search. Meet back here in one hour!" he said shortly as he motioned for several men to follow him. They quickly moved down the street.

Bonzwa sighed tiredly and turned to face the rest of his men. He selected two men to lead additional groups to search the numerous inns of the city. He took the balance of the remaining men and set off down a side street. Part of him sorely wanted to find the four travelers, while another part hoped they were miles away. If there was a vampire among their ranks, he really did not wish to face them again.

CHAPTER EIGHTEEN

THE HEART OF DARKNESS WAS the largest and oldest of taverns in Lirpa, situated near the center of the city. As the name implied, the tavern offered far more than simply providing a social gathering place.

It was widely known, yet rarely acknowledged, that The Heart of Darkness offered far more than just a wide selection of meads, wines, and ales. For the right price, just about anything could be purchased. Whores in just about any price range, all manner of weapons, and a rather large array of recreational herbs. One could also find ancient scrolls of incredible power. Of course, each scroll of uncounted seasons old and, if interpreted correctly, could unlock incredible power. The level of power was usually directly related to the amount of gold coins available.

Yet all of these were The Heart of Darkness's secondary trade. The tavern played host to the most valuable commodity in the realm — information. Very little happened in or around Lirpa that could not be discovered within the tavern... for the right price.

To the average person off the street, the interior of the tavern looked no different from countless others around the region. The first floor housed the bar, tables, booths and an area for dancing. The second floor housed a few rooms that were reasonably priced for very brief stays with a new acquaintance from the evening's entertainment.

Behind the main bar was where the real money was made. The back room was a notorious meeting place where all kinds of agreements were made, deals struck, and transactions were sealed in the comfortable blanket of secrecy.

Like most nights, the main floor was filled to capacity as people moved about drinking, talking, dancing, or seeking one of the unofficial products available at the tavern. Minstrels played their music loudly for the dancers on the huge dance floor. Every table and booth was occupied forcing the remaining patrons to resign themselves to standing.

The air of the tavern was thick with the smell of lantern oil, incense smoke, various blends of cigars and pipes, and the smoke of the fire. Add to the mix the aromas of ales, wines, brandies, cognacs, and other brews, and the air within The Heart of Darkness seemed to be solid enough to cut with the dullest of daggers. Yet there was a thickness in the air that could not be traced to any odor. It was the feel of the place. There was an air of seediness, as if the darker elements of the city were concentrated down to permeate every square inch of the building. Darkness, mystery, and danger were felt heavily while inside, and tinged with just enough seduction to make the atmosphere appealing.

At a corner booth, a man sat in silence, observing the large number of patrons. His sharp brown eyes took in each scene with good humor and wonderment at the perversity of the human race. With a wry grin, he acknowledged the same facets present within himself and welcomed them with open arms.

He was in his thirtieth season, yet his firm skin betrayed no telling of his true age. His features were rugged, a strong jaw framing his granite-like face. Although he spent most of his time immersed in the nightlife of Lirpa, his color was very tan. A mane of thick brown hair hung to his shoulders, parted off-center to leave wisps of hair hanging over his forehead. His sideburns were long, growing down past his ears while the rest of his face was clean-shaven.

He was a man who took care of his body. He stood over six feet in height and weighed well over two hundred pounds, every ounce pure hard muscle. This night he wore a white, loose-fitting shirt with a tan vest that he left unbuttoned. The loose fit of his shirt could not hide the bulging muscles of his upper arms and shoulders.

The sleeves of the shirt were rolled midway up his forearms while the collar of the shirt was open far enough to show the deep cleft carved into the hard muscles of his chest. There was an air of confidence about him that leaned heavily toward arrogance. It was clear that the man harbored no self-doubts and was capable of anything.

He sat with his back against the wall, his right foot in the seat bringing his knee up to provide a convenient prop for his right elbow. Between the first and middle fingers of his right hand was a long, thin cigar. The fingers of his left hand absently traced around the rim of a thick tumbler that held one of the finer blends of cognac. The thick square bottle of cognac was within easy reach, and the deep amber fluid within it absorbed the flickering yellow light from the candle on his table and threw it back out in a brownish gold aura that played upon the eye in a swirling, almost mesmerizing, pattern.

The man casually lifted his glass, dipped the unlit end of the cigar into the liquor, and took a long slow draw, savoring the mixture of flavors as they danced across his palate. He leaned his head back as the smoke from the tobacco mixed with the fumes from the cognac to elicit a sensation through his senses that caused him to close his eyes, breathe deeply, allowing the smoke to lazily curl from his nostrils taking its place with the already thick cloud of smoke which hung about the room. A sense of peace settled about him, and he reveled in the release.

"Excuse me, sir." A soft voice danced in his ears, and he slowly opened his eyes to see a young woman standing before his table. Other than opening his eyes, there was no other reaction from him. He had seen the young woman earlier in the evening and had noticed her stare following him about the room until he sat down.

She was obviously a whore, her dress and manner made that perfectly obvious. It was equally clear that she was new to the profession. A more experienced woman would have made her line of work less obvious in the hopes of gaining a higher class of customer, and therefore, a higher rate of payment for her services.

He regarded her for several moments, taking in her youthful features, not yet haggard by a long life of endless and meaningless embraces. Her hazel eyes still shone with the light of childlike wonder while her skin was supple and flawless. Her thick brown hair shone with luster, while fixed in a very appealing style.

Her gown, probably the only one she owned at this point of her career, was severe in its tailoring. Her body was trim and still blooming. Her breasts, while not very large, were full and had not yet begun to yield to the demands of age and gravity. Her hips, not yet stretched with the burden of childbirth, were well rounded, and he could just imagine that they slid seductively into long, well-shaped legs that rippled with enough muscle tone to be appealing. The skirt of the gown made it necessary for him to assume a great many things.

He felt a pang of sympathy for the young girl and immediately searched his mind for its source. He was not one who felt pity very often. It was a dangerous emotion, and he tried to understand its source.

He had known his share of whores in his life, and knew what an empty and lonely existence such a life was. Perhaps the thought of this young girl having her spark of youth doused by the cold, harsh blanket of the reality of that kind of life was the reason for his uncharacteristic feelings of sympathy.

Just as quickly as the sympathy appeared, he drove it down by reflecting that this was her choice, not his. Each person made their own path and could not hold another person responsible for their choices. As his eyes slid over her body, he felt himself begin to stiffen with anticipation. She was offering herself to fulfill a very basic need within him. Who was he to condemn her for such a thing?

"Yes?" he asked finally, bringing his head back down to its normal position. He felt a little annoyed at her intrusion upon his moment of peaceful solitude.

"Pardon my intrusion, but you look very familiar to me. Have we encountered one another before?" she asked, and he could hear the nervousness in her voice.

The man chuckled at the obviousness of her opening line. This one had much to learn about the more subtle arts of her profession.

She gave him a puzzled look that drew another small laugh from him. He kept his eyes trained on her as he took another draw from his cigar.

"I have said something to amuse you?" She was annoyed with his laughter, and she was trying valiantly to contain it.

"Indeed, you have," he replied, squinting through the smoke of his cigar. He pulled the cigar away and awarded her a wide smile and a touch of a reproachful expression.

"You have never laid eyes on me before this night, nor have you seen anyone who looks like me, and we both know this."

He watched, with no small amount of ruthless satisfaction, as she mentally scrambled to recover from his having so easily seen through her opening question.

"I fear I do not understand," she replied uneasily. She had been trained to expect a man to play along with her ploy.

"I have found that the best approach is the most direct one. You have something on your mind? A proposition, perhaps?" He instantly saw the blood flush to her cheeks as she realized he had seen right through her. The young woman quickly looked over her shoulder to a large bald man propped up against the wall, and the man followed her gaze.

He had seen the man before, hanging around the various taverns, peddling his small but growing stable of whores. While he did not know the man's name, he knew his type. He was the kind of man who fed his lifestyle from the toil of others.

The hairless man was watching them, yet trying not to appear to be doing so, and failing miserably.

"I fear I do not know what you speak of, sir. I simply thought I recognized you and wished to confirm or deny it. I have no other reason for coming to your table," she said as she shifted nervously before him. Her hands would hang at her sides one moment and then clutch nervously in front of her before she remembered what she had been taught, forcing them back to her sides.

He bit back on the chuckle that tried to rattle his throat and continued his mental torture of this apprentice whore.

He took a long draw from his cigar, letting his eyes roam over her form, and noticing how she winced ever so slightly at his gaze. Blowing out the smoke with an air of boredom, he decided to play with her for a bit longer. "What is your name, child?"

"I am not a child!" she said sternly, then remembered her place and smiled gently. Then, continuing in a softer tone, "Sir, I am in my twenty second season."

A lie. If she were one day beyond her fifteenth or sixteenth season, he would have been sorely surprised. This time the chuckle was unsuppressed as he lifted his glass and took a small mouthful of cognac, holding it there to let his taste buds absorb the flavor and essence of the liquor before letting it slide smoothly down his throat.

"Twenty second season," he said as though he believed her lie. "I see. My apologies, I meant no insult." He finished as he casually set the tumbler back to the tabletop and returned the cigar to his lips.

She gave him a smile that was as practiced as every move and every word she had said since walking over to his table. He wondered what she would be like if she allowed her true nature out. He did not find it hard to believe that it would be far more interesting than the front she was showing him.

"No insult was taken, kind sir. I am flattered that my appearance would lead you to believe that I am far younger than I appear. To answer your question, my name is Rhondella."

He caught the slight hesitation when she spoke her name and instantly knew that, like her age, her name was a lie. He watched her nervousness grow with each passing second as it became obvious to her that he had seen through her facade as though it were made of glass. To her credit, her chin lifted proudly in her determination to keep the front up for a while longer.

He found himself wondering why she was going to such pains to hide her profession from him. The large bald man came to mind, and he wondered if he were the reason. Perhaps, in his line of thinking, his girls stood a better chance of gaining a higher rate of pay if they pretended not to be whores.

His eyes narrowed, and a slight smile tugged at the corners of his lips. He knew the ploy well, and he had seen it played out by far more skilled practitioners than this young woman.

It would go something like this: the young girl would present herself to a client as a young, naïve village girl. She would entice him with her charms, hinting at pleasures that were well within his reach. At some point, she would tell the prospective client some very sad tale in the hopes of the clients' now overactive sex drive and any compassion he might possess leading him to give her money. Then, in what would appear to be an act of gratitude, she would bed him. If she were skilled enough at sex and convincing enough in her act, then perhaps the satiated client would give her even more money afterwards. It was an old ploy, and one seldom used because of the time involved in making it work.

He shook his head slightly. It was all an elaborate and unnecessary game. A man wanted sex. A woman could provide it for him. If the man wanted it badly enough, then the skill of the woman mattered not, and the woman could ask for any amount she wished.

Truly skilled professionals knew that the most direct approach was the best one. There were plenty of men who would shell out their last gold coin for the heated and very temporary embrace. He wondered why some people felt it necessary to take an arrangement that had worked very well for uncounted seasons and try to improve it.

He shifted his attention back to his subtle act of torturing this young whore. He let his eyes roam boldly and openly over her body, pausing at the more interesting attributes. She flinched and began to raise her arms over her breasts to hide them. With a mischievous twitch of his lips, he grinned at her movements. Raising her chin once more, she slowly lowered her arms to her sides.

"A pleasure to meet your acquaintance, Rhondella," he replied with an added thickness to his words. He could not deny the desires of his male drives, and the thought of bedding this young girl definitely had its promises, but the added thickness of his voice was deliberate. If she insisted on this false pretense, he felt he might as well play along. "Please, join me."

She hesitated a moment then looked back over her shoulder at the large man leaning against the wall. His face became hard and stern. With an obvious sigh of frustration, much like a child who was being forced to do something they did not wish to do, she sat down.

"You do not have to join me if you do not wish to." The man threw the bald man an obvious look of boredom, letting him know that he was not at all impressed with his control over this girl.

Rhondella realized that she had let her surface appearance slip and quickly forced the mature, sensual front back to the surface. She graced him with her very best smile.

"I would love to be in the company of one as handsome as you, sir," she replied with a forced huskiness in her voice.

The man resisted the urge to role his eyes at the empty compliment. He also resisted the urge to tell her to go back home, find an honest trade or a husband. She should leave this occupation behind for she was not very good at it. This was the time to leave, if she were able. Once she learned the skills of the trade, it would be too late for her to leave it behind.

The slow tones of the minstrels caught his attention and quelled the cutting remark that had been poised on his lips. A bright light entered his eyes, and he regarded Rhondella with a mischievous smile.

"Would you care to dance?"

Whatever she had been trained to expect from such an encounter, an invitation to dance had not been it, for her confusion was plain. He watched her mind shift into a near frantic search for what she was expected to do. Obviously, she had not been trained in the subtle art of increasing her price by "romancing" a potential customer with song, dance, and drink.

"I fear that I am not very skilled at dancing," she finally admitted with reluctance.

Despite her failures in the areas of her profession, the man found himself starting to like her. He sensed a wild and pure spirit that far exceeded the meaningless existence of the average whore. His sympathy returned. He knew that he could not save her from the choice she had made, but perhaps he could spare her one meaningless night out of the countless thousands that lie ahead.

This train of thought troubled him. He was not one to become involved in the business of others. He was a man who denied himself nothing. One of the many reasons he kept coming to The Heart of Darkness was to find the warm and temporary embraces of skilled practitioners. It surprised him that he would be wasting the mental energy in an effort to save this apprentice from a choice she had made of her own free will.

She was attractive, though her beauty had not reached its full potential. Her soft, yet firm curves enticed his male drives, and he mentally berated himself for having reservations about bedding her. It really was a very simple matter. She wished to give herself for a few coins, and he wished to take what she offered. Yet, he found such a desire disturbing.

Odd. He reflected to himself.

"Then allow me the honor of extending your knowledge. I am a very adept teacher of the finer arts of dance." He laid his smoldering cigar into a small glass tray, and then rose to his feet, extending his hand to her.

"Really, sir, that is not necessary. I find the quiet confines of conversation much more stimulating."

The man fixed her with a look that said he would not accept no for an answer. "I insist."

Finding no way to evade the dance, she slowly offered him her trembling hand. His was warm and large as he gently led her to the already crowded dance floor.

With a graceful spin, he swept her into a sudden, close embrace and began moving with the rhythm of the music. Despite her proclaimed inadequacy at dancing, she quickly picked up his movements and copied them exactly. As she became more familiar with his steps, she smiled up at him. He instantly knew this was a genuine smile and not the forced one from a woman of her trade.

"You dance very well for one who claims to be inadequate," he said warmly.

"Thank you, sir. I think it has more to do with the skill of my partner rather than any natural skill on my part," she replied easily, and the forced seductiveness in her voice was fading as she found release in the spirit of dance. He felt her rigid body begin to relax within his arms.

For several minutes, they simply danced and relished the release offered by the rhythmic movements. As more and more of her forced veneer faded and more of her true radiance began to show through, he found himself enjoying her company.

"You have not been doing this for very long, have you?" his voice low, it carried the knowledge of what she had laid out as her destiny.

She looked up into his eyes, and for a moment, he thought she would try to dismiss what he had said. At the last moment, though, her eyes dropped from his, and her face lost its animation.

"No," she whispered.

"Why?" His voice was nearly lost in the strands of music.

"Because I have no other choice," her eyes remained on their moving feet.

He smiled as a warm chuckle rattled his throat. "There are always other choices."

His easy reply caused her eyes to snap up to meet his, anger clearly burning in their depths.

"Easy enough for you to say! You are a man and in command of your own destiny. I am a woman of no stature, no wealth, and no consequence!" she replied bitterly.

Her outburst flew past him without ever even leaving an impression. He shrugged at her outburst and replied, "Nor will you ever be with such an attitude," he said evenly. There was no harshness, no judgment in his voice, only plain honesty.

"And what attitude would you suggest?" she snapped in irritation. "I feel I need not remind you of the state of things within this realm. Attitude is not what matters. Attitude will not fill your empty stomach or put linens upon your back or a roof over your head!" she retorted, the bitterness growing along with her raised voice.

He saw her pain and confusion, the utter despair at being forced to lead a life that disgusted her. She truly believed she had no other option.

"That would entirely depend upon your attitude. The right

attitude could lead you to accomplish all of those things and much more," he replied matter-of-factly.

She snorted in disgust. "Again, easy enough for someone to say with gold coins in their pocket!" she shot back, her anger mounting.

He guided her through a turn of the dance floor and continued his conversation without missing a step.

"Gold is the end result of what you seek, not the beginning. As long as you look upon physical wealth as the ultimate of attainable goals, you will be forever cursed to the sad limitations of such wealth. There is far more to your life than gold. The sooner you realize this, the sooner you will truly begin to live."

Rhondella snickered a disbelieving laugh, and her eyes flashed in annoyance. "Poetic nonsense! Romantic philosophy. You have the luxury of existing in the realm of dreams. It is a luxury I do not possess. What you suggest is nothing more than lofty dreams."

The man shrugged easily. "Dreams are the roots of reality. What you choose to call a lofty dream, others call their reality. It would seem to be a matter of perception and execution."

"Perception and execution?" Her brows knitted down in confusion.

"You perceive a dream, and you wish to make it reality, then you execute the steps needed to make it so. If it still seems as a dream to others, then so be it. Your reality is your own. Who is to say my reality is better or worse than yours?"

He watched her digest his words and, to his relief, saw her seriously consider their meaning. He smiled. Though she did not know it yet, a new thought had taken root, a chance for an alternate destiny that would take her from this dismal existence. Sadly, he acknowledged that he would never see it come to pass. It was enough that he had ignited the spark of change within her mind.

She had gazed off into the crowd of dancers as she considered his words. As they struck a chord within her, she turned her beautiful face back to his and smiled a very warm and very sincere smile. Her thick red lips parted to say something but the words never came. Her eyes shot over his shoulder to stare at something behind him. They grew wide and fearful.

"If you are going to keep her busy dancing all night, the price will be the same," a gruff voice spat out from behind him. He did not need to turn to verify it was the large bald man who had been propped against the wall, watching them closely.

"I believe the choice is the young lady's," he replied without turning, trying to continue the dance. Rhondella was rooted to the spot by fear, so the dance had been ruined.

"You are mistaken. She has no choice in the matter. Her time is mine to control. If you wish to spend my time dancing, fine. If you wish to take her upstairs and indulge in her young flesh, fine. The price is the same."

He stopped trying to dance, released Rhondella and turned to face the bald man. He did not fail to notice how he had to tilt his head back to look up into the man's rounded features. Up close, his face was cruel and seedy. The harsh lines spoke of a life fed by the toil of others.

"Price?" he blinked in an exaggerated expression of mock confusion. "There has been no talk of price."

The larger man snapped his hard eyes to Rhondella, and she immediately cringed as she took a faltering step back. The overabundant folds of flesh of the man's face flushed red in anger.

"Is this true? You have wasted this much time without setting a price?" his voice was low and dangerous.

Rhondella instantly slumped her shoulders as her gaze fell to the wooden dance floor. Her answer sounded small and weak. "Yes, I beg forgiveness. It was a slip of concentration that will never occur again."

"Perhaps she did not speak of price because she did not wish to levy a price on spending time with me," the smaller man injected with more than a touch of boredom.

The man swung his angry gaze to him. "That is not her choice! If you are stupid enough to believe she has any interest in you beyond bedding you for a price, then the fault is yours." He turned his angry gaze back to Rhondella. "As well as hers, and she will be punished."

He reached out to take her by the wrist, but before he could reach her, his own wrist was gripped and stayed with surprising force.

"I do not feel any punishment is due her. If punishment is due, I think it should yours for being arrogant enough to assume you can simply own and sell another human by brute strength."

Already there was a crowd forming around them. Couples abandoned their dances to focus on this much more interesting promise of entertainment.

The larger man regarded his hand before an evil smile crossed his thick lips. "You interfere in things that are none of your business. You obviously do not know with who you are dealing."

"Whom. With *whom* I am dealing," he corrected and watched with satisfaction as the already red flush to his jowls deepened at least two more shades.

"I am Cisab," the man snapped as if the mere mention of his name should be enough to make him realize what a dangerous path he was following.

"And?" he replied, raising his brows in an unimpressed bored manner.

Without warning and with surprising speed, Cisab launched a beefy fist at the man's face. With barely enough time to understand that he had underestimated Cisab's speed, the man realized he did not have time to duck or block the punch.

With a wet smack, the man's head snapped back a split second before the rest of his body followed as he was thrust backwards by the force of the blow. For a brief moment, the blow had sent him airborne. Suddenly the floor rushed up, and he hit hard. Air rushed from his lungs, and the inside of his skull ignited with hot throbbing lances of pain. Although his senses were numbed, he felt sure that when they returned he would find his skull fractured by the sheer force of the blow.

Over the ringing in his ears, he heard Rhondella gasp. Cisab's attention had turned to the young girl. "As for you, I see you are in need of a lesson. You will do what I say, when I say it!"

The man shook his head to clear it, rising to one elbow to see what was happening. Though his vision swam, it was clear enough to see that Cisab had roughly taken Rhondella by the arm. By her pained expression, his grip was unnecessarily forceful.

He reached up and wiped blood from the corner of his mouth. Examining the back of his hand, his gaze rose to Cisab who paid him no heed. With a broad smile, he climbed to his feet, gently refusing the offered help of the spectators. He willed himself not to sway as he took several steps toward Cisab and Rhondella. A wry grin parted his lips. He had hoped to experience something out of the ordinary this night; he was glad he would not be disappointed.

"Please, Cisab! It will never happen again, I swear it!!" Rhondella's plea was met with a vicious backhand that would have tossed her to the floor had he not had such a tight grip on her arm.

"Silence! I will hear no excuses!" Cisab shouted, roughly shaking Rhondella by only his grip on her arm.

Someone tapped Cisab on the shoulder, and he spun around to see who else would dare interfere in his affairs. He was not expecting the sight of a fist, less than a second before it made contact with his face. The impact rocked the big man so that he was forced to release his grip on Rhondella to keep himself on his feet. He staggered back a few steps before he was able to steady himself. He looked up to see who was stupid enough to strike him.

Cisab was surprised to see the man he had just sent flying across the dance floor, standing with a look of pure pleasure on his face. Cisab matched his smile as he wiped his sleeve across his bloody mouth.

"You are truly stupid! You do not know how bad a mistake you just made!"

The man smiled broadly and assumed a relaxed posture by folding his arms across his chest. He jerked his chin up in invitation. "Educate me."

"You arrogant bastard!" Cisab snarled.

Cisab's face twisted in brutal delight as he began to slowly circle the man, ignoring the sudden hush that had fallen over the tavern as customers and workers alike abandoned their tasks to watch.

To everyone's surprise, the man did not turn to keep facing Cisab. He stood still and confident; only his eyes moved to follow the larger man. When Cisab disappeared out of his line of sight, his eyes flashed forward, and a distant gaze fell across them, as if he were looking at something not in the room.

When Cisab was directly behind the man, he suddenly bolted forward, again with speed that belayed his large mass. He raised his large right fist above his head with the intent of striking the man square on the top of the head.

Just as the fist began its blinding descent toward the smaller man's skull, he sidestepped, turned, and caught Cisab's wrist. Instead of trying to hold it there, he turned, thrust out his hip, and used Cisab's momentum to carry him off his feet, flipping him through the air to land atop a table that collapsed under his weight. The table exploded, and he hit the floor with a bone-jarring thud that had many in the tavern wincing in sympathetic pain.

Very slowly, Cisab climbed to his feet and shook his massive head. When he looked up, his face bore the unbridled shock of surprise, then rage and humiliation. The man knew that Cisab would not be maddened into making a mistake. All the better.

Cisab moved slowly and carefully. He walked up to the smaller man and studied him for a moment. "Very good. What other tricks do you have up your--"

Before Cisab could finish his question, his adversary moved in a blur. He drove his left fist deep into Cisab's mid-section. Then he drove his right fist upward in a savage uppercut that carried Cisab to his back.

It took Cisab several moments to clear the fog from his brain, but he soon realized he had been downed. Quickly, he clambered to his feet to contain his humiliation and found the man in the same relaxed stance as before, as if he had never moved. Cisab tasted blood and spat angrily before fixing the man with a very dangerous stare.

"Who the hell are you?" he bellowed.

A deep voice answered from the crowd.

"His name is Raven Darkseed… the most arrogant, self-centered, self-serving bastard you will find in this or any other realm."

All eyes turned to the newcomer. The owner of the deep voice stood in a stance very much like Cisab's opponent. Cisab regarded the newcomer and snarled, "And who are you?"

Darkseed turned and regarded the owner of the voice, answering Cisab's question. "He is Daimion Devenshire, this realm's resident authority on bastards. I have heard he is a great lover though, so if any of you have any livestock in need of breeding, you are in luck."

Devenshire regarded Darkseed with an amused glint in his eye. "Pay no heed to his words. Darkseed is simply angry that the only way he can obtain sexual gratification is with the use of his right hand since no self-respecting animal would lower itself to be mated with him.

Cisab was astounded at the banter between these two apparent strangers, but he was nothing if not a man of opportunity. Perhaps if he allowed Darkseed to be caught up with the stranger, an opportunity would present itself.

A chorus of "ooohhs" went up from the crowd as they turned their collective gaze back to Darkseed for his reaction.

Darkseed smiled and shook his head for a moment. "I see that Devenshire, when not molesting farm animals, has resorted to his sad habit of peeking into my window at night to torture himself with a reminder of how he can, in no way, measure up to me."

Again, the crowd expressed their reaction to the insults and quickly shifted their attention to Devenshire; many waiting for what they hoped would be an equally vicious retort.

Devenshire arched one eyebrow and moved a little further into the circle formed around Cisab and Darkseed. Even Cisab became momentarily enthralled at the brash insults flying between the two men.

"Tell me, Darkseed, do you truly possess such a male organ?"

"Obviously," Darkseed answered with apparent boredom.

"Then I would advise you to release it since it must surely belong to someone else," Devenshire retorted.

Darkseed's features went slack for a moment, as if Devenshire had slapped him across the face. The crowd inched closer, anxious to see how Darkseed would handle both adversaries.

For several moments, Darkseed and Devenshire glared at one another, neither giving an inch.

Finally, it was Darkseed whose face softened then broke into a radiant grin. He strode toward Devenshire with his right arm outstretched, a hardy laugh on his lips.

"You son of a bitch! How long has it been?"

Devenshire smiled and met him halfway, clasping Darkseed's forearm. "Long enough for you to forget that in a battle of wits with me, you are unarmed."

Before Darkseed could come back with an appropriate retort, Cisab strode up beside the two men.

"Devenshire! You can reminisce with what is left of your friend once I finish with him. Or do you intend to interfere?"

Devenshire regarded Cisab with boredom before he stepped back and raised his hands in surrender. "What you do to him is no concern to me. However, I feel I must warn you that all is not as it appears, and you should not underestimate him simply by his appearance."

"Thank you for the warning,." Cisab replied before he suddenly spun and drove his fist deep into Darkseed's face. The wet pop of slapping flesh sounded again as Darkseed was sent sprawling to the hard wood of the dance floor.

Devenshire screwed his face into an expression of pain as he stepped further back into the crowd. "You are welcome."

Cisab wasted no time in crossing the distance to Darkseed who was struggling to regain his footing. The bear of a man jerked Darkseed to his wobbly feet, spun him around, and landed another meaty fist to the center of his face, which sent him to the floor again.

As Darkseed pushed himself up, he felt the old familiar pain across the bridge of his nose. As the blood poured from his nose and mouth, he realized that his nose had been broken again.

Darkseed was dimly aware of a pair of hands helping him to his feet. The owner of the hands spoke to him quickly, and he knew it had to be Devenshire. "If you cannot handle this fight, perhaps you should submit."

"Go find a lonely sheep, Devenshire!" Darkseed snarled as he tried to blink away the growing fuzziness from his vision.

"A lonely sheep would be far preferable to a fierce beating," Devenshire answered with thick humor.

Darkseed was about to launch a harsh reply when he realized his mistake. Instead of using those precious seconds to banter with Devenshire, he should have been clearing his battered senses and preparing for Cisab's next attack. Darkseed shot Devenshire a twisted look of anger as Cisab's large hand closed on his shirt collar and spun him around. Darkseed resisted the urge to close his eyes and wait for the next thundering blow and forced his crossing eyes to lock to Cisab's.

Cisab grinned and shook his head almost sadly. "What a foolish little man you are, Darkseed."

With a twisted smile, Darkseed saw his opening and wasted no time in taking full advantage of Cisab's arrogant ego. It never ceased to amaze him how large men felt the need to talk while they fought.

With a sudden jerking movement, Darkseed sent his right knee deep into Cisab's groin, and he was rewarded by an exclamation of pain from both Cisab and the male patrons who were watching. Cisab instantly released Darkseed and hugged himself as his knees bent and nearly buckled.

Darkseed paid the big man a silent tribute for being able to remain on his feet after such a blow. He gently placed his right hand on the back of Cisab's head before driving his knee up again. This time he smashed it into Cisab's face. The large man jerked upright to his full height. Darkseed moved in, firing a series of short, vicious jabs into the larger mans' mid-section. As Cisab bent over from the blows, Darkseed stepped back, planted his feet, and fired another savage uppercut that rocketed Cisab backwards to the floor, unconscious before he hit.

Another pronounced silence fell across the crowd. They were stunned at the sight of the smaller man standing triumphantly over a prone Cisab. It was obvious that the outcome was not the one they had expected.

Darkseed bent over and rested his hands on his knees, breathing hard and taking the time to clear his rattled senses. He found it easier to keep his eyes shut against the rolling waves of nauseating dizziness. He knew that Cisab might have a friend or two in the crowd and forced his head up and eyes open. He swept the crowd with a hard, questioning gaze, asking if any wished to take Cisab's place. Within the space of a heartbeat, the crowd began dispersing back into their previous activities. No one came forward to help Cisab, content to let the man come to in his own time.

Darkseed fought down another wave of dizziness and nausea as he finally stood upright and wiped the excessive blood from his nose and mouth, spitting the accumulated blood from his mouth to the floor.

Devenshire walked up, a beaming smile across his face. "Well done," he congratulated.

"No thanks to you!" Darkseed half snarled as he pulled a small linen from his pocket to mop at the blood pouring from his nose and mouth.

"I never interfere in the affairs of others," Devenshire replied with humor.

This drew an incredulous look from Darkseed. "Indeed."

"Indeed," Devenshire answered.

Finally, Darkseed smiled and clapped Devenshire on the back.

"It *is* good to see you again, Daimion."

"Aye."

"What brings you to my little corner of the realm?" Darkseed asked.

Devenshire's features went instantly grim, and Darkseed did not miss the transition, but simply waited for Devenshire to speak.

"Come with me. We must talk in private," Devenshire motioned for the door.

Darkseed nodded, and the two men began weaving their way through the crowd. Before reaching the door, Darkseed paused.

"One moment, Daimion. I have a final bit of business here."

Devenshire only nodded.

Darkseed turned and weaved his way back through the crowd to Cisab's prone form still sprawled near the center of the dance floor.

The minstrels had resumed playing, and a small handful of couples returned to their dances, mindful of the new obstruction in the floor.

He knelt and began patting down Cisab's trousers. He finally found what he sought and drew a rather large leather pouch from his pocket. Darkseed hefted the considerable weight in his hand as he stood up. He scanned the crowd, most of which were trying very hard not to notice what he took from Cisab. With a slight smile, he saw the face he had been searching for and quickly crossed to Rhondella who was still nursing a growing bruise on the side of her face.

Darkseed pitched the leather pouch to Rhondella. She caught it, staring at it before looking back up at Darkseed, her confusion plain on her face.

"A dream must begin somewhere," he replied softly giving her a brief warm smile before turning and walking back toward the door without hesitation or a second look.

When Cisab woke nearly an hour later, one of his women and a large piece of his wealth were many miles away on a horse bound for nowhere in particular, except in the direction of a dream.

CHAPTER NINETEEN

DEVENSHIRE AND DARKSEED slipped into the crowded streets outside The Heart of Darkness and began moving toward a less crowded section of town. As they weaved around the groups of people, Darkseed shot Devenshire a sideways glance and watched as his old friend tried valiantly to ignore the call of the city. It was subtle things, the glaze in his eyes, the way he repeatedly took in very deep breaths and the tiniest, fading hint of a smile at the corner of his lips.

Darkseed grinned through split and swollen lips. "Admit it Daimion. You miss this place."

Devenshire glanced at Darkseed quickly before sternly shaking his head. "Not in the least."

With his blood stained pocket linen, Darkseed gingerly dabbed at the blood that still trickled from his shattered nose, resisting the urge to sniff. "You may expect others to believe that, Daimion, but please do not expect it of me. I know you. You are a creature of the city."

Again, Devenshire shook his head, but kept his gaze locked forward, refusing to look at Darkseed. "Not anymore, Raven. Things change. People change. I no longer belong here."

Darkseed appreciated the honest sincerity that Devenshire had put in his voice. Someone who did not know Devenshire as well as he did would have believed the statement. However, he knew that Devenshire's soul cried out for him to loosen his rigid self-control and surrender to the darkness one more time.

As they walked the streets, Darkseed could easily recall many nights that he and Devenshire would prowl these very streets, searching out the evening's entertainment. A rather distant part of his mind found it interesting that he could remember such things so clearly since he and Devenshire spent more time drunk than sober in those days.

"I see," was his only reply.

Devenshire drew in a deep breath and quickly changed the subject. "May I ask what that was all about?" he asked as he jerked his left thumb back over his shoulder toward The Heart of Darkness.

Darkseed chuckled as he struggled against the rapid swelling of his right eye. "Simply a dispute over the value of a young lady's company."

Devenshire arched one eyebrow as he looked at Darkseed askance. "She must have been a very special young lady."

Darkseed smiled, which looked more like a snarl through his mangled lips. "She was... unique."

Devenshire smiled. "And the incident with the purse?"

It was Darkseed's turn to avert his gaze and quickly block all emotion from his face as he shrugged. "She was owed money. I was simply making sure she received what was due her."

Devenshire's smile broadened as he shifted his eyes forward, feeling certain he had caught Darkseed in an exceedingly rare act of kindness. It was his turn to simply nod. "I see."

Little else was said as the two men wound through the streets of Lirpa, searching for a less crowded street, if such a thing could truly be found in the city. After a time, they found a small tavern located on a side street that was barely wide enough to walk down.

Entering the dingy little tavern, they were pleased to find it was almost deserted and promised all the seclusion they would need. The few patrons that were seated at the bar looked far too drunk or were far to absorbed in their own troubles to worry about these two strangers.

A quick search revealed a small corner booth that would provide them more than enough privacy. As they seated themselves, Darkseed dug into his inner vest pocket to retrieve another cigar. What he withdrew from the pocket looked as bent and beaten as Darkseed himself appeared. The cigar was bent and one end was dangling by a thread of tobacco. Darkseed held the mangled cigar up and looked at it with deep regret. "Damn!"

Devenshire watched, with great amusement, as Darkseed detached the dangled end of the cigar and gingerly tried to straighten it. After several moments of effort, the cigar bore more of a resemblance to what it had once been, but still looked odd. Darkseed placed one end between his teeth as he reached for a candle sitting on the table.

Devenshire folded his arms across his chest and chuckled as he watched Darkseed try to puff the cigar to life through his horribly swollen and split lips. The wince on his face, coupled with the awkward smacking sound that came combined to provide a very amusing sight.

As the end of the cigar began to glow and the grayish smoke rolled from his mouth, Darkseed looked up at Devenshire with annoyance.

The expression was particularly effective since one eye had now swollen to the point that it was closed.

"I trust you are enjoying yourself," Darkseed said.

Devenshire smiled broadly. "Immensely."

A woman walked up to the booth. "What do you want?" she asked with nothing even close to warmth or welcome in her voice. Her expression, tone, and posture clearly communicated that she found their presence a terrible burden.

Darkseed gave her a hard look. "I would have preferred courtesy and welcome, but since you obviously cannot provide either, I will accept time and privacy!"

Devenshire measured the woman and instantly knew her type. Lirpa was filled to the brim with people like this woman. People who had surrendered to the hopelessness of their dismal existence and now just marked time until their era within this realm was over.

Whatever grand schemes and plans she had held in her youth were long gone as she approached middle age. She was a disappointed woman and with such soul-killing disappointment came anger, resentment, and deep bitterness.

The woman rolled her eyes. "You cannot just sit here. This is a business, not a rest area. If you are going to sit here, you must order something."

Darkseed glared at her. He was notorious for his impatience with rudeness from people who were supposed to be serving him. "Fine! Cognac!" he snapped.

Devenshire opened his mouth to order, but she cut him off, "We have mead and ale. That is it. You want something fancier? Go somewhere else!"

"I will take water," Darkseed said in tight, even, measured tones. "Providing you have any left after diluting your alcohol," he added in a final jab.

The woman gave him a very hard look before turning and heading toward the bar. Devenshire watched her go and chuckled as he turned back to face Darkseed who's glare followed her.

"Bitch!" he snarled.

"Maybe she is simply having a bad night," Devenshire offered with a tightly concealed smile. He took great delight in goading Darkseed when he became annoyed like this.

"She has no idea how bad of a night she is about to have!" he replied. After a few more moments, he snapped his glare off the bar maid and shook off the annoyance. "It is of no matter," he said as he made a gesture over the table before him. A tumbler of cognac wavered into existence.

Devenshire watched as he lifted the tumbler to his lips, and he instantly winced in intense pain as the alcohol touched his battle damaged lips. Darkseed set the tumbler down hard and gingerly covered his mouth.

"Damn!" came his muffled exclamation.

Devenshire's eyebrows rose slightly in amusement. "He could have injured you severely. You do know this, do you not?"

Darkseed tenderly dabbed at his lips with his fingers, attempting to remove as much of the alcohol as possible. The tip of his tongue eased out to probe the damaged flesh as he shrugged.

"That is what life is all about. The risk," he replied absently.

Devenshire cocked his head to one side, "Would you have let him beat you?"

Darkseed took another puff from the cigar, trying not to wince in pain from the act. Devenshire was having more than enough fun at his expense.

"If he had proven to be my better, I would have had little choice in the matter."

Devenshire cocked one eyebrow as he smiled. "Yes you would have."

Darkseed gave him a poorly concealed smile as a silent understanding passed between them. "Are you asking me if I would have used my powers had it appeared I was about to lose the fight?"

Devenshire nodded.

Darkseed considered the question for a moment before shrugging. "It is difficult to say. I have never been in that situation before, therefore I cannot say with any certainty how I would have reacted."

"I see," Devenshire replied as he deftly conjured a snifter of brandy.

Darkseed watched him lift the snifter and take a sip before smiling. "Still drinking that colored water, I see."

Devenshire grinned. "It is an acquired taste."

Darkseed chuckled as he lifted his tumbler, momentarily forgetting about his damaged lips, and tried to take a drink. As the alcohol burned across the raw flesh, he winced and gritted his teeth against the pain.

"Damn it to hell and back!" he exclaimed in anger.

"I suppose you will allow your injuries to heal naturally, as well?" Devenshire asked.

With his mouth hanging open, the tip of his tongue again eased out to tenderly caress the particularly large split in his bottom lip. Darkseed regarded him for several moments before smiling.

"Therein lies the difference," he replied with merriment replacing the annoyed pain.

"How so?" Devenshire asked, already knowing the answer.

"I already know how letting my injuries heal themselves will end. I have no need to experience it again."

Darkseed closed his eyes and slowly drew in a deep breath. His brow furrowed slightly as he called on his powers.

Slowly the split lip began to pull together, the flesh knitting itself back together while the swelling began to decrease. The enormous blackened swelling around his right eye began to lighten and shrink as the other forming bruises about his features began to fade away. The crook in the bridge of his nose cracked as the mystical forces re-aligned the cartilage, drawing a slight wince from Darkseed.

He lowered his head slightly as he continued to channel power into his self-healing. With his nose repaired, the swelling began to shrink and the bloodstain over his upper lip faded away, removing the last vestiges of the fight from his face.

Raising his head again and opening his eyes, he appeared normal. It was as if the fight had never occurred. As a finishing touch, Darkseed smiled and hefted his tumbler to Devenshire in a toast. Finally, he was able to take a sip and enjoy it.

Devenshire chuckled and shook his head. "You have a most unique approach to the application of the Mystical Arts."

Darkseed set the tumbler back on the tabletop and placed his warped cigar between his teeth, shaking his head as he replied, "Not at all. I have seen far too may practitioners of the Arts allow their physical bodies to lapse into disuse, relying too heavily on the Arts. I choose to test myself in areas outside the realm of the Mystical Arts."

Darkseed paused to pull a long draw from the cigar before removing it from his lips and letting the smoke drift from his mouth and nose.

"I manipulate the Arts, Daimion. They do not manipulate me."

Devenshire contemplated his answer. With an expression of appreciation for the wisdom of the answer, he raised his snifter in a toast. "Point well made and well taken."

Darkseed smiled and raised his tumbler to touch glasses with Devenshire. They each took a drink and locked eyes over the rims of their glasses in a silent understanding that can only pass between very close friends.

The moment passed and Darkseed took another deep drink from his tumbler before returning it to the filthy, faded tabletop. "So tell me, what trouble have you gotten yourself into that you need to seek me out?"

Devenshire's expression turned grim as he wrapped both hands around his snifter, gazing at the cracking paint of the table. "There is danger at hand," he replied solemnly.

Darkseed puffed on his cigar, watching his friend through the haze of smoke. "I gathered as much from your bearing. Are you going to tell me of it or am I to begin making guesses?"

Devenshire recognized that Darkseed was attempting to bait him, but he could not rise to the occasion, not with the grim burden on his mind. As was customary with the two of them, Devenshire didn't feel the need to ease into the conversation.

"Xavier has returned," he said matter-of-factly.

Darkseed crossed his arms, leaving the cigar clenched between his teeth. "Xavier? He was defeated seasons ago. He was killed at in the Battle of the Duvall Retreat."

Devenshire shook his head as he looked up at Darkseed, "No. He survived and has returned. Two nights ago he led a massive attack on a nearby village, massacring all who lived within it."

Darkseed shook his head, reaching up to remove the cigar from his mouth, "As vile as he was, Xavier did not possess sole claim to viciousness. There is no shortage of individuals within the realm capable of the barbarity that you speak of."

Devenshire locked his gaze deep into Darkseed's. "I have felt his presence. He lives and has resumed his path of evil."

The hard conviction in Devenshire's eyes left Darkseed no choice but to accept the truth of his claim. His brow furrowed as both absorbed and considered the fact that one of the vilest beings in recent history was still alive, well and once again, plaguing the realm with his existence.

Some of the constant merriment in Darkseed's bearing faded as his mind considered what he had heard, and its implications. His eyes narrowed slightly as he looked at Devenshire,

"There is more, Daimion. You would not have returned to Lirpa just to tell me of Xavier's return."

Devenshire looked deep into his snifter and nodded. "He has the Stones of Andarus."

Darkseed felt his eyes widen at that statement. "*THE* Stones of Andarus? Are you trying to tell me that the largest mystery in the history of the Mystical Arts has been right here all along? Countless quests have scoured every known corner of our realm searching for them. Thousands have died in the search for them with no one ever being able to even come close to locating them. All this time and effort, and they were in a tiny village to the south?" The lack of belief was thick in his tone.

Devenshire ignored the tone as he nodded again. "The village priest held them. He believed them to be a religious artifact."

Darkseed snorted a short, harsh laugh. "A religious artifact? That should go over well in the Afterlife." He paused to consider Devenshire's claim and then followed a thought that had occurred to him. "If Xavier has returned and claimed the Stones, how do you know they are the genuine Stones of Andarus?" The level of disbelief in his voice was as thick as the cigar smoke around them.

"I performed a spell of Mystic Knowledge within the ruins of the village's church. I felt Xavier's presence, as well as that of the Stones," Devenshire answered.

Darkseed shook his head, not truly wanting to accept, much less believe, what he was hearing. "Are you certain?"

Devenshire sat upright and locked eyes with Darkseed. "The spell of Mystic Knowledge does not lie, Raven."

"No, but what it reveals can often be misinterpreted," Darkseed replied.

Devenshire shook his head. "Not by me, not on something of this magnitude and importance."

Darkseed leaned back into the booth, almost as if he were trying to distance himself from what Devenshire was revealing to him. He felt a sense of crushing dread begin to settle about him. The thought of Xavier in control of the Stones of Andarus was nearly too horrific to contemplate.

"Does he know the secrets of the Stones?" he nearly whispered.

Devenshire shook his head. "The fact that everything appears normal tells me he does not. He will, no doubt, be heading back to the Duvall Retreat to unleash the power of the Stones. He will be using the time upon the trail to study them, contemplating how to tap into their power."

Darkseed had fixed his gaze to the table's candle, watching the tiny flame dance to inaudible music. "Surely not even Xavier is crazed or arrogant enough to think he can control the power of the Stones," he commented softly.

"We are speaking of someone who aligned himself with the Dark Mystics. Who led an attack on the Duvall Retreat and defeated the High Master Adept," Devenshire reminded him. "I do not think it beyond possibility that he would think himself skilled enough to accomplish what most feel is impossible."

Darkseed's features darkened as he ran the scenario through his mind. "The most terrifying prospect? He *IS* skilled enough to tap into them."

Devenshire nodded slowly. "I know."

"By the Lords..." Darkseed whispered as he slowly shifted his concerned gaze to Devenshire, hoping against hope that he would see his friends face break into a beaming smile and claim the whole terrifying story had been an elaborate jest. The dread that he both saw in his friend and felt coursing through his soul told him that such a claim would not be coming.

A long silence hung between them as each man contemplated what might come to pass if Xavier were successful in his attempts to tap into the power of the dreaded Stones.

Finally, it was Devenshire who found his voice. "There is no telling what direction the power will take or what form it will assume under

Xavier's attempt to control it."

"Do not be insane, Daimion!" Darkseed snapped angrily. "There is no way to control the power of the Stones. Any attempt to control it will only mutate it with no way to cancel it out. You have heard the legends and read the scrolls just as I have."

Devenshire nodded. "Aye. The power of the Stones mixed with the power of the Dark Mystics, both unpredictable and both uncontrollable. I fear that Xavier does not truly realize the depths of the evil he is toying with."

Darkseed didn't comment as he raised the tumbler to his lips, but he didn't drink as another thought occurred to him. With growing shock, he slightly lowered the tumbler to stare at Devenshire. "You intend to go after him," he muttered in growing disbelief.

Devenshire nodded slowly.

"Have you taken all leave of your senses?" Darkseed asked.

Devenshire didn't waiver. "I have to try. He must be stopped."

"You are no match for his powers, Daimion. You will only succeed in getting yourself killed... or worse!" Darkseed paused as another thought came to him. His eyes narrowed as he followed the thought. "You are going after him, and you want me to go with you," he said without any hint of question in his voice. He knew exactly what Devenshire was doing.

Devenshire held his gaze as he nodded again.

"You have gone insane. Stark raving mad," Darkseed replied.

"Perhaps. But I know I must try to stop him. If I fail, then at least I can pass from this realm with the knowledge that I at least tried to stop him. You are adept of the Mystical Arts; you can summon far greater spells than I can. Perhaps between the two of us we can..."

"Listen to yourself, Daimion! You are talking madness! If it were just Xavier, then perhaps we would have a chance at defeating him. But it is not just Xavier. He has aligned himself with the Dark Mystics and all the forbidden depths of dark magic that they offer. He was already a powerful mage BEFORE he went to the Dark Mystics. Now with the true power of the Mystical Arts combined with the powers of the Dark Mystics?" He shook his head. "I know I am no match for his hellish powers. This is suicide."

"There is no time to reach the Mystics of Solomenti, no time to reach any other mages. We have tracked Xavier, and I know he is heading for the Duval Retreat. While he may not attempt to tap into the Stones until he makes his Retreat, he will be using the time on the trail to study how to tap into them. He will be more vulnerable on the trail. An opportunity might present itself to finish this before he has a chance," Devenshire argued intensely. He had known it would be a difficult task to convince Darkseed to join him, and he now launched into what he knew would be his only opportunity to talk him into it.

Darkseed's heated glare told him he might have already lost the argument. "Will you listen to yourself? You speak as though we would have a chance to defeat him. What do you propose? Catch him relieving himself behind a tree and take him down with a single sword stroke? Or do you propose that we sneak into his camp and slit his throat while he sleeps?"

Suddenly his face beamed with mock surprise. "Wait! I have it! We will simply appear within his camp, within the midst of his Followers and demand his surrender, which, of course, he will readily do."

Darkseed layered heavy sarcasm into his voice and over-emphasized gestures as he continued. "I can see it now, he will come out of his tent, hand you the Stones of Andarus and kneel before us, begging for his life. Is that how you see it transpiring, Daimion?" Darkseed leaned forward, the mock merriment leaving his face and voice. "Need I remind you that we are talking about someone who dared to not only challenge the High Master Adept, but defeat him? Daimion, he took on the best mage in our ranks and defeated him. What possible hope would you and I have?"

Devenshire kept his face set as he absorbed Darkseed's rant and final assessment of their chances of success. After several beats, he replied, "We have conviction. That what we are doing is the right thing, the noble thing, the honorable thing. We also have determination, a trait that you have in great quantities."

Darkseed chuckled harshly and shook his head in disbelief. "Are you hearing yourself, Devenshire? Conviction? Determination? Have you taken complete leave of your sanity? Has madness claimed you?"

Devenshire felt the anger and frustration building within him and struggled to contain it. He still had a chance to persuade Darkseed to join him, but not by allowing his emotions to win control of the conversation.

"Perhaps, but I know that something has to be done to stop him. I know that if no one steps forward to stop him, then we are all doomed to whatever hell he unleashes upon our realm."

"And that someone is you, Devenshire? You? One who did not even complete to most rudimentary level of study of the Mystical Arts? You are going to stop him?" Darkseed shot back.

Devenshire's eyes narrowed slightly, and his mouth pulled into a tight line as he struggled against his frustration. "My level of skill is not the only factor to be considered."

"Ah, yes! I forgot. Your fantastic store of conviction and determination! Less we forget those! Listen to yourself! Conviction and determination. Lofty, dreamy words spewed by a dreamer! All the conviction and determination within the realm will not help you once you are confronted by Xavier's incredible power! He will reduce you to something your mind cannot even begin to contemplate could exist." He shook his head angrily. "It is suicide, and I will have no part in it!"

Devenshire studied Darkseed for a moment before continuing. "What has happened to you, Raven? Has the soullessness of this place finally claimed you? Have you finally become the empty shell that you so delight in studying night after night? You speak of testing yourself against situations where the outcome is unknown, and yet when a true unknown presents itself, you shy away from it."

Darkseed's eyes turned dark as they narrowed in anger from the sting of Devenshire's words. "Do not even attempt to lecture me, Devenshire! Do not forget whom you are speaking to! I know you far better than you know yourself, and do not think for a single heartbeat that I will sit here and be given a sermon on soullessness from someone who, not so long ago, was even more guilty of what you just accused me of being!"

The flare of anger came suddenly, much too quickly for Devenshire to even see coming, let alone do anything to stop it. He launched himself to his feet and glared down at Darkseed, a part of him wanting nothing more than to smash the man in the face repeatedly. Without his conscious effort, his fists curled into tightly balled fists and shook from his efforts to contain his suddenly boiling anger.

Darkseed glared back, daring him with the defiant lift of his chin. "Go ahead, Daimion. Do it! Give me a reason!" he muttered through clenched teeth.

"Be careful what you ask for, you may just get it," Devenshire rasped in return.

Both men glared at each other for several moments before Devenshire was finally able to wrestle his anger under control. Letting his breath out slowly he forced himself to relax, uncurling his fingers to release the fists. He reached down and picked up his snifter, draining the glass in a single gulp.

He tossed the glass into the air, and with a quick hand gesture, it vanished into thin air.

Darkseed leaned back in the booth and clapped slowly. "Amazing! Simply an amazing feat of Mystical work, Devenshire. Perhaps if you perform that trick in front of Xavier, he will yield to your awesome power."

Devenshire did not respond right away. He studied Darkseed for several moments before answering. When he did speak, the tones of anger were subdued, replaced with a slight undertone of sympathy. "You must act as your conscience directs you, Darkseed. Perhaps I have not always walked the right path. I have made mistakes and bad choices, and I am paying the tolls for those choices." He paused as a rare flash of pain flickered through his eyes and his voice grew distant. "Even now."

He quickly pushed the pain down and returned his gaze to Darkseed.

"I cannot change what I have done or who I was. All I can do is move forward, acknowledge my demons, acknowledge my shortcomings, and try to do better... to be more than what I was. Before condemning me for my choices, you should seriously reflect on your own past, present, and future. Farewell, Raven."

With that, Devenshire turned and began walking toward the door. Darkseed watched him go, feeling his own anger rising faster than he was prepared to acknowledge.

He jumped to his feet and downed the remainder of his cognac. He tried to make the thick glass vanish as Devenshire had, but the anger was distracting him, thwarting his efforts to focus his powers. This only served to infuriate him even further.

With a snarl, he dashed the glass to the floor taking satisfaction in the complete smashing destruction of it. He leveled a heated glare at the back of Devenshire's head. "To hell with you, Devenshire! I need not commit suicide to atone for past sins! I know exactly who and what I am, and I am more than content with that!"

Devenshire paused at the door and turned back to face him, his features arranged in the most sad expression he had ever seen. "Then may you rest easy with that knowledge when you face whatever damnation Xavier unleashes comes for you." Devenshire slipped out the door without another word.

Darkseed stood rooted to the spot, his limbs trembling with the incredible rage that was coursing through him. He didn't even notice the barmaid walking up to him, her bony hands resting on her skeletal hips. Her tired eyes took in the shattered remnants of the glass. "You are going to pay for that!" she snipped.

"Go away!" Darkseed hissed his eyes still locked on the spot Devenshire had just occupied at the door.

"You go away! I will summon a sheriff if you do not pay for that glass this instant!" she snapped in reply.

Darkseed turned slowly to tower over her, his rage now focused on her. Her eyes widened slightly, and she took an involuntary step back as his dark eyes bore into hers. His lips peeled back in a snarl as he hissed. "And I will summon the undertaker to bury your dead, broken, misshapen body if you do not leave me be!"

He turned on his heel and strode from the tavern, not really aware of a direction, but trying to put as much distance as he could between himself, the anger, and a growing sprout of guilt that was not entirely spawned from Devenshire's words.

CHAPTER TWENTY

DEVENSHIRE STORMED INTO the lobby of the inn, his mind churning in the storm of anger and frustration over his argument with Darkseed and ensuing failure to secure his assistance.

Raven Darkseed was a very talented practitioner of the Mystical Arts. His level of power and skill rivaled that of many Adepts, and yet he continued to turn his skills in directions that none could predict, not even those who knew him best. It was impossible to foresee which side of an issue Darkseed would come down on, but one thing was certain… once he did choose, there was no changing his mind.

His friendship was the first in Devenshire's memory. They had known one another since they were small children. The memories were plentiful, rich, full and served as the one and only surviving warm emotion from his childhood. There was no one in the realm that knew and understood him as well as Darkseed. The same could be said of the reverse, and it was that knowledge and understanding that helped fuel his anger. He, of all people, should have been able to sway Darkseed's mind to their cause, and yet he had failed.

With a tightening clutch of the anger, he understood that the very reason he had failed resulted from the same mind set within Darkseed. There was no argument that Devenshire could have launched that Darkseed would not have been able to see coming from miles away. His anger also stemmed from the harsh, yet truthful words they had hurled at one another. Each had been like an arrow and each had scored a bull's eye.

He reached the bottom of the staircase when a voice called out from behind him. "Are you Devenshire?"

He turned to regard the man behind the desk. It was not the older, kindly man who had been there before. This man was younger, rougher and his features did not share the warmth of welcome of his predecessor's. There was something not quite right about the man.

"Yes," he snapped in reply. He was in no mood for pleasantries.

"I have a message for you," the man behind the desk replied gruffly.

Devenshire released the banister and moved toward the desk, sighing heavily. His mind continued to churn over the epic failure of his meeting with Darkseed.

"Do not even attempt to lecture me, Devenshire! Do not forget whom you are speaking to! I know you far better than you know yourself, and do not think for a single heartbeat that I will sit here and be given a sermon on soullessness from someone who, not so long ago, was even more guilty of what you just accused me of being!"

The words echoed loudly in his mind and touched deeply buried memories, memories that were best left buried. Darkseed's words rang of a truth that he desperately wanted to erase. The guilt associated with those memories were part of what had driven him from Lirpa two seasons ago.

Now, with the return to Lirpa, and the confrontation with Darkseed, he had been shown just how very little distance he had gained from the phantoms of his past. A small part of his mind tried to focus on the disparity with the man behind the desk, but his rampant emotions prevented it.

"What is it?" he asked shortly.

Beware Daimion! All is not as it appears!

The thought slammed into his mind with such force that he stopped walking from the shock. He bowed his head and reached up to rub his forehead, half expecting to find an entrance wound of some kind.

The gruff man behind the desk tilted his head in confusion as he watched Devenshire's odd behavior.

Devenshire raised his head and looked about the lobby, searching for the owner of the thoughts, but no one was present. The thought had come so fast, and his mind had been so preoccupied, he had not had time to study the patterns.

"What is wrong?" the man asked.

Devenshire turned back to answer him and suddenly realized the source of the warning. He immediately chastised himself for his lack of attention. The glaring discrepancy before him was so obvious he should have seen it the moment he stepped through the door. Yet he had been so caught up with the fight with Darkseed that he had let his attention lapse. Such lapses could be deadly.

The man behind the desk did not belong there. His hair was mussed, his face had not felt the kiss of a blade for many days, and the pungent odor that prevailed about him said his body had not seen water for even longer. The rough cut of his clothes spoke of someone who lived in the outdoors, on the trail. The man looked very uncomfortable in his current position. His eyes would occasionally dart about, as though he were a cornered animal looking for the quickest path to escape.

Devenshire's eyes narrowed slightly as he studied the man and realized that of all the possible occupations this man held, the clerk of an inn was not one of them.

A Follower? Perhaps.

"What is the message?" Devenshire asked giving no outward indication that he knew his ruse had failed.

"Your companions will be joining you shortly. They wish for you to wait here for them."

Devenshire nodded, pretending to consider the message. He resisted the urge to look up toward the second floor. Were the others still here? Had they already been taken captive, or worse? Had they made good their escape? He had no way of knowing at this point, so he decided to play along for a moment longer.

"Who left the message?" he asked casually, his arms swinging behind him.

The question had caught the man off guard. He had not put much effort or preparation into his role as clerk. "Uh. The woman." He stammered out.

"Which woman?" Devenshire asked.

"What?" the man replied truly confused.

"I am traveling with two women. Which one left the message?" Devenshire took some small slice of delight in watching the man struggle to come up with an answer that would not give him away as the fraud he was.

"She did not leave her name," he finally answered.

Devenshire smiled and gave the man at least some credit for being able to think on his feet. "I see."

He heard the faint creek of floorboards to his right. He resisted the urge to look in that direction, but the man behind the desk didn't possess the same discipline as his eye darted quickly toward a darkened alcove.

Devenshire didn't need his powers to tell him that another man was hiding in the shadows just to his right. This was an ambush and the goal was obviously to capture him, since they had not attacked him in the open and made short work of him.

He turned and began walking toward the staircase. "Very well. I shall await their return. In the meantime, draw me a bath," he said with all the haughty air he could muster.

"What?" the man all but squealed. It was one thing to pretend to be a servant, it was quite another to actually perform the tasks associated with the role.

Devenshire turned back to face the man. "I wish to bathe while I await my party. You will draw me a bath."

The man's face darkened in growing rage. "I do not draw baths!" he snipped.

"I am a guest here. You work here. You will draw me a bath and do so immediately!" Devenshire shot back, turning back toward the staircase. He could barely conceal the smile as he heard the man's sharp intake of breath. For added insult he threw back over his shoulder,

"I expect the bath to be hot and ready by the time I return from my room."

The sound of the man's sword being drawn and the creak of the desk as he climbed on top of it were almost simultaneous.

"You can bathe in the fires of hell you bastard!" the man shouted as he launched himself toward Devenshire's back.

Devenshire ducked and spun away as the man landed in the spot he had just occupied.

The man snarled as he turned to find his prey. What he wasn't prepared for was to find the tip of Devenshire's blade pressed firmly into the skin of his throat. The harsh touch of the steel froze him for a second as he contemplated how the plan had gone so awry so quickly. He looked up the length of the sword to find the cool gaze of blue-green eyes staring back at him.

"It would have been better for you to have drawn the bath," Devenshire commented with an arched eyebrow.

The man's anger flared again, and he moved as though he were going to lunge at him. Devenshire twisted the blade ever so slightly, applying more pressure to the soft skin, threatening to split it. The cold touch of steel and the cold confidence of his eyes stayed the man's lunge.

"Drop your sword," Devenshire ordered. The man measured his will against Devenshire's and found he wasn't quite prepared to see if he would actually kill. With a clatter, his sword dropped to the floor.

"Tell your companion to come out," Devenshire ordered.

"I am alone," the man replied.

Devenshire's expression shifted into disappointment as he flicked his wrist, splitting the flesh and spilling a small amount of blood down his throat.

"Do not test my convictions," Devenshire warned. His lips held the slight smile while his eyes carried the cold hard truth of his willingness to kill him.

The man shifted his eyes toward the alcove next to the desk. "Bandella! Come out! We are discovered!"

Moments passed with no one appearing from the shadows. Devenshire shifted his gaze from the alcove to his target.

"It would appear that Bandella doubts my sincerity." Devenshire shook his head slowly. "Most unfortunate for you."

Devenshire drew himself up, as though he were about to drive the sword through the man's neck. Icy fear raced up the man's spine as his eyes flew open wide.

"Wait!" he squealed. "Please wait!"

The man took a brief moment to swallow against the hard bite of terror and forced his body to remain absolutely still.

"Bandella! Damn you, come out! He will kill me!" he shouted.

There was another moment of silence, save for the street sounds filtering in through the open doors. Finally, the creak of floorboards came followed by another man coming into the light, his sword held at the ready.

Devenshire arched one eyebrow. "Good evening, Bandella. Now, if you will be so kind, toss your sword away."

Bandella glared at him, but a quick glance at the tip of his sword tucked neatly into the gash of his companion's throat told him all he needed to know about who currently held the upper hand.

Bandella tossed his sword away and raised his hands to shoulder height, his angry glare locked on Devenshire.

Devenshire nodded, shifting his gaze between the two men. "Very good. Now, do yourselves a favor, and do not doubt my conviction to kill either one or both of you if I do not get what I seek. Where are my companions?"

The men looked at one another, trying to formulate a plan to extradite themselves from the positions they were in now. Devenshire applied a little pressure on his sword, which drew a wince from the man at the end of it.

"Where are they? If you lie to me, I will slit your throat and watch you bleed out." There was still merriment in his voice, but the cold determination in his eyes showed the true nature of the imminent danger the man was in.

"I do not know. They were not here when we arrived," he answered.

Devenshire gave no outward reaction, but at least he knew they were safe. It was annoying that they had ventured out when he had left word for them to stay at the inn, but their strong wills may have served to keep them out of harm's way.

"Why did you attack me?" he asked next.

"We were told to capture you," the man replied.

"By whom?"

The men exchanged glances once again. To Devenshire it appeared they were trying to decide which was worse: to tell him who wanted him captured and suffer that person's wrath or remain silent and suffer his. He resisted the urge to chuckle as he saw the inevitability of their situation dawn on them. It was a classic no-win scenario.

"Lordal." The man with Devenshire's sword at his throat answered.

Devenshire searched his memory and could not remember anyone he had ever encountered by that name. "Who is this Lordal, and why does he want me?"

"He seeks revenge for the men you killed last eve," the man replied slowly.

"Those men attacked us. We were only defending ourselves. Much as I will now if I am forced to." He paused to look at Bandella and then back to the man before him. Go back to Lordal and tell him you failed. Also, tell him that any other men he sends against me will meet the same fate as those from last eve. I will not play games with them, such as I have with you."

Suddenly, something shifted. Devenshire didn't know what or how he knew, but something in the situation had changed. He felt himself tense, preparing for whatever had altered the situation to make itself known.

Then he saw what had alerted him. The expression in the man's eyes before him had changed ever so subtly. The fear had faded, replaced with relief and the tiniest hint of a smile played at the corners of his mouth. The man had tried to keep his eyes locked to Devenshire, but they shifted to something behind Devenshire, something that gave him a sense of relief.

The sudden thud of a footfall and the ensuing creak of a floorboard from the doorway was all the evidence he needed that the tables had turned.

As the sharp twang of a crossbow rang out, he ducked and spun away. As he did, he heard the distinct meaty thud and sudden, sharp hiss of air being sucked in. He came out of his spin, his sword at the ready and his eyes turning toward the door.

Another man stood frozen in place, the discharged crossbow in his hands. His wide eyes were not looking at him, but rather at the spot he had just occupied. He turned his head to find the bandit he had held with the tip of his sword staggering back, his hands wrapped around the shaft of the crossbow bolt protruding from the center of his chest.

The timing couldn't have been more perfect or more deadly had it been wrong. Realizing that the crossbowman was stunned by his shot, Devenshire leapt into action. He quickly crossed the room and reached the man with the crossbow just as he reclaimed his senses. The man turned his head just in time to see Devenshire's angry snarl a moment before his fist filled the man's vision.

Devenshire's fist collided with the man's jaw with a wet, meaty smack. The man's head snapped hard to his left as the pommel of Devenshire's sword came crashing down on the back of his head. A brief but brilliant explosion of stars was the last thing the man saw as he collapsed to the floor.

Bandella recovered much quicker, and by the time Devenshire turned to see what had become of him, he was launching into an attack. Devenshire parried the thrust with a downward swing of his sword followed by a quick series of side steps that would give him more room.

"You bastard!" Bandella hissed as he slashed at Devenshire repeatedly. The attack was driven by emotion; therefore, there was no real skill. The thrusts and slashes were easily deflected and bought Devenshire time to decide if he would kill Bandella or simply seriously wound him.

"You will pray for death before I am finished with you!" he snarled, his face contorted in a mask of furry.

Devenshire arched an eyebrow and smiled as their swords collided with a sharp tang, separated, spun to new positions, and collided again. "You should save yourself humiliation and serious injury by surrendering now."

The man screamed in fury as he increased the intensity of his attacks. However, as the intensity increased, the man's skill decreased. Devenshire was able to parry every attack with ease. They moved around the lobby with Devenshire backing up in defense until he was backed into a wall or corner. He would then launch a counter attack that would send Bandella scurrying back, giving him time to move into a better position.

Devenshire had decided that it would be better for their passage through Lirpa if he didn't kill the bandit. He would wound him and then render him unconscious. The scene would explain itself, a man with a crossbow bolt in his chest and an unconscious man with a crossbow. Bandella would be wounded and left in an alley far from the inn.

Suddenly he felt the sharp, distinct tingling run up and down his spine meaning that someone was using magic very near him. The tingle was so sharp and intense that it was almost painful, which meant the proximity of the magic in use was very nearby, likely in the lobby with him.

A strange moan sounded from behind him. It sounded almost like a human moan, but there was no life in it. It was the most lifeless sound he had ever heard and it spoke of a danger all its own. Devenshire quickly executed a misdirected parry that caused Bandella to stagger and allowed him to step aside and turn toward the source of the strange moan.

Devenshire felt his blood run cold as he found himself staring into the wide-open eyes of the bandit who had taken the crossbow bolt to the chest. He felt his own eyes grow wide in shock. The bandit had obviously died from his wound, there was no way he could have survived a crossbow bolt to the heart. Yet he had risen, and his cold, lifeless eyes were now fixed on him.

The bandit's face was already ashen from the touch of death, and the gash in his throat no longer oozed blood. For a time, he simply stood from where he had risen, his empty stare locked on Devenshire.

Bandella also stood rooted to the spot, his mind unable to comprehend what his eyes were showing him.

Devenshire decided not to see what would happen next. He quickly stepped in, running his sword deep into the bandit's stomach until the tip of the blade sliced through his back, just to the right of his spine.

As the hilt of his sword touched the bandit's stomach, Devenshire found himself face to face with the deceased bandit. His face a tight snarl of the effort used to drive his sword through the body, the bandit's was absolutely blank, no expression at all.

The bandit looked down at the sword buried deep into his stomach, then raised his cold eyes back to Devenshire. Again, Devenshire felt his eyes grow wide with shock at the sight of the bandit standing before him with a sword run completely through his mid-section and showing no sign of injury. Without even so much as a blink, the bandit, with surprising speed, used both hands to strike Devenshire in the chest, hurling him back several feet before he hit the floor, his sword still in the body.

Devenshire propped up on one elbow and shook his head to clear the fog from his senses. The blow had been much more powerful than he had anticipated. He raised his eyes to see the corpse slowly, almost casually, reach up and pull the sword from his midsection. It was as though it were nothing more than a twig that had become tangled in his clothing. There was no pain in his face, no indication that the sword had so much as touched him, let alone sank deep into vital organs. The corpse tossed the sword away and returned its empty, lifeless stare to him.

"Turin?" Bandella asked cautiously, still not entirely sure what he was seeing. Turin turned his cold stare toward Bandella, but made no other response. Devenshire used the exchange to recover his senses and assess the situation. The corpse still responded to his name. He wondered if he would be forced to fight two opponents, one who obviously could not be killed by conventional means.

Bandella smiled at the sight of his comrade responding to his name. "Turin, are you well?"

Devenshire found the question odd, and had the situation not been so dire, might have even laughed.

The corpse didn't respond and continued to stare at Bandella with the same empty, unblinking stare.

Bandella turned his head to look at Devenshire over his shoulder, an evil grin spreading across his features. "I told you that you would wish for death." He snarled before turning back to the corpse.

"Let us strike, Turin. Together we can defeat the bastard and take him to Lordal." Bandella proclaimed as he stepped up beside Turin.

When Turin didn't respond, Bandella looked at his former comrade, question in his eyes. "Turin?"

His answer came in the form of a vicious and powerful backhand blow that sent Bandella flying backwards to crash into a table situated against the wall. The table shattered into splinters as Bandella's body hit with a loud thump. The bandit dropped to the floor and was still for several moments before a faint moan escaped his lips.

The corpse turned toward Bandella and froze. Devenshire knew his recovery time was over and quickly rose to his feet. He glanced around the room and found his sword at the base of the staircase. The distance wasn't too far, but he wasn't sure how agile the corpse would be, and the painful tingle wracking his spine convinced him that it was best to assess his opponent's abilities before taking any offensive action.

The corpse turned away from Bandella's addled form, and its empty gaze found Devenshire again. He knew he would have to use his limited store of spells to combat the corpse until a way could be found to dispatch it permanently. Magic had reanimated the corpse so it made sense magic would have to defeat it. He knew he would be hard pressed to combat the magic at work within the corpse with his very limited command of the arts.

He reached out with his powers, trying to gauge the strength of the magic at work. The aura surrounding the corpse was vague, hard to discern. This was very odd. Even with his limited abilities in the workings of the Mystical Arts, he knew he should have been able to learn more about the type and power of spell at work. He had no time to sort through the mystery, for the corpse began advancing on him and was moving with respectable speed for something that was dead.

Devenshire focused his attention and made a quick gesture with his left hand before thrusting his right hand, palm out, toward the body. A bolt of pale blue light shot from Devenshire's palm to hit the bandit square in the chest. For a moment, the body was bathed in the pale blue light. There was a faint crackling in the air as the two mystical forces collided. The blue light faded and the body staggered forward, almost fell, and then stopped. For several moments, it was frozen in a stooped position, and then it slowly returned to its full height and locked its gaze back on Devenshire before resuming its advance.

Fighting against rising panic, Devenshire took a deep breath and focused more energy into the counter spell. He repeated the gestures and thrust both hands out sending an even brighter shaft of light crashing into the body. The crackle in the air was more intense, and Devenshire could feel the power of the two spells struggle to cancel each other out. Again, the body of the deceased bandit staggered, but this time backwards as the aura of blue became tinged with red. The body gave no indication of any pain, any confusion, nothing that would tell of any consciousness that might remain.

The body swayed as the red and blue light faded. It took two staggering steps toward Devenshire before the body toppled forward to the floor. It did not move, did not so much as twitch as it seemed to relax into death once again.

The silence that followed was intense, and it was only moments later that Devenshire realized he was still in the position of casting the counter spell.

"By the Fates!!" came a whispered gasp.

Devenshire turned his head to find that Bandella had recovered and was standing in stunned awe of what he had just witnessed. His eyes were wide with fear, and his face pale. His terrified eyes moved from the body to Devenshire."What manner of demon are you?"

Devenshire stood upright, releasing the mystical energies he had gathered to battle the corpse. He felt taxed, and his arms tingled with tiny pinpricks, an after effect of channeling mystical energies through the body. He slowly shook his head. "That was not my work. I do not bring the dead back to life."

"Lordal was right! You are a demon!" Bandella cried out as he began moving along the wall toward the main entrance. His terrified gaze locked fast to Devenshire. "Stay, demon!" he almost screamed.

Devenshire shook his head tiredly and started to try to explain the truth. Before the words could come, the body before him began to twitch, as if nerve endings were expending their final energies. Yet the twitching did not subside, but only grew in frequency and strength until the body nearly jumped from the force of the movements.

Despite his fear, Bandella stopped to watch the body twist and writhe in hard convulsions. One convulsion gripped the body so hard that it flipped over onto its back. Devenshire stared into the lifeless eyes that stared at the ceiling and tried to ascertain what was happening. All he could sense was the strange magical force still at work within the body. He took an involuntary step back and prepared himself to cast another spell.

The tingling running the length of his spine turned to severe spasms of pain as the mystical energy within the corpse continued to build. Ignoring the pain, Devenshire continued to prepare himself, pulling in all the mystical energy he could. He found himself seriously wondering if every ounce of power he could muster would be enough.

The body thrashed about on the floor as the skin began to ripple like waves in a pond. The ripples seemed to be moving toward the body's chest, as though the energies were concentrating there. He winced as the ever-increasing spasms increased in connection with the energies coursing through the body. He wasn't sure what was coming, but it was a tremendous working of the Arts.

The crossbow bolt suddenly shot out of the chest, flying up to hit the ceiling. Blood gushed up through the gaping holed and the entire torso convulsed as though something was inside the body trying to escape. There came the distinct crack and snap of ribs breaking as the chest began to swell. The dead bandit's mouth dropped open and a haunting gasp rushed past his blue lips as the last bit of air was pushed from the compressed lungs.

Devenshire took another step back as the chest continued to swell outward, ripping the shirt at the seams, tearing it asunder. The chest was now bare and the sight of the massive knot forming just under the crossbow bolt wound was even more grotesque. The hard thrashing subsided, replaced by an almost subtle trembling. Blood stopped gushing from the wound as something suddenly blocked the hole. Devenshire squinted trying to discern what had suddenly appeared to block the wound. The answer wasn't long in coming as the hole suddenly exploded outward in a shower of blood and bone fragments.

Devenshire took up the edge of his cloak and quickly brought it up and around him as he spun away from the explosion, crouching low for added protection. He could feel the bone fragments pelt him through his cloak and clothing. He also heard the wet sound of chunks of flesh and organs impacting all around the small lobby.

Once the onslaught subsided, he carefully lowered his cloak and turned to see what had erupted from the body. Of all the things he had prepared to witness, what he saw was not among them.

A small reddish creature lay next to the mutilated corpse. The entire chest of the body was gone, leaving a hollow cavity, the contents splattered all over the lobby. The creature was in a fetal position, and once free of the body, began to rapidly grow in size.

It howled in what could only be intense pain as its body was subjected to rapid growth. Within seconds, it had doubled its size, and Devenshire found himself transfixed on the incredible sight before him.

The creature was bright red in color. He didn't know if this were its natural color or a result of being immersed in the body of the bandit. Its skull was round with a sharp jutting chin that came to a point. Its lipless mouth was peeled open in a howl of pain which revealed a double row of very short, sharp teeth that seemed to drip some kind of greenish ooze.

A row of boney spikes protruded from between its eyes and moved over the top of the skull to run down its spine. The arms and legs were very thin and boney in appearance. The creature's ribs and hips could be seen pressing against its taut skin as though it were malnourished.

Devenshire lost track of how long the creature had writhed on the floor as it quickly grew. When the growth convulsions subsided, the creature struggled to its feet and stood hunched over, breathing hard against what had to be intense agony. It stood roughly four feet in height. It opened its red, pupil-less eyes and began surveying its surroundings. The creature's hands were human looking, except that each of the ten digits ended in a long, lethal looking claw. Its toes also ended in shorter versions of the claws on its hands.

The red eyes came to rest on Bandella and locked there, its mouth opened in a long hiss as a forked green tongue flashed out as a serpents' would, sampling the air. It turned to fully face the bandit who was locked in the tight grip of shocked terror. With halting steps, it began moving toward the bandit.

Devenshire shook himself out of the morbid study of the strange creature and began focusing his power to cast a repeat of the spell he had used to defeat the corpse. Just as he was about to perform the hand gestures that would release the spell, the creature howled and launched itself at Bandella with eye-blurring speed. In a single bound, it had crossed the room to land in the center of the bandit's chest.

With the impact, Bandella was jarred out of his shock as he suddenly realized that he was under attack. He abandoned his sword to free up both hands and began to try to wrest the creature from him, but the creature's toe claws were buried deep in his chest as its hand claws began swiping at his face. He staggered back, letting out short shrieks of fear and pain as the attack commenced. He was so terrified, his body so gripped in cold, bitter fear that he couldn't even draw a deep enough breathe to scream.

Devenshire relaxed, letting the mystical energies he had gathered dissipate unused. There was no way he could release the spell now. With the creature in direct contact with Bandella, the spell would likely kill him as well.

The creature howled in a purely hellish sound as each swipe of its talons opened four deep gashes somewhere about Bandella's upper body. Bandella was finally able to draw in enough air to scream in a mixture of terror and pain as he fought to separate himself from the demon.

Devenshire spun around and moved quickly to where his sword

lay. Taking it up, he turned back to find that Bandella had stumbled in his backwards flight from the creature and now lay upon his back, his hands and arms mutilated in defensive wounds. Tendons had been severed and muscles snipped from their anchor on the bone. The damage was so extensive that his arms were now useless fronds of raw meat, which the creature swept aside to take another vicious swipe at his face.

Devenshire froze for a moment as he grimaced against the sight of Bandella's mutilated face. The creature paused after one hard swipe to examine something stuck to one of its claws. It was one of Bandella's eyeballs and the creature wasted no time in picking it off its claw with its teeth, devouring it hungrily. Even while it chewed on its delicacy, it resumed its attack, hacking and slashing at the mortally wounded man.

He set his jaw and quickly advanced on the demon, determined to behead it with a single swing of his sword. Just as he stepped up beside the body and drew his sword back, the creature suddenly spun at the waist, glaring up at Devenshire and screaming at him in a sound that could only be born of the underworld. The move and sound had come so suddenly that he reacted out of instinct and staggered backwards, bringing his sword down into a defensive position.

The creature spun back around and drove its face down into Bandella's throat, sinking its razor sharp teeth deep into already bloodied flesh. His screams were suddenly strangled, and his body went rigid. With equal force, the creature clamped its jaws shut and jerked itself upright, tearing a large chunk of the bandit's throat free. Blood gushed into the air as the creature chewed on its mouthful and then leaned forward to drink from the pulsating fountain of blood that erupted with each beat of the dying bandit's heart.

Devenshire felt his stomach convulse at what he saw and fought against the bile that rose up in his throat. Bandella may have been a bandit and intent on doing him harm, but he did not deserve a death such as this one. Drawing his anger to a fine edge, he stepped up and swung for the creature's head.

At the last moment, the creature hissed and sprung into a backwards summersault off Bandella's dying body. Devenshire was pitched off balance and staggered sideways as his sword swung through empty air. He recovered and spun back toward the creature to find it crouching where it had landed, breathing heavily, and hissing at him. It took most of his concentration to tune out the horrid gurgling sounds Bandella made as he died.

Devenshire stooped into his own defensive position as he watched the creature. He had seen the incredible speed with which it had attacked Bandella and was preparing himself for just such an attack.

The creature did not move. It hunkered where it had landed and continued to watch Devenshire with the hellish gaze. Devenshire resisted the urge to attack first. When fighting an unknown opponent it was always best to let them make the first move.

The creature began a slow walk toward the now silent and still form of Bandella, but its eyes never left Devenshire. Perhaps the creature thought to finish its ghastly meal. He was not going to allow the creature the satisfaction of dining on the remains and took a step to place himself between the creature and Bandella's body.

Just as Devenshire balanced his weight on both legs, the creature suddenly screamed out and launched itself at him with the same unbelievable speed with which it had attacked the bandit. Devenshire swung his sword up and stepped to one side, swinging as the creature flew past.

Just as Devenshire's sword cut deep into inhuman flesh, four razor sharp claws sank deep into the thick muscle of his upper right arm. Grunting in pain, Devenshire staggered back, trying to avoid any further attack while slapping his left hand to the burning gashes on his arm. He had tried to maintain his grip on his sword, but the reflex to being wounded had loosened it before he could summon the mental command to hold it.

Fighting back intense pain and ignoring the warm wetness that ran in rivulets down his right arm, Devenshire forced his eyes to look for his opponent. The creature lay against the base of the stairs with his sword buried deep into its midsection. The creature slowly rose to its feet and fixed him with a burning look of pure hatred. It took the hilt of the sword and violently jerked it free of its body before tossing it aside.

He saw purplish sludge ooze from the deep gash across the creatures stomach. It looked down at its wound then back at Devenshire. The burning hatred doubled as it began to slowly amble toward him as if it knew he was wounded, and would pose no further problems in killing. If there was any pain or damage from the sword strike, it was not apparent in the creatures bearing.

He did not know how deep the cuts on his arm went, but judging from the way the sleeve of his shirt was already soaked in his blood, the wounds were bad. He knew that he would have to act quickly if he were going to survive.

Fighting the creature hand to hand was out of the question. Not only was he already wounded, but also the creature was impervious to any traditional weapon. That left using his powers, which were already taxed from battling the corpse.

It was then that he noticed that the intense and painful spasms in his spine had eased considerably. It was back to the normal tingling sensation in which he was accustomed. Had he weakened the creature? Perhaps if he could conjure another spell like the one he had used to defeat the reanimated corpse, he might weaken it further, perhaps enough to destroy it.

He forced his racing thoughts to settle, to focus on the matter at hand. He blocked out the pain from his wounds and the fear that wrestled him for control. He took in a deep breath and forced his attention to a fine focus. It would take all of his control to gather the mystical energies he needed, and any distraction would be too much.

He took in another deep breath and let it out slowly, mentally calling on his powers. He felt the magical energies begin to gather about him, he could see their multiple colors within his mind. He slowly began performing the hand gestures necessary to focus the energy, and to channel it to his will. His injured arm screamed at him in protest as he forced the damaged limb to perform the needed gestures. He ignored the hot stabs of pain through the torn muscles of his arm. He would need everything he could muster. He also forced himself to ignore the fact that a release of the magnitude he was attempting would result in his being unable to focus his powers for several hours to come.

The creature cocked its head to one side as it watched him, as though it were curious about what he was doing. He was only vaguely aware of this as he continued to pour all of his concentration into one massive release of his powers. A part of his mind called to him, trying to remind him of his very limited abilities, and how it was very unlikely that he would be able to conjure enough energy to defeat the beast, but he ignored it.

The creature suddenly howled in its hellish voice as though it abruptly realized what its human target was doing. It leapt into the air with amazing agility and angled itself toward the human, its talons already raised to swipe at any part of him it could reach.

Devenshire took a precious second longer to complete his spell, and suddenly, he thrust his hands out, the heels pressed tightly together and the fingers splayed into claw-like positions. A massive bolt of blue energy shot from his combined palms to strike the creature in mid-leap and hold it in the air.

He held the powers as long as he could and when he could hold the spell no longer, he let his hands drop to his sides as he collapsed to his knees, his heart pounding in his chest, his breath heaving in his lungs as he fought to compose himself. His body felt as weary as if he had fought a hundred such creatures bare handed. Shaking his head once sharply, he lifted his eyes to find the creature still floating above the floor, encased in the blue aura of his magic. The massive release had left him drained, and now all he could do was watch and pray that he had managed to pull in enough energy to defeat the evil spawn.

The creature was encompassed in a shifting globe of mystical energy. Tiny lightning bolts danced an irregular pattern all around the globe as his magic sought to overpower the magic that had summoned the creature. It howled in rage, and perhaps pain, as it was caught between the two forces. The blue was tinged with red in several areas as the two forces battled for dominance.

For what seemed an eternity, and yet ended far too soon to give Devenshire even the remotest hope he had succeeded, the blue aura faded and the creature crashed to the floor. It curled into a tight ball, hugging itself against whatever pain it was capable of feeling.

Devenshire slumped forward in exhaustion. The creature was still here. It was drained, perhaps injured, but still alive and still a threat. There was no more power within him to strike out. It would be much longer than he had felt before he could unleash another spell. Perhaps, if he had his sword, he might be able to inflict enough physical damage to kill it, but his sword was on the other side of the room, and he knew he didn't have the strength to retrieve it.

Slowly the creature uncurled itself and struggled to get to its feet. Even without the ability to portray facial expressions, it was obviously in a great deal of pain. It stood hunched over, its arms hanging loosely in front of it as it continued to breathe heavily. It kept its eyes on Devenshire as it continued to summon its strength.

Devenshire felt a remoteness form around his perceptions, a sort of detachment from his senses. Had he already lost that much blood? It didn't seem like he had, and yet he felt his mind begin to loosen its grip on consciousness.

The creature pulled itself upright and took a step toward him. Devenshire knew there were no energies left within him. He looked about him for something he might use as a weapon or shield and found nothing useful. As his eyes swept the room, he spied his sword near the desk. It was tantalizingly close, and yet seemed a realm away.

The creature took another tentative step as though it were testing its balance and might. Its hissing breath was growing stronger, and the tremble in its limbs began to subside. It was regaining its strength and would attack very soon.

As drained as he felt, he knew he had to try to get to his weapon. Calling on his sapped powers, he locked his gaze on his sword and made a motion with his left hand. He felt the faint flicker of his powers deep within himself, and knew that it was not nearly enough to summon the sword from its resting place.

The creature howled in an ear-splitting shriek as it fought to reclaim its strength. It kept its burning gaze on Devenshire. It stood in a slumped position, its chest heaving as if it were having trouble breathing. It stood still, eyes boring into its' human opponent. Devenshire knew it was gathering its waning power to attack again, and he quickly turned his full attention to his sword and repeated the motion, forcing his mind to block out everything else save for his sword.

Again, there came a flutter of something deep within him, and the sword seemed to begin to rock back and forth, but it did not move from where it lay. Devenshire tilted his head forward and locked his eyes to the weapon before repeating the gesture and straining to force the steel to come to him.

The creature took two faltering steps toward the human, paused to take a deep breath, and then took two more steps. Its ragged breathing came as a hissing sound, no longer able to spare the energy to growl as it slowly raised its claws to attack position.

A wave of dizziness swept over Devenshire as he poured more concentration into his powers, forcing them to obey his commands. His stamina was fading quickly, and with it, the fading reserves of his powers. He briefly considered abandoning his abilities in favor of physically rising and crossing to where his weapon lay, but he doubted his physical strength would fair any better than his mystical strength.

Devenshire felt the cold bitter taste of his own fear and that angered him. The almost unresponsive flicker of his powers angered him. The frustration with Darkseed returned and added fuel to his emotions. He had faced so many opponents in his life, faced so many obstacles, and always managed to win. Now he was faced with defeat, true defeat, at the hands of a creature that was not even of this earth. The thought of so many victories, so many accomplishments being canceled out by this mystical creature of evil origins angered him most of all.

No. He would not submit. He would not allow death to claim him here, now. There was still much he wished to do, and wished to experience. He would be damned if he would let it end like this.

Suddenly, something within him flared up and began to burn as if his blood had become liquid fire. Rage raced through him unchecked, and he embraced it. It reminded him of the tingle of his powers, but this was so much stronger, so much more intense. It was a raw mystical energy that seemed boundless, and it coursed through him like fire.

Clenching his teeth under the tremendous weight of his rage, and with his limbs trembling in the grip of this newfound power, he thrust his left fist forward toward his sword then quickly opened his hand and flipped the palm up.

The creature took another set of weak steps and towered over the knelt man. The human did not even look up as it raised its claw and aimed for his throat. With a growl of pained satisfaction, it swung its claw with the intent of ripping the human's throat out.

Just as the talons were mere inches from their target, something struck its wrist and its claw suddenly separated from its arm to go spinning away, spraying the purple ooze in all directions. It screamed in agony as it staggered back. It saw the stumped end of its arm gushing blood and looked back up at the human to see him climbing slowly to his feet, his sword held before him dripping its blood.

Devenshire watched the creature pause to look from its clawless limb to his sword and back again, as if it could not believe what had just happened. Truth be told, he was having a hard time remembering exactly what had happened. Somehow, his sword had suddenly appeared in his left hand, and he had reacted out of instinct. It was faint, almost a blur.

He could not waste time on such matters. The creature was wounded, and his own rage drove him now. Without a second thought, he stepped forward and ran the tip of his sword through the creature's chest, jerked it free and ran it through the creature again. Each thrust resulted in the creature screaming out in that unholy voice and backing another step away.

Devenshire was not swayed by the creature's cries of pain as he repeatedly pulled his blade free of the creature's body only to perforate it again in another area. He hardly noticed that with each strike, the creature's howls grew weaker, and it no longer backed away, but simply stood on unsteady legs and took each new attack. Finally, he withdrew his sword and swung it around in a long arch that severed the creature's head from the rest of its foul body. Just as the last tendrils of flesh that held the head to the body were separated, there was a bright flash of red energy, and the sheer force of the released magic that had kept the creature alive momentarily overcame Devenshire.

He felt the cold evil of the magic wash over him and was staggered by its brute strength. He staggered back under the impact and called on his own regenerated powers to hold the foul energies at bay. Just as he felt that the raw power of the magic of the creature would overcome him, it faded leaving him drained, even more so than before, and he crumpled to his knees, unable to stand any longer.

The creature's headless body twitched and convulsed about on the floor, spilling more of its foul looking, and even fouler smelling blood into a large pool. Its head lay across the room, and the jaw worked as if it were trying to growl or suck in air it no longer needed. Then the head and the body both ceased moving, relaxing into death, if such a state existed for such a creature.

Devenshire felt weary, drained to his core, and he found himself wondering how he was even managing to remain on his knees as he studied the two pieces of the creature before him. Once his powers returned, he would have to perform a Spell of Knowledge to see if he could discern who or what had spawned the creature, although he already had a very good idea where the creature had come from.

Suddenly the creature began to shift, become transparent. Devenshire watched in weary awe as the two pieces of the creature began to fade in a shimmering red light until only the light remained which quickly faded out leaving no trace of the creature, not even the puddles of purplish ooze that had passed for its blood. There would be no examination, nothing to force his powers into to try to unlock the secrets of its origins. Whoever or whatever had sent the creature was taking no chances and had removed all traces of the creature's existence.

With a weary sigh, Devenshire bowed his head to try to gather his tiny remnants of strength. Now that the fury had passed, he was even weaker than before. He noticed the pool of red that dripped from his limp fingers to a puddle on the floor.

The white material was deep red from the four rips in the bicep to the rolled cuff at his forearm. He also noticed that the gashes no longer pained him and that his entire body seemed to have gone numb. His vision began to swim around sickeningly, refusing to focus. His head seemed to buzz, and he realized that he was on the verge of losing consciousness. Without knowing where the others had gone, and not knowing when they would return, he could not afford to black out now. For all he knew, the bandits may have already captured them, and if that were the case, they would need help very quickly.

Shaking his head violently, he tried to rise to his feet. Now was not the time for infirmities of the flesh. There would be time for rest and recuperation later. Halfway to his feet, something within him betrayed his will, and he felt himself pitching forward to the floor. His mind clawed at the slick walls of consciousness but could find no purchase.

He tried to push himself up, fighting to keep himself awake, but the last of his physical strength left him, and he collapsed back to the floor, his mind finally losing its last superficial grip on consciousness.

As the blackness claimed him, he wondered which would happen first: would he bleed to death from his wounds or would more of the bandits return, find their dead and mutilated companions, and decide to take retribution upon his dying form. With an odd, delirious based inner chuckle, he realized either scenario would end in his death, and he knew no amount of anger or rage would save him this time.

CHAPTER TWENTY-ONE

SHANTIRA WANDERED THROUGH the crowded nighttime streets of Lirpa in a true state of awe. She gave no conscious thought to her direction or any destination, just to walk through the streets that teamed with more life and variety than she had ever known, made such considerations unnecessary.

The feelings that had swam about her earlier this day as she looked out her window only multiplied and coursed around and through her. She knew her face bore the wide-eyed expression of a childish villager, but she didn't care. The rawness of the city, and those who lived within it, consumed her and swept her mind away to places her body could never go. She sensed the dark seductiveness of this place, and the power of that left her aroused in ways she had never even imagined existed.

Her eyes took in each face, each building, and each vendor cart she encountered, taking delight in each new encounter. With every step, she felt more and more as if she belonged here, as if her life to this point had simply been preparing her for her true existence... here.

The men she encountered were darker, more seductive than any man she had ever met... even Devenshire. Even the women bore a certain air about them that she had never seen. She recognized the women of the night for what they were, the noble women in all their radiant finery, and all the classes of women in between. They all touched her and none of their shortcomings registered on her mind, as if all her conceptions of right and wrong had been magically suspended. There were no good people here, no bad people - just people.

"It is quite a fascinating place, is it not?" a deep voice asked.

Startled, Shantira spun to find the owner of the voice that seemed to have singled itself out of the discordant chorus of voices around her to make her know the owner had spoken to her. A tall, thin, elegantly dressed man stepped from the shadows of an alleyway to walk to her with a grace that left her impressed.

"Yes it is. It is unlike any place I have ever encountered," Shantira replied as her eyes left the tall stranger to take in more of the city, feeling satisfaction at the sights, yet hungering for more.

"There is danger here, as well," the man stated.

With a crooked smile, Shantira nodded. "Aye. That there is."

A remote part of her mind acknowledged the multitudes of danger that were thickly layered around her, but she could not find the concern for such danger, only the thrill of excitement at being immersed in it.

"Be careful. Such danger should never be taken lightly," the man replied, a strange, low tone entering his voice.

Shantira turned her eyes to the stranger and noticed for the first time the very pale blue color of his eyes. Something deep in her mind called to her, trying to remind her of something she should recognize in the pale color of the man's face, the even paler hue of his eyes, but the recollection would not come. She felt as though she had recently seen this man, and the sight had troubled her, but the connection would not form in her mind.

The man tilted his head slightly as he locked his gaze deep into Shantira's and something within her fluttered with a sensation that raced to all points of her body. She could not stop the gasp of sexual sensation that rippled back through her.

"No... no... it should... should not be," she whispered, her eyes growing wide and her jaw going slack as her breath became shallow.

The man smiled a wicked smile and cast his gaze around the street, taking it all in with a majestic sweep of his arm. "But the danger touches you, does it not?" he asked, his voice low and husky. She tried to recall if she had seen his lips form the words. His voice seemed to caress her brain as if coming from her mind instead of his lips. She raised her trembling hand to her throat and felt her fingertips caress the suddenly warm flesh of her upper chest. She was remotely amazed at how her own touch seemed to fan the flames of her already mounting passion.

"Y-yes."

He turned his eyes back to hers, the intense gaze flowing hotly through her. It was as if he were inside her, touching every part of her with his eyes and leaving every area raw with pleasure, and the whispered hint of even greater pleasures just out of her reach. Her fingers traced a light trail down to the first fastener of her blouse, and without her conscious command, unfastened it to let the cool night air drift across her fevered flesh.

The man's eyes dropped briefly to the now exposed upper slope of her breasts and watched as they heaved under her heavy breathing.

As his eyes returned to hers she gasped again as another wave of pure passion rippled through her, and she found herself wanting to give herself to this man, to take his slightest whim and make it hers to fulfill to the ends of all else.

"You are untouched?" he asked.

She nodded slowly, unable to speak.

"You have never experienced the true pleasures that your body can provide," he said with no question to his tone.

"No... never," she whispered as she took an involuntary step toward the man.

"But you sorely wish to."

"Oh gods... yes," she almost cried.

"I can show you such pleasures. Both what you have imagined and ones you could not have possibly imagined."

"P-please?" she pleaded as she stepped even closer to him.

"It would seem that we have need of each other. You seek something from me as I seek something from you. We should come together and help each other obtain what we seek."

"Yes," she breathed heavily as she rose up on her toes to bring her face closer to his. Her lips ached to touch his, her body burned for his touch. It took what was left of her self-control not to rip their clothes from their bodies and force this mysterious man to take her now.

The man wrapped one arm around her waist and pulled her close to him. She whimpered as her body trembled and a mounting tension deep within her lower body doubled. She closed her eyes as the flames of her passion licked her body, burning, yet pleasing her. His lips touched her cheek, and she felt the chill of their coolness, but the oddity of this did not register on her fevered mind. The mere touch of his lips raced through her and added to the fire that burned through her, as well.

His lips slid along her jaw to her ear, and his voice sounded low and seductive as his other hand reached up, and his chilled fingers traced an intricate pattern across the skin of her neck and throat. She slid her arms up his back and pulled herself even closer to him. "Come with me. What I have planned for you is too exotic for the eyes of these paltry mortals."

She gasped as her thighs trembled with a sensation she had never known. It was as if some great tightening knot deep within her was swelling, threatening to explode, and she sought to release whatever was coiled tightly within her. Her mind swam as no alcohol had ever made it swim before. The pleasure that coursed through her was unlike anything she was even remotely prepared for, and she found herself submitting herself to it and the promise of release.

He released her and turned to walk back down the alley from which he had appeared. Shantira stifled the cry of pain that threatened to burst from her lips at the sudden separation from him. As he had stepped away from her, the sensations that had been raging through her had suddenly ceased and left her feeling emptier than she had ever felt in her life. She knew she would follow him, regardless of where he went. She had to have more of the feelings he gave her and would stop at nothing to have them again. Without hesitation, or a second glance, she found her trembling legs propelling her down the alley.

~*~

Brianna and Zandorth wound through the streets, intent on their near frantic search for Shantira. They both knew of the dangers that could befall her here and each imagined a danger more bone chilling than the one before it.

"Where in the realms could she have gone?" Zandorth growled as he scanned each face, each nook and cranny of the street around him, for any sign of Shantira.

"It is a large city, Zan," Brianna replied while she, too, continued to scan every area within sight.

"Of all the times for Devenshire to disappear! The one time his blasted powers could be of use, and he is not present!" he growled in growing frustration.

Brianna suppressed a smile at that comment. The more mischievous parts of her nature wanted to point out to the warrior that he was wishing for Devenshire to use the very powers he found so distasteful which, in turn, would simply infuriate him. The situation was too serious for such behavior, so she let the moment pass.

"We will find her," she replied instead.

They continued to search covering as much ground as quickly as possible. They had early on discounted the course of asking the citizens of Lirpa for any help in locating the missing woman. As a whole, the people of Lirpa were concerned with only their own ends and means. Everything else was of a secondary issue with them. They checked every tavern they encountered, each shop of whatever means and found no sign of her.

As the search progressed, and more time passed with no sign of Shantira, even Brianna had to acknowledge the panic that was growing within her. She had hoped to find Shantira quickly, but with each passing moment, the danger to her grew. She found herself agreeing with Zandorth in wishing Devenshire had been present. Even with his limited command of the Mystical Arts, he would have found her quickly, or at least pointed them in the direction they needed to go to find her.

Finally, the duo found themselves in the heart of the city, and they paused to gather their bearings and thoughts. The massive throng of people had been growing steadily as they neared the center of the city and now they found themselves amid a flood of bodies. Spotting Shantira in this sea would be near impossible.

Zandorth finally voiced what she had been thinking for the past hour. "We should separate, search for the child on our own. We can cover more ground that way."

She nodded as she continued to scan the crowd. "Perhaps you are right," she replied.

"I will go this way," his deep voice thundered as he indicated the direction he intended to go. "You go that way, and we will work our way back to the inn. Perhaps, by the time we return, Devenshire will have returned."

She knew the dangers in separating, but could not ignore the wisdom in his plan. She gave the plan only the briefest of consideration before nodding. "Agreed. Be careful Zan."

Zandorth gave a curt nod as he moved off to begin his search.

She watched him weave through the crowd and felt a sliver of trepidation slide into her mind. She was well aware of the dangers of the city, and was very capable of defending herself, but having the massive warrior at her side had been much more comforting than she had realized.

She shook off the concern and turned to begin her own search. She forced her mind to focus on only two things: Finding Shantira and keeping alert for any danger that might befall her.

She just hoped they found her before it was too late.

~*~

Xavier cried out in rage as he staggered back from the Orb of Vision. Fury washed over him in crimson waves and threatened to carry him away. It took all his fading control not to snatch up the Orb and dash it to the ground. Pure rage seethed from every pour as he stalked around the up righted log that held the Orb. His limbs trembled with fatigue and fury as he considered what had just transpired. With all his might, he wrestled with his anger, fought to subdue it, to channel it, to keep it from driving him.

Devenshire! The trap had been perfect; fool proof. Yet the bastard lived! He knew he should have been conserving his energy, saving his powers for the Stones. However, the temptation had been too strong, and he had thought to only use a small amount of energy to kill Devenshire.

Growling in barely subdued rage, he continued to pace and played back the events, searching for the flaw that had caused his plan to fail.

He had used the Orb to find Devenshire stalking toward the inn.

He learned of the bandits laying in wait for him and saw his opportunity to strike. He watched as the bandits attacked, and were quickly captured by Devenshire. The bungling fools had not put much thought into their attack, and he wasn't the least bit surprised when it failed. Idiots!

When he had re-animated the corpse of the bandit, he had thought the sight alone would shock Devenshire into immobility, and thereby allow the corpse or one of the other bandits to finish him off. He had not expected Devenshire to unleash a counter spell, which had canceled out his spell. It should have been impossible for Devenshire to do such a thing, yet it had happened.

In anger, he had conjured the demon and watched in delight as it attacked the bandit. He had to admit to the sheer thrill of the kill as it had ripped the bandit's throat out.

When it had wounded Devenshire, Xavier had felt his joy rocket to the heavens. Then the bastard unleashed an enhanced counter spell that had weakened the demon, allowing Devenshire time to retrieve his sword and kill the demon in short order.

How? Devenshire's skill and knowledge of the Mystical Arts was many levels below his own. There should have been no way for him to counter any of his spells, yet he had done it. Had he underestimated Devenshire? Had the rumors about him been misleading? With an angry shake of his head, Xavier discounted those explanations. The answer beckoned to him from the back of his mind, but he could not force himself to face that answer. To admit to that explanation would link him to a weakness he no longer believed himself capable. Yet the truth was there, and he could not evade it for long.

With a howl of rage, he stormed around the small clearing in the forest and let the anger claim him. His group had traveled all day, with Xavier lounging and napping in his carriage. They made good time and put more distance between themselves and Devenshire's group. Their diversion to Lirpa had taken them slightly off course.

They made camp, and after a hearty meal, Xavier had sought out another clearing in order to check on Devenshire's progress. That's when he saw his opportunity to strike out at him and had been handed a stunning defeat.

As he stalked around the clearing, the truth of how Devenshire had managed to best him haunted his thoughts and angered him even further. His previous concerns about Devenshire's presence deepened as he realized he could never allow him to reach the Duvall Retreat to confront him. He decided that he would have to be very careful, very calculating in dealing with Devenshire and use other means to stop him.

He stopped pacing and moved back to the small fire he had

conjured. He forced himself to try to relax as he reached out into the invisible Mystical Tides that moved about the entire realm. He was stunned to find he could not quite connect with the Tides. Normally, he had no difficulty, but now he wondered if he could even cast the simplest of spells with the level of difficulty he was having.

His anger, the rage coursing through him, was distracting and not allowing him to focus. He took several more deep breaths and continued to wrestle his rage under control. It was one of the few areas of his life he had yet to master completely. Once his temper was loosed, it was extraordinarily difficult to contain again.

It took a long time for him to finally tame the beast that was his anger. Finally, it howled in defiance one last time as he forced it under its chains in his mind. With the beast once again under control, he turned his mind back to the Mystical Tides and was delighted when his consciousness slipped easily into them. Once immersed, he was able to find the presence he sought and send out a mental command. *Cyrus! Attend me!*

After only a slight pause, the presence responded reluctantly. *Yes, my Lord, at once.*

Xavier smiled. Cyrus did not like serving him and made a very valiant effort of concealing that when they were face to face. Yet in the Mystical tides, there were no secrets, no lies, and it was obvious the level of dislike Cyrus held for him. It was amusing to watch the man try to conceal the truth.

"You underestimated him." a voice sounded.

Xavier spun, his connection to the Mystical Tides now severed. Someone had dared approach him unawares. Foolish to say the least. Xavier searched every nook and cranny of the clearing for the doomed soul.

No one was present.

Xavier scanned the clearing again, but could find no trace of anyone. His eyes narrowed as he considered if he had actually heard a voice, or if his own imagination were playing tricks on him.

He reached out with his powers and found no trace of anything out of the ordinary. There was no one here. After several moments, he turned slowly back to the fire and gazed deep into the flames, waiting for Cyrus' arrival. He continued to force his mind and body back to a calm, clear state.

"Devenshire will be the end of you," the voice sounded again. Xavier spun in the direction of the voice, his anger rising at the petulance.

"Who is here?" he demanded.

No answer came.

Xavier began formulating a proper punishment for whoever had decided to tempt their fates in this way. Xavier reached out with his senses for the location of the intruder, but felt nothing.

"You must destroy him," the voice said.

"Who are you?!" Xavier demanded.

"How soon you have forgotten," the voice replied, and Xavier began to feel a shift in the currents of the Dark Magic.

Then he knew.

Only one being could cause such a shift. A cold dread rippled through him as he considered the identity of his hidden visitor.

"Baldar," Xavier said without question. He stood still, waiting. He began pulling in on himself, preparing himself for what may come next.

A strange breeze began blowing about the clearing that seemed to draw all light from the area. The breeze grew into a wind that rustled the trees and caused the flames to flutter in angry response to the threat of having it extinguished.

Xavier squinted against the growing wind as leaves, twigs and other debris began to swirl about the vicinity. He forced himself to stand still, building his stores of dark energy should they be needed. Blackness enveloped the edges of the clearing, as if the trees, the sky, and the stars had suddenly been swept out of existence. The blackness began moving in toward Xavier, blotting out everything in its path.

He found himself having to exert more effort to keep from being moved by the growing wind. He steeled himself against the encroaching darkness, forced himself not to feel fear for the Dark Mystic would certainly sense that fear, feeding upon it.

"Enough! Show yourself!" Xavier shouted over the howl of the wind.

The wind only grew in strength and began shifting directions until Xavier felt himself being pushed and pulled in several directions as the wind continued to whip about him.

"I am not one of your mindless minions, Xavier! You do not command me!" the voice replied, seeming to come from every direction at once.

The wind continued to grow in strength until the force of it whipped the flames of the fire out, pitching everything into total darkness. Larger pieces of debris joined the maelstrom, and the force increased. The leaves and twigs that struck him stung more and more as the force driving them increased. Xavier raised his right arm to shield his eyes from the swirling cloud of debris. Along with the howl of the wind came a foul odor, one that was not born of anything of this realm, and Xavier knew that the Dark Mystic had come.

Xavier felt the air being sucked from the clearing, and the force of the wind began to push down on him. His lungs burned from the heat of the air, and his legs trembled under the weight of trying to remain on his feet as the storm continued to grow in strength. Pulling in his

THE DEVENSHIRE CHRONICLES

consciousness, he made several quick hand gestures, and a red ball of flaming light formed around him, sealing him off from the maelstrom of dark magic raging within the clearing.

"Nor am I one of yours!" Xavier replied, knowing he would be heard over the cacophony of the storm.

"You would dare use our gift against us!" the bodiless voice shouted back.

"I would dare defend myself against any who seeks to attack me!" Xavier challenged in return.

"You are very bold. Foolishly so."

"That is a matter of perception," Xavier replied calmly, silently slipping a little more power into his protective spell.

For several moments, the storm continued to rage, and Xavier could feel the dark powers probing his shield for any weakness. Obviously, there were none found as the storm began to fade. Xavier resisted the urge to smile triumphantly. There was a large difference between standing up to one of the Dark Mystics and being flagrantly arrogant.

As the maelstrom continued to dwindle, Xavier maintained his protective shield. One of the most important lessons he had learned from his long association with the Dark Mystics was to never let ones guard down, regardless of the circumstances. He had seen too many students of the Dark Arts lose their lives, or worse, by relaxing in the face of what appeared to be descent. The Dark Mystics had many zombie-like servants that had once been students of Dark Arts. Being condemned to such an existence, to have your soul trapped in a decaying body you could no longer control was certainly a fate worse than death.

Finally, the winds whispered into silence, and the clearing was silent, still and dark save for the faint reddish glow from Xavier's spell. Xavier sensed the Dark Mystic in the clearing even though he could not see him with his physical eyes. He could sense a hesitation in the Dark Mystic as if he were waiting for something. Xavier maintained an expressionless look on his face while inside he knew Baldar was waiting for Xavier to lower his shield.

"The storm has passed," Baldar finally said, and this time Xavier's eyes shot to the area of the clearing where he knew the Dark Mystic stood in complete darkness, waiting.

"Aye," Xavier nodded slowly, smiled, and lapsed back into silence. He could feel Baldar's irritation growing and calculated just how much further he could push this confrontation before he stepped across that unseen line between being bold and being arrogant. While he was sure enough of his skills that he would risk an occasional display of brashness, he was also wise enough to know that such displays could be taken too far.

278 | T O M   S E C H R I S T

"How far do you intend to carry this foolishness?" Baldar asked as the irritation carried plain upon the tones of his voice.

"Perhaps I could ask the same of you, Dark One. You attacked first," Xavier answered.

The irritation within Baldar crossed into the beginnings of anger and Xavier knew he had carried this display about as far as he could without risking the wrath of the other Dark Mystics.

"We have business to attend. We have no time for childish games," Baldar retorted.

"Agreed," Xavier replied and mentally released his hold on the spell. Within two heartbeats, the shimmering red of his protective shield faded pitching the clearing into utter darkness. Xavier glanced up and was relieved to see the black velvet of the night sky complete with the twinkling stars.

The small fire had been extinguished and the logs scattered. With a wave of his hand, the logs were brought back, stacked, and re-ignited. As the fire sputtered back to life, the light pushed the shadows back to a point where a tall, thin, dark robed figure could be seen at the edges of the light's reach.

The Dark Mystic stood still, arms folded into the sleeves of his black robes that were adorned with the various charms and symbols of the Dark Arts. Xavier allowed the smile he had been suppressing to spread slowly across his lips as he returned to his chair.

Baldar's black eyes bore into Xavier's back as he stepped from the shadows of the clearing. "You presume a great deal."

"As do you. Do not forget that you need me as much as I need you," Xavier replied.

"What makes you think that the Dark Mystics need a human, even one as skilled as yourself?"

"Because the Dark Mystics cannot manipulate the Mystical Arts, and it is the Mystical Arts which will be needed to unlock the secrets of the Stones," Xavier replied evenly, secure in the facts of his statement.

He could feel Baldar bristle under the reminder that there was something the Dark Mystics could not do and would need the help of a mortal to accomplish. Xavier knew he was walking an exceedingly tight line between being confident and foolish, and the thrill of excitement at doing so coursed through him like alcohol. Perhaps one day he would become too confident, too sure of his standing with the Dark Mystics and go too far.

But, he reflected with an inner smile, today would not be that day.

"I am glad you have mentioned that, for it is the Stones that bring me here. What is your progress?" Baldar asked, saving face and disarming a dangerous situation for both of them.

"I have made little progress since I acquired the Stones. I have had other matters to attend," Xavier replied calmly.

"Such as Daimion Devenshire?" Baldar asked.

Xavier felt himself tense under the mocking tone Baldar used in mentioning that name and fought to control his emotions. He knew that Baldar received the reaction he had hoped.

"You really should have disposed of him seasons ago when you had the opportunity," Baldar said absently, as he bent over to pick up the Orb of Vision and set it upright. He extended a gray hand with long nails to trace a small circle atop the Orb.

"I did not see the need in such an action at the time. He was harmless, of no threat to me. He still is not," Xavier said, trying to keep the tension from his voice, yet knowing that it still carried to Baldar's senses.

"Indeed?" Baldar asked swinging his black eyes to Xavier. "Perhaps you were merely toying with him earlier when you sent the demon after him,"

"Perhaps," Xavier replied evenly, locking eyes with Baldar.

"Or perhaps your tie to him makes it more difficult than you anticipated."

"That tie ceased to exist seasons ago. It is of no consequence now," Xavier replied.

Baldar chuckled as he straightened up and regarded Xavier with amused arrogance. "Is it? Then why not kill him now and eliminate that obstacle?"

"I will destroy him when I feel the time is right for such an action. He will not be a problem," Xavier replied.

"Find some other human to toy with, to amuse your sadistic humor. Do not take any chances with Devenshire. He poses a greater threat to you than you may or may not be aware of, and thereby poses a threat to us," Baldar said, then turned to fully face Xavier and leaned closer to drive his next point home... "And I can promise you that we will sacrifice you to him before he gets to us."

Xavier's eyes narrowed as his anger finally inched to a level he could not control. He bore his heated gaze deeply into the deep pitch of Baldar's pupil-less eyes.

"Devenshire is NOT a problem! I WILL destroy him long before he can interfere with my plans!"

The low cold tone of Xavier's voice was intense enough to reach through the superiority of Baldar's knowledge of his power and caused the Dark Mystic to mentally step back, but he maintained his dead lock with Xavier's cold stare. After a time, he smiled a cold smile as he turned to walk slowly about the clearing, pretending to examine the surroundings.

"Perhaps you will. However, do not toy with him. Kill him quickly. We have much grander plans in the works, and we will not have countless seasons of plotting and planning torn asunder by a paltry mortal!" Baldar said tersely.

Xavier bit down on his anger and called on his intellect. "He is dead already; he simply does not realize it."

Baldar paused to reach up and pluck a leaf from a tree. A cold grin spread across his deep blue lips, revealing blackened teeth. "Arrogant confidence. Very good. It is what drew us to you in the first place."

He examined the leaf. In his cold gray fingers, the leaf instantly began to brown and wither, and within seconds, the leaf had gone from green to brown and now crumbled into tiny fragments, scattering to the light breeze. He rubbed his thumb across his fingers to brush away the remnants of the leaf as he shifted his empty gaze to Xavier. "Do not let it lead you to failure and become the reason we cast you out."

"I will not fail," Xavier replied tightly, bristling under the implied threat issued through the destruction of the leaf.

Baldar's gray, scaled face lost all hints of merriment. "See that you do not. Failure will mean death... or worse!"

In the blink of an eye, he was gone, leaving Xavier with a distinct chill that had nothing to do with the temperature surrounding him. Shaking off the chill, he allowed a cruel smile to play across his features.

Baldar would be the last of the Dark Mystics to bow before him, and the last one to be obliterated by his newly found power; a combined force of the Mystical Arts, the Dark Arts, and his newly found power of the Stones of Andarus.

Let them think that he honestly believed that he would be rewarded for his work with the Stones. He knew the Dark Mystics had watched, and had learned their ways. He knew to the depths of his being that once he handed them the contained power of the Stones, they would destroy him.

Xavier smiled as he picked up the Orb of Vision and returned it to its canvas bag. What a horrible surprise he had in store for them.

His senses alerted him to the use of magic. He tied the bag closed and straightened. Cyrus was calling out to his presence in the Tides. Closing his eyes, he forced his concentration to a fine point, focused on slipping into the Tides.

A tiny blue ball of light formed near him, no bigger than a pea, hovering above the ground. Slowly, the ball began to grow in size as the shimmering blue light increased in brightness. Xavier opened his eyes and looked into the depths of the light.

"Come, Cyrus."

The blue ball expanded to an oval that would just accommodate a person. A man stepped through the oval and bowed to him.

The man was dressed in the robes of the Order of Wizards. It was a fading cult, a fading art, but one that had its advantages over the Mages of the Mystical Arts.

Wizards were a more passive group than Mages. A wizard only used his powers when all other paths failed, and then only enough to accomplish a marginal victory. Such had lead to their eventual downfall as more and more students turned to the Mystical Arts and away from wizardry.

Xavier had studied the Order of Wizards, and he knew that great powers lay within their craft, perhaps even greater than the Mystical Arts. A few wise students maintained their study of wizardry and learned the true depths of power that lay within that study. With a cruel smile, Xavier recalled how they all served him.

"You wished to see me, my Lord?" Cyrus said as he bowed. The wizard wasn't truly standing before him. This was a mystical projection brought to Xavier through their combined use of the tides. Cyrus was still physically at the Duval Retreat, but his mind - his consciousness - had left his body, traveled through the Mystical Tides and was now standing before him. The image was shimmering, transparent in some parts and very spectral looking, as though he were a ghost.

"Yes, Cyrus. I have a task for you," Xavier replied.

Cyrus was advanced in seasons. His once black hair was now streaked with more gray than black. Deep lines had creased the flesh around his brown eyes. While he appeared to be past his physical prime, Xavier knew that he was just entering the peak of his powers. The aging wizard was not very tall, not very muscular in build, and what build he did have, was hidden by the flowing dark blue robes of his order. There was no remarkable inner strength evident in his eyes or his stance, and to simply look at the man would lead one to think him to be of little consequence. With an inward smile, Xavier knew that he could not have designed a more perfect cover for a powerful wizard. Cyrus's appearance would lull an opponent into underestimating him and therein, would lay their critical error in judgment.

Cyrus tilted his head slightly and simply watched Xavier, waiting for him to speak. There was respect in his stance, but not with the soulless fear that his other servants regarded him. At first, Xavier had been angered by the older man's refusal to cower before him, but as time had passed, he had come to respect the way Cyrus could pay homage to him without degrading himself.

"There is someone who is following me with intentions of interfering in my work. I wish for you to destroy him," Xavier said.

Cyrus dropped his eyes to the ground briefly, as he slowly nodded. "I take it that this someone presents a unique problem for you to call on me to eliminate him for you."

Xavier felt his anger flash briefly at Cyrus's presumptuous attitude in his statement. It was another aspect of the wizard that Xavier had found himself growing to admire. While he served Xavier faithfully, he did not follow him blindly.

"You might say such."

"Who is it?" Cyrus asked in that ever-present calm that seemed to predominate every action the man took.

"A man by the name of Daimion Devenshire."

Cyrus's eyes widened slightly at the mention of Devenshire's name, and a faint smile tugged at the corners of his mouth. "Daimion Devenshire," he repeated as he slowly nodded. "A unique problem, indeed."

"Do not tell me that you fear him," Xavier stated with an edge to his voice.

Cyrus shook his head before answering, and Xavier wondered if there was anything the man ever said that was not preceded by a thoughtful moment.

"I do not fear him. He is a minor mage and poses no threat, at least not to me."

Xavier's eyes flashed at Cyrus. "What is that supposed to imply?"

Cyrus shrugged. "It is not supposed to imply anything. It was a mere statement of fact."

"Then explain yourself," Xavier demanded.

"I know of your unique ties to Devenshire. The very nature of those ties would make him a difficult problem for you," Cyrus replied.

"The ties you speak of were broken long ago, and Devenshire is not a difficult problem for me. I simply have other matters that require my full attention. If the task is too great for you, all you have to do is admit to such," Xavier said with a hard edge to his voice.

"I stand corrected, Sire. I meant no implication of weakness on your part," Cyrus quickly corrected. Xavier narrowed his eyes at the wizard as he considered if Cyrus truly stood corrected or was simply avoiding a confrontation that would gain neither of them anything. It was a common tactic used by wizards—seeming to surrender while truly not.

"Devenshire has set himself upon a quest to stop me from reaching my goal. See to it that he does not succeed," Xavier finally said.

Cyrus bowed again with the fluid grace of one who had performed the action for many seasons. "As you command. I shall depart immediately. Do you wish for me to return with proof of his death?"

Xavier considered the question for a moment before letting a hungry smile to come. "Yes. Bring me his head, preferably with a terrified expression frozen into his features by the touch of death."

Cyrus nodded and turned to step back into the oval, but Xavier stayed him with a raised hand."He is traveling with a Warrior of the Ancient Class and two women. Bring the women to me alive."

"Alive?" Cyrus asked with the closest thing to surprise Xavier had seen on his face.

Xavier smiled. "The women will provide excellent entertainment for me."

Cyrus nodded, and Xavier could feel the disapproval within the wizard. It was no secret that Cyrus found Xavier's eternal thirst for taking women distasteful. No doubt, another leftover by-product of the Order of Wizard's training.

"Anything else?" Cyrus asked.

"No," Xavier replied.

Cyrus nodded again and stepped through the oval, very quickly, Xavier recognized. The oval very swiftly collapsed in on itself and vanished in a tiny flash of light.

Xavier hoisted the canvas bag over his shoulder and summoned the power that would extinguish the fire. Wrapped in his beloved darkness once again, he set out for his camp. Walking through the darkened forest allowed his mind to finally reach the peace he had struggled for after failing to destroy Devenshire.

Thoughts of the future came to him, and he found the visions dancing in his mind very pleasant, almost delicious. Devenshire's preserved head hanging on his wall, Krahl spending the rest of his life fighting matches in his warriors' training circle, and the two women bound, naked, and begging for his male attentions. Other intoxicating visions came—Baldar on his knees, beaten and pleading for his life before Xavier and then...

...the rest of the realm.

CHAPTER TWENTY-TWO

EVEN BEFORE HE ROUNDED the corner that would lead him back to the inn, Zandorth knew something was terribly wrong. People were scurrying about, moving in any direction that would take them away from the inn. Vendors quickly moved their carts, and there wasn't a whore in sight.

Krahl stopped at the corner and took a moment to watch the people all but running away. It reminded him of the way a pack of rats would scurry for cover when suddenly thrust into the light.

He stepped carefully around the corner and instantly saw the reason for the citizen's quick departure. Five white steeds bearing the colors of the Royal Guard were tied outside the inn with a line of Lirpa sheriffs standing guard in the street to make sure no one entered.

Whatever had happened within the inn was serious, very serious, if the Royal Guard had been summoned. The Royal Guard was responsible for maintaining law and order within the kingdom. The men that made up their ranks were the best soldiers in the kingdom, and each one handpicked by King Lorderon for the purpose of enforcing his laws.

Each city had a constable with sheriffs under their charge to keep the peace. In most cases, however, the constable and his sheriffs were little better than the brigands they sought to control.

In Lirpa, the constable was a man of integrity, but his sheriffs were rogues, hardly above the criminals they had been charged to arrest. It was widely known that the sheriffs could be bought. They would turn their eyes from just about any crime, if enough gold coins were laid in their palms. Those who were not busy having their attentions bought were often involved in the very crimes they had been charged to stop. The Royal Guard served as the last line of defense in keeping something that resembled law and order. However, since the Royal Guard's numbers were exceedingly small for them to be everywhere all the time, they were only called out on the most desperate of crimes.

Moving toward the inn, Zandorth couldn't help but realize that one of the desperate crimes that would warrant the presence of the Royal Guard was murder. He needed answers. He singled out one of the citizens trying to disappear into the shadows and stayed him with a firm grip on his upper arm.

At first, the man tried to jerk himself free, but then he took in the sight of the behemoth that held him, and realized there was no way he could break free. Still, he had to try. "Release me!" he demanded, trying to make himself sound bigger than he was.

Zandorth's eyes never left the inn as he ignored the bravado. "What has happened here?" he asked.

"I do not know. Release me this instant!" the man snapped in reply. Zandorth increased the pressure he was exerting on the man's bicep and did not have to be looking at him to know the man was wincing in pain.

"My next unanswered questions will leave your arm shattered," Krahl said in a matter-of-fact tone.

"Ow! Stop it! You are hurting me!" the man exclaimed.

Krahl swung his massive head around and fixed his intense gray stare deep into the man's eyes, leaving no doubt in the man's mind about the level of pain he could expect should he choose not to cooperate.

"Death is rampant here! Evil death!" the man finally answered.

"What are you talking about?" Krahl asked tersely.

"Three men have been killed. Two have been horribly mutilated, their bodies rent beyond recognition," the man replied and resumed trying to pull himself free from Zandorth's steel grip.

"Who were they?"

"I do not know. None were from here. Please, release me. I know nothing else," the man squeaked.

Zandorth had many more questions, but he knew the man would not have the answers. He released the man's arm and continued toward the inn. He did not have to look back to know that the man had quickly vanished into the shadows of the night.

As he drew closer to the inn, Zandorth could see that four of the local sheriffs maintained a line outside the inn to prevent any from entering. Zandorth smiled inwardly as he noticed that they looked as anxious to be away from the Royal Guard as the citizens who were quickly scurrying away.

As he approached, one of the sheriffs saw him and stepped

forward to stop him. "Hold. No one may enter here," he said.

Zandorth stopped before him. The sheriff looked the warrior over, taking note of the massive build and the large broadsword at his hip. He looked over at his companions as if to reassure himself that he had some form of help should it be necessary to stop the large man from entering.

"What has happened here?" Zandorth asked as he looked through the open door to try to see what was happening inside. There were no windows on the front of the building, so he could only see what was visible through the door. All he could see were the members of the Royal Guard moving about.

"What concern is it of yours?" the sheriff asked.

"I am staying here. I have companions I am traveling with," Krahl answered shortly.

"You will be given passage to the inn when the Royal Guards have finished. Move along," the sheriff replied.

"I have heard that men have been killed here. Who were they?" Zandorth asked, ignoring the sheriff's order to move along.

"Do not attempt to interfere here or you will be arrested," the sheriff warned, but his voice did not carry the conviction of his words. The sheriff found himself wondering if he, the other sheriffs, and the combined strength of the Royal Guard would even be able to arrest this man.

Zandorth lowered his gaze to the sheriff in front of him and fixed him with a hard look, his gray eyes boring into the smaller man. "I do not seek to interfere. I seek information about my traveling companions. I wish to know if one of those who have been killed is one from my party."

"I do not have time to answer a lot of questions. I do not know the identity of those who have been killed. Now move along. This is your final warning," the sheriff replied. As if to make his point, the man placed his hand on the hilt of his sword, and the other sheriff's did likewise.

Zandorth regarded the other sheriffs before returning his gaze to the one before him. He did not doubt that he could easily fight his way through this line and gain entry to the inn. To do so would only arouse the attention of the Royal Guard and lead to a situation that he wished to avoid.

Zandorth stepped back and began to turn to walk on down the street, when one of the Royal Guards stepped from the door of the inn. "Hold. Did I hear you say you were a guest at this inn?"

Zandorth turned back to face the inn. "Yes."

"A moment of your time, then?" the Guard asked as he stepped out into the street past the line of sheriffs. When he was standing before Zandorth, he took a moment to size the warrior up. Zandorth

THE DEVENSHIRE CHRONICLES

sensed a different caliber of man before him. The sheriffs were undisciplined rogues who took the office of sheriff as only a means to increase their own personal wealth and enjoy a certain amount of immunity from the laws that applied to everyone else. He had gauged their skill with a sword to be no better than an average man.

The man who stood before him now was a different breed. He was dressed in the typical uniform of the Royal Guard; black boots, black breeches with the legs tucked into the boots, a white shirt of fine linen and a blood red tunic with King Lordoron's crest emblazoned across the chest. There was a look in his eyes, and a bearing in his stance that spoke of pride, of discipline, and the conviction of his office. There was no amount of gold in Lirpa that could buy this man's loyalty or skills. As his eyes took in Zandorth, Krahl could see how he was gauging not only the warrior's physical build, but his inner strength as well. This man would be a worthy opponent, and an even more valuable ally.

"What is your name?" the Guard asked.

"I am Zandorth Krahl."

"A warrior of the Ancient Class, I see," the guard replied.

"How do you know this?" Krahl asked.

The guard nodded toward Zandorth's waist. "The emblem on the buckle of your sword belt and the markings on the hilt of your sword," the guard replied, and Krahl found himself saluting the guard's attention to detail. He had missed nothing.

"And you are?" Krahl asked,

"I am Gregory Armand, Captain of His Majesties Royal Guard, Southern detachment, Donovan Province," he replied with all the pride his title deserved.

Zandorth nodded once. "Captain."

"How many were you traveling with?" Armand asked.

"Three. A man and two women," he replied.

"Their names?

"The Lady Brianna Standish, Shantira Dubrie, and Daimion Devenshire, all from Prothtow Province."

Zandorth watched the guard closely as he said each name, looking for some reaction that would tell him if any of those were among the deceased inside. There was definite recognition at the mention of Brianna's name, and of course, there should have been. There was no recognition at the mention of Shantira's name, but there was definitely recognition at the mention of Devenshire's name.

"Did you say Daimion Devenshire?" Armand asked, his brow furrowing deeply.

"Aye."

Zandorth watched as Armand tried to sort out where he had heard Devenshire's name before. It definitely rang a bell in the man's mind.

288 | T O M   S E C H R I S T

"This, Daimion Devenshire, how long have your known him?" Armand asked carefully.

"A little over one season now. Why?"

"Do you know if he has ever been to Lirpa before?" he asked, ignoring Zandorth's question.

"I believe he once resided here. I do not know for sure. I know very little of his past before I met him," Zandorth replied. "Why?"

"When do you expect Devenshire to return?" Armand asked, again ignoring Zandorth's question.

"I do not know. He left word with the clerk that he was going out and would return later this evening. I had assumed he had already returned. For the third and final time I ask, why?"

Armand didn't ignore the underlying threat in the warrior's voice this time. "My apologies, Sir Krahl, I meant no disrespect. I sometimes forget my manners when a particularly intriguing line of questions has me. Devenshire's name seems familiar to me. I cannot currently place where I have heard it before, at least not at the moment."

Zandorth didn't reply and simply stood watching the captain. Armand mulled over the mystery that the name Devenshire had awoken a few more moments before shifting it to the side of his mind for the time being.

"Describe the scene in the lobby of the inn when you departed this evening," Armand asked.

Zandorth relayed the events of earlier in the evening when they learned Shantira had ventured out on her own. He included the conversation with the desk clerk and their decision to venture out to find the girl.

Armand listened intently, and Krahl knew that every word was being etched into his mind. He would miss little detail, if any.

"You said you were traveling with Lady Standish. I can assume her honor guard is traveling with you, as well?" Armand asked.

Zandorth shook his head. "No. It is only the four of us."

Armand's expression shifted into a combination of suspicion and surprise. "She is traveling without her Honor Guard? How is that possible? Protocol dictates that any member of the Lordship must be accompanied by their Honor Guard at all times."

Zandorth features lightened slightly, and for a moment, it looked as though he would actually smile, but it was not to be. "Lady Brianna can be... determined when she sets her mind to a course of action."

"Zan!"

Zandorth and Armand turned to see Brianna walking toward them. Her expression was strained and Zandorth knew it was all she could do not to break into a run to reach the inn sooner. Obviously, she was experiencing the same dread he had upon reaching the inn.

"What is going on?" she asked when she finally reached him.

"Three men have been killed," Zandorth answered. He did not miss the way the Armand's eyes flashed to him as he said that.

"How do you know that?"

"A man on the street told me," Zandorth answered without looking at him, his gaze still focused on Brianna.

"Daimion?" she asked in controlled tones, but he knew there was far more to her question than she would like to have known.

"I do not know," Zandorth answered as he looked at the inn. "None are permitted passage."

"Shantira?" she asked, obviously wrestling with the growing dread and the stirrings of panic.

Zandorth shook his head. "I do not know."

"Who is this?" Armand asked, cutting into the conversation.

A small burst of anger flashed through her eyes as she turned to face the Royal Guard. "I am Brianna Standish," she answered quickly, letting it be known that she would not be talked about as if she were beneath notice simply because she was a woman.

The edge to her voice did not go unnoticed by Armand and he quickly and accurately executed the mandatory and customary bow when meeting not only a woman, but also a member of the Lordship.

"My most sincere apologies, M'Lady Standish. I meant no disrespect."

She nodded once and turned her attention to the inn. "Any word from Daimion? Any luck finding Shantira?"

Zandorth shook his head, his granite features betraying the dread growing within him as well. "None."

She bit her bottom lip as she studied the front of the inn, as if her piercing green eyes could somehow force it to tell her what she wanted to know. "Where in the realms could he be? Surely, it would not take this long to find Darkseed."

Zandorth caught the flicker in the Armand's eyes. Something in his mind clicked at the mention of Darkseed's name, and a piece of the puzzle seemed to have fallen into place. Zandorth could also see by the stiffening of his posture that the puzzle did not bode well for them.

"Raven Darkseed?" he asked.

Brianna nodded. "Yes. Daimion went out to meet with Darkseed."

Armand seemed suddenly very tense, as if the situation had just developed which caused him to become very alert very quickly. In response to the Armand's heightened sense of alert, Zandorth felt his own sense of urgent alertness form. The situation had just taken a turn that he knew he would not like.

"I must ask the two of you to join the other guests of the inn," he said as he turned and motioned toward the line of sheriffs. Three of them stepped forward and snapped to attention, albeit a very poorly executed form of attention.

"What do you mean? Why?" Brianna asked.

"It is only a matter of preliminaries. All the guests have been taken to the city jail where they are being housed pending further questioning," he replied in tight, controlled tones.

"Are we being arrested?" Brianna asked.

Armand smiled a forced smile and tried to make it seem warm and genuine as he held up his hands. "Oh no, by no means. This is simply a way for us to keep everyone together until we can question them."

Zandorth did not believe him. There was something in his tone that told him that the guard fully intended to hold them both, and the reason for that lay in something to do with Devenshire and Darkseed.

"You have already questioned me," Zandorth said.

"Aye, and I may yet have more questions. I must admit that the investigation has me somewhat preoccupied. More questions may come to mind later," he replied. Zandorth didn't feel as if Armand were out and out lying to them, but he was not being entirely forthcoming with all the details.

Armand turned to the sheriffs. "Escort these two to the jail with the other guests. See that no harm comes to them."

Zandorth took a half step back, his massive right hand drifting across his body toward the hilt of his broadsword. Armand didn't miss the action and quickly turned his full attention to Krahl. "Please, Sire Krahl. Do not be alarmed. You are not being arrested, simply taken to a place of safety until we can piece together what happened here this night."

"I see no need for us to be taken to the jail. We have no intentions of leaving Lirpa this night. We will be available for any questions you may have," Zandorth said resisting the primal urge to draw his sword, or at the very least, lay his hand on its hilt.

Armand saw the situation spiraling out of his control, and Zandorth could see his mind racing to find a way to detain them without the situation turning violent. But he had his duty to perform, and he would perform it regardless of the methods required to do so.

"Please understand. This is part of our investigation. We must talk to all who were present or have any information that may aide us in our investigation. You may have information that you are not even aware of that would be of help to us. You are not being arrested, but if you refuse to cooperate, then you will leave me no choice but to have you arrested."

Zandorth's eyes narrowed as he considered his words. They rang of truth and sincerity, but he could not shake the image of the Captain's eyes at the mention of Darkseed's name. There was something else afoot here, and it screamed at his warrior senses to be warned, to be alert for treachery. He felt his muscles begin to bunch involuntarily, his senses taking in everything they could reach, feeding him with knowledge of what now appeared to be his opponents.

"Very well. We will go," Brianna injected, stepping up beside Zandorth and laying her hand on his massive forearm. She addressed Armand. "Please do not detain us long. We have urgent business to the north and cannot be delayed for long."

Zandorth struggled against his instincts. They were screaming at him to not allow the sheriffs to take them to the jail. Yet there was something in Brianna's manner that seemed to tell him to at least, for the moment, go along with Armand's explanation of things.

"The delay will be as brief as possible, M'Lady. I swear," he replied, a flicker of relief flashing across his eyes as he realized that he would not have to undertake the daunting task of arresting the warrior.

The sheriffs stepped up as Armand took a step back. Brianna turned, drawing Zandorth with her as she did. She dropped her voice to a whisper. "Be still, Zan. Go along and perhaps we will learn something of what has become of Daimion and Shantira."

What she was asking of him went against his very nature, but he did what she asked. He had learned long ago that Brianna was one of the few people he could genuinely trust.

"Very well, but I will not be locked up as some animal," he whispered back, his voice carrying the warning as clearly as if he had spoken the words.

Brianna's soft laughter whispered to his ears as she patted his arm before withdrawing her hand. "I would hate to see the individual foolish enough to try."

~*~

Lordal stepped back into the alleyway, his anger seething from him as if it were a tangible thing, visible to all. He had watched the sheriffs take the warrior and the woman away from the inn. For a moment, he had thought that the warrior and the woman would move on after talking to the Royal Guard, and thereby, give him his opportunity to strike. Obviously, words had been exchanged that led the Guard to take them into custody.

He turned his angry gaze to Bonzwa. "Are you sure that those were two of them?"

"As sure as I can be, Sire. The light was very dim last night, and I only caught fleeting glimpses of their shadowed features. There is no mistaking the large one. His massive form could be seen even in the darkness. The woman?" He shrugged. "I am not sure. I am to assume she is one of them simply by her presence with the man," Bonzwa answered.

"What of the other two?" he demanded.

"No one has seen them," Bonzwa answered.

Lordal struggled under his anger as he turned to another bandit. The man huddled against the wall of the alley, hugging himself against a chill that no one else felt. His eyes were wide, tear-rimmed, and laced a deep fear that sent a sliver of a chill through those who looked into his eyes.

"Thed. Tell me how the demon escaped you," he demanded.

"He *is* a demon, Sire!! The very demon we seek!" The terrified bandit all but screamed. "The trap was set, it was impossible for him to have escaped. But he called on his hellish powers and killed Bandella and Sensal. He not only killed them, but he ate of their flesh, drank of their blood, and captured their souls!!"

Lordal's face shifted into annoyed impatience. "Calm yourself! You are speaking as a frightened child! Tell me what happened!"

Thed shivered as the memories came. He took several deep breaths before he closed his eyes and forced the words from his trembling lips. "Sensal was in place behind the desk. The dark one entered. Sensal drew him to the desk to put him in position for Bandella to come upon him from behind. I was just outside the door in case I was needed. But the demon knew. His dark spawned powers served to undermine our trap, and he drew Sensal into a fight.

"Bandella was discovered and drawn from his hiding place. I stepped inside and fired my crossbow, but the demon knew and stepped out of the way allowing my bolt to fell Sensal. The demon was upon me faster than any human could move and he knocked me out. When I came to, Sensal had been ripped to shreds, a massive hole ripped in his chest that left a hollow cavity.

"Bandella lay not far from him, his face destroyed, ripped away from the skull and most of his throat gone." Thed choked back sobs as he finished his recounting of the battle. Bonzwa watched in pity as the bandit tried valiantly to maintain his composure, but the horrors he had seen were tearing at his control.

"How is it that you survived?" Lordal asked suspicion clear in his eyes and words. Bonzwa looked at his leader in disbelief at his lack of concern and subtle accusation that Thed should have died as well.

"I do not know, Sire. I swear, I do not know," Thed replied in a shaky voice, tears slipping from his eyes.

Lordal seemed to consider thoughts that were known only to him and Bonzwa found himself holding his breath. The leader seemed on the verge of insanity, as if his anger and desire for revenge now drove him beyond the limits of rational thought.

They were in a very dangerous position at this moment. They were bandits—known bandits, and they were within very close proximity to a complement of the Royal Guard who would, no doubt, arrest them on sight. Yet the closeness of the Royal Guard seemed not to be among the thoughts the Bandit Leader was considering at the moment.

"Perhaps the demon sought to leave one alive as a means of warning us to break off our pursuit of him," Bonzwa finally offered, hoping to break the anger growing around Lordal.

Lordal considered this before slowly nodding. "It is possible. It would follow the arrogance of his breed to do such." Lordal's face twisted into an angry snarl. "But I will not be frightened away like some small child. I will not rest until the demon is dead at my feet!"

"Perhaps we should withdraw to the edge of the city and wait for them to continue their journey. We can ambush them much easier and with less attention drawn to our attack from there," Bonzwa offered, wanting to place as much distance between them and the Royal Guard as possible.

"I will not flee in fear from this demon. I know his kind, and I know his weaknesses. I will have him, and nothing will stand in the way of that!!" Lordal yelled, his face flushing with the hue of his anger.

Bonzwa felt his concern over his leader's behavior double. He became aware of the knowledge that Lordal would carry out his vengeance and would do so if it meant every man under him died in the process. While he admired Lordal and had pledged his loyalty to the man, he had no desire to become a pawn. He feared death as any sane man would and vowed that he would live to be a rich old man.

"What do we do now, Sire?" Bonzwa asked.

Lordal lapsed back into thoughtful silence. It was several minutes before he spoke again, "Pick five men and maintain your position here. Keep a watchful eye on the inn, and if the dark one or the other woman should return, follow their movements. Do not try to capture them or battle them. Send a man to our camp outside the city when you have them under your eye, and I will come with enough men to rid this realm of the demon."

Bonzwa nodded slowly, somehow knowing this course would have been the one Lordal chose. "What of the others?"

"Once the vampire is destroyed, we will deal with them, as well. I will personally show them the error of their ways and make them beg for mercy and forgiveness." Lordal locked a cold, angry and determined stare into Bonzwa's eyes. His voice was a dark whisper, as he finished with, "I will grant neither."

Bonzwa felt a chill ripple through him at the conviction of his leaders' words. Again, he felt a touch of sympathy for the other three travelers. Their deaths would be neither quick nor painless. He watched as Lordal straightened his cloak and pulled a necklace from under his shirt. He wore it always. It was a medallion of some sort, and its significance was considerable. A fond smile touched his lips as he gazed upon the medallion before he lowered it to hang by the chain as he stepped out into the street leading to the inn.

"Sire!" Bonzwa whispered harshly. "The Royal Guard is there. What are you doing?"

"I am going to enlist the help of the Royal Guard," Lordal spoke back over his shoulder as he strode toward the inn. Bonzwa watched in shocked disbelief as Lordal strode up to the line of sheriffs, showed them the medallion, and exchanged words with them. If any of them recognized Lordal, they gave no indication of it.

Bonzwa watched as the same member of the Royal Guard who had spoken with the warrior before came out and led Lordal aside to speak with him. After showing the captain the medallion, there followed a lengthy exchange. After a time, the Guard seemed to issue words of thanks, and Lordal turned and began walking back toward the alley.

As Lordal walked away, the guard summoned others of the Royal Guard, and they spoke in hushed, nearly frantic tones. Two of the guards quickly mounted their white steeds and thundered off down the street.

Lordal returned to his men with a look of true satisfaction. It was the closest thing to a normal expression the Bandit Leader had had in two days. Bonzwa looked from the sudden beehive of activity around the inn to his leader, his eyes asking the question his lips could not seem to form.

"Our task has just been simplified," Lordal said as he turned to watch the results of his visit to the inn.

"What did you tell them?" Bonzwa asked with disbelief evident in his eyes.

"The truth. They were seeking the person responsible for such horrendous acts, and I gave them a target," Lordal replied.

"I fear I do not understand, Sire," Bonzwa said.

Lordal took his eyes from the inn and placed them on Bonzwa. His lips formed a knowing smile, the smile of someone who knew a delicious secret, but wished to savor the flavor for a while before sharing of the feast of knowledge.

"You will, Bonzwa. In a very short passage of time, you will."

With a motion to the other bandits, Lordal began walking down the alley away from the street that housed the inn. Bonzwa motioned to five men to remain with him while the others followed Lordal, taking the still shocked Thed with them. Bonzwa watched until the shadows swallowed Lordal and the others before turning his weary gaze to the inn. Whatever Lordal had said to them had whipped them into a frenzy. More sheriffs and members of the Royal Guard were summoned, and within a very short time, the inn was fortified as if it were a fort or the King's castle itself.

A priest arrived, carrying with him all the wares of his trade. Other priests arrived shortly afterwards, and they all set about praying and performing odd blessings that Bonzwa had never seen before. Of course, he reflected, with his occupation and path in life, he would not be familiar with many of the religious practices being performed. His curiosity screamed out to be satisfied with what Lordal had said, how he had walked right up to the Royal Guard without being arrested, and even more, stirred them to a near fevered pitch of activity.

~*~

Armand stood in the lobby of the inn and considered just how deadly this investigation had turned. Once he had seen the mutilated states of two of the three bodies, he knew he was dealing with a very deranged mind. He removed his hat and ran a hand through his long black hair.

The conversation with the warrior, Zandorth and The Lady Standish had promised the capture of another pair of rogues who were wanted by the Royal Guard. Then the conversation with the Hunter, Lordalise, had shown him exactly what manner of beast they were facing.

He had doubted Lordalise's claims of being a Hunter, but he had produced the Medallion of the Hunter. Only members of the Order of Hunters possessed the pendant. It was used to identify themselves to each other and to local authorities. Armand had met a Hunter seasons ago and had been truly impressed with the beauty and majesty of the medallion.

When Zandorth had said the name of Daimion Devenshire, something had tugged hard at his memory, as if he should know that name. Then the Lady Standish had said the name of Raven Darkseed, and the puzzle completed itself. Several seasons ago, Devenshire and Darkseed had been involved in some dubious activities, and they were sought by the Royal Guard. However, the capture of both men had eluded them. Now, with the information supplied by Lordalise, he could understand how.

Devenshire was a vampire.

Armand watched as the priests knelt by each of the bodies, uttered their prayers, and performed the holy blessings, which would, hopefully, hold the forces of hell at bay until they could be destroyed. He watched his men keep a solemn watch over the proceedings and saw the fear in their eyes. They were soldiers, handpicked by the King for the serious task of maintaining the law in this region. There was no doubt in Armand's mind that any one of his men would fight to the death for His Majesty. They had all been trained and taught to do so. But none of them, he included, were trained to face the hellish powers and fears presented by a vampire.

Yet he had a duty, to not only the King, and those under his rule, but to himself and his family. This region had been free of the curse of the vampire for ages, and he would take whatever means were necessary to make sure it remained that way. Lordalise had sworn his assistance in ridding the area of the vampire. He had said he would need the help of the Royal Guard, and the Priests of this area. As he had sworn his help in ridding the realm of Devenshire, Armand had sworn his assistance in tracking the beast down, and detaining him long enough for Lordalise to perform a task as sacred as the one Armand himself was sworn to perform.

Devenshire, and those who followed him, were now the most wanted individuals in the land. Armand would not rest until Devenshire's hellish existence was eradicated, and those who followed him were hung from the highest gallows in the land.

CHAPTER TWENTY-THREE

DURING THE WALK TO the city jail, Zandorth could not shake the feeling deep in his gut that all was not as it appeared to be. Even though he trusted Brianna and her unique feminine instincts, he could not ignore his warrior's instincts, and at this moment, they were screaming at him to beware. Krahl glanced over his shoulder at the three sheriffs escorting them and resisted the urge to laugh. If he decided not to go to the jail, the three men would pose no resistance. He could see the lack of discipline in them, could see the boredom they felt with this assigned task. Their attentions were not on him or Brianna, aside from the occasional leering glances at her body.

"There is something wrong here," he whispered to Brianna, feeling confident that the noise of the street would mask his voice from the sheriff's ears.

"What?" she whispered back.

"I cannot explain it. But all is not as it appears to be," he answered.

"They simply wish to question us," she reassured him.

He shook his head. "No. There is more to it than that. When I mentioned Devenshire's name, Armand seemed to grow tense. When you mentioned Darkseed's name, something in him changed."

She gave Zandorth a sideways glance as she considered his words. "In what way?"

"It is something only a warrior would understand. He became suspicious, defensive," he replied. His features tightened as he struggled to find a way to articulate what he was thinking and feeling. Suddenly, the thoughts organized, and he turned his head to fix her with an intense gaze. "It was very much like a hunter who had found his prey."

Suddenly there came the sound of pounding hooves racing toward them. Zandorth's hand flew to the hilt of his broadsword as he swung his eyes to the direction the sound was coming from. Danger called to him, rousing his instincts to be prepared for battle.

Brianna spun to join Zandorth in watching for the approaching horses, and something seemed to be speaking to her as well, as her right hand raised to a position that would allow her to draw her own sword should it become necessary.

From around a corner came four white steeds bearing members of the Royal Guard. It was all Zandorth needed to see, and his sword sang as it cleared its scabbard. The sheriffs, startled by Zandorth's sudden movement, stepped back as their confused expressions darted about to find out what had caused the sudden shift in the situation.

"Be easy, Zan," Brianna called out, successfully resisting the urge to draw her sword, but keeping her hand near its hilt.

"I have not lived as long as I have by being easy!" Zandorth growled as he assumed a defensive posture.

The four members of Royal Guard maneuvered their mounts around the throng of people in the streets and quickly formed a circle around them. Brianna did not miss how two guards had their swords drawn, and the other two had crossbows at the ready. Some of Zandorth's uneasiness reached her, and she found herself wondering if perhaps she should not have trusted the warrior's instincts.

"Hold!" one of the guards shouted. "You are under arrest! Drop your weapons!"

Zandorth's eyes narrowed as he looked from guard to guard, seeking out the weakest link in their chain, and thereby finding his first target.

"What is the charge?" Brianna demanded.

"Drop your weapons!" the guard repeated.

When Zandorth did not drop his sword, the guard looked to the two men with crossbows, and nodded. They instantly shouldered their weapons and took aim at Zandorth and Brianna.

"I will not tell you again! I will not hesitate to fire!"

Zandorth locked eyes with the guard and saw the conviction there. His lips peeled back in a savage snarl as he tightened his grip on the sword. "Then you should pray they hit their mark for I will not miss mine!"

"Zandorth! Please! Drop your sword," Brianna pleaded. She felt fear course through her as she saw the conviction of the guards. She knew Zandorth, knew that surrender was a completely alien concept to him, and he would sooner die than yield.

"We have broken no laws! I am not a wanted man, and I will not simply submit on the word of this man!" he growled, tensing his muscles, preparing to attack.

Brianna looked about her and saw that the three sheriffs had finally recovered enough to draw their own swords. While she felt sure she could hold her own with the sheriffs, she knew her fighting skills were no match for the Royal Guards. Zandorth could, no doubt, handle the sheriffs, and quite possibly the guards as well, but even his incredible skill with a sword could not defend against two crossbows. She feared she would be forced to witness Zandorth's death if he did not yield immediately.

She quickly stepped in front of him, placing her hands on the tightly bunched muscles of his forearms. "Zandorth! Listen to me! There is no honor to be gained here! Your death will be meaningless if you do not yield now. If you must die, at least die for a reason! Do you honestly wish to face the afterlife not knowing why you were killed?" she asked hurriedly, hoping to calm the warrior before the guards opened fire on him. Honor was the main driving force in his life. He treasured it above all else, even his own life.

She watched as Zandorth's features changed subtly. He was considering her words, and she found herself holding her breath. She wanted to say more, drive her point home, but she feared that any further words would be useless and would only render her previous point powerless.

All she could do now was wait and hope that he realized just how empty his death would be if he resisted now. She sorely wished for Devenshire's ability to project her thoughts into the warrior's mind, to make him see the foolishness of fighting what probably was a misunderstanding or mistake on the part of the guards.

The anger in the warrior was mounting and soon, she knew, it would spiral out of his control save for directing his attack. Slowly he looked to each guard, then to each sheriff and finally, his gray eyes came to her. She saw some of his anger was toward her for saying words that disrupted his battle plans. She smiled warmly at him and slowly nodded, acknowledging his anger, and reassuring him that what he was considering was the right thing to do.

Finally, Zandorth returned his burning gaze to the first guard and slowly stood upright. With a reluctance that she knew tore at his soul, his massive sword tumbled from his hand to land in the dirt of the street.

Brianna slowly closed her eyes and breathed out a soft sigh of relief. With a trembling hand, she slowly drew her own sword, allowing it fall to the street next to his and took a step back from it.

She looked to Zandorth as she saw the warriors' angered gaze still locked to the guards. She shifted her gaze to the guard and saw the slight flicker of uncertainty there. She prayed that the guard had the sense not to push his temporary advantage by treating his prisoner with anything but respect. She knew she would not be able to stop

Zandorth again.

One of the sheriffs moved forward slowly, cautiously, as if he feared that the large warrior might change his mind. The sheriff slowly returned his sword to its scabbard before bending low to retrieve their swords. She saw the surprise in his eyes at the considerable weight of Zandorth's broadsword as he picked it up. She knew he was remembering how the warrior had wielded the sword as if its weight were nothing, and she took some small satisfaction in the fear that sprang from his surprise.

The Royal Guard nodded slightly, satisfied that they were now his prisoners. "Walk! Make no mistake, if either of you attempt to do anything but walk, I will kill you!" There was no hesitation in his words, his manner, or his expression. There was no doubt to the sincerity of his words.

Zandorth paused only long enough to make it known through his heated, hard stare, that he would not be treated as an animal, and any attempt to treat him as anything but a man would result in a most dangerous and deadly situation.

Brianna fell into step beside Zandorth and turned her attention to why they were being arrested. They had committed no crimes. Then she remembered Zandorth's argument of how Armand's demeanor had shifted at the mention of Devenshire and Darkseed's names. She knew that Devenshire and Darkseed had a history together, but she knew nothing of it. There was a great deal about Devenshire's past that she did not know, and she could not shake the feeling that she and Zandorth's arrest had something to do with that past.

She would go along for now, just to learn what the charges against them were, but if the time for escape presented itself, she would not even attempt to hold Zandorth back.

~*~

From a rooftop nearby, a lone figure watched the warrior and the woman being arrested. As the guards and their prisoners disappeared around a corner, the figure stepped back from the edge of the roof to consider her next course of action. As the night breeze rustled her dark cloak about her, she took a moment to close her eyes and concentrate on blocking out the distractions that called to her. Being in a large city like this was distressful to her, too many distractions. Her hunger stabbed at her and being in such close proximity to such large amounts of that which would quell the ever-screaming hunger made it difficult to stay focused. Her senses reached out without her bidding and returned with sounds, smells and thoughts that swam about her mind trying to intoxicate it with the teasing promise of what her nature demanded.

She could hear heartbeats... thousands of them. The pumping of warm blood, she could almost hear the river like roar of blood coursing through veins. She could smell the heat of it, almost taste it on the wind, and the hunger stabbed at her anew, tearing at her will, her determination. Thoughts came unbidden to her mind and she squeezed her eyes shut to try to block them out, ignore them. She could feel the change take place in her mouth and could feel the sensual desire and hunger growing quickly.

The pounding, nearly deafening explosion of each beating heart, called to her, teased her, coaxing her to give into what she was, what she needed.

The thoughts.

Dark, seedy, sensual, evil in nature, strummed into her brain, and the cool breeze of the night swirled around her, touching her skin as a passionate lover's hands would. She breathed in deeply and lifted her face to the sky. Her control was fading as the discordant sounds, smells, and thoughts slowly blended, mixed, and swirled with each other to form a song that lulled her senses and eased her tight resolve. For a moment, she surrendered to it.

With a sensual smile playing across her pale features, she turned and walked to the edge of the roof again. Her eyes burned brightly as she looked down upon the multitudes of humans below her and the visual stimulation added its own seductive chords to the ballad playing about her mind and body.

It would be so easy, ridiculously so. There would be no resistance. There were those below her who were not worthy of the precious gift that throbbed inside of them. In fact, she reflected, for many of those below her she would be doing them a favor in releasing them from the burden of an existence that was empty and meaningless.

There were those just feet from her, who would not be missed if they simply vanished into the night. There would be no questions, no concerns. They would simply be another of the countless others who simply walked off into the shadows of the night never to be seen or heard from again.

A man caught her attention in the crowd below. He was a fairly young man as human's measured it. He was strong and viral, and the thoughts she drew from him were darker and more evil than the rest. She squatted down on her heels, her elbows resting on her knees, and examined this man more closely. He took pleasure in the pain of others. He bought and sold women as if they were nothing more than objects. The younger and more attractive the woman, the higher the price he could fetch. His mind spoke to her of the many females he had taken, against their wills, and sold into slavery for those who could afford his price.

This night, his mind sang with satisfaction of his latest transaction—a young girl, barely in her sixteenth season, taken from a small village many miles from here. He had spent days in that area, watching and waiting, looking for a particular woman. His newest client had requested a specific type of prize.

Just as he was about to abandon his search and move on to another village, he had spotted her. He had found the young girl at a time when her mind and body were experiencing things she could barely understand, and he prayed upon that confusion.

He had romanced her, speaking empty words that, to her, held volumes of what she yearned for. Then he had taken her. Forced himself into her as her screaming pleas rang in his ear. The raw sexual satisfaction that those screams had wrought from him slammed into her mind, and she gasped involuntarily at the strength of them, leaning back on her heels as a ripple of dark pleasure fluttered through the very center of her.

The girl had resisted, fought with all her might to stop him. His back and arms still bore some of the deeper scratches she had inflicted on him that first night. The figure closed her eyes as his mind showed her the brutal scene. She sighed in sensual satisfaction and smiled. His memories were vivid and fresh.

The village girl had fought, but lacked the strength. As he had emptied his foul passions into her, she had cried out in shame, pain, and humiliation.

Afterward, he had beaten her harshly and taken her barely conscious form to his coach, bound her inside, taking her away from her home and family, never to return.

Over the course of the next several weeks, the verbal and physical attacks had been relentless and the girl's will broke quickly. When he had presented the girl to his client this very night, she was suitably subdued and submissive.

The man in the street smiled as his mind played back the massive mound of gold coins that had fallen into his pockets from the sale of the young girl. He had several clients in Lirpa, and he was on his way to pay them a visit, to see if his unique services were required.

From the rooftop, she watched the man saunter down the street, feeling very satisfied with himself. A very faint part of her mind felt total revulsion at the man, that the Fates would allow such a creature to walk the earth. The part that was in control was incredibly aroused by the craftiness of this one. He was a clever mortal with a very solid memory. Combined with a weak mental defense, it provided her with an exhilarating sensual excitement.

On one point, both parts of her agreed that if any deserved death, this man did. Her mind called to her, spoke to her of the countless women she could save by eliminating his foul existence from this realm. Her lips curled back from her sharp teeth in an angry snarl as she felt her muscles tense. She crouched low, gathering her strength to launch herself at him.

Just as she was about to issue the mental command that would sweep her down upon the man, something else called out in her mind causing her to pause.

A mental cry from deep inside sent the beautiful song back into the shrieking discordant noise of before. She shook her head, trying to force the song back to her, but that tiny part of her mind that cried out continued to disrupt the song. The sensual smile faded to be replaced with confusion.

Why could she not attack? Why could she not feed a dual need below her? It was right. No tears would be shed at the passing of the foul man below her. There would surely be no evil in eliminating him and the danger he represented.

"NO!" she cried out as she spun from the edge of the roof and strode several paces away, holding the sides of her head. She collapsed to her knees, tears tracing down her cheeks.

This was not right.

She could not.

She would not.

She cursed herself and her own damnation. That man's existence was not hers to determine. To follow her desires would make her little better than the man himself. Her mind frantically searched for something to grab hold of, to give her the strength to ward off herself. Then the image of another man sprang to her mind, and she embraced it with all the fervor of one being rescued from raging seas. The man she had followed here. The man that touched something within her that she had thought was long gone from her.

With a shuddering sigh, she wiped her tears and took several deep breaths to calm the trembling within her body. The hunger tore at her with ravenous teeth, ripped her mind, shredded her gut, and cursed her.

More tears flooded her eyes and flowed down chilled cheeks as she wrapped her arms about her mid-section, rocking against the intense waves of pain that racked her body. She needed to focus, to fight back against her nature, and stay her hunger.

The man would be waking soon, and he would need to know of the dangers that await him and his friends. She rose, unsteadily, to her feet and melded into the shadows of the night. As she moved toward the place that she had left the man, she hoped that she had enough strength to finish healing him for now was not the time for him to be weakened.

He would need all his strength for what was to come.

CHAPTER TWENTY FOUR

LORDAL RODE INTO HIS camp outside the city and wasted no time dismounting and entering his tent, leaving his men to tend the horses and set about preparing the evening meal. He issued no orders as what he expected was known and would be carried out without his having to say a word. For this, he was grateful for he had far too many other matters on his mind to trouble with trivial tasks.

Once inside his tent, Lordal shrugged out of his heavy cloak and unbuckled his sword to let them fall to the ground as he moved toward a chest sitting in the corner. The chest was one of his most prized possessions, and it traveled with him regardless of where he went. He knelt before the chest and let his eyes roam fondly over the leather that covered the pine construction of the chest. Thicker leather straps wrapped around the body of the chest and the lid, and above the locking hasp was adorned with an elegantly engraved L.

As his fingers played lightly over the inlaid letter, his mind replayed his discussion with Armand of the Royal Guard. Lordalise, he had told Armand was his name, and it was not a falsehood. His given name *was* Lordalise; he had simply shortened it to Lordal once he became a bandit.

A sense of grief washed over him as he considered his abandoned name, and the life that he had abandoned with it. His life had once been as different as day is from night. He had been a man of stature, of importance. His family's holdings had left him very wealthy, and very influential. He had carried out his sworn duties with the pride of a fine craftsman and, he reflected, he had been considered one of the best.

Yet things change. Life changes and one must be prepared to accept those changes and flow with the currents of the river of life. Forcing down the ever-present hint of bitterness at a life he had lost and could never get back, he unlocked the heavy padlock and laid it aside. Unclipping the locking hasp, he raised the lid of the chest and let his eyes dance across the contents, the tools of his trade, a trade that had made him almost a legend in his old life. As the nostalgia washed over him, his left hand rose to clasp the medallion around his neck. It was time to bring a part of that old life back. His skill was needed, and he felt justified in using the contents of the chest even though he was no longer a member of the Order of Hunters.

Hunters, or Slayers as some called them, were a group of men who had dedicated themselves to the eradication of the purest form of evil to blacken the landscape of this realm: vampires. Each member of the Order of Hunters had lost a loved one to the curse of the un-dead. In fact, it was one of the prerequisites of becoming a Hunter. It was felt that the thirst for vengeance would make one even more dedicated than someone whose life had never been touched by the foul stench of the evil vampires.

Lordal had lost a sister to the hellish embrace of a vampire. As he had watched her beheaded corpse burn, and bitter tears had stung his eyes, he had sworn vengeance, not only for the one who had taken his sister, but also for all who walked the earth of man with a life force they did not deserve and had, in his opinion, forsaken by choosing the dark path of the un-dead.

Within a week of his sisters passing, Lordal had sought out and joined the Hunters. Within a very short time, he became one of their best soldiers and rose quickly within their ranks. He had helped organize the Hunters, had brought a new sense of focus to their holy task, and many vampires had fallen before them.

Many Hunters were lost in those early days as well. Each loss cut, not only their numbers, but also their resolve. Lordalise traveled far and wide seeking out new ways to defeat the vampires while increasing their chances of surviving an encounter with the demons of the night. He visited distant lands learning of new methods and acquiring new weapons to use in their fight. Many of the weapons in use by the Hunters today could be attributed to him.

In one land, the very land where it was believed the first vampire had been spawned, he met several who had been fighting the plague of vampires for ages. From them he learned of even more ways to kill a vampire. They shared ancient scrolls, which told of a weakness of vampires that had been unheard of in his homeland. The contents of these scrolls were then adopted as standard procedure for dealing with vampires by the Order of Hunters.

In another land, he had learned of ways of forging weapons that were lethal to vampires. Forging a sword from the purest silver, and having the finished weapon blessed by the most devout of priests, could wound a vampire where ordinary sword strikes were inconsequential to the demons. The same was applied to crossbow bolts, tipped with blessed silver, and found to have the same effect. Where a vampire could walk through a thousand normal crossbow bolts and simply bare its fangs and keep coming, a single crossbow bolt made of silver would seriously injure the strongest of vampires.

On one trek into a foreign land, the ship Lordalise had been sailing on had met with a storm that rent the vessel to splinters. Many had died that night, and Lordalise had thought that he would be one of them. He had clung to a large piece of wood from the doomed ship and floated in the massive expanse of ocean for uncounted days before washing ashore in a land that appeared on no map. It was a strange land filled with strange beauties. The people of this land, while human, were different from any human Lordalise had ever encountered. They were a beautiful people, peaceful people, who devoted themselves to making their lives one with the world instead of trying to dominate it. The beauty of the land and the people touched him to this day.

Although their appearance had startled him at first, he quickly came to appreciate their difference from other humans, and in that difference, he found a serenity and beauty that was unsurpassed in his existence. The people of this land were short in stature and slight of build with raven hair and odd shaped eyes. Their language was as strange to Lordalise as everything else about them. Their language consisted of high-pitched chattering which bore no resemblance to the language that Lordalise had grown up with. Their written words were even stranger. It was made up of symbols, and even the manner of writing it was different. Where Lordalise scrolled words from left to right across a page, these people wrote top to bottom in columns.

The entire culture of these people fascinated Lordalise, and he spent three seasons with them, learning all he could learn from them. He had even managed to learn the rudimentary basics of their language that was exceedingly difficult to learn. Fortunately, one of the ancient ones among these people knew Lordalise's tongue and spoke it very well with only the slightest of hesitations in his words.

Through this old man, Lordalise was able to communicate with his hosts who took in his differences from them with far greater ease than he had taken in theirs. Many of their customs were strange, and some were nothing short of bizarre. His time with them had taught him that they were not bizarre, just different, and in that difference, was a kind of joy that he had never known.

These people were a peaceful people, yet they had a method of fighting which very rarely involved weapons, using only the body. It was not considered a fighting method to these people. It was a form of self-defense that required the mind and body to work as one. There was a beautiful serenity in the movements that brought a deep sense of mental and spiritual peace to those who practiced the art. There were many different forms and methods to this self-defense style. Lordalise had learned the basics and still, to this day, used many of the meditative methods to keep his mind clear and his soul at some semblance of ease. While he appeared to be a master of these martial arts to the people of his own land, to the people he had learned them from, he was nothing more than a struggling beginner and barely that.

The alchemists, if that term could apply to these people, were far superior in knowledge and skill to those of their counter parts in Lordalise's land. They developed many strange and awesome chemicals that performed unbelievable things. A vast majority of these potions and brews were made of herbs and plants or some ingredient derived from a combination of both. Lordalise still had many scrolls he had translated into his language with the help of the ancient one, and he used them when needed. They were among his most prized and closely guarded possessions.

From the alchemist of this land, he learned of a new weapon to use in his fight against the vampire. It was a very expensive and difficult thing to make, not to mention very dangerous. The slightest miscalculation could unleash the power of this invention and kill the maker. When assembled correctly, it would seriously injure a vampire just as quickly and easily as it would kill a human. The irony of this new device was that these people did not use the substance as a weapon, but as a form of entertainment. They used this strange powder to light up the night sky with brilliant colors and screaming explosions that were breathtaking.

On one particular night, he had sat and watched the multi-colored display of flaming light, delighting in each new and intricate pattern that each new explosion produced. At one point, he regarded the containers that held the strangely mixed powder. He noted that a thin cord extended from the base of the tube. When a flame was touched to the end of the cord, it erupted into a sparkling fire of its own, which hissed toward the tube. Once the strange sparkling fire disappeared into the tube, a deafening, screaming explosion sounded, which propelled a ball into the sky that sparkled like the cord from the tube. After a short while, the ball would erupt into the brilliant display of colored fire. Lordalise had noted that once the ball was launched into the air, the tube was utterly destroyed by the force of the explosion. On that night, within his mind, the Order of Hunters most lethal weapon was conceived.

With the aid of the alchemist and blacksmiths of this land, the conceived weapon was given life. He had posed a problem to them: to develop a portable tube that would launch the flaming balls without destroying the tube and thereby making it reusable. The tubes they used in their flaming displays were made from something they called bamboo, which, to his startled surprise, was a plant.

Various thicknesses of bamboo were experimented with, but the plant was simply not dense enough to withstand repeated explosions of the powder. Lordalise proposed using steel, much like the steel of swords. The blacksmiths forged tubes of steel, and eventually, a thick steel tube was developed that could withstand repeated explosions of the fire powder. Lordalise pointed out that thinner steel tubes could be used if smaller amounts of the fire powder were used. From this observation, smaller and shorter tubes were forged which could perform the same task, yet on a smaller scale.

While the alchemist and blacksmiths wrestled with the fascinating problem posed by Lordalise, he turned his attention to the sparkling ball that was hurled into the air. He considered the effect that such a ball would have on any object it might hit. He recalled the speed at which the ball was thrown into the air by the explosion and winced at what such a ball would do to a body. The sheer force at which the ball was propelled left no doubt in his mind that the ball would penetrate flesh as if it were parchment. He reasoned that a similar ball made of silver would wreck havoc on a vampires body, and the holy blessing of the purity of the metal would prove lethal once inside the foul essence of an un-dead.

The next obstacle to Lordalise's weapon was how to hold the steel tube while directing the path of the ball hurled from it. It did not take but one trial of the new steel tube to realize that the last thing one wanted was to have the tube in one's hand when the fire powder exploded. The explosion quickly heated the steel tube to a point that flesh would be seared badly. Lordalise flexed his right hand absently as he considered how that first trial had gone, and how the results had introduced him to another of these peoples potions of healing, an ointment which soothed the burn and helped aid in its healing.

Through many frustrating trial and errors, not to mention burns, a method was finally devised which would make it possible to hold the steel tube during the ignition of the fire powder. A handle was made of wood and affixed to the tube that made it possible to handle the tube while the powder exploded. His hosts welcomed the challenges Lordalise presented, and they embraced the problem with the fervor of new discovery.

Refinements were made, and after a while, a small tube with a wooden handle was fashioned that could be held in one hand, leaving the other hand free to ignite the cord that hung from the underside of the steel tube. The cord was nothing more than a thick twine dusted with a fine coat of the fire powder. While the weapon performed the task Lordalise wished of it, he did not like the time consuming method of setting fire to the cord. In his mind, he knew that if the weapon were to be practical against the eye blurring speed of the vampires, a quicker method of sparking the fire powder would have to be developed. A single spark was all that was required to ignite the fire powder

A spark like the one produced when flint was struck with metal.

Lordalise had presented this complex problem to the alchemist, blacksmiths, and others who had embraced the fascinating puzzles he was able to present to them. They seemed to revel in the challenge of taking a thought and turning that thought into reality. They were, Lordalise found, an imaginative people with an intellect that he found awe-inspiring.

Lordalise watched in amazement as they set about bringing this cordless method of igniting the fire powder into reality. He watched the progression of their thoughts as they started with striking a flint rock with one of the blacksmith's hammers that produced a large spark to smaller and smaller mechanisms that performed the same task without actually touching the hammer.

Thin rods of steel were found to exert a considerable force when they were coiled. These coils of steel could be stretched to a certain limit, and when released, they would return to their previous state with surprising force. Lordalise was amazed at how the rigid steel would, when stretched, spring back to its tightly wound coils. It was his observations that lead the people to call this new invention a spring. Of course, each new development they came up with was found to have many other uses, so splinters of the original group of inventors would follow these new possibilities.

A very small version of the new spring was attached to a tiny hammer which was fixed to a framework of steel in a manner that would allow the tiny hammer to swing in an arch to strike a small piece of flint rock which would result in a spark that was found to be enough to ignite the small amount of fire powder housed in the steel tube. Through many different versions of these mechanisms, one was finally developed that allowed the tiny hammer to be drawn back with very little force, but when released, the hammer would spring forward at incredible speed and force to strike the flint, producing a spark.

The next step was to find a way to affix this mechanism to the steel tube and wooden handle. The wood workers came up with a way to conceal all of the mechanism, save for the hammer, within the wooden handle of the tube. A small hole was cut into the base of the steel tube right under the tiny hammer. A tiny piece of flint rock was attached next to the hole, and the hammer would strike the flint in a glancing blow that would result in a spark that touched the fire powder through the hole in the tube. The handle was modified many times, and eventually, a handle was made that would allow someone to hold the tube in one hand and use the thumb of that hand to draw the hammer back, then release it to ignite the fire powder.

Lordalise had begun to notice that the elders began withdrawing from active participation in the development of his weapon. He had been very careful to conceal his true intentions for the new device since these were a very non-violent people. The thought of war and killing were abhorrent to them, and he had no doubt that had they known his true intentions for the device, they would have ceased all work on the project. The ancient ones, as they were called, knew, and they pulled their wisdom from the development of the device.

One day, Lordalise was in a field practicing with his new weapon. It was an awkward weapon and one that he had no doubt would take considerable time to get used to using. The explosion of the fire powder never ceased to startle him, which threw off his aim. Also, the act of holding the hammer back while he lined up his shot, then releasing the hammer also made accuracy difficult. While his mind pondered how to make the weapon more efficient, one of the ancient ones approached him.

"Lordalise. A word, please," the ancient one had said.

"Yes?" he asked.

"What is the purpose of this device you have developed?"

Lordalise felt dread spread through him at that question. It was one he knew was coming and one he had hoped that would not be asked. But it had been asked, and now he had the unfortunate task of answering it. He had made a vow to himself not to lie to these people. While he hid the truth behind the weapon from them, he did not consider that the same as lying. There was a sense of honor about these people, and they had gone out of their way to be hospitable to someone who was a complete stranger to them. They had opened their homes to him and made him welcome. He would not lie to them.

"It is a weapon," Lordalise answered.

The Ancient One nodded slowly, and Lordalise had the distinct impression that the Ancient One already knew the answer before he had asked the question.

"You are aware of how we feel about such things," he said.

"Yes. I am," Lordalise answered honestly.

"Then why?" the Ancient One asked.

"Because there is a need for such a weapon in my homeland."

"Can you not kill enough with your swords and crossbows? Do you need to find more ways to maim and kill each other?" the Ancient One asked the conviction and distaste obvious in his tone.

"I do not intend to use this weapon on my fellow man. The creatures that I will use this weapon on are deadly and common weapons have little to no affect on them."

"All creatures have a right to live. Who are you to decide which creature should live and which creature should die?"

"These creatures have already lived, once. They have traded their mortal life and mortal soul to the underworld in exchange for hellish powers. They prey upon humans and look upon us as nothing more than food. A way to sustain themselves," Lordalise replied, the bitter anger placing a sharp edge to his voice.

Lordalise could tell by the truly confused expression on the Ancient Ones' face that he had no idea of what he spoke. The dark blotch of the vampire had not found this land or hunted its people.

"You speak as if these creatures are dead, yet they walk about? They feed upon humans?"

"They are dead. Only the blasphemous power of hell keeps their soulless bodies moving about. The only sustenance that will sustain them is the blood of humans, and they drink rivers of it every night. Many times those they feed off become one of them, condemned to an eternity of never-ending hunger, never-ending violence, and a never-ending quest to dominate all humans everywhere," Lordalise answered

The Ancient One took a step back as his face paled and took on a horrified expression. Obviously even his great span of knowledge could not have conceived of such an evil within this realm.

Lordalise locked eyes with the Ancient One, conveying the truth of the nightmare of which he spoke. As much as he had dreaded being forced to reveal the truth behind the new weapon, he felt a sense of release in letting the truth out, of perhaps warning these good people of a danger that could very easily come to their beautiful shores. The Ancient One did not speak, his mind reeling under the revelation of such evilness within the world, and perhaps he was even pondering such a creature loose in his own land.

Lordalise took the pause to drive his point further. "If you run one of these foul creatures through with a sword, it will simply bare its fangs at you and keep coming. Shoot one with a crossbow and it will laugh at you as it drinks your blood until you are empty. Please believe me when I say that I have nothing but the utmost respect for you and your people, and I would not have hid my true intentions if the situation were not so dire." Lordalise paused for a moment and hefted the weapon in his hand and regarded it before returning his gaze to the Ancient One. "This weapon holds great promise. If I can perfect it, I can give my people at least a fighting chance against these demons."

The Ancient One alternated his aged gaze from eyes of Lordalise to the weapon before turning his wrinkled eyes to the horizon, and his face spoke of some deep train of thought he was following. It was several long moments before he spoke again. "What happens after you defeat these monsters?"

It was Lordalise' turn to be confused, "What do you mean?"

"What happens after you defeat these monsters? What will become of this terrible weapon you have created?"

Lordalise shook his head slowly as the confused expression spread deeper into his features. "I fear I do not understand your question."

"I may never have set foot on the soil of your homeland, but I have heard tales of it. I know men, I know what drives them, and I know what evilness men are capable of doing. The weapon of yours would give an unscrupulous man a tremendous advantage over others. It may have been developed with the purest of intentions, but this weapon of yours will unleash more evil and more evil deeds. Have you not considered this?"

Lordalise had to mentally agree with the Ancient Ones' assessment of man. An evil man with one of his weapons could wreak terrible havoc. He had never really considered the time after the vampire had been erased from existence.

"I will only allow this weapon to be used by those who are of my guild. I belong to a group of men known as Hunters. Only our ranks will have this weapon."

The Ancient One switched his gaze from the horizon to Lordalise and a thin smile spread across his lips. A low chuckle came from the old one, and Lordalise wondered what he had said that had amused him.

"I pray that you are not foolish enough to truly believe what you have just said. If just one of those weapons reaches your shores, then your homeland will forever be changed by its presence. The change will not be a positive nor productive one."

Lordalise lapsed into silence as he considered the Ancient Ones' words. There was wisdom within the old man and he found the smile and chuckle to suddenly have ominous overtones. He looked down at the weapon in his hand and considered his choices. With balls of blessed silver, he could eradicate many vampires. However, as much damage as the weapon would do to the vampires, the damage to humans would be far greater and more deadly. The design, in hindsight, was not difficult. The materials needed to make the weapon—the handle, even the fire powder was in abundance in his homeland, so duplicating the weapon would not be difficult.

For the first time since joining the ranks of the Hunters, he questioned the force that drove him. While the vampire was a deadly demon that stole the life beat from the chests of humans, this weapon could be just as deadly as the vampire. Would he not be trading one evil demon for another?

The Ancient One watched Lordalise for several moments before he gently laid his wrinkled hand on Lordalise' shoulder. "Contemplate what lies ahead, Lordalise. You can act only as your conscience directs you." The old man then turned and ambled off toward the village. Lordalise watched his frail form until it vanished from his sight. He then looked at his creation and felt the conflicting trains of thought battle within his mind.

Images of his younger sister came to his mind, images of her as an infant, then as a toddler, her blonde curls bouncing with each step, her deep blue eyes staring out at the world with the wonder that only a child could have; then images of her as she grew from toddler to young child to adolescence, and then to young womanhood. He smiled as various memories reminded him of her gentle and loving spirit and of how she always managed to find some form of beauty even in the most unpleasant of circumstances.

Without warning, the last two images flashed into his mind. The first was of how they had discovered her lifeless body, lying in a field of tall grass atop a hill that overlooked their town. Her eyes, which had always shone with the light of life, stared up at the dawn sky with an expression of terror, and a darkness that only the touch of death could make. The two puncture marks on her throat, which trailed the last precious drops of her life's blood, and the grayish tint that masked over the supple rich peach color her skin had always held.

The last image was of her headless, shrouded body burning in the flames of the funeral byre. Lordalise had lit the fires himself, had insisted upon it. By igniting the byre, he felt that he was releasing his beloved sister's soul from the cold grip of the vampire. That thought brought him no comfort as he watched his beautiful sister reduced to a pot full of ash. Bitter tears and thoughts came as he wept for the loss and mourned the precious gift that this world had been denied.

He considered the weapon through the blur of his tears and knew what he would do. The Ancient One spoke of what *might* happen if he took this weapon back to his homeland. It was speculation on the Ancient One's part. The threat of the vampire was real and would continue. There was no speculation in that truth.

Lordal wiped the fresh tears from his eyes as he stared into the contents of his chest, his thoughts returning from the memories of that beautiful land and beautiful people. It felt as if ages had passed since he had been there. A part of him longed to return to that land and lose himself in the serene peace. However, that was not possible, and he quickly forced his thoughts back to where they belonged—on tracking down the vampire and killing it.

He reached into the trunk and pulled out a sword and scabbard. The sword was laced with blessed silver, and it had sent many vampires to the fires of their true home. Next, he withdrew his crossbow and quiver of bolts, each tipped with a point of pure, blessed silver.

The next item he withdrew was a tunic. It was blood red in color, to represent the spilled blood of every human who had assumed the role of food for the vampire. Embossed across the chest of the tunic was the shield and arms of the Order of Hunters. It had been many seasons since he had worn it, and the memories of why he no longer did beckoned to his mind, wishing for him to recall them. A stern shake of his head refused them, and he turned his attention to one of the last items in the chest.

With a nearly religious reverence, he withdrew the weapon he had developed in that far away land. The steel tube had been polished until he could make out his reflection in its ebony surface. The wood of the handle had been stained and polished until it reflected the lantern light like the surface of a calm lake. To Lordal, it was a thing of beauty, the darkness of what it was capable of was masked by all the good it had accomplished. This weapon had destroyed many vampires. Lordal recalled each twisted face as the fire powder had sent a silver ball deep into their bodies and the look of shock and primal fear on each hellish face as the demons realized that their end was near. A sense of satisfaction had rippled through him with each victory the weapon had handed him, and each one strengthened his conviction that he had made the right choice those seasons ago.

Lordal gripped the handle of the weapon, which extended almost to the end of the underside of the steel tube. Thin bands of brass held the tube firmly in the cradle of the wooden handle. Lordal inserted his finger into the ring on the underside of the weapon and rested against the small lever housed within it. It had been the final refinement made to the weapon.

Lordal had recalled how a catapult operated and reasoned that the same theory could be applied to his weapon. The skilled people of that far away land had taken, again, his basic idea and quickly transformed it into a functional reality. Now the hammer could be drawn back until a faint click was heard. Once the hammer was drawn back, it would remain there until the lever was pulled which would release the hammer. It made the weapon far more accurate and much easier to operate.

It was the final refinement, and the one that led to Lordal being banished from the beautiful land, never to return. The Ancient One, along with what could be compared to a Council of Elders, had deemed that his violent nature, and the deceptive way in which he had built his weapon, were too negative a presence to their land. With a heavy heart, he had left that land, and for a brief moment, considered that the weapon had claimed its first victim.

With a sigh, he gently laid the weapon down and pulled another item from the chest. It was a leather belt with pouches attached to the right side. One pouch held an ample supply of silver balls, prepared in the tradition of his sword and properly blessed by a priest of high faith. Another pouch contained tiny bags tied tightly with twine. Each bag contained a measured amount of fire powder. Reloading the weapon was a simple matter of emptying the contents of one of the bags into the tube, inserting one of the silver balls and packing them down into the end of the tube with a thin rod which was housed in the handle of the weapon.

On the backside of the belt was a piece of leather, folded and stitched to the belt. This was the scabbard that held the fire powder weapon. Lordal had experimented with various designs and found that by having the weapon on his left hip and drawing it with his right hand, across his body, was faster than any other design but interfered with the drawing of his sword which also rode on his left hip. So he had stitched the scabbard to the back of the belt, which would require him to reach behind him to draw the weapon. It was not as fast as the other method, but it did allow him to conceal the weapon, and thereby allowing a small element of surprise.

Lordal rose to his feet and took up the belt which held the reloading materials for the fire powder weapon and swung it around his hips to buckle it securely in place. He attached the scabbard that held his Hunters sword to its place on the belt. Lordal took up the weapon and quickly loaded it. After making sure the fire powder and the silver ball were packed firmly into the tube, he checked the condition of the tiny flint rock and the action of the hammer/lever device. Satisfied that they were in good working order he slipped the weapon into its scabbard.

Next, he withdrew two of his silver daggers from the chest, slipped one into the top of his right boot, and tucked the other into the back of his belt, next to the fire powder weapon. After donning his cloak, Lordal returned the crossbow and quiver of bolts to the chest. Then he picked up the tunic and held it reverently in his hands before reluctantly returning it to the chest. He no longer had the right to wear the tunic, and he would not dishonor a true Hunter by wearing it. He kept it as a reminder of days gone by and of how one single lapse in his concentration, a slip of his judgment, had cost him the right to wear it.

After closing and locking the chest, Lordal turned to exit his tent, his mind turning over the confrontation to come and the part he had and would play in it. He did not know for sure if this Devenshire was a vampire, but he was somehow involved with one.

Devenshire, if he were not one of the demons, would tell him where the true demon was. Then, Lordal thought with a bitter smile, he would reap the consequences of his choice. It did not matter to Lordal if they were hung for their crimes or released by the Royal Guard to be dealt with by him. Either case would lead to each of them deeply regretting their choice as to ally themselves with a vampire.

CHAPTER TWENTY-FIVE

ZANDORTH PACED BACK and forth within the stifling confines of his cell with the nervous agitation of a caged animal. Cells of any kind did not sit well with him, and this one particularly angered him. He had spent a considerable amount of time in a cell many seasons ago, and the experience had left him with a permanent distaste for them.

Brianna sat on a small bench situated against the back wall of the cell and tried, as she had for the past hour, to ignore the warrior's pacing. Finally, she could stand it no longer. "Zan, would you please stop pacing like that?"

Krahl grunted in something resembling frustration and disgust. "I do not like this! Cells are for criminals or animals, and I am neither!" he snapped out curtly.

"I am sure it will only be a matter of straightening out a mistake with Captain Armand," she reassured him.

Zandorth shook his head, his right fist striking the palm of his left hand as he continued to pace, his angry state growing with each step. "I should never have listened to you! This is not as simple as a mistake. We are here because of Devenshire and Darkseed!"

"Now you do not know that for sure?" she replied, trying to ignore the stab of accusation in his voice.

Finally, the warrior stopped pacing and spun to face her. "I do know that we were not arrested until Armand learned that we knew of Devenshire and Darkseed!" He continued to bore his heated gaze into her as his rant began gaining momentum. "They have committed some crime, and we are being held, either as bait or to be questioned on their whereabouts. I need no mystical powers to put the obvious pieces of this puzzle together!"

He held the heated glare a moment longer before resuming his pacing. He paused at the front of the cell and took two of the bars in each massive hand. As he had done repeatedly since arriving in the cell, he tested the strength of the bars.

Brianna once again found herself silently agreeing with Zandorth, but something within her told her that it was not because of some crime Devenshire may have committed long ago or with his association with Darkseed. If that had been the case, then Armand would have arrested them immediately. Something else had happened after the sheriffs had begun escorting them to the jail.

The door at the end of the long row of cells opened, and Captain Armand with two of his men strode down the hallway. Brianna rose from her seat and crossed to join Zandorth.

Armand stopped before their cell and regarded each of them in turn. Gone was the warm pleasant nature he had used with them before. Now his expression and bearing was one reserved for criminals. Something had definitely happened after they departed the inn.

"I am here to inform you of the charges against you and give you the opportunity to present your defense."

Brianna regarded Armand and took stock of the man. He appeared to be in the mid part of his thirtieth season. His black hair hung to his shoulders while a very carefully groomed mustache traced a thin line across his upper lip. Only the faintest of lines could be seen forming around his hazel eyes and she could tell that age would only add character to his features instead of detracting from them. He was a handsome man and carried himself with the air of someone who was very sure of himself without being arrogantly so. He wore the uniform of the Royal Guard with pride, and Brianna could sense a determination within him that should not be underestimated.

"Why are we being held, Captain?" she asked.

"You are being held for associating yourselves with a vampire," Armand replied sternly.

Brianna felt her eyes grow wide. She looked to Zandorth and saw the same shocked expression playing across his face. She turned her stunned expression back to Armand. "A vampire?" she asked. As she considered his charge, the shock passed and the humor of it struck her, and she could not help but laugh. "Captain, I can assure you that we are not traveling with a vampire, nor are we in league with one. There has been some kind of mistake."

"Indeed there has been!" Armand replied sternly, his hazel eyes bore no humor nor did the stern set of his features. The hard look he gave her quickly stifled her merriment and the smile she wore quickly faded. "The mistake is yours for choosing to align yourself with a creature spawned from the bowels of the underworld!" Armand shot back.

"We have not aligned ourselves with a vampire!" Zandorth growled as his fists tightened around the bars until his knuckles turned white. It was obvious that he did not share Brianna's humor at the charge.

"You said you were traveling with Daimion Devenshire, did you not?" Armand asked in clipped tones shifting his glare to Zandorth.

"Yes. What has Devenshire to do with vampires?"

"My lords!" Brianna whispered as her right hand rose to cover her mouth. Her eyes grew wide in dawning realization and matching shock. "They think Daimion is a vampire."

"I have the word of a Hunter which is good enough for me," Armand replied. "Now tell me where I can find the demon, and perhaps I can intervene for you in your punishment."

"Do you realize how insane your claim is?" Brianna asked, still not truly believing what she was hearing. "I have seen Daimion in the sunlight, and I have seen him bleed when injured. I know little about vampires, but I do know enough to know that Daimion is not one," Brianna replied gently, trying to drive home the sincerity of her words with the softness of her eyes.

It failed miserably.

"I would have expected no other claim," Armand replied coldly.

"Are you calling me a liar, Captain?" Brianna asked, her eyes losing all trace of warmth and her voice taking on a hard edge."

Armand seemed to suddenly realize whom he was talking to, and taking a moment to consider his answer.

She took advantage of his silence. "I am the Lord of Prothtow Province and a member of the Lordship in the Court of King Lordoron. Tell me, Captain Armand, are you calling a member of King Lordoron's court a liar?"

Armand's disposition softened somewhat, and his demeanor shifted subtly into one more appropriate for addressing a member of the Lordship. "Forgive me, M'Lady, but I am under dictates to investigate this crime to its conclusion."

"That does not answer my question, Captain. Are you calling me a liar?" Her voice was now laced with a harsh, razor sharp edge, and her deep green eyes flashed with growing anger.

Armand drew himself up to his full height and launched into his reply. "Whether you are willingly being deceitful, or are under some sort of bewitchment at the hands of the demon, I believe you to be telling me falsehoods."

Brianna's lips almost vanished in the tight line of her indignation. "I see. Then I invoke my right as a member of the Lordship and demand an immediate audience with Lord Thallus!"

Armand's face grew grim as he considered the corner he had just painted himself into. He had hoped to gain the information without having to deal with Brianna's position and authority. Granted, her authority was limited since she was outside her own province, but all members of the Lordship carried certain rights and privileges, regardless of where in the kingdom they traveled.

He nodded once. "As is your right, M'Lady. I will send someone to summon Lord Thallus in the morning," he replied reluctantly.

Brianna shook her head sharply as she folded her arms harshly across her chest. "No Captain, you will send someone this instant!"

Armand's eyes narrowed. His pride had its limits and her behavior was rapidly pushing him to it. "While I am bound to honor your position and recognize your position within the kingdom, I am not required to answer your slightest whim. I will dispatch a courier at first light, and not one moment sooner. Let us not forget that you are currently under harsh suspicion of aligning yourself with a foul demon in the form of a vampire. That type of crime falls under my jurisdiction and will be handled as I see fit. Are we clear on our roles, M'Lady?"

Brianna's eyes narrowed dangerously. "Very clear, Captain. I sincerely hope this wild allegation of yours was worth your station in this kingdom. I will surely see to your ruination once this episode has passed, and you are revealed for the fool I now see that you are!"

Armand opened his mouth to reply, and quickly thought better of it. For the first time since his conversation with the Hunter Lordalise, he wondered if perhaps the man was mistaken and Devenshire was not, in fact, a vampire. If such were the case, his future was most bleak, indeed.

After taking a deep breath, he exhaled and turned to Zandorth, "Since Lady Standish has invoked her rights as a Lord and requested an audience with Lord Thallus, and I can no longer question her on this matter. That leaves you, Sir Krahl."

"Of all the things I can think of to curse Devenshire for, being a vampire is not one of them," he replied shortly.

"That is all you have to say on the matter?" Armand asked.

Zandorth locked a very intense gaze into Armand's eyes. "Only that I now give you my word as a Warrior of the Ancient Class that Devenshire is not a vampire!"

Brianna's jaw fell open as she spun to face Krahl. Armand's face, as well, went slack with shock. "Do you realize what you are saying?" Armand almost whispered.

The Warriors of the Ancient Class took their word as seriously as their honor, and it spoke volumes for Zandorth to have given his word in defense of Devenshire. She turned her eyes to Armand and could see that the captain recognized the form and underlying meaning of Zandorth's statement.

Krahl nodded once. "Very aware. You value the word of a Hunter. Are you going to show less respect for the word of a Warrior?" The challenge was definite, palatable.

"Hunters are a noble clan. Their holy work has helped keep the hellish grip of the vampire at bay for many seasons," Armand replied.

"The Warriors of the Ancient Class have been defending this realm for uncounted generations. I have given you the word of a Warrior, Armand. What is your response?"

Brianna turned her stunned gaze back to Armand. The Captain was in a most dire situation and his next actions would determine his and Zandorth's futures.

If Armand took the Hunter's word over Zandorth's, he would, in effect, be calling Zandorth a liar. Such an insult was bad enough for any normal person, but to call a Warrior of the Ancient Class a liar was as serious an insult as one could issue.

For Armand to accuse Zandorth of lying would cause the warrior to lose face before other members of the Ancient Class, a fate worse than death. The only way to save face were for Armand to either prove him to be a liar or give Zandorth the opportunity to take his honor back by fighting Armand to the death. If the latter came to pass, then an entirely new problem would surface for killing any member of the Royal Guard, especially a captain, as this was an offense punishable by death.

Armand shifted slightly, and Brianna could see the rapid thoughts playing through his mind. He had a very difficult decision to make. He opted for a third option. "I have no wish to offend you, Sir Krahl. You must be able to see my dilemma. I have the word of a Hunter that Devenshire is a vampire and now the word of a Warrior that he is not."

"I see that you have two choices, Armand. Release me, or call me a liar and grant me my opportunity to reclaim my honor!"

"There is, of course, a third choice," came a deep voice from the end of the row of cells.

They all spun toward the doorway to find Devenshire leaning back against the door, his arms folded casually across his chest. His dark cloak hung around his shoulders and allowed only a peek of his white shirt to peer out.

He was relaxed, almost comfortable, as he studied each stunned face now staring at him.

Brianna felt relief wash over her like the warm water of a hot bath at the sight of him. A thousand questions formed in her mind, and she had to fight the urge to ask them all at once. There would be a time for questions later, and Devenshire had damned well better answer them, she vowed.

"Who let you in here?" Armand demanded.

Devenshire grinned. "I let myself in. I did not wish to trouble your men with the tedious task of letting me in."

Armand's eyes narrowed. "Who are you?"

He arched one eyebrow, smiled a crooked smile, and bowed slightly, "I am Daimion Devenshire."

The three Royal Guards instantly drew their swords and took up defensive postures, which drew a chuckle from Devenshire, as he stood upright.

"A pleasure to meet you as well," he said with genuine merriment in his voice.

"You are under arrest! Surrender your weapons immediately!" Armand shouted.

"For what? I have done nothing wrong," Devenshire replied before he paused. His eyes looked upward shifting from one side to the other as if he were thinking. "Well, at least not lately," he finished with a wry grin.

"I will not banter words with you, Devenshire! Surrender immediately!" Armand replied and Brianna could see the genuine fear in his eyes and those of his men. It occurred to her that they genuinely believed Devenshire was a vampire.

Devenshire widened his smile as one eyebrow arched above the other, "Indeed? I will not surrender until I know of what I am being charged with."

"I have it on good authority that you are a vampire. Do you deny this?" Armand replied.

Devenshire's smile widened even further as his eyes considered the captain. The smile widened until it transformed into a good-natured chuckle. "Are you serious?" he said, humorous disbelief tinting his words.

"Deadly serious," Armand replied tersely.

"In that case, of course I deny the charge," Devenshire answered.

"Surrender!" Armand shouted with fear and anger mixing in his words. Devenshire's smile faded.

"I am not a vampire. If you have any doubts, then test me," he challenged.

"I intend to... after you have surrendered," Armand replied. Despite his fear at what he believed Devenshire to be, his eyes locked to his with a hardened glare.

Devenshire returned the hard stare as the humor he had shown vanished. For several moments, they stared at one another, each silently measuring the other. Devenshire's eyes left Armand to glance about the interior of the row of cells as he contemplated his current position.

Armand nodded. "You are indeed cornered. I know not how you

THE STONES OF ANDARUS

came in here without being noticed, but I can assure you that you will not leave that way. On the other side of that door is a complement of Royal Guards and sheriffs. One word from me and they will come barging through that door with weapons at the ready."

Devenshire regarded the door behind him briefly before turning back to face Armand. "It would seem I have little choice."

"Indeed," Armand replied steadily, feeling as though he might actually manage to capture him without losing a single man.

Devenshire's lips twisted in a poorly concealed smile as he shook his head. "Very well," he said as he raised his hands to shoulder level in surrender. "You have me," he finished and there was a distinct air of sarcasm in his tone and manner.

Armand looked over his shoulder at one of the guards and nodded. The man slowly sheathed his sword, his terrified expression never leaving Devenshire. He fumbled with the keys on his belt and finally managed to unlock the cell directly opposite Brianna and Zandorth.

Armand pulled the cell door open, its screeching hinges making an almost deafening sound in the ominous silence that had descended over them. They all stood behind the open door, as though to use it as a shield.

"In here!" Armand ordered, indicating the empty cell.

Devenshire almost chuckled, and his face was a mask of poorly concealed humor as he walked slowly down the aisle.

He paused at the open door and regarded Armand through the bars and, for a moment, it appeared that he would not walk on into the cell. Finally, Devenshire gave Armand a small wink and stepped inside the cell. Armand quickly slammed the door shut and locked it.

Only when the bolt of the door slammed into its keeper did any of the guards show any signs of relaxing. Armand, however, was not one of them. He seemed tenser now than before and there was something akin to suspicion in his eyes. He locked eyes with Devenshire and seemed to be contemplating something. When he spoke, he did not take his eyes from Devenshire's. "Go to the southern edge of town and summon Lordalise. Tell him we have the beast."

One of the guards quickly moved out the door, intent on his assignment and relieved, in no small part, in being given leave of being in the presence of true evil.

"Answer me this one question, Armand," Devenshire said, his voice low and as intent as his gaze. "If I were a vampire, would I have let you capture me like this? Would I not have killed the lot of you and had a feast?"

"I am no authority on your ilk. I do not know the depths of your damnable powers. You could have allowed me to capture you in an attempt to appear innocent. It matters not. Someone is coming who is

TOM SECHRIST | 323

TOM SECHRIST | 323

well acquainted with your kind and will be able to determine your true nature.

"If you are innocent, then you have nothing to fear. If you are, in fact, a vampire, then you will attempt to escape before Lordalise arrives," Armand replied.

Zandorth regarded Armand and had to admit to a grudging respect for the captain's tactics. By his last statement, he had all but guaranteed that Devenshire would not attempt escape. If Devenshire wished to have this dark charge dismissed from him, then he would have to remain in the cell until this Lordalise arrived and tested him.

Devenshire shook his head slowly. "You have been played as a fool, Armand. A true vampire would not need to waste time with such behavior. A true vampire, by now, would be drinking the last of you dry. This Lordalise is lying to you. He has some other agenda with me, and he is using this laughable accusation of my being a vampire to trick you into holding me here. By your own admission you know little of vampires, so how can you know if these tests Lordalise are to perform will reveal the truth?"

"Lordalise is a Hunter and would not dishonor his Order by using his office for revenge against a mortal enemy," Armand replied.

"You have also been given the word of a Warrior of the Ancient Class that Devenshire is not a vampire. I can see that you intend to take the word of this Hunter over mine. You have called me a liar, Armand, and I demand satisfaction," Zandorth said in hard, even tones, his cold stare never wavering from the captain.

Armand finally took his gaze from Devenshire and turned to regard Zandorth. "A great deal is at stake here. I cannot risk the fact that this demon might have duped you into believing him not to be a vampire. I have no doubt that you honestly believe what you are saying, but you must consider the fact that if he is a vampire, he could easily have tricked you into believing him not to be one."

"All I have to consider is that you have dishonored me, and you are bound to honor my demand for satisfaction," Zandorth returned with a harsh edge to his voice.

"I will wait for Lordalise to test this man. If it turns out he is not a vampire then I shall fight you and will let it be known that, in the event that you kill me, you are not to be charged with my death. However, if it turns out that he is a vampire then your word, by your association with him, will be meaningless, and I will be doing the Warriors of the Ancient Class a great service by having you killed," Armand replied calmly.

Zandorth's eyes narrowed as he bristled under the subtle accusation in Armand's words. Brianna saw the knuckles of his fists turn even whiter as he squeezed the bars tighter. "I shall see you on the field of honor, Armand!" Zandorth growled.

"We shall see," Armand said as he turned to regard Devenshire again. The Captain seemed to be trying to read Devenshire's mind as he studied his prisoner for several long moments. Finally, he looked at his men and began walking toward the door. "Post a heavy guard and let none enter."

The complement of guards exited the hallway and the heavy wooden door slammed shut behind them. The click of the lock echoed through the row of cells and the three were alone. Zandorth glared across the hall at Devenshire. "What have you gotten us involved in?"

"I am pleased to see you too," Devenshire replied with humor as he began surveying his own cell.

"Daimion? What is going on?" Brianna asked, trying to mask her own irritation.

"A very good question," he replied as he continued to casually study the interior of his cell. "One deserving of an equally good answer."

He regarded the rickety cot covered with a well-worn and very thin blanket in his cell with obvious distaste. The calm about him began to grate on her nerves. The man appeared not at all concerned that he was facing a very serious charge.

"I am waiting for that very good answer," Brianna said with a growing edge in her voice.

"Patience, M'Lady," he replied as he finished his study of his cell.

"Damn you, Devenshire! Answer her!" Zandorth demanded.

Devenshire regarded Zandorth with an amused smile. "First things first. This is no place for such a serious discussion."

"Oh? And where to you propose to hold such a discussion?" Brianna asked with thick sarcasm.

"I am thinking along the lines of a quiet tavern over a healthy tumbler of cognac," he replied.

"Unless they have opened a bar here, I seriously doubt you will get your wish," she said, the sarcasm still thick in her words.

"Then let us go and seek more hospitable surroundings," Devenshire said as he stepped up to the door and placed the palm of his hand over the keyhole. Within seconds, there came the very definite sound of the door's locking bolt sliding back, and Devenshire stepped out of his cell.

"Daimion! What are you doing?! If you escape you will all but be admitting that you are what they claim you are!" Brianna said in a harsh whisper.

Devenshire gently shut the door and relocked it in the same manner he had unlocked it. "They have already made up their minds. This Lordalise will make any test he administers come out to show me to be a vampire. To remain here is to be charged as a vampire and disposed of accordingly. Unfortunately, almost all of the ways there are to kill a vampire will also kill a human. Once they have killed me, they will hang the two of you for being in league with me. So, do you not see the need for our departure from here, and very quickly?"

"You do not know that for sure," Brianna argued.

"I know enough to know that I am not staying here to be given a series of tests that I have no hope of passing. Think for a moment, will you? A true Hunter would not risk the lives of others to trap a vampire, not even skilled soldiers. The whole point of the Hunter's existence is to protect humans from the vampires. A true vampire would have killed every one of those guards rather than be taken prisoner."

She digested that and had to admit to the logic of Devenshire's argument. She had little contact with Hunters and knew very little about them. What she had heard, spoke of the truth in what Devenshire had just said. She looked to Zandorth and saw the same thoughts running through his mind, as well.

"Then who is this Lordalise?" Zandorth asked.

"I am not certain, but we need to not be here when he arrives," Devenshire replied as he quickly stepped across to the cell holding Brianna and Zandorth and flattened his palm against the lock. Almost instantly, the lock clicked, and Devenshire quickly opened the door and stepped back to allow them to exit the cell.

"Who do you think he is?" Brianna asked. She did not immediately move to leave the cell.

"Will you stop with the questions?!" Devenshire almost hissed in irritation. "There will be time for that later. Now we must concern ourselves with getting as far from this building as possible."

Zandorth wasted no time in leaving the cell, almost knocking Devenshire out of the way as he exited. There came an instant expression of relief at being out of the tiny room.

Brianna fixed Devenshire with an annoyed expression as she stepped out into the hallway beside Zandorth. "Well, we are out of our cells. How do you propose to get us past the guards?" she asked as she folded her arms across her chest.

Devenshire smiled a very knowing smile as he turned his eyes to the door. "Guard!!" he shouted.

"What in the name of hell are you doing?!" Zandorth growled as he spun to face the door.

"Have you lost your mind?" Brianna echoed as she, too, turned to face the door.

"Well, I could not very well open that door the same way I opened our cell doors. They would have seen that, but if they open the door for us, then we can just walk out, and no one is the wiser," Devenshire answered calmly.

The heavy wooden door clicked, and then swung open to admit a guard. The man was nervous, and it was very obvious, for he had his sword drawn and there was a trapped animal look in his eyes.

"What do you want?" the guard asked looking toward the cell Devenshire had just occupied.

"Shall we?" Devenshire asked with a gesture of his hand toward the open door. Brianna looked at Devenshire, her eyes telling of her fear that he had lost his senses. Just as she looked at him she heard his voice answer the guard, but she noticed that his lips did not move.

"I wish for something to drink."

Brianna turned to see another Devenshire in the cell he had just left. She blinked in surprise as she alternated her gaze from the Devenshire before her and the Devenshire in the cell. When her gaze returned to the one before her, he smiled and winked.

"We have no blood for you, ghoul!" the guard shouted angrily and began to step back, pulling the door after him.

"I wish for something to drink as well, and I do not want blood," Brianna heard her own voice say, and she jerked her head around to see herself and Zandorth back in their cell. She looked back at Zandorth to see the warrior staring in the same shocked way she had no doubt she was.

Devenshire chuckled at their shocked expressions and began walking down the hallway toward the now open door. Brianna and Zandorth exchanged stunned expressions and turned to look at the Devenshire who was now standing next to the guard at the door. He gave no indication that he knew Devenshire was anywhere but in the cell.

The guard regarded her in the cell and seemed to be considering her request. "Water is all you will get!" he finally said.

"Anything will do," her duplicate answered from her cell. The guard mumbled something incomprehensible and stepped back inside the door to retrieve the water bucket and drinking cup.

"Shall we?" Devenshire repeated from the open door. "They cannot see us, so do not fear. If we do not leave while the door is open, we may have to use more attention drawing methods to leave."

Brianna gave their duplicates another astonished glance before she forced her feet to move her down the hall. Zandorth fell in step behind her, and with Devenshire in the lead, stepped through the open door and through the office of the jail that held five Royal Guards and four sheriffs. While Devenshire crossed to a large cabinet, Brianna and Zandorth stood in amazed silence in the midst of the guards, who gave no indication that they knew their prisoners were standing before them.

Brianna felt awe spread through her as she considered the power Devenshire was using here. She knew he was capable of magic, but she had no idea he possessed powers such as these. To create illusions of the three of them in their cells, while rendering their true selves invisible to the guards, was a considerable feat. She found herself wondering exactly what the limits were to Devenshire's powers.

She regarded her friend and lover as he made an odd gesture over the cabinet, then opened it and retrieved Zandorth and Brianna's swords. Again, the assembled soldiers did not react to the cabinet being opened or their weapons being retrieved. Devenshire quickly handed their weapons back to them and crossed to the open doorway of the jail. He paused at the door to turn to see them still standing in the midst of the room looking at men who could not see them.

"I am sure that I have surprised you with my gross display of power, but that display will not last long, so may I suggest we depart while the opportunity is present?" Devenshire said calmly, but with a slight sense of urgency to his voice.

Zandorth and Brianna shook themselves out of their awed state and quickly followed Devenshire out of the building.

Nothing was said as the trio wound their way through the crowded streets of Lirpa, putting distance between themselves and the jail. Zandorth and Brianna noticed that once they were away from the jail, the spell Devenshire had used to keep them invisible either had worn off, or had been canceled, for people began looking at them and moving around them. After a while, Devenshire led them down an alley, and once in the dark shadows, he stopped walking and turned to face them.

"That should do for now. The spell should last long enough for you to get as far away from here as possible, or at the very least, get an excellent head start on Armand," he said.

"What do you mean? You speak as if you are not coming with us," she asked.

"I am not," he answered, his eyes on the street they had just left.

"Why?" Zandorth asked.

Devenshire sighed in obvious irritation and shook his head. "How does Daimion stand it with you two always asking a million questions?"

"What?" she asked in confusion.

Devenshire closed his eyes and something strange began to happen to his body. It shimmered and waved as if they were looking at him through a veil of running water. Devenshire began to change; his clothes, his features, everything about him began shifting. Then, as suddenly as the change began, it ceased, and the man standing before them was not Devenshire. It was a man neither of them had ever seen before.

"By the Lords of Kuvol!" Zandorth uttered as he drew his broadsword. Brianna gasped in shock as she took several steps back from the sudden stranger, drawing her own sword.

"Who are you?" she asked breathlessly, her mind reeling from the shock of displays of powers she had assumed were beyond Devenshire's abilities.

The man regarded both of them with an expression of amusement as if their shock at his transformation was very amusing to him, and he took great delight in it. With a broad smile and a gallant bow, he said, "Allow me to introduce myself, I am Raven Darkseed."

"Where is Daimion?" she asked after finally finding her voice.

"I do not know," Darkseed replied as his amusement over the moment began to fade. "Listen to me, both of you. Get your mounts and get out of Lirpa as quickly as possible. My spell will fool them for only a short time, and once they realize they have been tricked, they will come for you in full force. Return to your homes and forget about this place and Daimion's suicidal quest."

"What are you talking about? Daimion and Shantira are missing, and we must find them," she argued.

Darkseed's face darkened as his irritation rose. "Are you deaf? Perhaps the seriousness of this situation is not apparent to you. If such is the case, then let me shed some much-needed light on it for you. Daimion has been accused of being a vampire. You and the other woman are known to be traveling with him. That makes the three of you the most wanted criminals in the city right now, and Armand will not rest until he has you again. Make no mistake about this: you will be put to death for your association with Daimion."

"As for this business with Xavier, put it out of your minds. Xavier is a fanatical mad man who is far too powerful for the three of you to stop. Leave the city now! I will try to find Daimion and get him out of the city as well, but you must leave now."

"I am not leaving without Daimion! As for him being a vampire, let this Lordalise test him, and he will be proven not to be a vampire!" she nearly shouted in return.

"Lordalise has some unknown wish for vengeance against Daimion and will do whatever he has to do to convince Armand that he is a vampire, and thereby be given full right to kill him! Armand, once convinced of Daimion's quilt, will have you put to death, and it will not be an easy death. Daimion has survived for many seasons before he met you, and he can take care of himself. Leave now! If you do not and are captured again, I will not help you a second time. I only intervened now because of Daimion," Darkseed replied.

"I will take my chances. I am not leaving Daimion behind," she shot back in anger.

"Nor will I!" Zandorth added.

"Daimion feels that Xavier must be stopped and feels strongly enough about it to act upon it. We are with him in this to the end," she amended.

Darkseed fixed each of them with an angry gaze for several moments before shaking his head in irritation. "Then you are as foolish as Daimion is! Do as you will! I have gone as far as I intend to in this matter. Indeed, I have involved myself far deeper than I had wished to."

"Devenshire came here to enlist your help in the Xavier matter! You will not help us?" Zandorth observed.

"You are very perceptive. I have no intentions of involving myself in someone's self appointed crusade into suicide," Darkseed answered tersely.

"I thought you and Daimion were friends," Brianna said flatly.

Darkseed looked her in the eyes and something akin to sadness flashed briefly through his as he sighed, turning his head away from her. "So did I," he mumbled in a tone too low to be heard.

"What?" she asked.

"Friendship has its boundaries, and Daimion has exceeded ours with his request for my help in what can only be certain death," he replied, forcing his anger back to the surface.

Her eyes narrowed as she considered Darkseed and his words. "So you will simply turn your back on him? Let him journey off into a battle where your obvious powers could mean the difference between victory and defeat? What manner of friend are you?"

"The kind who intends to stay alive," Darkseed answered with heated determination in his eyes.

"Let me tell you something. Friendship, true friendship, knows no boundaries. Zandorth and I are Daimion's friends, and we will follow him to the end, regardless. It appears that your 'friendship' with Daimion is based on something less substantial than true friendship," she shot back, the rage flashing in her green eyes with an intensity that made even Zandorth cringe slightly.

Darkseed's eyes narrowed as his anger mounted. It was plain that she had struck a cord within him and it irritated him. "Romantic nonsense! There is no such thing as what you speak of. Every man is only concerned with oneself, and that is a fact of existence that you would do well to learn. It will save you a considerable amount of pain and disappointment."

"Perhaps that is true of someone who ekes out an existence in the darkness of a place such as this. But where I hail from, friendship is much more, and is embraced when it comes along," she stated with controlled resentment bringing an edge to her voice.

Darkseed seemed to digest this, and it stirred something within him that he had sooner not have stirred. With an explosive sigh of heated frustration, he stalked past them, "Do as you will! I wish you luck in your dream reality... you shall need it!"

They watched as Darkseed strode down the alley to disappear into the crowd of the street beyond.

"What did you hope to accomplish?" Zandorth asked as he returned his sword to its scabbard.

Her eyes continued to stare at the point where she had lost sight of Darkseed. After several moments of silence, she sighed, slowly shook her head, and returned her sword to its resting place. "I do not know," she replied sadly.

"Understand. Men such as Darkseed have lived their entire lives in places such as this. They have a different way than we do," Zandorth said softly, a very unusual gentleness to his tone.

"How could Daimion consider him a friend?" she asked in frustration.

"You fail to remember that Devenshire once lived as Darkseed lives now. Darkseed is a part of his past that has carried over to his new life in our region. Perhaps, back then, Devenshire was not so different from Darkseed," Zandorth said.

"I cannot imagine Daimion being that cold and empty," she commented as she began walking down the alley in the opposite direction Darkseed had taken.

Zandorth watched her walk away and considered how she had lived her entire life in the same area, had never known what it was to live in a large city such as Lirpa, and what it took to survive in such a place. Perhaps it was one of the things he admired about her, the way she expected the rest of the world to live as she had.

He took his eyes from Brianna to the point in the street where Darkseed had vanished. With a slight grin, and a slow shake of his head, he mumbled, "I can."

CHAPTER TWENTY-SIX

SHANTIRA STUMBLED OUT of the darkened alleyway, holding one hand to her forehead while the other sought out the support of the stone wall beside her. Wave after wave of dizziness swept over her, and it took all of her strength to remain on her feet. She felt weak, confused, disoriented. She had trouble keeping some sense of balance about her, and in the short walk down the alley, she had been very thankful for the walls for she doubted her trembling legs would have supported her. Finally, she gave up and sagged against the wall, waiting for the dizziness and disorientation to pass.

With blurred vision, she began looking around her, seeking something that looked familiar, to give her some indication of where she was and what had happened to her. The scenery of the surrounding street looked vaguely familiar, and she barely remembered walking down it. She dug into her mind, dredging for any memory that would connect her to this place and the dizzying kaleidoscope of mental images that refused to focus into reality for her.

She remembered walking down this avenue, being lost in awe of the size and promise of the city. The emotions and thoughts that she had felt returned to her, and she fought to grab hold of them as if they could return her mind from the raging sea of disorientation to the firm shores of reality.

Ever so slightly, the dizziness began to fade, and she was able to hold her head up without nausea threatening to cause her to retch. She took several deep breaths and continued to lean against the wall until her strength returned. What had happened to her?

Shadowy images came. She had been walking and someone had

spoken to her. The image of herself in her mind turned to answer the person, and instantly, her memories blurred and spun away from the solid grip of focus. The next memory to come into focus was her awakening in the alley feeling weak and disoriented.

Shantira quickly checked herself and found she wasn't injured. Whoever had attacked her had rendered her unconscious without injuring her severely. Another check revealed that nothing had been taken from her. Her sword and daggers were still in place. Robbery had not been the motive for the attack. Then what could....

Cold dread took the warmth from her, as the alternative became an option. What if the attacker had taken something from her that was far more valuable to her than any material possession. She looked over herself and sought any confirmation of what she feared.

She did not feel as if she had been violated, and surely, she would if that had been the case. She had awakened fully clothed, and she felt sure that had rape been the driving motive of the attack, she would have woke to her clothes having been torn from her body.

As relief came over her, she found the puzzle of the attack remained unanswered. Who had attacked her and why? How had they rendered her unconscious so easily and been able to take her into the alley with all of these people around? It was then that Devenshire's, Brianna's and Zandorth's warnings to her of the dangers of this place returned.

The awe, beauty, and seductiveness of this place vanished to be replaced by the icy fingers of fear. What manner of people would allow a woman to be attacked, in plain sight and yet none would help? What sort of beasts, disguised as humans, inhabited this place? It was then it became clear to her how fortunate she had been. For she could easily have been robbed, raped, or even killed, in the midst of all of these people, and no one would have been the wiser. She suddenly desired to be far away from this place, to find the comfort of her friends, ushering them all away from this terrible place.

Forcing her still weakened limbs to move, Shantira pushed off the wall and took a series of slightly steadier steps to reassure herself that she could walk. Taking a few moments to get her bearings, she set off toward the inn with as quick a step as she could manage. She brought her senses to a fine point, looking for danger in each face around every corner. She silently vowed that the next vermin to attempt to attack her would meet with far less success.

As Shantira began walking quickly away, she did not see a tall thin man with ice-blue eyes step out of the very alley she had just emerged. She did not see the eyes follow her, or the slight smile that played across pale lips.

As the smile stayed on his lips, his mind considered what he had completed with satisfaction. He had considered taking from the woman what he had needed, but that would have aroused too much suspicion from Brianna's companions and made her useless to him. He was not used to controlling the urges of his nature, and he found the struggle to do so somewhat stimulating. He had always enjoyed testing himself against various situations as a way of measuring himself. But, he reflected, that particular test was not one he intended to take often.

Brianna was now a step closer to being his again. The young woman would be a useful pawn in his self-appointed game of chess with the Fates. They would not defeat him again. They would not take from him what was his, and the only thing he still yearned for.

"Greetings, sire. If you will pardon my forwardness, you appear to be one who is in need," a soft voice said to him. He turned to see one of the countless whores of this place, flaunting herself before him. The gaudy lavender of her thin gown did little to hide the flaws of her body, which time and the elements had not been kind to. While she was by no means old in the terms of the number of seasons she had lived, she was past her time for her profession.

"Do I? How very perceptive of you," he replied letting his eyes roam over her exposed flesh. His eyes briefly locked to her throat before returning to her eyes. He saw the emptiness of them; saw how there was nothing in this woman's existence, save for her nightly walk and countless embraces.

"What would you say I am in need of?" he asked letting his eyes swirl into hers. He saw the momentary glazed look spread through them, and he smiled. There was hardly any resistance within her to his will. This would be childishly easy.

For a moment, the woman's expression went slack as she became lost in the power of his strange eyes. She then shook her head quickly, forcing the fake smile back to her lips and allowing her long practiced look of seductiveness to return. "I would venture to guess that you are lonely," she replied.

"Lonely?" he asked as he pretended to consider her observation. Then he lowered his head slightly and locked his eyes deep into hers, making it impossible for her to look away. His voice sank low and steady, mesmerizing her just as it had the young woman before her."Loneliness is something you are very familiar with, is it not?" he asked softly.

Again, the glazed, slack expression returned to the woman's face as she stared wide-eyed into his eyes. She slowly nodded, a small piece of the massive loneliness within her floated to her eyes for him to see. "Yes," she breathlessly answered.

"It is a sickness to you. It makes your soul weary," he observed.

"Yes," she answered again.

"It twists and turns inside of you, feeds on what small amounts of happiness you manage to find for yourself. It is as a beast that lives inside of you, eating and tearing, leaving nothing but grief and emptiness in its wake," he said with the knowledge of what he spoke as the truth without her confirmation of it.

Tears pooled in her eyes as his words penetrated, not only her ears, but also every pore, every opening of her being. The soft deep timber of his voice spread through her, displacing the chilled presence of the very beast he spoke of. "Oh yes...." she whispered as a single tear fell.

"You wish to be rid of it. You pray for a release from it, yet none ever comes. Each night you come out and hope to find a way to escape from it, yet each dawn finds you with the beast having only grown larger during the night."

"Yes."

"So it would appear that you and I both are in need," he said.

She nodded slowly, unable to tear her eyes from the promise of comfort that his held.

"Come. Let us walk and find in each other what we need. What we have to have or we cannot survive," he whispered.

The woman slowly nodded and raised her trembling hand, which he took. Very slowly, the two of them began walking down the alley to disappear into the shadows.

~*~

The first thing Devenshire became aware of was the feathery cool brush of the night wind upon his skin. This struck his awakening mind as odd since he had fully expected never to wake again once his consciousness had left him so swiftly. The seriousness of his wounds and the rate of blood loss had led him to believe he would be dead long before anyone discovered him.

His mind lounged in the dream-like state of half wakefulness as he considered where he might be and how badly he was wounded. There was a strange tingling sensation starting to spread through his body, and he found no trace of the intense pain in his arm. Next he wondered who had found him and tended to his wounds. Brianna? Zandorth? Shantira? Whoever had found him had done an excellent job of caring for his injuries, and he made a mental note to thank whoever it was once he managed to come fully awake.

Then he considered where he was. It felt as if he were lying on his back upon lush grass, so he reasoned he was outside. The only sounds he heard were those of the night. The familiar song of the night mixed with the rustling of tree branches as they danced with the wind. There were none of the sounds of the city, and Devenshire reasoned that he was not only outside, but also outside of Lirpa.

With a soft moan, he rolled his head slightly to one side as he struggled to bring his mind back to full consciousness. A cool soft hand brushed across his forehead, and a melodious voice sang to his ears. "Lie still. You are safe."

The voice sounded familiar, but he could not place where he had heard it before. It was a nagging sensation that never failed to annoy him when it occurred. "Where am I?" he managed with a hoarse whisper.

"Outside the city," the soft feminine voice answered.

Very slowly, he forced his eyes to open. His vision blurred, started to focus, and then blurred again. He blinked several times, but his vision refused to cooperate. Obviously, he had been very deep into unconsciousness for him to be having this much trouble waking. His head swam against continuous waves of dizziness, and his limbs refused his mental commands.

"Fear not, your senses will return to you shortly," the voice said. The gentle tones of her voice swam about his awakening senses, and he found a strange comfort in them.

"Who are you?" he asked.

There was a soft laugh followed by another brush of her cool soft hand across his forehead. "A friend."

Devenshire smiled weakly. "Then I thank you for your help."

"No thanks are needed," she said.

Finally, Devenshire was able to open his eyes and images began to coalesce into sharp clarity. He could see the pale light of a full moon filtering down through the branches of many trees. The rich aroma of pine and earth filled his nostrils, and he inhaled deeply, savoring the naturalness of the smell and glad to be rid of the stench of Lirpa.

He rolled his head toward the direction the voice had come from, and the dim silhouette of a small woman wavered in the still unsteady focus of his eyes. Her features were concealed in shadow, but where the light of the moon touched her head, he could make out the rich thickness of her blonde hair. Again, that sense that he should remember this woman returned, and he dug in his memory for her identity.

"How do you feel?" she asked.

Devenshire smiled. "I have felt better. I have also felt much worse. I appear to be none the worse for the wear." Again, her soft laughter floated in the richness of the night air, and he wished to find a way to make that musical sound tangible, something he could capture and hold to himself.

Slowly, he raised himself up on one elbow and winced as a stitch of pain pinched his wounded arm. He looked down, but saw only the sleeve of his tunic over his limb. There was no bulge from a bandage; he could not feel any binding on at all, only the stiffness of the dried blood on his sleeve. He wondered how the woman had managed to stop the flow of blood or bind the wound with no bandage.

"Your wounds have been healed. Your arm will be sore for a day or two, and you may be weak from the loss of blood," the woman said.

"You are a healer?" Devenshire asked.

"No. Let us just say I have some experience in the subject," she replied.

Devenshire flexed his arm and was surprised that there was only a slight soreness instead of the searing pain he had experienced earlier. "My compliments. You are quite gifted," he said.

"Thank you," she replied gently.

With a mischievous smile, Devenshire regarded her silhouette, "No thanks are needed."

Although he could not see her face, Devenshire seemed to know she was smiling... could almost feel it. Devenshire rose to a seated position and looked about him. They were in a large clearing in a forest. He tried to dredge in his mind for the forest in relation to Lirpa, but the city was virtually surrounded by forest so the attempt was futile. It really did not matter to him at the moment, and the presence of the woman, he was sure, was why it did not matter.

"Tell me, where did you learn your healing gifts?" he asked.

"It was a very, very long time ago in a land far from here," the voice replied, and Devenshire caught the slightest hint of sadness in the underlying tones of her voice. It was with that realization that he knew who she was. He had heard that edge of sadness before.

"Nevertheless, it has proven to be of a valuable service to me, M'Lady Tambrey."

There was only the slightest of pauses in which Devenshire could feel her slight smile. "You remember me," she said.

Devenshire nodded. "Yes. You left an indelible mark on my mind."

"I am flattered," she replied.

"You have a unique presence about you. I find it difficult to forget," Devenshire said.

Again, there was a pause, and the underlying sadness within her seemed to flare briefly. "I am a unique person."

There was no conceit in her words. To Devenshire it was more like a condemnation of herself and that puzzled him. He felt the urge to delve into her mind to learn the secrets of such sadness, but resisted. "That sense of sadness about you remains," he observed.

"It is with me always. It is a part of me," she replied as she rose gracefully to her feet and began moving in a leisurely circle around him. She hugged herself as if she was cold, and her eyes seem to be fixed to something on the ground.

Devenshire's eyes narrowed as he studied her silhouette, trying to discern what could possibly make someone as lovely as her so sad. He rose slowly to his feet, making sure his sense of balance had returned. There was only a slight wave of dizziness, but nothing he couldn't handle so long as he didn't try to move suddenly. He watched her move around him, watching her features when they emerged from the shadows to be bathed in the moonlight. He had found her beautiful in the soft glow of lantern light in the tavern, but to see her countenance in moonlight made her earlier vision of beauty pale in comparison.

"What troubles you?" he asked.

A sad smile played across her lips as she shook her head slowly. "It is of no importance. Please, do not trouble yourself with it."

As in the tavern the night before, Devenshire sensed the deep soul-rending sadness that always seemed to hide just under the surface, threatening to break free. A touch of sympathy formed within him, and a desire to learn more.

"Remember in the tavern? How we discussed learning more of each other?" he asked.

Another delicate smile crossed her features as she nodded. "Yes, I remember."

"Do you still feel that I am too inadequate to deal with your phantoms?" he asked with a slight smile.

Instantly, he felt something change within her, as if she were pulling back from him, wishing to place as much distance between them as she possibly could.

"There is no time for that now," she replied with a definite dispassionate tone to her voice. A very marked difference from the warm tones he had heard from her earlier, and he realized that he had crossed some hidden line.

"If I have offended you, please accept my apologies. It was not my intention," he said.

"No offense was taken, Sire Devenshire. There is much that needs to be done, by both of us. You must depart now," she said in clipped tones.

"Of what do you speak?" he asked, feeling the confusion mount of what he had said that had sparked such a startling change in her demeanor.

"Much has happened since you lost consciousness. You and your friends are in danger and must depart Lirpa as soon as possible," she replied as she stopped her circular walk and turned to face him.

Almost instantly, Devenshire felt himself grow more alert, tenser. A sense of danger was calling to him, had been calling to him since he awoke, and he wondered how he had missed it.

"What kind of danger? What has happened?" he asked.

"The Warrior, and the lady have been arrested. The younger girl with black hair is missing, and you are wanted by the Royal Guard," Rachelle answered quickly.

"Zandorth and Brianna, arrested? Why? What have they done? Why is the Royal Guard looking for me?" Devenshire almost demanded, feeling a slight sense of panic trying to dominate his thoughts.

"The Royal Guard believes you to be a vampire and have arrested your friends for being in league with you. Make no mistake, Daim... Sire Devenshire, you are in a most dire situation," she replied.

Devenshire did not miss how she had almost called him by his first name and wondered why she had felt compelled to correct herself. There were a thousand other questions about her he wished to ask, but knew he didn't have the time. If the situation were as dark as Rachelle painted it, then quick and subtle action was called for.

"I do not understand. How could the Royal Guard believe me to be a vampire?" he asked.

"There is much about this situation that I do not know. I have told you all that I know. You must act quickly if you are to save your friends. But do not rush headlong into the city for you will be arrested on sight. You should go now," she replied, and that sense of her pulling away grew in strength. It puzzled Devenshire, but he knew he could not afford the time to ponder it now.

"Perhaps you are right. Let me, again, thank you for your assistance. I am in debt to you," he said.

"No, you are not. I do not collect debts. Just be very careful," she replied.

Devenshire's eyes narrowed as he studied her now stern features and felt himself longing for the warm smile she had graced him with earlier. Finally, he shook his head slowly. "Thank you, anyway. Which way to town?" he asked with an edge of his own.

"That way," she replied pointing in the direction that he would need to go. Devenshire nodded and walked away in the direction she had indicated. If she did not wish for his concern, then he would not force it upon her. Whatever drove her to behave in such a manner would remain a mystery. There were larger mysteries ahead of him that screamed for his attention. Just as he reached the edge of the clearing, her voice called out to him. "Sir Devenshire?"

There was just a hint of the warmness in her voice that he had heard before, and he paused to turn and look at her, his eyes asking what she wished to say.

"You are welcome," she said with a phantom of a smile playing vaguely across her lips.

Devenshire gave her a warm smile and a brief nod before turning and vanishing into the woods.

Rachelle watched him go, could follow his movements easily and admired the way he was able to put his weakness aside when the situation called for it. There was much to admire in him, and she had to fight the urge to rush off to join him, to lend him her abilities.

Then irritation claimed her, and she spun from the direction he had gone, forcing herself not to watch him go. What was she doing? She knew better than to engage in this type of foolishness. Experience had taught her that nothing but disappointment and pain lay along the path she was following. It had been a mistake to follow him. She should have remained in her own area, and left him to his own devices. It would have spared them the eventual horror, pain, and loss that were surely bound to come.

She did not regret helping him the night before by shooting the bandit who had addled him. He was a good man with good intentions, and this realm needed men such as him. She found she did not regret helping him this night, even though doing so had left her weakened, and the darker needs of her nature screamed at her so intently that she knew she could not resist them much longer.

She had exposed herself to a situation that tested a self-control she feared she would never master. The incident with the evil man she had observed from the rooftop when she had almost succumbed to her black nature was all the proof she needed of this truth. This was no place for one like her; she should not be here.

No, she should return to her own area, and spare both herself and Devenshire a pain they both could do without. The things she saw, felt and wished for from Devenshire were things she had forfeited any rights to long ago. Devenshire would soon forget her and move on to others who could give him what he needed far better than she and with less risk of pain.

With heaviness in her heart that surprised her, she turned to face the direction Devenshire had gone. A dark tear pooled in her eye as she adjusted her vision to just make out his shadow as it moved smoothly through the woods toward the city.

Farewell, Daim... Sir Deven... Daimion. You are a very unique and special individual. I shall treasure the honor of having known you, however briefly. I wish you well in your life, she thought, but did not project the thoughts to him.

She regretted vanishing from him like this, but she knew that it was what was best for both of them. As a tear traced silently down her cheek, she turned and began moving in the direction that would return her to her own area, a self-formed prison that she knew with each passing night she would never escape.

CHAPTER TWENTY-SEVEN

LORDAL FELT HIS HEART pound as his mount carried him toward the jail. The demon Devenshire was all but his, and a strange rush of excitement coursed through him at the thought of dealing out the holy justice of his cause on that vile ghoul. If it turned out that Devenshire was not the vampire he sought, then he would still suffer for daring to disgrace his race by allying himself with a dark one.

As for the others? He would leave their fate in the hands of the noble Captain Armand who, he had no doubt, would administer his brand of justice with the same fervor that Lordal intended for the vampire.

As with each encounter with a Dark One, Lordal felt the hidden hope rise that this one would be the one. The one who would reveal itself as the beast who had set him down his path of vengeance against the un-dead. With a bitterness that at times threatened to consume him, he recalled how he had failed to find the one who had taken his sister. He had gotten close on a couple of occasions, and one encounter had turned out to be a very dangerous meeting in which Lordal had nearly lost his life. The battle had been intense, and Lordal had nearly had the beast on two occasions, but the demon was crafty, very resourceful, and had managed to escape.

In the weeks to follow during his recovery, Lordalise strengthened his resolve to one day find that particular vampire, and he vowed that the next encounter would end much differently. The death he had in mind for it would be much slower, more painful, and more terrifying than the one it had handed his sister.

Although the journey from his camp to the jail in Lirpa was not long, it seemed to take an eternity. As he dismounted in front of the jail, he took a moment to calm his racing heart and his unsteady nerves. He could not afford to show weakness before the beast or those who observed his methods of testing it. Lordalise felt the comfortable weight of his silver sword and fire powder weapon, and took a deep breath to steady himself. He retrieved his pack that contained the tools he would need to test the vampire, and the methods he would need to bind the creature, so that he could move it from the jail to a place where he could leisurely set about destroying it.

As he stepped into the jail, he saw Captain Armand and a respectable complement of his men were on guard as were the Constable of Lirpa and many of his sheriffs. Lordalise noted, with satisfaction, that they all seemed to take the threat of their prisoner as seriously as he did.

"Lordalise," Armand said by way of greeting. "Thank you for coming so quickly."

"Thank you, Captain Armand, for your quick action in detaining the foul beast. I commend you and your men for such bravery and quickness of action," Lordalise replied, trying to seem at ease when his impulses drove him to bypass the pleasantries and hurry into the cells to confront the demon.

"Allow me to introduce to you the Constable of Lirpa," Armand said as he turned to indicate a man to his left. "This is Liston."

Lordalise smiled as he stepped forward to offer the Constable his hand in greeting. Liston also stepped forward and gripped Lordal's forearm with a strength that bellied his thin form. At first glance, Lordalise had wondered how the almost frail looking Liston managed to maintain any semblance of order or command of his men. But the firm grip of his hand and the hard look of his eyes told Lordal that this man commanded a strength that could not be seen and, thereby, made him a very lethal enemy or valuable ally. Lordalise made mental note to keep his raiding parties well clear of Lirpa for while his sheriffs may be vagabonds, Liston was a man to be reckoned with.

"It is an honor to meet you, Sire Lordalise. I have never met a member of your guild, but the Hunters reputation precedes you. Allow me a moment to say that I find your cause a noble one. In fact, I place its value second only to that of the Church," Liston said with a voice rich in deep timbre, which also contradicted his physical appearance.

Lordalise felt a stab of shame at being praised for work and an association that was no longer his. It was inappropriate of him to be presenting himself as a Hunter and accepting words of praise on their behalf. He still took the mission of the Order of Hunters as seriously as when he was among their ranks, and the justification of what lie ahead took some of the edge from the shame. Forcing a pleasant smile to his lips he nodded, accepting the praise. "My thanks to you, Constable." Lordalise released the Constable's arm and turned to Armand. "I am ready."

Armand seemed to become suddenly uncomfortable, and Lordalise felt a small dread rise within him. He had been in this situation before, and he could almost recite the next words that would come from the captain. "A moment, Lordalise. There is a matter we must clarify before we proceed," Armand said.

"And that is?" Lordal asked.

"What do you intend to do with Devenshire should he prove to be a vampire?"

Lordalise's features furrowed into confusion as though Armand had just asked what would happen if the sun set. "I intend to destroy it," he replied evenly.

Armand nodded briefly, his eyes darting to the floor before returning to Lordalise's. "And what of the other two?"

"Their crimes are beyond my jurisdiction, Captain. They will be yours to execute as you see fit," Lordalise replied and prepared himself for Armand's next argument.

"There is the touchy subject of overlapping jurisdictions here. Being a vampire makes Devenshire answerable to His Majesty as well as Constable Liston. There is some question about bringing Devenshire before a tribunal to face the charges against him," Armand said and Lordalise could see the uncomfortable regret in his eyes. Obviously, Armand was making this stand on orders from someone higher in rank than himself.

Lordalise nodded slowly before replying. "I see. If Devenshire proves to be mortal, then the point is moot. However, should he be shown to be a vampire, then I must insist that it be released into my custody for disposal."

Armand shifted his feet slightly and cleared his throat nervously. "The problem with that is where the matter of jurisdiction lies. Devenshire is guaranteed the right to answer to the charges against him according to the laws set forth by the King."

Lordalise forced a pleasant smile to his face, but he actually felt like striking Armand for being so ignorant as to say such a thing. Forcing his temper into submission, he locked eyes with the captain. "Captain Armand, you are applying guarantees that do not relate to these monsters."

"I understand that, Lordalise. However, Devenshire has yet to be proven to be a vampire. Until that proof is given, he has only been accused of being one and is still considered to have the guarantees given to all," Armand replied.

Lordal felt his pleasant smile fade as his anger and indignation rose. Just a few short seasons ago, Devenshire would have been handed over to him without question. But now there was a growing trend that Lordalise found alarming. This cry of guarantees for all. This growing habit of treating every criminal as if they were innocent until undeniable proof was submitted to the contrary. It was a waste of time and allowed many of the guilty to escape justice. Lordalise had found comfort and pride in the fact that this region had been free of the curse of the vampire, but now he wondered if perhaps these bleeding hearts needed a reminder of the terror that reigned under the dark cloud of the vampire.

He agreed that under certain circumstances, an innocent man could appear to be guilty, and every means should be exhausted to make sure that an innocent man was not punished for a crime he did not commit. But in the case of Devenshire and those like him, this growing concern with making a mistake was insane. There could be no doubt about a vampire's guilt. It was ridiculously easy to prove a vampire's nature, and no further consideration was needed.

"As I have said, Captain, if Devenshire is not a vampire, then this argument is null. I intend to perform the tests to show his true nature, and if he is a vampire, then these guarantees you speak of do not apply to him any longer for he is not human." Lordalise noted the tight tones of his voice and struggled to keep them from overpowering the calm words of his argument.

"But if Devenshire is a vampire, then he must still stand before the tribunals of this land and have proper sentence passed upon him," Liston injected.

Lordalise looked at Liston and suddenly knew where this insane concern for the rights of a vampire had come from. His initial impression of Armand had been correct, and the captain was only acting under the tight restraints of his office, not from any personal view of the situation. "Tell me something, Constable. Have you ever seen a vampire? Have you ever seen the results of an attack of a vampire?"

"No. I have not," he replied with no indication in his voice that he felt he needed to justify his lack of experience in the matter.

"Then you do not fully appreciate the service I am offering here. I pray to the Fates that you never have to learn, as I have, what a true blight on mortal existence a vampire is."

Liston considered this statement only briefly. "I have stated how I feel about your service to this region, Lordalise. I have nothing but respect and admiration for what your Order does, but I cannot ignore the dictates of His Majesty. While the Order of Hunters is a respected guild, they have never been officially declared as an office of the Court."

Lordal's eyes narrowed. "Are you saying you will not honor my right to take custody of this monster and dispose of it?"

"I am saying that your right to take Devenshire is not recognized by the Courts of the King. If you show him to be a vampire, then that information will be taken into consideration when he stands before the tribunal. Devenshire has been guaranteed the right to stand before a tribunal of the King to answer for the crimes against him."

This last argument sent Lordalise's calm spinning from his control. "Have you taken all leave of your senses, man? Do you not hear how insane your words are? A vampire will not allow itself to be hauled before any tribunal, lest it is to feed on a large number of humans. I can guarantee you, as dawn approaches, our chances of being able to handle this beast will diminish. I can promise you that once the sun begins to rise, Devenshire will not be in its cell and several men will lose their lives in the attempt to keep it there."

Armand shifted his gaze from Lordalise to Liston and found he wanted to intercede on Lordalise' behalf. He, unlike Constable Liston, had seen the results of a vampire attack and had no wish to witness such an occurrence again. The Constable, while a good man, simply did not realize the depths of the horror he held in his grasp. A grasp that the constable did not realize was as thin and weak as writing parchment.

"While I will admit that I do not have the knowledge of vampires that you do, Lordalise. I do know that we captured Devenshire, and he is tightly locked in his cell as we speak. Our jail is sturdy, and it has held many prisoners that were rumored not to be able to be held. Devenshire will not leave his cell until we are ready for him to leave it," Liston replied with controlled tones.

Whatever insanity claimed the constable's train of thought, lack of conviction was not part of it. "Devenshire will not be handed over to you for execution simply on your word that he is what you claim he is. A tribunal will be held, the evidence will be presented, and the tribunal will be given the opportunity to pass sentence upon him. Then, if he is found guilty, I will be more than happy to hand him over to you under the dictates of your Order."

Lordalise felt his face turn hot from the flush of anger, and his mind reel under the stark raving insanity facing him. Never before in his long association with the Order had a Hunter's word been doubted or set aside in favor of another judgment. It was understood that a Hunter was the foremost authority on vampires, and no challenge had ever been made to their right to take custody of and dispose of a vampire. He turned to Armand and grasped at his last chance to talk some sanity into the constable. Lordalise wished now that he had brought a complement of his own men along for he saw this situation quickly spiraling out of his control.

"Captain Armand, talk some sense to this man! Tell him what a large error in judgment he is making."

Armand was as uncomfortable as ever now. While he was a leading officer in the Royal Guard, it was also known that the local Constable could overrule such an official. It was hardly ever done, but it was possible. "Constable, let me personally vouch for Lordalise and what he claims rights to here. I have seen what a vampire is capable of and know a little about their kind. Lordalise speaks the truth. Sunlight is death to a vampire, and it will avoid sunrise at all costs. As dawn approaches, if Devenshire is a vampire, then not all of the men we can muster will be able to hold him in his cell."

Liston regarded Armand for a moment before a brief flicker of regret flashed through his eyes. Lordalise felt all hopes of resolving this argument fade away. The Constable had made up his mind on a course of action, and there would be no deterring it now. "Captain Armand, I have nothing but the utmost respect for Master Lordalise and the work he does. I am under the very strict and definite laws set forth by the King. ALL criminals, regardless of their crimes, are guaranteed the right to face the charges against them before a tribunal of the courts. Devenshire will stand before such a tribunal at the earliest possible time. Until that time, I cannot and will not release him to anyone."

Lordalise shook his head slowly. Liston would not release Devenshire to him, even if he proved that he was a vampire. The foolish Constable honestly believed his jail and his men capable of holding a vampire, and that faulty judgment would cause many deaths. Lordalise wrestled with his anger and focused his mind to summoning another train of thought and another course of action. He could not allow the beast to kill again.

"Very well. At least allow me to perform the tests. To show you what Devenshire is," Lordalise said, seeming to resign under the argument.

Liston smiled and seemed to relax, confident that he had won the argument and made his point. "Of course. You understand that several others and I must be present during these tests. This is to insure that the results of your tests can not be disputed due to a lack of proper witnesses."

Lordalise forced the pleasant smile back to his features and nodded his head. "Of course. We would not wish to make any rash judgments in this matter." He fully intended to show this foolish man what kind of creature he was dealing with. There were several of the tests he could administer that would force the vampire to reveal its true face. Once Liston sees that, Lordalise had little doubt that Devenshire would be handed over to him in short order.

Liston smiled again and turned to the pair of sheriffs standing guard at the wooden door. With a curt nod, one of the men turned and began unlocking the door. Liston was the first through the door followed by Lordalise, Armand, and a complement of men comprised of sheriffs and other soldiers of the Royal Guard.

Empty cells greeted their astonished gazes.

Lordalise felt the hairs on the back of his neck stand on end, and a strange chill soaked into the marrow of his bones. He felt his muscles draw up tight, and he strained his senses for any sign of where the ghoul had vanished. It would not be beyond the vampire to suddenly appear in their midst and begin killing them all.

"Be ready!" Lordal shouted, his eyes darting to the rafters and back. "It could strike from anywhere!"

Armand's face paled slightly as he, too, began looking all around for any sign of Devenshire, fully expecting him to suddenly appear from anywhere, fangs bared and ready. The fear was thick in the room. Armand could almost smell it. His men's, the sheriff's, and even his own fear was intense enough to cast a chill throughout the room.

"What in the name of hell?" Liston asked in utter shock as he studied the empty contents of the cells. Obviously, it was the last thing the constable had expected. "How?"

Lordalise did not look at the constable, but kept letting his wide eyes scan the area around them. "A vampire, Constable, a vampire."

"By the Fates!" Armand whispered as the meaning of two empty cells settled upon his mind.

"May the Saints preserve us," another man whispered.

Lordalise nodded in grim understanding. He not only had underestimated Devenshire, but he had let the demon capture his full attention, and thereby, forcing him to overlook another possibility that now came to him with sickening clarity: They were all vampires.

For uncounted moments, they all stood frozen in place. Fear held them in its icy grip, and the implications of all of them being vampires robbed them of the ability to move. Lordalise felt his anger rise, not only with the vampires, but also at himself. He had moved too quickly, revealed himself too soon. Now they knew who and what he was. The element of surprise so vital to a Hunter in pursuit of a vampire was lost. They would know, and they would be ready.

"Constable Liston! Captain Armand!" A cry sounded from the outer office as the sound of pounding footfalls broke the spell of fear. The assembled men turned to the open doorway to see another sheriff dash through the door. The man was pale and trembling. Even as he leaned against the heavy oak of the door, and his labored breathing racked his chest, the fear was as plain as the fear that permeated the row of cells. Something had scared the man to the point of incoherence.

Liston moved through the throng of men to stand before the winded, terrified sheriff. "What is it?" he asked.

"Come quickly. A woman has been killed!" the man gasped.

"What happened?" Liston asked.

The sheriff looked up at him, and they all saw the terror in his eyes. As a sheriff in Lirpa, the violent manner in which death struck was no stranger to them. It was almost a nightly occurrence. But this one was different, very different, and whatever the man had seen had terrified him beyond words.

"You should come and see for yourself, sir," the man's trembling voice replied.

Lordalise and Armand found themselves looking at each other, a sense of dreaded understanding passing between them. They each nodded to the other and then turned and began walking toward the door.

"Take us there," Armand ordered the sheriff, no longer concerning himself with who was in charge of the situation. The sheriff nodded briefly before turning and hurrying out with Armand, with Lordalise and the rest of the men on his heels. Only Liston remained behind, his senses addled by what he had just seen, and how sorely he had misread the situation.

He felt numb as he watched the men rush out into the night. How had he so badly missed the dangers here? Why had he not listened to Armand and Lordalise? It was obvious now that they knew of what they spoke. It was plain that this situation was far beyond his capabilities to deal with. He had heard of vampires, had heard the legends of what they were capable of, but he had always assumed these to be the dressed up stories designed to frighten and entertain. Yet what if the tales were true? What if vampires truly did drink the blood of humans and had powers beyond those of mortal men? What if they could do all of the things he had heard them capable of?

"Dear Lords," he heard himself whisper as he staggered back into the row of cells.

"Do not be too hard on yourself, Constable."

Liston spun at the sound of the voice, his breath catching in this throat, his heart seeming to cease beating at that terrified instant. His eyes took in the sight of a tall, thin, elegantly dressed man standing against the far end of the row of cells. The man wore dark trousers and dark jacket of a material that spoke of great wealth. Under the jacket was a red shirt of equally elegant linen. A black silk cravat encircled the man's neck. A pitch-black cloak was clasped with a golden fastener and swirled about his frame to almost drag the floor.

Liston noticed how pale the man looked, how drawn he appeared to be. Yet there was a severe handsomeness about the man that defied expression. Although the man did not appear to be too many seasons older than he, his jet-black hair was streaked with silver at the temples. There was a sense of power about the man, as if he commanded a strength that was not visibly apparent about him.

"A vampire is a difficult being to manage," the man said, and the deep richness of his voice seemed to sweep forward to encircle Liston with a strange sense of comfort and ease.

"Who are you?" Liston whispered, unable to force himself to recover from the start of finding himself not as alone as he had believed himself to be.

The man smiled, his ice-blue eyes seeming to dance with a light all their own. "Names. Such a tedious thing. Are names truly so important? Does the mere utterance of letters in a certain arrangement change who we are? Define who we are?"

Liston knew he should be alert, weary, and on guard. The very nature of his position demanded it. Yet there was something about this man that put him at ease. Even his odd answer about what he was called did not seem to alarm the constable even though he knew it should.

"It is how we identify ourselves," he heard himself answer.

The man nodded. "Yes. But is it truly that important? Will my name change who I am to you?"

"I do not understand..." Liston answered.

The man sighed sadly. "Alas. None ever do. It seems to be one of those eternal questions for which I will never find an answer. To answer your question, I am called Darius Thiberian."

"W-what is your business here, Sire Thiberian?" Liston asked nervously. He could not quite find the source of his nervousness, but it was there, calling him to be aware.

"Simply to pass a brief amount of time before moving on. I enjoy making the acquaintance of new people. For me, meeting a new person is like sampling a new wine. Some are rich and aromatic and full of hidden pleasures, while others are bitter, foul smelling brews that are difficult to swallow. Yet each should be enjoyed for their own unique differences. Would you not agree?"

"I have never given it much thought," Liston answered haltingly. A strange sensation was coming over him, as if a fog of disorientation had been settling upon his brain, and he was only now becoming aware of it.

"A shame. A man in your position has the enviable gift of encountering all kinds of beings, and in a city the size of this one, the variety must be mind staggering," Darius replied with a near sense of wonderment about him. "Close the door and let us discuss this at length."

Liston was dimly aware of his body turning and gently pushing the door closed. He had not wished to close the door, but he was acting under a compulsion he could not define. It seemed like it was his will to close the door, but he could not shake the sensation that he was simply acting out of the command of the stranger to do so.

"Take this Lordalise you just conversed with. He is a bitter man. He has a hatred within him that taints the rich wine of his being." He paused and let a wicked smiled play at the corners of his pale lips. "Yet that would not deter me from wishing to get to know him, to sample his wine." Darius seemed to be speaking as if his words held some kind of double meaning. But Liston's senses seemed to be dulled as he could not fathom what that other meaning might be.

"Lordalise is a noble man. He fights a noble cause," he answered.

"Noble? Setting about destroying beings simply because they are not like him is a noble pursuit? I think not," Darius answered with growing anger and indignation in is tone.

"Vampires are a foul lot. They kill innocent people for nothing more than to feed their own hellish appetites," Liston argued.

"Innocent?" Darius scoffed. "I think not! There is no such thing as an innocent man! All men are guilty of one sin or another, and each one seeks to justify their sins in the dubious cloak of humanity. Indeed, many men are more foul and hellish than you accuse vampires of being."

"There are many good men within this realm," Liston replied.

"The difference between what you call a good man and a bad man is only a matter of varying degrees of evilness," Darius observed. "What makes one man good and another man evil is simply a matter of perception."

"No. There are truly good men. Men who are above reproach," Liston argued.

Darius laughed, a hollow, empty sound that sent chills racing down Liston's spine. "Above reproach? You honestly believe this?"

His eyes seemed to darken to nearly black as he studied Liston. "My dear, Constable Liston, that is merely a comfortable blanket of hypocrisy that men often wrap themselves in. Tell me, do you consider yourself a good man?"

Without his conscious effort to do so, he looked deep into Darius' eyes and felt something take hold of him. It was not a tangible grip, but a grip nonetheless. He found he could not take his eyes away from the darkening gaze as he struggled to answer the question.

"Yes. I am a good man."

"Indeed. What makes you a good man?" Darius asked, his voice taking on a strange tone.

"I uphold the laws of the land. I ensure the safety of the citizens of Lirpa. I and my men, we are the barricade between the good people and the evil people," he answered. He had always thought of himself as he had answered. He had felt the truth of it to his soul. Now, under the strange dark gaze of the stranger, he felt as if he had just uttered the most ludicrous statement in the history of man.

Darius chuckled. It was a deep dark sound that raised gooseflesh on Liston and sent a cold chill to the center of his being. "A laughable statement. Tell me, Constable, do the fine, upstanding citizens of Lirpa know of your nightly habits?"

"What are you talking about?" he asked, feeling a sense of dread spread through him as if his darkest secrets had suddenly been thrust into the harsh light of knowledge.

"Do they know how you take your pleasures? How you delight in having young women from distant villages brought to you? How you prefer them to be bound, naked, and blindfolded? How you take sexual pleasure from nearly torturing them with unwanted touches and whispered desires that are yours alone? Do the people know how their barricade against evil forces himself upon these fair young maidens to empty his steaming 'goodness' into them? Do they know of how many of these young women are returned to their villages forever marked? Forever branded as something only slightly above that of a common whore? Let us not forget the numerous young women who are forced to bear the fruits of your steaming goodness alone. How their lives are forever altered as they are forced to bear life and be condemned to a life of caring for a child that was not of their wish. Do the good people of Lirpa know of this?"

Liston felt his already chilled flesh freeze under the revelation that he was sure none knew of. "I have no idea of what you speak!" he answered with a failing attempt at indignation.

"Oh, but you do, Liston. The thoughts are within your mind, the memories. I can taste each encounter as if I were there."

Darius paused, tilting his head slightly as more thoughts reached him from Liston. A wicked smile spread across his lips. "Just this evening you paid a man rather handsomely for a new girl. A village girl in her sixteenth season delivered to you bound and submissive. You ache to take her. Had it not been for this situation, you would be buried deeply within her even now. Delicious!

"Fear not, Liston. I am not judging you. I find no fault in what you do. Why else are these beautiful creatures placed here? The pleasures they hold so tightly to themselves should be enjoyed. I merely bring this to light to prove my earlier point: there is no such thing as an innocent man."

Liston thought to defend himself. To argue that what Darius spoke of were lies. Yet there was something in the man that told him that such a defense would be a waste of breath. He tried to find some way to dispel the dark truth he had been confronted with, but none came, and so he said nothing.

"Come, Liston. Let us speak openly here. Do you not find pleasure in such things?"

"Y-yes," he whispered as he fought to control the emotions of sheer excitement and soul rending guilt. Despite the shame of having his dark secret revealed, Liston could feel himself begin to swell at the memories that suddenly came to mind. The flicker in Darius' eyes said that he knew of the mounting excitement.

"You see? The memories excite you, even now. You wish to rush to your home and take the tender young maiden bound to your bed." Darius walked slowly toward Liston, his eyes having gradually darkened until there was nothing but blackness. All color had drained from his eyes; even the whites had darkened to pitch.

He took a faltering step backwards, encountering the solid wood of the door. His mind screamed at him to open the door and flee, but his muscles had turned to stone.

"You hunger for their tender flesh to yield under your touch," Darius whispered as he moved ever closer.

"Yes," he heard himself whisper in reply.

"You hunger for their muffled cries of protest as your mind turns them into cries of desire and pleasure."

"Yes."

"You hunger for their youth, their beauty, and the softness of their skin. Your hands ache to touch the swollen nipples of their breast, the damp heat of their loins." Darius' voice seemed to echo through the chamber and through the darkest recesses of his mind, and he found he could hide nothing from him. The chilling caress of his thoughts touched his mind, and his mind in turn, revealed all it wanted to know.

"Yes," he whispered as Darius stepped very close to him, his black eyes boring deep into his.

"You see? You and I are not so very different from one another. We both hunger, just for different things. Why should you be denied that which you hunger for? Why should I be denied that which I hunger for? You claim to be a man of justice. A man of honor. Do you not feel that if you are granted your darkest hungers then I should be granted mine?"

"Yes, of course. No one should be denied their soul's desires," Liston answered breathlessly. He blinked several times and managed to say, in a weak trembling voice, "What are you?"

Darius' dark eyes drifted down to Liston's throat and slowly back to his eyes. A smile as evil as any he had ever seen parted pale lips as Darius opened his mouth slightly. "Only one who seeks to have his desire's fulfilled... just as you do."

Liston's eyes darted to the open mouth, and they widened in terror as he saw two fangs hanging down from the row of even teeth. With a movement that he was not sure he could even follow, the fangs suddenly sank deep into his throat.

Liston grunted out in sudden pain as he brought his hands up to

Darius' shoulders and began struggling, fear finally breaking through to force his limbs into action, but the man held him in a grip of steel and all of his struggles, he knew, were in vain. As the sharp piercing pain faded, and an urgent sucking sensation replaced it, he realized that he had made another error in judgment, and this one, he reflected with his fading perceptions, would be his last.

CHAPTER TWENTY-EIGHT

STAYING TO DARKENED allies and side streets, Brianna and Zandorth were able to carefully make their way back to the inn. Several times they had encountered sheriffs and members of the Royal Guard. By the demeanor of the guards and sheriffs, they knew they were being searched for in earnest.

Zandorth had argued against returning to the inn, but Brianna reminded him that their few supplies were there, and they would be sorely needed in the days to come. She left unvoiced her hopes that Shantira had survived the streets of Lirpa and had made it back to the inn. She also left unvoiced her concerns that had the young woman returned to the inn, she would unwittingly admit to her association to Lirpa's newly most wanted criminals.

The duo finally made their way to an alley across the street from the inn. To their mutual disappointment, but not surprise, a large complement of Royal Guardsmen and sheriffs maintained a line outside the inn. They watched as anyone who attempted to enter the inn was questioned at length before being allowed to enter or being turned away.

"Did I not tell you that this was a waste of time?" Zandorth asked in clipped tones.

"We had to try," she grumbled.

"What are we to do now?" the warrior asked.

"Give me a moment. I am trying to figure that out," she replied.

"We do not have a moment!" he growled, his agitation growing by the second. "Darkseed's spell has no doubt worn off by now, and they will be looking for us in force. We should have left the city long before now."

Brianna turned her head to look at him with growing irritation in her eyes and voice. "And leave Daimion? Shantira?"

"Devenshire can take care of himself. Shantira may already be lost, and if she is not, she should have listened to us and not wandered off," Zandorth replied with equal measures of irritation. "This is foolhardy at best!"

Brianna could not contain her anger any longer. She spun on the massive warrior, her fists doubled at her sides. "Then go! Leave and bother me no more with your endless complaining!"

His eyebrows raised a notch in surprise at her outburst, and his eyes instantly narrowed in anger. He opened his mouth to reply but she cut him off. "I intend to remain here until I find Daimion and Shantira! I will not debate that point a moment longer! If you care only for the salvation of your own hide, then depart now! If not, stop complaining and help me! But do one or the other now!" Her nerves had been stretched to the breaking point, and she was tired to her soul of everyone saying that she should leave her friends behind. Enough was enough, she reflected.

"You put yourself in a dangerous position, woman!" he growled in reply.

Brianna did not so much as blink as she leveled a hard, angry glare into his eyes. "As do you!"

Zandorth studied her intently. At first, he thought her veiled threat implied the danger from her position of authority and power. As he stared back into the smoldering green depths of her eyes, he realized that she spoke of something that had nothing to do with her position.

He resisted the urge to laugh. Did she really think herself capable of doing battle with him? She was nearly half his size and did not have anything resembling his skill in combat.

Then he reflected on her inner strength and will of iron. He knew that once Brianna set herself to a course, there was nothing short of death that would deter her. While he acknowledged that he could defeat her easily, and she had to know this as well, he had to admit that if she decided to attack, she would not stop until he yielded or he killed her. It was as simple as that.

He searched his mind for a way to yield to her argument without losing face. He would never submit to anyone, especially a woman, governing lord or not. He knew he could easily escape Lirpa and deal with the damage to his honor once he was clear of the city. He felt sure that Devenshire could escape as well. Shantira, if not already dead, would eventually fall victim to one of the many dangers of this place. Brianna, in her stubbornness, would get herself captured or killed in short order.

The fates of the two women would be forever on his conscience and a mar to his honor and reputation. One of the many responsibilities of being a Warrior of the Ancient Class was to tend to the chivalrous duty to the women of the realm. To leave Brianna and Shantira behind to their own ends would deal an even more damaging blow to his honor than Armand calling him a liar.

Biting back on the frustrating truth of the situation, he sighed in irritation. "Very well. We will attempt to retrieve them." He locked his eyes deeper into hers, driving his next words to the center of her soul. "But know this—I will not be taken captive again! I will not yield to these false charges! Do not even attempt to stop me for that will make you my opponent, as well!"

The truthful intensity of his words and the glare in his eyes made her mentally take a step back. There was absolutely no room for any other interpretation of his words. They were as solid and unmovable as a mountain range.

"Fair enough," she replied before turning back to the inn. Once her back was to him, she allowed herself to softly sigh in relief. The situation had very nearly spiraled out of the control of either one of them. No matter how angry or determined she was, she knew she was no match for the warrior's skill. But she would be damned if she would let him intimidate her. No man... not even her father... not even King Lorderon... intimidated her. She had vowed to herself long ago when another man had tried to dominate and intimidate her that she would never, ever allow that to happen.

Shaking off the horrible memory, she shifted her eyes and attention to the inn. She searched intently for some way of gaining entrance without arousing the attention of the guards. Her thoughts were jumbling together, and it took great concentration to keep some form of order about them. Too much had happened and had happened too quickly for her mind to absorb and sort while trying to stay one step ahead of a massive man hunt that was probably already underway. Again, she wished for Devenshire's presence, his calm way of assessing a situation and always managing to find just the right course of action.

Just as the wish formed in her mind, she quickly swept it away. She was growing too dependent on Devenshire and that troubled her. She was independent, had been so for a very long time, and intended to remain that way. This growing dependence on Devenshire could only lead to more intense emotions that she would not allow herself to feel. She would find a way out of this predicament and do so without Devenshire's help.

"It is safe to assume that there are guards posted at the back entrance, as well," she thought aloud as she quickly dismissed the thought of sneaking around and going in the back way.

"Hmmm..." Zandorth replied absently.

She turned to see him looking upwards. She followed his gaze but could not find what had captured his attention.

"What is it?" she asked.

"They may very well be watching the front and back entrances. However, I doubt they have considered the roof."

She followed his gaze to the dark rooftop and felt a smile begin to spread across her face. "The roof!" she almost shouted, and a tiny giggle sounded as she quickly rose up on her toes to plant a quick kiss on his cheek.

"Zan, you are a genius!"

He stared down at her as he considered her sudden change in behavior. Not a handful of seconds ago she was ready to attack him, and now she was happy and nauseatingly giddy as only a woman could be. The warmth of her lips lingered on his cheek, and he wondered at how the obvious observation of using the roof as a means of secret entrance to the inn would spawn such a turnaround in her mood.

She drew enough control over her sudden elation to turn and make her way back down the alley with the proper amount of stealth, but with that ridiculous grin still spread across her face. Krahl watched her for a moment before blowing out a sigh of frustration as he turned to follow, shaking his head in irritated confusion.

"Women."

~*~

The journey was not an easy one. The path was fraught with perilous drops that could plummet one to their death or, at the very least, broken bones. They found a building with a short enough roof that a small stack of abandoned crates allowed them to climb up. They then climbed to another roof, and then began to traverse the distance.

It took considerable time and some backtracking to finally find a path that deposited them on a rooftop that was on the same side of the street as the inn. Zandorth, very early on in the journey, had taken the lead. He now paused at the edge of one roof, looking across the alley to the next roof. The distance was considerable.

Brianna, winded from the running, jumping, and climbing, paused to bend over, placing her hands on her knees. She eyed the distance and shook her head. "Too far. We will have to circle back around."

Zandorth shook his head. "I can make it."

"Maybe, but I do not think I can."

Zandorth regarded her briefly with only the tiniest hint of humor in his eyes. "Then perhaps you should wait here for my return."

She straightened up and fixed him with an annoyed expression. "Lead the way." She motioned across the alley.

Krahl backed up several paces and fixed his gaze on the neighboring rooftop. He launched himself into a dead run. Brianna watched in amazement at how quickly a man of his considerable size was able to propel himself across the roof.

For a moment, it looked like he would not jump, and she found herself holding her breath. At the last second, his foot hit the edge of the roof, and he hurled himself into the air.

Time seemed to stop as he sailed through the air, and she wondered if he would make the leap or if she would have to watch him plummet to the alley below. With a grace that bellied his massive form, he landed on the adjoining roof and instantly dropped into a shoulder roll to help absorb the impact of his landing.

She let her breath out in an explosive sigh as he fluidly rolled back to his feet. As though he had just walked across the street, he turned and walked back to the edge of the roof. It was hard to make out his form in the darkness, but she could see by his silhouette that he wasn't even breathing hard.

He stood on the next roof, his hands on his hips, waiting for her. She shook her head as she moved to the spot he had occupied to get his running start. She absently wondered how she always managed to land herself in situations like this. Were her brash displays of determination to convince others of her abilities or herself? She grinned at the answer — a little of both.

She locked her gaze on the next rooftop and took several deep breaths to prepare herself. The heels of her boots would make the leap difficult. They were taller and thinner than the heels of most boots. She had designed the heel herself and had them custom made for her. While they were attractive, they were definitely not designed for running across rooftops and leaping from one building to another. She knew there was no way she could get up to full speed and make the leap in them.

She quickly sat down and began unlacing them. She could feel Zandorth's irritated stare on her, but ignored it. Once she had the boots off, she stood up and clutched the boots securely in her left hand. She knew Zandorth would tell her to leave them behind, but they were expensive, and she liked the way she looked in them. She would be damned if she would leave them behind.

Shaking out the tension in her arms, she fixed her determined stare at the roof once again. She took another series of deep breathes and took off in a dead run toward the suddenly dark and ominous abyss between she and Zandorth. Her bare feet pounded against the rooftop as she poured on all the speed she could.

She switched her gaze from the alley to Zandorth. Looking at the distance between the two buildings stoked her fears. She gritted her teeth and poured the last of her strength into her pumping legs. The edge of the roof approached rapidly, and she quickly timed when to jump.

She planted her left foot and leapt. She had not counted on the debris under her foot to give way, causing her foot to slip as she pushed off.

The blackness opened under her as she sailed through the air. As soon as her foot had slipped, she knew she wouldn't make the leap. She bit back at the fear and panic that suddenly rose up within her. Hopefully, Zandorth would be able to keep her from falling to the packed earth of the alley, which seemed miles below her now.

She hit the roof at her midsection. The force of the impact knocked the wind out of her and dazed her. She felt herself slipping over the edge and told her hands to find the edge and hang on for dear life, but they did not respond through the haze of her stunned senses. At the last moment, the fingers of her right hand twitched as if to assure her that at least they had not abandoned her. She clawed at the edge and found purchase with the tips of her fingers. She hung for a moment before her weight proved too much for her fingertips to support and they slipped.

She felt the edge of the roof fall away and she braced herself for the impact. She closed her eyes and clamped her mouth closed, refusing to cry out in fear as her instincts demanded. If she had to die, she was determined to die with dignity.

Suddenly, something wrapped itself around her wrist and clamped down painfully. She winced at both the steel grip on her wrist and the sudden snap of her shoulder joint as her fall was abruptly halted. Her body swung forward and slammed into the side of the building, stunning her further. She knew the impact should have been much more painful than it was, but the remoteness of her senses shielded her from it.

As she hung in mid air over the alley, she looked up to see Zandorth's dark silhouette hanging half over the edge of the rooftop. She smiled and took a moment to relish in the fact that she would not die, at least not yet.

Moments passed, and yet he did not pull her up. Her shoulder cried out in pain from bearing her weight, and she was rapidly losing the shield of being addled from the dual impacts as her senses returned.

"Pull me..." she started to say and was instantly silenced by Zandorth's gruff reply.

"Be silent!" he hissed in a harsh whisper.

She was puzzled, but the answer wasn't long in presenting itself. Two mounted sheriffs entered the alley. One of them carried a torch to better illuminate the darkened alley. Without her mental command to do so, Brianna held her breath and relaxed, simply hanging and wishing for Darkseed's ability to render them invisible.

The sheriffs drew up rein directly beneath Brianna and took a moment to complain about their assignment.

"This is pointless!" one sheriff said, shifting his weight in the saddle. The creak of the leather seemed very ominous to Brianna as she watched them between her dangling bare feet.

"Agreed, but what choice do we have?" his partner replied.

"The Royal Guard has men searching for these demons! They are far more skilled in such matters. I say we seek out a hearty drink and the warm thighs of a whore."

The other sheriff chuckled as he reached into his cloak and withdrew a small leather drinking pouch. "I can aide you in your quest for one of the items you mentioned." He uncorked the pouch and took a deep draw from its contents.

Brianna felt Zandorth's arm begin to tremble from the exertion of supporting her dead weight. She wanted to look up at him, but she dared not move, fearing that even raising her head would somehow alert them to her presence directly overhead.

As the sheriff winced at the bite of the hard liquor, he passed the pouch to his partner who smiled at him. "And the other item I quest for?"

"For that? You are on your own."

The sheriff chuckled as he lifted the pouch to his lips and drank deeply. As he tilted his head back, Brianna feared he would see her. Fortunately, he had closed his eyes as he drank, and she resisted the urge to sigh in relief.

The sheriff winced at the harsh bite of the liquor, and nodded. "Very nice," he rasped out as he passed the pouch back to its owner.

"I know a man on the outskirts of the city who makes his own liquor and sells it for a reasonable price."

"Now you know that such an endeavor is not allowed. If he makes his own liquor, he must pay a distribution tax to be allowed to sell it within the city," the sheriff said with mock indignation.

The other sheriff chuckled. "He does pay a distribution tax. To me."

"Very nice," His partner said.

"It is much better. When he cannot pay the distribution tax, he allows me to bed his wife as compensation. She is a beautiful, sweet little morsel. It is the only time I can recall that I do not mind someone not being able to pay."

The other sheriff's eyes widened in shock. "He allows you to bed his wife?"

The sheriff assumed an air of deep consideration. "Hmmm... perhaps 'allow' is not an accurate depiction of the situation. I would have to admit that it is more a resignation to the facts of the matter than actually granting me permission."

The other sheriff laughed aloud. "You are a clever bastard, I will give you that!"

Come on! Come on! Brianna's mind shouted at the sheriffs. She didn't know how much longer Zandorth would be able to hold on to her. Half his body was over the edge of the roof so he was not only supporting her weight, but he had to use his strength to keep himself from slipping over the edge, as well.

"Now that we have conquered one phase of your quest, shall we search out the other?" the sheriff with the liquor asked as he corked the bag and returned it to its hiding place within his cloak.

"Indeed we shall, although, I am most intrigued by this man's wife you speak of."

The other sheriff nodded in mock thoughtfulness. "She is most delicious, and while she resists at first, she eventually submits to the inevitable."

Brianna seethed in growing disgust and anger at these vagabonds. She knew the sheriff's of Lirpa were brigands, but to be brought face to face with just how vile they were was unsettling and maddening. When she had hit the edge of the roof, her hand had lost its grip on her boots, and they had bounced across the roof. She sorely wished she had them to throw at these bastards.

"When was the last time he paid his 'tax'?"

"Yesterday," the sheriff answered and then grinned. "Perhaps we should go ahead and collect next week's tax now."

The other sheriff's face twisted into a wolfish grin. "If he paid the tax yesterday, it would be safe to assume he would not have the coins to pay the next one. Then we would have no choice but to accept compensation in some other method."

His partner's wolfish grin surpassed his, and Brianna felt the bile rise in her throat as he responded. "Indeed."

For a moment, she wished Zandorth would drop her. She would love nothing more than to land in their midst, and with her sword, make them wish to never see another woman for as long as either of them lived.

"Lead the way, sir."

Finally, the two disgusting men rode on, rounded a corner in the alley, and were gone. She blinked in the sudden darkness and looked upward, waiting for Zandorth to pull her up.

"Remain silent!" he whispered so softly she almost could not hear him. For a moment, she wondered why he was delaying, but then understood. He was waiting for the bastards to get far enough away that they would not hear any sounds he might make pulling her up to the roof.

After what seemed as hours, Zandorth grunted softly as he slid back onto the roof and began pulling her up. Her shoulder, which was already scolding her for forcing it to bear her weight, screamed out in retaliation at being pulled on.

As her head and shoulders cleared the edge of the roof, she used her left hand to take hold of the edge and to help pull herself up. She rolled over the edge and took a moment to lie on her back and stare up at the stars, forcing her trembling limbs to calm.

Krahl rose to his feet and began looking about. The only visible indication of what they had just endured came when he gently flexed his shoulder once. She marveled at his strength, especially since it had just saved her life.

"We must move!" he said in his usual heavy tones.

Brianna rolled to her knees and began looking about for her boots. It took some time, but she was finally able to retrieve them and set about putting them back on. A part of her mind made a note that once this was over, she would return to Lirpa, find those two sheriffs, and make them rue the day they were born.

The rest of the journey was laced with terrifying leaps, as well as moments of sheer terror as they crouched low waiting for a Royal Guard or sheriff to pass. Finally, they found themselves on the roof of the inn.

Zandorth quickly strode to the front edge of the rooftop and stole a glance over the edge to make sure their arrival had gone unnoticed by the Royal Guards below.

"Not a journey I would wish to undertake every day," Brianna whispered as she struggled to ease her labored breathing.

"I found it quite exhilarating," Zandorth replied absently as he set about finding a way to enter the building.

Brianna noticed that the warrior wasn't even breathing hard. With a tired chuckle and slight shake of her head, she stood upright and followed him. "You would."

They found a hatch situated inside a small enclosure that served to keep rain from leaking through the cracks around the small door. They also found a heavy padlock securing the door.

"That is just fantastic!" Brianna hissed at this new turn of bad luck.

"Calm yourself," Zandorth replied as he took hold of the padlock and twisted. The muscles of his right arm bunched as he continued to twist on the lock. With a loud crack, the nails that secured the hasp to the door ripped from the half-rotten wood. Zandorth turned to face her, the lock and hasp hanging from his hand.

Brianna regarded the broken lock with admiration. With a playful gleam in her eye, she smiled at Zandorth. "You know, if you ever tire of being a warrior, you could always lead a very prosperous life as a thief."

Zandorth snapped his gray eyes to her, and she could see that he had, once again, missed the joke. As his jaw tightened and his eyes narrowed, she raised her hands in surrender. "It was a jest, Zan. Just a jest."

"I found no humor in it!" he growled.

With a soft laugh, Brianna carefully opened the hatch and began lowering her lithe form through the opening. Just before she lowered her head out of sight she looked back up at Zandorth. "I was afraid you would not."

Brianna let herself drop the short distance to the wooden floor, landing on the balls of her feet to minimize the noise of her landing. As she gained her balance, she froze. She strained her hearing for any sign that someone below may have heard her landing and was now on their way up the stairs to investigate. No such sound came, and she slowly stood upright, checking both directions of the hallway. Finally satisfied that she had arrived without notice, she looked up through the hatch and motioned for Zandorth to follow.

"I cannot fit through this small opening," he whispered.

She suppressed a laugh and nodded in understanding. Using hand signals, she motioned for Zandorth to stay where he was and that she would get their supplies and return.

She went first to her room and retrieved her saddlebags and pack. After returning to the hatch and passing the items up to Zandorth, she went to each of their rooms and returning with their meager, yet vital supplies.

The last room was Devenshire's, and she found the room empty, save for his saddlebags and the mussed linens of the bed that still bore the aftermath of their earlier passions. Tightness clutched her chest as she considered how it appeared that Devenshire had never been in this room. How it appeared as if there was nothing but her memories of their love making to mark that the man had ever been here at all.

He had appeared in her life very suddenly, and she knew that he would disappear out of her life the same way. There would be no hint of his leaving; he would simply be gone one day. Such was his way. The thought brought sadness to her that she tried to ignore.

She walked slowly to the edge of the bed and looked down at the pillow she had last seen him resting his head upon. It still bore the indention of his head, and her mind could still see his face, smiling with satisfaction and contentment. She could still feel the heat of his body as she lay snuggled against him, her head upon his shoulder. She gently lifted his pillow from the bed and buried her face in it, inhaling his scent, and letting the memories flow.

Not only of this previous encounter, but of each and every one of their other passionate encounters, as well. Would she ever see him again? Or would that have been the last time she ever laid eyes upon his form and felt not only the physical sensations he stirred in her, but the other emotions as well. The friendship, the camaraderie, the...

She suddenly dropped the pillow to the bed. She called on her anger, her fury, her determination to never, ever let a man occupy that place within her heart.

I DO NOT love him! Her mind screamed in defiance of the emotions that threatened to run rampant through her. She refused to allow herself to even believe that such a thing could happen.

True, Daimion Devenshire was different. He accepted her independence and did not try to coax more from her than she was willing to give. There were many things about him that was so different from any other man she had ever known, but she would not fall in love with him. This girlish emotionalism was annoying her, and she struck out at it, forcing it back down beneath the layers of her control.

Perhaps it was time for her to put some distance between herself and Devenshire, to allow her time to gather her wits about her and redefine the nature of their relationship. She was getting too close to him, and it would drive him further away from her than she wanted him to be.

Taking a deep shuddering breath, she turned, took up his saddlebags, and strode from the room with determination. Now was not the time for such things. She promised herself that later she would begin to sort out her thoughts over Devenshire and try to return them to where they should be.

She returned to the hatch, passed up Devenshire's saddlebags up to Zandorth and prepared to leap up to the edge of the hatch. Just as she gathered herself to leap a voice rang out.

"Hold!!"

She spun to see a Royal Guard at the head of the stairs, his sword drawn.

"I should have known," she muttered.

CHAPTER TWENTY-NINE

"IS THERE A PROBLEM?" she asked, as she smiled disarmingly. She forced all the innocence within her into the tones of her voice.

"What are you doing up here? Who let you in?" the guard demanded.

"I am a guest here. I was merely returning to my room," she replied calmly.

"Who allowed you entrance?" the guard demanded again.

She studied the man's features and did not recognize them. She tried to determine if he was one of the Guards at the entrance of the inn, but was not sure, as the Guards had been a considerable distance from her. Finally, she decided to gamble that he wasn't one of the Guards at the entrance to the inn. She took a breath to answer and hoped her ruse was successful.

"The guards at the front entrance questioned me and allowed me to enter."

The guard studied her closely, suspicion heavy in his glance. There was not a second of hesitation about him, the slightest hint that he took her word for what she claimed. Brianna felt herself tense and hoped it was not as obvious to the guard as it felt like it was to her.

"Come with me. We will confirm what you say with the guards," he said carefully.

"Must I go through that again? All I wish to do is retire to bed and sleep. I have had a very busy night and am very tired," she answered.

"If what you claim is true, then it shall only be a matter of the front guard recognizing you and confirming your claim," the guard replied.

She hesitated only a second. Any longer would only raise more suspicion in the already suspicious guard. With a forced smile of resignation, she took two faltering steps toward the guard, stumbled, steadied herself and giggled as her eyes grew wide in surprise. "Ooooo… I fear the ale I consumed is catching up to me," she lied, hoping she appeared as drunk as she pretended to be.

"You are drunk?" the guard asked, and she finally saw a slight crack in his suspicion.

"Sir! I am not drunk!" she replied with the zeal she had seen in others who had denied their drunken state. "I am merely appropriately relaxed," she amended with slurred speech. She then staggered slightly toward the guard and adopted her most seductive smile. "I say. You are quite the handsome one, are you not?"

The guard seemed to grow uncomfortable as she approached. "Take care, M'Lady. You could fall and injure yourself," he said, and she heard the uncertainty in his voice.

"I will be very, very, very careful," she slurred in response as she drew nearer to the guard and paused to give him a very obvious head to toe appraisal with her eyes. "I do so love a man in uniform. May I say that you fill yours out very nicely?"

The man's cheeks flushed red as she weaved before him. She sloppily rested both hands on his shoulders and leaned very close to him, letting her drooping eyes look deep into his.

"Please, M'Lady. Such behavior is unbecoming of a lady," the guard replied casting a nervous glance over his shoulder.

"Oh? You do not find me attractive? My appearance does not stir your blood as yours does mine?" she asked without a trace of sobriety about her. She leaned her face very close to his and let all of her feminine qualities surface.

The guard cleared his throat nervously as he tried to avoid her gaze and failed. "Quite the contrary, M'Lady. I find you most… what I mean to say is that I think your appearance is very… that is…"

Brianna shored up her resolve and suddenly planted her lips hard against his. Her kiss was met with rigid unresponsiveness, and she silently cursed the tight resolve the Royal Guards kept over their more primitive male drives. Before the guard could separate himself from her forced embrace, she forced a very passionate moan from her throat and began pushing her body to his.

Again, there was not the slightest response from the guard, and she found herself growing annoyed. While she acknowledged that what she was doing had nothing to do with any genuine interest in the man before her, she was not used to having her charms met with such cold dispassion. With an even more aroused moan, she raised her leg up, pressing it tightly against his leg before curling it around his leg and pulling herself completely against him. As their hips met, she allowed a slight smile to form against his lips as she felt the one response that he could not control.

She wrapped her arms tightly around his neck and pulled back from the kiss, leaving her lips just inches from his. "I fear you may be right, sir. I am in no condition to be out in public. Perhaps you should escort me to my room before I make a spectacle of myself," she whispered breathlessly.

"I would be more than happy to do so, M'Lady. Just as soon as we confirm with the front guard that they allowed you entrance," he answered, and she could not help but notice the drop in the level of conviction in his words. There was hesitation there now, as if there was something else he would rather do.

"I have a better solution," she breathed into his lips and giggled as she ran her hand clumsily through her hair. "Why do you not escort me to my room, let me show you my appreciation for your assistance, and then we will go confirm my story with the front guard."

She saw the hesitation in his eyes. He was seriously considering her proposition. But there was still doubt within him, and she decided more persuasion was needed. She ran her hand lightly down his chest and let her eyes follow her hand until it reached his waist. She slowly raised her sleepy eyes back to his and saw his face pale under her touch. "Please?" she whimpered softly with just enough seduction in her voice to distract the guard even further.

"Please, M'Lady. I have a duty to perform, and I cannot lay that duty aside for personal gain," he answered as he closed his eyes, struggling with the two forces that were raging against each other in his mind. She mentally saluted his resolve to his duty, as inconvenient as it was turning out to be.

"Ah, but, my handsome warrior, you would be doing your duty. Escorting a lady who has obviously had too much drink to her room before she can fall prey to the many dangers of this city is well within the realm of your duties, is it not?"

"Yes. I suppose it would be considered as such," he replied cautiously.

She giggled again as she separated herself from him and turned slowly to walk down the hall toward her room, letting her hips sway more than usual. "Then come, my warrior. Duty calls."

"Hold, M'Lady. I cannot do this. Please come with me downstairs," the guard almost shouted, and she grimaced as she realized that this one would not be distracted so easily.

Brianna turned and folded her arms just under her breasts, lifting them for added effect, and let her features arrange themselves in a most seductive pout.

"Tis not fair! I have been alone for so long. My man left me weeks ago, and I find myself alone in this giant city with no warmth, no feelings of being needed or loved or desired."

"I assure you, M'Lady, such feelings are quite false. May I be so bold as to say that your man is quite the fool for leaving such a lovely creature alone? Just allow me to fulfill my duty, and I will make sure you make it to the safety of your room," the guard replied.

She allowed hardness to come to her face as the pout faded. She unfolded her arms and stood to her full height, albeit unsteadily. "Fine! Do your duty!" she said hotly, thick sarcasm coating the word 'duty'. "I find that afterwards I will not require your services to reach my room!" she snapped as she began staggering toward the guard who's face now bore the uncomfortable realization that his devotion to his duty may have just cost him far more than he was really willing to pay.

Just as Brianna reached the guard, she paused, letting her hand drift to her head. "Oooo..." she moaned as she began leaning backwards. Just as it appeared that she would topple over backwards, the guard bolted forward to catch her. Just as his free hand took hold of her wrist, she shifted her weight and suddenly jerked him forward, throwing him off balance.

He landed hard on his chest, his face smacking the floor with a dull thud. He shook his head once to clear it and bunched his muscles to launch himself back to his feet.

Before he could rise though, Brianna forced him back down by driving her right knee deeply into his back. She simultaneously took a handful of his hair in her left hand and jerked his head savagely upward while her right hand withdrew one of her daggers before pressing the cold blade firmly into the flesh of this throat just below his left ear.

"Cry out," she hissed harshly into his ear, "and the last sound you will hear will be your blood splashing onto the floor!"

She then applied just enough pressure to the hilt of the dagger to open a small wound in the guard's neck. He flinched under the sudden piercing of his skin, but did not cry out. "I know how men like to underestimate a woman's conviction to draw blood. That was just to show you that I have no qualms in that area," she whispered harshly.

The guard remained absolutely still.

"Very good. I see you are a wise man as well. I do not wish to harm you, but I do not have the luxury of being kind at the moment. Now, we are going to rise to our feet and walk down this hall to the hatch that leads to the roof. Please do not try anything foolish in the name of your duty. It will do nothing but get you killed."

The guard nodded slowly and carefully. He waited for her to begin rising before he moved. She maintained enough pressure on the dagger to remind him that a swift push would be all that was needed to send the cold steel deep into his warm flesh. When they reached the open hatch, she looked behind them to make sure no other duty bound guards had appeared.

"Through the hatch," she ordered in a whisper and stepped back to allow him to leap to the edge of the opening. The guard looked at her as she backed away, and she saw the anger burning in his eyes at having been duped so easily, and in such an obvious manner. But the depth of her conviction seemed to reach him through her eyes, and he did as she instructed.

When she joined him on the roof, she saw that the guard was secure under Zandorth's watchful gaze.

"We have begun taking prisoners?" Zandorth asked harshly as she gently eased the door closed. She stood upright and turned to look at the guard.

"Of course not. I could not very well leave him behind to alert the entire Royal Guard that we were here, however," she replied.

"What are we to do with him now?" Zandorth demanded.

"I thought you might help him to sleep. He looks very tired to me. Does he not appear so to you?" she asked with mischief in her eyes and voice.

A faint smile crossed Zandorth's chiseled features as her train of thought dawned on him as well. "Yes. He looks very fatigued," he replied and very calmly turned and unleashed a powerful right cross that took the guard on the jaw.

Brianna winced at the wet smacking sound as the guard spun from the impact. Without so much as a moan, he dropped to the rooftop and did not move again.

She regretted having to do such a thing to someone who was only doing their duty as their conscience directed them. But now was not the time to try to reason their way out of their current circumstance. She crossed to his prone form and knelt down, placing her hand under his nose and mouth. She was rewarded by his warm breath drifting across her hand. She nodded once. He was still alive.

"They will find him, or he will awaken and alert them. Either way, they will know we were here!" Zandorth protested as she stood up and shouldered his and Devenshire's saddlebags.

She nodded. "True, but we will, hopefully, be far from here before either of those events happen."

She picked up hers and Shantira's packs and saddlebags. It was a considerable amount of weight, and she recalled the path across rooftops that had brought them here. The return trip, she realized, would be even worse.

"Let us make haste to the stables and pray our mounts are not being watched," he said as he set off across the roof.

A commotion from the street below reached them, and they

hurried over to the edge to see what was happening below. What they saw gave them little comfort. A complement of Royal Guards and sheriffs pounded up to the inn to be met by the guards at the door of the inn.

"There has been a murder! The beast has struck, and his accomplices have escaped from the jail. Be on the look out!!" one of the mounted guards shouted.

"Who has been murdered?" one of the inn guards asked.

"A local whore. Her throat bears the marks of the demon Devenshire, and there is no blood left within her veins! I am riding on to our garrison to gather more men. These men will remain here to shore up your numbers should the ghoul return!" the mounted guard replied.

"May the Fates protect us!" the other guard said, and all of them seemed to be drawing back, fearfully scanning every shadow for the silhouette of the monster.

"Damn!!" Brianna swore in a harsh whisper.

"The Fates are not on our side this night," Zandorth observed with a hard, grim set to his features.

"The Fates do seem to be a fickle lot," she agreed. "Come. We must make haste. I doubt our mounts will remain alone for much longer."

As they made their way toward the stables, a thought haunted them, and by the third rooftop, it was Zandorth who finally voiced it. "Did you hear what the guard said? A whore was killed in the fashion of a vampire. Do you think it possible that there is indeed a vampire roaming this area?"

She did not break her stride, but her thoughts were staggering under what the implications of someone being drained of blood could mean. "Either there is one nearby, or someone is going to extreme measures to make it appear as if one is near and doing so to make it appear as if Daimion is the one responsible."

Any other fears or concerns that may have occurred to the warrior were left unspoken as they each confronted the mental phantoms of a vampire on the prowl.

CHAPTER THIRTY

SHANTIRA STAGGERED BACK away from the inn, staying to the shadows. Her mind, which had just begun to return to some semblance of its former self, was sent spinning into disorientation again at the words she had overheard from the guards. Devenshire was a vampire?

She found it hard to believe. He did not look like what she had always heard a vampire looked like, but then again, she had never seen one, so she had no way of knowing what a vampire truly looked like.

She had to admit that Devenshire being a vampire would explain a great many things. The air of mystery that always seemed to surround him, the subtle, yet strong seductiveness about him, and the way he could almost mesmerize with those incredible eyes of his.

Shantira quickly dismissed the thought. She had seen him about during the day light hours. In fact, the very first time she had ever seen him had been during the day. Of all the mysteries surrounding Devenshire, vampirism was not one of them.

Yet the point was moot. The Royal Guard and the sheriffs believed him to be a vampire, and that she, Brianna, and Zandorth were his accomplices. This meant they were all in danger of being arrested, and she understood all too well the penalty for being associated with a vampire.

Obviously, from what she had heard from the guards, Brianna and Zandorth had been arrested but had escaped. She doubted they would return to the inn. So where would they go? Where was the most likely place she could meet up with them? After a few seconds, the location came to her... the stables. No doubt they would return there, retrieve their mounts, leaving Lirpa as quickly and quietly as possible.

Shantira ducked into a darkened alley and took a moment to collect her thoughts and get her bearings. Though the disorientation still fogged her mind, she felt she remembered where the stables were in relation to the inn. Fading into the shadows, she made her way toward them.

~*~

Lordalise stood absolutely still. The faint breeze of the night was lost to him. The myriad of smells that wafted to his senses were ignored. He did not acknowledge the presence of terrified men behind him. The only thing he was aware of was the body of a woman at his feet.

The thin gaudy lavender dress covered an aging body that should have left that profession long ago. Her blonde hair was streaked with silver, and her face, even in death, bore the ravages of time. Under any other circumstances, Lordal would have thought that death would be a blessing.

The two jagged puncture marks below her left ear and the pale pallor of her skin reminded him of how she had died. It also told him of the hellish existence that could very well be waiting for her which was far worse than the one she had just departed.

"Master Lordalise?" a voice called to him, but he ignored it. His eyes bore hard into the corpse before him and willed it to reveal the identity of its attacker to him. But the dead eyes of the whore looked back at him and revealed only the emptiness of the shell that housed them. The look of near sexual release that was locked into her features made him sick, far more than the spread legged position the demon had left her body in. She sat against the wall with her arms open to her sides, her legs spread wide as if to invite anyone else to sample her charms, even in death. Leave it to a Dark One to be so grotesquely twisted of humor to do such a thing.

"Master Lordalise?" the voice harkened again, and he ignored it. It had been many seasons since the last time he had looked upon the remains of a vampire attack, and he was surprised at how the sights still managed to shock and sicken him to his soul. The longer he gazed into the dead eyes, the more blackness he felt seeping into his very being. As if the touch of death were attempting to ease into his body and claim his life force as well. There was a saying that claimed that the eyes were the mirrors of the soul. What he saw reflected in the eyes of the woman assured him that there was nothing within her soul... at least not yet.

"Master Lordalise. Are you all right?" the irritating voice beckoned again. Finally, he was able to tear himself out of his morbid reverie and turn to see Captain Armand studying him carefully.

"The demon's cruelty never ceases to shock me," he whispered as he returned his gaze to the woman.

"Her name was Lorinda. She was a well-known whore here. Well liked too, as the accounts go," Armand stated softly. "Are you certain it was Devenshire who did this?"

"There can be no doubt. Behold the marks upon her throat. Two very sharp fangs were driven deep into her neck, puncturing a vital vein. See how her skin has turned the ghastly pallor of death so quickly? You can cut her anywhere you wish, and you will receive little or no blood because none remains within her. See how the twisted mind of the demon wishes to further degrade his victim by leaving her in such an undignified position?" He shook his head and sighed softly. "There is no doubt."

"I shall summon the undertaker to dispose of the body," Armand said as he began turning to his men. Lordalise stayed him with a raised hand.

"Not yet. There is still a task to be performed here."

"Which is?" Armand asked.

"I must sever the head from the body. Then the body and head must be burned to ash and the ashes blessed by a priest of the highest faith. Once that is done, the ashes must be scattered to the wind. Only in this way can her soul be guaranteed to be free of Devenshire's evil influence."

"I do not understand," Armand said, truly confused.

Lordalise leveled a stern stare toward Armand. "We cannot deviate from the plan I have just laid out for you, Captain. To miss a step could very well mean she would return from the dead as one like Devenshire."

Lordalise did not miss the flicker of disgust that rippled across Armand's features. To the captain's credit, it was only momentary, and within a few seconds, the grim determination had returned.

"How long before she is turned?" the captain asked quietly.

"The time of transformation varies. She could become a vampire by the next setting sun, or it could be days. That is why we must act now, to ensure that she is spared the ghoulish existence that lies before her," Lordal answered as he slowly drew his sword.

Armand only nodded as he stepped back to allow Lordalise the room he would need. Without hesitation, Lordal took the woman by the hair and drug her away from the wall into the open space of the alley. When her body was clear of any obstructions, he calmly brought his sword up over his shoulder and brought it down with all the strength he could muster. The blade cut through skin and bone with a sickening meaty slush and the head bounced away. To mark Lordal's words, only the faintest trickle of blood seeped from the open end of the neck.

Several of the less experienced Royal Guards, and more than half the assembled sheriffs, quickly turned and began to vomit. Lordalise bore them no ill will for he remembered his first dealings with a victim of a vampire, and his behavior had been little different from theirs.

Lordalise bent low and wiped the blood from his blade on the lavender dress. As he stood and returned his sword to its resting place, he looked at Armand. "Have the remains taken out of the city and burned immediately. Take your best priest and follow my instructions to the letter. The sooner the better," the bitterness in his voice did not go unnoticed.

"What do we do now? We have no clue as to where to search for Devenshire," Armand asked.

"Have you sent for more men?" Lordal asked.

"Yes. More men should arrive by mid morning," Armand replied.

Lordalise nodded slowly. "Then we wait. Once the sun rises, we will begin an extensive search in and around the city. My men will join your men and the sheriffs, and we will search for every likely place that Devenshire could use to hide during the day light hours."

"But Master Lordalise, Lirpa is a large city, and there are nearly countless places that he could hide."

"I understand this, Captain, but unless you have another suggestion, then I see no other course of action. Many of your men have seen Devenshire and those who travel with him. Have them scour the city, talk to everyone, look everywhere. There is the slightest chance that he will become careless and allow himself to be seen," Lordalise replied as he began walking from the alley.

Armand picked out four of his men who were not busy vomiting and gave them stern, detailed instructions on the disposal of the woman's remains. He left no doubt of the punishment that would befall them if his instructions were not carried out to the letter. They nodded their understanding and quickly set about their gruesome task.

Armand stepped out of the alley with the balance of his men behind him. He looked up and down the suddenly empty street. Once word of the death had spread, the people had found other streets to occupy. The emptiness of the street only added to the grave-like chill that had suddenly descended upon them. Death, regardless of what summoned it, always left him feeling cold. With a touch of shame, he recalled how he had wasted valuable time arguing about jurisdictional rights and guarantees for Devenshire to stand before a tribunal for the charges against him. It was clear to him now that there would be no fair dealings with the demon. He must be destroyed, and on sight, with no time wasted asking questions. With a silent angry vow, he swore that Devenshire would not get the best of him at their next meeting.

~*~

To their surprise, Zandorth and Brianna reached the stables unmolested by the numerous detachments of Royal Guards and sheriffs they had evaded on their way. To add to their surprise, they found their mounts in their stalls with no sign of anyone about. They wasted no time in retrieving their saddles and preparing all four horses to ride.

"Perhaps the Fates have decided to lend us a helping hand," Brianna commented as she cinched her saddle tightly to her mount. She brought her knee up and pressed it firmly into the side of her horse, forcing it to exhale. She quickly pulled on the cinch, tightening the saddle to its back.

"Or they have lulled us into believing so," Zandorth replied as he followed suit. "I have learned never put full trust in the Fates."

"Good point," Brianna replied as she squeezed the nostrils of her horses muzzle so that the animal would have to open its mouth to breath, allowing her to slip the bit into its mouth.

Zandorth made quick work of saddling his mount and she reflected that he must have had call, on many occasions, to prepare his mount very quickly. She admired the way he moved swiftly despite his considerable bulk of muscle. As soon as his mount was ready, he retrieved Shantira's saddle and set about saddling her smaller mount.

Krahl was halfway finished saddling up Shantira's mount before Brianna finished her own. She quickly took up Devenshire's black saddle and approached his large black steed. The massive animal snorted its protest of her approach and began shifting nervously about its stall.

Brianna talked to the horse in soft, soothing tones, and the animal seemed to relax a little. As she opened the gate to his stall and stepped inside, the horse screamed out in protest and reared up on his hind legs, front legs pawing at the air with what appeared to be a genuine desire to cave her head in. She quickly backed away from the animal, dropping the saddle and barely avoiding the large hooves as they swiped the air where her head had been seconds before.

She stood outside the stall, her hands upon her hips as she regarded the horse with a stern glare. "You are as big a bastard as your master!" she scolded.

Zandorth chuckled as he finished with Shantira's mount. "You may wish to leave Devenshire's mount be. No one has ever saddled or ridden him but Devenshire. He trained the horse that way to prevent someone from stealing him."

Brianna shut the gate on the Frisian who snorted and pawed at the ground.

"Now is a fine time to tell me," she scolded.

"You did not ask. I assumed you knew," he replied with a poor attempt at hiding his amusement.

"You are a bastard, too. I seem intent on surrounding myself with bastards!" She looked back at Devenshire's horse. "What are we to do? Just leave Daimion's mount behind?"

Zandorth stepped out of the stall, retrieved his saddlebags and set about securing them to his saddle. "I see no other alternative. I am not about to attempt to wrestle with the beast just to saddle it. If Devenshire returns, he will have his own methods of retrieving him." As he turned, he caught the troubled look in Brianna's eyes as she scanned the open doorway of the stables. It looked as if she were waiting for something... or someone.

"We should go. Now," he said.

"I know. I was hoping Daimion and Shantira would find their way here before we were forced to leave," she replied.

"So you have come to your senses and have decided to leave without them?" Zandorth asked.

"No! I have not!" she snapped in reply. "I will not leave this area without them. But I will leave the city for the time being."

"To remain anywhere near this city is only asking for the Royal Guard or the sheriffs to capture us," Zandorth argued.

She fixed him with a cold stare. "I have already told you. If you wish to leave, then do so. I am not asking you to wait with me."

Zandorth watched her for several moments. While he understood where her motivations came from, that did not mean he agreed with them. It was folly to remain behind.

Suddenly, he tensed. Something was wrong. He turned from Shantira's mount and took a few cautious steps out into the main aisle, his hand drifting toward his sword.

"What is it?" she asked and her answer came from the doorway of the stables.

"Hold! Do not move! Surrender!"

She looked up to see four members of the Royal Guard at the open doorway, swords drawn and ready.

They were answered by Zandorth's broadsword singing free of its scabbard and the Warrior assuming a fighting stance. "Not this time!" he growled.

"Zan. Please!" Brianna said urgently.

"No! We have been through this once tonight and we proceeded in your way. This time, we proceed in mine!" he shouted as his hard gray eyes bore into the assembled guards.

"Make no mistake, Warrior! We will kill you if you leave us no choice!" one of the guards shouted.

Zandorth's eyes narrowed slightly as a hard grin spread across his face, but the gesture lent no humor to his features. "You are welcome to make the attempt."

The guards paled slightly at the ice in Zandorth's voice, but as with the guard at the inn, Brianna could see that they were bound tightly to their duty and would see it through to the bitter end.

"Listen to reason, man! We have no wish to kill you or the woman. Surely, you see that while we may have trouble subduing you, the woman will only get hurt or killed if you resist," the guard tried to reason.

Brianna arched one of her eyebrows. "Do not concern yourself with the 'woman'. She may yet surprise you!" she said in a frigid tone as she reached up and pulled her sword free.

For a while, they simply stared at one another, taking silent stock of their opponent, searching for any weaknesses that may be obvious. Finally, it was Zandorth who broke the silence by letting loose a deep throated battle cry and launching himself toward the guards.

"Here we go," Brianna muttered as she propelled herself to launch her own attack before the guards could outnumber and overpower Zandorth.

Steel collided with steel and the song of battle commenced. Two of the guards chose to fight Zandorth while the other two locked on Brianna, no doubt thinking to dispatch her quickly and then join their comrades in subduing the massive Warrior.

Brianna met the dual attack with a sweeping parry that took both guards by surprise. While they were off balanced by her defense, she pressed forward, slashing at one guard while she kicked out at the other. The heel of her riding boot dug deep into the man's stomach, and he grunted in surprise as the force of the kick staggered him back. The guard sagged to his knees as he realized the breath had been kicked out of him, and he sucked in desperately to re-inflate his lungs.

Brianna swept around the standing guard to position herself to where she could still fight one while keeping a watchful eye on the other. The guard snarled at her as he launched another attack that she found herself hard pressed to counter. The Royal Guards' skill with a sword had not been exaggerated, she reflected, as she was backed down the row of stalls. Their swords flashed faster than the eye could follow, so Brianna fell back on a battle tactic her father had taught her long ago... watch an opponent's eyes, they will tell you where they intend to strike next.

Zandorth had little difficulty in fending off the dual attack of the guards and simply parried about them, letting them hack and slash at him as he calmly deflected each blow. A genuine smile spread slowly across his face as he lost himself in the joy of battle, of testing his skill against a new opponent. He did not miss how the guards grew more cautious as it became obvious that basic attacks would do no good against an accomplished Warrior of the Ancient Class. As they moved on to more advance attacks, and Zandorth graduated to more advanced defenses, he felt the exhilaration grow as he realized this was going to be a good fight.

He had seen Brianna meet the attack of her two guards and quickly take one of them out of the fight with a graceful, yet powerful, kick to his midsection. Through the corner of his eye, he could see the guard on his knees, holding his stomach and trying to get enough air back into his body to re-join the fight.

Though he could no longer see Brianna and her opponent, he could hear their swords strike together, separate, and strike again in rapid succession. He felt concern rise within him for her safety, but he drove it from his mind; he could not allow himself to be distracted by concern for her. While he had no trouble defending against the two guards, he knew that should his attention wander too far, a critical opening might appear in his defenses.

With a mischievous grin, he decided to test the true metal of his opponents. He let loose a vicious growl and quickly swept his broadsword around in an apparent side attack, which both guards brought their swords around to block. At the last second, just as his blade met both of theirs, he drove his sword down, pinning the tips of their swords to the ground.

Their eyes met. The guards had a look of pure shock and astonishment at the swiftness and power of the move. Zandorth's face was hard, locked in granite. Then, slowly, a vicious snarling smile spread across his face, and he suddenly smashed a forearm into the two faces, sending both guards sprawling to their backs, their swords forgotten.

The two guards struggled to a seated position, their stunned gazes locked to Zandorth, and he could see the amazement in their dazed expressions. He had no doubt that they were wondering how they had so suddenly lost the advantage in this battle.

"Careless. Very careless," Zandorth commented calmly as he knelt down to retrieve their swords. He held their swords in one hand, his own in the other.

"Kill us! But I can promise you we will be avenged!" one of the guards shouted in defiance.

"I take no honor in killing those who simply make a mistake," Zandorth stated. "Shall we try again?" he asked as he tossed the swords to land at the guard's feet.

The guards wasted only a moment on amazed expressions before they took up their swords and climbed back to their feet. Zandorth's smile lapsed back into the stern look of concentration as he resumed his fighting stance. "When you are ready," he said.

"That will prove to be your fatal mistake. You should have killed us while you had the chance!" the other guard growled in anger as he closed in to resume the battle. As the combat resumed, he mentally saluted the now cautious, yet vicious attacks. He noted that they were now coordinating their attacks, forcing Zandorth to fight them individually instead of as a pair. This was going to be interesting, he reflected.

Brianna had backed almost as far as she could and was nearly backed against the far wall of the stables. Her opponent was an accomplished swordsman, and she was finding out just how difficult defeating him was going to be. She fought down the panic that tried to invade her thoughts, tried to maintain a calm mental state that would allow her to think clearly. She needed time to clear her thoughts and space to get herself into a better position to defend. Once the guard had her backed into the wall, it would only be a matter of clever sword strokes to disarm her or worse. One possibility called to her, and she grasped it for all she was worth.

As the guard attacked with a downward stroke, she turned her blade sideways. The two blades met and slid along one another until their hilts locked together and the guard pushed her hard against the back wall of the stables.

She hit hard and could feel a dazed sensation begin prickling at the edges of her perceptions. It was only through gritted teeth and sheer determination that she was able to maintain the lock with the guard. The guards snarling features loomed in to fill her field of vision. Their blades locked and his breath was hot against her face as he spoke.

"Surrender! I have no wish to kill or injure you!"

"Never!" she hissed in reply, feeling sweat pour down her face.

"I have no desire to mar or injure your lovely countenance. Surrender," he said in a softer tone. He exerted more force into pressing her into the wall. She felt her breath grow shallow in her chest, feeling her arms tremble under the sheer exertion of keeping the guard at bay.

"You concern yourself with matters that do not concern you. You are neglecting another part of me that should be of far more concern to you," she snarled.

"And what part is that?" he asked, the superiority of victory already shading his features.

"My knee," she replied calmly and almost smiled as she saw the thought dawn across his face with sickening clarity.

Before the guard could react, Brianna balanced herself against the back wall and brought her right knee up with a force and accuracy born of much practice. The bone of her kneecap sank into soft flesh as the guard's eyes flew open. With a sick moan, the guard instantly stumbled back to drop to his side, hugging himself against the hot, throbbing pain that lanced out at his body from his groin.

She sagged against the wall and began breathing deeply, taking a moment to rest and clear her mind. Although the maneuver was not considered good sword fighting etiquette, it was effective. She would concern herself with etiquette later as this was a matter of survival.

The first guard Brianna had felled with a well-placed kick had managed to regain enough of his air to stagger to his feet and take up his sword. Through teary eyes, he saw two of his comrades engaged with the warrior while his own partner had the black haired beauty backed against the far wall of the stables. Suddenly, his partner moaned horribly and collapsed to his side, and the woman sagged against the wall. Obviously, she was nearly spent and now was the time to strike, to disarm her without seriously injuring her. As he took a step toward the woman, something tapped him on the shoulder from behind and he spun.

"Shall we dance?" another dark haired woman asked as she pulled her sword back from tapping him on the shoulder with it.

"This fight is none of your concern, woman! Be gone!" the guard snarled.

"Oh, I disagree. You have attacked my friends, and I cannot simply let that pass," she replied as she took up the proper stance of attack and defense.

"As you wish, harlot!" he replied as he suddenly attacked.

Shantira parried his sloppy attack and countered with a maneuver that sent the guard leaping clear of a singing swing that would have certainty opened his stomach to the night. Taking advantage of his surprise, Shantira closed in with a flurry of swings and slashes that began driving him backwards.

Stealing a glance over the guards shoulder, Shantira could see Brianna standing full upright again and looking up to see her driving the guard toward her. She hoped Brianna could discern what she was doing and would act accordingly for she did not know how much longer she could keep the guard off balance with her flurry of attacks.

Just as the guard recovered from his surprise and began countering Shantira's attacks with moves that would soon put her back on the defensive, she suddenly jumped back and lowered her sword to her side.

"Have you had enough? Or do you wish for further humiliation at the hands of a woman?" she asked at his surprised expression at her sudden change in tactics.

"You are a child! You should spare yourself considerable pain by surrendering now," he replied. Then his eyes narrowed as he took in Shantira's far too innocent smile. Then he saw her eyes dart over his shoulder to something behind him, and he spun only to see the jeweled hilt of a sword rapidly filling his vision.

The hilt struck him with surprising force, and he staggered under the impact, tiny explosions of light filling his skull. The force of the blow spun him around to face the dark haired woman who had attacked him. She smiled sweetly at him before smashing his face with the hilt of her sword.

He spun a staggered turn to face the woman he had come here to arrest. His head spun, and he felt nauseated. His knees bent and threatened to buckle. Through the loud ringing in his ears he heard one of them speak. "Let this be an abstract lesson to you, sir," the woman snarled as she drove the hilt of her sword into the side of his head again, sending him to his knees. He grunted in pain as he tried to clear his senses, but just as he pushed up, he heard the other one speak.

"Never, ever underestimate the power of..." she started as she smashed him in the opposite side of his head, causing him to fall forward to support his failing strength with his arms, "...a woman," the other woman finished as she drove the pommel of her sword into the back of his head. The inside of his skull exploded in a shower of sparks as he pitched forward to land, unconscious, in a mixture of hay and manure.

Brianna watched the guard for several moments, making sure he was unconscious before looking up at Shantira. Through her heavy breathing, she managed a weak smile. "What took you so long?"

"Just wanted to make sure my help was needed before I interfered in your enchanted engagement with the men," Shantira answered with a smile, her own breathing labored from the fight.

"Enchanted? Of all the ways I could describe that encounter, enchanted would not be one of them," she answered breathlessly.

Shantira chuckled and turned to watch Zandorth as he continued to battle the other two guards. She was awed at how the guards were attacking with a skill and speed that she wondered if she could handle from just one of them, and how Zandorth met and countered each attack as if he were dueling with a practice dummy. While the two guards were drenched in sweat from their exertion, Zandorth appeared to hardly be breathing hard. She wondered how long the Warrior would be able to fend off the attacks before he made a mistake.

"Should we help Zandorth?" she asked Brianna.

Brianna regarded the warrior in silence for several moments before her face took on an annoyed look, "Zan! Will you stop playing?" she scolded.

"Playing?" Shantira asked in amazement.

Zandorth scowled and launched into a series of hacking thrusts that sent the guards back, their faces betraying their surprise at how a fight that they seemed to be winning had suddenly been knocked from their grasp.

"I... never... play!" Zandorth growled as he forced the guards back toward the open doors of the stables, his words coming between each violent thrust of his sword. One guard lunged forward and attempted to lock his sword with Zandorth's, but the warrior deflected the blow and quickly delivered a smashing punch to the guards face which sent him flying into one of the stable gates and then through it with a shattering crash of wood. Zandorth did not see the results of his punch as he immediately turned his attention to the remaining guard.

Shantira winced as the first guard crashed through the gate to land in a heap of hay, manure, and wooden splinters. He groaned, tried to rise, then collapsed to his back and did not move again.

The last guard fought with the ferocity of a true warrior, and Zandorth found himself forming a grudging respect for the guards. It was that grudging respect that saved the last guard from death. There would be no honor in killing this man.

With a finely executed disarming move, the guard's sword was ripped from his grip to spin off into one of the stalls across the way. The guard stood frozen for a second, his eyes searching his suddenly empty hands before turning them to Zandorth who had the point of his sword leveled at the guards throat.

The guard, realizing his defeat, straightened to his full height and prepared himself to meet certain death. His eyes locked to Zandorth's and never wavered. If there was fear within him, he did not let it show on his face.

"The fight is yours," the guard gasped between heaved breaths. He stared at Zandorth.

"You are a skilled and honorable opponent. I will spare your life."

The guard shook his head. "Make no mistake, Warrior. If you let me live, I will come after you."

Zandorth nodded slowly. "I would expect nothing less," he then stepped up and smashed the guard across the jaw, which sent him spinning to the ground. The man grunted and tried to push himself up. Zandorth stepped up quickly and sent another savage punch into the back of his head. This time the guard collapsed into unconsciousness. Zandorth watched the guard only briefly before he turned to face the women.

"Playing?" he asked angrily.

"A jest, Zan," Brianna answered with a smile.

Zandorth turned his hard gaze to Shantira. "Where have you been?!"

"I was merely taking a walk," Shantira replied defensively.

"You were warned of the dangers of doing so! You could have been killed, or worse!

"I do not feel that I need to explain myself to you!" Shantira nearly shouted. "I am fully capable of taking care of myself as my unharmed presence proves!"

"You were lucky! Leave us again like that, and you will be left to your own devices!" Zandorth growled as he returned his sword to its scabbard.

Shantira's reply was cut short by Brianna's hand on her arm and quick shake of her head. Shantira seethed under the anger brought on by Zandorth's scolding of her as if she were a child. But she restrained herself at Brianna's behest.

"Where is Daimion?" she asked.

"We do not know. He is missing and under suspicion from the Royal Guard," Brianna replied.

"I know... of being a vampire," Shantira replied. "What has happened?"

"I am not sure. Someone is going to great lengths to make Daimion appear guilty of being a vampire, and we are being hunted as his accomplices. We must leave the city and quickly. There are more guards where these came from and in larger numbers."

"You intend to leave Daimion behind?" Shantira asked in disbelief.

"Not leave him behind, just merely get ourselves out of the city until we can learn what has become of him, and how we can retrieve him," Brianna replied as she returned her sword to its scabbard.

The moans of the guard Brianna had sent to the ground were growing in strength and soon he would be back on his feet. She sighed heavily as she drew her sword again and crossed to the writhing guard.

"Sleep well," she said sweetly then sent the pommel into the side of the guard's head. With a mumbling moan, the guard was sent into the realm of dreams.

Zandorth was hauling the unconscious guard from the open doorway of the stable, heaping him on top of his partner in the stall. Next, he retrieved the other two guards, one in each hand, and piled them with their comrades.

Shantira checked her mount then swung herself up into the saddle. She tried not to think of the disturbing sensations that had been going through her at the sight of Brianna. The moment she had laid eyes on her, a strange sensation coursed through her, and she was trying to discern the nature of the sensation. She felt compelled to stay close to Brianna, to watch her closely, to make sure no harm came to her. The feeling went far beyond the normal concern for a friend's well being. She could not understand where this feeling came from and now was not the time to give it the careful thought it deserved.

Brianna mounted up next, followed by Zandorth. "We should stay to the outskirts of the city, circle around to the north, and proceed through the forest," Zandorth said as he gathered his reins.

"I agree," Brianna replied as she gave a wistful glance at Devenshire's black steed still in its stall.

"Let us make haste," Zandorth said as he urged his mount

forward. Shantira fell into place behind him, and as Brianna nudged her horse into motion, she looked again at the black stallion.

"Bring him to us," she whispered. The black horse snorted and bobbed its head as if it understood her words and was agreeing to do as she asked. Of course, the animal could not have understood her words, but it helped her to think he could.

CHAPTER THIRTY-ONE

LORDALISE AND ARMAND STRODE back into the outer office of the city jail, each man lost in his own contemplation's of how to track down the Dark One and destroy it before it struck again.

Lordalise's thoughts went to darker depths than Armand's, for he knew that each person Devenshire fed from that they did not discover was one more possibility of another vampire unleashed upon the earth. Of course, he knew simply killing someone did not guarantee that they would come back as a vampire, but the risk was simply too high to take. He knew the ample appetites of a vampire, and once they had discovered a large enough source of food, they would feed gluttonously.

"My men have taken Lorinda's body to the outskirts of the city and are disposing of her remains as you have instructed," Armand stated as he removed his hat and dropped it to a desktop before running his hands through his hair.

He sat down at Liston's desk and pulled open a bottom drawer, extracting a bottle of deep amber liquid. Next, he pulled out two small glasses and sat them on the desk before uncorking the bottle and pouring out a healthy amount into each glass.

Lordalise nodded as he crossed to the desk and took up one of the glasses. He wasted no time in tossing the entire contents of the glass down his throat. As the fiery liquor burned down his throat, he took a moment to collect his thoughts, to organize mental faculties that had gone too long unused. He had to force himself to think as a Hunter again, to force his mind back into the trains of thought that had been so familiar to him for so long but were now alien and took concentration to call into use.

"We should have Constable Liston summon the day sheriffs, as well. We must search not only for Devenshire and his companions, but any other unfortunate ones who might be attacked by him," Lordalise said as he poured another drink.

"I agree," Armand replied as he leaned back in the chair, his right hand holding the glass up as he looked about the office. "I thought Liston had remained here."

"Perhaps he has not the stomach for this type of work and has gone off to avoid it," Lordalise offered with bitterness tinting his words.

Armand took a sip of the liquor and winced at its bite. He shook his head. "Not Constable Liston. I have known him for many seasons and have yet to find the crime he is incapable of dealing with."

"Then maybe you have now found one. I mean no ill toward the good Constable, but his insane arguments of rights for Devenshire have tainted my opinion of him. How can any sane man even ponder offering mortal rights to a servant of the Master of Hell?"

"I understand how you feel, Master Lordalise, but I must remind you that this region has not been under the curse of a vampire for many ages. It was a lack of experience in these matters. I trust Constable Liston now understands the manner of beast we face and will pose no further arguments," Armand said as he took another, larger sip.

"I hope you are correct, Captain, for I will not yield to such arguments again," Lordalise answered, leaving no doubt in the tone of his voice.

Lordalise sipped his second drink as he walked to the window of the jail office and looked out upon the crowded streets beyond. It was still dark outside, but the torches that lined the streets made it possible for him to see the shadowed faces passing before him. His eyes took in each face, and it took several moments before he realized that he was trying to make each set of features re-arrange into Devenshire's. He blinked his eyes then rubbed them with the thumb and forefinger of one hand as he realized how tired he was becoming. He would have to marshal his strength, take care not to become fatigued, and thereby, careless. Such a mistake would be fatal. He cleared his eyes and turned them to the pitch black skies over the city. "It will be dawn soon. Devenshire will cease feeding and begin searching for a place to hide from the approaching day."

"He has already fed once this night. Do you believe he will feed again?" Armand asked.

"He will gorge himself on as much blood as he can obtain as quickly as possible. A single victim is not nearly enough to satiate his hellish appetite," Lordalise replied in clipped tones. "On a good night, a vampire can kill as many as a dozen people and still hunger for more."

"My Lords!!" Armand whispered. "And everyone he feeds from will become a vampire?"

Lordalise shook his head. "No. It depends upon the vampire. If he wishes to turn someone, then there is a different method of feeding. If feeding is all the vampire desires, then it will drink of a victim until they die. If it wishes to create another vampire, it will drain the victim to the point of death, leaving them alive. The poisoned magic of the bite will do the rest. It takes a single day, sometimes several before the victim finally succumbs from the bite. Either the body cannot produce enough blood to replenish what has been taken, or the loss of blood leaves the victim so weak that they succumb to any one of a number of ailments that can befall someone who is so weak. Either way, death will claim them, and the curse of the vampire will alter their mind and body into the ghoulish monster we now pursue."

"What manner of evil could create such a monster?" Armand asked.

"No one truly knows how the curse of the vampire began. There are many stories, some of which smack of truth, but none has ever been proven. Some say that a mage, many, many ages ago, was tampering with dark magic, and unleashed an ancient spell that converted him into the first vampire. Others say that a mighty warrior was facing a battle that he could not win and made a secret dark pact with Satan. The battle was won, and the Dark Master turned the warrior into the first vampire. There are many more stories," Lordalise answered sipping from his drink.

"A vampire is already dead?" Armand asked.

"Yes," Lordal answered.

"Then how do you kill something that is already dead?"

"There are numerous ways, none of them safe. Pure silver, blessed by a priest of the highest faith can injure and weaken a vampire. A wooden stake thrust through the heart can kill it. Exposing a vampire to sunlight will destroy it. Cutting its head off will destroy it. Ordinary weapons have no effect. A common sword or crossbow bolt will only amuse a vampire. A vampire cannot be physically detained for it has a strength that ten men cannot overcome," Lordalise answered evenly.

"I see that I have much to learn about the demons," Armand commented.

"You can never stop learning about the Dark Ones. The man who believes that he has all the knowledge there is to know about a vampire is a man who is doomed to making a mistake, and mistakes, where vampires are concerned, are always fatal," Lordalise replied.

The men lapsed into silence, each considering the evil that faced them. Lordalise remained at the window taking in the scene of the

THE DEVENSHIRE CHRONICLES

street before him, while Armand contemplated not only the vampire, but also what had become of Constable Liston. It was not like him to simply vanish, especially in a time of crisis.

Nearly half an hour later, their silent reverie was interrupted by one of the sheriffs dragging a manacled prisoner into the office. By the disheveled state of both men, and the multiple bruises that marked both of their faces, Armand reasoned that the arrest had not been a calm or easy one.

"Where is Constable Liston?" the sheriff demanded as he dabbed at his bloodied nose with a pocket linen.

"I do not know. He was not here when we arrived," Armand answered, "What did he do?" he asked nodding toward the prisoner.

"He attacked a whore in one of the taverns. When I tried to stop him, he attacked me, so I arrested him," the sheriff replied shortly.

"The bitch would not do her job!" the prisoner exclaimed with slurred words, and his breath reeked of the ale he had consumed.

"Just because she is a whore does not mean that she must practice her trade with one she does not wish to," the sheriff snapped in reply. "I cannot say that I blame her in her choice to refuse you."

"She is a whore. I have gold. Everything else is outside of consideration," the drunken man said.

"I will not waste time or words on you! Silence would be the trait that would best serve you at this moment!" the sheriff replied before he returned his attention to Armand. "I will lock this bastard in a cell and let Constable Liston determine what to do with him in the morning."

Armand nodded. He had no desire to become involved in an incident that clearly did not involve him or his office. He had served as a sheriff of a smaller town many seasons ago before being recruited by the Royal Guard. The memories of the human trash he had been forced to deal with were enough to dissuade him from taking any active participation or interest in this case.

The sheriff jerked hard on the chain between the manacles around the drunken man's wrists and began walking toward the large wooden door that led to the cells.

"You bastard child of a bitch!" the drunken man exclaimed as he recovered something that could pass as balance after the sheriff had jerked him forward. "Take these manacles from my wrists, and we will see how big a man you are!"

The sheriff turned and buried his fist deep into the ample expanse of the drunken man's stomach. As the man's breath was forcibly expelled from his lungs, which only thickened the stench of drunkenness surrounding him, he doubled. The sheriff grabbed a handful of the man's hair, jerked his head up, and smashed him across the jaw, which dropped the larger man to his knees.

388 | TOM SECHRIST

"I told you to remain silent!" the sheriff shouted. "Say another word, any word at all, and I will see to it that your day before the tribunal will have to wait until the healers finish trying to put your jaw back where it belongs!"

The drunken man simply continued coughing, trying to draw air back into his lungs. Satisfied that he had made his point, the sheriff turned and pulled on the ring that would open the door. He made to turn back to his prisoner, but something beyond the door stopped him. With a sharp intake of breath the sheriff suddenly froze.

Armand watched the sheriff for several moments, waiting for the man to take charge of his prisoner and escort him to one of the cells. But the sheriff did not move. Armand looked over at Lordal who also studied the sheriff for some sign of movement.

"Is something wrong?" Armand asked.

The sheriff did not answer, did not move from his place.

"Sheriff? What is the matter?" Armand repeated.

"By the heavens..." the sheriff whispered.

Armand rose to his feet and moved from behind the desk to be joined by Lordalise as they moved up behind the sheriff. What they saw beyond the door turned their blood cold in their veins.

Constable Liston lay sprawled on the floor, his head turned toward them and his eyes staring at them, but not seeing them.

"Liston!" Armand shouted as he moved around the stunned sheriff and knelt next to the constable. Lordal moved around the sheriff and stepped over the prone form of the constable to kneel opposite Armand.

"No!" Armand exclaimed as he placed his palm above the constable's nose and mouth, hoping to feel breath there but knowing he would find none. Liston's face was already the color of death, and the emptiness of his gaze had already told the captain that the man was dead and had been so for some time.

"Devenshire!" Lordalise proclaimed as he, too, knew the constable was dead before he had ever knelt beside him. When Armand looked at him with a questioning gaze, Lordalise pointed to the constable's throat.

Reluctantly, Armand lowered his gaze to find that a rather large gaping hole had been ripped in Liston's throat. Only the slightest trail of blood seeped from the wound to trace down the constable's neck to a tiny pool on the floor beneath him.

Armand slowly lowered his head and shook it slightly. Lordal studied the captain for several moments, wondering if the man would lose his senses under the burden of facing such brutality twice in the same night, and one of them having befallen someone he knew and liked.

"I am sorry," Lordalise whispered.

"Why him? Liston was a good man, an honorable man. Why would the Fates allow him to fall prey to that bastard?" Armand asked, his voice betraying the grief and anger that had begun to boil hours before and was only agitated further by this latest discovery.

"I wish I had an answer for you, Armand. I truly do. Death is indiscriminate. It comes to all in one form or another and leaves only questions in its wake. I swear to you that we will find Devenshire and make him pay dearly for the atrocities he has committed. I guarantee his ending will be as painful and horrible as his evil mind can contemplate," Lordalise replied.

If the captain took any comfort from Lordalise's words, it was not apparent in his grim look of grief and hatred. He raised his eyes to meet and lock with Lordal's. When he spoke, the grief was pushed aside in favor of the anger and hatred. "I want him, Lordalise! I want to be the one to send Devenshire back to hell. You track him, wound him, weaken him, but the death blow must come from me!"

Lordalise had seen such thirst for vengeance before. Death, especially death dealt by the fangs of a vampire, could stir the hot blood of vengeance quickly. He accepted Armand's grief and desire for vengeance with a slight nod. "I can promise nothing. If I encounter the ghoul and have the chance to destroy him, I will. I cannot merely wound him and wait for you to come to finish him. Such a thing would be very dangerous."

"Then I will travel with you until he is destroyed! I must be the one to cast it out of our realm," Armand replied.

"I cannot say with any certainty when or where we might again encounter it. What of your duties to the Royal Guard?"

"I will resign my commission if necessary! I will not rest until Devenshire's corpse is rotting at my feet, his foul blood upon my hands. If you cannot or will not aide me, then I will pursue him myself!" Armand shot back.

Lordal was silent for several moments as he considered the captain's words. It had been a very long time since he had witnessed the deep-rooted vengeance that a vampire could inspire in a man. A part of him reveled in it as one would revel in the first rays of spring sunshine following a harsh winter. Another part of him was frightened by it for he had seen too many people set off on a course of vengeance against a vampire only to end up as another in a long line of meals for the ghoul or worse, as one of their slaves.

Finally, he returned his gaze to Armand's burning eyes and sighed. "If circumstances occur that will allow what you wish for, I will grant it. But if I encounter Devenshire, and you are not about, then I will dispatch him myself as the dictates of my order command me to do. I can follow no other course of action."

"Fair enough," Armand replied.

"Be warned. If you set off after Devenshire alone, then you run the risk of ending up as Liston," he said indicating the corpse with a nod of his head. His eyes took on a deep stare of intense warning, and he continued. "Or worse... much, much worse."

Lordalise watched as Armand digested his warning, and he found himself praying that the captain could set aside his grief and his thirst for vengeance long enough for the true depths of his warning to settle deep into his mind.

"I understand. But, like you, I can make no promises. Just as you must act as the dictates of your Order commands you, so must I as the dictates of my conscience command me."

Armand and Lordal stared into each other's eyes for a moment, each man setting into granite what their words meant. Finally, Armand rose slowly to his feet, his eyes returning to the cold empty stare of Liston.

After what Lordal assumed was a silent farewell, the captain drew his sword and turned to the still stunned sheriff. "Constable Liston has been killed by a vampire. Do you understand?"

The sheriff did not answer but only continued to stare at the constable's body with the same wide-eyed look of terror his features had adopted upon discovering the constable's body.

"Sheriff! Did you hear what I said?" Armand demanded louder.

Finally, the sheriff was able to nod slowly. "Yes sir," his trembling voice replied.

"In order to make sure that he does not return as a vampire, there are certain things that must be done. They are not pleasant, and they seem disrespectful to the dead, but they must be done. Are you prepared to carry out these things?"

"What things? What do you speak of?" the sheriff asked.

"I must cut the head from the body. The head and body must then be burned to ash, and then a priest of the highest faith must bless the ashes. Once this is done, the ashes must be scattered to the wind. Do you understand?"

The sheriff's expression spoke of the horror he felt at these acts more clearly than any words he could have uttered. After a moment's consideration, the sheriff nodded.

"Gather your best men and the priest of the highest faith within Lirpa. Make haste, for every moment we wait is another moment that Liston could be slipping further into the clutches of the demon bastard that killed him," Armand said.

The sheriff nodded, but did not move.

"Go now! You do not want to witness what I must now do. When you return, the body and head will be prepared."

The sheriff was finally able to force his feet to move, and once free of the terror that had immobilized them, they carried the sheriff out into the night with surprising speed. Armand turned his attention to the drunken prisoner who still knelt where the sheriff had landed him. Like the sheriff, the drunken man stared at Liston's remains with the same terror, a strange sobriety having come from the fear.

"Be gone! Leave this place!" Armand commanded.

The man struggled to his feet and began backing toward the door, the fact that he was still in chains lost on his awareness. Once he had backed clear of the front door, the man turned and hurried down the darkened street.

Armand turned back to see Lordal standing across from him with his own sword drawn. The silver of the blade lay in the crook of Lordal's arm with the hilt toward Armand.

Again, the men locked eyes, and a silent understanding passed between them. Lordal nodded once, and Armand slowly returned his sword to its scabbard before taking Lordal's blade with the reverence of one taking hold of a sacred object.

Lordal took several steps back and folded his hands together in front of him. Armand looked down at Liston and slowly brought the sword up over his head.

"My friend. I swear upon the graves of my parents, upon the breath within my lungs and the beat of my heart that I will avenge you. I will not rest until the ghoul who has done this terrible deed to you has been returned to the fires of hell. Rest well, Liston, and may you finally find peace."

Without another moment's hesitation, Armand brought the sword down. With the singing of silver, the head of Constable Liston bounced free of his body. Armand stood upright and regarded the headless body of his friend for several moments before he cleaned the blade off upon his own cloak. With darkness in his eyes, he lifted them to Lordalise and offered the Hunter his sword back in the same fashion it had been offered to him.

Lordalise stepped forward and took his sword back and sheathed it. He searched his memory for any words of comfort he might offer the captain and came up with none. He knew from experience that there were no words for this moment, no words that would bring any comfort or ease to the grief and anger that burned within Armand.

"Do you wish for my help in preparing the body?" he asked softly.

Armand shook his head. "No. I will undertake this task alone."

"As you wish. I will wait outside until you are finished," Lordal replied as he stepped over the body and past Armand. Just as he reached the front door of the jail office, Armand's voice called out.

"Master Lordalise?"

Lordal turned. Armand stood with his back to him, still facing the decapitated body of his friend.

"Yes?" he asked.

"Thank you."

Lordalise watched the captain briefly before he nodded slowly and stepped out of the building.

Once outside, he noticed that the crowd had dispersed. Word did not take long to travel in a city this size. He sighed heavily, looked up into the star-riddled sky, and saw that the full orb of the moon hung low. Dawn was coming soon, but not soon enough to force Devenshire into hiding. There was still time left for the demon to foul the realm with his presence. Lordalise let out a sigh of frustration. While he harbored no deep feelings of regret for Liston's passing, he regretted Armand having to suffer the loss that was made doubly difficult by the manner in which the constable had died.

There were other sources of frustration and irritation within his sigh, as well. His passing himself off as a member was trampling upon the honor of the Hunters, which he held so dearly to his being. He was acting under the dictates of an Order he no longer belonged to, regardless of how deeply he believed that his actions were of the purest intent.

Also, acting as a Hunter and undertaking their tasks brought back memories that he had sooner not remember. There was a great sense of honor and accomplishment that went along with being a Hunter. There was pride as well. Lordalise felt all of these things and found himself sorely missing being a genuine member of the order.

He had acknowledged that he missed that life, missed feeling like his life meant something, and that he was performing a service to all of mankind. But over the seasons since leaving the Order, the sharp pangs of regret had dulled and softened only to be sharpened back to brutal clarity with his actions this night.

As with any time that he thought about his days as a Hunter, the other memory returned to torture him. The memory of his actions that had led to his being thrown out of the Order, the memory of the one crime that he should have been put to death for, but had been spared. The sparing of his life had not come from mercy, but from a desire to punish him in a way far worse than death ever could. It had been agreed that leaving him alive to contemplate what he had done, what it had cost him, was a far more suitable punishment, and they had been undeniably right in their thinking.

Desdemona. The name flashed unbidden in his mind, and with it, the mental image of a woman lovelier than any he had ever encountered. As much as he missed being a Hunter, he missed Desdemona with equal fierceness. She had come to him and brought with her feelings that he had feared he would never feel. The dark cloud of death and hunting the dead which had thickened until it permeated his entire being had been dispelled with but a single smile from her. She brought sunshine into the night of his existence, and he had loved her from the moment he had laid eyes upon her.

Before her memory could carry him down into despair, the sound of pounding hooves jerked him upright, forcing his mind to lock away the memories of a woman he should hate, should despise, but could not help but love.

A Royal Guard drove his mount toward the jail with an urgency that instantly brought Lordalise's senses to full alertness. Something had happened. Either another victim had been discovered or, and Lordalise dared to hope, news of Devenshire or his accomplices had been found.

"Master Lordalise! Where is Captain Armand?" the guard shouted before his mount had even come to a standstill.

"He is inside. Constable Liston has been killed by Devenshire."

The guards' harried urgent expression shifted for a moment into regret as he absorbed the news. Lordalise feared he would have to endure another tragic moment of witnessing more grief at the news he had been forced to bear. While he acknowledged the need for such grief, he also acknowledged that it could be costing them precious seconds they could ill afford to lose in their hunt for Devenshire.

"What has happened?" Lordalise asked, hoping to break the guard out of his despair at the loss of the constable.

"Devenshire's accomplices have retrieved their mounts and could be trying to leave the city."

"What?!" Lordalise asked in angered disbelief. "Were there no guards posted at the stables?"

"Yes, sir. There were. They were discovered unconscious a short time ago. We roused them, and they told us of how Devenshire's accomplishes had made good their escape."

"Any sign of Devenshire?" Lordalise asked quickly, his mind already leaping ahead to forming a plan that might allow them to be captured before they were able to leave the city.

"No sir," the guard replied.

Lordalise forced his thoughts to slow from their racing patterns. He had to remain calm, to think rationally. They had come into Lirpa from the south. He seriously doubted that they would be foolish enough to return to where they had come from. That left east, west and north as their possible directions of travel. The next nearest village lay to the north with nothing to the east or west that would not require many days travel.

Devenshire would require somewhere dark to hide during the daylight hours, and the trail to the north led into a mountainous region where numerous suitable hiding places could be found. Only dense forest range lay to the east or west. They must be heading north. They had to be.

"What steps have you taken?" Armand asked as he stepped from the jail. Lordalise found himself admiring the way the captain stepped from the grief of the task he had just completed into his role as commander of the Royal Guard. It took considerable force of will and control to set aside personal matters to tend to other matters such as the business at hand.

"I have pulled in our men from the inn, leaving it under the guard of a complement of local sheriffs. One regiment is heading to the northern edge of town to begin a searching sweep back into town. Another regiment is proceeding from the stables toward the northeastern edge of town. The final regiment is heading toward the southwestern corner of town to search back toward us," the guard replied.

Lordalise nodded in silent approval. That search pattern would put most of Lirpa under their sweep in the shortest amount of time. If Devenshire and his minions were still within the city, their chances of evading all of the guards were very slim.

"Very good. Recruit as many sheriffs as you can and have them meet me near the northern edge of town," Armand said.

"I have a few men of my own in a camp just south of town. I will summon them to join our search," Lordalise offered.

"Good. We will need all the men we can get," Armand commented as he stepped down from the walkway in front of the jail.

"Captain. Let me remind you of the danger your men face. They must not attempt to capture Devenshire without me. They are not armed to battle a vampire, and any attempt on their parts to capture or kill him will only result in more bodies for us to burn. Have your men, should they find Devenshire or his companions, follow and keep track of the ghoul's movements."

Armand stepped up beside his mount. Lordalise could tell that Armand did not like that particular course of action, but he recognized the need for it to be followed and followed closely.

After a short nod, he turned to the guard. "Instruct the men as you have heard Master Lordalise say. Make no mistake, Devenshire is a cold blooded killer of the worst kind, and all caution should be exercised should he be found."

"Yes, sir," the guard replied as he spun his mount around and spurred it off down the street.

Armand swung himself up into the saddle, gathered the reins and fixed Lordalise with an intense gaze. "May the Fates favor us this night."

"Yes. May fortune smile on us both, Captain," Lordal replied. "We shall sorely need it."

CHAPTER THIRTY-TWO

ZANDORTH JOGGED BACK to the women and horses hidden deep in a darkened alley. He had just ventured to the edge of the alley to take stock of their intended path out of Lirpa. By the grim set of his features, both Brianna and Shantira knew the news was not good.

"Yet another turn of events has taken place to further undermine our efforts!" he grumbled as he gathered his reins and mounted up.

"What has happened?" Shantira asked.

"I do not know. But whatever it is, there are Royal Guards and sheriffs everywhere. They are definitely searching for us."

"We cannot leave the city by a direct path. Perhaps if we circled back around to the east and tried that way," Brianna offered.

Zandorth considered her words carefully. "I do not know if we will have any more success that way. From what I have seen in the past, they are using a very detailed search pattern."

"What if we found a place within the city to hide? Perhaps they will tire of the search or think that we have managed to escape and leave a path open for us to use later," Shantira injected.

Zandorth's dappled gray horse shifted nervously beneath the warrior as he considered that course of action. He slowly shook his head. "They believe Devenshire to be a vampire. They will be expecting him to be hiding in the city during the daylight hours. If they do not find him before sunrise, then you can rest assured that they will intensify their search through the city tomorrow. Also, remember that a woman has been killed in the manner of a vampire." He shook his head with a very grim expression on his face. "They will not rest until they have him, and us. They will turn this city inside out looking for us."

"There has to be a way. There just has to be," Brianna commented.

"We must find their weakest regiment and fight our way out," Zandorth said.

"No. We may accidentally kill one of them and that must not happen. We are innocent of what they accuse us of, but if we kill one of the Royal Guards, then we will become the criminals they believe us to be. We must escape Lirpa without killing. We must also consider the possibility that fighting our way out will result in one or all of us being killed," Brianna argued.

"Better to die on our feet fighting than to be lead to the gallows and die the dishonorable death of a criminal," Zandorth countered.

"Zandorth! I am not going to argue this point with you. We will not kill!" Brianna shouted, her green eyes flashing in anger.

Zandorth's gray eyes turned to stone as his jaw muscles tensed. His eyes snapped around to bore into Brianna. "I do not believe that you have the choice of deciding my fate, woman. You are not in charge here!" he growled.

"I am not concerned with who is in charge. I am only concerned with getting us out of the city without further bloodshed!" Brianna replied in hard controlled tones.

"Now you are concerned with escape!" he exclaimed with sarcasm. "That should have been your concern the instant we escaped the jail," Zandorth shot back. "But you insisted on returning for our supplies. However, that was only a ruse, a tactic you used to stall for time in the hopes that Devenshire would turn up. I believe your feelings for him have clouded your judgment!"

"How dare you!!" Brianna hissed. "Who do you think you are that you can speak to me like this? My feelings for Daimion are none of your concern. Just because I am not a cold-blooded, self-centered animal, and wished not to abandon a friend in a time of need, does not mean my judgment is clouded!!"

"Hold!!"

They all spun in their saddles to see three Royal Guardsmen at the far entrance of the alley.

Zandorth slapped his hand to the hilt of his broadsword and turned his gaze to Brianna. "The time for talk has passed. What are your intentions?"

Brianna regarded the guards behind them and then to the open street in front of them. She gathered her reins and looked at Zandorth. "Let us hope we live long enough to argue about it," she said as she dug her heels deep into her horses' flanks. The mount lurched forward, breaking into a full gallop. Zandorth and Shantira followed suit, and the three of them bolted out of the alley. People were sent diving for cover as the three mounts sped down the street. The people's flight for cover was aided by the rider's shouts for them to get out of the way.

The protesting citizens of Lirpa made their way back into the street only to be sent diving for cover again by the blur of white stallions pounding after the first three. Their second pilgrimage into the street was slower and more cautious.

The trio rounded a corner and instantly pulled up rein, bringing their mounts to a staggering halt as their eyes showed them another complement of guards riding toward them. Zandorth swung his gaze around to see the first three guards closing in on them quickly from behind. With a snarl on his face, he began looking around for another path.

He spied a side street that appeared deserted and swung his protesting mount around. "This way!" he shouted as he kicked his horse back into a full gallop. Brianna and Shantira followed suit. Their flight down the side street deposited them into another main avenue only to encounter another detachment of guards.

With a growled curse, Zandorth spun his mount around and sent it racing off away from the guards. Sweat coursed down his face as his eyes searched for any signs of being cut off by more guards and for alternate routes of escape. Above the pounding of hooves, they could hear the shouts of the guards as they tried to coordinate their pursuit. Harsh clipped instructions were shouted only to be over ridden and changed. It also helped that the only light they had came from the street torches, limiting their visibility. Shadows were definitely their staunchest ally at the moment.

As they neared an intersection, Zandorth felt sudden alarm rise within him. Something screamed at him to avoid the intersection at all costs, and he was not about to ignore his instincts, not when they had kept him alive this long.

To Brianna and Shantira's surprise, the warrior suddenly pulled up and stopped. The two women shot past him and had to struggle to stop their mounts and then turning to rejoin him.

"What are you doing? They are right behind us!" Shantira shouted as she struggled to keep her shifting mount under control. The animals sensed the urgency in their riders, and they were nervous.

"The intersection! It is a trap!" Zandorth barked as his eyes swung around, searching for another escape. The streets were packed with people, other horses, and carriages. Maneuvering through the throng would slow them, and the guards could use the obstacles to their advantage. With this many trained soldiers in pursuit of them, more unorthodox means would have to be used.

Brianna allowed her high-spirited horse to prance nervously in a circle as she joined the search for another path. There were side streets and alleys within reach, but she reasoned that the guards would have them covered or would be within easy distance to cover them should they decide to make use of them.

"Well, if you have another alternative, now is the time," she said breathlessly.

Zandorth focused his attention, forcing his mind to remain clear and calm. Fear and panic tried to intrude upon his thoughts, and he savagely fought them down. He would make use of their added strength when the time called for it, but not now. Then his eyes spied what could very well be their salvation.

Unorthodox means, indeed.

"This way. Be alert, the path will be treacherous!" he snapped as he turned his mount and urged it toward a large warehouse.

"What is he doing?" Shantira shouted.

Brianna saw where Zandorth was going and smiled as she shook her head. "Surviving. Come on." She spurred her horse into motion, falling in behind Zandorth.

With a small complement of Royal Guardsmen very close behind them, the three raced for a warehouse.

Zandorth gauged the distance from the street, over the hitching rails and to the large double door entrance. He trusted his mount, knew the animal would perform any task he commanded of it. However, he found himself wondering about Brianna, Shantira and their mounts. He knew nothing of their horsemanship and even less of the caliber of their mounts. The near suicidal path he had chosen would require quick reflexes, not only from horse, but from rider as well. There was no time to worry about that now. Either the women followed him, or they were captured. He hoped they realized this and would use that fear to carry them through what was to come.

At the appropriate time, he tightened his knees to the shoulders of his horse and leaned down low. He felt the animal's muscles bunch and then the horse launched itself into the air, clearing the hitching rail, and landing with a solid thud upon the boards of the walkway in front of the warehouse. The boards creaked and groaned in protest of the sudden additional weight, but held their form. Without so much as a faltered step, the dappled gray stallion bolted through the open doorway and into the warehouse beyond.

Brianna had known what Zandorth had intended to do, but that knowledge did not ease the trepidation that raced through her as the Warrior jumped his horse up onto the walkway and then into the warehouse. She knew her turn was approaching fast, and she had a choice to make. Attempt the jump, or find another route. She had reasoned that the more obvious paths would be covered, and their only slim chance of escape lay in the way Zandorth had gone. There was really very little choice in the matter.

"Come on, boy. We can do this," she muttered as she drew herself up tight and urged her mount into the same leap as Zandorth's had made. Her eyes opened wide as she sailed over the hitching rail and angled for the open door. With a squeal of delight, she braced for impact. The sudden, bone jarring shock of landing came, and she feared she would be pitched from the saddle by the sudden stop.

With her heart pounding hard in her chest, she dug her heels in and urged her mount to follow Zandorth. Despite the fear that came with the flight from the guards, she could not ignore the exhilaration that accompanied the fear. As she pounded into the warehouse, she smiled with delight at not only having completed the jump, but at the thrill that raced through her.

Shantira watched as Brianna's mount sailed over the hitching rail to land nearly inside the doors of the warehouse and then disappear into the building. With a smile of her own, she prepared to follow. There was something about the danger of the jump, the danger of being thrown from her mount into the hands of the Royal Guard, that excited her. She knew she should be afraid, and a part of her mind acknowledged that she was very much so. But the fear was masked with excitement, the thrill of the chase, and the chance to test herself against a situation she had never encountered before.

As her horse's hooves left the dirt of the street, she heard herself shriek in a combination of fear and excitement. Like Brianna, her eyes remained wide open as she took in the brief view of the street from her position of flight. She saw the walkway rushing up to meet her and she tensed for the impact of landing. The hooves struck the boards of the walkway, and she felt the jar all along her spine. Only after she had steered her mount through the open doorway did she realize she had been holding her breath as she let it out in an explosive laugh of triumph.

~*~

The first Royal Guard stared wide-eyed after the trio as they had leapt up onto the walkway to disappear into the warehouse. It was suicide, but he was duty bound to follow. So he urged more speed from his animal and prepared himself to follow.

His horse leapt and he gritted his teeth as he landed hard upon the walkway. With his heart pounding in his throat, he turned his mount and gave chase into the warehouse.

The next man lost his nerve at the last moment and tried to pull up rein, but he had waited too long and his horse reared up on its hind legs. The animal slammed into the hitching rail, and the sudden shift in direction threw the guard clear of the saddle to fly into the warehouse wall. The guard crumpled to the walkway, dazed and nearly unconscious.

The next three men completed the jump and continued the chase. The remaining three, however, suffered varying degrees of failure. One horse decided that it did not wish to jump and stiffened its legs as it slid to a sudden stop, sending its rider careening into the wall to land next to his fellow guardsman.

The second rider had misjudged the distance and leapt too soon. The front legs of his mount hit upon the walkway while the back legs hit the street. The momentum of the leap carried the animal up and onto its' side on the walkway. In fearful panic, the horse screamed and began kicking, struggling to rise to its feet. The guard tried to remain in the saddle, but the animal was wild now, frantically fighting to regain its footing and flee. As the panicked beast found its footing, it bolted for the open street, dislodging its rider when his head struck the overhang of the awning and leaving him in a crumpled heap half on and half off the walkway.

The third rider, along with his horse, decided against the jump and pulled back hard on the reins. The mount grunted in protest and locked its legs, which sent the guard flying through the open door of the warehouse. The floor rushed up and snatched the man from his flight, and he bounced and rolled a considerable distance before he came to a stop, too dazed to even consider rising.

With the three failed attempts at the jump, the rest of the detachment found their path blocked. With shouts and curses, the remainder of the guards decided to split their numbers and attempt to circle around to the rear of the warehouse.

~*~Zandorth pounded through the warehouse, dodging crates and bags of various goods that lie in his path. At this time of night, there was no one inside the warehouse, and therefore, he did not have to worry about dodging people as well as the other obstacles. There were only a few lanterns scattered throughout the interior, which provided minimal lighting and an abundant number of opportunities for missteps and mistakes.

As the rear doors of the warehouse loomed ahead, the warrior considered his next path. Near the back doors was a set of stairs that led to the second level of the warehouse off to the left. To the right was a rampway used for rolling barrels of various goods up to or down from the second level. For a reason he could not understand, he suddenly jerked the reins hard to the left and sent his horse up the stairs. The animal's eyes grew wide and its ears flattened back. The steed bounded up the steps, but Zandorth could feel the uncertainty of the animal beneath him and urged it on with another vicious kick to the flanks.

"What in the name of all that is holy?" Brianna proclaimed as she watched horse and rider take to the stairs. So insane was Zandorth's actions that she pulled up rein despite the fact that guards were closing in on them.

"Has he taken leave of his senses?" Shantira asked breathlessly.

"Only the Fates know what he is doing," Brianna replied as she glanced over her shoulder to see three mounted guards racing toward them. "We have come this far. May as well see what madness Zandorth is following."

With a click of her tongue, she sent her own horse toward the stairs, trying to time her ascent to begin once Zandorth's mount was clear of the stairs. For a terrifying instant, she feared her mount would revolt and refuse to mount the stairs. But with only the slightest hesitation in its steps, the horse began climbing the stairs, which protested having to bear weight it was never designed to hold.

Shantira waited anxiously as Brianna climbed the stairs. She knew the stairs would never hold up to two horses at the same time, but she also knew the Royal Guard was closing on her fast. Once Brianna disappeared into the second level, she wasted no time in following. She did not worry about her horse following up the stairs for she had taken the animal on many rides into the foothills near her village, and the animal had proven to be very sure of foot. It took the steps as calmly as it had the rocky terrain of the foothills.

The four guards who had survived the jump from the street pulled up rein, their eyes wide in shock at the sight of the three horses mounting the stairs.

"They have lost their senses," one guard commented.

"They have trapped themselves. There is no escape from up there," another said as he urged his horse forward to begin a skittish climb of the stairs.

The second man followed and the third guard began his ascent too soon. As the second guard neared the top of the stairs, the third guards mount reached the mid way point of the climb. The load of two horses and riders proved too much for the lumber of the stairs, and with a loud groan, they gave way.

When the steps fell away from the hooves of the second horse, it whinnied out in protest, and its front hooves began pawing frantically, searching for some form of purchase and finding none. With a tremendous cacophony of cracking timber and screaming horses, the steps collapsed into a heap, a cloud of dust exploding outward in all directions.

The first guard spun his mount around at the head of the steps and looked down, trying to see through the cloud of dust. As the dust began to clear, he got his first glimpse of the results of the collapsing staircase. The second horse lay amidst the rubble of the stairs; it's front legs twitching. Occasionally, it would lift its head as if trying to rise only to let it fall back, unable to rise. The jagged end of a timber protruded from its side, just behind the shoulder and just below the backbone. Blood coated the jagged end, which pointed upward and bits of hide clung to its jagged edges. No doubt, the timber had severed the spine of the animal, leaving it paralyzed. The animal's weak snorts seemed deafening in the sudden silence following the collapse of the stairs.

The first guard caught sight of the third horse as it struggled to its feet from under a smaller pile of rubble. As the horse walked away from the debris, the guard saw how one of its front legs hung at an odd angle and how the animal limped badly. The leg was broken.

Before he could search for the two riders, the creak of wood and the click of hooves drew his attention behind him. He turned in the saddle and saw the three riders moving quickly away from him into the gloomy shadows. With an angry snarl, he jerked his mount around and urged it into a trot to follow.

~*~Zandorth had paused for only a moment at the crash of the collapsing stairs. A quick look back over his shoulder had told him that at least one guard had made the climb before the stairs collapsed. He knew they would have to get off the second floor of the warehouse for the flooring here would be hard pressed to hold the combined weight of all the goods stored up here and four horses and riders. Already, he could hear the timbers groan in protest of the additional weight.

"Stay close and be alert. The flooring could give way at any time," he said as he steered his mount around and behind a neatly stacked row of crates.

Brianna and Shantira said nothing as they fell in behind Zandorth, neither wishing to contemplate the results should the floor suddenly give way beneath them. Zandorth had scanned the entire second floor as soon as he had reached it and knew their route of escape lay in only one direction. He hoped he could get to it before the guard discerned where they were going and moved to cut them off. While he agreed with Brianna's argument that they must not kill any of the guards, he would not allow himself to be captured again. Memories of his short stay in the city jail had awakened memories of another time and another cell—he would not be locked up again... *ever.*

~*~

The fourth guard sat his mount and surveyed the shattered remains of the staircase. As the stairs had begun to collapse, he had barely managed to back his mount away from the falling debris. Now he regarded the dying remains of one horse and the maimed stance of another. Both animals would have to be destroyed, and that saddened him, for the horses used by the Royal Guard were the finest anywhere. They were proud and noble animals that were well trained. To have to kill one simply because it had done what it had been commanded to do seemed cruel. But, the man reflected, it would be crueler to let the animals suffer with the tremendous pain they both must be in.

"Stanwyck? Bontal?" the guard called the names of the riders of the two horses. He could see no sign of them within the piled debris of the stairs. When no answer came, he felt himself grow tense. Perhaps they were only unconscious, but the alternative could not be ignored.

"Stanwyck! Bontal!" he called again, more urgently. "Are you injured?"

Again, there was no answer to his call and he quickly dismounted and moved closer to the debris, hoping to spot some sign of either of them. Aside from the gouged horse half buried in the debris, he could see nothing of his fellow guardsmen.

The sounds of hooves pounding on wood above his head called to his attention, and he turned his eyes upward. When each hoof struck the floor above him, he could see dust dislodged between the floorboards. It made for a way to track the movements of the criminals, and it took him only a moment to learn where they were going. His eyes fell to the ramp that descended from the second floor. They would try to use it as a means of escape. He drew his sword as he crossed to the massive post that served as a support for the second floor and waited. The Royal Guard had lost two very fine mounts in this pursuit. It seemed only fair to the man that the criminals lose the same.

~*~

Zandorth weaved his way through the stacked crates and barrels in a path he hoped would keep them hidden from the guard behind them and keep their destination hidden as well. With each hurried step that his horse took, with each creak and groan of the flooring, he found himself growing more and more tense. The fact that there were no lanterns on the second level made the trip doubly nerve wracking. He was painfully aware that the next step his mount took could very well send him crashing through to the floor below to be followed by debris and most certainly a considerable amount of the crates around him.

As he rounded a tight corner in the path of crates, he spied the top of the ramp leading down. He also saw where another pathway led back toward where the staircase had been. In that instant, a plan formed and he pulled up rein.

"Brianna. You and Shantira go down the ramp and head back for the main street. I will join you shortly!" he whispered, keeping his voice as soft as he could.

"We cannot afford to separate now," Brianna argued in a harsh whisper.

"She is right! We must stay together," Shantira agreed.

"I seek only to gain us some escape time. The guard who followed us up here is right behind us. I will prevent him from following us," Zandorth said. He then began backing his horse down the path that led toward the opening where the stairs had been. From that position, he would be hidden from the guards view.

"We cannot kill them!" Brianna whispered urgently.

"I will not kill him. Merely render him unable to follow us right away. Now go! We have not the time to debate this!" he growled.

Brianna paused only a second as the sounds of the pursuing guards' hooves grew steadily louder. She gave Zandorth a hard look that she hoped carried a warning not to lose his control and kill the guard. Her hard look was met with the set determination of his eyes. She nodded once and urged her mount on with Shantira close behind. As they vanished into the isle of crates and barrels, Zandorth climbed down from his mount and prepared himself, his timing would be critical.

Within seconds of losing sight of Brianna and Shantira, the white steed of the guard came into view. The guard was moving quickly, and the opportunity to strike was already fading. With a snarl and low growl, he launched himself at the guard.

At the last second, the guard turned his head, and Zandorth received a very good view of his shocked expression. As his shoulder collided with the guards shoulder, he quickly twisted his body so that their flight would carry them both clear of the now startled horse, and any chance that a flying hoof would render his plan useless.

The guard hit the floor hard with Zandorth's massive frame on top of him. Zandorth wasted no time in straddling the stunned guard and drawing his right fist up to his shoulder.

"We are not guilty of what you think we are! Leave us be!" he snarled at the wide-eyed guard before smashing his fist down across the guards jaw. The man's head snapped hard to one side and his eyes rolled upwards into their sockets before the lids slid down.

Zandorth climbed to his feet and watched the guard closely. The man still breathed, but his eyes were closed, and he did not move. All of his training and experience told him to kill the man. Not to leave an enemy alive to strike again at some future time. But the sense of Brianna's argument not to complicate their situation by killing a member of the Royal Guard subdued his instincts, and he stepped away from the guard and turned to his mount. The guards horse had bolted as the guard had been swept clear of the saddle, and Zandorth had no idea where the animal had gone.

As he gathered his reins and gripped the pommel of the saddle to re-mount his horse, he heard the scream from below. It was the pain and terror riddled scream of a horse, and something within him regarded the sound with near panic. There was no way he could know which of the animals the sound had come from.

~*~

Brianna steered her mount carefully down the ramp. While she knew that haste was needed, she was not about to push her mount into what could turn out to be a very painful, if not deadly fall down the ramp. Her horse was not accustomed to the things she was making it do, and the horse was becoming ever more difficult to manage. Before this journey, the horse had only carried her out on occasional rides through the countryside. The animal was used to rolling plains and occasional leisurely winding walks through a forest, not the jumps and climbs it had been forced into this night. So far, the animal had performed as she had commanded it, but she could feel the tenseness in its muscles beneath her, could almost feel the fear the animal was feeling as it was forced into actions that were alien to it. With soothing words, she urged the animal slowly down the ramp, feeling pride in him for performing under such unknown conditions. She had wondered at the quality of the horse when she had bought it. This night had reassured her that she had made a good purchase.

Just as she neared the bottom of the ramp, something seemed wrong. She could not pinpoint what it was, but something was screaming at her to be alert. Her eyes scanned the dark shadowy interior of the warehouse for what was the source of her sudden unease. She saw the two rider-less mounts of the Royal Guard, and she wondered where their riders were. Then she saw a flash to her left. A brief glimpse of something shiny as it rushed toward her.

As she swung her head around to focus in on the flash, there came a wet thump just below and in front of her. Suddenly her horse screamed out and reared up tossing her from the saddle to land hard on the ramp, her wind gushing from her lungs in an explosive sigh. Pain lanced her spine and immediately shot out in all directions, causing her limbs to tingle as if they had gone to sleep. Dark speckles flecked her vision as darkness cut off her peripherals and her mind swam.

"Brianna!" a voice called out, but she could not recognize its owner through the sudden ringing in her ears. She tried to move, to regain her feet, but her limbs were numb, and her senses shrouded in a swirling fog. She dimly heard her horse running away, screaming in what sounded like pure agony, and she wondered what had injured it.

"Hold!" another voice called out. Then she felt something warm and wet touch her throat. "Drop your weapons and dismount slowly." She tried to pull her senses up from the soup of disorientation, but to no avail. Her limbs were useless, her vision blurred and her mind numbed.

"Do not harm her," the first voice pleaded.

"Drop your weapons and dismount, and she will not be harmed," the second voice replied.

Whoever the second voice had been speaking to seemed to obey his commands for Brianna heard the distinct sound of a sword clattering to the wooden floor followed by the creak of saddle leather as if someone were dismounting a horse.

"Let me see to her!" the first voice demanded.

"No," the second voice shot back. "Where is the other one? The Warrior?"

"He is upstairs," the first voice replied in tight tones.

"Call him down."

"Zandorth! Come quickly! Brianna has been injured," the first voice rang out, loud enough for even Brianna to gain recognition from its tone through the ringing in her ears. It was Shantira's voice, and she was scared to death. "Please! Do not harm her."

"She will remain uninjured as long as the two of you do exactly what I say," the second voice replied.

Shantira tried to rein in her racing fear while at the same time tried to determine why she felt so. Fear was normal, but this was not just fear. It was near panic at the thought of Brianna being harmed. She knew she had to gain control of her fear, to wrestle it under control, but she could not. As with the strange sensation that had passed over her at the sight of Brianna in the stables, this sensation coursed through her and acted with a will of its own. She felt her eyes begin to tear up at the sight of the Royal Guardsman with his bloody sword pressed to Brianna's throat. He had been hiding behind one of the support posts and had swung round it to run Brianna's horse through.

She feared for Brianna's life more intensely than she did for Zandorth's life, or even her own. She must not be harmed whatever the cost. She would sacrifice herself, Zandorth, even Devenshire, to keep her safe. She knew this as if it were a conviction she had held all along, but she could not shake the feeling that her actions were being dictated from another source.

"Call him again!" the guard growled.

"Zandorth! For the love of the Fates! Please come down now," Shantira called out without hesitation. She felt anger rising within her at the Warrior for not showing himself immediately. Surely, he would not gamble with Brianna's life in such a manner. She looked at Brianna and could see her eyes were barely open, and her breathing labored. She desperately wanted to go to her, to see if there were anything she could do to ease her pain, but she feared the slightest wrong move would cause the guard to send his sword through her throat.

The guard watched her intently, but she could see the tenseness about him, knew that his senses were tuned tightly to not only her, but also everything around her. She had no doubt in his conviction of killing Brianna if she and Zandorth did not surrender immediately. Something else tried to intrude upon her thoughts. Something about this being a waste of valuable time, time that could be better used for escape, and a part of her mind recognized this as the train of thought she should be following, but her concern for Brianna overrode this and shut it out from her consideration. All that mattered was making sure she was safe and unharmed.

The seconds ticked by, and there was still no response from Zandorth. Tears began trickling down Shantira's face as each second brought certain death for Brianna. She noticed how her hands trembled, and her mind was seized by the cold grip of fear. As even more of the deadly seconds passed, she felt herself growing sick at her stomach from the fear, feeling her knees begin to tremble and go weak. What was wrong with her? She knew she should be concerned for Brianna, but not to this extent. Not to the point of losing the ability to function.

"I swear to you! If the Warrior does not show himself now, I will kill her!" the guard said in a harsh snap of his voice, and the words sent Shantira to her knees, the tears flooding down her face.

"Please! I beg of you. Do not harm her. I will do anything you ask, just please do not harm her," Shantira replied with a definite tremble in her voice.

"Then you had better pray that the Warrior surrenders," the guard replied.

"What manner of man are you? That you would hide behind a half-dazed woman rather than fight for your honor," came Zandorth's gruff voice from the top of the ramp. Shantira spun around on her knees to glare at the warrior who still sat upon his mount. She could feel the anger burning within her, nearing hatred at the warrior for daring to jeopardize Brianna's life to save his own skin. She saw the odd expression in his eyes as he saw the fires of her anger reflected in her eyes.

"I need not, nor am I, hiding behind anyone. I am simply using every means at my disposal to arrest three criminals," the guard replied. "Surrender now or watch this one die!"

"NO!!" Shantira screamed and struggled to her unsteady feet. "Damn you, Zandorth. Surrender you, bastard!"

"He will not harm her. The men of the Royal Guard are bound by their ethics and own conscience not to follow such a path," Zandorth replied easily.

"Surrender, or I will kill you myself!" Shantira screamed back. "How dare you risk her life in such a manner!"

"Calm yourself, child! She will not be harmed," Zandorth replied tersely before turning his hard gaze to the guard. "Remove your sword from her throat, and step back."

"I am not bluffing. If you do not surrender, I will kill her," the guard replied.

"If you do, I swear by the Lords of Kuvol that the death that awaits you will be more hideous than you can comprehend," Zandorth replied.

Shantira felt her control slipping further and further from her grasp. She tried to maintain her composure, to find the reassurance that Zandorth knew of what he spoke. But the strange sensation concerning Brianna drove a wedge between her mind and the course of action she knew she should be following. Almost without her knowing it, she quickly drew the dagger from her boot, flipped it over to grip it by the point, and brought it back into a throwing position, aimed at Zandorth.

"Damn you!! If you do not drop your sword and come down here this instant I will bury this dagger in your skull!" she hissed.

"Take care, child! You play a dangerous game," Zandorth replied coldly.

"The game you play is far more dangerous! Brianna's life is not to be bartered with. Surrender!" Shantira replied.

Zandorth regarded the dagger in her hand, and then the guard with his bloodied sword pressed to Brianna's throat.

While he knew the guard would never kill in cold blood, even to secure the arrest of criminals, the strange cold glare that burned through the tears in Shantira's eyes was a different matter. If the woman were playing some sort of ruse to lull the guard into inattention, then she was playing her part to the hilt, for he felt a strange chill pass over him at the conviction he saw in her eyes. Slowly, he drew his broadsword and tossed it where it would land behind the guard. Then, with measured movements, he slowly swung his frame down from his mount.

Shantira turned and tossed her dagger away. "He has surrendered. Now please, let me see to her."

The guard's attention shifted back and forth between Shantira and Zandorth. He seemed to relax slightly after the warrior had surrendered his sword and dismounted.

"Very well. But be warned, at the slightest sign of treachery I will run her through," the guard replied as he eased the point of his sword back from Brianna's throat. Suddenly, Brianna's booted foot rose straight up and caught the guard in the groin. With a startled yelp, he staggered backwards, his sword dropping from his hand as it joined his other hand in cupping himself.

With a shrill scream, Shantira launched herself into the air and took the guard to his back with her coming to rest atop of him, straddling his waist. Before the guard could even think to react, she had his throat in both of her hands and her face twisted in the mask of unfettered fury.

"I will kill you, you bastard!" she hissed as she began squeezing with all of her strength. Her mind burned with anger and hatred, her vision became tinted with red, and all other considerations were lost to her save for the strangulation of the guard who had dared to even consider harming Brianna. The guard struggled to free himself from her grip, but she held tight. An odd gurgling gasp broke free of his lips, and his face began turning red as Shantira applied even more pressure to his throat.

Brianna struggled to her knees, as she was finally able to draw air into her lungs. Her head still swam, but her perceptions had returned. She had heard Shantira's words and found herself shocked beyond compare at the sudden change in the woman's behavior. It was completely unlike Shantira to lose such control of herself, even in the face of a friend in danger. She raised her head to see Shantira astride the guard, attempting to strangle him.

"Shantira! Stop it!" she called out as she shook her head, trying to clear it. But Shantira ignored her and continued to choke the guard with a fury in her face that startled her. She struggled to her feet and crossed the short distance between them to grab Shantira by the shoulder. "Damnit! Stop it!" she yelled, but again Shantira gave no indication that she had heard her words.

She turned her head to see Zandorth dashing down the ramp. "Zan! She is going to kill him!"

Zandorth pushed Brianna aside, took Shantira by the shoulders, and attempted to pick her up. As Shantira rose into the air in his grip, he was shocked to see the guard rise with her, her hands still locked tightly about his throat. The guard's struggles were becoming weaker, and his face was taking on a bluish tint. Only a few moments remained before the guard would die.

"Release him!" Zandorth bellowed, and as with Brianna, Shantira seemed to be oblivious to everything but her task of killing the guard.

"I do not wish to harm you, child. Release him now!" he barked. There was no time for this. At any moment, more guards could come crashing through either set of doors. Their opportunity at escape was fading fast.

Zandorth suddenly released Shantira. She and the guard crashed back to the floor with Shantira giving no sign that anything had ever happened. Zandorth suddenly backhanded Shantira hard across the face, and the woman's head snapped around hard. She hissed in defiance, as she shook her head once to clear it, and then resumed throttling the guard.

Zandorth slapped her again. Her eyes glazed over as the second slap had shaken her. Her grip on the guard's neck loosened, but was still tight enough to choke him.

With a snarl, he backhanded her a third time with more strength. Her grip on the guard's throat gave way, and she tumbled over backwards to lie in a dazed moaning heap across the guard's legs.

"We have no time for this foolishness. We must leave now!" he barked as he retrieved his sword and re-sheathed it. He quickly retrieved his horse and led it down the ramp while Brianna gathered Shantira's mount. He regarded Brianna who was staring down at Shantira as if she had never seen the woman before.

"Where is your mount?" he asked.

"I do not know. It threw me and ran off," she replied absently.

"Take Shantira's mount. Perhaps we will find yours as we go. We must not waste any more time. Move now!" Zandorth barked as he stooped down to pick Shantira's half-unconscious form up and tuck it underneath one arm. With one powerful movement, he was once again astride his horse with Shantira draped across the saddle in front of him.

Brianna shook herself from her shock and moved as quickly as her still stunned limbs would comply. She took up the reins of Shantira's horse and quickly mounted. There would be time later to sort through the mystery of her bizarre behavior.

Zandorth paused only a moment to consider which set of doors to depart from the warehouse through and decided on the ones they had used to enter. With a sharp yell, he forced his mount into a full gallop toward the door with Brianna close behind.

They bolted through the doors of the warehouse and leapt down to the street before pulling up to consider which direction to go. Zandorth spun his horse around in circles as his eyes took in the street. People were dashing back and forth in the confusion of their entrance to and sudden departure from the warehouse. There were only three guards in sight, and they were either stunned or unconscious from their failed attempts to make the jump from the street to the walkway.

"This way!" Zandorth finally barked as he turned his mount toward the direction they had come and buried his heels into the horse's flanks. The horse grunted slightly and seemed to instantly go into a full gallop down the street. Brianna followed his lead, trying to get used to the strangeness of Shantira's horse after having ridden her own for so long.

Two blocks later, they discovered Brianna's horse lying in the middle of the street. The animal nickered weakly as they approached, and it did not take but a moment to learn what was wrong with the animal. A gaping hole had been cut neatly into its side, just behind the shoulder. Blood poured from the wound and pooled in the dirt of the street. Brianna regarded her horse, and felt sadness and anger form within her. She had been very fond of the animal, and its loss would be terrible. For a split second, she wished Shantira had been successful in her attempts to strangle the guard.

"The animal will not live much longer," Zandorth said as he

studied the wound from atop his horse. "There is nothing we can do for it now."

"My supplies. I must retrieve them," Brianna said as she started to dismount.

"Hurry!" We have not much time!" Zandorth barked as he continued to scan their surroundings.

Brianna climbed down and quickly retrieved her saddlebags, a task made difficult by the animal laying on its side. After what seemed as an eternity, she was able to wrestle the bags free. She quickly slung them over Shantira's saddle and quickly mounted.

Zandorth nudged his mount onward.

With a small tear pooling in the corner of her eye, she smiled sadly down at the horse as it struggled weakly to rise, but no longer had the strength to do so.

"Farewell, my old friend. I will miss you. Thank you for the many pleasurable rides through the country," she whispered.

Although she knew the animal could not understand her words, the horse whinnied weakly to her, and finally laid its head down in the dirt of the street and stopped struggling. Its breathing was labored but it was already slowing as its life pulsed from the gaping hole with each beat of its slowing heart.

Brianna forced down the wave of grief and urged Shantira's mount onward. She did not wish to witness the horse's death.

CHAPTER THIRTY-THREE

THEY MADE THEIR WAY through the city, using side streets and alleys as often as possible and made respectable distance. As they moved from the center of the city, the street torches became less and the shadows more. Brianna actually entertained the thought that they would actually get out of the city after all.

Now that she was not jumping from one rooftop to another, sword fighting members of the Royal Guard, or riding for her life through crowded warehouses, she could think, and she found her thoughts jumbling under the numerous trains of thought that sought dominance within her mind.

Where was Devenshire? Why had he not appeared? Who was behind this ridiculous crusade to prove Daimion was a vampire? Why were they trying to prove Daimion was a vampire? What was behind this sudden and bizarre shift in Shantira's behavior? Why was Darkseed so set against helping them beyond their escape from the city jail?

Too many questions and not enough answers.

As their horses crept through the city, evading small patrols of either sheriffs or Guardsmen, Brianna struggled to make sense from her swirling thoughts.

Finally, Zandorth drew up and eased his mount to a standstill. As she stopped beside him, she noticed how hard the animals were breathing, noticed the lather that had formed on their coats. She also noticed her own labored breathing and the throb of her skull, which had met the ramp with respectable force.

"Our mounts are winded. We should let them rest," she said.

"No time. We must get out of the city as quickly as possible," Zandorth replied absently as his eyes scanned the area around them. They had made their way from the more commercial section of Lirpa and into a quieter, more subdued residential section. Very few businesses were located here with dwellings having slowly taken dominance as they had ridden. Most of the windows of the dwellings were dark, their inhabitants sleeping soundly in the safety of their walls. The tree-lined streets were nearly deserted and she found herself thankful to be away from the din and stench of the heart of the city.

"Which way now?" she asked.

"A moment. I have never been in this part of the city before," he replied.

"Perhaps we have evaded the guards," she offered as she joined him in scanning the street around them. Likewise, she had never been in this part of the city before.

"Perhaps, but I will not put a great amount of faith into that. If it were only the city sheriffs in pursuit of us, I would agree. The Royal Guard is nothing if not efficient. They will search the entire city until we are either captured, or they are convinced we have made good our escape," he replied.

Shantira moaned softly from her place in front of Zandorth. She moved her head slowly from side to side, tried to raise it, and then slumped back into unconsciousness.

"What came over her back there?" Brianna asked.

"I do not know, but you can rest assured that I will find out at the earliest possible moment," Zandorth replied tightly.

Suddenly, Brianna jerked her head up and raised her hand for Zandorth to be silent.

"What is it?" he asked.

For several moments she did not answer, but only lowered her head slightly as she seemed to concentrate on something. "Horses. Several of them. Approaching from behind," she whispered as she turned her head in that direction.

Zandorth turned as well and assumed the same listening posture. "Yes. I hear them. They are walking slowly," he whispered.

"Guards?" she asked.

"Most likely," he answered as he raised his head and regarded their choice of paths. They were very limited. "They will have an open field of vision from here."

Brianna scanned the street they were on which extended in an almost straight line as far as the dim lighting would show. Another street branched off to their left and continued in the same straight line as far as they could see.

"If we gallop away they will hear us. If we walk away they will see us," she commented dryly as the realization of their limited options came to her as well.

"We have been heading north. They may be expecting us to

continue along that path. If we were to change our direction, then perhaps they would be led astray long enough for us to escape by another direction," Zandorth said, thinking aloud more than actually saying anything to her.

"But that would involve going back through the heart of the city," she said with a dry twist of humor in her voice. "If it is all the same to you, I would rather prefer NOT to go through that again."

"We could attempt to run, but the Royal Guards' mounts are much fresher than ours. I do not know if we could outrun them."

"So we have returned to the starting point of this decision. Walk or run, and the risk of being seen is the same," she completed.

Zandorth simply nodded.

Brianna looked behind her and guessed that the riders would round the corner very soon. She looked down the street they were on which headed northeast, then regarded the street that ran directly north. With a sudden glint flashing in her green eyes, she smiled at Zandorth. "The shortest distance between two points is a straight line."

Zandorth watched her for a moment then allowed a rare smile to cross his lips as he pressed down on Shantira's body with one hand and held tight to the reins with the other. "Why would you walk when you can run and arrive at your destination sooner?"

Almost in unison, they dug their heels into their horse's flanks and yelled out to spur them into a headlong gallop down the street heading north. A short time later, Brianna chanced a glance over her shoulder and saw numerous white stallions pounding after them. The silver glow of the full moon was a mixed blessing. It gave them the light they needed to navigate by and see their opponents, but it also gave the same advantage to those who pursued them.

"We have company," she shouted over the thunder of pounding hooves and strained breathing of their mounts.

Zandorth gave one short nod in acknowledgment, and then let his head turn slightly from side to side as he scanned either side of the street. Brianna saw the look in his eyes and felt her stomach tighten as she recognized the look... it was the same one he had held when he led them on their frantic flight through the warehouse.

"Oh, no...." she moaned.

"Stay close, and be alert!" Zandorth shouted as he suddenly wheeled his mount sharply to the left away from her. With a sudden dread and a sigh, she jerked her reins hard to the right and peeled away from the street to follow.

What followed was a speed-blurred frenzy of jumping hedges, dodging trees that suddenly appeared out of the shadows of the night, hard sudden stops to avoid a house, or break neck changes of directions that threatened to toss them from their saddles if their attention wavered for just an instant.

Sounds reached her that enticed her to turn and look for they resembled the sounds of falling riders or horses screaming out in protest before they decided to abandon whatever suicidal maneuver their riders had attempted to command them to do. She knew that to look back would mean a similar fate for her in her lapse of attention to the path Zandorth was picking out with the discerning choice that resembled random chance and downright desperation.

"Duck low!" Zandorth yelled back as he suddenly leaned down over his horse's neck.

Brianna did not even question why, but instantly bent over in the saddle just as the line of twine that someone had strung between two trees to dry clothes upon sang over her back. As she straightened back up in the saddle, a twisted smile crossed her lips as she silently counted down the distance they crossed. Very faintly, but with enough clarity to make her chuckle, she heard the definite twang of the twine snapping, a strangled curse of surprise and the thud and roll of a body suddenly being dislodged from the saddle.

Without warning, they burst from the obstacle-laden path onto the street they had just left. With a frown, she saw that for all of the running, jumping and dodging they had endured, they emerged not very far from the point they had departed.

She did not have long to contemplate their minimal gains as Zandorth angled up the street toward the opposite side. To Brianna's near terror, she realized they were heading for a section of forest that intruded upon the city.

"Be alert!" he called back.

"You know, the jail really was not that bad after all," she called out wryly and was not surprised when the Warrior did not reply, but only seemed to draw more speed from his tiring mount.

They tore into the woods, hunched low in the saddle, and braced for the coming assault. Branches slapped them, briars tore at their clothes, and then their flesh, tangled in their hair and seemed to have a life of their own with no other purpose than to either rip them to shreds or tear them from their saddles, and hold them for the guards. Occasionally, their mounts would stumble as they stepped into a hole or misjudged a rise in the ground that the near blackness of the forest hid from their view.

Brianna shored up her resolve and tried to block out the pain and punishment she was forced to endure. Early on in their tearing path into the woods, she all but gave up steering the horse beneath her, allowing the animal to follow Zandorth or to pick its own path. She reasoned that the animal could do a much better job of it than she had been since her last attempts at guiding the animal had resulted in various slaps about her face and body by tree limbs.

"Prepare to jump!" Zandorth yelled, and she felt her eyes grow wide in disbelief.

Suddenly, Zandorth's mount gathered itself and leapt into the air. Brianna followed and felt her own mount tense, and then leap. The already darkened ground fell away sharply to show an empty blackness yawing out below her. It seemed to be reaching out for her, yearning to draw her into its never-ending blackness. Sweat poured down her face and into the multiple scratches and cuts, and stinging them sharply. She did not know why this sensation would come to her while she was airborne over only the Fates knew what.

After what seemed like hours, the sensation of descent came, and she found herself straining her eyes to see what they would be landing on, but only darkness loomed ahead. She felt panic swell within her as the possibility dawned on her that Zandorth had finally made the critical mistake by trying to jump something that was too wide. Just as she was about to squeeze her eyes tightly shut she caught the shadowy glimpse of some sort of brush.

The horse stumbled a handful of steps from the momentum of the landing then gracefully recovered its balance and resumed its headlong race into the unknown. With a slight nod, she admired the quality of the horse.

Not long after, the duo broke into a large clearing, and took the opportunity to pull up rein, and allow them and their mounts to catch their breath.

"Perhaps that should be enough to dissuade them from following us directly," Zandorth panted as he wiped at various tickles of blood as they mixed with his sweat and seethed down his features.

Brianna gasped for breath as she did the same with the hot stinging fluid on her own face.

"Did I say that I had rather not go back through the heart of the city? Perhaps I spoke out of turn," she said breathlessly. "The journey through the heart of the city was not so bad, after all."

Zandorth did not reply. His eyes studied the woods they had just emerged from, and she could tell that he was straining his hearing for any signs that they had been followed. She tried to do likewise, but all she could hear was hers, Zandorth's and their horses labored breathing. Even the sounds of the night were overwhelmed and canceled out by their heavy breathing.

After a while, Zandorth seemed to relax and actually allowed his normally rigid posture to sag slightly.

"It would appear that we have eluded them for the moment," he said.

"I hope so," she replied, as she was finally able to bring her breathing back down to a somewhat normal level.

"We will rest here for a short while before continuing on,"

Zandorth said as he slowly lowered himself from the saddle then took Shantira's limp form down and dropped it roughly on the ground.

Brianna dismounted and took a moment to squat low several times to work the cramps out of her legs. When the worst of the cramps eased, she began a slow walk about the clearing. The horses, their heads hung low in near exhaustion, began nibbling on the soft grass of the clearing, content to just stand still for a while.

While she stretched her legs, she regarded Zandorth as he stood in the center of the clearing, looking about the darkened woods.

"The sun will be rising soon. We cannot remain here long," he said.

She only nodded as she crossed to Shantira and knelt beside her prone form. She had come to trust Zandorth's instincts in these matters, regardless of how punishing they may be on her body.

Shantira bore the same ravages of their dash through the woods. Her shirt was torn in several places, as were her breeches. Leaves, twigs, and bits of briar were tangled in the thick mass of her black hair and a large bruise marked her jaw line where Zandorth had struck her. She winced at the already purplish tint of the bruise and knew it would be a bruise worthy of its kind.

Then her mind returned to the mystery of her behavior in the warehouse. Why had she lost her composure that way? Why had she focused on her safety even above that of her own or Zandorth's? Why had she turned on Zandorth with such venom? None of these things were typical of Shantira, and they both puzzled and troubled her deeply.

As if sensing her thoughts, Shantira moaned softly and began rousing. Her eyes fluttered several times before slowly opening. At first, they were dazed and Brianna knew that Shantira did not know what she was looking at. Then slowly the glassy eyes turned to her and slowly cleared. She gave her a slight smile. "How do you feel?"

Shantira closed her eyes and moaned again before answering. "Like I have been kicked in the head by a mule."

"Almost," Brianna commented dryly.

"What happened?" Shantira asked.

"You do not remember?" Brianna asked.

"It is very vague. Shadowy images at best," she replied softly.

"Allow me to bring the images out of the shadows!" Zandorth growled from behind Brianna. "You nearly sacrificed us all."

Shantira raised herself up on one elbow slowly and tried to focus on not only Zandorth's form but his words as well. "What?"

"Brianna was thrown from her mount after a Royal Guard ran it through with his sword. She was dazed by the fall, and the Guard threatened to kill her if you did not surrender. You immediately discarded your sword and called for me to do the same. When I tried to tell you that the guard would not kill her in cold blood, you became incensed and threatened me with a dagger if I did not surrender!" Zandorth replied tightly and Brianna knew it was taking all of his self-control not to jerk Shantira up and shake the answers from her.

Shantira's face twisted into a confused expression as one hand sought out her temple. "I remember... Brianna fell from her mount... the guard pressed his sword to her throat and... and... and..." her voice trailed off as the memories refused to surface.

"She is still addled. Give her some time," Brianna said as she looked up at Zandorth.

"Time is one thing of which we do not have a great deal of," Zandorth snapped back before turning his gaze to Shantira. "Be warned. I will be watching you," he then turned and strode off.

Shantira watched him walk away, her face showing her fear and concern over what Zandorth had told her. "Did I really do that?" she asked in a hollow voice.

Brianna nodded slowly. "Yes. I am afraid that you did."

Shantira's eyes grew distant as she tried to remember. After a few moments, she looked up at Brianna, taking in her severely disheveled appearance. "Are you all right?"

She laughed and looked down at herself. "None the worse for wear."

Shantira seemed genuinely relieved that she was safe. "Where are we? How was I rendered unconscious?"

"We are in a clearing in a forest north of Lirpa," she answered her first question, hoping to avoid the second one.

"How did I lose consciousness?" Shantira repeated.

"You were trying to strangle a Guardsman. Zandorth had to knock you out," Brianna replied softly.

Shantira's confused and concerned expression deepened as she struggled to remember. Finally, she sighed in frustration. "I believe what you tell me, but I honestly do not remember the events. I cannot believe that I would behave in such a manner."

"We have all been through a great deal in a short period of time. We need time to rest and collect ourselves," she replied.

Shantira eased up into a seated position, her knees pulled up to her chest, her chin resting on her knees. Her eyes took in the clearing and noted the presence of only two horses. "Where is your horse?"

"The guard you tried to strangle, killed him," Brianna replied.

"Any sign of Daimion?" Shantira asked, still struggling to put the fragmented pieces of her memory back together.

"No," she answered tightly. She had managed to make it through their mad dash from the city without thinking about Devenshire, and of what had become of him.

Zandorth strode back up to them, and said as he surveyed the tree line that surrounded them, "We should go. The Guards will be here soon and with one of our mounts having to carry two, our speed will be greatly reduced."

Brianna nodded and turned to Shantira. "Do you feel well enough to ride?"

Shantira nodded slowly, avoiding eye contact with Zandorth. She felt deep shame at what they had told her of her behavior. The truth be known, she did not feel well enough to stand, let alone ride, but she did not wish to agitate Zandorth any more than she had already.

Within moments, they were mounted with Shantira giving up the reins of her horse to Brianna and settling to ride behind her. As they moved out of the clearing, she pondered what they had told her and memories began to return. Very soon, she could recall the events in the warehouse clearly and found herself stunned by the way she had acted. However, the strange overriding concern for Brianna and her safety was as strong as ever, and she found herself feeling justified in her actions.

They wound their way through the dense forest, thankful to be walking through instead of having to crash through it. Silence reined as they rode, save for the song of the night and the rustle of their path through the woods. Each individual pondered their own thoughts, the strength and desire for conversation lost in those thoughts. Their respite was to be short lived.

Zandorth suddenly pulled his mount to a stop and raised his hand for them to be still. Brianna realized that she had let her mind wander among her own thoughts and had not been paying attention for any sign of pursuit. Silently cursing her lapse in attention, she turned her own excellent hearing for what had captured Zandorth's attention.

Then she heard it—the occasional rustle of leaves or branches, the snap of a twig, the sigh of a brush being gently pushed aside. The sounds seem to come from all directions, and she knew that several men were trying to move with stealth through the woods. Either a detachment of Royal Guards were approaching, or a group of bandits. Either alternative offered no promise of peaceful passage.

"Do you think they are aware of us?" Brianna whispered so softly she wondered if Zandorth heard her.

"They know we are here, but they may not know where," he replied softly.

She nodded as she tried to pin point the Guard's location. Several were on either side of them with another group coming from the path in front of them. Their only clear path appeared to be back toward the clearing. Brianna pointed in the direction she had heard tell tale sounds, and Zandorth nodded that he, too, had learned of their positions.

Zandorth jerked his chin in the direction of the clearing, and began the near impossible task of guiding his mount silently through the woods in the direction they had just come. Brianna fell in behind him as she, too, tried to steer the mount in the path that would release the least sound.

As they rode, each rustle of leaves, each swish of a displaced tree limb tightening their already bunched nerves, Brianna realized she had almost stopped breathing. The tension mounted quickly to a point that she could feel it surround her, pressing in on her. She could almost smell it in the air, could almost taste it. The pressure rose quickly, and she found herself feeling nearly panicked by it. The strain was tremendous, and she feared that the next tiny sound would send her rocketing into the sky in a panic riddled attempt to flee from the tension.

Every breath was shallow, every muscle bunched, each nerve stretched to its breaking point, but still they rode, slowly and carefully. Each rustle of a branch touched by the wind, each sound of an insect made her jump in a start. The cool breeze of the night air seemed to drop several degrees, and she shuddered under what she knew was just a result of her heightened nervous state.

She felt her eyes growing wide, trying to take in as much as she could, felt her breathing fade even more as she strained to hear any sound that would tell her where their pursuers were, and if they had been detected. Each shadow of a tree tried to meld into the form of a guard, and she knew she would have to calm herself for her imagination would surely provide the phantom of a guard and cause her to betray their position.

After an eternity of the torturously tense ride, the clearing could be seen through the thinning woods. Once in the clearing, they could then take stock of their situation and decide then if they could afford another dash through the woods in the hopes of finding another route out of town and out of the closing grasp of the Guards and sheriffs.

"There! They are there!" came a shout that nearly made Brianna jump from the saddle. The shout after so much silence was nearly deafening.

"Damn!" Zandorth swore as he realized they had been either seen or heard by a man who had been closer and had managed to keep his location hidden from them. There was no choice now, they had been found.

Before the echo of the shout faded, Zandorth had kicked his horse into a run with Brianna close behind. The clearing was just ahead, and so was their one last chance to evade capture. Shouts rose from all around them as they crashed through the underbrush. Once the alarm had been sounded, the need for stealth had evaporated and crashing sounds of pursuit exploded from all directions.

Just as his horse broke into the clearing, Zandorth realized he had been tricked. The tactic had been so obvious he cursed himself for not recognizing it sooner. They had been herded back toward the clearing as surely as cattle. Their pursuers had known that they had made it to the clearing and allowed them the time to gather themselves while they set up their deception.

Ahead of them, in the center of the clearing were a mixed complement of Royal Guards and sheriffs. With a sickening pit growing in his stomach, he realized just how completely and predictably he had acted. The chase was over.

"Surrender!" one of the guards in the clearing shouted.

Zandorth watched as a small handful of men materialized from the shadows of the woods behind them. The men that emerged from the woods were surprisingly small in number, and Zandorth realized that only a few men would be needed to create the illusion of many sneaking through the woods. The trap was complete.

"I will not surrender," Zandorth replied evenly.

"Then you will die," the guard replied almost instantly, as if he had known what his reply would have been.

"So be it," Zandorth said, his voice having grown low and monotone. He drew his sword and readied himself. "I may fall this night, but many of you will accompany me into the afterlife. The only decision left to make is which one of you will be the first to die."

"Your resistance only strengthens the appearance of your guilt," the guard said carefully.

"I have learned that you and your men are not inclined to listen to any words I have to say to the contrary of what you have already made up in your minds," Zandorth replied.

"It is not up to us to believe or disbelieve you. Our duty is to arrest you. You will be given the chance to claim your innocence before a tribunal of the courts," the guard said.

"Do not attempt to insult my intelligence!" Zandorth snapped. "The crime of which we are accused is a most severe one. By the time we stand before a tribunal, the minds of all will have already convicted us."

"I have no wish to kill you or the women. However, if you do not surrender, then you will have left me with no alternative," the guard said, and Zandorth found himself believing the man. The regret was plain in his words as well as his eyes.

"Nor do I wish to kill you or any man who is acting out of what his conscience believes is the right thing to do. But I will not surrender for a crime of which I am not guilty," Zandorth replied, letting the truth of his own words travel through his voice and eyes to the guard. Then he leapt clear of his mount and landed in a fighting stance, his eyes alert, and his senses ready.

The guard regarded Brianna and Shantira. "You ladies have the opportunity to surrender. I guarantee you that you will not be harmed in any way. You have my word that you will be escorted back to the jail, and treated with respect. You need not follow the Warrior into certain death."

Brianna studied the guard for a handful of moments before looking at Zandorth. She nodded slowly as she climbed down from the horse and moved up beside the Warrior, and drew her sword. "I am not what I have been accused of. I agree with the Warrior's assessment of what our chances are of a fair hearing before any tribunal. If I die fighting here or die under the headsman's blade, death seems to be inevitable."

Brianna heard the soft rustle of footsteps behind her and knew Shantira had dismounted and was moving toward them. When the young woman stopped beside her, she felt a small amount of pride swell within her. "I go with them," she said calmly. "Be it to freedom or to the afterlife... I go with them."

The guard seemed genuinely saddened by their decision. Then he noticed that Shantira held no sword in her hand, and his eyes found the empty scabbard at her hip. "You are unarmed. Surely, you see that you will be the first to die."

"Perhaps," Shantira replied evenly.

"Nay," Zandorth injected as he pulled Shantira's sword from his belt and passed it to her.

Shantira took the sword and felt tremendous relief wash over her. She had feared her father's sword had been lost to her.

The guard watched them, and as he watched them, his face showed his anger building at the waste before him. It was clear that he found their approaching deaths a waste, and the waste angered him. "Take them!" he shouted.

Men began closing in on them from all sides. The three of them turned and pressed their backs to one another's, forming a tight circle that allowed all three of them a view of the approaching men while protecting their backs.

They held their swords at the ready, waiting for the best moment to strike. The circle of guards and sheriffs closed in slowly. Apparently, Zandorth's question of who would be the first man to lead the journey into the afterlife had had its desired effects for none rushed in.

"It has been an honor," Zandorth muttered over his shoulder and with that statement, Brianna and Shantira realized that there was little to no chance that all three of them would survive the battle with so many opponents.

A thousand different sentiments flooded Brianna's mind. So many things she wished to tell Zandorth and Shantira, things she felt she should have already told them. Now was not the time for such things.

Her end was near, and she was determined to face it with the same fervor with which she had lived her life.

"See you in the afterlife," she whispered as she wrestled with her fear. She acknowledged her fear, acknowledged the regret at all the things she felt were left undone in her life. As she acknowledged all of these things, she set them aside and forced herself to focus, to concentrate. To her amazement, a strange calm descended upon her, and she found herself ready... for whatever was to come.

"Perhaps you will allow the guest of honor of this little party to join."

All eyes snapped around at the sound of a new voice in the clearing.

"Daimion!" Brianna shouted in surprise.

"Devenshire!" Zandorth shouted a second later.

Devenshire strolled easily into the clearing and smiled at his friends. "I apologize for being late. I had a rather nasty encounter with a tenacious little demon."

Brianna noticed how the right sleeve of his shirt was stained with blood and wondered how badly he had been hurt and what condition he was in now.

"Devenshire! Hold your place. You are under arrest," the guard shouted.

Devenshire arched one eyebrow as he stopped walking. "Indeed. May I ask the charge?"

"We have it on good authority that you are a vampire," the guard replied.

Devenshire studied the guard for a moment before he smiled. "Are you serious?"

He then saw the fear in the man's eyes, and in the eyes of the others. It was the kind of fear that spoke of the absolute truth he felt at his statement.

"Deadly," the guard replied with an attempt to add some bravado to his voice and failing horribly.

"You have never faced a vampire before, have you?" Devenshire asked.

"That is irrelevant," the guard replied.

"Oh, but it is. You see, if you had ever faced a vampire before, you all would be fleeing for your lives at this moment. If I were truly a vampire, I would not be standing here bantering words with you. I would be killing each one of you and feeding to my heart's content."

"You waste your breath, Devenshire. They will not listen," Zandorth grumbled.

"We have the word of a Hunter," the guard offered as though it were the final bit of evidence required to convict them and make their crime real.

"Who is this Hunter?" Devenshire asked.

"Master Lordalise," the guard replied, and said the name with such a reverence in his tone that he may as well have been speaking of a priest.

"Lordalise?" Devenshire asked with puzzlement. The name rang a bell in his memory, but it was a faint bell, and he could not immediately pull up where he had heard that name before.

"Enough talk. Do you intend to surrender or not?" the guard asked.

It took Devenshire a moment to pull his attention back to the present. His mind had been delving deep into his memories for where he had heard that name before and could not conjure up the source. "I will surrender if you allow my companions to go free," he finally answered.

"No!" Brianna shouted. "You cannot do that."

"No conditions, Devenshire!" Zandorth growled.

Devenshire ignored them as he locked eyes with the guard. "Consider it. I will lay down my sword and come with you peacefully if you allow them to leave this clearing unmolested. If you refuse, you may capture me anyway, but I can promise you it will not be until after many of your men have been killed. You can avoid senseless bloodshed with your decision."

The guard seemed to consider this. Devenshire watched the guard's eyes and could see his mind turning over the prospect of bringing him in without having lost a single man. Devenshire also watched as the guard tallied up the possible losses in a forced attempt to arrest him.

"I will not leave without you," Brianna said sternly.

"That is not your choice to make," Devenshire replied just as sternly, but never taking his eyes from those of the guard.

"Do I have your word that you will surrender if I allow them to leave?" the guard asked, and Devenshire had to call up all his will not to laugh. It was sadly obvious that the guard had no idea what type of creature a vampire was. It was useless to ask for the word of a vampire since the word of a vampire, on more occasions than not, was meaningless. But Devenshire saw an opportunity to put the guard's ignorance to good use.

"You have my word. I will not resist, I will not attempt escape, and I will not harm anyone. I will go willingly and face the tribunal for the crimes of which I am accused," he replied.

"A noble gesture, but meaningless."

Devenshire turned at the sound of a new voice to see another Royal Guard guide his white stallion from the woods into the clearing. Eight more guardsmen emerged from the depths of the forest behind him. Devenshire bit back a broad grin.

"Captain Gregory Armand," he said simply. He remembered several occasions when he and Darkseed were forced to match wits with the captain and while they won every encounter, each one had been a near thing. In a grudging way, Devenshire admired the captain as a worthy opponent.

The first thing that struck Devenshire was Armand's eyes. They burned into him with a hatred that he had not seen in a long while. This man truly hated him, and there would be no convincing him of his innocence.

"Captain Armand," the guard who had been on the verge of accepting Devenshire's proposal said.

The captain turned his burning gaze from Devenshire to the guard. "You were about to make a deal with this demon?" The acid that dripped from the captains words spoke of the intense anger the man was wrestling to keep under some sort of control.

"No, sir. I was merely confirming what he was offering," the guard replied nervously.

"Do not compound your crime with lies. Return to the garrison immediately and remain there. I will deal with you when I return!" Armand growled. His eyes gave no quarter for the guard, and any thoughts the man had held about arguing his innocence wilted away under the blaze in the captain's eyes.

"Yes, sir," the guard replied in small tones. With lowered eyes, he turned his mount and walked away into the woods.

Armand turned his fiery glance back to Devenshire. "I will accept nothing but your immediate surrender. You and your companions." The finality of Armand's words gave Devenshire no hope for resolving this without combat.

Devenshire studied Armand for several moments and did not like what he saw. The captain was set in is resolution to take him and his companions to jail, or kill them in the attempt. With a heavy sigh and slow shake of his head, he reached across his body and pulled his sword free. "If that is the way it must be," he said calmly.

"Take them!!" Armand shouted.

The men surrounding Zandorth, Brianna and Shantira instantly moved in. The three reacted with surprising speed and steel clashed upon steel. They had been anticipating this battle, and they had not been caught off guard by the rushing attack.

"Try not to kill!!" Devenshire shouted as he dropped back to face the oncoming attack of two sheriffs. He met their attack and parried it aside easily. Pulling his attention in on himself, Devenshire focused on the attack, feeling that part of him that reveled in the spirit of the fight rise up. As he remained on the defensive, simply blocking their attacks, he could feel the smile form on his lips.

Zandorth growled as two guardsmen closed in on him. They both thrust their swords forward viciously, hoping to impale the massive warrior quickly. Zandorth swung his sword around as he stepped to one side. The broad blades of his weapon caught the two blades of the guards and sent them into the ground with enough force to dislodge them from their grip. The guards looked at their empty hands then up at Zandorth. With a savage smile, he stepped forward and thrust his forearm, catching both men in the face. With a cracking of bone and cartilage, the men stumbled backwards, lost their footing, and tumbled to the ground. Before they ever hit the ground, Zandorth had already shifted his attention to another attack.

Brianna ducked beneath a sloppily executed swing of one of her opponents. As she dropped to one knee, she kicked out to her right catching another man's kneecap and thrusting it back with a savage snap. The man howled in agony and staggered back, his sword abandoned in favor of clamping both hands to his shattered knee as he toppled to the ground.

She had used the momentum of the kick to disable the man. She pushed her body to the left into a roll that brought her back up to her knees where she thrust her sword out and sliced another man deep across his inner thigh. As she propelled her sword out, she drew one of her daggers and swung it around behind her, opening a large slash across the back of the leg of another man. Without pausing to assess the damage, she had done, she quickly rolled to her left again and came to her feet, crouched low and ready for the next attack.

Shantira parried an attack from a sheriff and moved in a tight circle to gain an advantage. With another quick flurry of thrusts, they locked hilts. As Shantira held the lock, she began to turn to keep her back from becoming a viable target for anyone else. She felt the strange desire to protect Brianna trying to impose itself on her attention, and she fought to keep it at bay. If she let her attention stray from her own problems of the moment, then she was sure to be the first of their party to fall, and after her unbelievable behavior in the warehouse, she sorely wished to prove herself still a valuable member of this small party.

She knew she could not afford to remain tied up with one guard for very long, and quickly sought a way to disentangle herself from his lock. She acted upon the first thought that entered her mind, stepped closer to the man, and brought her knee up quickly. Her knee found the soft tissue of his groin, and she almost smiled as his eyes flew open wide. It was the momentary pause between impact, and the first wave of nauseating pain that would quickly race through him. She pushed off from the man as he began to double over, his knees coming together, and he began sinking to them. Just as his knees touched the ground, she balanced herself and kicked out with her right foot. The side of her boot smashed the man across the face, spinning him around and slamming him to the ground, face down and out of the fight.

Devenshire managed to dispatch the two sheriffs without injuring them severely. One man would have to nurse a shattered nose while the other would have to mend a nasty gash across his hip. As the last man fell, something in his instincts forced him to turn to meet the attack of two guardsmen. He parried their dual attack and quickly stepped back to give himself time and room to prepare for their next attack.

These two were more skilled and experienced in swordplay than the two sheriffs, and Devenshire found out quickly that he would have to be very careful with the duo. As his sword danced with theirs, a part of his mind studied them. They had obviously been partners for a long time. Each attack was fluid, graceful, and had the appearance of having been very well coordinated in advance. It was as if each man knew what the other was thinking and could predict what maneuver to execute to compliment, instead of detract from, the others attack. Devenshire found himself hoping that he would not have to kill either one of these men.

He did not wish to kill any of the guardsmen or the sheriffs for they were only acting as they felt they must. He did not feel that they should die for simply doing their duty. But duty or not, he could not allow himself, or the others, to be arrested. The burning hatred within Captain Armand spoke volumes to Devenshire, and he did not like what he read. With the appearance of Armand, the guarantees that he or the others would receive fair treatment, much less survive to face a tribunal were dwindling quickly.

The guard on his right suddenly shouted and brought his sword over his shoulder and swung it toward Devenshire with a slashing top to bottom slice. At the same time, the other guard brought his sword around in a horizontal swing. Devenshire let his instincts take over, knowing that he did not have the time to formulate a defense to such an attack. With barely a thought of performing the action, he suddenly leapt into a backwards somersault. The guardsmen's swords smashed together in the empty air he had occupied just a second before.

With his breath pounding in his chest and a thin sheen of sweat coating his face, Devenshire rose to his full height and saluted the guards by raising his sword until the guard of the hilt was in front of his face. Such a coordinated, lethal attack deserved some acknowledgment of skill. As the guards watched him, he jerked his sword down and to his side in completion of the salute. They almost smiled at him as they, too, saluted his agility and skill in evading the attack. With a slight smile, he launched himself at the guards and unleashed a flurry of quick slashing attacks that forced the guards to back pedal as they parried his attack. While they were on the defensive and backing up he knew now was his opportunity to disarm them and put them out of the fight hopefully without injuring them severely.

Stepping in with a furious back and forth slashing motion, he waited until the guard's swords were thrust in opposite directions from each other, and then locked his hilt with the hilt of the guard on his right, holding his blade at bay. While the momentum and element of surprise was on his side, Devenshire coiled his left leg up and to him, then kicked out with all his strength. The sole and heel of his boot snaked out and caught the other guardsmen square in the stomach. The guard flew backwards to the ground. The guard rose to his knees, both hands clutching his stomach. He tried to rise, but suddenly retched and collapsed to his hands and knees.

Devenshire followed the momentum of his kick, planted his left foot, and spun around away from the guard who stumbled slightly forward from the sudden absence of the force that had been pushing back upon him. Before he could regain his balance, Devenshire drove the butt of the hilt of his sword into the small of the guards back. As the guard grunted and arched his back from the blow, Devenshire suddenly spun back in the other direction while tossing his sword to his left hand. As he completed the spin, he launched his right fist to rocket into the guard's stomach. The guard grunted again as he doubled over under the punch as Devenshire grabbed a handful of the guard's hair, pulled his head up, and then drove it down as he brought his right knee up. Nose and knee collided in a wet crack of cartilage, and the guard fell to his back and did not move again.

Brianna found herself in a particularly challenging duel with one of the guardsmen. The man was one of the few she had ever encountered that treated her skill with a sword as just that: skill. The fact that she was a woman seemed lost on his perceptions as he fought her with the caution and regard that he would have fought a man.

In just the short time, she had been fighting the man she had barely escaped injury from with cleverly executed attacks. This man was patient, he was willing to let her counter his attacks and allow her to throw her best at him before countering it, and thereby gaining a very good feel of her style, which only added to the danger he posed for her. A patient opponent was a dangerous one.

Calling on all her training... all the other battles that she had ever fought... Brianna searched for a way to gain some sort of an advantage on this man, but each attack was met and countered with what appeared to be effortless ease and each counter attack was minimized. She seemed to be locked into the defensive with little or no hope of gaining the offensive.

Suddenly, the guard launched a thrust that Brianna sidestepped, and as she did, she felt her gut grow cold as she realized she had made a critical mistake.

The thrust was only half completed before it mutated into another slash that opened a gash on her left arm. With a sharp gasp of pain, she staggered back and almost abandoned her sword to let her right hand tend to her wound. It was only through sheer force of will that she maintained her grip on her sword and let her backwards stagger to carry her into a defensive posture.

White-hot pain lanced through her left arm and shoulder and the warm stickiness of her blood coursed down her arm. The pain screamed at her, tore at her attention, demanding that she abandon the fight to tend to her wound. Fear joined in trying to tear her focus from the fight. How bad was the cut? How much blood was she losing? How long could she continue? Then the one fearful question came, was she good enough to best this man?

Blinking back her shock at being wounded, Brianna regarded the man. For the first time since she took up the sword and began to learn how to use it, she felt doubt enter her mind. Not the casual self-assessment of her skills versus those of an opponent, but genuine doubt in her abilities, and that doubt fanned the fires of her fear. With shock born not of her wound, she felt herself begin to tremble in the vibrating grip of fear.

"Surrender. I have no wish to harm you further or to kill you," the guard said calmly. She saw in his eyes the near arrogant confidence in his abilities that had matched hers only a moment ago. She knew he saw the fear and doubt in her eyes, watched his body undergo the subtle changes that confidence in victory brought, and recognized them for the same subtle changes she had felt her own posture undergo when she had bested an opponent. It was a chilling sight, and she felt her resolve fading.

Another guard stepped up to her left and held his sword at the ready, watching the first man for any signal to join the attack. Brianna watched each man in turn and searched frantically for that part of her that seemed to have suddenly vanished. She felt fear, genuine cold fear turn her blood to ice, her nerves to twine, her mind to sludge. Why could she not come up with some appropriate verbal retort as she had always done in the past? Where was that firm blanket of sureness that she always wrapped herself in? She felt her heart thump hard in her chest, felt the sweat chill her already cold flesh, and felt her breath draw up into short gasps as her strength faded.

"No!" she tried to shout, but the words came out as a shallow whisper as she shook her head quickly. Her eyes had grown wide, and they dashed from one opponent to another as those of a wild animal that had suddenly found itself cornered.

"The fight is mine. We both know it. Yield before I am forced to hurt you more," the guard said evenly.

Brianna shook her head more violently as she brought her trembling sword up to the ready. She knew she lacked the conviction of her skills in the shake of her head. The sword suddenly seemed alien to her; it seemed heavy and awkward.

Snap out of it, Brianna! The thought echoed through her mind, and a small sliver of calm wedged itself into the fear. She gasped at the sudden appearance of the thought and jerked her head around to find the source, *Daimion?* Her mind asked.

Do not let the shock and fear of being wounded dull your senses! Fight! Devenshire's voice echoed in her mind. She felt his presence as though he were standing right beside her and the spike of calm drove itself deeper into the fear. Her frantic eyes scanned the area and found Devenshire engaged with a single guard. She realized how dangerous it was for him to be communicating with her while engaged in battle. It must be drawing his attention from the fight to send his thoughts to her.

I cannot defeat him. She thought to him.

Of course, you can. You have merely been taken by surprise, and that shock has numbed your mind, allowing fear to take over. Focus! Concentrate! I know you can do this! Along with his thoughts came a calming sensation that he, no doubt, was sending to her in an attempt to calm her raging fear. If you cannot beat back the fear, then use it!

How? she asked as her eyes darted back to the two men confronting her. She knew they would not wait much longer before they moved in for the finish, and the wave of fear tried to push the wedge of calm back at that realization.

Give into it. Let it guide your movements. Surrender to it as you do to your passion! his mind answered.

Daimion. I am frightened! she called to him.

Of course, you are. Who would not be? It is not a fault, a flaw to be ashamed of. Any sane person fears battle and the possibility of death. It is what makes us human. Reach deep inside yourself, Brianna. Find the core of your fear and lash out with it.

Brianna closed her eyes and took a deep breath, letting her resistance to the fear fade. Bitter cold, bone-chilling fear swept over her mind, cutting off her link to Devenshire, severing her perceptions of the world around her, blocking out all but the two men who sought to conquer her.

Only one other time in her life had she tasted fear this complete, when she was young, in the transition between girl and young woman. Another man had sought to conquer her, but not with a sword. She suddenly saw his lust-laden features snarled in sadistic pleasure as he backed her into a corner of a room. She had known his intentions, and that knowledge had brought her the first taste of this bitter fear. She had lashed out then, blindly fighting back against the source of her fear, and in the fear, she had found anger more intense and more consuming than any she had ever known.

Brianna's eyes narrowed slowly as her thick lips pulled back from the open jawed fear to a very animal-like snarl. The fear touched the core of that intense anger, and it flamed up, not dispelling the chill of fear, but changing it, mutating it into a completely different type of cold. The features of the two guards wavered and changed. Her mind wiped their faces away to show her the face of that horrible man so many seasons ago in that tiny room. For a moment, she was that half girl half woman, frightened beyond reason, and facing two of the men instead of one.

"No!" she snarled as the two copies of her attacker regarded her with uncertainty in their eyes.

"No!!" she shouted as the tremble of fear in her limbs turned to a tremble of pure, raw anger.

"NO!!!" she screamed as she launched herself at the man in front of her. Her sword moved without her commanding it, her body was no longer hers to direct. It was acting out of a command of thoughts far too primitive for her orderly mind to comprehend. She saw the man's features re-arrange to shock at the sudden brutal attack, just as the face had all those seasons ago.

The man tried to keep up with the near eye blurring speed of her attacks, and he was hard pressed to keep the edge of her blade from opening his flesh. He watched as her face twisted in rage, and at the effort that she was pouring into her attack. He searched her eyes for any sign of the cold, calm, calculating mind he had fought earlier and saw no trace of it. What he saw now was the piercing green eyes of an animal.

No sooner would he deflect a wild blow of her sword than he would be forced to step back and quickly swing his blade around to block another furious strike. He realized that she was not fighting by any set of rules of swordplay, but out of sheer desire for survival. There would be no etiquette here, not with her, not now. He sorely wished to raise his eyes to the other guard, to signal him to assist, but he dared not take his eyes from the woman-animal who snarled, hissed, and hacked at him.

Brianna did not think, but just moved as the fear and anger directed her. It was as if she were standing to the side, watching this battle instead of fighting it. The remoteness of her perceptions was strange, and she marveled at how she saw herself move without the slightest effort on her part to do so.

She suddenly shoved the man she was fighting backwards and spun on the other man who had thought to come up behind her. So swift and sudden was her turn that the guard stopped in shock. That moment of hesitation proved his mistake as she hissed at him and swung her sword across his chest, opening a gaping slash in his shirt and the skin beneath it.

The man yelped in pain as he backed away from the savagery. He looked from the red stain spreading across his chest up into the burning green fire of the woman's eyes and realized that there was only one option left to him that would guarantee his survival. Acting out of instincts that went beyond his control, he abandoned his sword and ran.

She spun back around and launched herself at the first man again who was trying to prepare himself for her attack. He did not have to wait long, as she came at him with a speed and savagery that he knew was not directed by any sane thought.

Steeling his resolve, he met her flashing blade with every defense he had ever been taught and a few that were devised out of sheer desperation for survival. There was no grace in her movements, no calculated misdirection's or feints. Just pure rage. Attacks that came from something deep within her that he could not fathom, and with that, he knew that he had little chance of besting her with skill.

As he was considering how to take the edge off her advantage, he saw her intentions of driving her blade deep into his chest and swiveled his hips so that his upper body turned aside as the blade flew past, opening his shirt just barely missing the skin below. Before he could regain his balance, a small cool hand reached up and entwined its fingers in his hair before a savage force jerked down hard. Where the hair went, so did the head, and the rest of the body soon followed until he found himself flat on his back with a black clad knee pressing down on his chest and the blade of a dagger at his throat.

He looked up into her face and saw his own end approaching quickly, "You think to defile me? You think just because I am female that I will simply yield my body to your sickening pleasures?!" her voice hissed. Her mind did not register the passage of time from that tiny room those seasons ago. Her mind told her eyes that the grass of the clearing was actually the dusty floorboards of the tiny room, the face of the Royal Guard that of the fat store keeper she had worked for. In her mind, she was in her sixteenth season again, trapped in that tiny storeroom in the back of the store, having been told to go there and finding that the storekeeper had followed her and secured the door behind him.

"What?" the guard asked with confusion.

"I am not a plaything for any man, least of all the likes of you!!" she growled as tears pooled in her eyes.

"M'Lady, I have no idea of what you speak. I am only doing what my duty directs me to do," the guard replied carefully, knowing very well that the slightest wrong word or inflection of word at this moment would send the edge of the dagger slicing across his throat.

"Lies!!" she screamed out, and he saw her body tense, preparing to open his throat to the night. He closed his eyes and prepared himself for death. Seconds passed and nothing changed. The cold steel of the dagger remained pressed to his throat, her knee remained in his chest, and her hot breath swept across his face. He opened his eyes into hers and saw something shift in their depths. Something was happening within her, and he found himself thanking the Fates, for whatever it was, it was sparing his life.

Slowly, the savagery left her eyes, the snarl relaxed, and he saw sanity return to sweep aside the primal glare in her eyes. She shook her head slightly, and then looked down into his face as if seeing it for the first time. Anger still shook her body, but not with the intensity of a few seconds ago. She leaned even closer to his face.

"I am not what you think I am. Devenshire is not what you think he is. We have done no wrong. You have been deceived, duped into believing us guilty of crimes we have not committed. Let this go. Do not force me to kill you," she said in tight controlled tones, but he could hear the anger and rage just under the surface. Before he could reply, she shook her head, cutting off his words.

"I know you do not believe me. I know you must act as you are commanded to. I just wished to tell you so that you may consider what you have been told about us," she said, and then quickly raised up to smash him across the face with the hilt of her sword. The man grunted once and then lapsed into stillness.

Brianna rose to her feet and felt her strength suddenly fly away from her. Her knees trembled with exhaustion, her arms became leaden weights, even her sword became too heavy to hold, and it slipped from her grip. She raised a trembling hand to her forehead as she tried to force her body to move.

The sounds of battle called to her, reminded her that her companions were still locked in a battle in which they were sorely outnumbered. She knew that they would be in dire need of her help that the loss of just one of them would almost certainly sweep aside what slim chance of victory they had. But in surrendering to her fear driven rage, she had used up all her stores of strength; once the fierce anger had been subdued, she had been left spent.

Just before her knees gave way beneath her, two sets of hands took her roughly by the arms. The hands on her left arm squeezed down hard on the sword gash, re-igniting the fire of pain that had been numbed by her rage. She cried out but could not struggle as one of the hands grabbed her hair and jerked her head back hard and the point of a dagger was placed against her throat.

"Move and I will bleed you like a slaughtered sheep!" a voice hissed in her ear. With a fogged sense of irony, she realized that she could not move even if she had wished to.

Zandorth staggered back and regarded the cut across his right forearm. The guard had scored a lucky strike and now he was closing in on Zandorth, feeling sure in his approaching victory by wounding the Warrior on his sword arm.

"Yield or suffer more pain!" the arrogant guard shouted.

Zandorth smiled at the guard, tossed his broadsword to his left hand, and swirled it before him. He had long ago learned how to use his sword with either hand in preparation for just such an occasion.

"The fight is only half yours," he said as he parried his sword about him. He did not miss the shocked look as it flashed through the guard's eyes. To the man's credit, the shock passed as quickly as it had appeared, and was soon replaced with shored determination.

Without a word, the guard stepped forward and began his attack, tentatively at first, testing the accuracy of Zandorth's left arm as it compared to his right. It did not take long for the guard to realize that the Warrior was as deadly and accurate with either arm.

As they parried and thrust about each other, Zandorth caught the flicker of something in the man's eyes that sent his instincts screaming alarm at him. Something was not right, and as the hilt of a sword crashed into the back of his head, he realized that the guard had seen one of his companions coming up behind Zandorth and had executed his attacks to keep him from turning.

Pain exploded inside his skull and pinpricks of light flecked his vision as he tried to move away, to gain room to engage both men. With a violent shake of his head, he sidestepped only to feel something solid strike him behind the knees. With a howl of pain, he felt himself pitch forward to his knees. Again, he shook his head, and by sheer force of will brought clarity back to his perceptions. As he pushed off the ground to his feet, another blow to the back of his head sent him sprawling back to the ground. Before he could rise again, he felt several men fall upon him, pummeling him with fists and butts of sword hilts. Each blow sent raw pain into his brain where it turned from lightning bolts of pain to an insubstantial fog that choked off coherent thought.

Shantira had just sent a sheriff into the blissful land of forced slumber when she turned to see the massive wave of guards and sheriffs sweep forward to take Zandorth to the ground where he vanished from sight.

"Zandorth!" she called out and took a step toward the mound of men. Whatever plan she had been formulating to aid the Warrior was sent spinning from her mind as something struck her across the side of the head. The blow had been well aimed and executed with enough force to send her careening sideways to the ground. The impact with the ground went unnoticed as her mind tumbled through the sudden disorientation that took her senses.

She was dimly aware of hands upon her, jerking her upright with no thought of her comfort. At least two sets of hands gripped her arms and wrenched them up and behind her, forcing her to stand on her toes to ease the stabbing pain in her shoulders. For a moment, she feared they would keep pulling her arms up behind her until they snapped from their sockets.

As the first spears of pain from her arms stabbed her brain, she cried out. She tried to open her eyes, but the pain forced them shut tightly as she clenched her jaw to hold back another cry of pain. She did not even bother to try to struggle. So swift and violent had her capture been that she knew resistance was useless, so she sagged in the grip of her captors and was rewarded by the easing of the pressure on her throbbing shoulders.

Devenshire knew that the tide of battle had turned against him. With each man he dispatched from the fight, two or three more were waiting to take his place. He did not know how long the fight had gone on, but he could feel the edges of his strength being reached. Already his breath came in ragged gasps, and his arms trembled from the continued exertion of continuous swordplay without even the briefest respite to gain his wind. Add to this the fact that he had still not fully recovered from his battle with the demon, and he was running out of time. He considered diverting some of his attention into a spell that would shore up his failing strength, but with so many opponents, he knew he could not spare the slightest bit of his attention to conjure the words of the incantation.

"Halt!!" Armand's voice rang out through the clearing, carrying over the sound of clashing steel. Almost instantly the guards fighting Devenshire fell back, resuming a ready stance should the captain order the fight to resume.

For a moment, Devenshire ignored the urge to look at Armand, but kept his gaze locked to the men closest to him. Beyond them, Devenshire could see more guards and sheriffs standing at the ready. With a sickening feeling, he realized that there were more men waiting to fight him than he could possibly overcome. Without giving any outward appearance of surrender, Devenshire turned his gaze to Armand who still sat astride his mount. The look of satisfaction on the captain's face made Devenshire realize that the situation was worse than he had feared.

"The battle is over. I have your companions," Armand said as he nodded his head toward another area of the clearing, inviting Devenshire to look. When he did, he knew the fight was indeed finished, and he had lost.

Two guards held Brianna by the arms with one holding a dagger to her throat. He did not miss the dazed and exhausted expression on her face nor did he miss the blood that soaked the sleeve of her blouse and coated her left hand. He had sensed in her thoughts that she had been wounded, but seeing the results first hand, he knew the wound was bad.

He shifted his gaze to where a group of four guards held Zandorth pinned to the ground. The Warrior was conscious, but Devenshire doubted he was aware of what was happening around him. Blood poured from his nose and mouth. Bruises covered his face where he had been struck repeatedly and with tremendous force. Already, the warrior's right eye was swelling and would be shut very soon. Various cuts, scrapes, and bruises covered the piled muscles of his torso that were visible through the rent remnants of his shirt that hung about him in tatters.

The last scene of defeat he looked upon showed two guards holding Shantira. They had her arms twisted behind her and were exerting just enough pressure to keep the woman from even considering any movement save those they wanted her to make.

"Surrender or I will execute them one by one," Armand said. The cold harsh tone of his voice told Devenshire that it was not a bluff. The hatred the captain held for him was overriding any calls of the responsibilities of his office.

Devenshire felt his own anger rising within him. It was more than wounded pride at having lost a fight, but was the brazen gall with which Armand used tactics to defeat him that were reserved for cowards. No honorable man would even think to use hostages to secure the surrender of an opponent. This course of action coming from Armand surprised him.

He had known of Armand when he lived within this city, the captain's reputation was widespread and well known, and what he had heard of the man spoke of honor and integrity. Whatever Armand believed Devenshire guilty of was stronger than his convictions and was now forcing him to act in a way that was entirely unbecoming of a man of his reputation.

"Is this the way of the gallant Captain Armand? To hide behind hostages? Do you really feel so inadequate that you must hide behind others to secure my surrender?" Devenshire asked with sarcasm thick upon his words.

"Do not even speak of gallantry to me, you bastard! How dare you even think yourself worthy of such considerations! Did you give the same to Constable Liston?!" Armand snapped back.

"Of what do you speak?" Devenshire asked, feeling off balance and at a severe disadvantage. Things had happened that he was unaware of, and without that knowledge, he was proceeding blindly.

"Just like one of you. To claim ignorance in the insulting attempt to claim innocence. I saw what you did to Liston and I can guarantee that his soul is now forever out of your reach!" Armand nearly shouted.

With dread, Devenshire realized that Liston had been attacked and killed, and that Armand believed he was responsible for the murder. Like Armand, Constable Liston had been well known and well thought of among the citizens of Lirpa. His death, and the subsequent blame being placed squarely on his shoulders, did not speak well of his chances of proving his innocence. But he felt he had to try.

"Captain. I had nothing to do with Constable Liston's death. I know not what you have been told or by whom, but I am not a vampire."

"Save your lies for your master in hell!! I will hear none of them!"

"Then I challenge you to test me. See for yourself that I am not what you think I am," Devenshire said, taking care to hold the anger he felt at bay.

"Oh, you will be tested," Armand said with sadistic glee shining in his eyes. "I will personally observe the tests and then I will be the one who sends your damned soul back to where it belongs. Trust me. You have feasted upon your last human! This is the last time I will tell you. Surrender or watch the Lady Standish die!"

Devenshire took only a second to assess Armand's conviction and found it solid and unyielding. There was no doubt that he would utter the command that would open Brianna's throat wide. With a hard look at Armand, Devenshire let his sword slip from his hand to land at his feet. Slowly raising his hands to shoulder level, he stepped back from his weapon and waited.

"Bind them all securely. Master Lordalise will arrive soon and I want all made ready!" Armand snapped as he dismounted and strode to where Devenshire's sword lay. With deliberate movements, he stooped down, picked up the sword, and studied it closely for several moments. While he did this, several men moved in to take Devenshire's hands and bind them tightly behind him. Though it went against his nature, he did not resist.

After his wrists were bound, he was forced roughly to his knees where another rope bound his ankles together and a third rope was used to connect his ankle bindings to his wrist bindings, securing him in a knelt position. With growing anger, he watched as the others were bound in the same manner. He did not miss the pain lancing through Brianna's features as her wounded arm was ignored while she was bound.

Armand stepped up to stand over Devenshire, his sword still in his hand. He followed Devenshire's gaze to Brianna, and smiled slightly. "Does that anger you? That she is treated so?"

Devenshire did not answer, but glared up at Armand, which seemed to delight the captain even further.

"Do not be angry with me, Demon! It is your fault that she is being treated so. Perhaps if you had not enlisted her to join you, then she would be somewhere else now. Safe and secure and free of the pain she is now in and the pain that awaits her for her crime."

"You are a blind fool, Armand!" Devenshire hissed. "If I were truly a vampire would I have allowed you to capture me? Would I care what happened to the others? Think man!!"

"I have fallen prey to one of your deceptions already this night. I have no intentions of falling for another one. If you are thinking of making yourself vanish from this place, consider the alternative," with a quick nod of his head, a guard moved up and placed the point of his sword between Brianna's breasts and readied himself to drive the steel into her at the slightest word from Armand.

Anger flared unchecked within Devenshire, and he scowled at Armand. "Damn you to the fires of hell, Armand. Unbind me, and I will kill you with my bare hands. Oh... but I forget... you have not the courage for one on one combat. You are a coward hiding behind wounded women in fear of a true opponent!"

Armand's face twisted into a snarl, and he doubled his fist and smashed Devenshire across the mouth. "Shut your vile mouth! You know nothing of honor or courage. You skulk in the shadows of the night and feed upon the unsuspecting. You feed upon women, noble men and the innocent people of this realm!"

Devenshire's head swam from the force of the blow, and he tasted blood in his mouth. As he forced his head back around to glare up at Armand, he felt a trickle of blood ease from the corner of his mouth and down his chin. "I bleed, Armand," he said with a bloody smile. "You brought blood. Does a vampire bleed so easily? Would your punch have even gone noticed by a true vampire?"

Armand watched the trail of blood as it moved down Devenshire's chin. Doubt tried to surface again as it had when Devenshire had been bound so easily. While he had to admit that from what he had heard of vampires, striking one hard enough to break their skin was not possible. There was a sincerity and conviction in Devenshire's words that called to his doubts and tried to give them form within his mind.

The reaction of Devenshire to the woman's harsh treatment surprised him as well. His impression of vampires told him that one would not be concerned with how an accomplice was treated. It sickened him to act as he had been acting this night. It was not in his nature to use hostages to secure the surrender of a criminal, nor was it in his nature to torture a prisoner once in his custody. But each time doubt crept into his mind, the image of Liston's body flashed again to drive the doubt from his mind and fan the embers of his anger and vengeance.

"With you? Anything is possible," Armand said forcing his flaring anger back under control. He turned and strode back toward the mounted guardsmen, Devenshire's sword still in his hand. "We will remain here. I have sent a rider back to bring Master Lordalise here."

Devenshire shook his head to clear the last of the dazing effects of the punch. Then he noticed one of the men guarding Shantira yawning, and the act struck him as odd. With the battle and ensuing victory of the guardsmen, a yawn was the last thing he had expected to see.

Another guard yawned followed by another and another. Devenshire watched as one man after another yawned followed by their eyes taking on the sleepy look of those who had trouble remaining awake. Devenshire realized that he had been so focused on controlling his anger and his concern for Brianna that he had been ignoring his senses. Closing his eyes, he reached out with his mind and felt the prickling sensation race down his spine. Someone was using magic, and it was a powerful spell. He had the initial inclination to counter the spell to keep it from rendering him unconscious, but he felt no effects from it. A quick visual check showed that none of the others of his party were showing any signs of sleepiness.

Armand caught one of the yawns and spun on the man, thinking to reprimand him then he noticed another man yawn followed by another. With mild horror spreading across his face, he spun around to watch one man slowly lower himself to the ground and curl up into a ball. Within seconds of assuming the position, the man was snoring softly. One of the men standing guard over Devenshire yawned for the third time before lowering himself to the ground to pass into peaceful slumber.

"What in the name of hell?!" Armand exclaimed as a man standing next to him turned, strolled to a nearby tree, and eased his frame down to lean against the tree and quickly fell deep asleep.

"Wake up! All of you!" Armand yelled. But none of the guards gave any sign that they heard him. One by one, they all found comfortable positions on the ground and fell fast asleep. Even the horses lowered their heads and closed their eyes as sleep claimed them, as well.

Armand strode to the nearest man and jerked him upright. "Wake up!! I order you!"

The man smiled sleepily at Armand. "Good night, sir," he mumbled as he lapsed back into slumber.

Armand spun around and glared at Devenshire. "What are you doing?!"

Devenshire smiled innocently at the captain and shrugged. "Not my doing, Captain."

"Damn you!!" he snarled as he drew his dagger and began moving toward Brianna who stared in wonder at the guards and sheriffs as they all were either sleeping or in the process of falling asleep.

"Armand!" Devenshire yelled in warning.

"Release my men from your damnable magic, or I will slit her throat!" he hissed over his shoulder as he approached her.

Armand showed no signs of the spell that had rendered the rest of his men fast asleep and alarm pierced Devenshire's mind. Calming himself, he called on a spell that sent his bonds falling to the ground, freeing him. As the last shred of rope touched the grass, he sprang to his feet. "Armand!!" he repeated and something in his voice halted the captain's advance on Brianna. Slowly he turned, and his eyes grew wide at the sight of Devenshire standing, free of his bonds.

Devenshire's right hand curled as if he were holding some small round object. With a poorly hidden snarl, Devenshire raised his hand to shoulder level and then dropped it with a jerking motion to waist level.

A small, bright blue ball of light formed in his palm, contained by his curled fingers. Tiny blue bolts of light danced around the surface of the orb. The bolts moved around Devenshire's hand and flashed up his forearm as the air crackled with the pent up energies within the ball. "Take another step toward her, and you will most definitely live to regret it!" he said in a low dangerous tone that turned Armand's blood to ice. The blue-green of Devenshire's eyes had taken on a dark blue glow as they bore into Armand, daring him to move against her.

"You are a vampire! I knew it!" Armand breathed softly as the warning Lordalise had given him hit home with sickening clarity. He realized just how poorly equipped he had been to face the vampire. He had been so bent upon avenging Liston's death that he had ignored Lordalise' warning, and now all was lost. Then he turned his eyes to the woman and saw his one chance of striking a blow against Devenshire. He obviously cared for the woman, and in that caring, Armand knew he could, with his final living act of this realm, hurt the demon.

"I shall see you in the hell, bastard! You and your whore!" Armand shouted as he flipped the dagger over to grip it by the point of the blade. With all the speed he could muster, he brought the dagger up and took aim at Brianna's throat. He only hoped he lived long enough to see the dagger quiver in her neck and perhaps even the shocked expression on Devenshire's face as he realized he had failed to protect her.

Just as he was about to the release the dagger into her frightened expression, something struck him with a force that carried him off his feet to sail through the air. His vision dimmed to match the glowing blue hue he had seen in Devenshire's hand, and he realized that he had not acted fast enough. A searing pain enveloped his body, and he felt it go rigid under the automatic response to intense pain. The tiny stabs of pain raced through his nervous system toward his brain and he struggled to fight it back.

As his body struck the ground, he found he could not move, his muscles tensed and locked as if in stone. The bolts of pain were racing through his nerves, his blood vessels, his very muscle fibers. In their wake, they left his body numb and cold.

So tightly locked were his muscles that he could not even open his mouth to scream. Panic rose within him as he realized that the wave of blue light was rushing toward his head, both inside his body and out. The first edges of the wave raced up his neck, past his jaw, around his nose and shot directly into his brain.

With a blinding flash of brilliant blue light, Armand felt nothing. No pain, no searing heat; nothing. As the flash of light faded, it left darkness in its path, and Armand knew that once the light faded, so would his life. He had not even time to fear his approaching death for the light was snuffed out suddenly, and with it, his consciousness.

Through the haze of pain and exhaustion, Brianna watched Devenshire's eyes and felt more than a little fear. He had looked wholly malevolent. The orb of blue energy in his hand, the intense blue glow of his eyes, the way his hair and cloak had been whipped by the mystical winds of his powers. It had been a truly chilling sight.

Slowly, the blue light faded from his eyes to leave them the same blue-green tint they had always had.

For a moment, he simply stood there, his eyes locked to where Armand lay motionless, and she could see the exertion he was under, considered how such a release of power would have drained him. Then he slowly swung his gaze to her, and he smiled tightly.

"Are you all right?"

"I think so," she answered unsteadily.

"Zandorth?" he asked turning to the warrior who only gave a curt nod in response.

"Shantira?"

"I will be fine," she answered slowly, obviously still somewhat dazed from her capture.

Devenshire closed his eyes and made several gestures with his hand. Almost instantly their bonds dissolved and they were free again.

"How did you do that? Put them all to sleep like that?" Shantira asked as she climbed slowly to her feet.

Devenshire looked about the clearing, his eyes searching. "It was not I. Someone else is working magic here."

Giving up the search with his eyes, Devenshire strode to where his sword lay near Armand's body. As he retrieved it, he studied the captain to make sure his spell had only rendered him unconscious and that he had not put too much power into the orb and accidentally killed him. The slow and steady rise and fall of his chest told him that Armand still lived, but the pain he would endure upon waking would make him almost wish for death.

"Is he dead?" Brianna's asked softly.

"No," Devenshire answered as he returned his sword to its resting place.

She nodded slowly, relieved that not one guard had been killed in the battle. True, several were wounded, but they would all live. She slowly retrieved her own sword and re-sheathed it. Her muscles ached, and her limbs still felt as heavy as iron, but she could move.

Devenshire walked up to her and carefully pulled back the tear in the sleeve of her left arm to examine the wound. With a slight grimace, he shook his head. "It is deep. It will not close on its own."

"We should leave! More men are sure to be on their way," Zandorth said as he sought his sword and tried to shake off the effects of the severe beating he had taken.

"A moment. Brianna's wound needs tending," Devenshire replied as he gingerly tested the flesh around the wound. She winced at the sharp edges of renewed pain his light touch ignited, but said nothing.

"Can you heal it?" she asked.

"I am not a healer. I have some basic knowledge of the healing arts, but not enough to heal this properly. I can stop the bleeding and help speed up the healing. But it will take someone more trained in the healing spells to close it completely," Devenshire answered.

"Perhaps I can be of assistance," another voice sounded from behind Devenshire.

"I wondered how long it would take you to show yourself, Darkseed," Devenshire replied with no surprise in him at all.

"You were so sure I would appear?" Darkseed asked as he walked up to Devenshire and Brianna.

"Yes," Devenshire answered as he continued to study Brianna's wound.

"And what made you so sure?"

"You never could resist a good fight," Devenshire answered as he finally looked up at Darkseed and allowed a slight smile to form.

Darkseed shook his head and surveyed the sleeping guardsmen and sheriffs. "Actually, I found this fight to be quite boring. It nearly put me to sleep."

Devenshire groaned and rolled his eyes but made no further comment about Darkseed's bad pun. "Are there more men coming?" he asked.

"Oh, yes. Several of them," Darkseed answered.

"How long?"

"Very soon," Darkseed replied as he joined Devenshire in

surveying the gaping gash along Brianna's arm. "That is a nasty one."

"Can you do anything?" Devenshire asked.

"Yes, but we have not the time for a true healing now. Stop the bleeding and bind it tightly. Once time permits, I will attempt a full healing," Darkseed replied.

"Once we leave this clearing, we are going after Xavier," Devenshire warned.

"I know."

"Then you have changed your mind about coming with us?" Devenshire asked carefully.

Darkseed shifted his gaze to the darkened woods and his gaze became unreadable. Only someone who knew Darkseed as Devenshire did realized that he had touched a nerve within the Adept and was forcing him to mentally deal with issues he would just as soon leave unattended. Finally, a glint of mischief had shown in his eyes. "As you said, I never could resist a good fight."

Devenshire smiled and clapped a hand to Darkseed's shoulder. "Thank you."

Darkseed shook his head. "Do not thank me yet. The time may come when you may wish you had listened to reason and abandoned this suicidal trek."

Devenshire nodded and turned his attention back to Brianna., "Are you ready?"

Her pale face turned from her own survey of her wound to regard Devenshire with eyes that spoke of pain and increasing faintness. "More than ready."

"This will feel a bit strange. Try to remain still," Devenshire said as he focused his eyes on the wound, which continued to seep blood. She watched as his brow furrowed, and his lips moved in the silent utterance of words. His eyes began to glow that eerie blue again, and she felt a strange tingle deep inside the wound.

Despite Devenshire's request that she remain still, she could not stop the flinch of her arm as the strange sensation formed deep inside of it. If her sudden flinch distracted Devenshire, he gave no indication of it as he made an odd gesture with both hands and began passing them over the wound.

Shantira moved up beside Devenshire and watched intently as he worked the Mystical Arts. A faint blue aura began to glow deep inside the gash, and Brianna gasped as a strange heat began to radiate from the deepest levels of the wound.

"Are you okay?" Shantira asked Brianna as she looked up at her.

"Just feels a bit strange. I am fine," she replied as she continued to stare at the blue glow of light that grew inside the open wound.

Gradually, the glow both in Devenshire's eyes and in the wound began to fade. Once both lights had faded from sight, Devenshire sighed slightly and looked up at her.

"How does that feel?"

Brianna flexed her arm cautiously. A mild look of surprise crossed her features as she flexed it a little harder. "The pain is not as intense. It is more sore than painful."

Devenshire nodded. "The bleeding has been stopped and some healing of the deeper parts of the wound has been done. It should be enough for now." He then turned to Shantira. "Find something to fashion a bandage and bind the wound tightly. Try to close the wound as you bind it."

Shantira nodded and set off to find something to use for a bandage. Devenshire caught the odd look in Brianna's eyes as she watched Shantira move off. "What is it?" he asked.

"Something is wrong with her," she said absently.

"What?" he asked.

"She is acting strange," she replied.

"How so?" Devenshire asked casting a look after Shantira.

Brianna seemed lost in thought for a moment before she shook her head. "During our escape from the city, we were cornered in a warehouse. A guard ran my horse through, and I was thrown from the saddle and dazed. Shantira became very agitated, almost frantic about my safety."

Devenshire smiled. "I can sympathize with her."

"Daimion, I am serious. She pulled a dagger and threatened Zandorth if he did not surrender to the guard who had me covered."

"She what?" Devenshire exclaimed in disbelief. "Pulled a dagger on Zandorth?"

Brianna nodded.

"That is odd. What do you think is wrong with her?" Devenshire asked.

She bit her bottom lip in a gesture Devenshire recognized as Brianna being in deep thought. Finally, she shook her head. "I do not know. But I believe we should keep an eye on her."

"Agreed," Devenshire replied as he began to walk away.

"Daimion. What happened to you?"

Devenshire paused, but did not turn back to face her. His thoughts turned to Rachelle and his awakening to find her sitting next to him. A sensation passed across his forehead as he remembered her cool touch as she had brushed his hair from his forehead. The mystery surrounding Rachelle Tambrey taunted him again, and he remembered how she had suddenly grown very dispassionate and distant from him. There was something about her that refused to depart far from his thoughts, and that irritated him somewhat.

"It is a long story and we have not the time for long stories. Perhaps later," he muttered as he resumed walking away.

She turned to Darkseed who was watching Devenshire walk away with an odd expression on his face.

"What is it?" she asked.

"I do not know. Something is on his mind though."

"Do you know what happened to him?" she asked.

Darkseed shook his head. "No," he continued to watch Devenshire, a quizzical look masking his face. "Has he resumed his study of the Arts?"

Brianna switched her gaze from Devenshire to Darkseed. "No. Not that I am aware of. Why?"

Darkseed continued to study Devenshire's shadow as he retreated. He then shook himself out of whatever train of thought he was in. "We should move out quickly. Do you feel well enough to ride?"

She smiled tiredly and brushed a stray strand of hair from her face. "Just so long as we do not let Zandorth lead the way."

She saw the confused expression cross Darkseed's face and she laughed. "Never mind. It is a jest between Zandorth and me. Well, actually, just me."

Devenshire strode up to Zandorth as he checked the condition of his mount. Devenshire watched him for a moment and saw how he favored his right arm, and how he seemed still slightly dazed from the beating.

"Are you all right?" Devenshire asked.

"I am fine," Zandorth snapped as he re-secured his saddlebags. "We should move and quickly. More guards are surely on their way."

"There are. According to Darkseed they should be here very soon," Devenshire replied as he continued to study Zandorth.

"Then each moment we stand here in useless chatter is a moment they grow closer to us," Zandorth snapped shortly.

"I could do a minor healing. It might help with some of your minor injuries," Devenshire offered, ignoring the shortness in his tone.

Zandorth turned and regarded Devenshire with a stern look. His right eye was swollen completely shut now and even in the pale glow of moonlight, Devenshire could see the unsightly color of the swollen flesh around it.

"Keep your powers to yourself! I have no need or use for them!"

"What is angering you, Zandorth?" Devenshire observed.

"Where were you?! Do you have any idea of what we have endured for the sake of waiting for you to appear?" Zandorth growled. "Brianna endangered us on several occasions by refusing to leave without you!"

"A trap was set for me at the inn. They were bandits, I suspect from the same group that attacked us last night. I was wounded in the ensuing battle and was healed by... a friend. I regret that it took me so long to rejoin you," Devenshire replied, opting to omit the part of his story involving the demon that had appeared from the corpse of one of the bandits. He had his suspicions on the origin of the demon, but he was not sure, and telling of the demon would only take up more time that they did not have.

Zandorth looked over Devenshire's shoulder at Darkseed. "This Darkseed. He helped us escape from the jail then left us. He said he had no desire to become involved in what he called your suicidal quest. Now he wishes to join us? I do not trust him."

Devenshire turned and watched as Darkseed stood conversing with Brianna. "I do."

"Then you shall be responsible for him. He has yet to earn my trust, and I will be weary of him," Zandorth replied as he turned and continued to prepare his mount for the coming journey. Devenshire sighed and turned to walk away only to be stopped by Zandorth's voice. "Heed my words, Devenshire. Darkseed and Shantira. Watch them closely... I know I will."

Devenshire studied Zandorth for several moments before he turned and walked away. As before, he felt off center by not having knowledge of events that had transpired in his absence. But now was not the time to catch up. They should leave the clearing and quickly.

Within moments, Brianna's wound had been bound, Devenshire's mount summoned, and one of the sheriffs' horses borrowed for Brianna's use. Once they were all mounted and ready, Devenshire moved to the front position, leading the way out of the clearing, conjuring a spell that would mask their passage from the clearing while creating a false trail that would show that they had left in the opposite direction from the one they were using. It was a weak spell, and one that would be discovered soon, but it would add to their lead-time on their pursuers, and he mused that every little bit would help.

~*~

They made it through the forest without incident and soon emerged on a trail heading north. They rode in silence, each contemplating what had transpired in the span of one night, how much everything had changed.

The faintest touch of gray could be seen on the horizon, heralding the arrival of dawn. Each considered the dawn, the birth of a new day and the death of the one before it. So much had happened, each wondered if there would ever be a normal sunrise again.

Darkseed rode up to Devenshire and slowed his pace to match Devenshire's. "Who is Lordalise?" he asked.

Devenshire shook his head. "I do not know. He obviously knows me and has formed some rather unflattering opinions of me."

"Unfortunately, he has convinced others of his beliefs. Now I am not one to worry overly much about other people's opinions, but when those others are the members of the Royal Guard," he paused to shrug, "then it might pose a problem."

He nodded. "Agreed."

Darkseed glanced over his shoulder at the others, making sure none could hear him. "Daimion, that spell you unleashed on Armand. Where did that come from?"

Devenshire glanced at him. "What do you mean?"

Darkseed shook his head. "That was a powerful spell. Well beyond your abilities as I remember them. Have you resumed your studies?"

He shook his head. "No. I simply reacted to the threat."

Darkseed nodded. There was something going on within his friend concerning the Mystical Arts. He could feel it, could sense it in the Mystic tides. He couldn't put his finger on it, but it was something to keep under watch.

Zandorth rode up on the other side of Devenshire, his heated gaze intent. "There are things you must know, Devenshire!" he scowled.

"I have never known you to be short on words, Zandorth," Devenshire replied.

"I have laid my honor on the line for you this night. I have acted out of preservation for myself, my companions and what I feel is best for the realm and will continue to do so."

Devenshire didn't reply and continued to look at him, knowing there was more to come.

"Know this! I have been associated with you, and you are accused of being a vampire. We have wounded several members of the Royal Guard and have fled capture as criminals would."

"You have a point," Devenshire remarked.

"Always. There is a complement of Warrior's of the Ancient Class nearby. Armand may call on them to assist in our capture. I will not raise my sword against my brethren!"

"What do you mean?" Darkseed asked and was rewarded by a harsh glare of the warrior's open eye.

"I will not fight other Warriors of the Ancient Class. Be prepared!" he snarled as he urged his mount forward.

Both men watched him ride ahead and each spent time lost in their own thoughts. Finally, it was Darkseed, who broke the silence. "Well, I will say this much for you, you certainly know how to go about a reunion. This has been simply a charming evening."

Devenshire turned his head to lock a serious gaze at his oldest friend. "Know that no matter how trying this night has been, what is to come is much, much worse. We may very well find ourselves at a point in time wishing for a night such as this."

EPILOUGE

"KNOW THAT NO MATTER how trying this night has been? What is to come is much, much worse. We may very well find ourselves at a point in time wishing for a night such as this," the old man said softly as he continued to gaze into the burning fire. He drew in a ragged breath and let it out slowly as he settled back into the thick padding of his chair.

Caleb scribbled the last words down and quickly set the page aside to dry with the thick sheaf of other pages that he had filled with the old man's story, thus far. His fingers throbbed with the pain of their frost bitten joints, and the cramping of quickly written words. He had no idea how much time had passed since the old man had begun his tale, and he did not care. The story the man had weaved of his first adventure with Devenshire had left him enthralled, suspending all thoughts, but the telling and recording of the story.

Within the deep, mellow tones of the old man's voice, Caleb had forgotten the pain of his existence. The loss of his fair Cassandra, the death of his companions on this quest to find something of Devenshire, and the pain of his soul all seemed faint memories in the magical tale.

Anxiously, he dipped the quill into the ink well and prepared to record the man's next words, to finish the story. After several moments, he realized that no more words came from the man. He looked up to find the storyteller gazing into the fire; his expression even more drawn than it had appeared before he had begun telling the tale.

"Well?" Caleb asked as the trembling point of the quill poised to jot down the next chapter of the tale.

"What?" the old man asked absently, still gazing into the fire.

"What happened next?" Caleb asked.

"That is enough for now. We both are in need of rest. I am weary, and you need to save your strength and heal from your ordeal," the man replied.

"There is no way I can rest now. There is so much more to tell. There are far too many unanswered questions for you to stop the tale now. I beseech you to continue!"

The old man chuckled wearily before he leaned forward to take up an iron poker and stoke the fire.

"You are young, Caleb, and being so you are cursed with impatience. True story telling is a lost art in this new world. More young people would do well to remember how a skillfully told story could stir the essence and refresh the spirit. All will be revealed in the course of time. But for now, we both need rest."

Caleb sighed in exasperation. "How, by the Fates, can I be expected to rest when you tease me with only a fragment of that which I came searching for?"

The ancient man slowly shook his head, a fond smile playing at the corners of his lips. "You have endured much to gain this fragment of the story. You have searched for seasons, have traveled hundreds upon hundreds of miles. You have lost all that you considered important in the search for this. Surely, you can endure another night in order to obtain the rest of that which you seek. Remember what I told you earlier, Caleb? I told you that all happens for a reason. The trials and tribulations you have endured to this point were not random occurrences of chance or some malicious toying game of the Fates. Everything you have endured to this point has been in the attempt to temper your patience."

"I don't understand," Caleb said curtly, as he realized the rest of the story would not be coming this night.

"Of course you do not," the man scoffed. "None your age ever do. You all sulk around and curse the Fates for the bad things that happen to you without ever truly taking a moment to consider the good that can come from even the direst of situations. If you take nothing from your trials you should look upon them as perhaps a lesson in endurance, of finding the true depths and limits of your will, of finding the strength of your spirit!

"Take the loss of your Cassandra for example. Perhaps it was destined for you to lose her heart so that when love finds you again, and it will despite what you may believe at this moment, you will be better prepared to appreciate it."

Caleb was silent for many moments as he contemplated the man's words. It pained him to consider the possibility that he had truly lost Cassandra to another, but he had to admit to the wisdom in the old man's words. Unknown to even Caleb, he began looking upon the treacherous journey to this cave as a measuring post of his will, spirit, and determination.

"So am I to take this pause in the telling of your story as a sign from the Fates to learn patience?" he asked.

"No. You are to take this pause as a sign that I am an old man, and I tire easily!" He scowled in return before mumbling to himself and shaking his head.

Caleb blinked in surprise several times before he allowed a smile to part his cracked lips. "And you are quick to become grumpy, as well."

"That too!" the man snapped as he slowly rose from the chair. "Before you retire, place more wood on the fire, and then go outside and gather more for in the morning."

Caleb watched the man slowly turn and begin to shuffle toward one of three other openings into this chamber of the cave. "You wish for me to gather wood from outside?"

"Of course! Do you think I am going to take you into my home, feed you, mend your injuries, and tell you Daimion's story for free? If such is the case, then your mind is severely frost bitten or you are insane!" The man lapsed into a grumbling tirade on young people expecting the world for free as he continued to slowly walk away.

Caleb found himself growing amused at the man's cantankerous behavior and smiled warmly as he caught only occasional words of his grumbling. "Good night, sir," Caleb called out.

"Whatever!" The old man threw over his shoulder as he reached the doorway that would lead further into the cave. Without a pause or another word, he shuffled on through the opening and was lost in the darkness beyond.

Caleb watched the now empty doorway for several moments before he chuckled softly and reluctantly laid the writing material aside, careful not to smudge the ink on the most recent pages.

His body still was not responding to his mind as he was accustom, so it took him longer to carry out the old man's instructions than it should. But he eventually had the fireplace loaded with fresh wood, and the firebox next to the mantle was stacked with ice-covered wood from outside.

His body ached anew from exposure to the bitter cold while gathering the wood from outside, and he took several more moments to warm his throbbing joints by the raging fire.

As he warmed himself, Caleb looked up at the portrait of the woman over the mantle. She seemed even more beautiful and even sadder than the first time he had looked upon her. He switched his gaze to the other portrait, finding her even more beautiful and alluring than before.

He found himself believing that the woman over the fireplace was the mysterious woman who had helped Devenshire twice so far in the tale. The other woman? She had to be the Lady Brianna Standish. He felt sure of it.

For several more moments, he continued to warm himself by the fire and gaze upon the faces of the two women who knew Daimion Devenshire, perhaps even better than he had known himself. In them, he found a link to the man he had hoped to find and now knew that he would never meet. In that link, he felt as if he had touched a fleeting part of Devenshire, and in that fleeting touch, a tiny sense of completion seemed to settle upon his troubled soul.

With a majority of the new chill finally displaced from his bones, Caleb made his way to the furs he had first awakened. Crawling beneath the furs, he curled himself into a tight ball to ward off the deeper aching chill in his bones. Despite the restlessness of only having heard a part of the old man's story, he found himself drifting off into the warmth of the furs and the pull of his own fatigue.

As his mind, reluctantly, released its last tenuous grasp on consciousness a single thought came to him. He knew not what the rising of the sun would bring, or what lie ahead in the days and seasons to come, but for this moment, for this night, he had the beginnings of this story and a wondrous sense of magic.

A sense and wonder of magic that had never been known to his life and had all too soon left his world.

Now, a sneak peek at the next book in
The Devenshire Chronicles Series,
"Predator & Prey"
Book Two.

SNEAK PEEK

DEVENSHIRE CROUCHED LOW, straining his senses for the location of whoever was trailing him. A full moon overhead, filtered by the canopy of branches, made it possible to navigate the forest with care, but it also provided deep shadows that any manner of predator could hide in. He was far from the campsite they had made earlier in the evening and therefore on his own. He had an arrow nocked in his bow and the tension of the bowstring provided some marginal comfort. Twisting his head around, he searched the shadows and patches of bright moonlight for any indication of where his stalker might be. He found it ironic that in the span of a heartbeat he had gone from predator to prey. Absently he acknowledged that he wasn't a huge fan of irony.

Their escape from Lirpa had been harrowing and left a great many unanswered questions in its wake. To better increase their lead over Captain Armand and the Royal Guard, they had pushed on through the next day and well into the evening before stopping to rest. Brianna's arm needed tending to, the mounts needed to rest and they all could use a moment to take a breath that wasn't being listened for by a guard or sheriff. While camp was being made, he had taken his bow from his pack and set off on a hunt for mountain hares. They were camped at the base of the Mt. Kil'tafore range and the large hares were plentiful in this region. He didn't particularly like the bow, but it was the only weapon he had to take the wild animals at a distance. He was, by no stretch of anyone's imagination, an archer, but he possessed enough skill to hunt with the weapon, which was all he ever used it for.

He had been well into the hunt before he became acutely aware of being watched. He softened his breathing and willed himself to remain calm as he continued to search his surroundings while straining his senses for any indication where the stalker might be. He could hear the faint breeze rustling branches and bushes, mixed with the constant chirping of crickets. Occasionally an owl would call out and in the distance a wolf could cry out in its' solitude, all normal sounds of the night. His eyes strained into the darkness, but showed him nothing but shadowy images and insubstantial masses that could be anything. He gently took a deep breath and then released it softly, calming his nerves and readying himself to summon his powers. His mortal senses were useless. Half closing his eyes, he released his powers and reached out, searching. He detected the presence of several rodents, insects, several meat serpents on hunts of their own, and even some of the mountain hares he had come to hunt, but no trace of anything that shouldn't be here.

Closing his eyes completely, he applied more power to his search and expanded the perimeter of his spell. All he found was more of the same, nothing that shouldn't be here and nothing with any malevolent intent; at least not towards him. He was about to pull the spell back when the outer edge of it touched something, something that did not belong here. He focused the spell, pulling the power from a wide circular search to a fine line that surrounded the object that had caught his attention. It was a person, but that was all he could glean from the spell at this distance. Whoever it was, they were at the outer most limits of the reach of his powers, which made discerning details difficult at best. Maintaining a tight mystical lock on the person, he opened his eyes and turned in the direction the person lie in. He rose slowly and quietly to a standing position and began moving slowly towards the person, using great care to keep his steps light. His hope was to bring them further within the range of his spell and, thereby, learn more about who they were.

The familiar tingle of his natural sense of the Arts began running up and down his spine. Whoever the person was, they were now using magic to keep a mystical lock on him. He paused to kneel, laying the bow on the ground. He quickly, but quietly, slid the quiver of bows from his shoulder and laid them next to the bow. Standing upright again, he gently drew his sword, feeling more confident in his abilities with it over that of the bow. Moving with all the stealth he could muster, he continued towards his invisible target. It was going to be a difficult hunt because he would need his physical senses to navigate the darkened forest and using them would detract from his mystical senses. The person began to solidify in his mind, he could make out a cloaked figure crouched low in the brush. He could not make out any weapons, but that did not mean they didn't have any. As he moved around a tree and stooped low under a branch, he focused on the figure's face. It was a grey, featureless blob at the moment, but he knew that as he drew closer, he would be able to make out more detail. Devenshire paused to concentrate on his vision spell, abandoning his physical senses in favor of his mystical ones. As he did, more details began to coalesce in his mind. The figure was just below average height. The heavy cloak they wore made details of their physical build hard to make out so he focused his attention on their head. Slowly the grey mass shifted into a face-shaped oval. Indentions for eyes and a mouth began to sink inward as a bulb in the middle of the face began to grow outward to form the nose. He resisted the urge to hurry the image to form. Working the Mystical Arts was meticulous and time consuming and impatience was one of the quickest ways to ruin a spell. More features formed and soon he would be able to discern if the person was man or woman and once he had their face locked in his mind, he would be able to search the Mystical Tides for their identity. He closed his eyes and forced more concentration into make the face solidify. Just as the eyes began to come into focus, the figure shifted and was gone.

Devenshire's eyes snapped open, instantly locking in the direction the figure had been. They had moved, as if they had known he was about to learn their identity. By having so much of his energies focused on the figures' face, all they had to do was move and they would be outside the reach of his focused spell. He quickly expanded his focus outward and just barely picked up the impression of the figure retreating into the woods at a brisk walk.

Mumbling a curse, Devenshire set off after the fleeting figure. Again, he was forced to divide his attention between keeping a mystical lock on the person while using his physical sense to navigate the perilous path in the dark. It was a taxing bit of work and he could already feel the beginning barbs of a headache working its' sharp tentacles into his brain. The person knew he was on the move for they quickened their pace to stay just on the edges of his ability to sense them. This troubled him as much as if someone were stalking him. Was the fact that they were at the outermost limits of his powers because of a limitation on their part, or were they luring him into some form of trap? His opponent increased their pace and Devenshire had to quicken his pace even further to keep up. The added task of using his physical body and senses took away from his mystical ability to find out who the person was. At this point, all he could do with his powers was to keep a fleeting lock on their position. His mystical gifts were being taxed to their limits with trying to keep up with them and the path they were following was physically demanding as well. It was almost as if they were testing him, trying to see just how much concentration he could spare for the spell while navigating a treacherous path through the dark. Several times, he stumbled or caught a grazing slap of a branch as he bounded through the dark. His breath heaved in his lungs and it took all of his concentration to keep the duel demands on his focus under control.

Suddenly, whoever it was stopped and turned back to face him. Devenshire instantly slid to a stop and crouched into a defensive posture. For whomever it was, to be so intent on escape and then suddenly stop and turn back, meant that they either were making a stand, or were ready to spring their trap. The maneuver had been sudden and had taken him by surprise. Devenshire tightened his grip on the sword and released some of his hold on the mystical energies, opting to concentrate more, now, on his physical senses. So far, all he heard was the steady song of the night and his taxed breathing. Nothing else was registering on his mystical senses save for the mysterious person just ahead. What it was waiting for, he had no idea. The element of surprise for a trap was lost, but that did not mean one was not waiting for him.

An immeasurable amount of time passed with Devenshire and his opponent squared off against each other across a distance far outside either of their fields of vision. Devenshire studied his options, weighing his next course of action. This was a dangerous game and not one he intended to lose. He decided to increase the power of his spell and make another attempt to find out whom this person was. He grimaced as he realized that using more power on the spell would increase the strength of the already pounding headache.

Then, they were gone.

Devenshire blinked even though the action would have no bearing on his spell. The person had not turned and moved out of range of his spell, they had simply vanished, as if into thin air. He felt himself tense, preparing for the attack. Surely, it would come now, as the person would use the distraction of an attack to cover their escape. Time passed and nothing happened. Devenshire's joints began to ache from holding the defensive posture and waiting. It became obvious that whoever it was who had been following and watching him, was gone now. He straightened up and turned a slow circle, searching with all of his senses, and found nothing that wasn't supposed to be there. With more than a little irritation, he noted that most of the mountain hares had scattered with his driving run through the forest. It would now take longer to track them down and with his throbbing headache, it promised to be a very unpleasant hunt.

Moving off through the woods with stealth, he moved back towards the bow and arrows so he could resume the hunt. He was unaware of the cloaked figure that stepped from the shadows to occupy the spot he had just left. They watched him move through the darkness as a tight smile graced their lips.

"Very good," they whispered softly before turning and melting into the night.

From The Author

There have been many pivotal moments in my life:
March 5, 1965, the date of my birth (kind of a big one there.)
May of 1983 I graduated from High School.
June of 1984 I dropped out of college and returned home.
October of 1984, the date of my first marriage.
June of 1985, the birth of my son, Johnathan.
October of 1987 and the death of my father.
April of 1988 and the birth of my daughter Nikkie.
March of 2003, the unofficial official end of my first marriage.
January of 2007, the birth of my first grandchild, Blaine Alexander Sechrist.

Two and a half months later, when we lost little Blaine. (Papa loves and misses you, little man.)

September of 2008 when my granddaughter Allie was born and came to live with me 5 weeks later.

October 15, 2008 when my granddaughter Tara was born.

July of 2008 when my mom went to take care of Blaine in heaven.

October 25, 2011 when my second granddaughter was born, Jaelyn Shon Love (Opa's wittle Jammin' Jaelyn.)

September 30, 2011, the day I met the woman who would literally, and figuratively, save my life. Renee Martin and I had coffee at Denny's and talked the night away.

December 26, 2011 when I saw Allie for the last time (I love and miss you terribly, little Allie!)

June 30, 2012 Renee Martin became Renee Sechrist. This also marks when my family expanded with the addition of Damen, Brittney, Christopher, Michael and little Marley (Knarley Marley!!!)

There are some dates and events I left out on purpose, and some I'm sure I simply just forgot (not very pivotal if I forgot them.) There's one other event that is just as pivotal as most of the above dates:
September 28, 1998.

This was when Daimion Devenshire was born somewhere in the recesses of my mind. This marked the day that my dabbling in a hobby of writing became an obsession for a life-long career. It has been, and will continue to be, an obsession that has taken me through some of the darkest times of my life and has been with me through the most glorious ones, as well.

Daimion quickly formed a personality all his own. Of all the characters that I have created and all the stories that I've dreamed up, none are as real to me as Daimion and The Chronicles. This story, and these characters, are deeply embedded in me, and at the risk of sounding schizophrenic, are part of me.

Some have said that I patterned Devenshire after me. This isn't entirely true. I'm sure some part of my ego tried to influence me to make him like me, but Daimion quickly soared beyond anything I had ever imagined for him. These days I like to say that there are parts of Daimion I wish I had, and some I hope I never get.

There have been several times over the past 14 years that Daimion was very close to becoming a useless character in a discarded storyline. My first foray into becoming published was an anguishing lesson in how hard it was to realize a dream.

In the early 2000s, e-books were just starting to come into being. There were several who saw a day when e-books would be the norm and not the exception. Unfortunately, none of those visionaries was in control of the publishing industry.

I quickly learned that print publishing was not the way to go, not unless I wanted to lament in a queue somewhere for years on end with the spaghetti thin prospect that some editor in some giant publishing house would pick up my manuscript and give it a shot.

I turned to e-books, and the first publisher I chose turned out to be a scam run by con artists. Many promising and ambitious authors were hurt in that scam.

The second e-book publisher I went with kept putting my book in queue, shuffled from one editor to another. The last editor who had my book said she was working on it but had limited time. All the while, her e-books were rolling out one after another while mine sat in queue for month after month after month.

So, I decided that perhaps I had been too hasty with my critical analysis of the print publishing industry. I spent the next six months being reminded by agents and publishing houses just how spot on my earlier evaluation of them had been.

Throw into this mix the breakup of my first marriage, and the beginning of an eight-year relationship that shouldn't have lasted eight seconds. These eight years served to sink me even further into the abyss that I had determined would become my existence. This was to be my purpose in life, and I should simply surrender and accept it... and for a while I did.

At this point, my dreams of being a published, successful author had withered and died. Daimion Devenshire and his story faded away and became fond memories of a life I had left behind and would never return. My future was set.

Or so I thought.

Daimion Devenshire can be one stubborn bastard. Something in him (and in me) refused to die, and refused to be forgotten, or even ignored. For those eight years he simply stood in a dark corner of my mind, arms folded patiently across his chest, that one eyebrow cocked and waiting. He would not pursue me and force me to write his story, but neither would he simply walk away into oblivion. He waited and watched, and when the moment was right, made his return.

That moment was September 30, 2011 when Daimion met his staunchest supporter, strongest ally, and my future wife. Renee came into my life at a time when I had decided that romance was truly dead and love was nothing more than, as Al Pacino put it in *"The Devil's Advocate"*, *"Overrated. Biochemically no different than eating large quantities of chocolate."*

Or, as Daimion puts it in the book, "Love is an over romanticized state of insanity."

Fortunately, they were both wrong. Renee reminded me of what love, true love can be, and what it can inspire in a man. She brought the sunshine back into my world that had been overcast for many years. She gently and lovingly brought me back into a world I had turned away from. By the time January of 2012 came along, I began feeling the stirrings of my craft calling to me. It took me a while to realize what the feeling was since it had been so very long since I had felt it. For the first time in years, I wanted to write, and I wanted to write Daimion's story.

As with other events in my life, it wasn't going to be that easy. I had lost the original manuscript and knew there was no way I could ever re-create it from memory. That's when Renee suggested that I at least try. "Who knows," she said, "maybe you can re-write it better than it was before?"

So I rewrote the epilogue, and it wasn't too bad. Better than I remembered. I rewrote chapter one and it was pretty good. While there were elements from the original missing, it was quite high-quality on its own. It felt good to write again.

Then, as luck would have it, I found an old copy of the original manuscript on a disk I had put away. At that moment, Daimion stepped from the shadows of my mind, arched one eyebrow at me and said,

THE DEVENSHIRE CHRONICLES

"Now. Are you ready?"

Yes, I am. It's past time, and now there is no stopping me. Not with what I have been given and what I have learned. It's my time now! This is my destiny and purpose. I won't deny it any longer.

There are so many people that need to be thanked. To give them the praise they deserve would make the forward longer than the book. However, there are a few whose contributions must be acknowledged.

Angie, for all the nights you were roused from a deep sleep and asked to read a passage of the book. For your support in my dreams of becoming a writer.

To my son, Johnathan, for your outstanding artwork on the cover. For being such a strong young man in the face of some adversities that most people could not handle. Your writing is very good, and I hope you continue to pursue it. You have the gift.

My daughter, Nikkie, for being the proud, determined young lady that continues to inspire me. You have been my confidant, my friend, and on more than one occasion, my counselor. I love you and Johnathan with all my heart.

A-Game Amber for being my feedback source. Our long discussions about the book were invaluable to me. I look forward to more of the same with the books to come.

A big thanks to Kay, as well, for her contributions to the editing and revision process, your help was invaluable.

To my editor, Rogena Mitchell-Jones. You are Daimion Devenshire's new best friend. You took his story and polished it up to the diamond it has always been in my mind. Your words of encouragement and support were also invaluable, and I can't begin to thank you enough. I truly look forward to working with you on the other books in the series! Thank you!!

Finally to Renee: As a writer, it's my job to come up with words and phrases to describe things so that my readers have a vivid image of what I'm trying to convey. With you, though, I'm at a loss. My craft fails me. I don't have the words to describe or express the depth of my love for you.

You have given me so much, have shown me a life that I would have never had thought possible. In your gentle, warm, and loving way, you are drawing me out of my self-imposed prison. You have saved me from myself and continue to heal my wounds and sooth my battle scars. I never imagined a woman like you existed and never thought I would ever feel a love like ours, not in a thousand lifetimes.

You are everything I ever wanted in a best friend, a lover, and a wife along with a few things I didn't even know I needed or was looking for. This seems so inadequate in comparison to everything you've done for me but,

Thank you!

I must also say a giant "Thank You" to you, my reader. Without you, this is all kinds of pointless. I hope that you had as much fun reading this book as I had in writing it. The story is just beginning, and so is our adventure together – writer and reader.

Until we meet again, from Daimion, Brianna, Raven, Shantira and Zandorth…

Farewell and safe journeys.

 Tom Sechrist

www.ingramcontent.com/pod-product-compliance
Lightning Source LLC
Chambersburg PA
CBHW060758030726
47503CB00002B/296